Som̶ Happene̶ ̶n the Way to Heaven

C000244566

Something Happened on the Way to Heaven
Edited by Samantha M. Derr

Published by Less Than Three Press LLC

Sunburnt Country edited by Caitlin Penny
A Better Ending edited by Caitlin Penny
One for Sorrow edited by Caitlin Penny
The Lost Angel Copyright edited by London Burden
Watch as My World Ends edited by Caitlin Penny
On Wings Not My Own edited by Courtney Davidson
Made for You edited by Samantha M. Derr
Angel Eyes edited by Ania Love
Angel Fever edited by Courtney Davidson
The Book of Judgment edited by Samantha M. Derr

Cover designed by Lainey Durand

First Edition February 2013

Printed in the United States of America

ISBN 9781620040904

Something Happened on the Way to Heaven

Edited by
Samantha M. Derr

Table of Contents

Sunburnt Country

LJ LaBarthe

James groaned as his alarm clock went off and sleepily hit the snooze button, dozing until it went off again ten minutes later, just past five. James stretched and blinked up at the shadows of the ceiling fan above him, the sound of the blades comforting in the dimness of his room. Light from the rising sun leaked through the cracks between the curtains and the wall.

James sat up and yawned, running his hands through his sandy blond hair. Getting out of bed, he padded barefoot to the tiny bathroom of his cabin and took a quick shower beneath the spray of lukewarm water, then dressed in loose jeans and a plain t-shirt. Donning his Akubra hat and grabbing his sunglasses, cell phone and keys, James tugged on his worn and scuffed work boots and headed outside.

The bright blue sea of the Great Australian Bight caught his attention as it did every morning. It made living in the tiny town of Ngapa bearable. Ngapa was a tiny desert town nearly equidistant between the capital cities of Adelaide and Perth that served to provide travelers along the Nullarbor Plain with a place to rest. Sometimes people stayed for several days or a week, or the drivers of road trains would take a day to rest before continuing on to their destination. It was a town with a fluid population, people coming and going on a near daily basis; those who lived permanently in Ngapa were owner-operators or employees of the few amenities in the town.

Today, the sea was teal with patches of rich, dark, navy blue indicating depths and flows of the current, with no whitecaps on the gentle swells of the waves. The red desert with its uneven patchwork of grey-green saltbushes ran along the flat plain to the seashore where the sand turned white, and then the brilliance of the water began.

Touching the silver Celtic cross around his neck, James put on his sunglasses and turned towards the building that was a motel, truck-stop, restaurant, gas station and caravan park all in one. This was where he worked, living on the premises in one of the cabins that the owners, Marge and Bert, kept for their employees. Also living in Ngapa was Bill, who owned and ran the bar; Tommy, his wife Rita and their children, Indigenous Australians who worked for Marge and Bert and lived nearby in a small cabin they had built on the edge of the caravan park. James had been living in Ngapa for nine months and had come to think of the small community as family.

"G'day, cobber." Tommy grinned at him as James walked into the office of the motel building to check his roster for the day. "Sleep well?"

"Not too bad. At least it isn't humid at night." James grinned back. "How's Rita this morning?"

"Pretty good. She's setting up for class with the kids. We had to get Bert out early to set up the satellite dish for School of the Air to come through properly. She doesn't trust that internet thing at all."

"Don't blame her. Is the coffee hot?" James nodded towards the coffee urn.

"Hot as a tin roof, mate." Tommy moved out of the way as James made a beeline for the urn and mugs. "How you can drink that stuff is beyond me."

"Too early for beer," James shrugged. "And I need to wake up properly." As he prepared his coffee, he leaned back against the counter. "What's on the schedule for the day?"

"Not a lot. It's gonna be a quiet one. Few road trains scheduled to stop for gas and probably a beer or two, but that's about it." Tommy consulted the large notebook with the details for the week's arrivals. "You've got a light day's work today. Just a bit of cleaning up in the gardens Marge likes so much and manning the gas station in the afternoon."

"Okay," James nodded. "Sounds fine. No tourist groups?"

"Not this week." Tommy flicked through the pages of the notebook. "Not next week neither. Makes a nice change. So, you want to join me and Rita and the kids for tea tonight?"

James smiled at the invitation. "That'd be great. Thanks, mate."

"No worries. You always seem to like Rita's food."

"And the homebrew," James laughed. "You make a mean lager, Tommy."

"Hey, a man has to know how to use his talents. And I have many," Tommy joked. "Say seven?"

"Sounds good." James drained his coffee, pulling a face. "Okay, time to clean then ... see if Marge or Bert need me for anything else, I guess. I'll see you tonight."

~~*

It didn't take long to rake the scant leaves and clean up the gardens that Marge had put in the year before, giving overnight guests somewhere to sit if they didn't want to stay indoors, go down to the beach or the motel's pool. Finished, James hummed to himself as he put the gardening implements away in the shed and turned to head inside when a headache came out of nowhere.

"F-fuck," James gasped, squeezing his eyes tightly closed. He pressed the heel of one hand to his forehead as he groped blindly with his other hand for the wall to steady himself. The headache was the worst he'd felt in some years—when he'd been a teenager, he'd suffered from cluster headaches and they were the sort of thing he wouldn't wish on his worst enemy. But this was awful: the pain was intense and he thought he could hear something like a confused babble of voices—harsh, unpleasant voices that sounded akin to nails scratching down a chalkboard. The sun was pounding on him like boiling knives and the headache made every part of his body sensitive. James dropped to his knees, crying out raggedly as the pain grew even more intense. The voices seemed to grow louder, the sound of raucous, ugly laughter accompanying them.

The next thing James knew, there were hands on him; warm, gentle hands, and the sound of urgent conversation. He couldn't figure out if the words came from the voices in his head or from someone else. All he knew was pain, the sensation similar, he imagined, to having a herd of buffalo stampeding back and forth over his skull.

"Get him out of the sun."

"Quickly now!"

"Bert, go get Maggie."

James felt himself being half-lifted, half-dragged indoors to the blessedly cool and dim interior of the staff room of the motel. He heard a rough sound that seemed almost as loud as a gunshot and realized that it came from the venetian blinds being drawn closed. James felt a cool towel press against his forehead, and with a gasp, he reached blindly for something, anything, to anchor him to the real world.

"There now, there's a lad."

James recognized the voice as belonging to Rita, her soft timbre soothing to his ears. "Rita?" he managed to grit out. "What ... "

"Shh, lie down."

He moved unresisting to the sofa, lying back and groaning with relief when he suddenly found himself inhaling the strong, pleasant scent of eucalyptus. The pain in his head subsided a little and he moaned. "Shit."

"Can you tell me what's wrong, love?" That was Marge, James thought fuzzily. He nodded slowly, and then winced, wishing he hadn't moved his head at all as it throbbed.

"Headache," he muttered. "A really, fucking, bad one. Worse than a migraine or a cluster headache."

"Here." Rita again, he thought. "Inhale. Gently, mind."

James did as he was told, smelling more eucalyptus and accompanying spearmint. It didn't ease the pain entirely, but it was enough for him to open his eyes without crying out.

"Drink this." Rita handed him a chipped mug full of steaming liquid.

"What is it?" he asked, even as he sipped it.

"Tea," she said calmly. "Rock fuchsia bush: it's good for soothing headaches. It's an old bush remedy my Gran taught me years ago. It'll help."

He grunted in reply, still drinking even as Bert entered the room with Maggie, the local nurse, in tow. James flushed slightly, embarrassed by the commotion he'd caused.

"I'm okay," he began, but he was hushed by Maggie as she moved to examine him carefully. "It's just a headache," he added lamely.

"A bad one," Maggie said thoughtfully. "Do you have a history of migraines, James?"

He nodded slowly. "Yeah, I used to get cluster headaches when I was younger. That was years ago, though. Last one I had was when I was nineteen, so ten years ago."

"Cluster headaches." Maggie shook her head. "Those things are the worst. I think you'd better spend the rest of the day in bed with the fan on and the curtains closed."

There was a murmur of agreement from the assembled as Maggie rummaged through her bag and pulled out the necessary pills for headache relief. "Take these," she ordered. "Two now, then one every two hours."

"Yes, ma'am." James managed a wan smile, taking the pills from her and setting down the now empty mug.

"Water." Marge handed him a glass.

"Thanks." Still embarrassed by the fuss he had caused, he swallowed the pills and pulled a face. "Ugh, pill-coating tastes revolting."

They all chuckled, the tension broken. The sound of a loud air horn outside made them all jump and Bert swore.

"Shit, it's the first road train. A sixteen-wheeler, I think. C'mon, Tommy, give me a hand, mate."

Tommy nodded. "Will do. Jimbo." He turned to look sternly at James. "Go to your cabin and rest. We'll look after things. You're lucky we've got light traffic today."

"Okay, okay, fine, I'm going." James held up a hand in surrender. He didn't wave off Rita, Marge and Maggie's help to stand or to walk the short distance from the motel building to his cabin. They left him alone with water, the headache pills and the ceiling fan turned on high, the venetian blinds and the curtains drawn closed. James groaned as he lay on his back with his eyes shut and tried not to think.

~~*

How long he'd been asleep, he had no idea, but James came awake with the feeling that he was no longer alone. Thinking it was Rita or Marge (Maggie would have to go back to work, checking on other patients who lived along that part of the Nullarbor) he pulled a face as he sat up slowly.

"Couldn't leave me alone, huh?"

"I think," said a soft male voice, "you're mistaking me for someone else, James Marlowe."

James blinked, turning to stare at the owner of the voice. Sitting in a chair at the foot of the bed was a man who appeared to be near to James own age of twenty-nine—or perhaps a little older. He had dark, shoulder length hair and pale skin, and wore simple blue jeans and a dark grey t-shirt. His eyes were a bright, piercing blue, a color that reminded James immediately of that navy blue of the deeper parts of the sea. They were beautiful eyes, almost mesmerizing in their intensity and James felt himself inexplicably drawn by them.

"Who are you?" James asked. Ngapa was remote enough that random strangers wandering into his cabin was practically unheard of ... at least until now.

"My name is Raziel," said the man as he stood up. "And I am the Archangel of Secrets and Mysteries."

James stared at him incredulously, suspicion turning immediately to skepticism. "Right. Sure you are. And I'm the pope."

"Very droll." Raziel rolled his eyes. "Your headache. Is it still bothering you?"

"A little," James admitted, and then he frowned. "What the hell is this? Who are you *really*?"

"As I said," Raziel shrugged. "I could prove it to you if you wish, but you humans seldom enjoy such demonstrations."

"Yeah, well, no." James crossed his arms over his chest, completely unconvinced by Raziel's words. "Prove it."

Raziel let out a heavy sigh, the sound of one who is truly put-upon, and before James's astonished eyes, a pair of russet brown wings were suddenly visible, unfurling and stretching. The room seemed suddenly tiny with those large, magnificent wings revealed—not fully spread, however, for they would not have fit. There was a faint sheen of bronze light around the feathers, a light that both drew James and filled him with fear. He gulped.

"Okay, I believe you." James was amazed at how even his voice sounded.

Raziel quirked an eyebrow. "Well now, that was easy. I thought I'd have to levitate you to the top of the motel building or something else equally tacky."

"No, no, the wings are ... well, the wings are bloody amazing; that's good enough for me." James couldn't take his eyes off them. "But ... I don't believe in God, sorry. Or the Devil or demons or angels or, well, you."

"That's all right," Raziel smiled, and James noticed a flicker of that strange bronze light in his eyes. "You don't have to believe in us. We believe in you."

James had no reply for that. The words made the hackles on the back of his neck stand on end and he shivered, even though it wasn't particularly cool in his bedroom. It wasn't simply the words, however: James couldn't help but stare at Raziel, taking in his slender form, the warmth of his smile, the way his cheeks dimpled. Raziel was beautiful, beautiful and intriguing and a million other clichéd words and phrases that James didn't want to dwell upon, for fear of turning crimson in embarrassment and feeling like a horny teenager. It wasn't just the wings or the smile or his body, James realized, as Raziel carefully furled the wings against his back where they faded from sight: it was those intense, otherworldly eyes and the voice and ...

Oh God, he was doomed. He was lusting after an archangel. James forced himself to pay attention to Raziel's words as he continued talking.

"Now, I am not my brother, Raphael, who is the healer of my family, but I do know a little of the healing arts, and we need to talk, you and I. So I am going to fix your headache so that you can concentrate on what I have to say, all right?"

"If you can get rid of the headache, I'll concentrate on whatever you want," James promised.

Raziel chuckled and moved to stand in front of James, resting his hands on top of James's head. "Just listen to me is all I ask."

James nodded, falling silent again as he felt the warmth of Raziel's touch cascading through his skull like a comforting blanket. There was the sense of muscles being relaxed, of pain being sponged away and soothing caresses on his mind by invisible fingers that left little trickles of what felt like electricity in their wake. James's eyes fell closed as he relaxed completely, lulled by the power of Raziel's touch.

Finally, Raziel stepped back and looked into James's face critically as he opened his eyes, then nodded once. "Good." Raziel sat down again, pulling a packet of cigarettes from the pocket of his jeans and lighting one with a lazy snap of his fingers. "So. Let's talk."

James leaned back against his headboard. "Okay." He realized that he had no idea what to say. And yet ... "Why is an angel smoking?" he blurted out. "Isn't that sort of a sin?"

Raziel chuckled. "I enjoy my vices, James. They aren't many, really—cigarettes, the occasional beer, sex. My father is much less strict about these things than you humans would otherwise believe. Our duties are such that these little ... tastes of ours are forgiven as a necessary evil if you will—something we do to wind down, to relax or to cope. What we do, after all, is rarely pleasant or easy." He took another drag of his cigarette, exhaling slowly and gazing steadily at James, his expression unreadable.

"I need your help, James," Raziel continued, taking another deep drag of his cigarette. "A book has been stolen from me, a very important book—a book that I wrote a very long time ago. It's been stolen and hidden by some very unpleasant creatures. Now, before you ask me what this has to do with you, I shall tell you. For I am just that awesome." He grinned boyishly and James couldn't help but laugh.

"Okay, Raziel the Awesome, tell me."

"Raziel the Awesome, huh? I like the sound of that." Raziel's expression grew serious. "The book is called the *Sefer Raziel*, which is, essentially, the book of me. I wrote it and gave it to Adam. Yes, the Adam who was married to Eve and lived in Eden, before you ask. It's a book of magic and a guide to taking care of this planet. It's been stolen from the place I have kept it in for eons by a rather nasty little archdemon named Adramelech, who seems to think he can use it to start the final battle and give Lucifer an advantage over my oldest brother, Michael. I'd really rather he didn't do that—I'm sure you can understand why. I don't particularly want to see Dad's—*God's*—creation destroyed or watch my big brother die, even if he is a stuffy, uptight, pain in the ass sometimes."

"What's this got to do with me?" James asked.

"You can hear demons." Raziel exhaled a cloud of cigarette smoke. "That's the reason for what you call cluster headaches—which are a very real thing, I hasten to add—but not what you yourself suffered. The headache today is worse because Adramelech is close. This barren wasteland you live in suits his needs. I can't find him, but you can."

" ... what?" James blinked. "I what now?"

"Hear demons," Raziel repeated patiently. "Like ... internet radio for Hell."

"Gee, that doesn't make it sound any less psycho or, pardon my language, fucked up!" James got to his feet, raking his hands through his hair. "I hear demons?! What the hell!"

"It does not mean you are evil, James," Raziel said calmly. "Some humans can hear angels, others hear demons, and still others hear both. Those unfortunates who hear both inevitably end up in institutions. The human mind is not designed to cope with the sounds of Celestial and Gehennan voices simultaneously." His expression grew sad. "I like humans," Raziel went on, "and it grieves me to see the effects that the sound of those voices have on human minds. The human mind is an amazing, remarkable thing, capable of infinite ideas, concepts, inventions. Seeing such potential torn apart by the agony of noise like that is ... well. It saddens me." He shook his head. "Anyway. To return to the point. You, my friend, hear demons. Congratulations!" Raziel grinned, the display of his quixotic mood-swings not lost on James, although he chose not to comment on it. There was, after all, a bigger issue to discuss.

"I hear demons. Do you have *any* idea how fucking fucked up that is?" James was shaking—with shock or anger, he wasn't sure. "So, wait. Let's say I believe you. You want me to tune into demon radio and figure out where they are and what they're planning, is that it?"

"More or less," Raziel agreed smoothly. "For now, though, I think you need to eat. You must be hungry."

James waved a finger at Raziel. "Don't think you can fob me off, mate. We're coming back to this topic."

"Of course." Raziel stood up. "However, I have found humans tend to deal better with a new situation if they are regularly fed."

"Oh good, now I feel like a fucking sheep or a cow." James rolled his eyes.

"Nonsense." Raziel smiled brightly. "If you were a sheep or a cow, it would be cannibalism."

James gaped at Raziel. "You are fucking weird," he said finally. "I mean that in the nicest way, of course."

"Quite." Raziel's grin grew cheeky. "You also think I'm attractive and are having lustful thoughts about me. I'm flattered."

"You're reading my thoughts? Don't! Don't read my thoughts!" James blushed to the roots of his hair.

"As you wish. Shall we go and eat?" Raziel gestured towards the door.

"Fine." James shook his head. "This is ... the most bizarre day I have ever had. I can't believe I believe this shit."

"Stranger things have happened. Come." Raziel gestured again. "You require nourishment."

James rolled his eyes and moved towards the door. "How am I going to explain you to my friends here?"

"However you like." Raziel's expression was serene as he lightly touched James's elbow. "I'm sure you're inventive."

"Great," James muttered. "Just fucking great."

~~*

Tommy intercepted them on the short walk from James's cabin to the restaurant. James smiled at his friend as Tommy clapped his shoulder, grinning from ear to ear.

"You look much better, lad," Tommy said, nodding to emphasize his words.

"I feel it and all," James replied.

"I didn't know you were expecting a mate, though." Tommy was looking at Raziel now, his expression curious.

"Oh, right, yeah." James nodded. "This is Raz, a friend from the UK; I forgot he was coming today, what with the headache coming out of nowhere like it did. Raz, this is Tommy."

"Understandable." Tommy's expression cleared, and he offered Raziel his hand. "Nice to meet you, Raz. Any friend of James is welcome here."

Raziel shook the proffered hand, nodding politely. "Likewise, Tommy." As he looked around, James could see that Raziel was taking in the facilities and the landscape, and that his expression was growing more and more puzzled by the moment.

"Where's the nearest town?" Raziel asked, turning back to James and Tommy.

"You're standing in it," James said, trying not to laugh.

Raziel blinked, turning in a small circle. "But ... there are no houses or streets or anything of that sort. Just that long road that I assume is a highway."

"Yup. Welcome to outback Australia." Tommy was starting to chuckle now and James couldn't hold back his own amused grin.

"How many people live here?" Raziel sounded incredulous.

"Fifty, officially," Tommy shrugged. "The population changes because the tourists and some of the drivers of the road trains stop overnight. Or longer, in some cases."

"What is a road train?"

"Big truck," James supplied. "Usually a twelve- or sixteen-wheeler, carrying goods from one capital city to the other. They usually supply the big chain grocery stores and places like that. Or they carry cars or sheep or cattle."

Raziel frowned in confusion, looking out toward the highway and the desert on the other side. "And no one lives out there?" He pointed towards the scrub.

"No." Tommy shook his head. "The tribespeople who lived here when this place first got settled died out." His voice was clipped as he spoke, and James smoothly interjected before Raziel could ask another question.

"There's a history museum of sorts just up the highway, Raz, if you're interested in that."

Raziel quirked an eyebrow but didn't press the issue, instead shaking his head as a small car whizzed past, sending up a cloud of dust in its wake. "Barren place," he remarked.

"Desert is like that." Tommy was smiling again. "C'mon you two, you must be thirsty." He gestured toward the restaurant attached to the motel and gas station. "Unless you want to go to the pub?"

"Restaurant is fine," James nodded. "I'm hungry anyway. Which is a good sign, because those headaches usually make me hate food and throw up when I smell it."

"Bloody awful, mate." Tommy pulled a face in sympathy. "Rita'll be glad to hear you're feeling better. Raincheck on dinner, though; I think you need to get an early night."

James didn't protest. Truth be told, an early night sounded like a good idea. He was still tired, and despite Raziel removing the pain of the headache, the experience had worn him out. He nodded and smiled at his friend gratefully. He was about to say something when Raziel stopped dead in his tracks and stared, pointing.

"What on earth is *that*?"

"It's a big blue whale," Tommy said calmly.

"I can see that, but ... why is it here?" Raziel stared at it.

"It advertises beer, mate." Tommy stifled a laugh behind a cough.

"It's made of solid concrete," James added helpfully, grinning broadly at Raziel's astonishment.

"But ... but ... why? Why is it here? Why at all? Why a big, blue concrete whale?" Raziel's confusion was obvious.

James and Tommy shared a grin.

"Why not?" Tommy chuckled.

"That's not an answer," Raziel frowned, looking at Tommy.

"Sure it is, mate," Tommy laughed. "It's just not an answer you like."

It was an astute remark, James thought, as Raziel's eyebrows shot up in surprise. Raziel was wise beyond imagining, but such things as giant, concrete whales advertising beer in the middle of the Australian Desert were beyond his ability to rationalize. That seemingly flippant answer of 'why not' was, James thought, a very good answer to most of the questions of why anyone did anything at all. And, he realized suddenly, Raziel, a creature of nearly unlimited power and knowledge, would find the answer of 'why not' as frustrating and unsatisfactory as James found the knowledge that angels and demons were real. For both of them, the information only led to more questions and the answers to those questions were equally frustrating and unsatisfactory. It was like a mental Escher painting: no matter how much information they had, it still led to only more questions and tangents and ultimately, more confusion. It was something he had in common with Raziel and that made Raziel more human and less alien. It was comforting.

"There are loads of big things around the country," Tommy was saying. "A big orange, pineapple, rocking horse, macadamia nut, barramundi, River Murray cod, you name it."

"Why?" Raziel blinked in confusion.

"Again, why not?" Tommy laughed. "C'mon, mate. Come inside and eat. Don't think too much about it; it's not really supposed to make sense. It just is."

Raziel opened his mouth, and then closed it again, looking at James in bewilderment. "This is ... very strange."

"You've not been to Australia before, then?" Tommy asked as he walked to the door, holding it open for them.

"Not in many years, no." Raziel nodded his thanks as he entered, James on his heels.

"Don't mention what you are," he hissed to Raziel.

"I wasn't intending to," Raziel replied mildly. "I'm not a complete idiot, you know. There's no reason to say what I am to these good people and confuse or upset them. This place ... " He stopped, gesturing to the restaurant, the big blue whale and the town of Ngapa as a whole. " ... is remarkable. Strange and confusing, yes, but remarkable."

"I like it," James said. "Let's get some food. I don't know about you, but I'm starving."

Raziel chuckled. "I don't actually need to eat, James, but I will do so, to preserve the fiction that I am human."

"Good on you." James rolled his eyes.

"I thought so." Raziel, undeterred by sarcasm, merely grinned.

"You're a brat," James declared.

"Yes, yes I am." Raziel winked and James laughed, unable to stop himself.

~~*

James sat on the edge of the bed, watching as Raziel moved around the room. Raziel was doing something, but what that something might be, James had no idea. It appeared to be quite complicated, involving little bursts of that alien bronze light. When they had returned to the cabin from the motel's restaurant, Raziel had walked around the building, doing whatever esoteric thing it was that he was now doing in James's bedroom.

"I think that will hold it," Raziel said finally, moving to sit down in the chair by the window.

"I hope you know that I've got no Earthly idea what you've been doing for the last hour." James lay down on his side, his weariness beginning to overtake him.

"Protecting the town and your abode," Raziel sighed, running a hand through his hair, mussing it and making him appear even more attractive than he already did to James's eyes. "I told you there are demons around, under the command of an archdemon."

"Adramelech," James nodded.

"Quite." Raziel flashed a small smile at James remembering the name. "Adramelech is the equal and opposite, if you like, of my older brother, Uriel. He used to be an angel, once upon a time, but decided he liked Lucifer's ideas of how things should be more than our father's. So when Lucifer was sent to Hell, Adramelech and a good two thirds of our brothers and sisters went with him."

James blinked. "I didn't know that."

"Read the Bible, James." Raziel's blue eyes locked on his and James couldn't suppress the slight shiver at that intense gaze. "It's all in there. More or less."

"I don't really have time for that," James shrugged, before changing the subject. "So you've protected Ngapa and my place from them, which is awesome, great, thanks. But now what? I mean, I bet you don't just pop out of the ether to humans on a whim, do you? You said I hear demons and I might be tired after that bloody headache, but I'm not an idiot. You said you wanted me to tune into demon radio and find Adramelech. You want me to do that so you can go into wherever he is and kill him."

"Astute." Raziel stretched his legs out in front of him, pulling out his cigarettes from the pocket of his jeans and lighting one. "You are, of course, correct," he went on. "That is what I need you to do for me. Killing Adramelech isn't my job, however; that's Uriel's task as ordained by our father, and I wouldn't dream of depriving my favorite brother of something he's been looking forward to since before the advent of time. No, I need to get my book back. The spells within are not for use by demons or fallen angels. They're not for use by humans really, not anymore. The book is a curiosity mostly, but in the wrong hands it could be used to destroy this entire planet."

James gaped at Raziel in shock. "Are ... what ... seriously? The information in it is that deadly?"

"I rarely joke about potential genocide." Raziel's gaze was unblinking and sent a shiver down James's spine. "The book contains words of power, James. And those words of power are not meant to be used for evil deeds."

James digested that, shaking his head slowly. "This is going to take a while for me to process."

"I understand," Raziel nodded. "For what it's worth, though, you're taking everything remarkably well."

"I'm numb," James said drily. "Also really bloody exhausted."

"You should rest. We can talk tomorrow."

James opened his mouth to protest, then sighed and nodded. "Yeah, okay. Do you ... I mean, I only have the one bed ... " He trailed off, blushing furiously.

Raziel laughed. "I do not require sleep, James. I will read while you slumber."

James couldn't stop the faint pang of regret at that, but he simply nodded and stood up, walking to the bathroom. In the doorway, he paused and looked at Raziel for a long moment. Raziel held a book, taken from who knew where, and as he turned the pages with long fingers, a lock of dark hair fell into his face. Raziel was gorgeous, James thought again, and maybe a little terrifying, but the attraction he felt outweighed the fear. With a soft sigh, James went into the bathroom and closed the door behind him, trying not to think about Raziel's bright blue eyes containing that flicker of bronze light or the shadows of those enormous, russet brown, wings.

~~*

The next day dawned clear and sunny, and James woke feeling refreshed. He sat up in bed, blinking in the dim light of the room, his eyes immediately searching for Raziel. He was standing by the window, gazing out over the saltbush scrub towards the sea, his expression inscrutable.

"Did you sleep well?" Raziel asked, not turning away from the window.

"Yeah, thanks." James yawned and stretched, rolling his shoulders and making a contented noise. "Quiet night for you, was it?"

"One cannot complain." Raziel turned away from the window and faced James, a small smile tugging at the corners of his lips. "I have breakfast for you." He indicated the table in the corner of the room.

"How did ... actually, no, I don't want to know." James wriggled out the bed and ran a hand through his hair, looking at the table laden with food, neither of which had been there the previous night. The smell of bacon and eggs assaulted his nose, making his mouth water. Standing up, he moved to the table and tucked into his meal.

"While you were sleeping," Raziel began, moving to sit beside James, "I took a walk around this place where you live. It is very flat, isn't it? The land, I mean."

James nodded. Swallowing a mouthful of eggs, he cleared his throat. "Yeah. The whole of the Nullarbor Plain is flat. A lot of people call it the Nullaboring."

Raziel quirked an eyebrow. "Droll."

"I guess." James resumed eating.

"Why did your friend Tommy grow ... restrained in his conversation when the former indigenous residents of this place were mentioned?" Raziel rested his chin in the palm of one hand, propped on the table, his other arm on the formica and brushing James's own.

James shot Raziel a quick look. "You don't know about the avoidance speech?" As Raziel shook his head, James took a drink of his coffee and sat back in his chair, although he didn't move his arm away from Raziel's. Setting the mug down, he shrugged one shoulder. "It's Aboriginal tradition not to speak of the dead when they've passed. It's a sign of respect."

"I see. Thank you for telling me. I do not want to give Tommy or his family or people any offence." Raziel was serious. "I understand there are many different tribes here?"

"Mhm." James talked between mouthfuls. "Australia's a big country, Raz. A lot of it is desert, but that doesn't really matter to the indigenous peoples—they've lived here for a very long time and they know how to live off the land, how to live in harmony and respect with it."

"Like the indigenous peoples of the Americas," Raziel mused, nodding thoughtfully. "Or New Zealand."

"Yeah, exactly."

"My brother, Gabriel, is very fond of New Zealand," Raziel smiled. "He spends a great deal of time there when he is not working, at a place called Mount Aspiring."

"Never heard of it." James grinned. "New Zealand's a pair of small islands, but there's a lot on those islands. Just like Australia is a big, red, sunburnt country that's also an island and a continent."

"You love your country," Raziel noted.

"Yeah," James shrugged. "I do. So." He finished his breakfast and turned to look at Raziel. "What do we do today?"

"Today we see if you can tune into Adramelech, and find out where he has hidden himself and my book." Raziel's voice was all business now, his eyes glittering. "I need to get that book out of his fallen angel hands and hide it. Matter of fact ... " His voice became a low, angry growl that sent shivers down James's spine. " ... I want to know *how* he found it in the first place."

James looked away, swallowing hard. Raziel's tightly controlled anger, the growl in his voice, the glitter of *other* in his eyes were more than a little bit of a turn on. To try to focus on something else, James stood up and moved toward the dresser. "I should get ready for work."

Raziel shook his head. "Not necessary. I spoke with your employer while you were asleep, and he felt that you deserved a week off to spend with your good friend Raz from the UK." He grinned impishly and James gaped at him in surprise.

"You spoke to Bert?"

"Indeed. And his wife. Lovely couple."

"Yeah, they're cool," James agreed, reaching for the coffee pot and pouring himself another cup.

"And what of your own family?" Raziel's head tilted to one side curiously.

"They're dead." James's voice became clipped, cold. "There was a bush fire accident several years ago. I'd rather not talk about it, thanks."

"Understood." Raziel hummed for a moment. "Do you not have a partner? A wife or girlfriend, perhaps? A lover?"

"*He* died, too." James sighed. "Seriously, Raz, I don't want to talk about it. He was a soldier; he died serving our country."

"I'm sorry for your losses," Raziel said softly, his voice full of sincere compassion. "I know how it feels, for what little it may be worth."

James nodded, not trusting himself to speak, and sipped his coffee. Silence stretched out between them as James tried not to think on the losses in his life: his mother, father and little sister in a bushfire, his lover in an insurgent attack on a military convoy in the Middle East. He wished desperately for something to take his mind off thoughts of the dead, but nothing sprang to mind. Enough time had passed that his grief was no longer all-encompassing. He couldn't deny that he missed his family and his lover, but he was honest enough with himself to know that life was for living and that dwelling in the past did him no good. It had taken him some time to come to terms with everything, and moving to Ngapa had given him a sense of hope for the future, the knowledge that yes, life was still good and he had the right to be happy and loved. There were moments of sadness, and James knew there always would be, but they no longer defined him or his life. That was all in the past and James was determined to keep it there. He wanted a good future, a happy future, a future with someone who he loved and loved him in return. He didn't think that was so much to ask.

Raziel pulled him from his momentary melancholy. "Perhaps today you'd show me around the outlying areas? One can only see so much on foot or from the air, and when one is not familiar with the land, it means little. In the process, perhaps you can see if you can hear Adramelech or any of his familiars?"

Nodding, James stood up. "Yeah, I can do that. Sure thing. What about the headaches, though? And ... does Adramelech know about me?"

"You shouldn't experience them again. I took care of that, all being well, and no, in answer to your question. Adramelech does not know about you specifically. He is aware that there are humans who can hear demons and angels, but not that you are one of them. It requires a certain kind of power to identify a human mind capable of that, and my power is connected to secrets, mysteries, the things that are hidden. Therefore, as your talent is hidden and a mystery, mine is the power that can identify individuals such as you." With that, he also stood up and James realized that Raziel was a few inches shorter than him. Standing close to each other, James was able to see that Raziel's bright blue eyes were rimmed with bronze, the flicker of that color in his irises giving him an otherworldly, exotic appearance. His dark hair fell in mussed waves to his shoulders, and there was a slight upward quirk to his lips that suggested a sense of humor. Idly, James wondered what Raziel would look like when he laughed.

His gaze was drawn again to Raziel's mouth and James sucked in a sharp breath through his nose. He moved a little closer, aware that Raziel was watching him intently.

"Raziel," James began, "I ... "

"You may," Raziel answered the unspoken question.

James closed the small space between them and, trembling with nerves that he hadn't felt since he was a teenager, kissed Raziel softly.

Raziel responded to the kiss slowly, gently deepening it, and James felt a warmth spread through him, a heat that made him want more. He responded with an eagerness he hadn't felt for what seemed like an eternity, a hand tangling in Raziel's dark hair as he kissed him harder. Raziel's own hands rested on James's shoulders, thumbs brushing his neck. James shivered in pleasure, pressing closer.

They kissed for several long moments before Raziel ended it, reaching up to cup James's cheek with one hand. His fingers were calloused, James realized, and his palm was soft and warm. "We have work to do," Raziel said gently.

"Oh, right, yeah." James forced himself to step back from Raziel.

"Later, though ... " Raziel trailed off suggestively, and then waggled his eyebrows.

James burst out laughing. "Later for sure."

"Good." Raziel grinned broadly. "You have nice lips."

"Uh, thanks," James blushed. "I'll just get dressed, and then we should go. Work, remember?"

"Of course," Raziel nodded, and politely turned his back to give James some privacy.

Watching Raziel out the corner of his eye, James stripped off his boxer shorts and t-shirt, and then tugged on a pair of clean jeans and a thin, blue shirt. Rolling up the sleeves, he pulled on socks and his work boots, and then announced, "Ready."

Raziel turned back to him and smiled, moving toward the door. "Let us take care of work then."

"My van is parked in the motel parking lot," James said as they walked outside, close enough that their arms brushed together. "It's probably better to drive around than to walk, especially with the heat in the middle of the day—that's the worst time to be out if you don't have a car or sunscreen, or both."

"Whatever you think is best," Raziel replied equably. "This is your land, after all. I have not been in Australia for a very, very, long time. It's changed considerably."

"How long is a very, very, long time?" James asked curiously, leading the way towards his van.

"I believe human dating conventions would put it around the mark of two thousand years BC." Raziel lit a cigarette as they walked. "As I said, a very, very, long time ago."

"Wow. Uh, yeah." James shook his head. To change the subject to something that felt safer and didn't make him feel small and insignificant, James gestured toward the strip of grey asphalt that was the highway that stretched in a long line as far as the eye could see. "East or west?"

"Either." Raziel looked around as they reached James's van. "I suppose westward would make more sense, assuming it's less inhabited in that direction."

"Yeah, it is." James slid into the driver's seat, unlocking the passenger door for Raziel. When Raziel was inside, he started the engine and pulled out of the parking lot. "I'm not sure where an archdemon would hide, though," James mused. "I mean, it's really flat out here. No caves, no underground structures, not really. There's a sort of smuggler's cave in the cliffs of the Great Australian Bight, but it's pretty popular with tourists, so it'd be a bad choice of hideout."

"I confess that I'm perplexed as well." Raziel hummed thoughtfully. "As you say, there's little in the way of natural structures that would work as a place to hide. Are there any ruins from human habitations?"

"A few," James frowned. "Not that they'd be much use either; they're full of sand. Depending on the winds, you can either see a little of the walls or actually be able to go inside the ruins, but a lot of the time they're so full of sand that you couldn't stuff a magpie feather in them."

Raziel idly drummed his fingers on the armrest of the door. "Curiouser and curiouser. I can understand why he chose this part of the world—it's quiet and empty and hot—but the lack of concealment ... it is not like him at all."

"Maybe he buried your book underneath a saltbush," James suggested as he drove out onto the highway.

"I highly doubt that," Raziel replied, snorting in amusement. "These bushes, do they literally contain salt?"

"I don't think so, but you'd have to ask Rita." James quickly checked the rear-view mirror. The road before and behind them stretched empty and silent, just like the desert.

"Salt is repellent to him and demonkind," Raziel explained. "Which again begs the question of why here, considering the proximity to the sea."

"Maybe the pros of silence and emptiness outweighed the cons?" James was looking at the desert with a new appreciation for its flat, unchanging landscape. "I mean, there really is no one for miles. There used to be a military installation further north, but that's still a bloody long way from here."

Raziel shook his head. "It's a mystery," he mused, and then grinned boyishly. "I like mysteries."

James laughed. "I guess you do, considering that's what you said you are—Archangel of Mysteries and Secrets, right?"

"Indeed," Raziel nodded, before pointing at the thick white lines painted on the surface of the highway, like a zebra crossing. "Why is that there?"

"Hm? Oh. That's a landing strip for the Flying Doctor Service," James explained. "We're too small to have an airport or anything. The Cessna airplanes they use are small enough to land on the highway, and then they taxi down it until they stop and berth in those side bays on the edge of the highway there." He nodded towards the large bays that were obviously carefully maintained on each side of the road.

"Fascinating," Raziel looked at everything with great interest. "Humanity is truly remarkable. To settle out here, in such a remote area with little to sustain it ... humanity has achieved remarkable things in order to continue to survive with ease. I'm extremely impressed."

"You really mean that, don't you? You're not just humoring me?"

"I really mean it," Raziel confirmed quite seriously. "I know ... well, I know nearly everything there is to know about everything, but there are still things that surprise me. Humanity's tenacious determination to survive is one of them. It gives me hope for the future."

James quirked an eyebrow at that, but decided to say nothing. Instead, he sped up and drove for some time in silence. Finally, he slowed and pulled the van over onto the shoulder of the highway.

"I don't know how much further you want to go, but if we drive for another two hours, we'll hit the next town," James explained. "So, what do you want to check out next?"

Raziel sighed. "You are getting no sense of Adramelech at all?"

"Not a one."

"Then I suppose we should turn around and try the opposite direction." Raziel considered it as James started the van and turned around. "Can you show me these ruins you spoke of?"

"Yeah, I can do that. We'll have to hike a bit, though."

"I believe I'm able to hike quite satisfactorily," Raziel drawled. "I am not going to faint in the heat of the sun or become weighed down in the sand."

"Did I hurt your archangel pride there, Raz?" James grinned. "Sorry."

"It's of no matter. I forgive you," Raziel declared grandly. "For I am awesome."

James laughed. "Yeah, you're pretty awesome."

"And sexy," Raziel continued, a sly note in his voice.

"And really fucking modest," James teased.

"Compared to some of my brothers, I really am." Raziel laughed softly. "However, you think I'm sexy, do you not?"

James felt his cheeks grow hot and knew he was blushing. "Uh, yeah."

"Thank you." Raziel was silent for a moment. "You are also attractive."

"Thanks." James shook his head, amused. "You're not used to dealing one-on-one with humans, are you?"

"What gave me away?"

"Just a hunch." James shot Raziel a quick look.

"Don't mistake me." Raziel's voice was serious. "I spend a lot of time with humans, but they are ... deferential. It's rare that I am out among people who don't know what I am and don't speak to me formally. Frankly, it annoys me. I don't need to be worshiped or venerated. I am not my father. I have a job to do and I do it well, but obeisance toward me is neither required nor appreciated." He shook his head and James, watching him out the corner of his eye, thought that he seemed more than a little frustrated.

"Here, however," Raziel's tone lightened considerably. "I am treated as an equal to you and that is refreshing. I like it a lot. It means I can do my job without humans bowing and scraping to me, and I feel more like myself. Just Raziel. Not Raziel, Holy Archangel of Secrets and Mysteries, He Who Stands Beside the Throne of God."

"That's your full title?" James wrinkled his nose. "It's a bloody mouthful."

"It is and I much prefer Raziel. Or Raz. It's my name and I've been hearing it forever, so I do recognize it, more or less."

James chuckled. "I'll bear that in mind, then, and not call you the Grand Poobah of Mysteries or something."

"I appreciate that," Raziel nodded. "Because Poobah sounds ridiculous."

Laughing, James drove onward, back in the direction of Ngapa and the ruins on the outskirts of town.

~~*

They trudged through the sand together. James shielding his eyes with one hand as the wind blew, sending up clouds of yellow grit. The treeless plain of the Nullarbor made walking annoying since the wind that blew in from the sea met no resistance and the sand was always moving and shifting.

Raziel seemed to be unaffected, but James felt that little would affect Raziel. The hike to the ruins of what had once been an old telegraph station was never easy, given the nature of the ever-changing sands, but today it seemed as if the wind was conspiring against them to make the hike even more unpleasant than usual.

As they crested a dune and looked down on the shallow hollow containing the ruined buildings, James felt a strange tug on his mind and heard a sound similar to white noise, followed by the welter of voices that had previously filled his head prior to his headache. Tensing immediately and steeling himself for the pain that he expected, James was therefore surprised when none came. Instead, the babble of voices evened out and he could pick out individual words and phrases, but nothing that made any sense to him.

"James?" Raziel's touch on his elbow made him jump, and James let out a startled noise. "Sorry." Raziel looked contrite. "I did not mean to surprise you."

"No, it's okay. I can hear them, that ... weird sound, like radio static. Where I can hear words, but they're mingled with white noise." James rubbed his face. "It doesn't hurt," he hastily added, "but it feels uncomfortable."

Raziel nodded, his hand still on James's arm. "I see. This is a good sign. Are you getting anything of Adramelech himself or simply his underlings?"

James frowned, concentrating and realizing that he was beginning to sweat. Reaching out with his mind was an alien concept for him, and it was extremely difficult. He closed his eyes and found it a little easier, but there was nothing other than the sounds of voices and white noise. With a sigh, he relaxed and opened his eyes, shaking his head at Raziel. "Nothing specific."

"Never mind." Raziel smiled encouragingly. "This is a good beginning."

"I don't think he's here right now." James frowned in confusion. "I don't know what makes me think that, it's just ... just the impression I get from what little I could understand."

Raziel's expression became calculating. "Indeed? Well, well." He snapped his right hand and suddenly he held a sword, the blade shimmering with a nimbus of bronze light.

James gaped. "Okay, now that's something you don't see every day."

"James." Raziel turned to face him, resting his left hand on James's shoulder. "I want you to listen very carefully and do exactly what I say. There may be fighting. Don't get involved, no matter how much you want to. I know what I'm doing and it's best for both of us if you keep out of it. There may also be a point where I shall tell you to close your eyes and keep them closed. Do not argue with me. Trust me when I say that if you open them before I say it's safe to do so, you will forever lose your sight."

James gulped, nodding. "Eyes closed until you say otherwise. Got it."

"And no rushing to my aid in a fight," Raziel repeated.

"Okay."

"Okay." Raziel lightly squeezed James's shoulder and let go. "Shall we?" He gestured toward the ruins with his sword.

"Yeah." James wasn't about to say that the situation had suddenly taken a very surreal, terrifying turn. Instead, he concentrated on walking forward instead of following his increasing desire to run away.

The largest ruin had been the main office of the telegraph station and wasn't full of sand, although small piles of it filled the corners, while the wind whistled through the remnants of corridors and rooms. It was a large building that James had never really examined before, never appreciating the construction of something that had lasted so well with nothing between it and the sea, other than wind and sand. In the back of his mind, he could hear the now almost-constant chatter of voices that contained high, shrill notes and harsh, scratchy tones, like nails running down a chalkboard. He was overwhelmingly relieved that Raziel had made sure that the sounds wouldn't debilitate him, as James had no doubt that he'd be a writhing mass of pain on the ground otherwise.

Slowly, they made their way through the skeleton of the structure until they reached the last room—a room that had, much to James's surprise, a door. He exchanged a long look with Raziel that spoke volumes: a ruined shell of a building with a mysterious door suggested that whatever lay behind it was what Raziel sought.

"On three," Raziel whispered, his voice so soft that James had to strain to hear it. "One … two … three."

As Raziel shoved the door open and stepped into the room, James followed him. He was entirely unprepared for the sight that lay before him, but clearly Raziel was not. Raziel's expression was forbidding and his sword shone with a light that hurt James's eyes, the bronze nimbus seeming to increase in intensity. There were four people in the room, three men and a woman, and they took one look at Raziel before screaming in terror, surprise and rage.

"Hello, everyone," Raziel greeted them urbanely. "How are you all this fine day? I see you have something of mine and I'd really like it back. So you can either do this the easy way or the hard way. The choice is yours."

The four looked at each other before changing in front of James's horrified eyes. Their faces grew elongated, skull bones becoming narrow and almost visible through skin that resembled rice paper. Jagged teeth were exposed as they grinned nastily at Raziel, their eyes turning a solid, glistening black and deep red, flame-like scars appearing on their cheeks and foreheads. Their hands, held out in defiance, were tipped with long, yellowed, pointed nails, the fingers longer than a human's and narrower.

"Raziel," growled the female-shaped creature. "How did you find us, you feathery freak?"

Raziel grinned nastily. "That would be telling." Implacably, he continued, "My book. Give it to me."

"And what if we don't?" she sneered at him.

"Then your death will be very unpleasant and my dear fallen brother will be ever so fucking pissed off." The last three words came out as a growl that made James shiver. Something that held the promise of unspeakable violence should *not* sound that sexy.

"Adramelech isn't scared of you," the female countered, her body language and tone of voice holding little more than bluster and bravado.

"Oh, but he should be," Raziel laughed scornfully. "Even if he isn't, he is extremely scared of Uriel, who, if I am not mistaken—and I rarely am—is only one shout away."

The mention of Uriel gave the demons pause. They exchanged a long look and the female turned back to Raziel, defiantly raising her chin as she looked down her nose at him.

"Do your worst, Archangel. You're not a warrior, like Michael, Gabriel, or Uriel. We aren't afraid of you."

"More fool you, then." Raziel said with a shrug, and before the demons could reply, he was moving.

James watched in fascination, despite the terror of the situation, as Raziel moved with a rapid grace between the four demons. They lashed at him with their nails, snarling as he swung his sword, the blade cutting into their bodies and making them howl with anger and pain. James began to perceive that it wasn't just the keen edge of the sword that caused them pain, but the bronze light that surrounded it like a glow of power. He suddenly realized that was exactly what it was. The bronze light he saw flicker in Raziel's eyes, surrounding his wings, and now his sword, was the color of Raziel's power.

There were agonized screams as Raziel cut down two of the demons, the other two falling back, one tightly clutching a cloth-covered book. His face grim as death itself, Raziel advanced. "My book," he stated. "Give it to me."

"We'll tell you where Adramelech is!" cried the female demon.

"You will, yes, but you'll also give me my book." Raziel leveled his sword-point at her throat. "Now."

"Curse you!" the demon yelled, and then she and her companion unfurled dull grey, leathery wings and tried to fly to safety. The demons were clearly not going to give up the book if they could help it.

Raziel growled and lunged, his sword swinging in a wide arc. It sliced through bone and sinew as he slashed at their legs, distracting the two demons from their attempted escape. Howling, they crashed to the sandy ground, the male demon still clutching the book as the female started chanting in a language that sounded full of all the hate and misery in the world. James clapped his hands over his ears in a futile effort to keep the words out, but his ability meant that he could hear her chanting in his head.

"Close your eyes," Raziel barked over his shoulder. "*Now!*"

James obeyed.

Later, Rita and Tommy would tell him they'd seen a beam of bright white light shoot towards the sky, and then disappear in a sudden swell of storm clouds and a thunderous downpour of rain. Rain in the middle of the Nullarbor Plain was rare enough, but rain like this was unprecedented. The residents of Ngapa scrambled indoors, staring out the windows as the rain came down in torrents, hitting the tin roofs like a rapid staccato of drum beats. The midday sunlight vanished behind thick clouds that scudded overhead, rain pounding relentlessly against the ground and the buildings.

That, however, would be later. At present, James struggled to keep rain out of his face as he resolutely kept his eyes closed. The rain was cold and oddly comforting, washing away the sweat and the sand and the stench of fear, and the other odors that James hadn't noticed until they were gone: blood and death, pungent herbs and candle wax.

"You can open your eyes again," Raziel said after what felt like forever, his voice gentle in James's ear and his hand warm and reassuring on James' arm.

Cautiously, James did so, blinking against the torrent of rain as he looked around the room. That it was unroofed was only a detail; the rain was washing away everything that the room had once held, cleansing it entirely.

"You did this? The rain?"

"I did this," Raziel confirmed, his hand sliding up to James's shoulder. The sword was gone and his hair was plastered to his head, but his eyes were bright above his grin. Tucked beneath his arm was a cloth-wrapped book.

"You got your book back," James noted.

"I did," Raziel chuckled. "Are you all right?"

"Yeah, I'm fine. I'm going to have new fuel for my nightmares forever, but I'm fine." James straightened, pushing his sodden hair back from his face and leaning against the ruined wall. He took a deep breath to steady himself and willed his heart to stop pounding. "Do we have to stay here?"

"No." Raziel gently steered him outside and toward the side of the road where the van was parked. "We may return to Ngapa. You require rest and I must speak with my brothers."

"This isn't over yet, is it." It wasn't a question.

"I'm afraid not," Raziel sighed. "Adramelech is still out there and he will be ... annoyed."

"Understatement of the century, Raz, I'd put money on it," James chuckled wryly, moving on shaky legs to the driver's side of the van. "Let's get out of here."

~~*

The rain had gentled to a drizzle by the time they returned to Ngapa. James parked the van in front of his cabin rather than in the motel parking lot. He was soaked to the skin and starting to shiver, a combination of receding adrenaline and the cold. Beside him, Raziel was silent.

Together, they entered the cabin, James locking the door behind them. He took a deep breath as he leaned against the wall, toeing off wet boots and socks. "I think I'm going to have a shower," he said, looking quickly at Raziel.

Raziel nodded. "A good idea."

James bit his lip, wondering what to say next. Raziel smiled at him gently, an understanding expression.

"Go bathe," he said. "I will make use of the facilities after you, if that's all right."

"Yeah, that's fine." James tugged off his shirt and tossed it on the bed, before turning and walking into the bathroom, closing the door behind him.

Stripping off the last of his clothes and kicking them aside, James turned on the shower. Once the water was hot enough, he stepped beneath the spray and stood there, his palms pressed against the cream tile of the shower recess wall. He took several slow, deep breaths, gradually starting to relax. The experience at the ruined telegraph station seemed less and less real as the minutes ticked on, and James didn't want to think about it anymore than necessary. Demons, angels, magic—it was too much. James didn't want to dwell on the reality that there was more to the world than what he had thought only a few days before—before he had met Raziel.

Sighing, James stepped out of the shower, dried himself off and tugged on the loose pair of sweatpants that he kept hanging on the back of the door. Walking into the bedroom while toweling his hair, he looked at Raziel, who was carefully examining the book he'd taken from the demons.

"It's all there, then?" James asked, more for something to say than anything else.

"Yes." Raziel smiled and James smiled back—the smile was infectious, wide and bright, and full of an almost innocent delight. "Whole and complete, safe and sound. Thank you, James."

"What are you saying thank you for?"

"You helped." Raziel closed the book. "You didn't have to."

James shrugged. "It was the right thing to do."

Raziel stood up and moved to James, stopping bare inches away from him. "It was, but that would not motivate others to help."

James's breath caught as he gazed into those deep blue eyes. They were clear, no flicker of bronze light in the irises; just a deep, deep sea blue. "Raziel ... " James began, trailing off as he realized he had no idea what to say.

Raziel took a small step closer and James shivered as he felt the heat of Raziel's body radiating against his own. He wanted Raziel, wanted him a *lot*. He reached up to touch Raziel's cheek, fingers moving to trail through that dark hair. Raziel stepped even closer and James leaned in, kissing him.

Raziel's lips were soft and warm, and for a moment, the kiss was gentle. James groaned low in his throat and Raziel pressed firmly against him, deepening the kiss. Warm hands ran over his sides and back, fingers teasing along the line of his waistband. James groaned again a little louder, want and need burning through him. His own hands slid down Raziel's body to his hips and they both moaned as their cocks rubbed together through their clothing.

"You're wearing too much," James panted between hot, hungry kisses, tugging at Raziel's shirt with one hand.

"Agreed." Raziel paused only long enough to tug off his shirt, and then resumed kissing James.

James tugged him toward the bed and they fell onto the mattress in a tangle of limbs, laughing breathlessly as they kissed and touched. James wriggled out of his sweatpants, his hands going immediately to Raziel's jeans as Raziel's own hands roamed over James's body. With fingers made clumsy by desire, James finally got Raziel's jeans open and shoved down, causing Raziel to growl and roll on top of him. James groaned, too turned on and caught up in the maelstrom of passion to realize that Raziel had removed his jeans with his power, those talented hands still roaming over his body, fingers gently tweaking nipples and skating over lines of muscle down to his cock.

"Raz," James moaned, tangling a hand in Raziel's hair as he shifted, their cocks dragging together through the slick slide of sweat and precum. "Raz, please." He wrapped his legs around Raziel's hips, bucking up into him, the meaning unmistakable.

Raziel's groan only made James want him more. As Raziel groped blindly for lube and a condom, James rocked into his body, kissing his neck artlessly. His hands ran down Raziel's back, following the line of his spine, and when a moment later Raziel's slicked cock slowly pressed into him, James let out a soft cry, arching into the penetration. There was a moment as muscles protested, but Raziel's hand wrapped around James's cock and stroked in time with his slow thrusts. Pleasure shot through James and erased all other sensation and thought.

James rocked back onto Raziel's cock and forward into his hand, his groan turning into a hungry growl when Raziel's mouth captured his mouth in a hard kiss. The thrusts gradually sped up and James cried out, clenching down on Raziel's cock as he came. Raziel groaned, trembling, and after a few more thrusts, came as well, collapsing on top of James and panting.

James felt sated, relaxed and content. Their passion had done a lot to chase away the lingering darkness of the encounter in the ruins, and he felt almost back to normal, his mind free of shadows and fear. James's hands slowly caressed Raziel's back, eliciting a pleased hum from the almost dead weight on top of him. James chuckled and teased, "You weigh a ton."

"Thanks awfully," Raziel laughed, slowly pulling out of James's body and rolling to lie on the bed beside him. He discreetly used his power to get rid of the condom. "Are you okay?"

"Yeah. You?" James rolled onto his side, propping himself up with one hand as he gazed fondly at Raziel lying beside him.

"Yes." Raziel's smile was soft. He ran a hand down James's chest and James hummed happily at the caress.

"Will you get into trouble for this?" James bit his lower lip. "I mean ... sex with a human? Are you allowed to do that?"

"If I were not, I would not have done it," Raziel said in a reasonable voice. "No, James, it is as I said before: we are permitted our vices, few though they are. And, too, my kind are barren and unable to procreate. Not since the days of Eden, when a choir of angels called the Grigori were punished for raping the daughters of men and making them bare their half-breed children, the Nephilim. Father was resolute in those days and unforgiving. He changed us after Uriel released Noah's Flood, so that no children could be borne of our passions and suffer the pain of being not entirely human or angel.

"I have taken lovers over the millennia," Raziel mused quietly, "some human, some angel. God is love, James, all love. He does not discriminate and neither do we. As humans have learned and grown, so have angel-kind. I remember them fondly, as you remember your past lover, and I know that as long as I remember them, they will never truly be lost. That is the great gift of memory. That is the great gift of father's love. Love keeps us alive." He chuckled. "I believe I have just recited Gabriel's speech on the subject almost word for word."

James was silent for several moments, digesting that. "Okay," he said finally, "I just don't want to be the reason you got into trouble, that's all."

"You're not," Raziel hummed, a melodious sound.

"I like that idea," James continued, his voice very soft and reflective. "That as long as we remember the ones we lost and love their memories, they never really die. That's kind of poetic."

"I'll pass that onto Gabriel. He was the one who came up with it." Raziel ran a hand down James' back in a fond caress. "He is the most warlike of my brothers, but he also has a remarkable gift for explaining the love of God."

"We don't have to be anywhere, do we?" James asked. He wanted to delay going anywhere, just enjoy the calm, relaxed somnolence that filled him.

"No, why?" Raziel raised an eyebrow.

"Because," James laughed a little sheepishly, "with everything that happened today and really great sex, I need a nap."

Raziel laughed. "Sleep," he said. "I will watch."

"You'll be here?" James's eyes followed Raziel as he slid off the bed, standing up and stretching, the muscles in his chest rippling with the movement.

"Yes." Raziel leaned over and pressed a soft kiss to James's forehead. "Now sleep."

James smiled and shifted around to get comfortable, yawning and letting his mind drift, not focusing on anything other than post-coital contentment and the comfortable feeling of relaxed weariness. He was asleep in moments, not even hearing the sound of the shower as Raziel went to clean up.

~~*

"Hell of a downpour yesterday," Tommy remarked, as James and Raziel walked up to him. With Bert and Rita's help, he had been cleaning the sandy mud from the buildings and the concrete blue whale. Now he stepped away from the whale and ran a hand through his hair, his smile easy and relaxed.

"It was, yeah," James agreed. "Was there much damage?" He looked around the complex.

"Nah, just dirt," Tommy replied. "It all blew over during the night."

"And today we're back to normal weather, lots of heat." James shook his head, amused. "Do you guys need me for anything today?" He waved to Rita who was walking over to join them.

LJ LaBarthe

"Nope, you kids are free to do whatever you like. The blokes at the border radioed in to say that the road trains there are staying put until tomorrow, and the folk further west did the same, so we're all at a loose end." Rita smiled. "Just cleaning up Old Blue here, then we'll be done."

"Are you sure?" At their nods, James grinned. "Okay, well, I thought I'd show Raz the beach."

"You two enjoy yourselves," Rita winked, as she looked knowingly at them. James had a feeling that she knew more about him and Raziel than she was letting on. But he found that he wasn't terribly embarrassed—Rita's calm good nature and Tommy's geniality told James that his relationship with Raziel, however it could be described, was not a problem; rather, it was met with approval. "If you stop by the office, Marge will make sure you've got something to eat for lunch," Rita added with a warm smile.

James blushed a little, even as Raziel nodded politely. "Thanks, Rita."

"Welcome. Have fun, you two." She ruffled James's hair affectionately, patted Raziel's shoulder and turned back to work on the concrete whale.

James dragged Raziel towards the motel office before Raziel could say anything. "I won't be a minute," he said, as they reached the door.

"Very well." Raziel seemed amused as James went inside the office, but then Raziel often seemed amused. He supposed that to a creature like Raziel, humans *did* seem amusing.

Marge was at the reception desk, straightening up piles of paper and files, and she smiled at James as he walked up to her. "Hello, lad. Didn't get too wet yesterday?"

"A bit, but I think we managed to miss most of it." James quickly changed the subject. He didn't really want to talk about the rain or the visit to the ruined telegraph station. "Rita sent me over, she said something about lunch?"

Marge laughed at that. "Just a mo'." She ducked out of the office through the rear door and returned ten minutes later with a grocery bag. "Here." She held it out to him and James took it, raising an eyebrow in silent query. "It's just some sandwiches, a bottle of water, two bottles of beer." Marge made a shooing motion with one hand. "Take your friend and show him around."

"Okay." James moved around the reception desk and gave her a quick kiss on the cheek. "Thanks, Marge."

"Get along with you," Marge chuckled.

"I'm going, I'm going," James grinned, and then went outside to join Raziel.

"So we are going down to the beach?" Raziel was smoking when James rejoined him.

"Yeah. Marge gave us food, so we're good for the day." James started toward the path that led down to the beach. "Didn't you want to see the Great Australian Bight?"

"I did," Raziel concurred. "I think Adramelech might be in a cave or somewhere similar."

"I don't know of many caves in the cliffs, apart from that one I told you about," James said thoughtfully as they walked. "Not that that means anything, really. There're a lot of cliffs. Parts of the cave system that are underwater are popular with deep-sea divers and marine biologists, which would probably interest your secretive and mysterious self."

Raziel chuckled. "Some humans have referred to me as Doctor Science," he said. "Friends in the past, they seemed to think I was something of a science geek."

"There's nothing wrong with that," James grinned. "I kind of picked you for a Doctor Science type to be honest."

"Oh really?" Raziel looked surprised. "How?"

"Just the way you focus in on something, the way you ask me questions about things you don't know much about. It's ... it's almost scientific, like you want to study it, examine it, pull it apart and put it back together, see how it works. No specific 'it', I add," James finished.

Raziel considered that. "You are very astute, James. Very observant. And correct. I do like to study things I know little about. I tend to bore my brothers, sometimes, but I am what I was made to be. One of us has to be and I rather enjoy it."

They walked in companionable silence onto the pristine white sand of the beach, the rotting wooden jetty jutting out over the clear blue water of the sea. It was difficult to believe that there had been a ferocious storm the previous day. The sea was calm and seagulls flew overhead, calling raucously to each other. The cliffs of the Great Australian Bight loomed in the distance and the scent of brine was strong. James walked to one of the pylons of the jetty and sat down, leaning against it.

Raziel was staring hard at the cliffs, his expression serious. "Can you hear anything?" he asked without turning away from his rapt concentration of the landscape.

"No, not a thing." James pulled the bottle of water from the grocery bag and took a long drink.

"Hm." Raziel said nothing further for a long moment, looking at the cliffs for what seemed like an eternity. "Pity his minions told me nothing of worth regarding his location before I killed them. I did try to get them to reveal the information, but they refused. They were more stubborn than I had thought they would be." Raziel shook his head and sighed. "I think he is shielding himself."

"That seems like a safe bet," said a new voice from just behind James.

James jumped, swearing as he turned. He gaped at the newcomer as the man walked forward, looking at the cliffs and ignoring James entirely.

"Uriel," Raziel grinned broadly. "I was wondering if you would show up."

"And miss a chance to kill Adramelech? Hardly." The newcomer, the Archangel Uriel, wrinkled his nose. "Do we really need him?" he jerked a thumb in James's direction.

"Yes." Raziel's voice was determined. "We do. Uri, this is James. James, this is Uriel, one of my brothers."

"Pleasure," said Uriel in a voice that suggested that it was anything but. He flicked a quick, almost contemptuous glance at James. "You're the human who hears demons. Lucky you."

"Yeah, it's real awesome," James drawled. "I really love hearing Hell in my head; it's a fucking laugh a minute."

Uriel's eyebrows rose, and then he laughed. "I like you," he said. Clapping Raziel's shoulder with one hand, Uriel added, "The human's got spirit, Razzy."

"I rather like him," Raziel demurred. Uriel snorted.

"I can tell. Right then, as much as I love these little moments of small talk, I do have better things to do. Where's Adramelech?"

"Over there, I believe." Raziel pointed at the cliffs in the distance.

"You got your book back?"

"Yes."

"That's something." Uriel gazed at the cliffs, his brow furrowing. "Odd. That's sacred land. Adramelech's probably feeling really itchy. Good—I love making him uncomfortable."

"Sacred land?" Raziel raised an eyebrow.

Before Uriel could speak, James interjected. "The Aboriginal tribes have a lot of respect for the Bight. There are Dreamtime stories about it—creation myths."

"What he said." Uriel pulled a cigar from thin air and lit it with a snap of his fingers. Flame curled around his hand, bright orange and sending a nervous frisson down James's spine. "I'll take care of Adramelech. It's my fight, anyway—I was ordered to kill him and I'd do it regardless. I've wanted to gut him since the dawn of time. You, little brother—" He looked sternly at Raziel. "—will protect those humans in that town ... thing. With the giant, blue, concrete whale."

"I don't know what it's for," Raziel said. "Before you ask."

"I wasn't going to ask because I don't care." Uriel ruffled Raziel's hair in a gesture of fond affection. "Go back there and keep your human here safe. Protect the place and I'll go skin Adramelech and make myself a pair of shoes with what's left of him."

"Charming as ever." Raziel wrinkled his nose, but he moved to Uriel and hugged him, the older archangel hugging him back. "Thanks for coming, Uri."

"What are brothers for?" Uriel grinned. "You—" He looked at James. "—don't leave the border of your little home until Raziel says otherwise."

"Yes sir," James said without thinking. Uriel's voice was not one to be disobeyed.

"An obedient one; the world really is ending," Uriel said dryly, shaking his head. "I'm off. Take care of your end of things, Razzy."

Before Raziel or James could say anything further, he was gone with a rustling of feathers.

Raziel shrugged helplessly. "He is ... blunt."

"To say the least." James scrambled to his feet. "He doesn't like humans much, huh?"

"Not really," Raziel sighed. "Anyway, we should get back to where it's safe. Uri fighting Adramelech is going to be ... loud."

James raised an eyebrow, but Raziel refused to say anything more on the subject, instead leading the way back to Ngapa and stubbornly keeping his silence.

~~*

A few hours after their return, James's head began to throb. It wasn't bad at first, just a slight pressure in his temples, but it quickly blossomed into a headache the likes of which James had hoped never to experience again. The pain was incredible as he squeezed his eyes closed, clutching his head and panting harshly, sweat beading on his skin.

"James," Raziel's voice sounded very far away and James groaned, pain alternating between nausea and vertigo. "James, focus on me." He sounded anxious, James thought, as he feebly tried to concentrate. But before he could say or do anything, there was that familiar screeching in his head and he dropped to his knees, letting out a soft cry of agony.

"Well, well, well," purred a cultured, urbane voice. "How fascinating. I thought we had managed to capture all of the humans who had this talent, but it seems not."

"Adramelech." Raziel's voice was a low growl. "How did you get through my wards?"

James forced open one eye, taking in the form of the Archdemon Adramelech. He was handsome in a cruel, self-indulgent sort of way, his hands in the pockets of tailored slacks as he leaned against the wall. There seemed to be a nimbus of blood red light glowing around his form, and James gritted his teeth as he felt wave after wave of unspeakable evil and contempt roiling from him. Adramelech was the personification of the old adage that beauty was only skin deep. James was aware of the danger he and his friends in Ngapa were in—the archdemon would no doubt feel no need to refrain from maiming or killing them all to get what he wanted.

"Quite easily, actually," Adramelech said in answer to Raziel's question. His openly mocking smile held no warmth. "Dear old Dad left my kind and me a little loophole. Fallen angels, dear Raziel, means that we can—if we wish—tap into that part of our being." He waved his hand airily. "Of course, most of my brothers don't wish to do that, but it's a useful tool, like any other. Especially when I want something like your book. Give it to me." He took a slow step forward, exuding malice and indefatigable determination. James shivered as he watched Adramelech through narrowed eyes.

"No." Raziel moved slowly away from James, who sat heavily on the floor, trying to focus on something other than the pain burning through his skull. Raziel and Adramelech were the same height, he noticed absently, and nearly the same build. They were both slender and muscled, light on their feet, their shoulders unbowed. Raziel glowed with a soft bronze light, just as Adramelech glowed red, and James blinked against that shimmer, not wanting to look too closely at it. There was something about it that promised the unspeakable horrors that Adramelech would delight in inflicting. Adramelech was an archdemon who most likely enjoyed his hellish work.

"You will eventually. Probably sooner rather than later, or I will destroy this place and eviscerate your little human lover." Adramelech smirked as he spoke. "Honestly, Raziel, do you really believe you can defeat *me*? You're not a warrior; you're a scientist. You should have stayed in your laboratories and left the fighting to the grownups."

James took a deep breath and pushed himself to all fours, slowly crawling over to the table where Raziel's book lay. Each movement was a nightmare of almost unbearable agony, pain shooting through his entire being as he got closer to the book and the two elemental creatures near it. He was shaking almost violently as he reached up and grabbed the book from the table, crawling away as fast as he was able. Neither Raziel nor Adramelech seemed to have noticed.

"You'd be surprised what I can do," Raziel was saying. "Science and mysteries and secrets, yes, but you're an idiot if you think none of that involves warfare."

"Precisely why I want your book." Adramelech snapped his fingers and a long, wicked-looking dagger with a hooked end and serrated blade appeared in his hand. "It will unleash a war like ... nothing that has been ever seen before. And it will be glorious." The last words were spoken with an almost childlike wonder. "Rivers of blood, Raziel, mountains of bones and sinew and flesh, the screams of these parasitic humans will be a hymn to celebrate Hell's victory."

"Which is precisely why you won't get it. I'll destroy it first."

"Nonsense," Adramelech laughed. "You, Raziel, destroy the written word? It goes against your very nature."

There was a flutter of wings as Uriel appeared suddenly. "You are a total idiot."

James blinked, relieved. Uriel was clad in full armor, reminiscent of the fifteenth century knights he'd seen in books when studying history at school. The tiny room seemed to shrink in on itself with his additional presence and Raziel moved back to drop down to his knees beside James, his arms going around him.

"Are you all right?" Raziel asked in a concerned undertone.

James managed a weak grin. "No, but at least I can sort of function."

"We have to get you out," Raziel said grimly.

"No one is going anywhere," Adramelech interrupted. "I want the book and I will be not denied. Not even by you, Uriel."

"I was so hoping you'd say that." Uriel grinned wolfishly and swung his sword in a slow arc. It whistled through the air, the blade glowing the color of the setting sun.

Adramelech growled and moved, his dagger extending and crashing loudly with Uriel's sword. James closed his eyes and clutched the book as tight as possible. He could not close his ears, however, and even with Raziel holding him close, the battle was loud, both aurally and psychically. The clash of steel on steel was accompanied by grunts and swears, by flashes of power, both red and orange, as the Archangel Uriel and the Archdemon Adramelech fought each other with power as well as blade. Although Uriel had said he was looking forward to this fight, James could not imagine it. Uriel was doing what he was commanded to do and doing it with relish, to judge from the sounds of the combat, and James hoped desperately that Uriel would win.

There were other noises too: a choir of voices rose to the holiest of all things, mingled with the howls of rage,determination, and hate, filled with all of the loathing of the universe. The noises grew louder and louder until James was forced to turn away from Raziel and throw up. Raziel's touch on his skin was soothing, but it wasn't enough to stop the pain. As Raziel touched his face with warm, gentle fingers, James took a deep, shaking breath and passed out, still clutching the book tightly to his chest.

~~*

The first thing James became aware of was cool sheets beneath his skin. The second was the refreshing scent of eucalyptus and spearmint, and finally, the soft breeze from the overhead fan. His eyes blinked open and he let out a soft groan of relief, stretching languidly. Free of the pain in his head, he felt relaxed and comfortable, with no lingering sign of discomfort.

"Raz?" James called quietly, not sure who else might be in the room. He looked from side to side, blinking in the dimness; the curtains and blinds were closed, allowing no sunlight to leak into the room.

"You're awake." Raziel sat beside him on the bed, lightly touching his forehead. "Good."

"I'm awake," James agreed with a small smile. "How long was I out?"

"Two days." Raziel shook his head. "I had to get Rita to help. She has some truly remarkable bush remedies that I am looking forward to studying." He smiled. "Are you feeling all right?"

James nodded. "Yeah. What happened?"

"After you passed out, Uriel grabbed Adramelech and moved them both away from here. Teleportation, you would call it," he elaborated at James's confused expression. "I got you onto the bed, and then went to seek help. Rita and the nurse ... Maggie? Yes, Maggie. Anyway, they were of great assistance."

James frowned, pushing himself up into a sitting position. "They didn't see Uriel or that demon?"

Raziel shook his head. "No. I said you had experienced another headache—a very bad one. Which was true enough." He regarded James inscrutably for the longest moment, then much to James's astonishment, grabbed him in a tight hug. "Don't do that again," Raziel muttered, shaking James gently. "Promise me, James."

"Uh, okay." James awkwardly patted Raziel's back. "I won't save your amazing book of super magic from the big, bad demon bloke. No problem."

Raziel huffed an exasperated sigh and let James go. "I cannot deny that your assistance was invaluable, but you were in a great deal of danger."

"The book's okay, isn't it?" At Raziel's nod, James shrugged. "Then it was worth it."

Raziel was staring at him again as if he was something Raziel didn't quite understand, and James shifted a little beneath such scrutiny. He changed the subject. "So Adramelech is gone?"

"Yes, dead. Uriel killed him. The explosion was quite ... large."

"Where?" James gestured vaguely with one hand. "I mean, where did they fight?"

"Out there." Raziel nodded in the direction of the desert. "Where there are no humans to see or hear. No doubt the light from the explosion will be reported as some sort of strange aberration of the weather or a product of global warming or, perhaps, UFOs. I noticed that there seem to be quite a few humans who feel the urge to pin the unexplained on such phenomena."

James laughed, reaching over to take Raziel's hand in his own. "So long as that's all it is. I'm glad Adramelech is gone and you've got your book."

"I will need to take great precautions when hiding it," Raziel said slowly. "So I will be leaving soon. However ... " He took a deep breath, looking down at their hands. " ... I was thinking, perhaps, if you are of a mind, that maybe you would be like to spend time together once I have completed that task?"

"Are you saying you'll come back when the book's been hidden?"

"If you agree, yes." Raziel smiled and looked up. His cheeks were faintly pink and James found the light blush to be utterly endearing. "I have duties, you understand, so I cannot always be here, but in between those duties I would like very much to be with you. To get to know you better as a person and ... to pursue our ... relationship?"

"I hope more hot sex is included in that," James grinned.

"Oh yes, definitely," Raziel said eagerly, and the blush deepened.

James laughed, tugging Raziel down for another hug. "I'd like that a lot, Raz," he said. "I really would."

Raziel shifted and gazed into James's eyes for a moment, a smile tugging at the corners of his lips. "I am very glad to hear that, James."

James reached up to curl a hand around the back of Raziel's neck, pulling him close for a kiss.

A Better Ending

Isabella Carter

"In other news tonight, the police are on a trail of a murderer. His victim, a young woman, was found near a dumpster behind a popular restaurant early this morning. Sources claim that the level of brutality shown by the killer hasn't been seen in this area for decades. The police are investigating the circumstances of the young woman's death; however, they ask for our viewer's help in identifying this woman."

The knife slipped through Ainsley's hand as he stared in horror at the sketch that flashed up on the screen. He'd come home from classes half an hour ago and decided to make himself dinner. The news had been on only for background noise until they'd begun highlighting the brutality of the killing. He wasn't even sure why it had caught his interest, other than pity for the poor victim, but he had stopped in the process of slicing tomatoes to look up at the picture on the screen.

It showed a woman with short dark curls, her mouth a bit too wide for her face, her eyes just a little too big. She could have been anyone, but Ainsley recognized that face. He could only stare at the screen in shock as they flashed the picture up one more time, asking for anyone that knew her to please call the number.

"Eleanor?" There was no way that could be Eleanor. What were the chances of recognizing one of those quickly flashed pictures from the television? The police line was probably receiving a dozen crank calls and half a dozen worried relatives that thought the picture looked like a long lost relative. Ainsley's call would be another irritation they'd have to sort through and reject while the woman went unidentified.

It couldn't possibly be her, but still Ainsley's hand fumbled for the phone. He'd call them and they'd go confirm that Eleanor was fine, and he'd feel silly later. Eleanor would call him, and scold, "You're wound up way too tightly, Ainsley."

He'd call and this would all be a mistake.

~~*

"You knew her well?"

Eleanor was dead. Ainsley had kept telling himself that it would all be a mistake right up until the point they'd asked him to come in and confirm it was her. The sight of her body lying pale and lifeless on that slab, though, had made it impossible to deny. Eleanor was dead. Afterward, the detectives in charge of the case had sat him down to ask a few questions.

Ainsley squirmed in the hard plastic chair, before finally answering, "Not well, exactly. We were more than acquaintances, but not quite close enough to be called friends either." The older detective, Keller, if he recalled correctly, gestured that he should continue. "I helped her out a year or two ago—well, not her. Her brother."

Unsurprisingly, those few questions had morphed into what felt like an interrogation. They'd offered him a cup of coffee and he'd accepted, before remembering he didn't actually drink coffee. At least the cup gave him something to do with his hands. He was beginning to regret it now, however, as he wondered if it made him seem guilty.

"She has a brother?" Keller wrote that down in his little notebook. "Do you know where he is?"

"David?" Ainsley shrugged. "I believe he decided to go into the military. A second chance." He wrapped his hand around the cup of coffee and let the warmth seep in. The air conditioning had been cranked up high and he hadn't thought to grab a jacket when he'd left his apartment.

"Second chance?"

"He used to spend a lot of time with a bad crowd. Ended up in jail with someone else's stash. I volunteer time to check over prisoner's cases, see if something was missed that might make a difference. It's how I met Eleanor." Keller didn't look impressed and Ainsley sank further in his chair, before glancing over at Keller's partner. Since the man had entered the room ten minutes ago, he hadn't said a word, but Ainsley was startlingly aware of him. He'd looked up, just once, and their eyes met, Ainsley noticing the startling green of the detective's eyes. The detective had continued to stare at Ainsley, but it wasn't that that had made Ainsley uncomfortable at first—it was his expression, as though he could see everything inside of Ainsley, as if there was some part of him that the detective imagined would be delectable and not at all in a sexual way. Ainsley had looked away quickly, but he knew the detective was still watching him.

"Mr. Moore?" Ainsley turned to see Keller giving him a confused look. Obviously he had missed a question or two.

"I'm sorry. I'm having a hard time believing that she's dead." And it wasn't a lie, because Eleanor had been so vibrant that it was difficult to believe that she could possibly be gone. He could remember the first time he'd met her. Her attempt at a strong and hardened attitude hadn't hidden the desperate hope in her eyes that her brother would be coming home soon. Eleanor's sun had risen and set around David, and she hadn't known what to do with herself when he was put in prison. The day he was freed, Eleanor had burst into tears and thanked Ainsley until she'd run out of words. Ainsley wondered if they'd be able to track David down.

"You said the two of you weren't that close." Keller closed his notebook as he studied Ainsley.

"Some people make an impact on your life." Ainsley pulled himself up straight, lacing his fingers together on the cold metal table. "Who will take care of her? Until her brother can, I mean."

Keller frowned. "If he can't be located within enough time, then she'll be buried by the county."

That didn't sound right. "I'll take care of her." At Keller's raised eyebrow, Ainsley faltered a bit. "When you release her, I'll take care of her. She should be somewhere nice, for when her brother comes back."

"Seems like an awful lot to do for someone you weren't close to."

"Everyone deserves the dignity of a proper burial." Ainsley could feel the tension hanging in the room. He knew it was like pulling a scab off a wound, but he looked up again. The detective was still staring at him, although his expression had changed into mundane polite interest. He was handsome enough, dark wavy hair in need of a cut and well-built physique. His tie was hanging loosely on his neck, though, and Ainsley's hands twitched with the urge to fix it. However, he didn't want to make any sudden movements. He wondered if the detective thought he was guilty, if he was simply waiting for Keller to extract a confession, or perhaps intended to force one through the weight of his stare.

Ainsley quickly turned back to Keller, dismissing the thought from his head. It didn't matter what they thought;

there was no confession forthcoming. He wanted to make sure that Eleanor was treated properly. "Do you need anything else from me?"

Keller tapped his pen on the notepad. "Just a few more questions."

Ainsley could feel the weight of the younger detective's stare on him, but he was determined to keep staring forward. "That's fine."

Keller nodded and opened the notebook again. "Do you know of anyone who might have wanted to hurt her?"

"I didn't know her other friends, but she could be rather harsh sometimes."

"Harsh?"

"Outspoken. A bit rough. A man cut her off once, and she chased him down to his workplace and shouted at him about how he should be more careful, how he had almost killed us." Ainsley could remember that day clearly. He'd been terrified that the man would pull out a baseball bat or a gun. Later, Eleanor had explained that one had to rip into men like that; otherwise, they thought they could always get away with being ignorant and rude. "One day," Eleanor had ranted, "he's going to kill someone driving like that. Hopefully the next time he's about to do something like that, he'll remember the crazy woman who screamed at him." Ainsley hadn't had the heart to point out that the driver would likely chalk the encounter up as much more than a crazy woman screaming.

"So she was confrontational?"

"Well, I don't mean that. I mean … She believed in standing up for herself. There's nothing wrong with that," Ainsley added defensively. He hadn't meant to put her in a bad light. He had only wanted to explain a facet of her personality.

"You admired her." The low rumble sent shivers down his spine. Ainsley lifted startled eyes to meet the steady green gaze. Those were the first words the detective had spoken since Ainsley had arrived.

"I did. She was a good person. There's nothing wrong with speaking your mind; she was still a good person." Ainsley once again looked away first.

Keller gave his partner an odd expression, before asking, "Would you happen to know the name of any of her other friends or relatives?"

"I don't think she was close to the rest of her family." Ainsley's fingers played restlessly with the cuffs of his shirt. This whole situation was making him nervous and nervousness made it impossible for him to sit still. "And Eleanor was kind of a loner. She didn't have many friends—or at least, that was the impression I got." Keller paused, his pen hovering over the blank paper when Ainsley stopped speaking. Ainsley hurried to continue. "I mean, her world was all about her brother, and he was a handful. She just didn't have enough energy for other people."

"And yet the two of you were friends."

Why was he harping on that one statement? Did he think that Ainsley had killed her? Killing her might have been a bit difficult, considering he hadn't even seen her in about a month. "Yes."

Keller nodded and wrote something else in his little notebook, and Ainsley couldn't help staring at the notebook suspiciously as he wondered what exactly Keller had been writing. Making observations of his guilt? Drawing bunny rabbits? Ainsley refused to be intimidated by a stupid memo pad. *Or maybe*, the sane part of his brain kicked in, *he's writing down what you're saying since you came forward about Eleanor.*

"Thank you for your time," Keller was saying as Ainsley tuned back in. "You'll be notified when the morgue releases her."

Was that it? After all the questioning, the sudden end seemed almost anticlimactic. Not that he'd wanted to be dragged away in irons. "Oh. If you need anything else, I'm happy to help," Ainsley offered tentatively, and Keller nodded again, clearly dismissing him. Well, okay. Ainsley stood and carefully pushed the chair in before grabbing his jacket. As he turned to leave, he felt a hand wrap around his upper arm. When he looked up, he found himself staring up into green eyes.

"I'll walk you to your car." The statement let no room for argument. Ainsley didn't want to be alone with the detective, much less alone in a darkened parking lot. It seemed less like that he was ready to eat Ainsley, but he still continued to stare and Ainsley didn't know what to do in this situation. If it had been anywhere else, he would have assumed that the guy was hitting on him. Very few had persisted the way Morgan seemed to, in meeting his gaze … but something about the detective terrified Ainsley. Unfortunately, Ainsley had never been especially good at saying 'no'.

"Okay," he responded weakly, praying that this wouldn't be the last in a long line of questionable decisions.

The hand slid down to his back, gently encouraging Ainsley to continue his exit. "Morgan?" Warning was clear in Keller's tone, although Ainsley couldn't fathom about what Keller might be warning Morgan. Maybe he knew Morgan was going to take him out back and kill him? If so, Ainsley sincerely hoped he'd put a stop to it.

"I'll be back," Morgan responded, and gave Ainsley a light nudge when he might have stopped. Morgan's hand fell to the side once Ainsley started moving and silence fell between them.

Desperate to end it, Ainsley began talking. "You'll catch him right? The person that did this to her? I mean, she was a good person. She took care of her brother." Aware of Morgan at his side, their hands nearly brushing as they walked, did something funny to Ainsley's gut. "And she took care of me, too, since I don't really know anyone here." Shit. He shouldn't have said that. Now Morgan knew that if he killed Ainsley, no one would realize he was missing for a long time.

"We'll find him."

"Is that something you say to people to make them feel better?" They'd stepped outside by then, and with the evening had come a cool breeze.

"I don't make promises I don't mean." Ainsley looked up at him. "I promise you Ainsley. We'll catch him." Ainsley wanted to believe him when he made statements like that.

"It's just that this is the only thing I can do for her." The thought made him frown and his gaze shift downward toward the gravel. This was all he could do for her, other than lay her to rest. It was funny—he'd known Eleanor for two years and had never been sure whether he could call her friend. For a moment, he hated the insecurities that had kept him from letting their friendship grow. Ainsley had liked her when he first met her; she'd been funny and determined to help David. When he was released, she'd cried. Now she was dead. Maybe the part Ainsley was having the hardest time wrapping his head around was that she was really gone. He'd known her and now she was gone. There were so many lost opportunities.

Morgan didn't respond right away, but when he did it was to say, "I'm not especially good at this. I'm sorry."

"At what?"

"I don't know what to say."

Ainsley paused. "Sometimes listening is enough." When he looked up, Morgan's gaze was elsewhere. His eyes scanned the parking lot. Ainsley was still a little afraid of him—he hadn't gotten that hungry expression out of his mind—but Morgan had walked out here with him to offer a bit of comfort. "Morgan." Morgan looked down at him, and Ainsley gave him a small smile. "Thank you."

Morgan seemed stunned by his smile. Slowly, as if outside of his control, Morgan's lips quirked upward into a halfhearted copy of Ainsley's. "What for?"

They'd reached Ainsley's car, but rather than answering Morgan's question, Ainsley asked one of his own. "Do you think he's hunting tonight? Eleanor's killer."

He expected that Morgan would lie, like one of those small white lies designed to make him feel better. "Probably."

"But you'll stop him."

"I promised, didn't I?"

"Promises aren't guarantees."

"Mine are."

Oddly enough, Ainsley found himself wanting to believe him. He pulled his keys from his pocket and unlocked his door. "I'm holding you to it, then." He climbed into his car and started it. Morgan stepped back, but continued to watch as he put the car in reverse. Ainsley allowed himself one last look through the rearview mirror. He'd probably never see Morgan again, after all, and he wasn't sure he wanted to, but Morgan was still nice to look at, and in the end, his kindness had made Ainsley rethink his initial impression. The truth was that Ainsley wasn't quite able to help himself.

His eyes widened as he took Morgan in, standing beside the car next to where Ainsley had been parked. He was still handsome … and he was glowing. Ainsley's foot slammed on the brake as he blinked rapidly. When he checked again, Morgan seemed perfectly normal. It had just been his imagination, combined with the fact that Morgan had been standing in front of the lit station.

Weird.

~~*

By the time Ainsley walked into his apartment, he had managed to convince himself that the glowing had been a trick of the light, a product of his overactive imagination. Looking around his apartment was strange, however; he'd left his dinner—*still uneaten*, his stomach reminded him—

lying unmade on the counter and the television was off, but his school bag lay across the couch where he'd dropped it after class. A couple of hours ago, he hadn't even known Eleanor was dead. Weird to come back to his apartment and see that things were the same—the world hadn't ended, the earth hadn't stopped turning. People died and life went on.

What a depressing thought.

Ainsley walked to the couch first, grabbing his bag and sorting through the books, taking out the ones he needed to get his work and studying done the next day. He debated turning on the television, but memories of the news broadcast made him set the remote back on the stand. He went through the fixings he had set out for dinner earlier, throwing away what couldn't be eaten after being left out and pulling enough together to make himself a sandwich. As he settled himself in the quiet living room, Ainsley debated trying to call David—but he didn't know what to say, and he was sure the police had people trained in that sort of thing. It sucked feeling so useless.

Ainsley finished his sandwich off as fast as he could and made his way to the bedroom. He took out his contacts and changed his clothes, before settling on the bed. Morgan had promised to catch the killer, but as much as Ainsley felt inspired to trust him, he knew he had to accept reality. Morgan and Keller would try their best, he was sure, but so many murders went unsolved every year. Ainsley knew the statistics. The chances were high that they'd never find her murderer. It wasn't likely to have been a random killing; Eleanor didn't hang around that sort of area. Somewhere, Eleanor's killer was wandering free, hunting his next victim, and the police were no closer to finding them than they had been when they'd found Eleanor. At least she had a name in their files now—and she'd have somewhere to rest.

Ainsley let out a small groan of pain as the questions circling in his mind coalesced into a headache. He shouldn't be thinking about all of this right now; what he should be dealing with were his revisions on the paper he had due in less than a week or studying for the test coming up at the end of that week. There wasn't anything further he could do to help the police; he had given them everything he knew about Eleanor. It was out of his hands—they'd either catch the killer or they wouldn't.

Ainsley couldn't afford to fall behind on his studies, not if he wanted to look at internships. But his eyes closed even as he chastised himself. The last thing he needed right now was to fall asleep. Although, maybe a short nap wouldn't hurt—a half hour of rest and Ainsley would be wide awake and ready to focus.

Before he knew it, he had already slipped under.

~~*

Ainsley awoke in front of a fast food restaurant, which was odd enough in itself, considering Ainsley hadn't visited a fast food restaurant since he was eight and his mother had decided that he was far too chubby for his age. He glanced down and immediately grimaced when he noticed all of the trash on the ground and a napkin attached to his shoes. His favorite shoes, too.

Grumbling, Ainsley lifted his foot, leaning his weight against the car beside him so he could pull off the napkin. Now that that had been attended, he could take a long look around the area. He sort of recognized it, although he couldn't recall from where. The whole area was fairly empty. Figuring that he probably wouldn't get any answers from standing around, Ainsley started toward the restaurant, the lights from the sign garish and nearly blinding in the darkness.

As he approached the building, squinting against the lights, Ainsley saw some movement from around the back.

From there, Ainsley was torn: continue toward the safety of the building or back toward the potentially dangerous alley? Well, to be honest, one of those ideas sounded terrible.

"But you want to know what's back there, don't you?"

The voice came from nowhere and Ainsley turned to check behind him. No one was there. Then where had the voice come from? It didn't sound like Ainsley's conscience. Still, it had a point: Ainsley did want to know what was back there, even if the whole idea seemed like a horror movie cliché.

As he walked toward the alley, the silence struck him as odd. His shoes weren't making a single sound upon the gravel street.

No sound of cars on the road or people talking, not even the sounds one would expect standing right next to a fast food place.

All he could hear were soft, pathetic sobs.

Fear hit him then, fast and sudden, making him want to fall to his knees. Something was wrong here, so very wrong, and Ainsley was right in the middle of it. He continued forward because he couldn't stop now, not when the voice was calling him closer, calling him to see what it had done, like a small child with a crayon drawing.

It was only when Ainsley rounded the corner that he could see that he'd been right to fear. Eleanor lay on the ground, blood caked in her short dark curls and on her shirt. For a moment, Ainsley almost believed the bloodstains were simply paint and this was some horrible game in poor taste. But then Eleanor let out a tiny whimper and shifted, and Ainsley's eyes were drawn to the shadowy man standing over her. He couldn't make out the details, only knew that the man was cutting into Eleanor's arm with a clinical look in his eyes. His nail drew down her arm and he lifted it, tongue darting out to taste the blood he'd drawn.

Ainsley was sure he was going to be sick.

"Sweet, sweet Eleanor," the monster sang. His voice was sweet, nigh on angelic, even when he leaned in to whisper in Eleanor's ear, loud enough for Ainsley to hear. "I will make a feast of you."

His other hand, which had until then simply been resting on Eleanor's chest, began to push down. Eleanor screamed until her voice went hoarse. Why wasn't anyone coming to stop this? Why wasn't Ainsley stopping this?

At that realization, Ainsley moved forward to help Eleanor. The monster looked up then and Ainsley found himself pinned in place by a pair of intense green eyes. "Please wait your turn," he requested politely. Ainsley's mouth half-opened to tell him to stop hurting her, but the monster had gone back to crooning to Eleanor. "Sweet, sweet Eleanor, you don't understand. You're but a pawn in the bigger picture." Eleanor's screams had stopped, her eyes staring glassily upward.

He leaned down and rubbed his cheek against Eleanor's own. "Don't worry, dear, you're going somewhere better. No more corruption or pain for you. I envy you." His arm twisted and he giggled like a child, the sound high and sweet. "Well, maybe just a bit more pain."

He continued what he was doing, rooting around in her chest. Ainsley began praying that he would be sick, that he could fall unconscious so he wouldn't have to witness this anymore. But that would be the easy way out. That would leave Eleanor, who had always only tried to do the right thing, alone and suffering. So he sat and made himself watch, willed Eleanor to know that she wasn't alone.

"I guess it's time for this all to end, then." He pulled his hand back, and just when Ainsley thought he might be finished, he noticed something dark and red clutched in the killer's hand.

Eleanor's heart. He'd pulled out Eleanor's heart. "The heart is so many things," the man started, and it took Ainsley a few moments to realize that the man was talking to him. "Humans attribute so much symbolic meaning to the heart. If you're a good person, then your heart is good. If you're evil, then it's dark and corrupted. The truth is, I've tried a variety of hearts, and when you really get down to it, all hearts are the same at the core."

Ainsley couldn't suppress the disgusted shiver. "So you pull them out to check them?"

"No, silly boy," the man laughed. "I pull them out to eat them. Check them? Really; how ridiculous."

Whatever blood that was left in Ainsley's face quickly drained. "You eat them?"

The man smiled. "You see, if you have the ability, you can find something extra in them, get a special little boost." He looked greedily down at the heart in his hand. Ainsley could only watch in horror as the man began to devour it. He knew then that this had to be a nightmare. "Not a nightmare—or more than a nightmare. I can never untangle them in my head."

"I—you—what are you?" Ainsley hated the stammer in his voice. If this thing was going to kill him, then he didn't want to die stumbling over his words like a coward.

"I won't kill you, not yet."

Ainsley wasn't sure why he asked, why his lips even formed the words. "Not yet?"

"No, that would ruin the fun." The monster gracefully got to his feet. "Souls like yours, they must be cherished. In comparison to you, she's just an appetizer." He kicked at Eleanor's body to emphasize to whom he was referring. "But you, I'll take my time with you. Not until the time is right, though; it won't be complete until he sees it, too. Until he suffers."

"Complete?" Then the other part of his statement occurred to Ainsley. "Who suffers?"

"The other player of our game of course. Consider this your formal invitation."

"Who are you?"

"You may call me Le Monstre."

The Monster. "I don't want to take part in this game."

He giggled again. "It's adorable that you think you have a choice." Ainsley could hear his voice fading. "Spend your last days wisely, Ainsley Moore."

Ainsley woke suddenly, nearly tripping over his rug in his rush to get to the bathroom and revisit his light dinner. It was just a dream, he tried to tell himself. Just a dream and that monster couldn't hurt him because he wasn't real.

But even as his brain tried to rationalize it, his heart knew the truth: the monster was real and he was coming.

~~*

The next day found Ainsley picking dejectedly at the sandwich in front of him. He hadn't been able to sleep after the nightmare, his thoughts plagued with memories of the monster as he'd killed and devoured Eleanor. No matter how much he'd tried, Ainsley hadn't been able to erase the picture of that thing smiling at him. He'd tried studying, but his thoughts wouldn't focus. The terms and facts had all blended together until Ainsley had thrown the book in frustration. Afterward, he'd picked up the book and checked to make sure he hadn't done any damage to it. Feeling appropriately ashamed as he returned it to his bag, Ainsley decided to go out. Fresh air would clear his thoughts.

At first, he'd walked around his neighborhood under the illusion of window shopping, but when he'd started seeing monsters out of the corner of his eye, he'd dropped the pretense and wandered into a nearby restaurant. He hadn't been hungry at breakfast, memories of his visit with the toilet still hanging around in his mind, but his stomach made it clear that he needed to try to eat.

Ainsley tried ordering a sandwich, figuring it would be light enough to not disrupt his stomach, but it had obviously been a poor decision. The more he stared at it, the more he was reminded of the sandwich from the night before—and that brought back to mind the nightmare. He was morbidly curious if the nightmare had any grounds in reality ... if Eleanor had truly been torn open. When he'd identified her, he had only seen her face. Of course, she probably hadn't been torn apart like that; it was just a dream after all. Likely it was a bit of subconscious guilt over the fact that Ainsley felt like there was nothing he could do to help her. Identifying her body didn't seem enough, even when he logically knew that there was nothing more that he could have done.

With a sigh, Ainsley pushed the food away and stared up at the ceiling. It had been a dream, nothing more, and he needed to get over it. There were worse things than having a bad dream. Eleanor would be shaking her head at him if she could see him right now, calling him pathetic. She'd never had much patience for self-pity.

"Hey."

Ainsley's eyes flew open, a shriek of surprise nearly leaving his lips before a warm hand clamped down over his mouth to muffle it. He struggled a bit before he managed to identify Morgan through his panic. Morgan was looking increasingly nervous, glancing around the restaurant as if checking to see if anyone was staring. When Ainsley calmed, Morgan tentatively lifted his hand.

"What the hell?" Ainsley hissed, the minute he could.

"You would have disrupted the other diners. Rather high strung this morning." Morgan rationalized. "May I sit?"

Ainsley took a few more calming breaths until he thought he could answer Morgan without cursing. "Sure."

Morgan sat across from him and laced his hands on the table. He didn't say anything, leaving Ainsley to study him. He hadn't gotten any less handsome in the light of day, although there was a bandage on his chin where, Ainsley could only assume, he'd nicked himself shaving. His tie was yet again tied incorrectly, and his hair was rumpled and brushing against his collar. He was a mess. An attractive mess, but a mess nonetheless.

Ainsley's hands twitched to fix the tie, but he told himself that it wasn't his job, instead wrapping his fingers around his mug of tea to give them something to do. "So, what are you doing here?" Sometimes the most direct questions were best.

Morgan looked at him like he hadn't really noticed him before. "You wear glasses."

Ainsley's hands went to his glasses automatically, pushing them up his nose. He'd been forced to put them on that morning, since his eyes were too puffy from his lack of sleep. "I do."

He wasn't sure with what he expected Morgan to reply, but it certainly wasn't, "They're cute."

The statement made Ainsley flush. "Thank you."

After a moment, Morgan asked, "Are you alright?" Ainsley's eyes widened, for how could Morgan possibly know about his dream last night? "You seemed unhappy last night and I was worried."

Oh. "It's still a bit of a shock. Weird to think that someone I know is dead; that I'll never see her again."

"It'll take some time. I know it sounds cliché, but it'll take time. I don't want to interrupt your meal for too long."

He made to stand up and Ainsley reached out to stop him before he even realized he wanted to do so. Morgan looked baffled and Ainsley blushed. "You can stay. You're not interrupting me."

Morgan stared long enough that Ainsley thought perhaps he should take back his invitation, but then Morgan gave him another of those half-smiles and sat. He glanced down at the plate with which Ainsley was playing. "Shouldn't you eat?"

Ainsley glanced down as well. "I guess, but I'm not really hungry."

Morgan frowned. "Well, I don't really care for turkey, but I guess I can make the sacrifice this once."

"What? Hey!" He snatched the plate from where Morgan had been about to steal it. "Leave my food alone!"

"You're being wasteful. I'm trying to help. It's a sacrifice on my part, really." He stole a chip and ate it happily.

"I paid for it. It's my food to waste." Morgan started eyeing his plate, as if he might steal another chip, and Ainsley placed his arms in front of it to protect it, then took a large, purposeful bite of his sandwich. When he glared up at Morgan defiantly, Morgan seemed pleased with himself. Ainsley blushed and swallowed his food before asking again, "So why are you here, anyway?"

"Like I said, I was worried about you." Morgan leaned back in his seat and started rooting through his pocket. "There are any variety of killers, muggers, and just plain bad people running around."

"Do you follow every witness to make sure they aren't attacked?" Ainsley asked doubtfully. Now that he'd taken a bite of his food without getting sick, he felt ravenous. He polished off the last bite of the first half of his sandwich and looked up to see Morgan staring at him. For a moment, there was something almost inhuman in his eyes. Unlike the day before, however, it didn't terrify Ainsley; instead, it made him feel warm and protected. Something brushed against his arm and he checked, expecting to see feathers.

"You're special, Ainsley." Ainsley's eyes darted up, staying around the vicinity of his nose. It was a nice nose and Ainsley wasn't sure he could meet Morgan's eyes again. There were too many strange things going on.

"Special?"

"I'm not the only one who realizes it." Actually, Ainsley was pretty sure he was. He'd been in this city for three years and apart from Eleanor, there was not a single person he'd gotten closer to than merely acquaintances and he hadn't considered himself particularly close to Eleanor.

"Just because he's out there doesn't mean that he's coming for me."

Spend your last days wisely, Ainsley Moore.

Ainsley shivered and reached for his tea, but a warm hand wrapped around his and stopped him. Suddenly, he wasn't so cold anymore, but certainly startled by the goose bumps that the touch sent across his skin. Ainsley tried to calm his racing heart, tried to remember how much Morgan had terrified him when he first saw him ... but all he could think of was whether or not Morgan felt this thing between them, too.

"Doesn't mean you should take the risk."

Ainsley pulled his hand away quickly and started on the second half of his sandwich. "Let's change the subject." He could feel Morgan studying him. When he heard the flick of a lighter, his eyes shot up, noticing that Morgan was lighting a cigarette. "You can't do that here." When Morgan looked confused, Ainsley pointed at the sign above them. It was one of the main reasons he liked this restaurant: no risk of cigarettes ruining the enjoyment of his meal.

Morgan followed his finger up to the sign and shrugged as he took a drag of his cigarette. Ainsley watched in horrified fascination. There was absolutely nothing sexy about cigarettes—they were miniature cancer sticks—but why oh why couldn't he look away as Morgan blew out a plume of smoke? Ainsley was so focused on his lips that when Morgan asked, "Are you okay?" he started, his sandwich nearly slipping between his fingers.

"I'm fine." To prove that was true, Ainsley took another bite of his food.

Morgan looked like he might disagree, but let Ainsley be. "So why are you studying to become a lawyer?"

"Huh?" It took Ainsley a few seconds to change tracks, even though he'd been the one to request the change in subject. In his defense, Morgan continued smoking his cigarette, which Ainsley thought should be banned for a variety of reasons, health concerns being only one among them.

"Why did you want to become a lawyer? I mean, I assume that it's what you wanted, not something you were forced into."

"No, no one forced me into it." Ainsley nearly answered him, and then stopped to think. This was a good opportunity. "But I'm not telling you anything unless we make a deal."

"Deal?" Morgan tapped the ash off the cigarette onto the edge of Ainsley's plate.

"A deal." Ainsley glanced down at his plate and was reassured to realize that it was still completely disgusting to him. At least Morgan wasn't driving him out of his mind along with everything else. "I'll tell you if you'll tell me something." Maybe then, at least, he could find something out about Morgan, some detail that might put Ainsley more at ease. He couldn't help feeling nervous around Morgan. At first, it had been because Morgan completely terrified him. Ainsley didn't do well with bigger men in general, and a few times the night before, he'd found himself comparing Morgan's expression to the monster in his dreams. They'd been so similar, the look of avarice on their faces.

Morgan hadn't worn that expression since and Ainsley could feel a bit more of his guard slipping every time Morgan seemed concerned for his sake. Common sense told him it was a stupid move—he was letting his attraction to Morgan make rationalizations for things when he knew he should be walking away.

"An exchange of secrets?" Morgan went to tap his cigarette on Ainsley's plate again and Ainsley moved it away.

"That's disgusting, and that's right, an exchange of secrets."

Morgan rolled his eyes. "I've gotten rid of every other vice. Let me at least have this one." Ainsley gave him a bland look and Morgan sighed heavily. "Fine. Let me have the plate." He stubbed out the cigarette. "Happy?"

"Getting there. Why do you do it anyway?"

"It's an excellent stress reliever."

"It's an addiction."

"So is hand sanitizer." Morgan pointed to the little bottle Ainsley had used before he started eating his lunch. "But I'm not judging you."

"That's not an addiction! It's a compulsion. Besides, do you know how many germs lie in the average public space?" Ainsley felt sick thinking about it.

Morgan looked unimpressed. "I feel compulsed to smoke cigarettes."

"That's not a word!" Ainsley cleared his throat and picked up his napkin to make sure he hadn't left any crumbs. "Anyway, I have a question—"

"You already asked your question."

"What?" Ainsley thought back. "That doesn't count!"

"I answered it. Anyway, why are you studying to become lawyer?"

Ainsley frowned, and then sighed. "I'm good at it, and it's a practical skill. I have a business degree, but I wanted to do something so that I could help other people. I wanted to contribute, I guess."

"You could run a business and still give back."

"I guess." Ainsley thought about it. "It wasn't what I wanted to do." No one had really asked before. His parents certainly hadn't cared; it seemed like they were willing to pay any amount so long as it kept him from getting underfoot. They paid for the apartment, for his schooling; so honestly, he had nothing about which to complain. Soon enough, Ainsley would be able to support himself. "Why did you become a detective?"

"I like to detect things."

Ainsley glared at Morgan. "What kind of answer is that?"

"You said I had to answer; you didn't say you needed a full and detailed one." Morgan looked so pleased with himself that Ainsley wanted to kick him. "Maybe you should have specified— Ow!" Ainsley didn't quite manage to resist the urge.

"You're cheating, Morgan."

Morgan sighed again. "I'm correcting my karmic balance."

"You did something wrong in a past life?"

"I wronged a lot of people in my past life. It would take lifetimes to start making up for it. Now seemed like a good time to start," Morgan replied unhappily. Ainsley worried that he'd ruined the mood with his line of conversation, but when he opened his mouth to apologize, Morgan asked, "How did you meet Eleanor?"

Ainsley was stunned by the question. "I told you and Detective Keller earlier. I met her when I helped her brother out. She demanded my presence at dinner the first day I met her and proceeded to drill into my head that her brother was innocent." Ainsley shrugged. "After I got her brother out of trouble, she'd call up every once in a while and decide that I needed to get out."

"But you didn't consider her a friend?"

"I ... " Ainsley trailed off and looked down at his tepid tea. "I guess I've always been very careful about how I define my friends." It was because friends mattered, and it hurt even more to be used by them in the end.

"You shouldn't be so guarded, Ainsley." Ainsley looked up into Morgan's eyes. "You'll miss out on all the important things."

What were the important things? Hadn't they always been good grades, a good job, and complete independence? Looking at Morgan, he couldn't help but worry that he was missing an important thing right now. "Do you want to do this again sometime?"

"What?" Morgan asked, completely confused, and Ainsley was struck by the fear that maybe this had all been one-sided from the beginning.

"Get food or something. Maybe do something afterward. A date." He was absolutely sure he hadn't been reading Morgan wrong.

Morgan's face went through a variety of expressions and Ainsley was glad to note that disgust wasn't one of them. Ainsley sighed and his mouth tilted downward in a frown; that wasn't much better to be honest. He knew he was going to be rejected before Morgan even said the words. There was no way to brace against that kind of rejection, though. "Ainsley, I can't. Even if there wasn't the issue of you being involved in our case, I just … can't."

"Right. Of course. I'm sorry. I don't know why I asked." Ainsley knew he was babbling, but he didn't know how to stop. He wasn't sure he wanted to stop. If he did, Morgan might realize how mortified he was, and he wanted to leave this situation with his dignity intact. "I'm just going to go to the restroom." Shit. Why had he said that? "Thanks for … umm … checking in." Ainsley stood, intending to beat a quick retreat. He knew that it only made it more obvious how much Morgan's rejection had bothered him, but he needed to be out of there.

Before he could make his escape, however, Morgan grabbed his arm to stop him. "Ainsley." Ainsley stopped and looked down at him. To his surprise, it wasn't pity in his eyes or apology; it was regret, and that left Ainsley feeling even more confused. "Be careful." He reached into his pocket and pulled out a pen and a card, writing on it before handing it to Ainsley. "If you're ever in trouble, call me."

The card was going into the trash the minute he got home, but for the time being, Ainsley nodded and tucked it into his pocket before making his escape to the restroom. When he returned, the mess had been cleaned off of the table and Morgan was gone. It was for the best—Ainsley kept repeating that to himself as he walked out into the sunlight.

An hour of chatting with Morgan and the lingering traces of his nightmare had almost been completely wiped from Ainsley's mind. Now if only he had a distraction to wipe Morgan from his mind. Trying to change the train of his increasingly depressing thoughts, Ainsley joined the group of people waiting to cross the street.

It started with an odd feeling that he was being watched. The feeling brought back to mind Ainsley's nightmare and he glanced around, not even trying to be subtle about seeking out the monster from his dream. Nothing seemed out of place, though; no glowing eyes met his, no lips dripping red with blood. He was imagining it. By even thinking on it in passing, he'd brought the paranoia with him in full force.

Not comforted by the thought, but needing to believe it, Ainsley turned to watch the light. That was when the whispers began. Nothing distinct, but he could swear they were coming from around him. Yet again, when he glanced around, he saw nothing. ... but the whole feeling creeped him out enough to make him take a step away from the crowd, just in case. Now if anyone was hiding in there, he'd be able to see him if he made a move. Maybe he wasn't hiding in the crowd? Maybe it was a passerby? Maybe it was the guy standing beside his vehicle, sorting through his change for quarters to feed the meter? Paranoia made his skin crawl, and the longer the light took to change to walk, the antsier Ainsley began to feel.

This wasn't like him at all. Usually, he could deal with these strange situations. Usually, a dream wouldn't affect him this much. He wasn't a child, after all, still searching for the monster under his bed. Yet, Ainsley couldn't help but be terrified that this monster was real.

The light finally changed and the crowd surged forward. Keeping a tight grip on his messenger bag, Ainsley started forward to join them. When his body didn't move, he didn't panic right away. His first thoughts were confusion. Why wasn't he moving? Why did the world seem to be swimming in front of his eyes? Was he about to pass out? When the walk light changed to a blinking hand, he started to panic. He couldn't move, couldn't say anything, as though he'd lost control completely. He could barely keep a hold of his thoughts.

"Shh. Calm down." The sweet melodic voice was the only thing he could hear. He couldn't even make out the usual white noise that should have been buzzing around the street corner. "Don't panic. Everything will be okay." How could everything possibly be okay? He couldn't move. He couldn't think. "This might hurt a little, but it will all be over soon."

That was when his body started to move forward on its own. Noise came back in a rush. A woman screamed. A man yelled out a warning. A car horn blared. Brakes squealed. He felt pain as the car hit him. It seemed unfair that he'd still feel pain when everything else was fuzzy, but he felt his ankle twist and send pain shooting up his leg. He felt himself fall, and his head crack hard against the pavement.

Just before he lost consciousness completely, Ainsley saw a glowing figure standing above him. It was the wings that caught his attention, large and wide as they reached toward the heavens, a blinding white, save for the gray creeping in at the edges. Ainsley could swear he saw it move further through the wings as he slipped into unconsciousness.

~~*

Noel Morgan realized that he was an idiot. He hadn't needed to see the rejection in Ainsley's eyes to recognize that fact. He couldn't let himself get involved with Ainsley, though, not with Cian on the loose, not with everything at stake. He'd done that once; trusted that everything would be okay and tried to focus on his own happiness. It had ended in death—and it was still ending in death.

Morgan had a feeling that until he stopped him, Cian would keep killing. Either Heaven couldn't stop him or they simply didn't care. The sad thing was that either answer sounded equally likely.

When Morgan had first seen Ainsley, he'd nearly been blinded by the brightness of his soul. It had been clear to even someone as tainted as Morgan that Ainsley was destined for Heaven. For a moment, Morgan had wanted nothing more than to reach out and grab him. Ainsley wouldn't have put up much of a fight; it had been clear from looking at him in his prissy, button-up shirt and tie that Ainsley wasn't much of a fighter. Still, even if Ainsley had hidden the strength of ten men, he wouldn't have been much of a challenge.

It had been such a clear image in his mind, Ainsley's startled look fading into shock, then finally into the slack of death. For that moment, to devoure Ainsley's essence, his soul, he could close his eyes and remember Heaven. The light. The warmth. For that one moment, he'd be able to experience perfection. Of course, the problem was that Ainsley wouldn't be enough: once Morgan had seen Heaven again, he wouldn't be able to stop until he could see it again and again.

He would have become the same as Cian.

Morgan had been willing to risk it, though, until Ainsley had turned to look at him with those wide, startled blue eyes. The hunger had faded then, replaced by a feeling of warmth. It hadn't faded as Ainsley had continued to shoot him nervous glances while Keller questioned him. It had only gotten stronger when Morgan had touched Ainsley.

He'd tracked Ainsley down in the restaurant to make sure he was safe, but in his heart, he knew the truth: Morgan had tracked Ainsley down because he couldn't stay away. He hadn't expected Ainsley to invite him to stay, hadn't expected the conversation that had followed. They'd talked about his addiction to cigarettes, but the truth was he was afraid that he was quickly becoming addicted to Ainsley himself.

The feeling hadn't faded when he'd talked to Ainsley, as he'd hoped it would. Morgan had hoped that a few minutes of talking would convince him that Ainsley was a dud, an idiot or a ditz with a pretty face. Then Ainsley had spoken so passionately about his urge to help people. He'd blushed when Morgan had called his glasses cute, and Morgan knew he was in trouble. It didn't help that Ainsley himself was gorgeous, even with his preppy, button-up shirts, making him look so prim and proper that Morgan was afraid to do so much as slump in his presence.

Not that it would be much of a worry anymore; he'd seen the hurt in Ainsley's eyes when he'd said 'no' and he'd almost explained everything then—Cian. Trionne. Everything.

He'd almost convinced himself Ainsley would understand.

Yet, bright soul and kind heart excluded, Ainsley was only human, and Morgan wasn't sure he could stop himself so easily next time. What if he really did attack Ainsley? That was why he had to stay away, even though that task was appearing harder and harder.

So Morgan had gone back to work and tried to explain away his long lunch break. He had a feeling Keller was onto him, but kind enough to let him pretend to keep his secrets. When his cell phone rang loudly while they reviewed their notes, however, Keller looked startled— Morgan rarely got phone calls. In fact, there were only two people that had his cell phone number and one of them was currently in the room.

Trying to quash the surge of hope, Morgan excused himself and stepped out into the hallway. "Hello?"

"Detective Morgan?" The voice on the other end didn't sound familiar at all, which confused Morgan even more.

"Yes?"

"This is Sacred Mercy Hospital. We're calling to inform you that Ainsley Moore has been involved in an accident—"

For a second, it felt as though Morgan's heart stopped. "Is he okay?"

"He's conscious." He heard the nurse's irritated tone, and took that to mean he was conscious and causing trouble.

"I'm on my way." Life was conspiring against his good intentions.

The nurse told him which floor to come and he hung up. When he stepped back into the room, Keller seemed especially interested in the phone call. "I have to go to the hospital."

"Emergency?"

"Sort of." Morgan grabbed his coat and noticed that Keller was looking at him expectantly. "Someone I know was in an accident."

"Oh." Morgan understood that to mean that Keller hadn't been aware Morgan even knew anyone, much less well enough to be summoned to the hospital. He felt compelled to explain. "It's Ainsley Moore."

"You gave him your cell phone number?"

"I was ... " *worried that the serial killer might get him.* No, that wouldn't be good to say; then Keller would wonder why Morgan felt certain that the killer was after Ainsley and it would open a whole can of worms Morgan knew he didn't want to handle. "I wanted to."

Keller sighed and waved his hand. "Whatever. Just go before Adams gets back and demands your time again." Morgan thought of the lead detective and cringed, taking

Keller's advice and leaving while he had the chance to escape.

The drive to the hospital was filled with worry. What had Ainsley done to land him in the hospital? Morgan had left him an hour ago. Had Cian found him in that time? At least that was one question to which Morgan could be sure he had the answer—if Cian had found Ainsley, then Ainsley likely wouldn't be in the hospital. Cian wouldn't take chances that they'd be caught; he'd kill Ainsley before anyone had a chance to realize anything.

Morgan made it to the hospital and, once he'd made his way upstairs, he saw that the nurse he'd spoken to was the one manning the desk. She looked so relieved to see him that Morgan began recalculating his estimate of exactly how much trouble Ainsley was causing.

"Hopefully you can calm him down a bit."

That wasn't very likely; not after how he'd rejected Ainsley the last time they'd spoken. In fact, it was more likely that he'd make things worse. He didn't say anything to her, however, not wanting to say anything that would result in her maybe not allowing Morgan to see him. He wanted to make sure he was all right. Afterward, if Ainsley wanted him gone, Morgan would leave without argument. "What happened to him?"

"He walked in front of a moving car."

That didn't sound like Ainsley at all. To be honest, Ainsley seemed more the type to check both ways three times before he even took a step into the street. "Was the car speeding?"

"I'll let him explain the story to you." With that, she turned a corner and stopped in front of a door. The nurse gestured that Morgan should precede her and he walked in to see Ainsley staring grouchily down at his foot. He looked up when the door opened, and whatever diatribe had been about to leave his lips stopped when he saw Morgan. Morgan took advantage of his surprised silence to study the damage. His left leg poked from under the blanket, the foot in a brace. There was a web of bruises already beginning to color further up on the leg, which disappeared under the thin blanket. His arms were scraped up and his eyes looked a bit glassy. Morgan was overcome by the sudden desire to have his powers back; not for himself, but for Ainsley, who was moving his head with care as he looked between his leg and Morgan.

Ainsley's expression of shock faded into a frown. "What are you doing here?"

"You asked the paramedic to call him," the nurse reminded him as she bustled in and started to check on him.

"I don't remember that."

"I assure you, you did," the nurse informed him dryly.

"Are you okay?" Morgan walked tentatively closer. Ainsley did seem to be calmer now, staring between the nurse and Morgan.

"Do I look okay?" This wasn't a side of Ainsley that Morgan had imagined existed. With his hair rumpled and that perpetual frown on his face, he looked adorable. The petulance only made Morgan want to tell him that everything would be okay. He shoved his hands into his pockets before he could give in to the urge. Ainsley's eyes suddenly lit up. "Are you here to take me home?"

"You're not going anywhere, Mr. Moore. You're staying here for twenty-four hours. Doctor's orders."

"I'm fine," Ainsley argued, as he tried to wiggle away from her. He stopped and winced. The nurse gave him a doubtful look. "I can't stay here." The nurse sighed and looked at Morgan as if to say, *"See what we've been dealing with?"*

Morgan walked up to Ainsley's right side, hand coming down to lie gently on his shoulder. "Ainsley, if the doctor says you need to stay here to feel one hundred percent—"

Ainsley looked up then and Morgan could see that it wasn't stubbornness making him argue; it was fear. What was Ainsley afraid of? "I can't stay here," Ainsley insisted, his voice low and urgent.

"What happened, Ainsley?"

Morgan could see Ainsley debating whether or not to tell the truth. Finally, he settled on, "I wasn't paying attention; I walked out into the street after the light had changed." But he couldn't meet Morgan's eyes as he told the obvious lie. "Morgan, I can't stay here."

"I'll stay here with you, then."

"Why would you do that?" Ainsley looked honestly baffled and the look, coupled with his rumpled hair and the overly-large hospital gown, made Morgan's resolve melt. "You don't even like me."

"Ainsley, not liking you was never the problem," Morgan sighed, as he searched around for a chair. Once he'd located one, he pulled it over and sat down. The nurse said nothing, but he could sense her relief when Ainsley seemed to relax slightly. "Besides, knowing I was the person you called when you were in trouble means something."

"Don't read too much into it. You're the only person I know here. Other than ... " He didn't finish the sentence, but they both knew he meant Eleanor.

"Well, that makes it even more necessary, doesn't it?"

"You can't protect me all night."

"I'll figure it out." Morgan trailed his hand down until he could lace his fingers through Ainsley's own. "Have you called your parents?" As soon as the words were out of his mouth, Morgan wondered if he might have stepped into the wrong thing. Ainsley hadn't mentioned them before, but when he and Keller had done a background check, he'd found that they were both alive and well.

Ainsley's grip tightened, then released. "Please don't bother them." Why would knowing that their child had been injured have been a bother? Ainsley must have sensed his confusion, because he added, "I'll call them later. I don't want to worry them."

Morgan resolved to ask later and changed the subject. "I promise you, I won't let anything happen to you."

"Why are you even here?" Ainsley asked again. The nurse finished her check-up and left the room after giving a nod to Morgan. "Not even an hour ago, you were telling me you weren't interested."

"I lied. I thought some distance would be best."

"Why?"

"There are so many things going on Ainsley, some beyond your comprehension. I thought I was keeping you safe."

"I feel safe when you're around," Ainsley stated sleepily. "But sometimes you scare me."

That startled Morgan. "I scare you?"

"A little." Ainsley mumbled, then his brow furrowed, "My head doesn't hurt as much anymore."

Morgan looked down at their intertwined hands. He'd thought that the warmth was from Ainsley's hand, but maybe his prayer had been heard, after all. "Go to sleep, Ainsley."

"You'll be there."

"I will."

"We should talk," Ainsley yawned.

"We will. Go to sleep." Even as he drifted to sleep, Ainsley kept a tight grip on his hand. For the first time in a while, Morgan felt needed.

Each time Ainsley woke during the night, Morgan was there, still holding his hand. The one time he wasn't, Ainsley was startled fully awake, feeling the panic and fear coming back, even after the nurse assured him that Morgan had just stepped away to the bathroom. By the time Morgan actually returned, Ainsley had nearly worked himself into a full blown panic attack and he wasn't sure why.

All Ainsley knew was that he was afraid, and when Morgan had promised to keep watch, Ainsley had believed his promise that nothing would happen. Waking up after the accident had been the single most terrifying moment of the whole experience; he could still feel lingering traces from the thing that had taken control of his body. It hadn't felt like the monster from his nightmare, but that was all the more frightening—it had felt like a presence he could trust, a presence he should trust. And lately, Ainsley was starting to feel that he couldn't trust anyone but Morgan.

That was dangerous, relying on a person like that. Ainsley had learned that lesson multiple times.

Still, he felt better when Morgan was in the room. It wasn't just the rampant paranoia that eased, but also the pain in his head and ankle. When he shifted, nothing ached. Ainsley couldn't explain it; he just knew that everything felt better when Morgan was there—which was why he couldn't let himself linger over the fact that Morgan wouldn't be there long.

Soon enough, Morgan would remember that he didn't actually feel anything for Ainsley, and then Ainsley would be alone again. Unlike last time, where he'd convinced himself that he and Eleanor had time to develop a friendship, he didn't intend to let this chance slip by without enjoying the time he had with Morgan, even if Morgan was only sticking around out of pity.

When Morgan returned to the room, Ainsley's heart calmed. Morgan took his seat beside Ainsley's bed, his hand sliding automatically into Ainsley's as he spoke in hushed tones to the nurse. Ainsley didn't bother to listen; he didn't need to hear the words to know the nurse was telling Morgan about his little freak out. Then Morgan settled back beside him and the nurse left, and everything was right in Ainsley's world. Well, almost—he was still wide awake.

"Morgan, I can't fall asleep."

"Close your eyes," Morgan suggested, and Ainsley might have hit him if he hadn't been afraid of hurting something in the process.

"I tried that. It's not working." Ainsley squirmed on the bed until he found a more comfortable position, staring forlornly at the blanket until Morgan sighed and moved it to cover his injured foot. "Talk to me."

"About what?"

"I don't know. Anything."

"Why do you think that you'd be bothering your parents by calling them?"

Ainsley frowned. "Anything else."

"Ainsley."

"Fine," Ainsley huffed. "It's not some depressing story of neglect and abuse. I was a late baby."

"Why would that—"

"My parents had already had my brother—he'd grown up and given them grandchildren." Ainsley continued over the interruption. "Then during their thirtieth anniversary, they conceived me. And I mean, they weren't neglectful or anything; it's just that they didn't know how to deal with a young child. When I started taking care of myself, they seemed so relieved. So I try to bother them as little as possible."

"So you think they wouldn't care?"

"What good would it do to tell them? It's not like they could come and help. I'll tell them before the bill comes." Morgan's pitying expression was depressing him. "Let's talk about something else."

Morgan sighed again. "Once upon a time—"

"I don't want a bedtime story! I'm not a child."

"Then stop acting like one." Chagrined, Ainsley didn't comment further when Morgan restarted his story. "Once upon a time, there lived an angel who believed he could change the world. He came down from Heaven at the request of a friend. His friend had gotten into terrible trouble and hoped that the angel might help him find his way back to Heaven. The angel couldn't refuse; he thought that he could guide his friend back to the light. Only, when he saw his friend again, he realized how corrupt the former angel had become.

"Rather than seek guidance, the angel arrogantly believed that he could still help his friend on his own. Finally, he realized the difficulty of his task and decided to pray for guidance. However, before he could bow in front of the altar, he saw her: a beautiful woman that seemed so bright to him, it was as if she carried Heaven itself inside of her. In the time he had been on Earth, the angel had come to miss Heaven and found himself drawn to her. She was kind, listening to his problems and offering advice. Before he knew it, he had fallen in love with her.

"And that was where the problems began: the woman had already promised herself to another. She was married to the priest of the church and she would not break her vow to her husband. The angel's heart was heavy, but he promised her he understood. He went to his friend and cried out his sorrows.

"Seeking to help him, the friend chose to take matters into his own hands. Late one night, he killed her husband, believing that if he were gone, the woman might return to the angel. When the priest died, the friend devoured his soul, not wanting it to escape to Heaven and give tale of his misdeeds. And that was the beginning of the end, for it is impossible to taste a pure soul and not desire more. When the angel learned of what his friend had done, he was horrified. He prayed then for guidance, but the friend was already tainted for his part in the incident.

"Unable to return to Heaven, the angel became a broken man. Surprisingly, the woman he'd fallen in love with did not blame him for her husband's death. She could never be with him, not the way he wanted, but she promised to stay with him and help him seek forgiveness. He fell in love with her all over again. He grew so distracted with her that he forgot his tainted friend. In his loneliness, his friend tuned more and more to the darkness. Since the angel would no longer help him, he turned to devouring souls. If he could not return to Heaven, at least he would see it in every good soul he devoured.

"It soon reached the point where the former angel could no longer ignore his friend's actions. He sought him out, confronted him; but without the power of Heaven flowing through him, he could not face his friend, who had grown stronger with each soul he had taken. His friend left him alive, but unconscious. When he awakened, the angel returned to the church, intending to pray for the power to stop his friend. The woman he'd fallen in love with, had come to call a friend, was now a steward of the church. He hoped that seeing her would lift his spirits as well, give him hope that he could stop his friend.

"When he returned to the church, however, all he found was death—those who had sought shelter at the church had been slaughtered. In the sanctuary, he found the woman he'd loved butchered, his friend standing above her. When he demanded to know why, his friend informed him that he'd grown tired of the angel's inattention, that he'd grown tired of being ignored and forgotten by Heaven. He'd decided to make his way to Heaven on his own. He offered to let the angel join him, reminding him of their friendship and of the promise the angel had given him.

"The angel refused—he had no desire to see himself tainted that way. His friend asked if the angel wished him dead, and although the angel wanted so badly to take his vengeance, his friend once again defeated him. He made a promise that they would meet again and left the angel there to bury the bodies."

"What did he do then?" Ainsley asked.

"He mourned them and his friend stopped for a time. The angel fooled himself into believing it was over. He could not find his friend, but neither did he hear tell of the monstrosities his friend was capable of committing. Then it all began once more. The angel had grown comfortable in his belief that his friend had subsided to quietly seek redemption. It took him a year to hear of it and five more to track down his friend at last. In that time, he sought guidance. He prayed desperately to Heaven that they might stop his friend at last ... but his prayers fell on deaf ears.

"So he left to confront his friend himself, willing to doom himself to whatever fate Heaven had decided. He nearly died that day, but his friend realized the damage he had done and stopped, leaving once again. The angel realized that he could not allow himself to become comfortable again and sought him out."

"He stopped him in the end, right?" When Morgan didn't answer right away, Ainsley demanded once again, "That can't be the end."

"I don't know," Morgan shrugged. "I haven't come up with the ending."

That wasn't satisfactory. "The angel found him and stopped him! That's how it's supposed to end. You don't end with him failing. He finds his friend, he stops him, and then he goes back to tell the victims that he's gotten the bastard!" Morgan looked bowled over by his outburst and Ainsley sat back, embarrassed. "Sorry. It's your story."

"It's fine." Morgan didn't add anything else, until, "Stopping him, huh?"

"It's not the end, but it's a good start." Ainsley shrugged. "I just think you should find a better ending for your story."

"I'll do that." Morgan squeezed Ainsley's hand, and Ainsley smiled.

"And when you do, tell it to me again; I'd like to hear it." Ainsley closed his eyes.

As he started to slip away, he thought he heard Morgan mumble, "I can't see a place where this doesn't end in blood. Please give me the strength to make the right decision."

Ainsley spent the next day worrying. Morgan had had to leave in the morning, citing work. He'd yawned hugely, and then leaned down to kiss Ainsley on the forehead before he left. His intimate gesture hadn't even seemed to occur to him until he'd started to walk away. Then he'd paused and Ainsley had almost been able to hear the loud buzz of thoughts in his head as he tried to sort them out. After a second, Morgan had seemed to deal with them and moved on, but then he paused again near the door and turned back to Ainsley.

"I'll figure things out." He'd left before Ainsley could question whether he meant the case or this thing between them. Either way, he hoped Morgan figured them out soon.

The day crawled by slowly. Ainsley worried about his classes, worried about his foot, worried about this thing with Morgan—worried about the fact that he was almost certainly losing his mind. By the time Morgan returned, the doctor still hadn't come by to let him know if he could go home, and Ainsley had worried himself into a near panic attack.

When Morgan walked through the door, Ainsley was grateful to see him, if for no other reason than the fact that it gave him something else to focus on. "Did you come to take me home?"

"I said I would." Morgan seemed to think that his word should be enough. He glanced around the room. "Hasn't the doctor been by yet?"

"I've been waiting for *hours*."

Morgan snorted at his dramatics. "I'll go check." He stepped out of the room.

Ainsley noted that Morgan hadn't stepped any closer to him than was required, a big difference from the man who'd held Ainsley's hand through the night and given him the quick kiss that morning. Obviously, he had come to give some answers, but Ainsley wasn't sure he wanted to hear them.

Morgan slipped back into the room a few minutes later. "She said the doctor should be along shortly."

"She said the same thing to me two hours ago," Ainsley groused.

Obviously the nurse had been more charmed by Morgan than she was by Ainsley, because the doctor showed up a few minutes later with nary an apology. He checked Ainsley, gave him some instructions for home care, and then released him with a bid to check twice when crossing the road. Ainsley tried not to wince at that last piece of advice.

After Ainsley changed, Morgan got him situated in his car. Once they'd gotten onto the road, Ainsley closed his eyes, hoping that this trip would pass quickly, so he could get back to his normally scheduled life. The past three days had been a trilogy of weird.

"Lee, what really happened?" At first Ainsley didn't respond, but after a moment's pause, he realized that Morgan was referring to him. A nickname? No one had ever given him a nickname before—he wasn't sure how he felt about it.

"What do you mean what really happened?" Then it occurred to him what Morgan meant. "I accidentally walked out in the road, that's all."

"You're lying."

Ainsley didn't have the energy to be offended at Morgan catching him in a lie. "You wouldn't believe the truth." Ainsley could barely believe it himself. The more he thought on it, the more he managed to convince himself that it was a concussion-created illusion. Giving voice to it might drag it into reality.

"Try me," Morgan challenged, and Ainsley finally gave into the temptation to do just that.

Without opening his eyes, he explained, "After I left the restaurant, I felt like something was watching me.

Then I lost control of my body." It sounded even more ridiculous outside of his head. When Morgan didn't respond, Ainsley opened one eye and peeked at him. Morgan didn't seem to be laughing or trying to scoot away to ensure that he wouldn't catch Ainsley's insanity. Rather, he seemed to be considering something, and for some reason, that thought scared Ainsley even more.

"Did you see anything out of the ordinary?"

"You mean the evil demon laughing his head off at my misery?" Morgan slowed down at a yellow light and gave Ainsley a look. "It's just my mind playing tricks on me. Otherwise, I wouldn't be seeing angels in the middle of the street." Morgan slammed on the brakes hard enough to send Ainsley pitching forward and nearly slamming his head into the windshield. "Morgan, you can't slam on your brakes like that!"

"Oh, sorry." When he looked up, Morgan was wearing a grim expression. "You saw an angel."

"Just my mind playing tricks, remember?"

"Right." Ainsley had the feeling Morgan was humoring him.

"I don't want to talk about it anymore." Thankfully, Morgan let the topic drop and they drove in uncomfortable silence for a few minutes more. Ainsley cleared his throat to try and end the trip on a more positive note. "Thank you for sitting with me last night." He wanted to add something else, but he really was grateful, no matter how irritated he was at Morgan. He had been honestly terrified the night before.

"I didn't mind at all. I ... " Morgan seemed to be searching for the right words. "With everything else going on right now—Eleanor's death, your accident—I'm not sure it's—"

Ainsley cut him off before he could finish. "Morgan, we're not dating. You don't have to break up with me."

"I'm not—"

"Don't worry. I'm not going to imprint myself on you. I just wanted to thank you." Ainsley didn't have time for this, not if Morgan was going keep wavering. He was lonely, not desperate, but the more he tried to tell himself it didn't matter, the more it did. Even when he turned to stare at the window, he was completely aware of Morgan glancing between him and the car in front of them.

When the car finally came to a stop in front of his apartment, Ainsley nearly cried with relief. "Thank you for the ride. I'm fine getting up there on my own." Before Ainsley could even finish his first sentence and realize that he was alone in the car, however, Morgan had gotten out and grabbed his crutches. He opened the door before Ainsley could gather his wits enough to do it himself. Ainsley got out of the car with a huff of irritation— irritation that only grew when he ran into Morgan's solid chest.

" I can open the fucking door myself, you know." Crap. He hadn't meant to let his anger get the best of him. If he'd kept his mouth shut until he'd gotten upstairs, he could have been home free. Now he was left to stare upward at Morgan's face and hope Morgan moved back far enough that he could breathe without every part of his body rubbing against the man who hadn't only rejected him once, but twice.

The first time had been humiliating, but the second was worse somehow; as if Ainsley was all the more foolish for thinking that it would work the second time. It would have been better if Morgan had been a complete asshole, but he'd held Ainsley's hand and told him a story to try and help him sleep. He'd been kind and sweet, which had made it ten times worse when he'd tried to explain to Ainsley that it wouldn't work. In Ainsley's experience, "It's not going to work" usually translated into "I've lost interest in you". Of course, if Morgan gave him half the chance, Ainsley would be well on his way to making a fool out of himself a third time.

When Morgan didn't move, Ainsley gave him a little shove. Of course he would be built. It was obvious that at this very moment, life only existed to make Ainsley look like a complete and utter idiot. "Please move."

"Are you done your tantrum?"

Ainsley wanted to knee him in the balls. It wouldn't be fighting fair, of course, but it would have been oh so satisfying to watch Morgan curl up on the ground and cry like a girl. He knew a lot of that was the bitterness talking, but sometimes the bitterness had some awfully good ideas.

Ainsley took a deep breath and repeated, "Please move."

Morgan offered the crutches and Ainsley managed to take them without snatching them from his hands. "You don't need to escort me upstairs. I'm perfectly fine on my own."

"Why are you acting like this all of a sudden?"

He couldn't be serious. Ainsley didn't bother to answer as he hobbled his way across the lot, tripping a few times on unstable pavement. By the time they made it to the elevator, Ainsley was ready to call it a day. His arms hurt, his side was hurting again. His foot hurt from accidentally putting weight on it. Ainsley slumped against the wall of the elevator and dreaded the next few steps to his apartment door. When the doors opened, Morgan took his crutches from him and picked him up without a word. While Ainsley was sputtering, he asked calmly, "Where are your keys, Lee?"

"I hate you. You are not carrying me across the threshold of my apartment like a fucking bride."

"If we keep standing around here, one of your neighbors is going to come out and see me carrying you like this."

That was an even worse threat. Ainsley squirmed around until he could free his messenger bag from his shoulder. Morgan picked it up to root through it, locating the keys and unlocking the apartment. After the door was shut and secured, Morgan deposited Ainsley onto the couch.

"Thank you," Ainsley managed through gritted teeth. "You can go now."

"No. Not yet." Oh God. How much longer did this humiliation have to continue? "What's wrong with you, Ainsley?"

"Are you serious?" When Morgan blinked in confusion, it was all Ainsley could do to not slam his head against something—except that that last thing he needed was to make his concussion worse. "You just told me you weren't interested in me. Again."

"But you said you were—"

"If you say 'okay with that', I will risk serious injury and kick you."

"Ainsley." Morgan dropped down to his knees so that they could look at each other face-to-face. "I can't even begin to try and explain all the reasons why this is a bad idea."

"Try." Ainsley was totally going to ignore the fact that Morgan had placed himself close enough to send Ainsley's imagination into overdrive.

"Maybe it's not even you and your issues; maybe it's me and mine."

"But you admit you think I have issues." Morgan looked at him pointedly. "A dislike of germs is not an issue. It's common sense."

"Regardless." Morgan brushed Ainsley's hair out of his face, his hand lingering. Ainsley could see where this was going, could see it so clearly, and yet he was hesitant to stop it. "This isn't a good idea. I have no clue about relationships, and you're just latching onto me because you're in danger."

"And you're making up excuses about your job." Ainsley leaned into the touch, willing to allow himself to be petted.

"Lee, I've done some things I don't deserve forgiveness for."

"Like what?"

Rather than answering his question, Morgan continued, "And I don't think I can stand falling in love again."

"It's not love, Morgan." Not yet. "Sometimes relationships aren't about dramatic declarations. Sometimes they're about finding someone you like being around. Someone that makes you feel safe."

"Do I make you feel safe?" Morgan sounded baffled by the thought.

"You kept your promise, didn't you? You stayed."

"Ainsley ..." Morgan took a deep breath. " ... I like you."

"Then stop running away."

"I don't deserve any of this."

Ainsley rolled his eyes. "Stop being dramatic, Morgan. There are some who would say that being with me isn't exactly a prize."

"Then they're the ones that don't understand." Morgan closed the distance between them and caught Ainsley's lips like a starving man. Ainsley opened his mouth to gasp and Morgan took full advantage, pressing closer until their upper bodies were pressed flush together. The hand that wasn't tilting his head had wrapped around him, holding him so close that breathing became a serious worry.

Ainsley pushed him away slightly so that he could get a gulp of air, before Morgan pulled him back, loosening his grip and letting his fingers splay against the small of Ainsley's back. As they kissed, his hand found its way under Ainsley's shirt to lie against his skin. The feel of skin on skin, Morgan's callused fingers, sent tremors up his spine. Morgan broke the kiss, although he didn't pull back entirely.

"You'd better not come back in the morning acting like you don't know how to handle this."

"Huh?" Morgan seemed dazed.

"I swear, if you give me another 'you don't understand how bad this is' speech, I'll hurt you."

Morgan made a noise of agreement and moved forward again, this time to lay a soft kiss against Ainsley's lips. One kiss turned into a flurry of kisses, each one growing more intense until Ainsley was moaning from pleasure. Morgan's fingers started to slip lower until they started to push below his waistband, but Ainsley gathered enough presence of mind to push him back. When Morgan stared at him blankly, Ainsley had a moment of pity for him. "I'm not that easy."

The trill of the phone interrupted whatever Morgan's response might have been, but he didn't rush to answer it. Instead, he lingered, hands moving upward to a safer zone as he leaned in once more to press one last lingering kiss. When the phone let out its third ring, he leaned back and pulled it to answer it. Ainsley fell against the couch as he tried to process everything that had happened. He was aware enough to register Morgan's grunts of agreement.

Ainsley opened his eyes and studied Morgan, blushing when he realized that Morgan had begun studying him as well with a hungry gaze that gave away the direction of his thoughts. "I'll be right there," he promised the person on the phone before hanging it up and sticking it back into its case. "I have to go."

"I know."

"I don't want to, though." Morgan leaned forward to give him yet another kiss that made it clear exactly where he preferred to be.

"I'll call you." It wasn't the first time Ainsley had heard those words, but for some reason, he believed Morgan when he said them. "We need to talk." Talking had gotten them into trouble in the first place, so Ainsley wasn't sure he liked that idea. Morgan laughed at his expression and kissed him again, as if he couldn't help himself, before pulling away and leaving.

Ainsley sighed and looked up at his ceiling, trying to will away his erection. It was going to be a long night.

~~*

Ainsley didn't often dream of churches. It was his first clue that something was wrong—his second was the feeling that he wasn't alone. He turned quickly to see the monster standing at the end of the aisle between the pews. Ainsley studied him in a way he hadn't had a chance to before. He was physically handsome, all blond hair and rippling muscles, but Ainsley had seen past those red-rimmed eyes; he knew the truth about the darkness that lived inside of him.

"Resting well?" the monster asked, and Ainsley could almost believe he was a normal civil person, if not for the aura of malice he exuded.

"I was." His brain screamed that this was just a dream—that there was no reason to be afraid of the monster when it couldn't touch him in the real world. "What are you?"

"'What' is such an unimportant question; perhaps 'who' would be more accurate. 'Where' would certainly get you past some confusion, but 'what' would just be giving you an answer you already know."

Ainsley felt like he was talking to the fucking Cheshire Cat. "Did you shove me into traffic today?" 'Shove' was such a saner way of saying it.

The monster looked baffled, then oddly enough, hurt. "Why would I do that? Getting hit by a car is painful."

"So is having your chest ripped open." Memories of what he'd watched this monster do to Eleanor made bile rise in his throat.

"That's art."

Ainsley had the distinct feeling that he was talking to someone who wasn't completely sane. "Why? Why Eleanor? Why are you coming after me?"

The monster seemed to stop and think. "Why," he finally repeated. "That's a good question. Why." He started down the aisle and Ainsley gave serious thought to backing up ... to running away. But he wasn't going to give the bastard the satisfaction and he had no intention of letting the monster see his back. So he stood, shaking but unmoving as the monster approached. Finally, when they stood toe-to-toe, Ainsley staring up into dark eyes, the monster answered. "Eleanor glowed so brightly, like a beacon lighting the way. When I devoured her soul, I saw perfection once again. In comparison to you, though, she was merely a nightlight." The monster's eyes flicked downward, and Ainsley shivered in revulsion and fear.

"Morgan is going to catch you. He'll stop you."

"You think?" The monster looked almost hopeful, before the hope faded into doubt. "He's promised before, and every time he's failed. What makes you think he'll succeed this time?" Ainsley didn't answer right away, and the monster continued, "Do you know where we are? Some tiny village in France, I forget the name, because the name isn't important. What happened is important."

"What happened?"

The monster looked delighted, as though Ainsley had answered some secret cue. "This is where I destroyed him. Where he wept and begged for me to kill him. This is where he fell." The monster frowned. "But he didn't stay. He was alone: Heaven had forsaken him and I was here for him, and he didn't stay."

"So you kill people?"

"There are some who say it's an addiction, you know, the need to see Heaven. In every soul, I find just a bit of perfection, but it got lonely. Because why did I do all of this if he wouldn't stay?" The monster seemed to be talking to himself more than Ainsley.

"Maybe it's because you kill people," Ainsley suggested.

The monster glared at him. "So he's replaced me with you? I could perhaps accept Trionne, but never you."

"I don't know who you're talking about."

The monster grabbed Ainsley's shoulders and shook him hard. "Be wary, Ainsley Moore; I have more reason than ever to want you dead. You have what I want most." Ainsley could taste blood in his mouth. "And be careful to whom you give your trust so blindly—because he's the same as me. Under that veneer of suffering and nobility, he's exactly the same. One day, he won't be able to stop himself. His conscience will fail to protect him, and he'll reach out and take a piece. Just a taste. Then he'll never be able to stop."

Ainsley realized who the monster meant. "He'll never become that." Ainsley shoved back, catching the monster by surprise and sending him stumbling back a few steps. "I don't know what sort of evil made you, but Morgan doesn't have that sort of darkness in him." He remembered the warmth of Morgan's hand when he'd held Ainsley's hand through the night.

"We all start as good people; it doesn't mean that there isn't darkness inside all of us, waiting to be freed." The monster laughed harshly. "Don't fool yourself, Ainsley Moore; Morgan sees the same thing I do. He sees you bright and pure, and he wants it for himself. He can deny the urge all he wants, but it won't change the inevitable. He'll keep you around, until one day, he devours you.

"Morgan isn't like that," Ainsley insisted once again, but he wondered who he was trying to convince: the monster in his dreams or himself?

"If you don't believe me, ask him. Ask him what went through his mind the day he first saw you. Ask him how much he desires to return to Heaven again. What he would do for just one small taste of that perfection again." Ainsley raised his arms to shield his face against the sudden wind, only tentatively lowering them when it had faded. The monster had grown wings, black wings that towered above them, the feathers dripping in blood. "You ask him how I came to be, and how long it will be until his sins show as dark as mine."

Ainsley awoke suddenly, shivering as he remembered his dream. A dream; it was only a dream. But when he looked down and saw a black feather clutched in his hand, he knew the truth: the whole nightmare had been real from the beginning.

Ainsley had questions to which he wasn't sure he wanted to know the answers.

~~*

The call concerning another killing had turned out to be a bust. It had been a reasonable enough copy, but when Morgan had touched the body, careful to keep it hidden from fellow detectives, he'd known in an instant that this woman's monster had been a human one. Still, Adams remained convinced and her picture went onto the board as the team tried to figure what linked this woman to all the others. Morgan could have explained to them that the one thing linking all the victims of the serial killer wasn't something they'd easily see, but if he explained it to them, it was highly unlikely that they'd believe him. Even if they did, they wouldn't stand a chance against Cian.

So Morgan wasn't able to return to his apartment until the early hours of the morning. He tried not to yawn as he approached his door, checking his cell phone and wondering if he should call Ainsley. It wasn't likely that Ainsley would appreciate being woken up. In fact, he'd probably throw a fit.

Morgan shouldn't have been so happy about that; he knew he shouldn't. Giving into anything in regards to Ainsley would make him a bigger target. It would weaken

Morgan's focus. It should have been more important that he catch Cian than starting a relationship with Ainsley, something Morgan realized after he was some distance from the hospital. But again, the minute he'd gotten too close, he had been unable to stop himself from falling all over again.

Ainsley had been right: he needed to make a choice. He'd chosen Ainsley.

For all the good it had done him—likely the minute Ainsley learned the truth, he would drop Morgan so quickly that Morgan would never see it coming. What had he said to Ainsley? If he gave up before it even started, he might miss out on something that could become important. Maybe he could stop Cian without Ainsley ever having to know. It was a long shot, but he couldn't stop himself from praying desperately that that would be the case.

As he put his key in the door, a feeling of apprehension went through Morgan. Someone was in his apartment, but not a human someone. He paused to feel out his visitor. Whoever it was didn't have any ill intent, so it couldn't have been Cian. Although if it was, it might have been nice to have Cian turn his anger on the appropriate target for once, rather than the mass of innocents he had targeted. Morgan took a deep breath and did his best to lock his thoughts away. With his weakened strength, he had no way of telling how powerful the person on the other side of the door might be. He might not have been an angel any longer, but he didn't want his weaknesses used against him; he didn't want Ainsley involved in this at all.

Morgan unlocked the door and entered.

The angel was sitting on his couch, staring at the television with an expression of distaste. When he saw Morgan, a smile spread across his face. "Noel!"

Morgan couldn't have explained why the angel inspired animosity in him, but he wanted the man gone. It was strange; seeing another angel should have made him ecstatic, but there was something about him. "Can I help you?" He didn't even recognize the angel. In human form, he looked much like every other angel might, which meant absolute perfection. No part of him looked quite real, especially the grey eyes that narrowed in suspicion.

"Well, yes. I wanted to talk to you." The angel gestured that he should sit. There was something about his manner; too smooth, too polished. It was no wonder he grated on Morgan's nerves.

"Perhaps you should introduce yourself first," Morgan suggested, as he threw his coat onto the back of a chair and walked over to the closet. He took care to remove the cigarettes from his pocket before hanging the coat up. He wanted one so badly that he could already taste the nicotine.

The angel seemed at a loss for words, simply staring while Morgan leaned down to open his gun safe and set the weapon inside. He'd have preferred to be armed, but it wasn't like the bullets would do much against the other angel, anyway.

"I am Micah." Morgan even hated his name. "I have been told that you are after the nephilim. I had thought we could work together."

What Morgan wanted to do was tell him where he could go and how he could get there, but he had to remind himself that he was trying to turn over a new leaf. That probably meant not cussing out angels who hadn't actually done anything to earn his ire, yet. "How did you think we might work together?" He kept his tone neutral and respectful. He'd at least hear Micah out; then he would tell him to get the fuck out. His fingers twitched for his pack of cigarettes, but he managed to stop himself.

Micah gestured again at the chair beside him. "Sit. Let's talk." Morgan wanted to sigh, but sucked it up and, after checking to make sure the safe was secure, closed the closet door and walked over to sit in the chair. "I have heard how difficult life among the mortals can be. How are you?"

"Fine," Morgan answered succinctly. "What is your plan regarding the nephilim?"

Taken aback by his abruptness, Micah stumbled a bit, before managing to reply, "I have located his final target."

"Yes. So have I." With a soul that bright, there was no doubt as to his last target.

"Oh, have you?" Micah deflated a bit. "Well, I have come up with a plan to lure the nephilim out into the open." At Morgan's silence, he continued, "Since it has become obvious that he needs to devour their souls in order for his ritual to be complete, if his prey is in danger of dying before he is ready, surely he will come out and prevent it."

Morgan thought that over. "So you put his prey in life-threatening situations in hopes that he'll swoop out to save them." Micah nodded eagerly. "What if he doesn't? Save them I mean."

Micah obviously hadn't considered that possibility. He shrugged. "Then I suppose we shall be forced to find a new plan."

"Meanwhile, a person dies."

"All mortals die eventually."

"And you think his guardian will let you get away with this."

Micah waved his hand. "Oh, that's no problem—I'm his guardian."

Something occurred to Morgan. "You've tried this already."

Micah frowned. "Well, I was less than successful today, but I anticipate that next time will go better. Perhaps he knew that the car would almost come to a stop before it hit him? I was surprised by how little damage it caused."

"You almost killed Ainsley."

"But I didn't kill him." Micah looked confused, as if surprised to realize that Morgan knew his charge's name. Not only was he attempting to kill Ainsley, but Micah was a pretty half-assed guardian, as well. "It would have been for the greater good!" The worst part was that Micah sounded like he honestly believed that.

"You're a piss-poor excuse for a guardian."

Micah's pretty face flushed angrily. "Oh, that's rich coming from you, Noel. I've heard tales of your fall."

Morgan refused to show how much those words affected him, how deeply those memories stabbed into his heart. "My fall has nothing to do with this." The fall wasn't the worst part; it was what had happened afterward that weighed on his soul.

"Please. You should be happy that a servant of Heaven even deigns to talk to you after that mess you caused with Cian."

"A servant of Heaven would never carry as much taint as you do." Although Micah didn't have them out, he could see the creeping gray swallowing his wings. It reminded him so strongly of his own. He'd stopped pulling them out, not wanting to see the once pure white feathers covered in gray.

"What?" Micah looked confused.

"In your attempts to stop Cian, you're going down the same path he did." Morgan might have been sad for him if he weren't so angry. "Stop now before your turn around and realize you can never go back."

"I don't need your help," Micah sneered. "I'm sure we both remember the last recipient of your counsel."

All those bodies—innocent people trying to get away from the cold wind. Yes; they both remembered the last recipient of his advice—and what he'd done in the end. "Get out." The words were whispered softly.

"I don't understand you, Noel; you should be ecstatic at this opportunity. This could be your chance to get back into Heaven. To be honest, we were rather surprised

when you didn't join your friend in his newfound ... "
Micah paused. "Habit."

Funny; there might have been a time when he'd have done anything to earn just a little bit of Heaven's forgiveness. However, time had taught him that before he could even try to seek Heaven's forgiveness, he needed to start with finding something worthwhile within himself to forgive—and that started with stopping Micah from making a mockery of his purpose. "Get out of my house." Micah wouldn't be touching Ainsley again. Morgan would kill him first and deal with the consequences later.

It was time that the little neophyte learned exactly with whom he was messing.

"You can't talk to me that way!" Micah gasped and fell back when Morgan released his own wings. They were dove gray from his sin and a bit ragged from lack of use. But they were far larger than Micah's; an obvious display of his power.

Micah seemed stunned. Obviously he hadn't done his research and had come expecting a weak, desperate creature. Perhaps at one time, Morgan had been that, hiding from his shadow and praying that Cian would stop, but he'd changed; he was going to find a better end for his story—and his ending didn't have room for cowardly angels that risked other people's lives for their own gain. "Leave my domain."

"Your domain is a crappy little home in a crappy little city," Micah responded snidely, then whimpered when a crackle of power cut into his arm.

"If you touch Ainsley again, I will make sure that every piece of his pain is revisited upon you." If Micah was lucky, that was all he would do. If he hurt Ainsley, Morgan could easily see tearing him apart and dragging Micah's soul down right along with his to the deepest bowels of Hell.

Micah didn't respond and Morgan could see a spark of defiance in his eyes. Part of him hoped that Micah would give him the excuse he wanted to vent his rage, but Micah didn't say anything; just turned and left.

With a sigh, Morgan let his wings fade away. It was the worst part, letting them fade into nothingness. It was when withdrawal felt the worst. He closed his eyes and lay on the couch, praying for the craving to pass. He would stop Cian this time, help or not. He'd humbled himself after he'd fallen, praying as he'd never prayed before on the floor of that little chapel Trionne had cherished. He'd begged Heaven for help so that he could stop Cian. Never again would he cry to Heaven as he had that night.

Unlike the angels sitting carefully on their clouds, he hadn't sat around watching for fifty-five years as Cian killed. He'd saved who he could, buried those he couldn't; everything he could have done without Heaven's grace, he'd done. And still his wings had grown darker with every life Cian took; nothing he did made it better. The only way to stop it would be by killing Cian, and killing Cian was the one thing that would damn him for sure.

He'd do it, though; Morgan would accept Hell if it meant he could at last correct his mistake. Cian would die or Morgan would die trying. This was why it had been a bad idea to get involved with Ainsley: Morgan would likely be gone by the end of all of this.

~~*

The next morning, Ainsley was almost afraid to leave the house. It was the weekend, which meant that he didn't have to worry about classes. He still needed to email his professors to explain his absence, however; but, hey, maybe if he waited a couple of days, the soul-eating monster would finish him off and he wouldn't have to worry about whether or not he could pass his test next Wednesday.

No, he couldn't think like that. Even as a joke.

It concerned him, though, that the man in his dream had been so quick to deny responsibility for walking him into the road. In fact, the monster had seemed bothered by the implication. Of course, the man was also an insane serial killer, but Ainsley had a feeling that whoever had been responsible was still out there. They obviously weren't following the monster's focused plan, either.

But Ainsley couldn't hide forever. That wasn't the kind of person he was. On top of that, he dreadfully needed food. The sandwich he'd made four days ago had been the last bit of his food supplies, so he needed to go to the grocery store. He could either go out and pray that nothing happened, or he could stay in and starve. That was perhaps putting it a bit more dramatically than needed, but he wasn't allowing himself the coward's way out and ordering in. Of course, going out wouldn't be easy with his foot the way it was, but the grocery store wasn't too far away. Maybe staying in wouldn't be the coward's option; maybe it was just the smarter option. But at this point, Ainsley had built it up so much in his head that he couldn't back down now.

Of course, his common sense chimed in, he could always call Morgan. After last night's dream, he was having difficulty getting behind that idea. The monster in his head was a liar; he was trying to destroy whatever Ainsley and Morgan had started a few days ago. He'd said as much in fact. But the fact remained that even if he was making this all up in his head, Morgan had secrets he wasn't sharing and Ainsley's dream had only made him more concerned what they might be. If he called Morgan, he might have to face that truth.

With a pained grunt, Ainsley hopped over to his crutches and, using them, made his way out the door and to the elevator. Just getting to the elevator had him out of breath and he panted as he leaned against the wall of the elevator. But Ainsley had already gotten this far; He couldn't turn back now, not when he just needed to make it to the car. Then he could sit down and take a rest. He wasn't even going to bother trying to think about how the hell he was going to go from aisle to aisle once he actually made it to the damn store.

When the elevator stopped, Ainsley took another deep breath and managed to make it out of the lobby and down the short set of steps to the parking lot. He'd just started to make his way to his vehicle, when he had the sudden feeling that he wasn't alone. The feeling combined with all the fear and paranoia circling in his head, until he had almost managed to convince himself that the monster was right behind him. He could smell the darkness, hear his laughter, his calm insistence that Morgan was going down the same path.

A hand landed heavily on Ainsley's shoulder, and Ainsley jumped and stumbled around to face his attacker. Morgan stood behind him in casual clothes, a couple of plastic grocery bags in his hand.

"Morgan, you startled me." Ainsley leaned heavily against one crutch and put a hand over his racing heart. When he had calmed down a little, he looked up to see Morgan staring at him angrily. "What happened? What's wrong?"

"You're an idiot," Morgan growled, and Ainsley blinked in surprise at the growl.

Then the words dawned on him. "Why are you —" But before he could finish, Morgan took a step forward. Ainsley automatically stepped back and hissed in pain when he nearly landed on his injured foot. "You'd better not pick me up again."

"Why the hell are you down here if your ankle is broken?"

"Sprained," Ainsley corrected him.

"Whatever." Morgan shifted, and held out one of the bags in his hand. Morgan had brought him lunch. Before Ainsley could even begin to feel moved by the act, however, Morgan quickly moved and took the crutches from him, swinging Ainsley easily over his shoulder.

"Let me down! I just told you not to pick me up!"

Rather than listening to him, Morgan made his way up the steps and into the apartment building. "Obviously, you're not in your right mind. I don't have to listen to your demands." Ainsley contemplated kicking Morgan, but with his luck, he would have ended up doing more damage to himself. Truth be told, he hadn't really been sure how much further stubbornness and determination would carry him. "Where were you trying to go, anyway?"

"I didn't have any food." The very same statement that had made so much sense when he'd left his apartment made absolutely none now.

"Why didn't you call me, then?"

Because of the nightmare. Because he wasn't sure he could trust Morgan. Because he didn't want to be that needy guy. They hadn't even decided where this thing was going, yet. Ainsley hadn't ever developed the philosophy that it was okay to rely on other people; especially when it was something he needed to do himself. "I thought you might be busy." He knew that embarrassment and guilt had crept into his voice. "I didn't want to bother you."

"It would *bother* me more if you hurt yourself worse and ended up back in the hospital because you were too stubborn to call for help."

Ainsley was glad that Morgan couldn't see his face as he flushed with shame. "I'm sorry." It had been a while since he'd had to say those two words—since he'd even cared enough to try.

Morgan sighed and set Ainsley down, allowing Ainsley to lean against the wall beside the elevator. Ainsley tried to look everywhere but at him, until Morgan forced him to look up with a gentle grip. "Ainsley—"

"I'm scared." Just saying those two words was freeing in a way. "I'm scared and I don't like it. I thought if I just dealt with it, I wouldn't be so scared anymore."

Morgan's eyes softened. "Why didn't you call me?"

"I can handle things!" At Morgan's telling look, Ainsley sunk further back, his face flushed with embarrassment. "I can."

"You'll have to learn to start relying on someone someday, Ainsley. You can't do everything on your own." Morgan leaned forward to brush a soft, lingering kiss against Ainsley's lips. "I've tried that; it doesn't work."

Ainsley closed his eyes and tilted his face upward, leaning into Morgan's next kiss. Unlike the night before, these kisses weren't rushed; they were slow and thorough. And somehow, that fact succeeded in driving Ainsley mad. His foot didn't hurt, and when he wrapped his arms around Morgan—as much for support as to pull him closer—he realized that his arms, which had ached from the crutches, didn't hurt either.

Morgan pulled back and Ainsley whimpered, tugging on Morgan to bring him closer, when they were interrupted by the elevator doors opening. While Ainsley tried to scramble back, an attempt that proved unsuccessful since he was already against the wall, Morgan didn't bother to hide what they'd been doing, standing close enough that even if Ainsley tried, he wouldn't have been able to make it look innocuous.

A small group of people departed the elevator. An older man Ainsley remembered seeing from time to time walked past them without even looking. So did a woman Ainsley was sure had moved in recently. The two young men stopped and stared however, lips curled in disgust.

"Go find a room. Fucking queers."

"Seriously. Doing that shit in public."

Ainsley had never felt like he needed to apologize for himself before, but he had always tried to avoid confrontation. He wasn't quite sure what to do in this situation. He glanced up at Morgan and gasped in horror.

Anger would have been a poor word to describe Morgan's expression. Darkness had spread across his face, his green eyes rimmed with red. It was the second time Ainsley had been truly afraid of him, especially when he turned to face the two idiots. Ainsley could swear he saw wings rising from his back, large and gray as they reached toward the vaulted ceiling. He knew this feeling—his nightmare. The monster.

Before Morgan could take another step forward, Ainsley reached out to grab his shoulder. He wasn't sure what had made him do it, other than the knowledge that he needed to stop Morgan before someone got hurt. Morgan turned and Ainsley winced at the feeling of all of that hatred targeted at him.

When he opened his eyes, Morgan seemed to have calmed, a sheepish look on his face. "I'm sorry. I guess I let their comments get to me."

"Morgan. What are you?" The monster had said that Morgan was the same as him. But Morgan couldn't possibly be the same; he was making up for bad karma. He'd dealt calmly with Ainsley's mood swings. He'd held Ainsley's hand through the night and Ainsley hadn't felt so alone. There was no way Ainsley wouldn't have been able to tell by now that there was something dark in Morgan. But he had seen it, hadn't he? That first night, Morgan's eyes locking onto him hungrily; as if he was a hunter and Ainsley the prey.

"What do you mean?" Morgan asked innocently, but Ainsley could see the truth. He knew that Ainsley had realized and dreaded having to face the truth.

It would have been so easy to let it go. So easy to tell himself that he'd imagined it all. But he was supposed to be facing his fears—and Morgan was quickly becoming one of them. "What are you?"

Ainsley could see the moment he won, when defeat shone in Morgan's eyes. "Can we not talk about this here?"

The first words out of Ainsley's mouth were nearly that he wasn't sure he trusted Morgan in his apartment, but he knew that wasn't the truth exactly; he didn't trust himself alone with Morgan. Didn't trust that once Morgan gave him some bullshit answer, he'd accept it in the hopes that he wouldn't lose what he'd only just gained. The truth was that Ainsley didn't really want to know the answer to his question—didn't want to face the implications.

He didn't want anything to tarnish what he'd had for less than a day.

Ainsley shuffled awkwardly to the elevator, clinging to the wall. He could see Morgan fighting the urge to help him, but he was glad when Morgan decided against it. When he finally did make it into the elevator, he slumped in a corner. Morgan handed him his crutches before pushing the button to the correct floor, and they rode together in heavy silence. It wasn't until after Ainsley had slowly limped his way back to his apartment and Morgan had made sure that he was settled on the couch that Ainsley attempted again. "What are you?"

"I'm an angel."

Ainsley opened his mouth to demand that Morgan stop playing around and tell him the truth, but then he thought of the wings he'd seen earlier. He thought of the wings the monster had displayed in his dream. "An angel," he repeated, and then something occurred to him. "Your story from earlier."

Morgan looked pained. "Yes."

"How much of it is true?" What part had Morgan played?

Morgan seemed like he'd rather be anywhere but there. "Cian and I were friends." There was something in the way Morgan said the word that made Ainsley wonder just how close of friends they'd been. "But we'd gone our separate ways. In that time, apparently Cian had come upon a small village where he decided to stay. Then he fell."

"Why did he fall?"

"He killed a man. Murder is among one of the most cardinal of sins."

"And then he called you."

"Yes," Morgan sighed sadly. "And then he called me, and instead of helping him, I became distracted with Trionne. It was my fault. I was his friend, I was the one he'd come to for counsel, and I didn't see the darkness that had overcome him until it was too late. He slaughtered Trionne's husband as a warning. That was the day I began to fall.

"I tried my hardest to make it back into Heaven's graces, but it is so easy to fall and so hard to seek forgiveness. Not to mention that I could never make myself feel repentant over my feelings for Trionne even if she never did return my feelings."

Morgan paused, and Ainsley tentatively encouraged, "What happened?"

"Cian had gotten a taste for human souls. He started with the ones closest to him, those that had become his friends. One day, I returned and he had slaughtered everyone in the church. As we stood over Trionne's torn body, I begged him to allow me to join them, but that was my punishment, he told me: I would live, fallen as he was, until my soul turned as dark as his had. Only then would he grant me release."

"You'd fallen, then?"

"I share responsibility in every life Cian takes. Every soul he takes weighs on mine, as well. It was a fate I believed I deserved."

"But why haven't you tried to stop him before now?"

"I have tried. I tried prayer when force didn't work. I tried force where prayer wouldn't work. After Cian killed those people, he vanished. I buried them. Then I prayed for Heaven to stop him. He wasn't as powerful then as he is now; it would have been possible. Then he stopped and I thought that maybe Heaven had heard my prayers. So I began working on my penance. For twenty-three years, I worked for forgiveness. Then out of the blue, Cian came to me again. He was supposed to be dead." Morgan's head sank into his hands. "Like a demon, he'd returned with the same promises as before. And they were so very tempting. It is far easier to fall than it is to seek forgiveness, you know?" He looked up, his eyes imploring Ainsley to understand.

"Morgan—"

"I said no, of course. Nothing had changed about him; his wings were still black as night, his soul heavy with corruption. He promised me he'd changed, but I knew he hadn't. Perhaps he had managed to hold in the urge, but it didn't change things. It didn't bring all of those people he'd killed back to life. I told him to go away and he grew angry.

"Do you know they blamed the first body on me?" Morgan's laugh was bitter. "I sat in prison for thirty-six hours before Cian killed again. When they released me, I sought him out. It took me years to find him. He'd become a master of hiding his presence. Acted like it was some silly hide and seek game.

"He almost killed me, then."

"And you gave up?"

"No. I never gave up. Cian got better at hiding. I'd hear occasional whispers, of course, but by the time I arrived, he was far gone. Until I received an invitation."

Somewhere, the full story was starting to come together for him. "He sent you an invitation?"

"An invitation to the end." Morgan sighed. "I thought he'd come after me."

Silence fell between them. "I understand that this changes things." Yet despite Morgan's words, Ainsley could see the acceptance twining with regret. Ainsley wanted to tell him that he was wrong, that this didn't change how he felt. Didn't change where they were going, but it would have been a lie. The full story changed everything; not how he felt necessarily, but certainly where they were going.

"Why did he say you were the same?"

"He said?" Morgan asked, confused. "When would you have spoken to Cian, Ainsley?" There was something in his voice, but Ainsley couldn't figure out what it was.

"My dreams. I've had nightmares in this apartment since the night I learned Eleanor died. He—" The first dream didn't bear mentioning. He couldn't even think about it without seeing Eleanor ripped open. "He told me that you would inevitably become the same—that you wouldn't be able to stop yourself from devouring me."

Morgan's eyes closed, and for a second, Ainsley assumed that he wasn't going to answer. "Angels desire nothing more than to return to Heaven. The same can be said for fallen angels, as well. To see Heaven is to see perfection and to be denied is akin to withdrawal of the worst kind. The ache to see Heaven is almost a physical pain in my body."

Ainsley's heart started beating faster as he eyed the distance between the couch and the door. As if he'd even make it in time without crawling. He looked back to Morgan, who still had his eyes closed; but oddly, despite the story, Ainsley wasn't afraid of him. He controlled himself at the police station, and in all the time that he and Ainsley had been in each other's presence the past couple of days, he hadn't once tried to hurt Ainsley; not even when Ainsley had been asleep and vulnerable in front of him. "I don't think you're capable of it."

"Hmm?"

"I don't think you're capable of becoming Cian."

Morgan's eyes opened and he regarded Ainsley strangely, before answering, "It doesn't matter; even if I don't start devouring souls, I'm as bad as he is for not stopping it."

"Morgan, I can't grant you the forgiveness you're looking for. You're not the one who killed those people."

"But I stood aside and let it happen."

"Then do something now. Don't sit around and whine." Morgan opened his mouth to argue and Ainsley kept going. "The more time you spend thinking on your own failure, the more Cian hurts people. You'll have eternity to reflect on what you didn't do."

"But I need to make a better ending, right?"

"Right." Ainsley's stomach growled and he blushed. "I'm hungry."

Morgan looked happy to have a change in subject, although Ainsley knew that they'd have to revisit it. "I bought food." Morgan sounded so proud of himself, even if the food was likely lukewarm by now. "I bought Chinese."

Ainsley's nose wrinkled, but he didn't say a word. It was the thought that counted. Still, when Morgan walked back in with a salad, he was pretty sure he could easily develop lasting feelings for this man.

~~*

Micah hadn't expected Noel to say no to his offer. In his experience, fallen angels craved the approval of Heaven, after all. He had imagined that the only way Noel had managed to keep his sanity was through the belief that one day he'd be able to return. Micah couldn't begin to fathom the thought of having to deal with the idea that one might never return.

It was understandable why many angels who were cut off from Heaven lost their minds.

But it could not be borne. Cian had killed so many that might never be able to see the gates of Heaven, now. So long as he lived, they would be forever left to wander on the mortal plane. Micah couldn't count the number of angels that had simply watched sadly, but done nothing as the dead suffered. Then he'd overheard an angel discussing how the person who stopped the grigori would most likely be regarded as a hero. As a guardian angel, Micah was simply one of many, but the chance to be a hero?

That was when Micah had started his plan.

When Cian had come to this place to hunt Ainsley, he'd seen it as a sign from Heaven itself. Obviously, he was meant for greatness. If one human had to be sacrificed so that he would finally be recognized, well, at least Ainsley Moore would arrive in perfection and there was nothing wrong with that.

Then Noel had gotten in his way. If Noel could have just agreed, then they could have made a great team. Micah had heard stories of Noel's power, but when he'd actually met him, Noel had seemed so human that Micah had grown disgusted. Even if he had retained a good amount of his power, one had only to look at the gray wings to know that he had not earned the right to be as arrogant as he was. Regardless of his strength, he'd still fallen in the end—which meant that Noel would always be weaker in Heaven's eyes.

Yet he'd seen fit to lecture Micah on his behavior. The hypocrisy grated.

Micah wasn't afraid of Noel; not by a long shot. He had retreated, then, just so he could form a strategy. The way Micah saw it, he had the righteous light on his side: powerful or not, Noel would fail. What was one human life compared to the many Cian had killed? If Noel wanted to protect this one human, then he should have started centuries ago by destroying Cian the moment he'd found him.

Micah watched Ainsley's apartment from his hiding place. He'd seen the other man hobble out earlier, but Noel had already been there. For a fearful moment, Micah had worried that Noel had somehow gotten wind of his plans. Then Noel had simply taken Ainsley back inside and Micah had breathed a sigh of relief, but Morgan hadn't left. Why hadn't he left?

He watched as the lights went out and everything settled, and wanted to scream. Apparently, Noel planned to add one more thing to his list of sins. Micah seethed as he moved away from the building. Fine. Noel might be able to protect Ainsley now, but he wouldn't be able to protect him forever. So what if Noel obviously hadn't lost all of his power when he had fallen? He'd seemed off his guard when he had walked blindly into Ainsley's apartment. Maybe Micah would wait there for him and give him a little surprise.

He was almost to Morgan's apartment when a strong grip yanked him back into the alley. "Who do you think—" Micah stopped mid-sentence when he got a good look at his captor. The darkness of his soul made Micah gasp and back up until he hit the wall.

They'd spoken about it in Heaven, what happened when an angel fell. There were some who said they lost their wings and would spend centuries earning them back. He'd heard tales that the soul turned so black that even the Devil wouldn't take it. However, rumors couldn't have prepared him for the sight of Cian's soul, dark and evil even as the man himself wore a pleasant grin.

"You're poaching," Cian informed him calmly.

This was what he'd wanted, the thing for which he'd planned, but now that he was staring Cian in the face, Micah was terrified. Cian's soul was darker than any demon's and stained with so much blood. Such a thing shouldn't have even existed. To Micah's untrained eyes, it felt like looking directly into Hell.

"No response?" Cian asked. Micah whimpered and attempted to back up further. "Then I suppose it is time to eat, which is rather sad since your soul is barely pure enough to satisfy."

"Wait!" Cian paused in the act of reaching forward. "You can't eat me. You can't eat an angel!"

Cian laughed and the sound made his fear rise. "I've eaten priests and beggars. I've eaten monks and great thinkers. I've eaten volunteers and misers. What makes you believe that you are so special?"

"There has to be some good left inside of you. Some part of Heaven."

The smirk that twisted Cian's lips was cruel and mocking. "My experiences with Heaven drive me, and you are further proof of their indifference. How can I be the one who falls and yet scum like you are still allowed among their ranks?"

"I haven't sinned," Micah argued.

"You sin every day you look at the human world with disgust and elevate yourself above them. You sin with your willingness to sacrifice others to suit your own purpose. You sneer at the humans, but yet they possess brighter souls than you." Cian sighed. " I grow tired of explaining a concept you have no ability to understand. They've sent others, you know; others before you to stop me." Micah had not known that, although in retrospect, it made sense, and explained how Cian had grown so powerful in the first place. "And now you'll join them."

When Cian reached forward this time, he moved quickly enough that Micah had no chance to raise his power to fight back. The angel fell dead before he could so much as speak another word. Cian sighed again and leaned down. When had this whole game become so very boring? Cian had hoped that if he did enough damage, someone would come along to stop it. Yet, even with the many people he killed, no one bothered to stop him.

At least now Noel was in the game and they could put an end to this one way or another. If the stakes were high enough, he wouldn't run away again. Cian sat down and plunged his hand into Micah's chest to retrieve his admittedly anticlimactic prize. With his other hand, he flipped open his phone and dialed the police.

"Hello? I'd like to report a murder."

At two in the morning, Ainsley found he couldn't sleep. It wasn't the nightmares keeping him awake, but

Morgan in his living room. He hadn't brought up Cian again that night, but the subject had hung between them. When Ainsley had finally decided to go to bed, Morgan had asked to stay.

Ainsley's cheeks had gone flaming red. "Morgan, it's a bit soon for that and not quite the right mood."

Morgan had rolled his eyes. "I mean I'll sleep on the couch, Ainsley. Cian is after you." As if Ainsley could have forgotten that fact. "Maybe if I stay here, you can get a good night's rest. Unless ... " He'd looked tentative, then. "You're afraid of me ... "

"It's a lot to take in, Morgan; anyone in their right mind would be afraid." Morgan's face had fallen. "But not of you. I'm not afraid of you." Morgan's smile had been sweet. "Let me go get you some blankets." Morgan had followed behind him as he'd walked to the linen closet and Ainsley's mind had continued to spin. He could have invited Morgan to stay in his room, but that would have been too fast, too soon. There was a part of him that worried whether Morgan had been right, whether this whole thing would fade once the danger vanished.

But this all seemed just too right. Having Morgan around was quickly making him want to forget how he'd handled it before, being by himself. It made him think of Eleanor's last words to him. They'd gone out to lunch close to where Eleanor lived and Ainsley had been steadfastly ignoring the waiter's attempts at flirtation. When Eleanor had asked him why, he'd told her that he didn't date, that he simply didn't have the time. What he hadn't said was that most of the time, even when he tried, it didn't take long for him to chase them away. It had just gotten easier to not even bother trying. "One day," Eleanor had warned, laughing, "you're going to find someone that makes you want to try a bit harder."

"I try hard enough," Ainsley had scoffed.

"One day you're going to meet someone who makes you not want to be alone anymore." Ainsley had dismissed the statement at the time. Then he'd found Morgan, who not only had come the minute the nurse had called him, but had held his hand throughout the night. Had brought him a damn salad because he knew Ainsley would have issues with Chinese food. Who'd gone and stocked his damn refrigerator with fruits and vegetables and all of the things he assumed Ainsley ate. Ainsley hadn't had the heart to remind Morgan that he wasn't a vegetarian.

Ainsley had finally met someone who didn't make him feel so alone anymore and he was on a damn suicide mission. Ainsley had turned and Morgan had reached out to grab the blankets from him, expression becoming puzzled when Ainsley hadn't let go. "Ainsley?"

"Morgan, you don't have to do this alone, you know."

"What?"

"You reminded me that I should learn to rely on people, but you should do the same. I won't let Cian kill you."

"Cian killing me would be the least of what I deserve."

"Fine, then." Ainsley had shoved the blankets into Morgan's arms hard enough to send Morgan off-balance. "Even if you don't care, I do. Don't die."

Morgan had laughed disbelievingly. "Is that an order?"

"You can consider it one."

Morgan had looked down at the blankets in his hand, then back up to Ainsley. "Fine, then consider yourself ordered in return." He had leant in, over the pile of blankets squished between them, and laid a soft kiss on Ainsley's lips. "Good night, Ainsley."

Ainsley had gone to his room and gotten ready for bed with the help of the crutches, but the minute he'd gotten into the bed, all he'd been able to think of was Morgan so close, and yet so very far away. Finally, a few minutes past two, Ainsley gave in and climbed clumsily out of bed. It was ridiculous; hadn't he been the one to tell Morgan that they should slow down a bit? Yet here he was, limping clumsily to the living room so he could watch Morgan sleep.

Sleeping, Morgan looked like, well ... like an angel. His hand rested just under his cheek, dark curls falling into his face, somehow having managed to fold his tall body onto Ainsley's admittedly short couch. Ainsley sat on the arm, setting his crutches to the side, and watched him. Sadly, the sight didn't last long before Morgan started to wake.

"You ever feel sometimes like things are moving too quickly?"

"Things always move at the pace they're meant to." Morgan answered sleepily. "What are we talking about?"

"Like, we only met four days ago and we're already telling each other our deepest secrets."

"Deepest secrets?"

"I let you use my pillow, Morgan." Ainsley pointed to the pillow Morgan was laying on. "Do you understand how big of a deal that is? Do you know how many people drool in their sleep?"

Morgan self-consciously checked his cheek. "I think you have the unfair advantage of being far more awake for this conversation than I am." But Morgan sounded like he was catching up, so Ainsley didn't feel so bad for him.

"I lied earlier," Ainsley stated. "Did you really love Trionne?"

Morgan looked surprised by the question, but he answered, "I did." He sat up and finger-combed his curls, gesturing that Ainsley should join him on the couch. Ainsley thought it might be safer to stay where he was, however.

"So you're bisexual, then?"

For the second time that day, Morgan looked as though he wished to be anywhere else. "I'm not defined by one or the other, Lee. Love isn't that easily defined."

Ainsley nodded. "You loved Cian, too." It wasn't a question.

"What makes you think that?" The question came out quick and fearful.

"What happened, Morgan?"

"I don't love Cian, not anymore," he insisted.

"Love isn't that easily defined, Morgan."

Morgan crumbled. "He wasn't always this way. He was once a guardian angel, just like I was. He was my best friend. Eventually, we became more to each other. Everything was fine. Perfect. But then he started to question."

"Question?"

"Everything," Morgan exploded. "He questioned whether Heaven was truly perfection or whether that idea had been ingrained into us since birth, whether there were times when killing shouldn't damn a man's soul, whether Heaven was right in its rules and strictures. He questioned everything." Morgan seemed to deflate. "And I couldn't handle it. I couldn't follow him down the path he'd chosen to take. I asked him so many times to stop, to give me a chance to understand, but he refused. He'd grown tired of the rules and regulations. Tired of risking himself to save humans that were often ungrateful for his assistance. He grew tired of the atrocities we'd both witnessed during the war and been helpless to stop. But I still had faith. I wanted to believe that he was wrong. So I left."

"And he fell."

Morgan nodded. "And something broke inside of him. I don't love him."

"Maybe not the way he is now, but you still love the memory."

Morgan sighed. "I'll always love the memory," he admitted.

"Would you go back if you could?"

"To Cian?"

Ainsley resisted the urge to roll his eyes. "To Heaven."

Morgan thought about his answer before giving it. "There are so many things I miss. It's perfection. It's home." Morgan reached out to curl a finger in Ainsley's hair. "But when I'm with you, it doesn't hurt so much and I don't miss it quite as badly."

"Wouldn't you get that from anyone with a pure soul?" Ainsley was letting himself be drawn in until he was curled against Morgan's side. He could hear Morgan's heartbeat like this. He wondered if it was beating just a bit faster, as his was.

"A part of it, yes. But I would never get from anyone else what I get from you." When he leaned in this time, Ainsley didn't block him. This time, when their mouths met, Ainsley didn't passively let Morgan control the kiss. He nipped at Morgan's lips and teased until Morgan growled and threaded his fingers through Ainsley's hair, grip just tight enough to keep Ainsley reasonably still, while Morgan plundered his mouth.

Ainsley started to curl his hands around Morgan's shoulders, not sure if it was okay to explore. Morgan's hand slipped under his robe, coasting down his back. The gentle caress drove Ainsley near out of his mind, until he was arching into it, practically begging without words for Morgan to explore further. Some small part of his mind reminded him that he wasn't supposed to be this easy. Morgan hadn't even officially asked him out anywhere, yet.

Then Morgan pushed him back and stood from the couch, taking a couple steps away. Ainsley was confused, his lips still tingling. "You're stopping?"

"You're not that easy, Ainsley, remember?" Morgan's lips curved in amusement.

Ainsley kind of hated himself right that moment. "I'm not," he replied, trying to gather his dignity about him.

"Go to bed, Ainsley, before I remember just how easy this can all be." His look along Ainsley's body made him feel like Morgan had already mentally stripped him of his clothes.

"Right. Good night." Ainsley fled as fast as his crutches would allow him.

An hour later, Morgan knocked on the bedroom door. For a moment, Ainsley thought he'd changed his mind and decided he did want to prove exactly how easy Ainsley was—the thought shouldn't have made him happy. But when he opened the door, Morgan was fully dressed, even if his tie was crooked. It was the tie that drew Ainsley's attention as Morgan started talking. "I need to go. It looks like they've found another body."

"Oh." Reality sticking its nose in once again. "Was it Cian?"

"I won't know until I go have a look."

Morgan took a step back and Ainsley stopped him by grabbing his tie. While Morgan watched bemusedly, Ainsley untied it and wrapped it around his own neck to do it properly. "Do you think he's coming here next?" Ainsley was surprised by how unconcerned the question sounded, even when he could feel terror rolling in his stomach.

Morgan's voice sounded calm, but Ainsley could see his hands clenching hard enough that he'd likely leave marks in his palm. "I won't let him touch you, Ainsley."

"Is that another promise?"

"It is."

Ainsley finished doing the tie and took it off so he could put it around Morgan's neck, setting it under the collar and tightening it. This was all so domestic. The thought terrified him enough that he yanked his hands back quickly, folding them together so he wouldn't fidget. "Be careful." At Morgan's raised eyebrow, he elaborated, "Cian is after you as well."

"What makes you think that?"

He'd seen Cian's eyes when he'd talked of Morgan; love had mixed with hate. "Just a feeling."

Morgan sighed and Ainsley gave in to his impulse to lean forward and give him a quick kiss. "Come back when you're done. We can have breakfast." It would be almost like a second date. Ainsley had already gone further than he normally did for a second date. Did the hospital count? Maybe he could consider this a third or a fourth. "I'll make pancakes."

Morgan's smile was slow to bloom, but once it set in, it was radiant. "I really like pancakes," he confessed.

Ainsley laughed. "Then you'd better hurry back."

Morgan nodded and leaned forward for one more kiss, before he turned to leave. "Don't open the door for anybody."

"What if someone is coming to tell me the apartment is on fire?"

Morgan rolled his eyes, "Nobody."

Ainsley sighed. "Fine. I'll wait here for you to return, even if I end up burned to death." Morgan shook his head, but didn't bother to respond, locking the door behind him as he left. Ainsley followed and slid the deadbolt into place. With Morgan gone, his apartment felt less somehow. Since he'd moved away from home, he'd always been alone. It hadn't been sad, because that had been the way he preferred it. When he'd met Eleanor, she hadn't been pushy about her presence and it had been nice having someone that he could see when the mood to be social struck. Now in the past four days, he'd been almost constantly around Morgan, and the few times he'd been alone had been haunted by terrifying nightmares. Ainsley was finding that he didn't much care for loneliness anymore.

Ainsley should hate it, being dependent on someone else for company. One of the problems with depending on others was that they'd inevitably disappoint. How many times had he told himself that one person would be the exception to that rule in the past and found himself utterly disappointed when he was yet again alone? It seemed as though he was setting himself up for failure, because at this point, it didn't matter. Even if he tried to convince himself not to fall for Morgan, his heart had already decided. He found himself wanting so badly to trust Morgan when Morgan told Ainsley that it was okay to depend on someone.

However, no matter how much he let his thoughts turn in his head, Ainsley knew he wouldn't find an answer that night. Instead, he turned off the lights and crawled back into bed.

~~*

The next morning found Ainsley fiercely regretting his stupidity the evening before. Everything ached. He could only be thankful that he didn't have classes for the day as he took some aspirin and tried to go back to sleep. It took a few hours for the aspirin to work, and by then, Ainsley had gotten bored of trying to fall asleep. He debated making himself something to eat, but he was looking forward to making something for Morgan and pancakes were his best recipe.

After eating a small snack, Ainsley wavered for all of a minute before turning on the television. He hadn't watched the news since this whole mess had begun. But if he turned on the news now, chances were high that they'd be showing the face of the latest victim and Ainsley was absolutely sure that he didn't want to see them. It would make the truth all the more real—Cian was coming for him. The previous night had settled a lot of things, emotionally, but it had made it all the more real to him. The monster had a name and he was coming.

Part of Ainsley raged at the idea of sitting around like this, waiting for Cian to come and eat him. But Morgan had trusted him with his story, and now it was time for Ainsley to trust him in return. Morgan wouldn't run away and leave him to face Cian on his own.

Ainsley heard his phone vibrate and reached for it, thankful for the disruption. It was a text message.

Going to take longer than I thought. Stay safe.

At some point last night, when he'd left his phone on the table, Morgan had typed his name and number into his address book. *Just sitting around studying. No fires yet.*

Ainsley smiled once he'd hit send. Almost right away, his phone lit up again. *Good. I'm still expecting my pancakes.*

With a snort, Ainsley quickly typed back, *Who says you get pancakes? Maybe I ate them.*

The response took a few minutes this time. *You'd know better than that.*

Is that a threat? It took Ainsley a few minutes to realize that the giggle he had heard had come from him.

Five minutes this time. *Stop texting me Lee. People keep asking me why I have a stupid smile on my face.*

Ainsley was tempted to keep going, but he dropped the phone into the pocket of his hoody. He gave up studying as a loss and had just started to reach for the television remote when a knock at the door came. The first thought was that of his earlier comment to Morgan about a potential fire. The memory made him snort, even as he limped to the door to peek through the security peephole. He didn't recognize the man standing outside of his apartment at first; then he realized it was the detective he'd spoken to the first time, the one who had questioned him about Eleanor's death. "Detective Keller?"

"Morgan sent me to check on you."

The first thought through his head was excitement that Morgan had thought of him, then suspicion. Morgan had just sent him a text; why would he do that and send someone to see if Ainsley was still there? "Can I see your badge?" Ainsley's paranoia had already been triggered. He reached for his phone and typed out a quick question to Morgan. *Did you send Keller to my apartment?*

The response was gratifyingly quick. *No why?* Before he could even finish typing a reply, the phone vibrated in his hands. *Hide.*

Ainsley wasted a minute staring at the screen as his horror grew. He looked back through the peephole. Keller had pulled out his badge to show and it certainly looked genuine. Morgan's advice circled through his head. "Are you going to let me in?"

"No."

The badge came down and Keller looked surprised by his answer. Then his expression morphed into annoyance. "Ainsley, I understand that you might be a bit worried since the accident a couple days ago, but I'm here to help you."

"Help me?"

"Yes. We found the person responsible for your accident. Did Morgan tell you that?"

If Morgan had known, why wouldn't he have told him? "No."

"See? I'm just here to give you some information. May I come in?"

"You can talk through the door."

Keller looked confused. "I can't give out this sort of information through your front door." He sounded almost offended by the idea that Ainsley wouldn't let him in.

"Why not?"

"It's information concerning an ongoing case. I can't just shout it out here for all your neighbors to hear."

Ainsley frowned—he didn't like this. "Then Morgan can tell me when he comes back."

"You two have grown that close, huh?" Keller's voice was low, dangerous. Ainsley took a step away from the door, just in case. "How unsurprising that he would forget me so quickly."

"It's been decades." Ainsley was glad they'd dropped the pretenses, but he was still thrown off-guard; he'd expected anger. The jealousy threw him and he wasn't exactly sure why. He'd known Cian felt something for Morgan, but he'd imagined, for some reason, that the love had been eclipsed by hate.

"Decades," Cian scoffed, pacing the hallway in Keller's pudgy form. "Love is supposed to last forever. When did it start having an expiration date?"

"When you took pieces of him with you with every person you killed."

"He was supposed to stay. Then I thought—" Cian took a deep breath. "But that doesn't matter. I was wrong, I suppose." Ainsley peeked one last time through the peephole to see Cian-as-Keller lift his foot. Ainsley stumbled back, clinging to the wall for support when Cian's boot heavily hit the door. Ainsley started looking around, but there were no weapons immediately at hand.

Ainsley stumbled back further when Cian kicked the door and he prayed that no one would approach Cian outside. Likely, Cian would kill them. Ainsley looked down to the phone he still clutched in his hand. Would it do him any good to call an emergency number? Would he just be sending more to the slaughter? He hit the power button and the phone came out of sleep mode. He had a message. Hell, he was going to die, anyway; might as well take a chance to read his last message.

I'm on my way. Ainsley glanced at the time stamp on the message. Morgan had sent it just after his other two. Morgan was on his way and Ainsley had no idea whether he would make it in time or not. But it gave Ainsley a bit of hope, enough that when Cian kicked again and the door flew open, Ainsley grabbed for one of his crutches. Cian came stomping down the foyer and Ainsley swung the moment he came into sight. He cringed to hear the crutch hit against the wall. The cost of that was so coming out of his deposit if he got out of this alive.

Cian looked stunned, but when Ainsley swung again, he caught the crutch in his hand and pushing it back hard enough to make Ainsley lose his precarious balance, before throwing it to the side. Ainsley cringed at the sound of the crutch hitting the wall, sending picture frames to the floor. Cian had dropped Keller's form and now wore his own. He stalked closer and fisted his hand in the front of Ainsley's hoody, lifting him up easily. "Nuisance." Ainsley bit his lip against a whimper of pain when Cian slammed him into the wall. Nothing hurt; he was flying high on adrenaline and he was about to die.

"I won't kill you now. I'll wait until Noel comes."

"Why?"

"Again with the 'why'. The 'why' doesn't matter." Then Cian seemed to consider. "But I'll answer your question, regardless. All I ever wanted Noel to do was stay. If I couldn't keep him there, then I thought Trionne would. If I freed her, Trionne would love him back, and then he'd stay. But of course, the bitch was too pious for her own good." Cian's other hand punched the wall beside Ainsley's head. "She didn't want to be with him, just wanted to help him get back to Heaven. And of course, he blamed the whole mess on me. If I hadn't done anything, he'd have been lost to me forever. He had to stay. So I killed every last one of them, and Heaven placed the blame squarely on Noel's shoulders."

"But why would they blame him?" Ainsley didn't know why he tried to speak. Cian's grip was tight enough that he could barely get in air, just enough to keep from getting too lightheaded. "He didn't kill them."

"But he was just as guilty as I was because he failed to save my immortal soul." Cian's face fell as he remembered. " Even then, he didn't stay with me. We were both fallen together. No more Heaven to worry about, and even then he pleaded with me to kill him, too. He can't kill me, you know; he's tried. It'll end this time, though."

"You'll drag him down to Hell with you."

"At least then he won't leave. Besides, it's not like Heaven cares enough to stop me or save him."

"Cian—"

"Do you know why Heaven cut me off? I came across a man beating a prostitute. He wouldn't stop when I demanded, so I hit him. I didn't know my own strength." Cian laughed. "Or perhaps I did. But no one could say that the man didn't deserve death. That was why they cut me off from Heaven."

"Even if they were wrong, you made it worse each time."

"Why should I be loyal to them when Heaven was willing to throw me aside for even the smallest of infractions?"

Ainsley thought Cian was rather missing the part where he'd killed a man. "Then you didn't have to drag Morgan into it."

"Morgan," Cian sneered. "He took her last name when she died, you know; some sort of homage to the dead. I tried reminding him that it wasn't her name. It was his name he was carrying, but the martyr didn't care." He shook his head. "It doesn't matter, though; he'll come back and I'll either kill you and push him that one last step to finally fall over the edge, or I'll kill *him*."

"He'll stop you this time."

Cian stopped and looked at Ainsley. Then a smile slowly curled his lips. "Do you think you'll give him the strength to kill me? How very romantic of you. What do you think inspires him, hmm?" Cian pressed uncomfortably close. "Do you think it's your looks? Perhaps your constant need for control? What do you have, Ainsley Moore, that I don't?"

"A conscience." Cian backed off, eyes widening as he took in that answer. He let Ainsley fall to the floor and Ainsley curled up, trying to make himself as small as possible against the wall. Cian looked like he might say something more when they both heard running footsteps down the hall.

They watched quietly as Morgan made his way up the foyer, stopping when he saw the two of them. His eyes locked onto Ainsley first, and Ainsley could see worry and relief at seeing him alive warring in his eyes. Then he looked at Cian. His expression changed,—sadness was definitely present, and guilt. "Cian."

"Noel. I see you've replaced me at last." Cian gestured down to Ainsley and Morgan sighed.

"Not replace. Never replace." He sighed again. "Why Cian? Why still?"

"The same questions," Cian sneered. "Maybe you and the pretty boy are well-suited for each other, after all. Besides, didn't you know? I'm an addict."

"You're not an addict," Ainsley cut in. "You stopped for twenty years. You don't even care for Heaven, so why would you want to see it?" Cian shot Ainsley a hateful look that promised a slow and painful death. "I don't want to kill you."

"But you will." Morgan nodded and Cian let out a huff of laughter. "Then try. And if you fail this time, he'll be the one to suffer. I can see already how close you've been dragged to Hell. I'll bring you those last couple steps and you'll have no choice. Once I bring you to Hell with me, there will be no turning back." Cian pulled a weapon from the sheath in his jacket, a long, wicked-looking knife that made Ainsley gasp. "I won't kill you. I'll kill him and make you watch." His wings came out, then, black, monstrous, and corrupted. Feathers fluttered to the ground, a few of them landing in Ainsley's lap.

"If your real fight is with me, then why bring all these humans into it? Why bring Ainsley into it?"

"Because they've always mattered more. You would have never been happy with me, turning your back on Heaven. That's why you left."

Morgan's eyes darkened. "It is."

"Bastard!" Cian leaped at him and Morgan didn't bother to try and dodge. Instead, he allowed Cian to bowl into him and they tumbled backward together, crashing through to the foyer. There were grunts and curses as they struggled together, and Ainsley thought he heard the clatter of the knife falling to the ground. Ainsley struggled to his feet, not sure if his presence would make things better or worse, but needing to do something more than sitting there, waiting.

He managed to pull himself to his feet, but a soft hand against his shoulder stopped him. His spine stiffened and he turned slowly, ready to find almost anything behind him. Eleanor stood there, her expression sad, but determined. Ainsley's eyes widened as he took in her transparency. "Eleanor?"

Eleanor didn't speak; instead, she mouthed something to him. Ainsley couldn't make out her words, but another loud crash drew his attention toward the fight. Morgan let out a wounded cry when Cian caught him in the side with the knife. He'd brought his wings out now, large and gray, just like Ainsley remembered from the evening before. Was it just his eyes or was that gray growing just a bit lighter?

Ainsley turned back to look at Eleanor, but she had vanished. Shrugging, he started to make his way over to the fight. Even if he could do nothing more than throw himself onto Cian in hopes that he could give Morgan the advantage. Regardless of what Cian claimed, Ainsley remained confident that Morgan would stop Cian.

A strange feeling came over him, then, something sliding into his skin. It reminded him of the feeling he'd had before the thing that had taken over his body had walked him into the street. But this time, instead of being completely aware of his actions, he found himself slipping away. The last thing he heard was Eleanor's soft voice: "I'm sorry, Ainsley."

Cian smirked and stepped back. "Is this the best you can do, Noel? It's no surprise you've failed all these years. All those people dead because you're weak."

Morgan roared and threw himself at Cian, uncaring of the knife. Morgan landed on top of Cian, the knife skittering beyond either of their reaches. Despite being pinned, Cian's smile was still cocky. "Go ahead and kill me, Noel."

"Why, Cian? I just want to know why."

"Seems we're both doomed to never get what we want, then, huh?" Cian's fist caught Morgan in the chin, throwing him off-balance. Morgan grunted as Cian's next fist caught him in the stomach. While he was struggling to catch his breath, Cian reversed their positions. Morgan looked into his eyes and it hit him finally that there was not much left to save in Cian. He didn't resemble the angel Morgan had once loved in the least bit.

Cian's grin turned manic. "The thing I regret most is that you won't get a chance to see me kill him. I won't get to see your pained expression." His fingers stroked Morgan's cheek, pushing a few stray hairs out of his face.

"I hate you." Cian's grin melted slowly from his face, his hand paused. "Rest assured. If I'm going to Hell, I'm dragging you with me."

"For him?"

"For him. For all those people you killed. All those people you will kill. But mostly for him."

Was it possible to hear the very second a heart broke? Morgan imagined he could. He watched as Cian's eyes widened in shock, as his fist clenched and his teeth gritted together violently. Had Cian truly believed all this time that there was any way they would be together again? "Then don't let me stop you from being a martyr again." Cian slammed his fist into the floor beside Morgan's head and Morgan could hear the hardwood crack.

Cian raised his hand and Morgan could see the blood dropping from his fist, turning black before it hit the floor. "I'll grant your wish, then."

Cian's wings extended to their full span and Morgan realized he wouldn't be able to keep his promise to

Ainsley. Darkness coalesced around Cian's fist into the form of a wickedly sharp claw. Blood continued to drip onto Morgan's cheek. Looking up, though, he realized that not all of it was blood—Cian was crying.

Then his fist started to descend and Morgan closed his eyes, awaiting certain death.

When it didn't come, Morgan carefully opened his eyes to see Cian's fist hovering just about his chest. Cian seemed preoccupied with something protruding from his own chest. It took Morgan blinking until he was able to focus. Was that Cian's knife? Cian turned at the same time Morgan raised his eyes to see Ainsley standing above them both—but it wasn't Ainsley. Something was off. The eyes.

"You?" Cian's voice wavered.

"Who's the nightlight now, asshole?" The voice wasn't right either. Ainsley had been possessed. Again.

The feathers began to molt from Cian's wings as he whipped his head back to Morgan, eyes panicked. "Noel." Then he couldn't talk. The many souls Cian had taken over the past fifty-five years poured free from his mouth, the resulting light so blinding that Morgan had to close his eyes. He felt a caress against his face, the touch all at once warm and comforting, before it drifted upward toward Heaven. When the light faded, he slowly opened his eyes again and found himself staring into a blank red gaze. Cian's wings were nothing but bone. He thought for a moment that Cian was gone, but then he heard him whisper, "When did everything go so wrong, Morgan?"

"When you started killing." Cian continued to stare. "Every time you killed one of them, you took a piece of me, too."

"All I wanted ... " Cian stopped himself with a hoarse laugh. "It doesn't matter what I wanted, does it?" He let out a groan of pain and clutched his chest. "Looks like I'll be alone in the end, after all." He fell backward, then.

When his back hit the floor, he started sinking, until there was nothing left of him.

Morgan could only stare at the spot where Cian had disappeared. He sat up and tried the space with his hand, but there was no give. Cian was gone. The thought should have made him happy. Cian was gone. His victims were free. Ainsley was safe. So why did Morgan feel as though he wanted to cry?

A shuffling sound made Morgan look up to see Ainsley standing there, an expression of vindication on his face. Then he seemed to notice Morgan was looking at him. "I notice," —Morgan was proud of the fact that his voice managed to stay calm— "that you didn't join them." He gestured upward to make it clear to whom he was referring.

The person in Ainsley's body followed his finger upward, then smiled, "Yeah, I suppose vengeance isn't high on their list of approved actions."

"Is that what it was?"

"Take care of him. He was a good friend to me, even if he never realized it." Ainsley's eyes closed and his body fell toward Morgan.

~~*

Ainsley sat on the bench beside the cemetery and watched as David stood beside his sister's grave. He'd stood beside David through the funeral, but he'd thought that David and Eleanor needed some time alone. He hadn't been sure exactly how far away he should go, though, so he'd settled on the bench.

"Nice day, huh?" He looked to his left to see Eleanor sitting beside him.

"I suppose."

"I never imagined I'd be attending my own funeral."

The statement sounded so surreal. "Was it okay?" Normal people didn't have to worry about things like this, whether or not their friend approved of their funeral. Or maybe they did have to worry, but the person wasn't in attendance to personally critique it.

"Ainsley, the fact that someone cared enough to give me a funeral made it perfect." She sighed. "I never thought about this part, you know? There was supposed to be plenty of time in my future."

"Isn't that what we all believe?"

"It's true." She stretched her legs out, foot going through a leaf. It bothered him, but he didn't want to bring it up. "They all went to Heaven when he died."

Ainsley didn't have to ask about what she was talking. He'd awakened after that encounter with his head cradled in Morgan's lap, and when he'd sat up, wanting to know what had happened, Morgan had tugged him back down. He'd held Ainsley so close that Ainsley had worried about whether he could breathe, but he hadn't told Morgan to stop, doing a bit of clinging of his own. It was over and even the thought of that was hard to believe.

"So what about you?" Ainsley asked her.

Eleanor shrugged. "I guess I haven't earned my wings yet. Although you would think that killing a monster would have done that."

"Do you regret it?"

"Not one bit. Your boyfriend would have killed him, you know. He would have regretted it later, but he would have done it. The last straw was when he threatened you, I think." Ainsley didn't remember any of this. "There were so many souls, Ainsley. So many people that he'd killed. Look at David." She gestured to her brother. "Who will take care of him now?"

"You will, I guess." Eleanor turned surprised eyes on him. "Don't tell me you weren't thinking about that."

"It's true. I mean, I know he can handle himself, but he's my little brother, you know? I practically raised him. I just want him to be happy." They watched as David coasted his hand along the casket. " What about you, Ainsley?"

"I want him to be happy, too?"

Eleanor rolled her eyes. "I mean, why are you here by yourself? Where's your boyfriend?"

"He's coming to pick me up." Ainsley gestured to his foot. "He couldn't come because ... " Ainsley didn't finish his sentence.

Eleanor picked it up, though. "It's fine. I understand. He still mourns Cian."

Ainsley frowned. "He understands that Cian had to die. He was ready to do it himself. I think the reality was just a little ... " He shrugged. "I don't think he'd prepared himself for the actuality."

Eleanor nodded. "But everything else?"

"Everything's fine." Ainsley blushed as he spoke.

"Is that so?" Eleanor giggled. "Are you finally putting some effort into it?"

"Well, after all that happened in my apartment, he was going to let me stay with him." It had worked for all of a day, when Morgan had returned from work to find Ainsley organizing his silverware by their size and width. " That didn't work out too well, so he helped me find a sublet."

"Can't stay there?"

"A portal to Hell opened up in my apartment. I wouldn't be able to sleep there."

"Ask Morgan to stay with you; maybe you won't have to worry about sleeping." Eleanor followed that statement with a suggestive wink. Ainsley did his best to ignore her and she laughed again. When she'd settled, she asked, "So you got your happy ending, then?"

"I miss you, Eleanor."

"Why miss me? I'll still be around, popping in to check on you." She winked again and Ainsley blushed.

"Please don't," he begged, and she laughed again.

"It's not how I wanted things to end, but I'll do the best with what I can." She tilted her head as if listening for something. "So, everything's good? You're happy?"

"I am." It was weird to realize that he was, even if Morgan had taken to dropping him off at the library rather than leaving him in his apartment alone. Right after Cian's death, Morgan had disappeared for a day. He'd returned the next, a bit moodier, but gradually getting better. Ainsley wondered if Morgan had been to visit Trionne's grave, but chose not to ask. There were some secrets better kept.

"Good." Eleanor stood, her eyes tracking her brother's progress toward the church. "You deserve it. I'm glad we were friends—are friends. Thank you for taking care of me." She glanced down the path. "Tell Morgan I'm sorry."

"Don't say things you don't mean."

Eleanor gave him a wry smile and vanished. Not long after she disappeared, Ainsley watched Morgan walk up the way. He was careful not to look in the direction of the cemetery, instead keeping his eyes focused on Ainsley. When he got to the bench, he commented, "Beautiful day."

"It was."

"Did everything go okay?"

"According to the guest of honor, it was perfect."

Morgan repeated his words quietly, and then it seemed to dawn on him to whom Ainsley was referring. He smiled and offered Ainsley a hand. "Ready to go?"

Ainsley took his hand and let Morgan help him to his feet. "I think I've found the perfect ending for your story."

"Oh?"

"And they lived happily ever after."

"Bit presumptuous of you, isn't it?" Morgan laughed as he dodged Ainsley's punch. He handed Ainsley his crutches and Ainsley was a bit sad. This moment felt like a hand holding moment, but his stupid crutches would stop any attempt.

Not quite perfect, then, but Morgan smiled at him and Ainsley thought to himself that it was pretty close.

One for Sorrow

Sylvia A. Winters

Suriel has been around death for a long time. Reaping souls has never been an easy job, but it's all Suriel has ever known. There have been times when her purpose has been brought into question, when she has looked at a mother with her face raised to the clouded sky, begging for her child's life, and Suriel hasn't wanted to have to take that soul away; but she never relents, because death is eternal and every living being, including herself, belongs to it.

There are others like her, angels of death, reapers and ferrymen, working across the world. Suriel has her favorite haunts and this place is one of them. The church itself is old, first built in the 1540s, burned down in 1658 and rebuilt from the ruins a hundred years later. The graveyard is older than the church. When they dug the foundations, they found the bodies of sacrifices to ancient gods. Suriel doesn't know what happened to the souls of those people; perhaps another angel took them or perhaps they belonged to someone else, some other god that demanded blood in payment for his favor. Suriel knows little of such mysteries.

She watches from the trees as a little girl in a blue dress, hair uncombed and pulled back in a messy ponytail, lays down a bunch of sunflowers on her mother's grave. Her father watches her with reddened, deeply shadowed eyes. Suriel knows the look well. The small baby in his arms starts to wail and he looks lost, stares down at it as though he doesn't even know what it is, let alone what to do with it. The girl takes the baby from him and bounces him gently in her arms, looking as though she's had as little sleep as her father.

The baby goes quiet and the girl sits down with him in a sunny spot, while her father kneels beside the grave. For a moment, Suriel's heart goes out to the girl and she wishes things were different for her. The girl turns to look into the trees and seems to stare right at her for several moments, until her gaze passes over her and she turns back to the baby in her arms.

Suriel sees the girl a few times between her parents' deaths, as she waits in the trees for dark to fall, so she can reap souls unseen and unheard. The girl, Corrine, often sits in the graveyard, scribbling furiously in a brown leather notebook. It's as peaceful a place for her as it is for Suriel; unlike most people Suriel sees in graveyards, she seems almost happy here.

Fifteen years after her mother's death, Suriel watches Corrine bury her father, the baby, Alec, now grown and standing beside her. They take comfort in one another and Suriel almost feels as if she knows them. She held their mother's soul as a part of herself once and she knows their names, knows Corrine's love of books and animals and pretty clothes. Corrine is beautiful, and her heart is pure and full of love. Suriel doesn't need to hold her soul to know that; she can see it in the way she cares for her brother, in the way she moves, in the way she speaks. For

Suriel, it is only a small spark of feeling, but it is enough to make her wish that things were different.

~~*

Corrine has always thought this a beautiful place, visiting many times before to lay flowers at her mother's grave, and later on, her father's, too. Now, despite the beauty of it, the grass all lit up with a warm, golden glow, Corrine finds it grey, drab and cold.

She wraps her scarf tighter around her neck and mouth, blinking away the tears that blur her brother's name on the headstone. They laid him beside his mother and father, a family again in death. Corrine begins to cry every time she looks at their names etched side by side in stone.

A magpie pecks idly at the ground and, finding nothing, takes wing and settles over Alec's grave. It seems to stare at her and she stares back, her gloomy expression melting into a weak smile as the bird chatters at her and flies off into the trees, its feathers glinting green and violet in the setting sunlight.

Corrine's knees feel numb, the legs of her jeans damp and muddied from kneeling on the wet earth. It's November and she shouldn't be spending all day out in the cold, but her body refuses to move. She's been here for the better part of a week, arriving first thing in the morning when the gates open and leaving last thing at night, long after the sun has set. The caretaker is a nice old man whose wife is buried here, right in front of the house. He brings Corrine hot tea and sandwiches at lunchtime, but she is rarely hungry these days and doesn't eat much. Still, she makes an effort to accept his generosity.

A little over a week ago, she watched the last remaining member of her family being lowered into the earth. There weren't many people at the funeral; both of her parents were only children and she has no other relatives, but a few friends of her mother and father came to pay their respects, people she hadn't seen since her father's funeral three years ago. A small handful of Alec's old friends huddled together, bringing white roses to place on his coffin. Corrine doesn't have any friends; she has acquaintances and co-workers, people with whom she might have a drink with down the pub, but as for actual friends ... she was always too busy looking after Alec to ever maintain any firm friendships. It was hard enough to scrape decent grades in school and college, let alone socialize on top of everything else.

Corrine thinks she understands now how her father felt when their mother died in childbirth, as if nothing could ever be good again. She cried for her mother, but her father practically disintegrated, grieving for so long that he became incapable of being anything other than a man who had lost his wife. He was never much of a father after that. Corrine remembers him lifting her up and making her soar through the air, the ground a blur of colors beneath her. She remembers him reading her bedtime stories about gods and devils and giants and dwarves, and kissing her goodnight. Alec had no such memories of their father; instead it was Corrine who played with him and read him stories and tucked him in at night.

She remembers the stories of the underworld, of the Norse Helheim, the rivers of ice and sharp blades that no man can pass through without suffering, the only bridge over guarded by a formidable giantess. She wonders if Alec is there now, faced with the half-living, half-decomposed figure of Hel. Perhaps he is elsewhere, having his heart weighed against a feather to see whether it will be eaten by Ammut. Corrine used to believe in these stories; as a young child, every one of them was true, but now she isn't sure what she believes, or if she even believes anything at all. There are many places Alec could be now, but how many of them would be kind to a person who took their own life?

She yawns; having grown accustomed to the chill of the winter air, it no longer feels invigorating and her eyelids droop. She rests her head on her arm, close to the headstone, and begins to talk, to tell a story, not of Hel or Ma'at, but Alec's favorite, which she made up just for him. In it, the two of them are eagles, soaring high above the Earth and looking down on their mother and father in the past, where they were happy and smiling. The two of them land on top of the house, and they flap their wings and become human again. They knock on the door to the house and their mother answers. She is beautiful and welcomes them inside where it's warm and happy. Corrine falls asleep before she reaches the end of the story, where they become eagles again, and their mother and father join them in the sky.

A few minutes later, Corrine is woken by a rustling sound to her left. Although it feels as if only a few minutes have passed, it must be closer to an hour, because the sun has set. The graveyard is gloomy now, lit only by the dim light from the gates and the caretaker's house. She sits up, rubbing a hand over her face and trying to stifle a yawn.

The rustling comes again and she scrambles to her feet. She isn't a person prone to jumping at every little sound, but it's dark and she can see the caretaker's television flickering, the blue light seeping through the thin curtains of the living room. She turns away from the house and looks back at the grave. She's further away from it than she thought; she must have rolled in her sleep. She rubs her eyes again, growing accustomed to the dark.

There's a shadow over Alec's grave. At first, she thinks nothing of it, but then realizes that it isn't cast by any tree or stone. The shadow moves and begins to take shape, the shadow slowly filling out into a human form. It appears male, with strong, muscular legs and broad shoulders, but as Corrine's eyes adjust, she realizes that it's a woman, her long, black hair tied into tight braids and pinned around her head in a crown. As she leans forward, a large pair of soot-black wings emerge from the shadows, the most beautiful thing Corrine has ever seen—and the most terrifying. She presses against the trunk of a tree, a knot digging hard into the small of her back. The woman bends down in the mud at the foot of Alec's grave and (God, she must either be dreaming or going mad from grief, because this can't actually be *real*) parts the earth with nothing but a gesture.

Corrine doesn't move, barely breathes, as she watches the woman jump into the grave. She hears the wood splinter, and then someone wheezes and coughs. When the woman climbs out, she's carrying a body in her arms— Alec, his arms wrapped tightly around her neck. The woman whispers something and Corrine leans forward, eyes wide.

Alec moves, twitches in the woman's arms, and Corrine is deafened by the sound of her own pulse. The woman sets Alec down and he stands by himself. Corrine is ready to run to him, to hold him, kiss him, tell him everything will be alright, but then he screams and Corrine's body seizes up with fright. The scream becomes a wail and his body is jerking violently, the woman holding him still and running a hand over his face as his cries increase in volume and desperation. Corrine moves, pushes herself forward until she's clutching at Alec's back, crying and yelling with him. She doesn't know what's happening, but she sees the woman lean forward and kiss him, before he grows still and falls to the ground.

Corrine falls with him, her ankle twisting painfully under her, making her cry out. Alec lies limp in her arms once more. Corrine wants to scream, to shout at this intruder, this strange and unnatural grave robber. She wants to hit her and scream her grief as she does so. Instead, she demands, "What the fuck is happening?" and the words grate in her throat, emerging strained and hoarse.

If this is a dream, then it's the most vivid and terrible dream Corrine has ever had. But the pain in her ankle is too real for it to be the product of her imagination.

She blinks up at the woman and almost chokes on a sharp intake of breath. The woman is bathed in a soft, bluish light, her eyes black and set in a soft, milk-skinned face. She looks surprised, not angry or malicious, and her face deepens into a confused frown, before relaxing and smoothing out again.

"Don't be afraid," the woman breathes. "I came to collect your brother's soul."

"Who are you?" Corrine asks, still clinging to her brother's body. "What have you done to him?"

She looks down at Alec, her hair falling forward and hiding her from the strange, winged woman. His eyes are empty, black sockets and his mouth hangs open loosely. Corrine takes in a shuddering breath and tears her gaze away from his face and back to the woman.

"You shouldn't be afraid of me—what has been done is necessary to extract the soul. I'm the angel Suriel. You are Corrine Thompson; you were born in this city and when you die here, I shall collect your soul, too."

Corrine laughs, the sound building to a hysterical crescendo. She shakes violently and clings to Alec's body for support, trying to ground herself. Finally, the shaking subsides and she looks up at Suriel, her face streaked with mud and tears. "You're mad," she whispers, shaking her head.

Suriel just smiles, and so Corrine tries again. "How do I know you're an angel? You expect me to take your word for it because of those?" She gestures at Suriel's wings, biting back another laugh. "You could be a demon or a mutant or ... or anything."

"Trust me, Corrine. I'm no demon."

"But how do I *know*? You're out robbing graves, for fuck's sake!"

"I steal nothing. His body will be placed back as I found it. I take only that which belongs to us."

"No!" Corrine shouts, almost screams, and Suriel's eyes widen in surprise. "He doesn't belong to you! His soul isn't yours to take. I don't care what you are, you can't have him!"

"Corrine, this choice isn't yours to make. I have to take him or his soul will remain here, cold and alone and scared while his body rots in the ground. Look." She rests a hand against Corrine's cheek, her skin cool.

Corrine feels a wave of warmth wash over her. Behind her eyes, she sees stars blinking into existence, sudden blazes of light and heat emerging in the darkness over billions of years, sped up before her.

"All life comes from God, and to Him, all life must return," Suriel whispers against her ear, and one by one, the stars explode, bursting outward and falling in on themselves, falling back into darkness.

Suriel steps back and Corrine's vision is her own again, the graveyard swimming back into view, seeming much lighter than before.

"You haven't answered anything," Corrine says softly, feeling calmer and even more resolved. "So you're an angel; I get it. Except I don't know what that *means*. You talk about God as if that means something; you show me the stars, but *why*? God gives and he takes away, is that it? Well, I don't give a fuck about God; I just want my brother. He wasn't even eighteen years old. He never had a fucking chance and you want to take him away?"

"It's his time. Once a body is dead, the soul must return to its creator. I have no power over this."

"You have no power? You're an *angel*; you just proved your power. All things return to their creator? Sure. But Alec hasn't even lived. What does it matter to you if he gets another chance, if he returns to his 'creator' a little later? It makes no difference to you, but it means *everything* to me. Please, Suriel, just give him back." She hears her voice crack on the last syllable and fights to regain control.

Suriel studies her for a moment and Corrine wants to hide from those deep, black eyes, wants to bury her face in her brother's body, curl into a ball and never look up. Instead, she holds her gaze. Then, Suriel nods, just once.

"There is something I could do," Suriel says, her voice barely a whisper in the dark. "But I shouldn't; it's not supposed to work this way. I don't have the authority."

"But you *can* do it?" Corrine clings to the grain of hope offered to her, and her hands fly from Alec's body to Suriel's shoulders, her flingers clutching at the rough material of her tunic. "You can bring him back?"

The angel shakes her head. "Not to this body; it's dead. But I can put him into a new one. Souls are often reborn, but I'm not supposed to act without higher authorization."

"Please," Corrine breathes, meeting Suriel's eyes with fierce determination. "I don't care. Just do it."

Suriel nods and kneels in front of her, closing the last inches between them and pressing their mouths together. The kiss is neither romantic nor refined, but after the initial shock of it, Corrine loses all resistance and opens her mouth under the press of Suriel's tongue. Her vision blurs and the ground seems to disappear as Suriel's arms wrap around her, enveloping her in warmth. Her face grows hot and she's dimly aware that there are tears running down her cheeks again, and then the warmth is gone and Suriel is standing by the graveside, lowering Alec's body back into his coffin. She claps her hands and the earth falls on top of him, appearing undisturbed.

Suriel moves towards her and lays a hand on her shoulder—in the dim light Corrine can see that her face looks strained and worried—and then the graveyard is empty again. This time, Corrine doesn't wait for the caretaker to send her on her way before limping slowly back to the flat she had shared with Alec only a few weeks earlier. She tries to keep her weight off her injured ankle, but savors the pain as the rest of her is overwhelmed by a deep-seated numbness.

Corrine doesn't bother undressing before she falls face down on her bed, grabbing her teddy and clutching it to her chest. As she falls asleep she desperately hopes that when she wakes up the last four weeks of her life will have all been a dream and she'll be able to manipulate Alec into making her bacon sandwiches in the morning.

~~*

Wrapped in a thick, black cloak of darkness that would be stifling if she weren't used to it, Suriel flies through the night and into the void between Earth and Heaven. It is cold here; a living human being would not survive the journey, but it is a path Suriel has travelled many times before. Here, she catches glimpses of events she only half-remembers, swimming behind her eyes and melting back out into the void. She doesn't question them; she knows that the void will eventually eat away everything she remembers. So many of her memories have already been lost here, but she doesn't miss them, doesn't need them; she has seen many things and many are irrelevant to her existence. Prolonged exposure is dangerous, but no one ever remains in the void longer than they must, although Suriel often feels the pull of it. She finds the darkness soothing, something about the quiet and total absence of life calming to her spirit.

Suriel is on another path, a dangerous path that makes the void seem like a charming country trail. She isn't sure why she did what she did; for many long years, she has gone untested, but now there is someone that exists who can not only see her, but is able to reach out and challenge her. Everything of which she was ever certain has been shaken. She knows that it's a weakness, a flaw that has been buried deep and widened over the years, but she doesn't regret her decision. She knows she will come to, but for now, she can't help but feel as though she has done the right thing, that she has, for the first time, done something fundamentally good. The problem with good deeds, of course, is that angels aren't supposed to be good or evil. Suriel knows that it doesn't matter which side she chooses—both ways only lead downward.

She could return to Heaven and admit what she has done, or she could return to Earth and wait until they drag her back. Or she could remain here, in this no-place for eternity. They would never find her, but she knows that she would lose herself. Even the wrath of Heaven would be preferable to the fate that awaits her here if she remains too long.

Suriel stops for a moment, her wings silent in the empty air. Now is not the right time to return to Heaven—she needs to think. She knows that she will have to return and that it won't be long before she can no longer ignore the pull of home and duty, but she also knows that little good awaits her there. Perhaps if she can reap more souls before she returns, they'll be more forgiving. God rarely forgives disobedience from His angels, but if there is one thing Suriel knows for certain, it's that His will cannot be predicted.

The doorway opens out over four hundred miles from where she entered and she emerges into a white flurry of snow. It's high up here, but her feet are on firm, albeit rather cold and wet ground. She sits on a rock jutting out from the hilly surface of the small mountain, crossing her legs beneath her and folding her wings close to her body. The cold is a welcome feeling after the emptiness of the void. She goes unseen here, always unseen when she wishes. Always, that is, until Corrine Thompson saw her collecting her brother's soul. Suriel doesn't know why that should be, can't begin to understand how divine purpose could be thwarted by the tired eyes of such a girl. Suriel must be growing old, weak; already there are small sparks of feeling that run through her being every now and then. They scare her, even the smallest emotions overwhelming.

There is a man climbing the small mountain and Suriel watches him for a while, submerging herself in his ascent, listening to his ragged breathing as he makes his way up the steep slope. Many people enjoy the walks up here; many more take the train up and just walk back down again, but it is not the descent Suriel values—no, it is the upward climb that is the most remarkable, the stretch and push of limbs, the sweat and heavy gasps for air. The ascent is slower; it takes time and it is difficult, even on a small journey such as this one. The descent is easy, albeit dangerous, and the trick is only to slow the fall.

Suriel feels the gentle tug of the dead, a hook beneath her ribs pulling her forward, and she takes flight once more, coming to land in a small graveyard in a Welsh village. A soul is calling to her, screaming, his voice lost in the void and re-emerging inside Suriel's head. The soul is that of a young boy, and he is easy to pin down as he screams and writhes. They always struggle when Suriel revives them, but they have to be brought back, just for the few moments while their souls are extracted.

It's a painful process, the body still dead, but the mind awake, alone in the bitter cold and the dark. Their souls are in the no-place of the body, neither truly dead nor truly alive. Suriel wishes she knew they were going to a better place, but that information has always been denied to her. She passes a hand over the boy's face, digs her fingernails into the sockets of his eyes and plucks them out, blocking his exits should he try to escape. Then she kisses him and feels his soul enter her body, everything that made this boy special and unique, everything that ever made him happy or scared or angry. His body stills, and reverently, she places it back in the grave. The soul within her churns, a warm fire in her chest; she takes a moment to soothe it with her thoughts, waiting until it goes quiet before she moves on.

In Venice, a woman of ninety-six is interred in the earth after dying from kidney failure; in New York City, a man of forty-three dies from pneumonia whilst living on the streets; in Vancouver, a three-year-old girl is run down by a car; in Damauli, a fourteen-year-old boy has been beaten to death. She reaps them all and keeps them safe within her, calming their fears until she feels them settle. Suriel is almost ready to return home, to take the souls for their judgment, but there is one more thing she needs to do—she has to see the girl, Corrine. In her grief and misery, Corrine seemed the most beautiful thing to have ever crossed Suriel's path—a human that could see her and communicate with her. Suriel might never return to Earth, and before she leaves, she must see her, just one more time. One glance, just enough to determine whether or not she made the right choice, and then she will fly once more into the darkness.

Suriel had expected to wait a while before finding Corrine, but as soon as she enters the graveyard, she sees her sitting cross-legged on the grass. She's reading aloud from a book of poetry, her voice crisp and light on the warm spring air. She's smiling, one hand resting on her swollen stomach where a new life is still growing; she no longer seems the broken, desperate creature Suriel met the last time. Instead, she appears to have returned to her old self, the quiet, peaceful girl that Suriel has watched over the years.

Suriel knows that while it has only been a short time since she last saw Corrine, it has been months since Corrine last set eyes on her. Time moves differently in the void and the same journey can take as little as five minutes or as long as five years.

~~*

Corrine glances up from her book, placing the marker between its pages and setting it aside, the smile fading from her face. In the golden light of the evening, Suriel is even more beautiful, her features sharp and angular, and wings lit up with the sun's rich glow. Corrine sees that they are not black as she thought, but dark with iridescent purples, greens, and blues that seem to shimmer as she moves.

Corrine eyes Suriel warily as she sits down beside her, tucking her bare feet beneath her. It has been a while since Corrine last saw her, but she hasn't forgotten that night—Alec's anguished wailing, Suriel's figure emerging from the shadows. It's a scene that has plagued her dreams for months.

In the daylight, Suriel seems almost fragile, but Corrine knows better. She feels the earth beneath her hand, twists her fingers in the uncut blades of grass to reassure herself of its solidity, its reality.

"He grows strong," Suriel smiles, reaching out and laying a hand on Corrine's stomach.

Corrine's breath catches in her throat, the touch unexpected. "Yeah, thanks."

Weeks passed and she didn't know what would happen, had no idea if Alec would return to her or if she had dreamt the whole thing. It was worse, in a way, than anything that had come before—the confusion, the feeling that she might be going mad ... It was almost too much to bear. Then she found out she was pregnant, and suddenly she *knew* it had all been real. Corrine laughed, falling into a long bout of hysterical laughter and tears, alone in her flat with the test still in her hand. She thought it ridiculous, the idea of a ... well, not a *virgin* birth, but what basically amounted to the same damn thing.

Suriel looks confused for a moment. "I'm sorry, I thought you knew."

"How could I possibly have known? I mean, I asked for him back, but this? It's kinda creepy, you know?"

"You want me to take him back?" Suriel frowns, her fingers twisting together in her lap.

"No," Corrine says quickly. "No, I don't. I just ... you could have warned me."

Suriel looks almost lost, vulnerable out here in the open. "Oh. I'm sorry," she says quietly. "I just assumed."

Corrine sighs and leans forward a little to rest a hand on Suriel's shoulder. "It's fine. I'm just happy to have him back ... even if it is weird."

"There was no other way. I can't create a new body or bring an old one back to life. Only God can do that."

"What's he like?" Corrine asks hesitantly. "God, I mean ... "

"I wouldn't know. Only two angels, the Shekinah and Metatron, have direct contact with Him. But Heaven ... it's full of His love ... and His wrath. It's a place of beauty. Nothing spoils it."

Corrine thinks for a moment, picturing a perfect garden like the one her grandmother used to keep. She never met her grandmother, but her photo albums contained many pictures of the garden, the grass always kept trim, the flowerbeds neat and tidy, not a single twig or leaf out of place. It was beautiful, yes, but Corrine never much liked the look of it. It was no fun playing in gardens like that, where you could look, but not touch. The fields by the lake near their house were much better, with tunnels through the hedgerows, ditches, and long grass that came up to her waist.

"And you live there?"

"I live everywhere." Suriel smiles softly, and Corrine belatedly realizes that she's telling a joke, or what could pass for one. "But yes, that is my home."

"And this," Corrine gestures at the space around them. "This is, what ... your workplace?"

"I go where I'm needed, which is primarily places like this— graveyards, battlefields, wherever the dead lie."

"Can't be much fun."

"No, but it's important." Suriel's voice is firm, resolute. "Angels were not made to fulfill their own needs. We work, and without us, this world would fall apart."

Corrine has nothing to say to that. She feels sorry for Suriel; it must be lonely for her, having only one sole purpose, and ignoring all her own needs and desires. Corrine smiles, then, and the confused look on Suriel's face only makes her laugh; she doesn't have to imagine how it feels, because she knows first-hand: her whole life has been spent putting aside the things she wanted for herself—friends, university, everything—and for all that Suriel is strange and different, they actually have something in common.

"So why did you help me?" Corrine asks, tilting her head to one side and watching the way Suriel's lips press together in a hard line, her dark eyes avoiding Corrine's gaze. "I mean ... you're an angel. You could have just ... I don't know, ignored me or knocked me out, or something. But you didn't; you helped me."

"You believe I'm an angel now, then?"

"Yeah, I believe. I mean, I still wasn't completely sure ... but this ..." She waves a hand at her stomach, a smile spreading across her face. "Well, I guess it's as close to a miracle as you could get; and you're avoiding the question."

Corrine is pretty sure she sees a blush spreading across Suriel's cheeks. "I don't know. I've been around death for a long time, my whole existence. I've never created life before. No one has ever challenged me before ... no one has even seen me before unless I wanted them to. Why did you?"

Corrine thinks for a moment. "Why did I see you or why did I challenge you?"

"I understand why you would challenge me. Grief is a powerful thing. I understand that, but I don't understand how you could have seen me."

"I don't know," Corrine shrugs. "I just woke up and there you were." She shivers at the memory, the cold reminder that Suriel isn't human.

Suriel frowns and shifts her wings, folding them around her shoulders like a cloak. Corrine reaches out a hand before her mind even registers what she's doing.

"Can I?" she asks, her voice low and tentative.

Suriel doesn't say anything, just shifts a little closer and inclines her head slowly.

Suriel's wings are beautiful, delicate at first sight, and Corrine's fingers stroke through the soft feathers. It's soothing, the feel of them against her skin, and she can't help but wonder what they would feel like wrapped around her back.

She shifts forward, almost pulling herself into Suriel's lap, the movement slowed by her pregnancy. Suriel's wings shift beneath her hands and she curls her fingers over the muscled frame, awed by the solid strength of them. Suriel leans forward and their lips meet, a soft press of their mouths, before they pull apart, and Corrine's free hand comes up to trace the line of Suriel's jaw.

Suriel sighs and closes her eyes, her lashes long and dark against her skin, her hands coming up to rest on Corrine's arms. They stay like that for a while, sitting together in the warm spring evening, their kisses gentle, almost reverent at first, deepening as the sun sets and the sky darkens.

Then Suriel is pulling away. It feels as though only seconds have passed, but Corrine knows it has been much longer.

"I have to go," Suriel murmurs, eyes downcast.

Corrine wants to pout and demand that she stay, just for a little while longer. She wants to understand Suriel's world, to question her about Heaven and the things she has seen. She wants to pull Suriel to her and bury her hands in her dark feathers and her hair, to give her something that isn't about duty, but she knows that Suriel has important things to attend to. Besides, Corrine has already asked too much of her, she doesn't want to ask for more. Instead, she asks, "When will I see you again?"

Suriel shakes her head sadly. "I don't know. I'll return when I can, but there is much to be done."

Corrine grasps hold of her hand, forcing a smile and pressing a parting kiss to Suriel's lips. "Thank you." She steps back, missing Suriel's departure when she looks down at her feet for a second. When she looks up again, Suriel is gone, leaving her alone in the darkening graveyard.

~~*

Suriel locates a doorway amongst the branches of an old oak tree overlooking a lake. The water is dark, seeming still in the cool of the night, the leaves of the tree whispering gently in the breeze. Suriel lands on the thickest branch, ducking her head solemnly. This is a sacred place and she takes a moment to flatten her palms to the rough bark, to feel the tree breathing beneath her skin, before she slips down and into the darkness once more.

Here, in this no-place, she feels the crushing, suffocating weight of the darkness, no longer a familiar, quiet blanket of solace. She is completely alone here. It has never made her afraid before; cautious, yes, but never afraid. Now, she thinks of Corrine, of her smile and her purely human soul, so beaten and damaged, but healed to its limits by Suriel's hand. She could lose her in this place; the darkness would claim all memory of her and it would be as though she never existed. Suriel would never see her again and she wouldn't even miss her. Corrine would be wiped from Suriel's mind. There is nothing that Suriel has ever had cause to miss before, nothing that was so precious she could not regain it elsewhere, but now she clings desperately to the feel of Corrine's fingers running through her feathers, of Corrine's mouth on hers, the sensation of being truly alive at Corrine's smile and at her touch. She would relinquish everything to the darkness—everything but this.

A small glimmer of orange light flickers in the black and she feels that she's close now, but knows that in the void, distance is just as irrelevant as time. Flying here is not like flying on Earth, with the wind brushing through her feathers, and it's not like flying in Heaven, with love and warmth and purpose guiding her. Really, it is not much like flying at all and more like floating, just under the water, eyes closed and not knowing which way is which. To a new angel, freshly created, it would be unimaginable, but Suriel knows how to navigate through it. She doesn't remember her first time—perhaps the void took that away too, or perhaps it just faded naturally with time.

She reaches the door and passes through before she can even register that the darkness has fallen away and been replaced by the bright light of the sun. There is no door directly into Heaven, and instead, she finds herself at a set of silver and iron gates, two gargoyles—the gatekeeper angels of the sixth Heaven—perched high on either side. As she approaches, the gargoyles move, stand tall with their stone wings stretched out behind them. They both wield swords of fire, the flames flickering and curling around the heavy metal of the blades. Suriel bows low and they nod once, before the gates swing open and she is allowed to enter the kingdom of Heaven.

The first garden she passes through stretches further than she can see in all directions. There is no grass here and red dust swirls under the gust of her wings as she sets herself down, taking a moment to breathe in the pure air. She does not stay long and takes wing once more, heading onward until she reaches another gate. This one is much smaller and the angel that guards it is not made of grey stone, but of a reddish rock. He holds no weapon, but still no angel would dare cross him. He shows her through with a gesture of his wings, and she stands in a hallway; the walls, floor and ceiling are a rich marble with greens, reds, blues and golds threaded through the off-white.

There are many doorways leading out from the hall, each of them sealed. Suriel heads down to the very end of the hall, presses her hand to the smooth expanse of marble, and waits for the door to reveal itself. A thin line of gold stretches around the outline of her hand, and when she removes it, the handprint begins to glow and spread outward, until the wall disappears, leaving only bright space. Suriel steps into it, and instantly, the light dims.

She stands in the large waiting room and stares at the ceiling for a long time, watching the clouds dance around each other, blown apart by a wisp of her breath and reforming again, taking on new shapes and patterns. They are never the same and she takes great pleasure in the knowledge that every time she breathes, she is creating something new and ephemeral. For a little while, at least, she can play at being human.

A door opens and an angel wrapped in a dark cloak with ashen wings spread out behind him descends the pearly staircase at the far end of the room. The angel is genderless, but he is brother to Suriel, as are all angels. Suriel knows him well: Cassiel, Angel of Solitude and Tears, ruler of the seventh Heaven, whose duties are far more precious than Suriel's own. Cassiel will take the souls into the realm of the seventh Heaven, of which this room is only an antechamber. There they will be judged and, if they have not yet reached the ends of their journeys, their next lives will be determined.

Suriel bows and waits until Cassiel stops before her to straighten again. The souls squirm inside her, reacting to this new presence and immediately growing afraid again.

She tries her best to calm them, but she can still feel them quaking. Cassiel reaches forward and cradles her face with skeletal hands. Suriel reaches for him as well, reverently, and pulls back the hood of Cassiel's cloak. The face beneath is a blank space, part of the void pulled apart from itself and molded into form. The eyes that burn within are of white fire, dancing deep in the darkness.

Suriel waits, the souls growing increasingly desperate with each second that passes, until finally, Cassiel leans in and kisses her. The burden grows lighter as the souls are sucked out of her, one by one. They will move on and be judged. Suriel doesn't think about what might happen if any one of them is found lacking; that is not her purpose here.

Cassiel bows and retreats back up the stairs, while Suriel leaves through a small wooden door to the right of the staircase. She has had very little cause to ever remain long in this part of Heaven. The grass here is green and lush, the flowerbeds tangled with all manner of unearthly plants, as well as roses, marigolds, tulips and forget-me-nots.

A huge willow tree stands in the center of the garden and three angels kneel beneath its shade, their hands pressed to the trunk of the tree. She recognizes them instantly as Jabniel, Rabacyel and Dalquiel, but in their prayer, they are only part of the tree through which they pass their worship to God. They are humming and their song fills Suriel, until she, too, is kneeling, pressing her hands to the rough bark of the tree and humming with them.

Through the tree, she can feel them, these three angels whose purpose is to serve the third Heaven and to worship here at the tree; their hearts beat in unison, their minds synced and blank. They think only of the tree and the tree rewards them, gives them visions that Suriel will never experience, no matter how long she kneels and prays here.

Suriel shows the Shekinah her weaknesses, her failing in the graveyard, her desire for Corrine. Everything, she gives to the Shekinah—and the Shekinah speaks. The voice inside her head is for her and her alone.

She feels her body slip away as the Shekinah pulls her into itself. She does not feel afraid; there is only peace here as she awaits her judgment, happy that whatever is decided will be righteous and just. The Shekinah is thoughtful, its wispy branches blowing in the breeze of the four angels' breath. The humming is not only from the angels now, as the Shekinah sings with them, its purpose clear. Suriel presses her face to the trunk, dropping delicate, reverent kisses to the bark.

You have failed in your duty. You have acted against the laws of Heaven and of God.

"Yes, I know, I'm ... " Suriel was going to say 'sorry', but she cannot lie here. She falls silent and waits for the Shekinah's next words.

You are old now, and yet you are young. There is a secret that no one ever tells, but I shall tell it now. Suriel stares up into the high branches of the tree, waiting with bated breath. *Angels are not infallible. We fight, we fall. You do not remember the war, yet you fought in it, killed in it. The void has taken it from you and it is a blessing. I remember everything.*

Suriel has heard stories of the war, rumors passed down through the angels, and even reaching mankind, but they had always been stories, a history of a time before she was created. The void took the memory from her, and she doesn't know if she should be grateful or distraught. The Shekinah's calm washes over her and she feels nothing.

Since Man was born, you have been here, Suriel. You have never once neglected your purpose; you have never once forgotten your charges or made a mistake, until now. You have forgotten your place and broken the highest command in choosing the next life for a human soul. Law dictates that you should be bound in the fifth Heaven for eternity.

Suriel nods slowly. She will be bound in heavy chains to always mourn the loss of her divinity, so close to God's presence, and yet so far away, forbidden to see anything but the darkest depths of her tainted soul.

But God forgives, Suriel. Not only Man, but us as well. You will not be punished, although you deserve to be.

"What will happen?" Suriel asks, her question a melody, barely leaving her lips before it is answered.

That is up to you. You have strayed onto the path of free will and you shall decide your own fate.

The answer, when it comes, is simple and not a little surprising. Suriel has spent her whole existence serving God. She *loves* God, loves Heaven, but her first thought is of Corrine. She knows that a life of servitude would be a lie that she would only come to resent.

"I want to be with Corrine," she says. "I want to live."

Then you shall live. You have created life and you will care for it. You will not return here until you die a mortal death. Then, like all other mortal souls, you shall be judged. You may go.

Suriel is almost ready to leave, but there is still a question that burns within her and she cannot leave without asking. "Why could Corrine see me?"

You understand so much, and yet so little. No human is capable of seeing an angel unless that angel reveals itself. Whether by conscious intent or by unconscious accident, she saw you because you wanted her to.

Suriel breaks away from the tree and feels its power drain from her. She presses a firm kiss to the trunk once more, a symbol of her gratitude, and then she leaves, walking back through the door and away from the singing of the angels, away from the unsurpassed beauty of the Shekinah; unsurpassed, except by God.

~~*

Corrine holds her newborn baby in her arms, his lungs strong and his cries loud, tiny arms waving up at her, hands grasping. She presses him to her breast and he clamps his mouth over her nipple, going quiet instantly. It's a strange feeling and she can't quite bring herself to think of this small new life as her brother; he's her son now, and although she spent most of her life looking after him, everything is different now.

She won't call the baby Alec, because Alec was her brother—the same soul, but in a different body, and she wants this to be a fresh start for both of them. Corrine spent a good part of the last month and a half thinking about names, but still hasn't thought of one that fits. As she looks down at him now, one name returns to her: René. Gentle and soothing, and more than anything else, fitting.

Corrine doesn't know where Suriel is now and has no idea if she'll ever see her again. She hopes she will and that Suriel isn't in trouble for this, but even given the chance to go back and redo it, Corrine wouldn't change her decision. It's been over three months since they last met and Corrine can't stop thinking about that evening, about the soft feel of Suriel's wings, the warmth of her body and the softness of her mouth. Despite how perfect this moment should be, something is missing. Through childbirth, there was no one to hold Corrine's hand, and it wasn't her parents for whom she longed—it was Suriel.

It isn't long before Corrine's ready to leave. She hails a taxi, shifting in her seat because it's uncomfortable to sit up at all at the moment. René cries almost the whole way home, and Corrine can see the taxi driver's frustration growing. When they arrive at her building, both of them are glad for her departure.

The nursery is decorated and ready. It hurt to tear down Alec's old posters, to clean the room of his things and pack them away into boxes for storage, but realistically, half-naked model pin-ups just aren't appropriate for a new born baby. Corrine changes his nappy, wrinkling her nose at the smell. She always hated doing this as a kid, but she got used to it then and she'll get used to it again now.

Looking down at him lying in his cot, making little snuffling noises as he sleeps, he doesn't look much like her brother. René's eyes are a dark violet, while Alec's were hazel, and the fine hair that clings close to his head is black, while Alec's was the same sandy color as her own. She struggles to remember how Alec looked on the day he was born, whether his hair and eyes had changed over time, but it was a long time ago and her memory of that day is marred with grief at the loss of her mother.

Weeks pass, and with them, René changes. His eyes lose their purple hue and fade to a green-flecked brown and his hair fills out a little. The Christening is a fairly quiet affair. A year ago, she would have thought that a naming ceremony would be just as good, but after all that had happened, she knew it was wrong for René. His life may not have been given by God, but he was a gift from something divine.

~~*

Suriel flies back the way she came, the gates leading off the third and seventh Heavens closed to her now. She knows it won't be forever, but she won't be the same when she returns—no longer angelic or divine, but human.

Instead of flying, Suriel walks over the red earth, the dust kicking up under her bare feet, the ground warm against her skin. She savors the journey, and when she reaches the gates, she wishes she had walked slower, that it had lasted longer.

As the gates shimmer into sight, she notices that the stone gargoyles have left their platforms and are standing on the ground, facing her. Together the angels preside over the Heaven. While one sleeps, the other watches. The only time both sets of eyes are open is when someone attempts to pass through the gates. At the moment, their swords hang at their sides, but the flames still crackle against the metal. She bows low as she reaches them, and this time, they return the gesture.

"Suriel," says Sabath, the angel on the right. "Many times have you passed before us into the kingdom."

"You shall be missed," finishes Zebul.

Suriel nods, touched by their emotion.

"Know that when you pass by us, it shall be the last time."

Suriel doesn't think about what her fate might be as a fallen angel. She was given this gift, and she takes it as a chance to start anew. She will not waste the life the Shekinah has given her.

As she passes by the gatekeepers, they each lay a rough, stone hand on her shoulders. Seconds pass, and then she slips back through the void, her wings too heavy to keep her on a straight path. The darkness all but consumes her and a numbing pain eats its way through her flesh, into her bones, through her skull and into her head. Somewhere, she loses her way and her flight becomes a fall.

When she awakens, Suriel is still in darkness, but it isn't the total dark of the void. There is a dim light filtering through a crack above her, and she's sprawled out across something hard and lumpy. The stench is terrible; she has long been used to the smell of freshly decaying bodies, but this is something else, a composting reek of old food and soiled nappies. She wrinkles her nose and pushes out her arms, lifting off the lid of the container. She pulls herself out and falls to the ground, gravel scraping her skin. Looking up at the large red container, she laughs out loud. The sound of her voice is strange, almost bitter. The doorway opened up into a large rubbish bin.

Suriel pulls herself to her feet; her body feels sore, her muscles weak and aching. Something is wrong, and she stumbles after letting go of the bin. She's off-balance, and it's only when she catches sight of herself in a small puddle of rainwater that she understands why: her wings are gone. Nothing remains of them, not even bloodied stumps or ribbons of sinew and feather. It's as though they were never there. She falls back to the ground, landing hard on her knees, skin tearing. Her eyes sting and she hides her face in her hands, giving in to the frightened shudders that rack through her body. It's the first time she has ever cried and it only frightens her more, making her want to curl up in the bin where she landed and hide away from the world, from her pain.

She doesn't. Instead, Suriel takes a deep breath and hauls herself back into a standing position, then takes a few tentative steps forward. Once she has a sense of her altered balance, she finds it a little easier to move.

There is only one place she needs to be, only one place where she has ever felt a connection to a living human being. She has to find Corrine. There is no one else in the whole world who can help her now. Suriel is no longer angelic; she needs to eat, drink. There are so many things she doesn't understand, all the fine intricacies of human society that she cannot simply soar over anymore. She needs Corrine, and she needs to take care of her and the baby. It isn't just a personal need now, but a duty that she has to fulfill, to take care of the life that she created.

She reaches the end of the alleyway and leans against the damp surface of the stone wall. Outside is a rush of bright colors, cars zipping past, one after the other. She realizes she must smell like the inside of the bin; her rough-hewn tunic is filthy and torn in places. She steps out into the street and immediately a car horn blares at her, even though she's standing close to the buildings and away from the road, one hand against the rough brick to support herself.

She needs a sign, a marker to tell her where she is. The doorways of the void are volatile at the best of times; only a skilled servant of Heaven can travel through unharmed and predict the region of the next doorway. Somewhere in there, Suriel lost a piece of herself and her flight through was more of a fall. She has no way of knowing where she is now.

A yellow neon sign in a doorway says 'open' and she realizes that she must be in an English-speaking country. She heads down the street toward a row of brightly lit shops and steps into the first one she sees. The smell of frying meat hits her in a wave and she suddenly feels very hungry.

There is a man behind the counter, his narrow eyes distrustful. "Can I help you?" he asks, his tone guarded. He wants her to leave, but she can't, not yet.

He is unnaturally quiet, his voice the only thing Suriel can hear from this distance. She cannot hear the steady beat of his heart or the wordless whisperings of his soul. He is closed to her and the silence is terrifying.

The fear is like a solid object lodged in her throat and her breath catches as she attempts to speak. She tries again, summoning her strength and pushing past it. She has more important things to do before she can let herself crumble around it.

"I wondered if you could tell me where I am." She knows the words sound strange and that the man won't appreciate her question at all, but it's more important that she knows than that he gets to keep his night an easy one.

"East Mount Vernon," he says. "You can get a taxi across the road."

"Thank you," Suriel replies. "Could you tell me which town and which country this is?"

The man looks at her as though she's grown a second head, and maybe it's worse than having a second head—people try to ignore physical deformity, but the appearance of madness scares them. The man is clearly unnerved now and his frown is so deep that a person could hold cards in the creases of his forehead.

"Somerset, Kentucky," he finally answers dryly.

"America?"

"No, Mozambique. Of course America. Go on now, get the hell outta here."

Suriel respects his abrupt request and leaves with a courteous "Thank you." Kentucky presents a problem, or rather, America presents a problem. Corrine lives in England and Suriel has no way of contacting her.

Suriel's tired; more than tired, she's exhausted, the feeling seeping deep into every pore of her body. Suriel has never slept before; angels don't need it. She finds herself drifting off even as she walks, and eventually, she finds a couple of bins, slips into the space between them and the wall, and allows herself to fall into unconsciousness.

She dreams. In the dream she's falling, her wings in tatters, and the Shekinah is laughing, its voice deep and mocking.

A woman shakes her awake, her face wrinkled and kind. "I'm sorry, honey. You can't sleep here," she says, her voice soothing.

Like the man Suriel spoke to before, the woman's heart and soul are silent.

Suriel blinks, and mutters, "Sorry."

"It's alright, honey, but you come on now, you can't stay here."

Suriel stands, her muscles protesting. She feels as though they're creaking beneath her skin.

"Listen, if you head west onto Columbia Street and keep going on Ohio, there's a place you can go there."

Suriel nods and the woman points her in the right direction. She drags her bare feet over the rough tarmac on to Columbia Street. It feels longer than it is, and when Suriel finally finds the building—an unassuming grey brick—she feels as though she could collapse.

She has to queue in line with five others, all of whom smell as bad as she does. What lives have they have lived to end up here? she wonders. They are her kin now, her brothers, but she doesn't speak a word to them, just waits until they've been shown through to another room and it's her turn to talk to the woman behind the glass screen. Suriel gives her name and improvises a second, Crawford, remembering a street she passed on the way.

Eventually, she's led through to a room filled with tables, where she's sat down and given soup, bread and milk. After devouring the meal, a man in his late forties hands her a small pile of clothes and a bar of soap, and shows her into the communal showers. He leaves her to strip away the material of her tunic, all that's left of her service in Heaven, and step under the warm spray from the shower. The hot water feels good on her skin, the soap even better.

When she emerges, Suriel feels more awake. The clothes she was given are too big, but a belt holds up the trousers, and she rolls up the cuffs of her shirt. She slips her feet into a pair of green socks and ties up the old, worn trainers. They fit well enough and she heads back out into the dining room.

She sleeps on the bottom of a bunk-bed, the springs creaking every time she moves, and the frame rattling as the occupant above her rolls over. A woman in the next bed is snoring loudly. Despite the distractions and the overwhelming sense of being utterly lost and alone, Suriel soon finds herself falling asleep again.

In the morning, she's sent on her way with a ham sandwich wrapped in paper. She eats half as soon as she leaves the building, but holds on to the other for later. The woman behind the glass, a different one from the previous night, drew her a map leading from the building to a bus station. It takes her a while to find it, and then they won't allow her to travel without any money, despite her best attempts to wring some sympathy from them.

Sitting on a small patch of grass at the curb outside the station, Suriel eats the rest of her sandwich, feeling incredibly small and lost. There's a huge expanse of ocean separating her from Corrine and Suriel has no idea how to get across it. She knows that humans can fly, but she has never taken the time to understand how. She's watched the airplanes overhead, leaving trails of white cloud behind them, but she has no idea how to find one—and even if she did, it would probably be like the bus and require money she doesn't have.

She briefly considers abandoning her plan and starting a life here in Kentucky, but one night on Earth as a human was hard enough, and she doesn't know how to find a job or shelter or food, or any of the things human beings need. What she really needs, more than anything else, is Corrine. Corrine is the only person who knows who she is, what she used to be. Suriel fell because she couldn't refuse Corrine's plea. Corrine is the reason she walks now and will continue walking until she finds a way back to her.

"You need a lift someplace?" A blonde young man, jaw working over a piece of chewing gum, sits down beside her. "I got an uncle pickin' me up in ten minutes. Where you headed?"

"England."

The man laughs, his voice light and free from age or concern. "Well, we can take you a ways, but I think my uncle won't like to take his truck swimming. What's in England, anyhow?"

"Home, maybe ... " Suriel bites her lip. She isn't even sure if Corrine will want her there. After all, it has only been a few days for her, but for Corrine, it might have been months, if not years. But Corrine owes her and she needs a place to stay, just for a little while if Corrine doesn't want her.

"So you're an English chick, then? That's awesome. I ain't been to England. Went to France once, though. Nice place, 'though couldn't understand what anyone was sayin'. What's your name? I'm Ed Martin."

"Suriel Crawford."

"Huh, strange name. Still, I got a cousin called Pancake 'cause her mom just craved loadsa pancakes when she was carryin' her."

Suriel smiles. She likes Ed Martin and his chatter, and finds it comforting. The road here is dusty and quiet, and the sunlight reflects off the windows of the bus station, making Suriel angle her face toward Ed to avoid the glare. His face is thin, but there's muscle in his bare, tanned arms.

A battered red pickup truck pulls up on the other side of the road and Ed pats her on the back. Suriel flinches a little, unused to the sudden touch.

"C'mon Suriel," he says, running the i and e together so it sounds like 'Suryel'. "My uncle's here. He'll give you a ride."

Ed's uncle, a tall man standing a good half a foot above them, gets out of the driver's seat and helps Suriel into the back of the pickup. He introduces himself as Martin, and for a moment, Suriel thinks his name is Martin Martin, until Ed explains that he's his mother's brother and his last name is Ellis.

Suriel doesn't have anywhere to go or stay, so Martin offers to drive them all down to his ranch to give Suriel a place to stop a while. Suriel accepts, although she privately thinks his offer might have been less generous had Ed not introduced her as a friend rather than a stranger he met five minutes ago.

The ranch is a little over an hour's drive away and the road is rough, forcing Suriel to hold on tightly to the side of the truck as she's jerked back and forth. Her hair is coming undone from its tight knotting around her head, and the long strands of it fly out in the wind and into her face, covering her line of sight and getting into her mouth.

It's annoying and she keeps trying to push them out of the way, but they don't stay put for long.

The ranch house is huge, and they pass six different rooms before reaching the guest bedroom where Suriel will be sleeping.

"You hungry?" Ed asks. "I bet you're hungry. Dinner won't be a few hours yet, but I can make you some soup."

Suriel nods eagerly. Her stomach is making odd little growling noises, the sandwich from earlier not doing a whole lot to sate her hunger.

Ed talks constantly while he peels potatoes and chops vegetables to make a quick soup. "I'm down for the summer. Mom and Dad live in Tennessee, but I go to college in New York. I enjoy the work here, ranch work. It's good. Hard, I mean, but I've practically grown up on this ranch. It's good to be back, you know? I think my uncle's gone out to mend the fence that blew down last week. He'll be back in no time, or leastways in time for dinner."

The soup turns out to be the most delicious thing Suriel has ever tasted, not that she has much for comparison. There are rolls of thick, crusty bread and she wastes no time in sinking into it all.

Ed just laughs and watches her eat, helping himself to a bread roll and talking about how much he loves this place, and how it'll be good to ride a horse again. Apparently, there's not much call for horses in Manhattan.

"So how come you got no place to be?" he asks finally, and Suriel gets the sense that he was working himself up to the question, torn between curiosity and the fear of intrusion.

"I have no money," Suriel shrugs, eating another spoonful of soup. "I need to find a plane, but I have no way of paying for it."

"You got any relatives you can ask for money?"

"I know no one. Only Corrine, but I don't know how to contact her."

Ed grins. "Well that's easy. You eat up and we'll get on the computer. There's nothin' you can't find on the internet."

Suriel smiles. "So how long have you been taking in strays?"

Ed laughs, his cheeks dimpling. "Since I was a kid, I guess. Started small, kittens and stuff. My parents hate it, but I figure, hey, if I'm lost or hurt or whatever, I damn well want someone to help me out."

After dinner, Ed opens what he calls a laptop and switches it on. Suriel is amazed at the vibrancy of it and the way the images change at the click of a button. She has seen a lot in the history of mankind, but almost all of it has revolved around the fundamental existence of life and death.

Despite Ed's confidence in the machine, they can't find Corrine Thompson anywhere on it. They try typing in her parents' names, her brother's, but although they find almost eight million results for each of them, there are just too many to determine one Corrine Thompson from another, no matter what combination of names and locations they try.

~~*

There's a suitcase by the front door when Corrine gets home from work. Her job is part-time, twelve hours a week in a place where tourists can paint their own ceramics. Daniel is at the kitchen table, his expression glum. Corrine glances from him to the door of the nursery.

"Is—" she begins, but Daniel interrupts.

"He's fine," his voice is hard, the muscles in his neck taut.

"You're leaving me." Corrine's mouth is suddenly dry. It's not like she hasn't been expecting it; their rocky patch seems to have stretched out for miles and things haven't been right for months. She thought about ending it herself, had even screamed at him to leave in their last argument, but somehow, the reality of it is harsher and it feels as though a weight has settled in the pit of her stomach.

Corrine liked Daniel when she first met him a little over a year ago. He was kind, generous and sweet, and she thought she was in love with him. He moved in, was great with René, played with him, changed him, and fed him. Something about that grated; in the back of Corrine's mind, it just felt wrong. Daniel would be a wonderful father for René, but she couldn't help but feel that he *shouldn't* be. She was being unfair, she knows, snapped at him too many times and threw too many insults when they were fighting. It didn't really matter how many times she said sorry, they'd always just revert back to the same pattern.

"I'm sorry," Daniel says without looking at her, staring at his clasped hands.

Corrine considers asking Daniel to stay, knowing he might not leave if she does, but something stops her—she isn't sure she *wants* him to stay. He's nice, a better guy than she knows she deserves, but he's just … not enough.

"I'm sorry, too," Corrine says, and she *is* sorry, because she just couldn't bring herself to let him be what he wanted to be. Corrine thought she could make it work, thought that this was what she wanted—a boyfriend, a dad for René, a normal relationship with another human being. But she was wrong.

"It's okay," Daniel says, standing. He picks up his suitcase and kisses Corrine on the way out, as if he's just on his way to work and will be back later. He won't be. Corrine knows she'll never see Daniel again. He'll go back to London while she stays behind in the small, country-side city where she's spent her whole life, living alone for the rest of her life because she'll never be able to maintain a normal relationship. Of course, she won't really be *alone*, because she'll always have René.

Corrine opens the door to the nursery and looks at René, his face hidden in the pillows. She perches on the edge of his bed and lays a hand on his back.

"René," she whispers. "Hey, sleepyhead, it's time to wake up."

René stirs and groans in the back of his throat.

"Come on, kiddo. You know you won't settle tonight if you don't get up now. Wake up and we'll go to the park, okay?"

He pushes himself up at that and rubs his eyes sleepily. "Park," he repeats, yawning.

The park is a little play area set in a large field framed by ash trees. There are swings, a slide, and a small roundabout. Corrine remembers the roundabout she used to go on when she was a kid. It seemed very high at the time and went very fast, because the older kids would spin it round and not always stop when asked. The council had taken it down when Corrine was about fourteen, because too many kids had fallen off and broken bones, herself included. Pushing René on the swing now, she's pretty glad he won't be riding that one. She isn't sure her nerves would be able to handle it.

She still wishes she could have made it work with Daniel, that they had been different. Was she wrong to let him go like that? But asking him to stay would have been a lie. She doesn't know what she'll say to René when he asks where Daniel is, how she's going to explain that he isn't coming back.

When she looks at René, with his black hair that never belonged to her brother (or to anyone in her family), she thinks of Suriel. Suriel didn't just give Alec back his life that day—she gave Corrine back her life, too. She's happy, or content at least, and whenever she looks at René, she knows that everything she does is worthwhile. She makes him happy, looks after him. That's her purpose in life and she intends to fill it to the best of her abilities.

She has found that being a parent is far more sociable than her previous life. For the first time in her life, Corrine has friends that understand her priorities, others with their own families. Gloria and George, René's godparents, moved up to Edinburgh a few months ago, but they keep in touch. Corrine finds herself with a firm, albeit small, set of friends from René's playgroup. Her life is different now, has changed for the better, but she can't help but wish that Suriel was still around to share it with her. Suriel said she'd return, but it has been over three years and she wonders what happened to her. Did Suriel just forget about her or was she forbidden from coming back to Earth?

Corrine helps René out of the swing and goes to sit on a bench while he runs around, taking turns to push the roundabout with a girl a little older than him.

A man, presumably the girl's father since the rest of the playground is deserted, sits at the other end of the bench. They remain in silence, watching their children play and laughing occasionally when they squeal in happiness, riding the roundabout or skidding down the slide. Corrine thinks for a horrible moment that René is going to knock the girl right off the end of the slide, but she jumps up and out of the way just as he reaches the bottom. She glances at the man, who's biting his lip. Apparently, he'd had the same thought.

"That one yours?" the man asks, nodding toward René. He's clearly attempting to start a conversation, since it's pretty obvious whose kid is whose within the almost empty playground.

"Yeah."

"Cute kid. How old is he?"

"Three," she replies proudly. "Yours?"

"Almost four. She'll be starting school come September. Time flies, eh?" he chuckles.

"Yeah, it does," she agrees. "She have a name?"

"Emily Rose. Emily after her grandmother, my mother, and Rose after her mum."

"Oh? Where's her mum?" Corrine can't help but ask, despite a creeping suspicion that she already knows the answer. People rarely name their kids after themselves these days.

"She died when Em was born. Still, you gotta be thankful for what's left, and I've got the most beautiful daughter in the world. Her mum would've been proud of her, I know."

Corrine smiles and nods. "Yeah, I think she would have been."

"Thanks. It's probably not good manners to over-share like that, huh? It's always been a flaw of mine, I'm afraid."

Corrine laughs. "It's fine. I like to hear peoples' stories. You obviously love your daughter very much."

The man nods. "She's my light. Cheesy, huh?"

"Just a bit." She smiles. "I'm Corrine."

He shakes her outstretched hand. "Brian. We'd best be going now, but maybe I'll see you around sometime."

She smiles as he leaves, and shortly after, takes René home, wishing that her father had been more like Brian, that he'd been able to see just how much he'd really had. After all, he might have lost their mother, but he'd gained a son at the same time. She hadn't thought it then, but now, when she looks back, all she sees is a bitter selfishness and self-pity that he wallowed in for fifteen years, until it killed him and later killed his son. She understands, of course, knows too well the grief that consumed him, but it was a character flaw in her father, having neither the strength nor the desire to pull himself out of his own pain, even for his children.

René will know the name of his grandfather and the story of their family, but he will never know the pain of it. It will be distant from him, something that happened once upon a time. He will never know the pain of a father who blamed him for his mother's death. Corrine will make sure of that now. She will always keep him safe, warm and happy.

~~*

Suriel likes Ed, enjoys his company and enjoys the atmosphere of the ranch. After just a few days of staying with Ed and Martin, she insisted on helping out around the place. Martin laughed at first and refused, didn't believe that Suriel wasn't the delicate flower he assumed her to be, but she insisted and he gave her a trial. It's hard work and her muscles protested after just the first day, but since then she's more than proven herself to be capable.

Ed teaches her to be a better rider in their spare time and she finds that she enjoys it, the horse seeming to understand her despite her inexperience. Suriel's happy here in the heat and dust of rural Kentucky, and almost feels as though she could have a home here.

But after the heat of the day has died down and she's lying in her bed in Martin Ellis' spare room, she can't help but think of Corrine and wonders how Alec is doing, how tall he is now. She learnt on her first day at the ranch that the year is 2011, four years from the inscription on Alec's gravestone. She wonders what Corrine is like now, if motherhood has changed her, if she's happy. She still searches, spending a couple of hours each day on Ed's computer, clicking each search result in the hope that one of them will give her Corrine's address or phone number or *something*.

Ed told her that she needs more than money to fly—she needs a passport, and to get a passport, she needs all sorts of records that she doesn't have. She's pretty sure she'll have that sorted soon. Ed said a person could find anything on the internet. Although Suriel has found that to be a little inaccurate, he wasn't entirely wrong. Suriel has found a lot of things on the internet. She has, among other things, discovered a love for videos featuring cats, but the most important find is a website that makes fake passports. She doesn't know if they'll be real enough to enable her to fly, but she knows she has to do *something*. As much as she enjoys her time here, she can't stay forever.

Suriel shivers, the skin of her shoulders tingling as she thinks about how it felt to have Corrine touch her wings, spread her fingers through her feathers. She wishes it had lasted longer now that she knows she'll never experience that feeling again. She wishes she hadn't left so suddenly, but there had been the souls churning inside of her and she couldn't keep them waiting.

It's late September, the heat of the summer beginning to cool, when Ed hands her a small, brown paper parcel. "This it?" he asks.

She told him about the fake passports and he told her it was worth a try, that he'd compare it with his own to make sure it was potentially passable. They've become firm friends over the two months she's been staying with him, and she would trust him with her life. Hell, if it wasn't for him, she might not even have a life right now. She hasn't told him about her past, although he kept questioning her about it for the first few weeks—she might be new to the human side of things, but she isn't stupid. She felt bad though, meeting his generous hospitality with such refusals, but she didn't want to lie to him either.

Suriel tears open the paper and can't help the excited fluttering in her stomach as she sees the blue cover with 'PASSPORT' printed across it in bold lettering. It's enough to get her across to England, but she knows that she might not ever be able to come back to America. It's too much of a risk, and without any nationality of her own, she has no idea what would happen to her.

"I'm going home," she says, a grin spreading across her face.

"Yeah." Ed suddenly doesn't sound quite so enthusiastic, his voice wavering.

"What's wrong?" she asks, stepping back and studying his face.

"Nothin'. Just that I was hopin' you might stay."

"Why?" Suriel asks. "You're going back to college in a couple of weeks. This is perfect timing."

"Well, you coulda come with me."

Suriel shakes her head slowly. "No, I have to go. I can't spend all this time thinking about it and not being there."

"You love her, don't you?" His expression is neutral, but carefully so.

"Yeah, I do."

"That's good." Ed smiles, slow and cautious. "I guess we better find you a flight home then, huh?"

The flight they do find leaves at six the next morning. The tickets are expensive due to their last-minute booking, but Suriel finds that now that she has the means to go, she just can't stomach the idea of waiting any longer. She's earned enough money over the past two months by working on the ranch to cover it, although it costs her most of her savings.

Suriel has her things packed in ten minutes. She doesn't own much. Martin gave her a set of boots, a hat, two shirts and a pair of jeans when he realized that she didn't have anything but the clothes on her back. She also packs a small, leather-bound book of poetry by Percy Shelley that Ed let her keep. She recognized one of the poems as the same one Corrine had been reading aloud the last time Suriel had seen her—*be it joy or sorrow, the path of its departure still is free*. Every time Suriel reads the line now, she hears Corrine's voice as clearly in her head as if she were really there.

As most nights, they all eat dinner together, the farmhands without families joining Martin, Ed and Suriel at the table and digging into a whole table full of rich foods. Ed seems a little less talkative than usual, but his voice is still the most frequently heard.

After a short night's sleep, Suriel is woken by the high-pitched beeping of her alarm clock, the luminescent digits telling her that it's one in the morning. She finds Ed in the kitchen, brewing a pot of coffee, and Martin busying himself making bacon and pancakes for breakfast.

By two, they're on the road, Suriel wearing a thick coat of Ed's to protect herself from the cold of the late night. She savors the feel of the air on her face and watches the dust and the rocks speed away beneath them. It might be the last time she sets foot in this place and she wants to remember it forever.

By five, Ed is hugging her goodbye.

"You come back and visit us sometime," Martin says.

Suriel cranes her neck around Ed's shoulder and smiles at him. "I'd love to," she says, and she means it.

She knows she'll miss Ed and his constant chatter, the stark contrast between him and his soft-spoken, quiet uncle. She'll miss the ranch and the constant bustle, riding out under the heat of the day to milk cows or fix fences that had blown over in the night. They've all been so kind to her, done more for her than she could have ever expected and treated her like family when she was little more than a stranger.

"Thank you," she says, and can only hope that her voice truly shows the gratitude that she feels toward them both; words suddenly feel so inept.

"It was my pleasure," Ed grins. "I hope you get your girl."

Suriel hopes so too. She walks away, then, taking one last look over her shoulder to see Ed saluting her with an awkward, somewhat forced grin plastered on his face. Like him, Suriel doesn't much feel the smile that she returns.

The flight to England is long, and Suriel feels small sparks of fear whenever the plane jolts unexpectedly. It feels unnatural flying like this, entombed within a narrow metal trunk when she should be outside, carried on the wind and her wings, feeling the air whip through her feathers. She feels cramped, her knees jammed against the plastic back of the seat in front of her. She stares out at the earth beneath them, marvels, not for the first time, at how it can look so tiny and picturesque from up here, and yet seem so huge and unfathomable when her feet are on the ground.

Suriel sleeps fitfully on the flight, frequently waking up in a sudden panic, expecting to have missed their landing and find herself back in America. The elderly woman sitting next to her smiles in exactly the same warm and amused way each time, but doesn't speak.

Eventually, a voice announces that they'll be approaching the UK momentarily. Suriel looks out of the window to see the green edge of land stretching out into the blue like a tail beneath them. A wave of excitement floods through her with the certain knowledge that, yes, this is how everything is supposed to be, the tendrils of her existence finally beginning to twine together.

The sky is a darkening grey when they touch down at Heathrow. Suriel steps off the plane and is herded along with the other five-hundred-odd other passengers toward the gates. Once out of the airport, she finds herself confronted with a busy street, hundreds of people walking along at a fast pace, taxis collecting those standing still and driving them away. She makes her way down the street, following signs for the bus station. She pays using some money that Ed converted into pounds for her. Silently, she thanks him dearly for it as she hands it over and gets her ticket in exchange.

The coach is almost empty when it arrives, slowly filling with the people around her. Half the seats are still empty by the time they pull out of the station. The man in front of her falls asleep almost as soon as the engine starts and the rest of the journey is punctuated by his snoring.

They leave the straight, smooth roads of the capital and the motorway, the coach winding its way through the bumpy country roads. Suriel stares out of the window at the hedgerows, rivers, lakes, and fields they pass. Everything here is so green and quiet. Even through the towns, the roads are quiet, only the occasional car rushing past them in the opposite direction. She dozes off somewhere after their brief stop in Bristol, where she was able to step outside and stretch her legs for a few minutes, while the driver finished off his cigarette and showed a couple more passengers on board.

The coach jerks to a halt and Suriel doesn't wake until the driver taps her on the shoulder, his moustache twitching as he smiles at her. "Think this is your stop, love," he says, and Suriel yawns at him in reply, before picking her bag off the floor, thanking him and heading out into the streets.

It's a strange feeling, being so close to Corrine, and yet having no idea where she is. She feels suddenly very small out here with the shadows of grey stone buildings towering over her in the dark. She knows this place and it doesn't take her long to find the graveyard, but still she feels lost, tethered to the only place through which she knows Corrine might pass.

A clock hanging on the side of the church tower tells her that it's just past two in the morning. She doesn't feel as though she's been travelling that long and remembers that of course the time zone shift will have added extra hours. Would Corrine still be awake at this time?

The gate to the graveyard is locked, but the walls are low enough for Suriel to hoist herself up and climb over. She waits, chewing her lip in a feeble attempt to stave off the anxiety and anticipation that threatens to bubble up and out of her mouth in a shout, or a bout of nervous laughter. She recognizes it as a very human habit, one of many that she seems to have picked up easily and all too quickly. She's glad of the comfort of it now as she waits in the dim orange light of a streetlamp, her shadow blending with the vertical lines cast by the gates.

"Hey! What do you think you're doing?" A man is making his way across the graveyard towards her, old age slowing his stride to a shuffle.

"I'm sorry," Suriel says hastily, not wanting to do anything to anger the man.

As he approaches, Suriel realizes she recognizes him. He's the caretaker here, has been cutting the grass and tending the graves since he was thirty-five. Suriel took his wife after she'd been interred in the earth beside their little house, and she has seen him often throughout the years. She knows him to be a kind man, his soul a good one, although it's silent to her now.

"I was looking for someone," she tells him.

He looks annoyed; he must have been tucked up in his bed when he saw someone climbing over the wall through the window. He's still wearing a maroon dressing gown and slippers.

"Well, you aren't gonna find anyone living in here," he says firmly, removing a key from his pocket. "You just go on out of here now." His voice is rasping and he wheezes a little. Suriel wonders how long he has left to live.

"I'm not going to be any trouble," she says gently. "I just want to wait for my friend. I have nowhere else to go."

"Maybe you ought to show some respect," the man says, his tone angry, but his eyes betraying a hint of fear. "This isn't a hostel, it's a sacred place. Now go on." He opens the gates wide and gestures for her to leave.

Suriel frowns and crosses her arms. She's spent many nights here; almost every soul in this graveyard has been taken by her. She was here when this church was built, when the first humans were given Christian burials here, before this man was alive, before his house was built. She doesn't want to leave, but she knows that fighting will only make it worse, and he has been loyal to this place. He has kept it well over his lifetime and looked after the graves in the same way that Suriel looked after the souls.

A thought occurs to her, so simple it's infuriating and she doesn't understand why she didn't think of it before. "Perhaps you know my friend," she says quickly. "Corrine Thompson. She spends a lot of time here."

"Yeah, I know her. She's a good girl, been through a lot. What do you want with her?"

Suriel doesn't blame him for being suspicious. She's learnt that most people aren't all that receptive to strangers at the best of times, let alone in the dark when that stranger is perceived as a trespasser.

"She's a friend of mine. I need to speak to her, but I don't know where she lives."

The caretaker is still frowning deeply, but he lets go of the gate and his shoulders relax a little.

"If I phone her up, you gonna leave quietly? Even if she doesn't answer?"

"You can do that?" Suriel breathes.

"Sure. She runs errands for me sometimes when I'm not so well. Like I said, she's a good girl."

Suriel follows the caretaker back to his house. He doesn't let her inside and she sits down on the step, the closed door at her back, straining to hear as he dials Corrine's number.

~~*

Corrine groans and pulls the duvet further over her head. A peek out at the clock sitting on her bedside table tells her what she already knew: that it's arse o' clock in the morning and she should still be dreaming of Jessica Alba fighting crime in a bikini.

She groans again and flings out a hand to switch on the bedside lamp, wondering who could possibly be ringing her at half past two in the morning. It's probably Ted next door, drunk again, having lost his keys to the building. She throws back the covers, and then waits a moment in the hope that Ted will just fall asleep in the bushes and leave her to her nice, warm bed. She listens for René and hears nothing. The jammy bastard has always been the deeper sleeper, except as a very small baby when he would start screaming at so much as a whisper. Now he could probably sleep through an air raid, were one to occur.

The telephone keeps ringing, its tone harsh and grating against her skull. She climbs out of bed and makes her way into the hallway, picking up the phone and almost dropping it before she gets the receiver to her ear. "Hello?" Her voice is thick with the remnants of sleep.

There's silence on the other end, and she's about to put the phone back on the hook when she hears a rough "Hello?" crackle through.

"Hello," she says, her patience thin. "Who's this, please?"

"It's Jacob Foster. Sorry to trouble you so late, but—"

"What's wrong? Are you okay?" she asks hurriedly, knowing that Jacob would never phone her so late unless it was an emergency.

"Nothing's wrong," he reassures her, and her concern melts back into confusion and mild annoyance. "I've got a girl here and she says she knows you. Wanted me to call you. I know it's late, but she seems agitated and I thought I'd better check, you know."

Corrine nods, before remembering that he can't see her. "Of course, what's her name?"

"Hold on a sec." There's a clicking noise and a rustling as he presumably goes to check the girl's name. "Err … Cereal. Oh, sorry. Suriel."

Corrine fumbles and almost drops the phone for a second time, her hands trembling slightly. She hopes against hope that she heard right and isn't still dreaming. "Suriel?"

"Yeah. You know her?"

"Yeah," she breathes. "I do. I'm on my way over."

She doesn't wait for his reply before slamming the phone back in its cradle and rushing back into the bedroom to pull on a pair of jeans and a shirt.

It has been three and a half years since they last saw each other, a brief moment that has replayed in Corrine's mind insistently over the years. It's faded only a little in her memory, decreasing in frequency but never disappearing, not really.

René rubs his eyes sleepily and whines when she shakes him gently awake. He's still half-asleep as she pulls on his coat and hoists him into her arms, grabbing the pushchair from the hall cupboard and making her way quickly but carefully down the flights of stairs to the front door.

It isn't far to the graveyard, but suddenly it seems like miles, the pushchair's wheels clicking over the bumps in the pavement as she half-walks, half-runs. René fell asleep again almost as soon as she sat him down, his thumb tucked neatly into his mouth.

The gates to the graveyard have been left open for her and she only has to push them a little, the chain clanking, to get the pushchair through. She can hear her heart beating at an almost alarming pace, and her hands are sweaty against the plastic handles of the pushchair, despite the chill of the night air. The lights are on in Jacob's house, a warm yellow glow spreading out from both the kitchen and living room windows.

Corrine hoists the pushchair up onto the step and slams her fist down on the door, much harder than she intended.

Jacob answers with a bemused expression on his face. "It's a lucky thing I don't sleep much," he says with a smile, showing her into the cramped hallway. "I'll put the kettle on."

He leads her into the living room—a small room crammed full of books, family photographs and odd knickknacks he's accumulated over his life—and wanders back out into the kitchen to make the tea.

The woman standing in front of her doesn't look much like the Suriel she remembers. That Suriel had huge wings that stretched out above and behind her shoulders, thick black hair that was plaited and tied perfectly around her head, not a single strand out of place. This woman has no wings and her hair is shorter, pulled back in a tight ponytail. She's dressed not in the rough-hewn tunic of their first encounter, but in t-shirt and jeans. The first few signs of age show in the corners of her eyes and her skin isn't the pale white Corrine remembers, but a golden-brown. But her eyes are Suriel's eyes, exactly as they are in Corrine's memory, a deep and seemingly impenetrable black. They both stand there, staring at one another, drinking in the changes of each other's appearances.

"You're not … " She finds herself at a loss for words, her hands feel heavy and limp at her sides. "You're not an angel."

Suriel shakes her head. "I had a choice," she says, her voice rougher than Corrine remembers it. "I chose you."

Corrine isn't sure what that means, but right now, it's all she needs to hear. Questions will come later. At the moment, all she wants is to wrap her hands around Suriel's waist and pull her close, grinning stupidly up into her dark eyes and cataloguing the changes in her face. She leans in and kisses her, Suriel's mouth soft and warm against her own.

~~*

Suriel loves this place and has been coming here every summer for the past few years. She and Corrine sit side-by-side on Martin Ellis' front porch, arms wrapped around each other. They both smell of sweat, dirt and manure, but after a hard day's work, neither of them care. They watch René grinning happily, laughing as Ed gently kicks the horse into a trot. Corrine leans forward, worried that he might fall off, but Ed has his arms around him and they both know he's perfectly safe, that Ed would never let him fall.

Sometimes, when Corrine looks at Suriel and the light hits her the right way, she thinks she can still see the shadow of those black feathered wings. Then Suriel will move away and they're lost once more in the light. She misses them, Corrine can tell, when she lifts her head and watches the birds in the sky with a mournful expression on her face. Suriel is old, has spent eons in flight, her life pledged to serve Heaven, and yet here with her feet on the ground, in a mortal skin, she often seems much younger than she really is.

They laugh a lot these days, more than either of them can ever remember laughing in their lifetimes. René is growing up. At seven years old, he doesn't look much like Alec, but Corrine sees her brother whenever she looks into his eyes, hears him when René speaks. They have the same soul, but René is so much more alive, more vibrant than she ever remembers Alec being.

There are times when she wonders if Suriel regrets it, times when Suriel freezes outside a church and looks longingly at the graveyard around it. Suriel often prays, and Corrine knows it's stupid, but she always feels as though it's a judgment upon her when she does. Then Suriel will smile and pull her close, whisper her love into Corrine's ear and prove it beneath the sheets.

The summer is long, and Corrine can afford to sit in the sun and relax as it sets below the horizon. She has a job writing for a magazine and the month she spends working here will make its way into her next article. Suriel flits from job to job, but they always manage to stay afloat. Martin always insists on paying them for their work on the ranch, although they're both just glad for the break, of the change of scenery and the chance to visit the place Suriel thinks of as a second home.

As the sun sinks, René abandons his riding lesson and curls up against Corrine's side, his thumb tucked obstinately into his mouth, despite her chastising. Ed sits with them, his knees tucked up to his chin, talking into the night. They stay outside until the air grows cold and the moths flutter around them, pulled by instinct toward the light of the porch lamp. Together like this, it feels like home, like family. Corrine lets the feeling wash over her, basks in its warmth, secure in the knowledge that all of this is hers now, and she never has to lose it again.

The Lost Angel

Elizah J. Davis

Alex was five the first time he saw an angel—young enough that the fantastical was still possible, and therefore not much of a surprise. The angel appeared at his grandmother's hospital bedside to take her away. It all seemed quite glorious as far as Alex could see, and it wasn't until years later that he understood why everyone else in the room had been crying.

His mother thought that Alex started making up his imaginary friends to cope. The truth of the matter was, once word got out that he could see them, angels started flocking to him as a matter of course. In an age when so many people had stopped believing in them altogether, human recognition was something they seemed to crave.

A normal life had never been in the cards for Alex, but that didn't mean he didn't occasionally resent his celestial company.

"In ancient times you would have been considered an oracle," Annie told him one night, after ruining what had been up to that point a *very* promising first date.

"Yeah, well, in modern times I'm just considered a nutjob. Thanks for that, by the way."

Annie shrugged, not at all put off by his irritation. She had appointed herself his guardian angel after a minor car accident when he was nineteen, and, as such, wasn't deterred by anything he might throw at her. That wasn't the case with all of the angels. Alex had hurt his share of angel feelings before he realized that some of them were ridiculously sensitive.

"You may save your ire. I only meant to illustrate that you are one of a chosen few open to a higher calling. Many in your position would be using such a gift to help people. Instead, I am forcibly reduced to vetting your dates."

"Despite my repeated requests for you to stop," Alex pointed out. "I don't actually think our taste in men is compatible."

"Taste is entirely irrelevant in this instance," Annie said dismissively. "That man was not interested in you in any respect beyond carnal."

Alex groaned and only barely refrained from beating his head against the wall in frustration. Despite the many ways in which he'd tried to explain to her that, sometimes, interest on a purely carnal level was okay, the stubborn angel refused to understand it. She did it deliberately, as far as Alex was concerned. She certainly wasn't stupid to the ways of mankind.

As much as he'd like to claim noble intentions and the overwhelming desire to help his fellow man as his motivation, that wasn't exactly the case. The fact of the matter was Alex had opened *The Lost Angel* in an effort to get Annie off his back, which would, with any luck, lead to him getting laid again someday.

"Historically, many oracles kept their purity intact in order to remain open to the divine communications."

A guy could hope, anyway.

The basic business plan for *The Lost Angel* was fairly simple: It was a space where angels in need of someone to save could connect with people most in need of saving. Also, Alex had always been a little bit enamored with the idea of being a neighborhood bartender. He'd grown up watching a lot of *Cheers* reruns on Nick at Nite, and it had always seemed like fun.

Alex's talent, beyond being able to see and talk to angels, was in matching them up with people who had lost their way. He wasn't entirely sure if it was the angel mojo that drew troubled people to him, or if was part of the gift he had that allowed him to see the angels in the first place. It worked out either way, and on good days, he felt like his life had purpose. On bad days, he felt like a glorified matchmaker. Most days he was somewhere in between, happy to help where he could, and fascinated by the people he got to meet.

The Lost Angel wasn't in the best neighborhood, stuck in a mostly-industrial area, just off the interstate, nor did it get many repeat customers. The people who found their way to his humble establishment were those who had nowhere else to turn, those who had nothing but their last shred of hope. Even the few customers he got who lived in the area didn't stop by more than once. Once people had been set back on their rightful path, they tended not to return to the place where they'd been at their lowest. That was okay by Alex. Repeat customers meant they'd failed, and so far they had a one hundred percent success rate.

"If ever there was a soul in need of saving ... " Annie said, sounding way more excited than she ought to.

It had been a slow night.

Alex sighed. "You know, when I opened this place, I didn't really expect for it to become such a meat-market.

Your people need to get a hobby. Learn to knit or something."

"You should be ashamed for implying such a thing, Alex, when we desire only to help," Annie said primly, but Alex could see angels all over the bar perking up at the newcomer. It was too eerily similar to the way people reacted to a hot piece of tail for Alex's peace of mind—which, in this case, was also pretty accurate.

The man walking through the door was downright gorgeous and, despite Annie's claim, he didn't look like a man clinging to his last shred of hope so much as a man in need of a drink. He had a square jaw, deep blue eyes, and wavy brown hair that couldn't possibly be as soft as it looked. Short of being wrapped up in a big red bow, it was like someone had tapped in to Alex's wet dreams and created the man especially for him. In fact, if they didn't spend so much determined energy in ensuring his celibacy, Alex would've suspected some angelic manipulation in the man's presence.

But they *did* spend a distressing amount of time keeping him single, and it was all Alex could do not to shift under the blatantly disapproving stare of every angel in the joint. It was his damn bar. If he wanted to ogle his customer before passing him off to one of them that was his freaking prerogative, because holy *shit*, the guy was hot.

Annie's head snapped in his direction as soon as the thought crossed his mind and Alex could perfectly picture her frown, but he really couldn't help it. It had been a long dry spell.

"What can I get you?" Alex asked, hoping his voice didn't betray his thoughts.

After a moment, the man laughed and looked down. Shifting to one side, he reached in his pocket and pulled out a crumpled five dollar bill. "The strongest shot this will get me."

Alex waved the money away. "What do you *want* to drink?" He shrugged at the man's skeptical look. "It's a slow night and I need someone to talk to. I'd rather have the company, if it's all the same to you." There. That sounded reasonably smooth. "Alex," he said, holding out his hand.

"Finley. Finn. Either works," he replied, shaking Alex's hand after only a slight hesitation. "Though I'm not sure you want me as company." The smile he offered was small, but genuine. "Bad day. Week. Whatever."

"Let me get you a drink and you can tell me about it."

Finley looked like he wanted to refuse, but he only nodded, seemingly too weary to argue. "Whiskey, whatever your bottom shelf is."

Ignoring the last part of Finley's request, Alex grabbed a bottle from his personal stash under the counter and poured a glass for each of them.

"Lucifer too was beautiful," Annie said beside him.

Alex tried to hide his scowl, unable to shoo her away with Finley watching him. The best he could do was to ignore her, leaning against the counter with his back to her as he slid Finley's drink to him. He knew without looking that every angel in the room was focused on them, waiting for Alex to decide who should take Finley under their wing. For the first time in his life, Alex resented it, and he realized with some surprise that he very much wanted to help Finley himself.

If they didn't like it, they could find themselves another angel pimp. Alex was officially off-duty for the night.

~~*

Were someone to ask Finley's mother what his worst quality was, she would tell them without hesitation it was his impulsiveness. It would be a fair answer, too. Finley had a habit of rushing into things without thinking them through beyond the initial, 'Oh, that sounds like fun!' He'd always been that way, and he'd long since given up hope of outgrowing it.

That wasn't his worst quality in Finley's estimation. He was, in all honesty, rather proud of his adventurous spirit, and *that* was his actual downfall: pride. Pride was why he was sitting at some shitty dive bar in the middle of nowhere with five dollars left to his name. It was why he'd been living in his car for the past two weeks, driving around the country quite aimlessly instead of halfway home after Robert had left him high and dry.

Finley didn't like admitting his mistakes, and Robert had been his biggest yet. Worse was that his mother had told him so from the start.

"So," the bartender—Alex—said as he handed Finley his whiskey. "You wanna talk about it?"

Alex was apparently the type of guy who could pull lines like that off, because it didn't sound nearly as lame as it should have. He seemed sincere, even, his expression sympathetic and open. Finley guessed Alex was in his mid-twenties; there was something charmingly boyish about him. Under different circumstances, Finley might've been interested. With short, dark hair and pretty hazel eyes, he was good looking enough by anyone's standards. At the moment, however, Finley had had his fill of charming, pretty boys.

"Let's just say life hasn't worked out the way I expected it to," Finley finally said. Smirking, he added, "Never date a musician." He slouched down in his seat, pleased that he'd hit the right wry note with that statement. Finley was nobody's sob story, and if that's what Alex was expecting, he was going to be sorely disappointed.

Alex only nodded, his smile a mix of amused and ironic, and Finley felt something in his chest unclench. "So what brings you to my humble establishment?"

That he did not pursue the dating line of questioning raised Alex a little higher in Finley's esteem. "Just passing through. Or, I dunno." He smoothed his fingers over the five dollar bill he'd left sitting on the bar, considering the sad state of his current financial situation. His credit card was nearly maxed and he doubted he could get another one with no job or residence to speak of. He knew if he called, his family would send him all the money he needed to get home. "I might stick around for a little while and see if I can pick up some odd jobs. You wouldn't happen to know of anything, would you?"

"Actually ..." Alex shot a dirty look over Finley's shoulder, but when Finley turned around, nobody was there. "I've, uh, I've actually been meaning to hire someone. If you're interested?"

"Seriously?"

Alex nodded. "I pretty much run this place by myself, and I've been thinking it would be nice to foist some of the grunt work off on someone. I'm not saying it'll be the most glamorous job ever, but—"

"Yeah!" Finley said, cutting him off before he could rescind the offer. "No, yeah. That's okay. That's great. I can do grunt work."

"Cool." Alex smiled and scratched his chin. "We can work out pay and job description stuff tomorrow. The only major thing is that we get shipments in throughout the day, starting pretty early in the morning. There's a little apartment in the back, where I used to live, but then I bought a place down the street." He made a vague gesture with his left hand and shrugged. "I mean, you aren't required to stay here or anything, but if you wanted to, I mean, for shipments and stuff, rent and utilities would be included in your compensation."

Bullshit. Finley bit back the desire to actually say it out loud, but it seemed like too good an offer to be true; which, in his experience, meant it was. He wondered what the catch might be. Maybe Alex was some sort of pervert and there were cameras set up all over the apartment. "That seems like a good offer for someone you just met. How do you know I'm not a total psycho?"

"I have kind of a knack for reading people." Alex slid his hand along the bar, making a face when he hit a puddle before wiping his palm against his jeans. "Comes with the territory."

Finley nodded. "Okay, then. How do I know *you're* not some sort of psycho?" He smiled to take the edge off the question, but not enough to make Alex think he didn't expect an answer.

"That's a much better question," Alex said, and he seemed to be seriously considering it. "You can ask my mom? I mean, not right now, because she's asleep and she'll kill me if I wake her up for a character reference, but—"

"Yeah, okay," Finley said, cutting into Alex's babbling. "I mean, egg on *my* face if you turn out to be Norman Bates, but any grown man whose first thought is to use his mom as a reference is probably okay." He grinned and added, "Maybe a little socially stunted, but ..."

Luckily, Alex laughed. "Where I'm from, we respect our mommas. Ain't nothin' to be ashamed of."

Finley smiled widely at the hint of southern drawl that had crept into Alex's voice. It sounded natural, though Finley couldn't place it precisely. "Where are you from?"

"I was born in Mississippi, but I've moved around a bit. Military brat."

"What made you settle here?" Finley asked, genuinely curious. There was something interesting about Alex, beyond his pretty face, though damned if Finley could figure out what it was.

Alex shook his head, though he didn't seem offended by the question. "Long story, best left to another night."

"Fair enough," Finley said, nodding and touching the brim of an invisible cowboy hat. "Another night, then."

Elizah J. Davis

"Deal." Alex's smile was bright. "You can stay here tonight if you want. There's a bed and stuff back there. I sometimes crash if I have a late night and early delivery. Since you've been drinking and all, you probably shouldn't drive." He winked and poured Finley another shot.

Proud though he might be, Finley was grateful for the offer and the easy excuse Alex had provided him with to accept it. The truth of the matter was, he had no place to go. "Yeah, that'd be good, thanks. I should ..." Finley looked around and realized he was the only one in the bar. "I have some stuff that I shouldn't leave in the car."

"Sure." Alex handed him a set of keys. "Just lock up when you come back in. I'm gonna—" He nodded toward the kitchen.

There wasn't actually much Finley had to bring in. Most of his stuff fit in his trunk, so he only bothered to grab his shaving kit and a clean shirt before heading back inside. Locking the door behind him, he headed toward the kitchen, Alex's keys in hand.

"Yeah, well, I'm the boss, so it's my call," Alex said suddenly, making Finley jump.

Finley stopped short, confused. "Don't tell me I've pissed you off already." He couldn't help but smile when Alex flinched and turned around, clearly startled.

Alex rubbed the back of his neck and gave Finely a sheepish grin. "Yeah, I've run this place alone for way too long so I have a tendency to talk to myself. I'm hoping you'll find it quirky and charming?"

It was probably safe enough to guess that most people did. He surprised himself by wondering what Alex must've been like as a kid. He probably got away with everything. "Quirky and charming is exactly what I was thinking," Finley said dryly, making Alex laugh.

"Come on, I'll show you the apartment."

The apartment could be accessed through the storage room, though it also had a front door, Alex explained. It took up the entire back half of the building, and was surprisingly nice considering the neighborhood.

"I only have one set of sheets here," Alex said apologetically as he flipped on the light in the bedroom. "But I think I only slept on them once. They're mostly clean."

"It's cool," Finley said, dropping his stuff on the dresser. Up until an hour ago he'd been planning on sleeping in the car, so he considered an actual bed a luxury. He looked around the room, and raised an eyebrow in question at the calendar hanging next to the door. "Firefighters?"

"Yeah, I'm a fan of their work. Y'know, putting out fires and stuff." Alex laughed then, and Finley found himself utterly charmed by the ease of Alex's humor. He couldn't remember the last time he'd been around someone who could genuinely laugh at themselves. Alex seemed to be in a state of perpetual amusement.

"So, bathroom's down the hall." Alex pulled out his wallet and handed Finley a business card. "My number, in case you need something. I keep weird hours, so don't worry about waking me up."

Finley nodded. "Hey, Alex?" He looked up and then back down at the card, suddenly struck by the magnitude of what Alex had so readily offered him. He'd gone from having no one and nothing—on the brink of having to slink back home, tail between his legs—to having a place to recoup and lick his wounds, dignity as intact as he could hope for at that point. "Thanks. For this." It seemed inadequate, but Finley had never been great at expressing such a significant level of gratitude.

"Sure." Alex hesitated for a moment, like he wanted to add something, but he only said, "I'm gonna go finish closing up. We'll go over everything tomorrow."

"Yeah, sounds good."

Smiling, Alex turned and headed back into the bar.

"Goodnight," Finley added as an afterthought. He wasn't sure Alex even heard him.

After brushing his teeth, Finley shucked his jeans and shirt and crawled into bed. He pulled the blankets up around his shoulders; they smelled like fabric softener and cologne. It was surprisingly comforting, and Finley slipped off to sleep with no trouble at all.

~~*

As a kid, Alex had found the angel names to be too much of a mouthful and had very quickly taken to nicknaming them after his favorite characters, which was how he found himself currently being scolded by Annie, Bert, Ernie, and Paddington. He supposed he should be grateful that it was only the four of them who had followed him home.

"What precisely do you think you're doing?" Paddington asked, his wings flapping in agitation. He was the largest of the angels present, and generally quite teddy bear-like in both manner and appearance, hence the name. The other angels leaned back as he turned, in order to avoid a face full of feathers. It would've been funny if they weren't all so upset, and therefore intent on being a pain in his ass. "You don't honestly think you can help this boy?"

"He's older than I am," Alex pointed out. That was as far into the briefing as Annie had gotten before Alex stopped her, feeling that if Finley were going to be there awhile, getting his heavenly dossier might be a little unfair.

"Exactly!" Paddington shouted, apparently feeling that the two year age difference between Alex and Finley summed up everything that was wrong with the situation.

"Look, I know y'all are bored, but I don't think this guy needs the full angel brigade on his case. He just seems like he needs some time and maybe someone to talk to, and I can help him out with that." Alex spread his hands, closer to pleading than he would prefer, but they generally reacted well to that. "Does it really matter that I'm the one to help him, just so long as he's helped? That's what we're after, right?"

"Have you considered how it will affect your helping of the others?" Ernie asked. "Finley can't see us. How shall you go about helping us make the appropriate connections while keeping our existence a secret from him? Will he not find you odd?"

Luckily, Alex had at least though that far ahead. He pulled out his cell phone and held it up. "If you need to talk to me and I can't duck into the back room or whatever, just make my phone ring. We can work out the details from there."

"That's not the only problem we face," Bert said. "Surely you must—"

"This is acceptable," Annie said, surprising everyone. "Finley will come to no lasting harm by Alex trying to help him, and if he doesn't succeed, we will be there to step in and set things to right."

"Thanks, Annie." Alex grinned at her, touched by her defense of him. By her standards, that speech was downright warm and fuzzy.

"The matter is settled for now. Alex needs his rest." Annie nodded, and the others disappeared without further protest. Once they were gone, she turned to him, her mouth set in its usual disapproving frown. "I am of course pleased that you want to take a more active role in the service of others. Only, be sure that it is Finley's interests that you serve, not your own."

With that, she disappeared; though Alex knew she was still within reach should he need her. He rubbed his eyes tiredly and headed to the bathroom to get ready for bed.

Despite being surrounded by sanctimonious, overbearing guardians who would be watching his actions more closely than ever, he couldn't help but smile as he thought of Finley. There was something about him that appealed to Alex. The ironic edge to his humor despite the fact he was going through a rough spot, maybe? The fact that he was easy on the eyes didn't suck either, but that wasn't the main draw by any means, no matter what insinuations Annie made about Lucifer.

Alex would feel him out, and if Finley were in any sort of serious trouble, he would assign him an angel. The fact that Annie was letting him try, though, led Alex to believe the situation wasn't quite that dire, and he fell asleep looking forward to seeing Finley again in the morning.

~~*

Alex woke up with a renewed sense of purpose. He really did want to help Finley, and it had nothing to do with his pretty smile. His resolve lasted through picking up breakfast for them and heading back to the bar; it lasted right up until Finley answered the door, barefooted and adorably sleep-rumpled.

Only the fact that Alex's hands were full kept him from reaching out to attempt to tame Finley's hair, which was sticking up every which way. "I got you some coffee," Alex offered instead, holding up the carrier. He was pretty much screwed. Any second, Annie would show up and catch him panting after a barely coherent Finley and decide that he wasn't up to the task of helping him.

Finley grunted and backed away from the door to let Alex in, shooting him a grateful look when he handed over one of the coffees.

"I didn't know how you liked it," Alex said, which was only half true. He wasn't *sure*, but the *cream, no sugar* scrawled across his foggy mirror when he stepped out of the shower that morning gave him a pretty good idea.

"It's perfect." Finley's voice was way too appealing, all scratchy and pleased as he shuffled into the kitchen after Alex.

Alex's mind happily came up with other scenarios where Finley might sound like that, and it had obviously been way too long since Alex had known someone in the biblical sense. He felt like an awkward, horny teenager.

"Sorry, I'm not really a morning person," Finley said, as though it weren't quite obvious. He made another delighted noise when Alex handed over his breakfast. "What is this?"

"A bacon and egg panini." That he had guessed at, though he figured any guy who turned down bacon wouldn't be worth his time.

"Okay, you are officially the best boss ever." Finley slouched into one of the kitchen chairs, thankfully too focused on his food to notice Alex flinch at the reminder that he was, technically, Finley's boss.

This whole endeavor was going to be an exercise in self-torture, but Alex was still determined to help if he could. He grabbed his own sandwich out of the bag and sat down across from Finley. "Just to give you fair warning, I'm kind of curious by nature, so feel free to tell me to mind my own business if I start getting too nosey."

Finley took another sip of his coffee and smirked at Alex, looking a little more awake. "I'm Finley, I'm an Aries, the youngest of three boys. I enjoy movies and long walks along the beach ..." He shook his head. "Actually, I've never lived near the beach."

"Pisces, with a Sagittarius rising," Alex said. "No strong feelings about the beach one way or the other, but I do enjoy movies."

"Look at you, Sagittarius rising." Finley grinned. "I have no idea what that means."

"I have a friend who's into that sort of thing." It was actually Babar who had explained to Alex how the movements of the stars affected and shaped people, though those conversations often devolved into a tirade about how most human-interpreted astrology was crap. "It means I'm a good listener, and that I'm incredibly charming."

"Yeah?" Finley held his gaze long enough to kick Alex's pulse up a notch. "Yeah, I can see that," he said softly.

Before Alex could think of a good way to respond, Annie popped into the room right behind Finley, startling Alex enough that he nearly knocked over his coffee.

"Sorry, uh. Muscle spasm," Alex said, wiping the splashed coffee off the back of his hand with his T-shirt.

Finley shrugged, and the moment was gone. Alex shot Annie a dirty look once Finley's attention was again on his breakfast. He wasn't dumb enough to think her timing was random, nor was it all that subtle.

~~*

Finley had actually worked as a bartender for a while back home, one of the several odd jobs he'd had before Robert had convinced him to join him on the road. He'd done it long enough that he knew the basics, and it only took an hour or so for Alex to show him the specifics of *The Lost Angel*. It made Finley wonder once again exactly how much of what Alex told him was true. Did he really need the help, or was Finley some sort of charity case?

Unfortunately, at the moment, Finley needed the job too much to ask.

"I guess it doesn't seem like much right now," Alex said. He scratched the back of his neck and looked around, as if hoping that some other task might present itself. "The first few years I spent so much time here. I haven't had a real vacation since we opened. Now that I can afford it, it'd be nice to have someone to help out if I want a night off."

"Understandable." Finley nodded. It did make sense when Alex put it that way, and Finley felt mildly better about the whole situation. "You seem to be a little young to have been doing this for a few years already."

Alex shrugged. "Yeah, I guess so. I don't know. It always seemed like a cool job when I was a kid. My parents helped me out when I went to start it up, so, y'know."

Finley took that to mean Alex's family was fairly well-off, but he wasn't quite so uncouth as to ask him that directly. "Are they not around to help you out if you need a day off?" he asked instead.

"Nah, they moved to Florida when they retired. They visit every now and then, but mostly it's just me."

"Your parents are retired already?" Finley asked, surprised. His parents still had a few years until retirement, and he was the baby of his family.

"Uh, yeah." Alex grinned. "I was a very unexpected miracle baby. My parents had long given up on having kids when I came along."

"So you were an only child?" Finley frowned when Alex nodded and tried to reconcile the new information with the impression of Alex he'd already formed. He tried to imagine Alex as a little kid growing up all alone with wealthy, elderly parents. "Wasn't that sort of lonely?"

"I was actually very rarely alone." Alex seemed amused by either the question or his own answer, though Finley didn't think either one was particularly funny. "Extended family," Alex added, and Finley guessed that maybe there were some adventures with his cousins that he was thinking about.

"What about you?" Alex asked when Finley didn't respond right away. "What, uh—What's your family like?"

"A little *Leave it to Beaver*-ish, maybe," Finley said, ignoring the pause that made him think that wasn't the question Alex originally wanted to ask. "I was sort of the wild child of my family, and, some bad decision-making aside, I wasn't really all that bad. Just ..."

"Lost?" Alex looked mortified as soon as he said it, which made Finley want to laugh.

"Maybe a little. My brothers both had very clear ideas of what they wanted to do with their lives growing up. I'm still trying to figure that out."

Alex grinned. "Well, you've come to the right place for that."

"Have I?"

"Yep."

Finley would have argued the point, uncertain how a part-time bartending job would help him figure out his life, but Alex seemed so pleased, he found he didn't have the heart. Hell, maybe he was even right. Stranger things had happened.

If he'd thought *The Lost Angel* was a little odd before, Finley's first night of serving cemented that impression. There was something unusual about the atmosphere, though Finley had yet to pinpoint what that might be. It wasn't bad—In fact, Finley felt completely at home in the bar, which was unusual for him. It was just *different*.

One thing was for sure, Alex was truly in his element. He chatted easily with all of his customers, making sure to spend at least several minutes with everyone who walked into the bar. Finley spent nearly as much time watching him as he did working, and while Finley didn't intentionally eavesdrop, he was amused by the bits of conversations he did overhear.

"If I had to choose between Bert and Ernie, I would definitely go with Bert," Alex said to one woman. How they'd gotten to that point in the conversation, Finley couldn't even begin to guess. "I mean, Ernie's got his good points, but you've got to wonder about a guy who's that happy all the time."

"Well, sure," the woman said with a sly smile that was all the more impressive given that she'd looked like the whole world was ending when she'd walked in. "But Bert was always 'doing the pigeon,' and that can't be sanitary."

Alex had cracked up at that, and Finley had to duck into the backroom to hide his own laughter. Later, he overheard Alex insisting to another patron that Paddington could 'totally kick Pooh's ass' in a bar brawl.

It made Finley wonder if it was some sort of game that Alex had invented to amuse himself on slow nights, or if the customers themselves were that random. He was so preoccupied with the question that it wasn't until well into the night that he realized everyone who walked into the bar came in alone and they all, without exception, left the same way.

In fact, aside from Alex, and Finley himself if he was serving someone, there was very little interaction between people, even when the bar was at its busiest. The weird part was that it wasn't all that awkward. The music playing through the overhead speakers kept the bar from being dead silent, and everyone seemed content to keep to themselves.

"Is it usually like this?" Finley asked after they'd locked the doors for the night.

Alex gave him a curious look, like he wasn't sure what Finley was referring to. Finally, he said, "There are better places around here to go to hear music, or dance, or meet people. I think people come here to ... Reflect."

Finley considered that as he wiped down the tables. Hadn't he, in fact, been drawn there for that very reason? He wondered if it was something Alex had intended all along, or if it had developed organically from the atmosphere and Alex's particular way with people.

It didn't matter, Finley decided as Alex handed him his tips for the night. "Holy shit. I didn't think we had that many customers," Finley said as he thumbed through the bills again.

"People tend to tip well here." Alex shrugged like it was no big deal, but it had been awhile since Finley had had that much cash to his name.

"Hey, man, thanks again," Finley started, but Alex stopped him with a wave of his hand.

"Don't mention it. It's good to have some help." The smile Alex gave him made Finley feel warm all over. "I think this will end up being good for both of us."

"Yeah." Finley nodded. "Yeah, I think so too."

~~*

Alex would be the first to admit that having Finley around made his work a little more complicated. But, for the first time in a long while, he also had something to look forward to. He liked spending time with Finley, even if they were both busy doing other things. Having him around made Alex realize that he *had* been a little lonely over the past few years. If nothing else, it was nice to have someone normal to talk to on a regular basis. Unfortunately, Alex's daily weather chat with the barista at the coffee place next to his house didn't really count, sweet as she was.

"To a successful first week," Alex said, pouring them each a glass of whiskey on Saturday night after they'd locked up.

Of course, Finley had no idea how successful they'd been, but Alex was feeling quite pleased with his new system. Sure, some of the customers might've found him a little odd for bringing up Grover or Elroy Jetson out of the blue, but the angels got it and that's what mattered. It wasn't as though the customers would be back and, with few exceptions, most of them responded well to the random, whimsical turns in conversation.

All in all, Alex was feeling pretty awesome, and he wanted to celebrate.

Finley dropped the rag he was using back into the bleach bucket and picked up his glass. "To *The Lost Angel*," he replied tapping his glass against Alex's. He slid onto the barstool Alex kept behind the counter and sighed. "I can see why you decided to stay closed on Sundays. I'm actually kind of exhausted."

Alex laughed. "You get used to it. It's good to have a day off, though." He sipped his drink and watched as Finley closed his eyes and leaned his head back, exposing the long line of his throat. He looked tired, beautiful, and oddly vulnerable like that. It made Alex's chest ache, and he forced himself to look away before Finley opened his eyes to catch Alex staring like a creep. He was surprised Annie wasn't standing over his shoulder frowning at him for it.

"I'm not used to actually working, I guess," Finley said. He sighed and straightened back up in his seat. "It might take a few more days."

"What were you—Sorry. Nevermind." Alex pulled the last load of glasses from the dishwasher and started to dry them off to distract himself from asking things he shouldn't. He was determined to wait until Finley was ready to tell him on his own.

"It's killing you not to ask, isn't it?"

Alex set the tray of glasses down on the counter a little harder than he meant to. "Like you wouldn't believe."

Finley chuckled and slumped against the wall again. "Robert, my ex, was a touring musician. He asked me to go on the road with him last summer. At the time, I thought it meant that he missed me when he was gone and he wanted me around. In retrospect, I think he just wanted someone who would do all the booking and merch stuff without wanting a cut of the profits."

"So what happened?" Alex asked, watching Finley as he swirled the whiskey around in his glass.

"When we first got together, Robert was only in town a few months out of the year. He was very good looking and very charming." Finley shrugged, looking a little embarrassed by the confession. "I was flattered that he wanted me. Figured he had plenty of options. Once we were on the road and together all the time, I realized he wasn't who I thought he was." More than anything else, Finley sounded resigned. "What I'd mistaken for charming self-confidence was actually raging narcissism, and once I stopped thinking he was perfect, he stopped caring what I thought."

"So you broke up with him?"

Finley gave him a rueful grin and tossed back the rest of his drink. "No, I stayed with him for another six months until my money ran out. Hope springs eternal, I guess. I kept waiting for him to turn back into the guy I thought he was. The good times were really good at first. It made the bad times harder to reconcile."

Alex fished around for something useful to say. Unfortunately, when it came to actual human relationships, he was woefully lacking in experience. The best he could come up with was, "I'm sorry."

"Don't get me wrong," Finley said, waving the apology away. "I'm not broken up over him. He wasn't worth that sort of energy. But, I don't know. I don't think I'll ever not be mad about it."

"Because he lied to you?"

"Because I wasted so much time on someone who never actually existed. It was all fake, and I bought into it for longer than I should have because I wanted to believe it." Finley nodded when Alex offered him another drink. "That fucks with your head a little, and I hate that he's still able to affect me even that much. I hate that it makes me question my own judgment."

"You didn't know," Alex said when Finley didn't continue. "Some people are experts at only letting others see what they want them to see. You can hardly blame yourself for that."

Finley looked at him like he was trying to figure out what Alex's angle was. "Maybe," and was all he said.

"All I'm saying is, don't let one jackass screw with your faith in other people. There are honest guys out there."

"I know," Finley said, and the smile he gave Alex was completely genuine.

It made Alex feel weirdly guilty. The feeling only compounded when Annie showed up a moment later, her assignment for the night apparently finished.

"Anyway." Alex cleared his throat and started to dry off the glasses again. "Do you have anything exciting planned for tomorrow?"

Finley gave an amused snort. "Besides sleeping? I don't know, I thought I might drive around a little and get a feel for the city."

Alex nodded and, despite the warning look Annie was giving him, asked, "Would you maybe want to go to breakfast with me? There's a place a few blocks from my house that does a great Sunday brunch."

"Yeah, actually. That sounds good." Finley gave him a goofy grin. "This is probably lame to admit, but I love going out for breakfast. I don't know what it is, exactly, but there's something really appealing about it."

"The bacon," Alex supplied, and grinned when Finley laughed. He knew he was walking a dangerous line, but he couldn't seem to help himself. Finley was way too appealing by half, and after so much time spent on his own, Alex couldn't deny himself the pleasure of his company.

"And what will you do if he decides he wants more than just friendship?" Annie asked over Finley's laughter. She was obviously not expecting an answer, and Alex wondered what her purpose was in asking.

The better question to Alex's mind was what would he do if Finley decided friendship was the only thing he wanted? Unfortunately, he had yet to come up with an answer that didn't hurt like hell.

~~*

It didn't take long before Finley genuinely felt at home at *The Lost Angel*, comfortable enough that he finally told his mom that he and Robert had broken up. Though, he *may* have implied that it was because he'd found a great opportunity in town, and not because Robert had been the waste of time she'd always suspected him of being.

At home as he felt, though, Finley still had the sense of waiting for the other shoe to drop, try as he might not to indulge in that sort of useless worrying. He was pretty sure that he still would've noticed the strange things at the bar, whether or not he was looking for them.

For one thing, there were no repeat customers. Ever. Finley had been there for nearly a month, and he had yet to see someone come into the bar who'd been there before. Admittedly, he wasn't always great with faces, but every bar had its regulars, didn't it?

And, the thing was, Alex was great. A little quirky, sure, but he was honest-to-God *nice*, which in Finley's opinion was a rare enough quality in people as to make it blatant in everything Alex did. He listened to people, and seemed to genuinely care about what was going on with them, regardless of the fact that he was unlikely to ever see them again.

Finley found it truly baffling. If Alex not offered him the job, Finley might've shown up every night anyway just to be around him. He couldn't believe that Alex's kindness hadn't managed to generate any sort of customer loyalty for the bar; not that it actually seemed to affect business, and that was weird too. Finley really tried not to think about it unless he had to. It gave him a headache.

"Look, I don't care how you decide. Both you and Dale are more than capable of getting the job done."

Unfortunately, ignoring it wasn't always an option.

Finley froze on his way into the backroom at Alex's comment. He peeked around the corner to see Alex standing there on the phone, his back to Finley.

"I don't care." Alex sounded exasperated. "I don't think it's necessary, but if you both want to go, that's fine. Just make sure you get the job done. Tonight. He's unstable, and I don't trust him not to do something stupid while you two are busy standing there arguing semantics."

Before Finley could back away, Alex turned and spotted him. He looked panicked, then irritated. Finally he sighed and said, "Its fine. Just go, please." With that, he ended the call and slipped his phone back into his pocket. "So, you're probably wondering what that was about."

Finley shook his head. No matter what it sounded like, he was ninety-nine percent sure Alex hadn't just ordered a hit. "It's none of my business." Even if all the weirdness might be explained if *The Lost Angel* was some sort of front for mob activity. Surely they wouldn't have hired him if that were the case. *He* wouldn't have hired Finley. There was only Alex, no shadowy 'they'.

"Oh my God." Alex blinked at him and then started to laugh. "Your face! Man, I don't even want to know what's going through your head right now. That was my cousin. One of our other cousins just went through a bad breakup and since she and her brother only live about an hour away, I wanted one of them to go spend some time with him over the weekend."

"Oh." Finley grinned, embarrassed. "That's really nice of you. Not everyone would think to do that."

Alex shrugged, looking uncomfortable. "All I did was order my cousins around. It's not that amazing."

"But it kind of is," Finley insisted. For all that Alex cared about people, he didn't seem to realize how significant that was. "You're really—"

"I should get back out there," Alex said, cutting him off. "Customers." He walked past Finley back out into the bar, leaving him standing there feeling a little stupid.

"Yeah, that went well." Finley sighed and went into the backroom, hoping it would jog his memory as to what he'd been headed back there for in the first place.

They didn't talk much for the rest of the night, and they were halfway through the closing list before it really got to Finley. "Hey, I'm sorry about before." Finley waited until Alex actually looked at him before continuing. "I'm sorry I was eavesdropping. It was none of my business, and I'm sorry if I made you feel uncomfortable. You didn't really owe me an explanation or anything."

"Don't—" Alex sighed and then smiled at him. "You don't need to apologize, you didn't do anything wrong. Low-level drama is sort of a constant thing with my cousins, so I'm used to it. I just didn't want you to think, I don't know, that I'm drama-prone, or that I was fanning the flames or something. What?" he asked when he caught sight of Finley's grin.

"Nothing. I was just trying to think of a scenario that would make me think less of you. It involves ordering a hit on someone, just so you know."

That only seemed to confuse Alex. "A hit?"

Finley shook his head. "Nevermind. Family drama is universal, I think. Your cousins are lucky to have you, whether they realize it or not." When Alex shrugged and looked away, Finley realized it was the praise that made him uncomfortable. He couldn't keep himself from adding, "You're a good guy, Alex Monroe. And here I thought those were a myth, like dragons or narwhals." He laughed and ducked as Alex chucked a bar towel at his head.

"Narwhals are real, idiot," Alex said, making Finley laugh harder. "You aren't all that bad yourself," he added as Finley retrieved the towel. He smiled when Finley handed it back over, and Finley realized with a start that what he really wanted to do was lean across the bar and kiss the hell out of him until neither of them could think.

Oh.

That's where the other shoe was.

~~*

Saturday night had fast become Alex's favorite part of the week. He and Finley had easily fallen into a post-work routine, sharing a drink and—after Alex had brought over his old TV and a VCR he'd found at a garage sale—watching crappy movies on VHS.

"Man, I can't believe you have this," Finley said, pawing through the box of movies and pulling out a *Care Bears* video. "I totally remember this one."

"It's from when I was a kid. Don't knock nostalgia, man." Alex grabbed it and threw it back in the box in favor of something else. "Oh, *Spaceballs*! Come on, you know you want to."

"Sure." Finley smiled indulgently. It was a good look on him. "Put it in, I'll do the popcorn."

Alex popped the video in the VCR, but didn't start it. Watching the old previews was half the fun, after all. He always felt surprised that the videos still worked; somehow he'd assumed with all the new technology that they would just stop.

"Hey, I got some Coke from the grocery store," Finley called from the kitchen, just loud enough to be heard over the popping of the corn. "Do you want to do drinks or just have soda?

"I'll grab the rum," Alex said, ducking into the bar to get some.

That was probably their first mistake. By the time they were halfway through the movie, Alex was drunk enough that he couldn't quite remember who'd suggested doing a drinking game, nor could he recall what the 'take a shot' criteria had originally been. They'd abandoned any real rules almost immediately.

"Hey, do you believe in destiny?" Alex asked after they did a shot for Rick Moranis being onscreen.

Finley snickered, looking up at Alex from his seat on the floor. "What's that got to do with the Millennium Falcon?"

"No, seriously. Like destiny, like ... Destiny." Alex waved his hand for emphasis.

"Seriously?" Finley sighed and pushed himself up, turning to crawl onto the couch. He flopped around until he was sitting on one leg facing Alex, his hand braced on the back of the couch for balance. "Fuck those guys. I say, do what you want."

Alex couldn't keep from laughing. Finley looked so earnest. "No, I mean like, shit happens for a reason, y'know? Like a butterfly flaps its wings and somewhere else gets crappy weather."

"I don't think that's destiny," Finley said.

"No," Alex agreed, shaking his head. "But I mean, like, if you didn't have a dick boyfriend, then you wouldn't be here and we wouldn't know each other. So maybe that had to happen so we could watch *Spaceballs*, right?" He broke off with a sigh, frustrated. He wasn't explaining it right.

"I'm not sure the universe is concerning itself with our Saturday movie." Finley patted Alex's leg with his free hand. "We could've watched *Care Bears*."

"The movie doesn't matter. I just think things work out and that you're supposed to be here." Oh, crap. He was making a mess of the entire conversation. He was about to tell Finley to forget it, and turn back to the movie when Finley leaned forward, his hand still braced awkwardly on Alex's leg.

"You want me to be here? Like, in a destiny way?" Finley was close enough for Alex to feel his breath, hot against his cheek.

"Yeah," Alex said. It felt so obvious to him, he was surprised by the question. Was it possible Finley had missed that completely? "Since, like, five minutes after you got here."

"Tonight?"

Before Alex could punch him for asking stupid questions, Finley leaned in the rest of the way and planted a sloppy kiss at the corner of Alex's mouth.

"Like that?"

"More ..." That was as far as Alex got with his instructions before Finley was climbing on top of him. He managed to turn enough to stretch out on the couch without incident, groaning happily as Finley settled against him, his movements surprisingly graceful, considering.

"I can kiss you now, right?"

Alex nodded vigorously, not really caring how stupid he looked at that point. He was rewarded with another kiss, far more serious than the last. Finley tasted like rum and salt, hot enough to make Alex's head spin. He pushed his fingers through Finley's hair like he'd wanted to do since day one, and Finley rumbled like a big cat. Alex wanted to pet him all over.

"We should have done this way sooner," Finley mumbled against his lips. "We should be doing this all the time."

"Is this truly the consummation you were hoping for?"

Alex flinched, bumping his nose against Finley's as he turned. He groaned when he saw Annie standing there in all her terrible, cock-blocking glory. "Come *on*."

"Come on what?" Finley leaned down and kissed a wet stripe from Alex's jaw to his ear. "Wanna go back to my bedroom? The bed is kinda small, but I think we can make it work."

That was exactly what Alex wanted to do, but he could tell by Annie's severe frown that it wasn't about to happen short of Alex developing an extreme exhibition kink in the next few minutes. He wasn't *sure* Annie wouldn't leave if he and Finley kept going, but it wasn't a game of chicken he was eager to play, no matter how drunk he was.

"We shouldn't. I shouldn't."

Finley brought his head up, obviously having realized Alex had stopped responding. He frowned. "Why?"

"I'm drunk. We're drunk, and I—" He shot Annie a dirty look. She couldn't even give him a private minute for this? "I really like you," he whispered. "I don't want us to fuck this up before we've even gotten started."

"Oh." Finley's frown melted away, though he still looked confused. "Yeah, that's—okay. We could go to sleep?"

"That's probably not a great idea. I outta go."

"You're drunk," Finley said as he rolled off of him. "You can't drive home."

"It's not that far." Alex sat up and shoved his feet back into the sneakers he'd kicked under the coffee table. "The walk will do me good."

"You're going to walk home at this hour, through this neighborhood?" Finley shook his head like he couldn't quite process what Alex was actually saying.

Alex was pretty sure the *'Just to get away from me*?' was implied in the curve of his frown. "Don't worry about me," he said, feeling his own fair share of bitterness. "I'll be safe."

"Yeah, okay," Finley said sullenly as he walked Alex to the door. "I guess I'll see you then."

"Tomorrow? Afternoon," Alex added, swaying a little. He really was pretty wasted. "We could ..." He sighed and looked at Annie, who was still waiting for him like he was a particularly troublesome child. Turning toward Finley, he grabbed his shoulders and pressed him against the door. He leaned in and kissed him hard, more desperate than seductive, but Finley didn't seem to mind.

Pulling away, Alex looked at him as steadily as he could manage. "You have no idea how much I want to stay."

Finley nodded, clenching his fingers against Alex's shirt for a moment before letting him go. "Okay," he finally said, looking at least somewhat mollified as Alex backed towards the door with the promise that he would call after he'd sobered up. "Talk to you tomorrow, then."

"I hate you," Alex said when they were a block away.

Annie retaliated by zapping the drunkenness out of him and saying, "That was unkind."

Sobriety really didn't improve his mood, but Alex apologized anyway. He didn't hate Annie, as much as he wanted to. Ultimately, he didn't want his first time with Finley to be a drunken fuck. He did hate the fact that she'd been right to stop it, but that was really neither here nor there.

He silently took back his apology when he woke up with a raging hangover and spent the first two hours of the morning puking.

Petty, meddlesome angels.

~~*

Alex called the next day as promised, though he sounded as miserable as Finley felt, and they'd both agreed that neither of them would be good company. For his part, Finley had spent the better part of the day curled up in bed, very much wanting to die. He was grateful Alex hadn't been around to witness that.

By the time Alex showed up for work on Monday, Finley had mostly recovered. Unfortunately, by that point, it had been just long enough that seeing him again was awkward.

"So, uh. Rum," Finley said as an opening gambit. "Probably not our best idea ever."

"Right?" Alex laughed. "Man, I hope nobody orders any rum drinks tonight. I'm not sure I can even pour it right now."

"I know, huh," Finley offered weakly. He wanted to say *'So, we should try that again without the liquor sometime,'* but when Alex gave him a wary, hopeful smile, he chickened out. "I guess we should get going on prep."

"Yeah, that sounds like a plan," Alex quietly agreed. From there they didn't speak beyond what was strictly necessary to do their work.

It was pretty much the longest, suckiest night Finley had spent there. By the time last call rolled around, he was ready to do something stupid, just to break the tension.

Decision made, he followed Alex into the backroom after the closing. Too quietly, evidently, because Alex jumped when he turned to find Finley standing there, making Finley jump as well.

"Sorry, I didn't mean to—"

"Naw, it's cool, you just—"

Finley ran his fingers through his hair and laughed. "I just wanted to ..." He took a step forward, and when Alex didn't move away, he leaned forward and pressed a chaste kiss against his lips. "Wanted to do that while we were both sober," he said with more bravado than he really felt.

"Yeah." Alex let out a shaky breath. For a moment, it looked like he was going to reach out, but he stopped himself. "Yeah."

"Okay. So, there's that." Finley backed up a little when Alex didn't say anything. "Um."

"I meant what I said the other night." The corner of Alex's mouth quirked up as he looked down at his feet. It was pretty cute. "I really like you, and I haven't really liked someone in a while. I'm not sure where to go from here."

"Well, maybe we could do the movie night thing again, but with less of the rum and more of the kissing." Finley waggled his eyebrows and gave Alex an exaggerated leer, feeling the need to cover for how exposed he already felt by the conversation. "I really like you too, you know."

"Yeah?"

Finley shrugged, expression teasing. "Sure. I mean, you know, *Spaceballs* always gets me a little hot and bothered, but that was at least seventy-five percent you, baby."

"I like those odds." Alex shoved his hands in his pockets and rocked back on his heels. "A shower, shave, and the right pair of jeans and I'm pretty sure I can knock that up to a solid eighty."

"Saturday night, then?"

Alex nodded. "I mean, I sort of have standing plans with this guy from work, but I think I can weasel out of them."

"You should totally ditch that loser." Finley reached out and grabbed Alex's hand, tugging him closer. "I'll make it worth your while."

"That wasn't really a concern." Alex leaned in close, bringing his other hand up to curl around the back of Finley's neck. "You make things worthwhile no matter what."

They were close enough to be breathing the same air, and Finley was all ready to say screw Saturday night when right now would work too when Alex flinched and took a step back, his hands falling back to his sides. His eyes slanted to the side, and for a moment he looked irritated.

"We should probably finish up," Alex said after a weird pause. "I'm not sure I'm fully recovered from our adventures with rum yet."

"Sure," Finley agreed, and that, sadly, was that.

Saturday night took forever to arrive. Finley was fairly certain there had never been a week longer in the history of the world. After agreeing on a date, the awkward tension between him and Alex had disappeared, only to be replaced by an anticipatory sort of tension that was driving Finley crazy.

It was a good kind of crazy, but crazy was still crazy. They spent their time at work flirting in a way that probably would have disgusted Finley had he been subjected to it by someone else. Smiles and little touches, Alex's hand on Finley's hip if he had to walk around him or reach past him behind the bar, a few quick kisses in the backroom.

Finley couldn't remember the last time he'd wanted someone like he wanted Alex. He wasn't sure he ever had. Alex was different in everything he did, a tantalizing mix of brazen and shy. He watched Finley when he thought Finley wasn't paying attention, and Finley wondered how long that had been going on without him realizing.

The difference now was Alex didn't look away when Finley caught him at it, and it made Finley feel flushed and overheated. Nobody had ever looked at Finley like that, like they saw every part of him and approved of everything.

Really, it was a testament to Finley's self-control that he didn't try to pounce on Alex every time they were alone together. By the time they shut the doors Saturday night, Finley's self-control had worn paper-thin.

"So, I was thinking—I mean, we don't have to, but would you want to go back to my place?"

At another time, maybe, Finley would've laughed at the fact that Alex seemed unsure of what his answer would be. As it was, he just said, "Let's get the hell out of here."

To his credit, Finley kept his hands to himself until they were in Alex's house, the front door securely shut. As soon as that task was completed, however, all bets were off. Alex made a satisfying 'oomf' noise when Finley pushed him back against the door, a weird sort of desperation kicking in. He was so close to where he wanted to be, he didn't want to give Alex a chance to have any second thoughts.

"Is it just me, or has it been an incredibly long week?" Finley asked against his mouth. Assuming Alex agreed with him, he continued on to the actual kiss.

His hunch was confirmed when Alex groaned and clutched at Finley's hips, pulling him closer.

"I, uh," Alex said dazedly once Finley gave him a chance to breath. "Um, bedroom?"

"Yeah." Something unclenched in Finley's chest at the suggestion. Grinning, he stepped back enough to let Alex move away from the door. "Lead the way."

Alex grabbed his hand, lacing their fingers together before he started through the living room and down the hall towards his bedroom. He stopped abruptly once they reached the door, and Finley bumped into him, making them both stumble.

"So, I have sort of a confession." Alex turned to face him, looking a little hesitant. "Not a *confession* confession, but it's definitely—"

"Alex!"

"It's been awhile," Alex said in a rush. "I mean, I remember how it goes and all, but ..." He trailed off and shrugged.

It took Finley longer than it should have to realize that Alex was *nervous*. Oddly enough, it made the rest of his own tension disappear, leaving a giddy sort of playfulness in its wake. "That's fine," he said nonchalantly. "We can take it easy tonight. I mean, I don't even have my handcuffs and ball gag with me, so, y'know."

"Thanks, I feel much better."

Finley grinned and stepped around him, tugging him into the room. "Come on, I bet all my buddies I could at least get to second base with you."

Alex snorted and let himself be led to the bed, which had obviously been made for company. Finley toed off his shoes and sat down, not bothering to pull back the covers. After a moment of hesitation, Alex did the same, kneeling on the bed next to Finley.

Finley scooted back to give him more room, tugging on his shirt until Alex settled on top of him.

"I'm glad you're here," Alex said, balancing his weight on his elbows as Finley ran his hands up the back of his shirt.

"Here like destiny here?" Finley teased.

"Shut up."

"Make me."

When focused solely on the task, Alex, as it turned out, was even more of an excellent kisser than Finley had believed. He kissed like he couldn't bear to stop, one leading into the next and the next until Finley lost track of everything else he'd wanted to do. He couldn't think of anything beyond Alex's mouth and the feel of his hot, smooth skin under his fingertips.

They made out like teenagers until Finley's lips were sore and tingling and, except for the desperate need for something to drink, Finley could've happily continued on like that for another few hours.

"Not gonna lie, man," Finley said when they finally broke apart. "If that's you out of practice ..."

Alex laughed. "Yeah, well, you bring out the best in me, I guess."

Finley wondered if he would ever get used to that sort of frank sincerity. He didn't feel worthy of the compliment, and he had no idea how to respond other than to pull Alex into another kiss and hope that it was enough of an answer for the moment.

It was good and easy and hot and comfortable all at the same time. When they finally crawled into bed to go to sleep for the night, having done nothing more than kiss and feel each other up, Finley didn't feel frustrated by it at all.

"Hey, Alex?"

"Hmm?" Alex sounded out of it already, his arm a warm, solid weight across Finley's chest.

"Goodnight."

"'Night." A minute later, Alex's breathing evened out, and Finley could feel the puff of each exhale against his neck.

It took a while longer than that for Finley to slip off to sleep. Alex stirred up a tangle of things in him that Finley had yet to sort through. Lust had been the easiest to focus on, and somehow Alex had managed to twist even that around into something else. Beyond all of that, Finley felt content, which was a frightening thing in itself. Finley hadn't meant to fall so deep so quickly, but he couldn't muster up the energy to panic about it. The contentment was too strong with Alex pressed up against him like he belonged there, and when Finley did finally fall asleep, he was smiling.

~~*

Alex wasn't sure what woke him up—he was usually fairly resistant to consciousness first thing in the morning. The arm he was laying on was asleep and his other arm was wrapped around Finley's waist. For about two seconds, Alex felt completely awesome. Then he realized that Annie was sitting at the foot of the bed.

"What is wrong with you?" he hissed. "This is private time. We talked about this." They'd talked about this. Alex had sworn up and down he'd take things slow in return for Annie's promise that she'd give him the space to do so. He'd honestly believed she trusted him enough to honor the agreement.

"It is safe to talk. He'll remain asleep while we do so."

Which, okay, wasn't the most amazing angel power he'd ever seen, but it was definitely the creepiest.

"What do you want?" Alex asked as he sat up. If Finley was momentarily awareness-impaired, he might as well get the feeling back in his arm. "What is the problem now? Please tell me how I'm taking advantage of the situation."

Annie gave him her patented blank stare, like she had no idea what he was talking about, which actually meant she knew exactly what she was doing and was willing to stare him into compliance in order to get her way. "I believe it will be best if you tell him the truth before your relationship progresses any further."

Alex eyed her warily. "What truth?"

"The truth about your gift. If you care for him as I believe you do, you should be honest with him. Such love and trust will be rewarded." She said it all so matter-of-factly, Alex was sure he'd misunderstood what she was getting at, given that the idea of telling Finley the truth was completely insane

"Are you *trying* to make my life more difficult? I mean, really. Is it a hobby for you? Something to keep you from getting too bored?"

Annie frowned at him. "You have a rather frustrating habit of assuming untoward motives where there are none to be found." She actually had the gall to look hurt. "Your happiness has always been my primary concern."

"Right. That and me using my 'gift' to help others," Alex pointed out.

"You say that as though they are not two parts of the same whole."

"Whatever you say." Alex wasn't in the mood to argue that particular point. "And how exactly would getting dumped make me happy?" Alex asked. "Because I guarantee you, I tell him I can see angels, and that's exactly what'll happen."

"You should have more faith in us, Alex. I understand your need for secrecy with those we help, but that should not extend to Finley if you mean to share your heart with him. The longer you wait to tell him, the more difficult it will be."

Alex shook his head. "He'll think I'm crazy."

"Give him the chance to trust you." Annie seemed more weary than exasperated, which was different. "You cannot spend your life lying to the man you love."

"Whoa, hey." Alex held up his hand. "We haven't even had an actual date yet. I think you've jumped ahead a few pages."

And *there* was the exasperated look Annie was so fond of. "I often find myself worrying that you're rather stupid and simply very good at hiding that fact." She disappeared without giving Alex a chance to respond.

"I know you are, but what am I?" he muttered as Finley started to stir.

It wasn't like he wanted to lie, but lying was one of the occupational hazards of being an angel pimp. Alex didn't make up the rules. He just had to live by them, especially if he wanted Finley to stick around.

"You talking to yourself?" Finley mumbled, half his face still pressed against the pillow.

"My guardian angel. She likes to meddle."

Finley snorted. "Tell me you're not a morning person. I don't banter pre-coffee."

"I'll try and keep that in mind." Alex reached out and traced his fingers down Finley's side, grinning when Finley smiled and batted his hand away in response. "You feel like going out for breakfast?"

"Hmm." Finley rolled onto his back at that and blinked his eyes open, rubbing at them with one hand. "Will there be coffee?"

"Always," Alex promised.

~~*

Instead of the usual coffee shop breakfast, they ended up at Alex's favorite little diner a few blocks away.

"This is what I needed last Sunday," Finley said, making a little noise of appreciation as the waitress dropped off his biscuits and gravy.

"I'm not sure you'd have been this excited about it last Sunday," Alex said dryly.

"Touché." Finley knocked his foot against Alex's under the table as he dug in.

It was so casually flirtatious Alex was struck anew that this was actually happening. They'd fooled around and woken up together, and they were having a breakfast date. Sort of. That didn't mean he was assuming Finley was going to stick around for the rest of his life, but Alex could admit, at least to himself, that he wanted him to.

"So, what were your plans for the rest of the day?"

Finley seemed surprised by the question. He looked up and then back down at his food, shrugging. "Didn't really have anything specific in mind."

"What about coming back to my place for a nightcap?"

"A nightcap?" Finley raised an eyebrow as he sat back in his seat, stretching out until his knee rested against Alex's leg. "What happened to taking our time?"

"Oh, I still plan on taking my time." Alex took a sip of his coffee to cover his embarrassment at having actually uttered that line, but it was worth it when Finley sat up and motioned for their check, his breakfast not even half-eaten.

After his morning conversation with Annie, Alex felt sure enough that they'd have no angelic interruptions to keep his word on that. He'd wanted Finley for too long to rush it, and Finley, for his part, seemed content to let Alex take the lead.

"Okay, you may ravish me now," Finley said as they stepped into the bedroom, spreading his arms wide before flopping down on the bed.

Alex bit back his sarcastic reply in favor of stepping between Finley's knees and reaching down with one hand to push his shirt up over his stomach. It was more a tease than anything else. There were so many things Alex wanted to do, he hardly knew where to start.

He stroked his hands over Finley's sides as he pushed his shirt up until Finley took the initiative and pulled it off completely. The pants came next, and Alex could feel his hands shake a little as he undid the button. He felt oddly reverent—Finley was so beautiful, so exactly what Alex wanted, he seemed unreal.

When Alex didn't go any further than unzipping his fly, Finley scooted back on the bed, wriggling out of his pants as he went, giving Alex a look as he settled back against the pillows. Alex shucked his own pants, shrugging out of his shirt at the same time in what had to be the least seductive striptease ever. Finley didn't laugh at him, though, and Alex was thankful for small favors.

The first press of Finley's bare skin against his was a shock to Alex's system. It shouldn't have been possible for something so simple to feel that good.

"What, um … What do you like?" Alex whispered hesitantly, nuzzling Finley's throat and refusing to look directly at him while he asked such a stupid question.

Finley gave a strangled-sounding laugh and said, "You. Everything else is just gravy."

It was the worst possible moment for an epiphany, especially one of the 'Annie-was-right variety, but Alex had never had great luck with timing. He was very much in love with Finley, and he was going to have to tell him the truth. He just hoped that Finley would believe him, and forgive him for waiting until *after* for his confessions.

~~*

Finley made a noise that he hoped sounded disapproving when Alex started moving around somewhere beside him on the bed. His whole body ached deliciously, and he was disinclined to move until he absolutely had to, or until it was time for round … Whatever round they were on now.

"Does that mean you're awake?" Alex asked.

They were really going to have to have a discussion about this talking in the morning thing, Finley decided. He would have to nip it in the bud before Alex started expecting regular responses from him. Then he cracked an eyelid and realized from the slant of the sun that it wasn't actually morning yet.

"What time is it?"

"Little after five," Alex said. "I thought you might be hungry. I was gonna order some pizza."

"Pizza's good." Finley rolled onto his other side and squinted up at Alex. He was thumbing through his phone, totally focused on the task at hand, and Finley was content to watch him.

Finley ran his thumb along the edge of the sheet where it rested against Alex's stomach as he ordered, grinning to himself when Alex smacked his hand to get him to stop. He wondered how long the pizza would take, if they should fool around while they waited, or if the time would be better spent in the shower.

Of course, they could always fool around in the shower.

"Half an hour," Alex said, ending the call. "Which will likely be closer to forty-five minutes."

"Yeah, I can work with that," Finley said.

Alex tangled his fingers with Finley's before Finley could succeed in tugging the sheet down lower. "Actually, I had something I kind of wanted to talk to you about."

"You're pregnant?"

"No."

"*I'm* pregnant?" Finley laughed when Alex rolled his eyes. "Okay, I'm sorry. This is serious?"

"It's not serious like, y'know, worrisome," Alex hedged. "It's just a thing, a sort of personality thing, I guess?"

"Okay." Finley pushed himself up into a sitting position and folded his hands in his lap. "Lay it on me."

"You trust me, right?" Alex asked.

"I wouldn't be here if I didn't, Alex." Finley frowned at the question, his playful mood fading. He couldn't begin to guess what would have Alex so worried.

"You know how I told you about my family, and how they're always having some sort of drama?" Alex waited for Finley to nod before continuing. "Well, that wasn't exactly the whole story. They aren't so much my family as they are, um. Angels."

"Angels."

"I can see angels?" Alex gave him a hopeful grin. "I've been able to see them since I was a kid, and now I help them help people, because I can see them and others can't."

Finley's lips twitched into a confused smile. "I don't get it."

"It's not a joke. I opened the bar to help match up the angels with people who need them. I'm not explaining this well, am I?" Alex groaned, running a hand through his hair. "People don't believe in them anymore, and that makes it harder for them to help. So, I talk to people and sort of give them an in. I'm not sure exactly how it works on their end."

"You …" Finley stared at him with the horrified realization that he really wasn't joking. "You're serious. You actually believe that."

"I believe it because it's true." Alex grabbed his wrist when he moved to get out of bed. "Look, you think I don't know how crazy it sounds? I know how crazy it sounds, trust me, but I'm telling the truth."

Finley shook him off and stood up, searching for his boxers. When he couldn't find them, he pulled on his pants, his back to the bed. "You expect me to believe that angels are real, and you're the only one who can see them, and they've decided the best use of their time is hanging out at a bar in the middle of nowhere hoping that people who need help will just, what? Wander in?" He pulled on his shirt, realized it was inside-out and pulled it off again. "Yeah, no, that sounds completely plausible."

"They don't all hang out there. It's a specific class of guardians that I can see. They were created to look out for people. Finley, *please*." Finley turned to see Alex standing on the other side of the bed, zipping up his jeans. "I didn't want to lie to you. They don't generally interfere with me. I mean, except for Annie, but she wanted me to tell you."

"Annie. Annie the angel?"

Alex winced. "I nicknamed them as a kid."

"Sure. Of course you did. Who doesn't have nicknames for their pet angels?" Finley stalked out into the living room and shoved his shoes on, not bothering to take the time to straighten the crumpled heels. He needed to get out of there. God, he felt so stupid.

"Finley." Alex sounded so heartbroken, it was almost enough to make Finley turn around. "What can I say that will make you believe me?"

Finley shook his head. "You have proof that angels exist?"

"I—It's pretty much a faith thing."

"Right." Finley gave a bark of bitter laughter and let his head fall back, staring up at the ceiling as he tried to put the whole thing in a context that made any sort of sense. He couldn't come up with anything other than, "You're either crazy, or you're amusing yourself at my expense. I'm honestly not sure which is worse."

That time, when he went to leave Alex didn't try to stop him.

~~*

For whatever reason, Finley ended up back at the diner they'd gone to that morning. He wasn't particularly hungry anymore, but he didn't want to go back to *The Lost Angel* at the moment either. He ordered coffee and a piece of pie, and tried to get beyond feeling like a complete idiot long enough to plan out what he was going to do next. Obviously he couldn't continue living in Crazy Alex's bar-apartment. He probably had enough money that he could leave town entirely.

The thought of leaving made him feel sick.

"I didn't read you as a fool, Finley Cooper, and I am rarely wrong."

Finley glanced up to see a woman sitting down across from him, a determined look on her face. She looked young at first glance, but seemed less young the longer Finley looked at her. It was disconcerting.

"If you walk away from Alex, you're a fool. Alex is a good man. You won't find better, I can promise you that."

Great. Crazy Alex had sent one of his crazy friends after him. "Yeah? And who asked you?" Finley took a bite of pie, not really tasting it.

"What?" The woman blinked at him, clearly startled.

"What business is it of yours whether or not I walk away? Who the hell are you to tell me what to do?"

She beamed at him. "I'm Annie. Alex's guardian."

Finley shut his eyes and took a deep breath. Then another. And another, until he didn't feel like his head was in danger of exploding. When he opened his eyes, the woman was still there. "Is this some sort of sick game with you guys? Do you get off on fucking with people's minds? Are you serial killers? What the hell is wrong with you?"

"Sir?"

"I'm good, thanks," Finley said, waving the waitress away. "Unless you wanted something. Annie, was it?"

"Sir?" the waitress said again, a little more slowly.

When Finley looked up, she was watching him with a very concerned expression. "Yeah?"

"Who are you talking to?" She shook her head when Finley gestured toward Annie. "There's nobody there, sir."

Finley looked around the restaurant, then, and realized that several people were watching him, murmuring to each other. "What, is everyone in on it? There's no way—"

"I think you maybe shouldn't be out on your own," the waitress said. "Do you have someone who can come and pick you up?"

"I'm fine, thanks. I'm ..." Finley dug out a twenty and slapped it on the table, scowling when Annie gave him a smug look. "I'll go now."

Annie followed him outside, trailing along after him as he started towards his apartment. "Do you realize what this means, Finley?"

"You're not real."

"I am, and you can see me. You gain nothing by denying it."

"Nope." Finley shook his head. "This is a breakdown. I'm having a breakdown. Or Alex drugged me. Oh, god, you guys are serial killers."

"Why do you find the truth so difficult to accept?" Annie asked.

"The truth?" Finley stopped and turned back to face her. "What? That angels exist, but Alex is the only one who can see them? Except that now I can too?"

"Yes."

Finley snorted and started walking away again. "Right. I suppose he has magical sperm that lifted the veil from my eyes."

"I do not believe that to be the case. Physical intimacy alone has never been enough to allow his other—"

"Shut up!" Finley snapped, cutting her off. The last thing Finley wanted to discuss was Alex's previous lovers.

"What, then, is your answer, Finley?" She touched his shoulder and Finley felt his anger drain away, leaving nothing but confused misery in its wake. "What is your reasonable explanation for what has happened today?"

"Well, obviously I'm so stupid in love with a complete nutjob that I would rather be crazy with him than sane without him." Finley shrugged. "I've had a psychotic break."

"I suppose that is a possibility." Annie sounded amused. "My belief is that your faith in Alex runs deeper than your skepticism and you are being rewarded."

"Rewarded with what?"

"Proof that angels exist." Annie raised her arms and Finley realized that what he'd dismissed as a really tacky backpack was actually a set of pure white wings. "I am the proof you asked Alex for. The question now becomes, what are you planning to do with it?"

~~*

Alex felt a brief, painful flare of hope when he heard the doorbell until he remembered that he'd ordered pizza. Right on time. He paid the man and shut the door, setting the pizzas on the coffee table untouched. Where they could sit there and mock him for how very alone he was. Even the angels were keeping their distance, which, truth be told, was probably a good idea at the moment.

It'd been stupid to try and tell Finley the truth, as disastrous as he'd known it would be. Except, Alex hadn't wanted to continue to lie and he'd allowed himself to hope for the best, despite knowing how Finley would react, that he wouldn't believe him. Who in their right mind would?

"So what am I supposed to do, you giant cowards?" Alex asked the empty room. He had no idea how to fix things. There wasn't a graceful way to come back from "I can see angels" that he knew of, if he could even get Finley to talk to him again. Was he just supposed to suck it up and accept that he was meant to be alone? What good was it to have an in with heaven if it screwed up all of his human relationships? "Why couldn't you let me have this?"

The doorbell rang again just as his phone chirped in his pocket, and he fished it out absently as he walked back to the entryway. Maybe the pizza guy had forgotten the cheesy bread? He stopped short, his heart pounding in his throat when he actually looked at his phone and saw that it was from Finley. The message read, *Do you believe in destiny?*

Alex was still staring at the phone as he fumbled with the door handle. Despite the text, he wasn't expecting to look up and see Finley actually standing there. Annie was standing behind him, peering over his shoulder, a very self-satisfied look on her face.

There was no way that could be good.

"Can I, uh. Can I come in?" Finley looked hesitant. After a moment, Alex realized that he'd been standing there, staring like an idiot.

"Yeah. Sorry. Yeah." Alex stepped aside, giving Annie an exasperated look as she followed Finley inside.

"You know, my parents have been married for like thirty-six years." Finley walked into the living room, but didn't sit down. "They're … Well, they're pretty adorable. They know everything about each other. They are also the least romantic people on the planet, I think, but it works for them."

"Okay," Alex said, completely nonplussed. He'd been under the impression that Finley wanted nothing more to do with him, unless he'd been woefully misinterpreting their previous conversation. He was almost certain that wasn't the case, and he couldn't account for Finley's current calm.

"I always kind of wanted that, but not, you know?" Finley asked, and he was *smiling* of all things. "Like, I've always wanted to have that closeness with someone, but I also wanted something a little more epic. I guess that sounds kind of dickish, right?"

"I don't understand." Alex opened his mouth to say more, then shut it again, figuring that pretty much covered it. He tried to squash the feeling of hope blooming in his chest, still too off-balance to trust what Finley seemed to be telling him.

Finley shrugged. "I'm just saying, I don't think I'm going to get more epic than angels conspiring to get us together. Unless you're also a superhero or something. You're not a superhero, right?"

"I—What?"

"He can see me," Annie said, sounding both excited and smug.

"Seriously?" Alex asked.

Finley nodded, his smile fading. "I'm sorry, Alex. About before." He looked away, scratching absently at the back of his neck. "I knew who you were – who you are. I should've trusted that. I shouldn't have walked away without even giving you a chance to explain."

"I wouldn't have believed me either, but you came back." Alex glanced at Annie for confirmation. "You can really see her? You believe me?"

"Well, she made some good points." Finley shrugged. "Then I got tossed out of the restaurant for arguing with myself. Also, the wings are pretty convincing."

Alex laughed, still feeling more than a little dazed. "Welcome to my world."

"Yeah?" Finley took a few steps toward him, his hands shoved in his pockets. "Does that mean I can stay?"

"I'm pretty sure once you're part of the club, there are no take-backs." Alex closed the remaining distance between them, wrapping his arm around Finley's waist, grateful for the solid proof that he was actually there. "I think you're stuck with us. There's no way I'm letting you walk away twice."

"Good," Finley said, leaning into the embrace. Ducking his head, he asked, "That's the big secret, right? The angel thing? Do you have anything else you want to get off your chest? An evil twin brother, perhaps?"

"You sound way too interested in that possibility."

"That's not a no," Finley pointed out.

"No twin brother, evil or otherwise." Alex brushed a kiss against Finley's mouth and added, "As for anymore secrets ... I love you, if that counts."

"Yeah," Finley said, returning the kiss. "That counts for just about everything."

~~*

"Say it."

"No."

"Say it!'

"Ow!" Alex frowned and rubbed his arm where Annie had pinched him. She'd *pinched* him.

"You must admit that I was right," Annie demanded.

"Isn't gloating against angel code or something?" Alex asked, still rubbing his arm. There was going to be a bruise there, he was sure of it.

"You have said many hurtful things to me over the years regarding your romantic escapades. Now you will apologize and tell me I was right for making you wait." Annie glared at him, and Alex couldn't help but laugh.

"Okay, yeah, fine. You were right." He glanced behind him as he heard the door between Finley's apartment and the bar open. "He was worth the wait. What I don't understand is he didn't really need an angel intervention. How did he get here in the first place?"

Annie's wings flared open behind her in an exaggerated expression of her irritation. "Finley didn't come for our assistance. He *was* our assistance." She stared at him and sighed. "For you. You were the one who needed us, Alex. We guided him here for you. Idiot," she added as he stood there gaping.

Finley joined them before Alex could think of an appropriate response to that. "Holy crap," he muttered, looking at the crowd of angels already in the bar. "Okay, that's going to take some getting used to."

As soon as the words left his mouth, the angels turned as one to look at Finley, having just realized that he could now see them.

"Are they all looking at me?" Finley whispered. "I'm not imagining that, right?"

"It's 'cause you're so pretty." Alex turned to the angels then and said, "Guys, try to watch the creepy intensity until he gets used to you, okay?"

The angels started talking amongst themselves at that, and Annie told him he had no tact whatsoever, as though that were somehow news to her.

"So, what were you talking about?" Finley turned to him, possibly still disconcerted by the angels watching him.

"Evidentially, you are my reward for good behavior." Alex leaned in and kissed his cheek. "Lucky me."

Finley considered that for a moment, then said, "I always suspected I was God's gift to someone. It's good to have outside confirmation on that."

Alex laughed. "So you're really okay with this? I mean, it's not what you signed on for."

"I admit, *this*," he said, gesturing towards the group on the other side of the bar, "is on the creepy side of things, but I'm assuming that will fade with time. That will fade with time, right?"

"More or less?" Alex hedged, trying not to laugh at the worry obvious in Finley's voice. "I'm sure you'll get used to them."

Finley *humphed* and crossed his arms over his chest. "I guess I'm lucky you're worth it, then, huh?"

Alex pulled him in and kissed him hard, unconcerned with who might be watching. "Luck ain't got shit to do with it."

"No?" Finley's eyes sparkled with amusement. "What, then? A butterfly flaps its wings and I end up meeting Mr. Right?"

"Something like that," Alex said. "Don't you believe in destiny?"

"Yeah, actually," Finley said as leaned in for another kiss. "I'm starting to."

Watch as My World Ends

Kayla Bain-Vrba

If Nathan Homestead took the time to think back, which he purposely never did, the utter emptiness of his existence would have eaten away at what remained of him. He had been hollow, incomplete, somehow wrong, since the day of his creation.

There had been no birth for Nathan Homestead—Ephraim, as he had been christened by his creator. There had been no nine month incubation, during which he and his mother had been joined mentally and physically; there had been no extensive labor where he and his mother had fought for his right to live, allowing him to come screaming into the world.

No, there had been none of these first rites of passage for Nathan Homestead. Instead, he had been created. One day, he had not existed, and the next, he was fully grown, fully conscious, created for a purpose, and what a purpose it was! With the Tribulation of the Apocalypse in full swing, angels were being created in waves to fight for God and Michael. The Antichrist and his armies of blasphemous, wretched worshippers were fighting tooth and nail, and there were not enough God-created angels to go around. Nathan—Ephraim, still, at the time—was created in the third wave and immediately trained to fulfill his purpose.

There had been no childhood for Nathan Homestead, no boyhood love for his doting mother; there had been no manly upbringing by his emotion-repressing father. Nathan hadn't gotten any of these rites of passage, either.

He hadn't seen the Rapture; that had been before his time, between the first and second waves of angel creations. His first taste of Earth had been when his wave of angels was marched out of Heaven and sent to the battlefields as reinforcements.

He wasn't a spectacular soldier: he did his job, it was true, but he just wasn't anything special—just another competent soldier. It hadn't been his techniques on the battlefield that set him apart; it had been his mindset. He didn't believe in what they were fighting for. Day after day in the hellhole purgatory that Earth had become, squashing beneath his boots those that were already crawling on their bellies, deprived, mistreated, neglected … He could empathize with that, with being denied the most basic experiences because of the circumstances of birth—or creation.

Nathan—still Ephraim—couldn't help but notice that God, the One who had started this whole war, the One who had announced the Rapture, the One who had released the horsemen, was surprisingly absent, doting on His favored children in Heaven while He sent His angels into battle to fight on His orders. People were corrupt; that was the law of the land. Humans were vile, uncouth, unclean, uneducated, greedy, lustful, sinful … The humans still on Earth, that was.

God had made His choice, had rewarded those believers who had somehow managed to stumble upon Christianity during their short time on Earth and had condemned those who had committed the great crime of being uneducated. The slaughter went on, angels obliterating the souls of humans who had done nothing wrong, killing them instead of educating and saving them.

Nathan (then still Ephraim) had stood up to his officers, to his angel slave-drivers, had told them what he thought and felt, had told them that he wanted to help these people, not condemn them. He had been flatly told that God had condemned them long before the angels had come to do His bidding, and it was his purpose to carry out God's will. He had questioned that, questioned God's decision, had refused God's order.

The angels had ripped out his wings in a blaze of fire and cast him out, sending him to live among the wretched humans for which he had stood up. It never would have worked for a true angel, the removal of his wings; only God, the creator of the angels, had the power to revoke His blessing. Angels could not die. However, the waves of angels created for the war were demi-angels: imperfect, lesser, a half-existence whose final solution had not yet been thought through to conclusion.

Nathan—Ephraim—had wandered the earth, blinded with the burning pain that wracked his ultra-sensitive body, spreading from the gaping wound between his shoulders, blinded with the emptiness, the loss, the lack of purpose that had only grown stronger since his banishment.

He had been lost, completely and utterly, having nothing to his name but his name itself, a constant reminder of his past. He had renamed himself 'Nathan' after seeing it written in graffiti on a church, thinking that perhaps there was something metaphorical or ironic there, something obscure about being able to write over the memories of the past from which he so desperately needed to distance himself. The surname 'Homestead' came from a street sign.

War waged on, both Michael and the Antichrist throwing soldiers at each other in a fruitless battle that, no matter how many lives were lost, could not end until the seven years of the Tribulation had run their course, as prophesized centuries before. Michael, God, Heaven—they would be victorious, but the Antichrist and his greed-filled followers wouldn't give up without a fight. The Earth was a wasteland; any surviving cities belonged to the Antichrist, and agreeing to serve him—a requirement to live in his thriving cities—was an irreversible decision for all eternity. Anyone that still had hope for their immortal souls kept away. Some joined Michael's army, where they would at least be fed and clothed before they died. The remainder of the population, hoping to escape the war, hid in small communities that had sprung up. Biblical terrors—earthquakes, volcanoes, fire storms, oceans of blood, locusts—had destroyed the Earth and war overran it. Anyone who didn't find a community to protect him was dead.

Nathan wandered aimlessly on his own, some gut instinct of self-preservation the only thing forcing him to keep living, until he found one of these communities. Brilliantly called 'Civilization,' the town had high walls, a strong protecting force, and a leader modestly referred to as 'the Savior.'

The Savior took special interest in Nathan, who, as wrecked as he looked, still gave off the thrill of terror that only angels could emit; there was something about the thought of having an angel at his will that gave the Savior a rush of power. He gave Nathan a tour of the town, talked about how it was one of the few remaining civilizations in the area, and told him that to be allowed to stay in Civilization, it was required that all citizens held some kind of job: a laborer, a guard, a farmer. For every job that Nathan offered his services, however, he was denied. Finally, the Savior graciously agreed to allow Nathan to stay if he let the Savior fuck him whenever the mood arose. With no other option, Nathan agreed.

While his regular rounds with the Savior's dick allowed him to stay in the city, they did nothing to cover his other necessities: food, shelter, clothing. When no one would hire him, he sold himself to anyone who would trade with him. The amount of men was obviously disproportionate to the number of women in the city and Nathan's services were always in demand. It didn't mean Nathan ever had a constant roof over his head or a steady source of food, but he always had the eyes of a town in desperate need to be entertained by some poor sap worse off than they. The fact that he had once been an angel soldier, attempting to wipe them into oblivion and falling even lower than they, only sweetened their sick thrill.

~~*

Nathan grunted as the Savior pounded into him, dropping his head down between his arms. He was kneeling on the Savior's bed, an item he didn't have the privilege of owning, getting fucked for the second time that day. That morning, it had been Sean, a farmer who had traded him breakfast for his services—now it was the Savior's turn.

There came a knock on the door and the Savior paused, buried deep inside Nathan's body. He roughly called out, "Who is it?"

"Dakota," came the concise reply. "You sent for me?"

The Savior pulled out of Nathan, and then shoved back in, making Nathan swear. "Come in."

As Dakota came in, closing the door behind him, Nathan glanced sideways through the hair in front of his eyes. Dakota Walker—black haired and gorgeous—was a hitman, a well-off favorite of the Savior, who Nathan had seen once in passing, and then purposely kept his distance. Most significantly, Dakota was an angel, the only angel Nathan had come across since arriving in Civilization. The citizens gossiped about Dakota's recent arrival, but Nathan had hoped to avoid him—preferably, until the world ended. Behind him, Nathan felt the Savior stiffen ever so slightly. Angels put humans on edge; it was in their genetics. To humans, angels were mesmerizing, captivating, thrilling, terrifying—heartbreakingly beautiful, aloof, and untouchable.

The Savior had felt it when he had met Nathan; Nathan could easily remember the way the Savior's arm hairs had all stood on end and the way his breath had quickened. Nathan reasoned that this was one of the main attractions the Savior felt for him. Fucking Nathan was his way of overcoming his fear, of declaring dominance, of assuring himself of his position. Nathan assumed that this was the same reason many human men treated their women poorly: an inferiority complex and fear of the mysterious unknown.

As the Savior resumed thrusting into him, Nathan dropped his head back down, concentrating. It wasn't the first time he'd been fucked in front of an audience, but Dakota looked uncomfortable.

"Are you … ? I can come back. I should come back." Dakota began inching toward the door.

"No, no," the Savior replied, voice firm and even, although sweat was running down his face. "I'm almost done."

With his audience captive, the Savior set up a brutal pace, slamming in and out of Nathan's tight body with a new speed and force, making a show of it. Nathan swore, clutching at the bed, tensing his shaking arm muscles to keep himself upright.

It didn't last. He crashed down on the bed, the Savior holding his hips up as he continued to fuck him to his content. It wasn't always like this; sometimes the Savior even let him come. That wasn't to say that the Savior did anything to help his orgasm, such as hitting his spot or touching him, but sometimes he let Nathan jerk himself off. There were times when the Savior even got off on the way Nathan's muscles would clench and spasm around him.

This was not one of those times.

When the Savior finally came, deep and hard inside Nathan's body, he continued thrusting into him a few more times, spreading the come around and making a mess, bruising Nathan's already tender hole.

Eventually, the Savior pulled out and cleaned himself up. He ignored the gasping and wincing as Nathan pulled his worn jeans back up and stumbled past Dakota, giving him as much berth as possible as he left the room.

Downstairs, Nathan cleaned himself up in the bathroom, being as gentle as possible and doing his best to keep his only pair of jeans unsoiled. He took his time, too, seeing as no one was banging on the door to take their own turn in there.

When Nathan finally did leave, he ran into a few of the Savior's slaves—they were actually household servants, but the title wasn't what mattered—unsuccessfully trying to move a heavy desk. It was a frivolous piece of furniture, but as the dictator of Civilization and savior of lives, the Savior was entitled to whatever he wanted. Nathan helped them move the desk to its new location in exchange for a loaf of freshly baked bread, which he sat outside to eat. He didn't have anywhere else to be, the sun was shining, and if he didn't move his hips at all, it didn't pain him to take the time for himself.

Nathan looked up when the estate door opened and Dakota came out, looking out of place among the filth of the world. Nathan felt his heart speed up, felt his breath catch in his throat. This was the first angel he'd had contact with since leaving the army and it was frightening. Dakota emitted waves of power, strength, insight, Godliness. His looks didn't put Nathan at ease, either, his hair sawed off at the chin, green eyes sharp, and body clad in black.

Nathan had to turn away—even watching another angel, especially one who made him feel like this, was just too consuming, too overwhelming. He tried to steady his breathing and calm his heart.

"Doesn't that hurt?" Dakota asked, jerking his chin at Nathan's seated position and sounding genuinely sympathetic.

Nathan shrugged. "I'm fine."

"Dakota Walker." Dakota held out a hand.

Nathan raised an eyebrow, trying to determine what Dakota was thinking, but shook the hand anyway, even though he wasn't sure physical contact was the best choice. "Nathan Homestead."

"Nathan Homestead," Dakota repeated.

"Yup, that's my name," Nathan retorted. "Feel free to scream it as loud as you need to." He couldn't help the dry tone; it had become his natural, and only, form of self-defense.

Dakota glanced away, for some reason looking slightly off-kilter. "You look wrecked. Come back to my place with me; I'll fix you up."

Nathan got to his feet, wincing but trying to hide it. Call it intuition, call it the fact that Dakota hadn't seemed too keen on watching him get fucked through the bed, but Nathan got the feeling that his pain wasn't much of a turn on for Dakota, even if it seemed to be for most men. "I can blow you, but I can't be fucked yet. In a couple hours, maybe."

Dakota's eyes widened in his pale face and he shook his head quickly. Nathan was blunt. "I don't want that."

"Okay." Nathan waited, but Dakota didn't continue. "Well? What do you want from me?"

"Nothing," Dakota said softly. "I'm not here to take anything from you."

Nathan rolled his eyes. He'd been having an alright time and now it was ruined, thanks to Dakota fucking Walker and his mind games. Angels. Nathan had no desire to stand here and pretend as though they didn't both know exactly what Dakota wanted and exactly what Nathan could give him—which were the same thing.

"Whatever, Walker." Nathan left, trying not to appear bowlegged, a trick he was sure he would never master. He certainly hadn't managed it in his year and a half in Civilization.

~~*

Once outside the view of Civilization's guard towers, Dakota took to the air. Not only did flying help to clear his mind, but it made it easier to keep an eye out for soldiers. His target was in a small community several days to the south. Their leader had agreed to hand over a large supply of hoarded medicines in exchange for the Savior's warnings before biblical catastrophes. The Savior had warned of an approaching plague on Antichrist worshippers, but no medicines had exchanged hands. Both traders and diplomats had failed in negotiations, so Dakota had been called in.

As he flew, his mind—which was supposed to be clear—kept coming back to Nathan. He was an angel who had fallen from grace, big deal; Dakota had seen and killed plenty without a second thought. He couldn't understand why Nathan was whoring himself out; all angels had skills, military and otherwise. There were a dozen other jobs for which he would be suited—better suited than most humans. There was something about him that set Dakota off, a feeling of self-loathing countered by a tiny desire for life. It made no sense to him and he tried to clear his mind.

The community Dakota's target led was small, but well-protected; even under the cover of darkness, Dakota still had to knock out two guards before they could raise the alarm or try to stop him. He landed on the roof of the leader's home, kicked in his bedroom window, and was greeted by the sound of giggling, rather than screaming. Two naked girls lay in bed with the man, all smoking something pungent.

Dakota wrinkled his nose at the sight and the smell. This was how these people were choosing to spend their last three years alive?

He leaned over the giggling blonde to grab the man's hair and yank back, baring his throat. It was obvious what he was about to do, but the three imbeciles just kept laughing. Disgusted, Dakota didn't bother wasting his breath to remind the man why he was about to die; he just slit the man's throat with one pull of his knife, the warm spurts of blood coating his fingers. The two girls gasped, wide-eyed, then erupted in laughter, even as their former leader and lover lay choking between them.

The return flight was filled with thoughts of Nathan. It was strange that for all of the dirty things about Nathan, all Dakota could see was the possibility in his eyes. Maybe this was God's plan, he realized; maybe Nathan was the redemption he was seeking.

~~*

Nathan's week had gone from shitty to shittier since his run-in with Dakota. He hadn't eaten for two days because no one was 'in the mood,' whatever the hell that meant. In an attempt to distract himself, he went to see Amber.

Amber Mason was pretty and blonde, still sweet in spite of her kick-ass demeanor, and was the only thing similar to a friend that Nathan had. He certainly didn't call her that, though, and it had taken him the better part of a year to finally trust her as much as he did.

Amber smiled and welcomed him with a hug when he showed up on her doorstep, and although the strength in her hug shouldn't have surprised him anymore, it still did.

There were three types of women in Civilization: the Savior's women, who he refused to share; married women, whose husbands guarded them religiously; and women like Amber, who were exclusive and so threatening that no one without matrimony on their mind came near them. Amber's family had been military and she had been able to take down a fully-grown man since she was six. She had offered to teach Nathan, but he had turned her down. He already had all the fighting skills he could need, but he numbed them down so he wouldn't scare off potential customers.

They sat at the table, but Amber didn't offer food or drink. She had learned quickly that Nathan didn't accept handouts.

"Find anything new?" he asked. "About angels after Trib?"

She shook her head. "No, sorry. There's a million and one cheesy stories about a thousand awesome years with Jesus, but they don't say if that's for angel survivors, too. No one really has much to say about any angels, Bible times or after. Humans don't really care, I guess."

Nathan snorted. "No shit."

There wasn't much to say to something like that. "I'm sure you'll be with us. They say that all believers—"

Nathan stood so suddenly that he almost knocked his chair over. He couldn't stand listening to prophecies or judgments, couldn't bear to have Scripture recited at him.

"Nathan?"

"I—I can't. I've got to go." He stumbled back and almost felt bad about the sad look on her face. "I'll come back another time." He ran from her house.

Nathan ran until he came to an abandoned alley. As dank as it was, at least he could be alone, but that was when his thoughts caught up with him.

The past four years had been structured and planned, organized and prophesized, so that everyone knew what was coming. First was the rapture, then the Antichrist, then World War III ... It was exact, timely enough to build a calendar around.

The future looked like that, too. When the seven years of Tribulation were over, Michael would chuck Satan into the pit, Jesus would descend, and a thousand year party would start for the humans. It seemed that no one gave a rat's ass about the angels. Maybe they were invited, maybe not. No one could be bothered to give a definitive answer.

The entire world was waiting for the end. There wasn't much else to do for the remaining three years, unless the humans wanted to join the angel army and head up to Heaven early. They had survived this long; they might as well stick around 'til the end, even if the second half was going to be the worst. There wasn't much to do while waiting, other than try to be as comfortable as possible. There wasn't really any point in creating any kind of lasting relationships—most people would be dead within months, and those who lived long enough had a huge party to look forward to with all the survivors, not just the few they managed to be stuck with during Tribulation.

Nathan had realized that that was why he was so popular. Sex with him was easy: no commitments, no strings attached. It was easier to go fuck Nathan than to waste time wooing the neighbors. Besides, if they settled for someone in their Community, they were going to be stuck together for a thousand years. Jesus wasn't big on divorce, supposedly. He wasn't big on having sex with multiple people, either, so everyone had to get that in before the party started.

No one gave a shit about Nathan—not the town, not God, not even Nathan himself. He was waiting for the end, but unlike most people who had an idea of the future—

party!—there was no Scripture about angels. They said that all believers got to live forever, but what about the outcasts? What about those who'd already turned their back on God once before?

The only thing he could think of was that maybe—maybe—if he suffered enough, maybe he could hope—

"Wanna blow me?" The approaching man—Nathan thought he recognized him as a city raider—put an end to Nathan's doomsday thoughts.

If this wasn't a sign saying he needed to suffer more, Nathan didn't know what was, so he got to his knees and let the man smack him around a bit before fucking his face, and then dumping him in the mud.

Exhausted, Nathan just laid there afterward, pushing the traded meal token into his pocket, spitting up blood and come into the gunk around him. He didn't even bothering to pull up the hood of his brown zip-up when the near-constant storms picked up. The way he saw it, his clothes were already ruined, and there was just no point in moving until he was forced.

That happened sooner rather than later.

"Nathan?" Dakota, recently back from his mission, bent down beside him.

Even in his semi-conscious state, Nathan managed to groan. Of course. Of course. Of all the people in all of Civilization, who else could have come across him? God didn't just 'not care' about him; He hated him.

"Nathan, I'm going to lift you up."

Even with Dakota's warning, Nathan hadn't expected to be plucked off the ground like a small child and carried away in Dakota's arms. He wasn't sure if he should be humiliated or not. Probably. Definitely. He was most certainly humiliated by this, being carried by an angel like a helpless child. This was going to be the ruin of him. This angel was going to be the ruin of him. He tried not to notice the firm definition of lean muscles in Dakota's chest and arms, the way he could feel Dakota's heart beating beneath his breastbone, the feel of the expansion and compression of his lungs with every breath.

Too late.

~~*

Nathan found himself in Dakota's home, a house in the nice part of town, not the alleys and shacks where Nathan usually ended up. Dakota cleaned him up, helping him shower and bandaging up the cut across his cheek, before bringing him a clean set of clothing. Nathan took this without too much complaint, honestly too exhausted to put up a fight or pay much notice to just how intimate these gestures were, especially when shared with another angel. He just accepted that he'd pay what he owed when it was over.

Nathan slept on Dakota's bed, for ages, it seemed. Soft linen, a sturdy but gentle mattress, warm blankets. God, how he'd missed these things … The slip into unconsciousness, like a gentle sea wave crashing over him, was the most blissful thing in the memories he allowed himself to visit.

~~*

Looking over at Nathan, lying asleep in his bed, Dakota couldn't help but realize how young he looked. It was true that everyone said people looked young, innocent, and carefree when they slept, but it really was true about Nathan. His boyish features smoothed out, all the pain and suffering slipping away.

He really was beautiful, Dakota decided, inside and out.

Dakota hadn't come across many angels since leaving the Lord's army … not like this, anyway. Not angels who emitted such horrible pain of tragedy and desperation in waves like Nathan did; not angels who were so broken and lost that it filled their eyes when they let their guard slip for just a moment. Nathan's eyes weren't completely dead, not yet, and that gave Dakota hope; the small spark of anger, of resistance, of self was the only thing keeping Nathan from being completely gone.

Dakota had met other angels, ones who had left the army or had been kicked out, who had turned to greed and lust and wrath, who had encompassed all of the seven deadly sins and radiated them into the souls of those surrounding them like a cancer. They were dark creatures, vengeful, deceitful, power hungry. On more than one occasion, Dakota had been sent to find these rogue angels and destroy them. He didn't want Nathan to end up like those soulless things, incapable of happiness even when they were rich and powerful and had everything they could possibly want or need. He didn't want to see Nathan destroy himself, throw himself away, lose himself.

Maybe this was God's plan for his redemption, for him to save Nathan. Whether it was or not, Dakota actually wanted to help him. Some heartless killer he was—which, he supposed, was a good thing, considering he wanted redemption and all that.

Dakota was good at reading people, at knowing them and understanding them. All angels were good at that, but Dakota was even better. He could only imagine how difficult things must have been for Nathan, to have spent all this time hiding himself from the perception of humans only to suddenly have an angel staring at his soul. But Dakota couldn't help it; he wanted Nathan, wanted him in a way he hadn't wanted anyone in a long time, in a way he hadn't realized he could. It was spiritual, primal; a magnetic connection of souls, drawing him to Nathan. Nathan was so beautiful, so tragically and heartbreakingly beautiful, that Dakota almost felt privileged to witness it, if only Nathan would let him in. That was why Dakota couldn't give up on Nathan; because when he looked at Nathan lying on his bed, clean hair falling softly around his gentle face, slender and slightly skinny body curled comfortably on one side, he thought that he remembered this feeling as love.

~~*

When Nathan finally woke up, it was dark. Had he really been asleep all afternoon? He sat up, turning to look around. Dakota sat nearby, reading a book by lamplight, but he glanced up when Nathan cleared his throat.

"Nathan! How do you feel?"

Nathan shrugged, honestly not giving a damn. "Alright. Okay. Better."

Dakota smiled. It was a nice smile, Nathan admitted, straight, white teeth, warm and sincere. His own teeth were a little less on edge, his skin barely crawling. Still, he doubted that he'd ever be comfortable in an angel's presence, particularly this angel, who could see so much of him.

"Good. I was wondering how long you'd sleep. It's been hours."

Nathan shrugged again, and muttered, "It's been a while since I slept in a bed. It was nice."

Dakota's smile faded a little, the walls in Nathan's eyes shooting up sky high. "I'm sorry."

Nathan shrugged once more. This was becoming his standard, his all-purpose response to anything life—or Dakota—could throw at him. "It's fine. It's the way it is. Not your fault." He gripped one wrist, lifting his arms above his head and arching his back until it popped comfortably, and then sighed. "So, you wanna fuck now? I mean, you obviously stayed awake all this time because you've been waiting. You ready to go?"

Dakota raised his eyebrows—perfect eyebrows, Nathan thought, strong and fierce and perfect, out of place in this haggard world. "I don't want to fuck you, Nathan."

Nathan gave him a doubtful look. "Yeah, right," he replied dryly. "Half the town wants to fuck me." Even angels have needs. "You want me to blow you, then?"

Dakota snorted. "I don't think blowing me will save you or me."

Nathan pulled a face; 'save' was not a word he liked—too much responsibility, too unlikely, too much like God. "What the hell are you talking about?"

Dakota shrugged. "Salvation. Redemption. Saving you to save myself."

"Look, I'm not here to save anyone and you certainly can't save me. So let's get on with this trade so you can take your missionary somewhere else."

"This wasn't a trade."

Nathan sighed. Was Dakota trying to be difficult or was he just a pain in the ass by nature? "Yes, it is," Nathan forcefully replied. "Everything is a tradeoff; life is a tradeoff. You gave me something, now I give you something back. That's the way it works."

Dakota shook his head. "I don't want you playing whore for me."

Playing whore? He was one. Nathan shook his head, frustration beginning to boil over. "I have to pay you."

"No, you don't."

No pay? Take something without giving anything back? What kind of man did Dakota think he was? That wasn't the way this world worked; it wasn't the way things were. Give and take, tradeoffs, that was his life. He was taking something without paying for it; he was stealing. He felt the guilt and disgust creeping up inside him, clawing at his chest and throat.

"Take me, Dakota. Take what's yours."

"You don't belong to me. And I told you, I won't take anything of yours that you don't want to give."

"I want you to—"

"No, you don't." It was a simple fact, the way Dakota said it. "You don't want it, not now, and I certainly don't want it this way. When you actually want it, when you can make me believe it, then we can have it."

This was Dakota's thing—feeling like he was in a relationship or some shit? Fine. Nathan slid off the bed, crawled on his knees to Dakota, and buried his face in Dakota's crotch, all without warning. "I want you," he moaned. "I want you so much."

Dakota pushed him away. Dakota rejected him, turned him down. "I said no." His voice was hard, fierce, as though Nathan had hurt him. "No, Nathan."

It sunk in then; Dakota really wasn't going to let him pay. He couldn't be in debt to Dakota like this; he couldn't owe him something forever that he would never be allowed to pay.

Nathan ran from Dakota for the second time since meeting him, grabbing his dried hoodie and jeans, before disappearing off into the dark town to find an alley to sleep.

~~*

The Savior stood at the window of his bedroom suite and looked out at his community. It was hard to see without his glasses, but he didn't need any help observing what he'd built out of nothing. Long gone were the days when he was Thomas Ackley, the skinny, washed-out boy who had been teased and tormented throughout his school years. Gone were the years he'd spent poring over Bible passages, the only thing his Jesus-freak parents would let him read. It didn't matter. Their idiocy had taught him that God was not power—the fear of God was what truly mattered. This refusal to worship God was probably what had resulted in him being left behind during the Rapture.

If only all those high school teachers and college professors, who all said he'd never amount to anything, could see him now. No one had ever believed in him—not parents, not teachers, not classmates—yet here he was, a god among insects. He had two angels at his beck and call, one of which was completely subservient and crushed beneath his thumb. He was overlord to a community of two hundred and sixteen people, all of whom answered to him and hung on his every word. They hated him sometimes, hated his power, hated his decisions that took advantage of them—his lowly peons. They needed him, needed his knowledge of Bible lore to read signs and predict catastrophe, needed his leadership to govern the eight-man council that kept them safe and fed, needed his charisma and power to keep them all orderly. As he watched the town come to life, he knew that it was because of him that they lived.

Turning away from the spectacle, he looked over at the two beautiful women tangled on his bed. Chelsea, the ginger-haired one, had found the community—and the Savior—on her own. His spies had taken the twins, Rachel and Emily, from a distant community to be his own. Emily, unfortunately, had been ill lately, so Chelsea and Rachel had had to entertain him without her.

The Savior slipped on his silk robe and decided against getting dressed just then. Perhaps the girls could be coaxed into a morning show.

If only his parents could see the world he had built. His ma would give him an earful about indulging in sin—sex before marriage, polyamory, fucking a boy, and a whole lot more—and his pops would back her up. His little sister would act prim, pure, and beautiful, as usual, and soak up praise.

Actually, on second thought, he was glad to be rid of them. All of them getting sucked up in the Rapture had been the best thing to happen to him. Almost immediately, people began rallying to his predictions and charisma, willing to do as he said in order to live.

He sat down with a smile as his two women began to stir. He had three more years before he had to answer for his indulgences, and in the meantime, life was good.

~~*

Dakota couldn't stand to see Nathan hurt. He couldn't stand to see Nathan give himself away, and people take from Nathan his very soul. If they were gentle, if they cared ... then he could forgive them, he could almost look the other way and forget it happened. He could.

But when they were rough, when they hit Nathan, when they took him hard, when they were brutal and inconsiderate and purposely malicious ... Dakota couldn't handle that. If someone hurt Nathan, then Dakota hurt him. It was just that simple. When he heard Nathan's raspy, barely-there voice after the butcher had used his mouth, Dakota knocked out two of the burly man's teeth. When he saw bruises across Nathan's throat after a quick fuck, he broke the farmer's fingers. When Nathan was staggering and wincing after rough sex, Dakota made it so the carpenter would be pissing blood for a month.

People started to leave Nathan alone after that. Not just being gentle with him—leaving him alone altogether. That suited Dakota just fine. It did not, however, suit Nathan.

Business slowed to a trickle, and then died out altogether. It even got so bad that Nathan thought about going to Amber. She hated doing it, but when he wouldn't take food from her any other way, she'd let him finger her. He knew she didn't exactly like the situation, but as long as she got off and seemed to enjoy it, he didn't feel as bad taking food from her.

He wasn't at that point, not quite. People didn't just stop needing sex, particularly not an entire community altogether, and unless there was an easier whore out there—Nathan knew the few other occasional ones, but they had nothing on how easy and convenient he was—there had to be a reason for the sudden dry spell.

He went around asking direct questions and all answers pointed to a fear that 'that angel hitman, Dakota Walker' would come for them if they touched Nathan. Clearly, Dakota hadn't given up on his little game and was trying to destroy his livelihood, so that Nathan had no choice but to accept Dakota's charity.

That was great. Just great.

~~*

"What the hell are you trying to do to me?" Nathan demanded, as soon as Dakota opened the door to his house.

For a moment, Dakota blinked at him in confusion, then stood back to let Nathan in.

"Do you want me to die?" Nathan strode past him, eyes livid, not caring that he was taking on an angel. "Is that what this is? Some kind of game?"

"What are you talking about?"

"You're killing me, Dakota! Thanks to your little 'lord protector' stunt, no one in Civilization will touch me! And if they don't fuck me, I don't eat. I don't have clothes; I don't have anywhere to sleep. I have nothing. Do you know what you're doing to me?"

Dakota looked surprised, shocked even. "I didn't ... I didn't mean to ... "

Was Dakota really this naïve? Really? "You didn't mean to starve me? Cuz you have. I haven't eaten in four days. Four days!"

"I ... I don't know what to say. I'm sorry, Nathan. I didn't ... "

"You don't get how it is here, okay? I get fucked and I get to eat. I get food and clothes. Without that—"

"I can get you that."

Nathan immediately shook his head, on to Dakota and his game. "No. Not unless you let me pay."

It was Dakota's turn to shake his head, returning to their same old argument. "I don't want it like that. I want to be your only one. I want you to want me. I don't want to share you with the entire community."

"Fuck you! You want to be my only one? I haven't been touched in days! Even the Savior hasn't had his way with me lately. You want to be the only man inside me? Go ahead and take me."

"I won't take anything from you, Nathan. That's not how redemption works."

Nathan rolled his eyes, sick of this game that he didn't understand. "I'm no one's redemption, okay? Leave me alone."

He left Dakota standing there, staring after him, something that had become just another everyday occurrence between the two of them.

~~*

Nathan sat beside Amber in the crowded hall, listening as the Savior droned on about Revelation omens he was tracking. The Savior was good at tracking signs; Nathan could admit that. Really, though, the Tribulation had been so heavily documented that there were practically calendars laying it all out and anyone with a head on their shoulders could figure out the basics. It seemed that people just didn't want to do the work, preferring to get a summarized version from someone else. How original.

"And just as I predicted, the Antichrist's supporters have been struck with plagues!"

The room gasped at the Savior's announcement—as if any of his signs and portents were ever wrong.

"My spies have brought word from two Antichrist cities, both infected. They say that the other cities are accursed as well. But here in Civilization, you are safe because of me!"

Nathan's snort was lost as the room erupted in applause. They were safe because they weren't Antichrist supporters—duh. How did people so ignorant survive four years of Apocalypse?

As parasites on the Savior's back, obviously.

~~*

"What idiots!"

Nathan smiled as Amber closed the door of her house, keeping their conversation from prying ears.

"Honestly." She led the way further into the house and sat down at the table, her only real piece of furniture other than her bed—and she wasn't bringing Nathan there. "Does he think he's the only person in the world who can read a Bible or any of the fifty thousand books with a timeline of this shit?" She reached over to her bookshelf, picked up one of the Revelation books she collected, flipped to a bookmarked page, and read, "'The first bowl of the bowl judgments: foul and loathsome sores on those bearing the mark of the Beast!' What do we care? If any of us were Devil worshippers, we'd be living comfy lives in the city. He saved us from judgment that wasn't even coming for us. Ooh, what a guy!" She snorted and set the book back.

"I've got this sign reading thing down," she said. "Have since I got stuck here. And the Savior? He irks me, sitting pretty in his damn mansion, while the rest of us work to keep him safe and comfy. I could do his job twenty times better." She leaned closer. "I've been thinking about it, starting my own community. If I could get enough people to go with me, so we could get ourselves started... " She sighed. "It's silly, I guess. There's three years left, might as well just stick it out. Still, it's nice to dream, right? Just imagine what it would be like in a new community."

Nathan shrugged. "Wouldn't matter for me. I'd still be me, doing what I do, no matter where I end up."

~~*

Dakota sat across the glossy maple table from the Savior, eating a lavish meal on gilded dishes. It was ridiculous, really; the entire room, the Savior's entire estate, was ridiculous. The world was ripped apart by war, the people of the community struggling just to get by. But here in his private estate, surrounded by the best that could be acquired, the Savior reclined in absurd comfort. What place did gold dishes and velvet curtains have in this world?

The Savior himself was a frivolous and idiotic man. He was power hungry and charismatic, flawed and corrupt. Being left behind in the Rapture had probably been the best thing that had ever happened to him. He had been surrounded by the pathetic and needy, those desperate to be led, guided, and protected. For a fee, he had 'provided' for them, but in reality, they were providing for him. He was an idiot who had no concern for others or for progress—only for power.

A servant poured more wine for Dakota, and then bowed his way out. Bowed, like the Savior was some kind of king or god. Dakota repressed a sigh and reached for his goblet.

"I don't have a new mission for you, not yet," the Savior said around a delicate bite of red meat, "but I will soon. The diplomats have been having difficulty renegotiating the trades with Haven, and I might need you to step in and prove a point before they attempt to make a military stand."

Dakota nodded absently. This was what he did, 'step in' before things escalated to violence or 'step in' to put an end to violence or threats to Civilization or its Savior. 'Step in' to punish people who wounded the Savior's pride ... or people he just didn't like. Without a direct order from the Savior, there was nothing for Dakota to do but be prepared to leave in the near future.

"I'm also keeping a wary eye on the north community."

The tiny thrill that raced through the Savior and laced his words caught Dakota's attention, and he set down his fork.

"What north community?"

The Savior gave a small shrug, trying to act nonchalant, even when Dakota could taste the fear radiating from his skinny frame, see the fear in his thin, pale eyes. Even his naturally pallid face lost color. "A community of angels to the north of here."

Dakota's eyes widened. "An entire community of angels?"

The Savior gave him a peculiar look. "Looking for family?" He attempted to sound snide, but ended up sounding desperate, as if his prized hitman was going to leave his control.

Dakota forced a bark of laughter. "Angels don't have families. We're born soldiers, we die soldiers." That was unless they made themselves into something more.

The Savior nodded, comforted enough to explain the situation. "The angels to the north have gathered in a town of sorts. They don't trade with us; they have made it clear that they want to have no dealings with our community. I worry about what that may mean for us, if they go hostile."

"Maybe they just want to keep to themselves."

With a look, the Savior said, as if he were speaking to a child, "That's why I run this community and you follow my orders."

Bristling, Dakota said nothing and let the conversation drift for the remainder of the meal. Afterward, he shut himself up in his house, trying to shake the uneasy feeling that was leaving him nauseous. There was an entire community of angels nearby? Angels living with the sense of family and belonging he had never been able to grasp? That was where he belonged, with his own kind, with people who would understand him. Dark, greedy angels didn't flock together; they couldn't stand the judgment or competition for authority. This community must have been wonderful ...

But he couldn't go, even though he didn't agree with Civilization or any of the other communities he had come through. Every angel there would judge him for what he'd done, and he could never live with the intensity of an even more constant guilt trip.

Never before had his quest for redemption seemed so vital or elusive.

~~*

Dakota was dreaming. He told himself this again and again, but it didn't wake him or make the dreams feel any less real. Normally, when angels dreamed, they saw prophetic visions. Just like every aspect of their waking lives, their senses were heightened so acutely that no human body would survive the overwhelming trauma. Angels were built to endure much more and still live.

He was on the battlefield. Putrid smoke burned his eyes and lungs; screams and battle cries rang in his ears. All around him, people were dying, angels and humans alike, all crying out for God and mercy with their final breaths. He couldn't save any of his brothers and sisters, just like he couldn't stop slaughtering the humans. Projectiles exploded; Heaven's fire rained down. The screams, the pain, the smells, the sights all warped together around him until he thought he was going to lose his mind.

He was in the city—that city. It was too quiet and too still; the people knew they were coming. He walked side-by-side with Laren, their footfalls audible in the dark silence of the city that shouldn't have been empty. Automatic gunfire rang out and he heard Laren gasp, felt his pain and shock as he fell to the asphalt. He dove for cover as the shots continued, watched as Laren choked and squirmed alone in the middle of the street. The fire was too heavy; he tried to get to Laren, but couldn't. Laren died, his eyes wide and staring into Dakota forever.

He was in the back of a truck. The truck was loud and rough as they drove through the burned lands, picking up any survivors. They came to a community and took away anyone strong enough to fight.

The faces came next; he knew it before they started. Angels and humans, men and women, all the lives he was responsible for destroying flashed before him. Dead, empty eyes. Bloody bodies. Pieces of people. Crying women. Screaming children. On and on they came, all blaming him as he blamed himself.

When he finally, blessedly, woke up, Dakota could hardly breathe. Tears soaked his skin, his body shook, and he felt so ill that he thought he might throw up. The dreams clung to him, hanging on like some eternal ball and chain, and he moved to sit on the floor, desperately hoping the uncomfortable position would keep him awake—and out of the dreams.

~~*

Since the war had started, Nathan had quickly learned that good things came and went. *'You get what you pay for and you pay for everything you get' was the motto of his existence.*

When a busy cook traded Nathan a hot slice of meat for him to deliver food to Dakota, Nathan didn't think twice. He would pop by, drop off the delivery, and then be on his way. No need for words to be exchanged; no need for their usual fight to recommence. Plus, he was getting a nice meal as payment. Win-win all around.

Nathan wasn't quite sure what he had expected to find at Dakota's house; perhaps Dakota reading or not even there, but it wasn't to find Dakota was slumped in a corner, tears staining his face, eyes red ... a complete wreck.

Not knowing what to do and feeling more than a little uncomfortable, he stood awkwardly in the middle of the room. "Dakota?"

Dakota looked up at him through thick lashes, green eyes shining with pain. He made no attempt to hide or stop his tears. "Nathan."

"What ... are you ... okay?"

Dakota shook his head.

"Can I help?" Where did that come from? He didn't owe Dakota anything but the same trouble he'd caused Nathan.

Dakota just looked at him. "How?"

Nathan knelt beside him. "I know how to make a man feel good."

Dakota immediately pushed him away, hurt and anguish and fury in his eyes. "Fuck, Nathan! Can't you understand that you're more than just a hole? You were born an angel, not a whore!"

Nathan blinked at him, taken aback by the suddenness of Dakota's attack. "I don't ... I don't have anything else to offer you."

"You think you don't," Dakota replied, watching him carefully, weighing him with his all-seeing eyes. "Will you listen?"

Nathan nodded, still unsure of just what was happening.

Dakota leaned back, resting his head against the wall. His eyes slid away from Nathan's, but it looked to be in a way that meant he was remembering, not trying to avoid him.

"I was born to be a soldier, created in the first wave of angels they made. I remember the Rapture. I don't know if you were around, yet, but I can still remember it like it happened this morning. I remember standing on this hill with my lover, Laren … God, he was beautiful … " Dakota closed his eyes for a moment, and for the first time in a long time, Nathan felt something, felt Dakota's pain and loss at the memory bringing tears to his eyes.

"We stood there together, watching these bodies being raised up to Heaven, and it was like our entire troop wasn't there, as if there was no one in the world but the two of us and this amazing spectacle before our eyes. It was just … too much to be real, you know? This mind-blowing experience … It was humbling, the awe-inspiring power and glory of God. Laren was moved, too, more inspired and dedicated than I'd ever seen him before. He started volunteering for special missions and I went with him, of course.

"Laren was killed on one of the special ops." Dakota's voice had become broken, as if he was fighting not to fall apart, and he spoke in a detached way, trying not to get lost in the pain of the memories. "He got shot by some Antichrist idiots. God, all the missions we'd gone on … We'd been captured before, just the two of us prisoner to an entire camp of seculars, for Christ's sake, and nothing like this … We'd been roughed up, shot, but never … " Dakota ducked his head, the tears falling freely down his strong face. "Laren was just so beautiful, so crazy, so full of life. He was so perfect, in every way. He was the strongest man I'd ever met, the most sensitive, the funniest, the … everything. He was everything."

Dakota let the tears fall freely for a little while. He owed Laren that much. Laren would have cried for him, he knew that, and he would let himself cry for Laren, for the man he had been, for what he'd lost, for everything they could have been.

Nathan tentatively rested his hand on Dakota's forearm, feeling awkward. It had been so long since he'd touched someone else with this intention.

"And then it was just me. I became a machine so fast. It was almost effortless, stripping myself of everything I had been and locking it away, becoming a mindless killer." Dakota spat out, "And I was good, so fucking good. I was on special ops and sniper missions all the time, because they just couldn't use me enough." He tilted his head back, resting against the wall, waiting for the rage to subside. "After slaughtering innocent people for two years, they got worried about me. I was freaking out, having these breakdowns, so they sent me to pick up kids for a couple months ... That was even worse than the killing. I was sending these kids to become monsters, to kill, to destroy their souls.

"I ran. I ran and didn't stop running, didn't look back. I killed a man who tried to mess with me and that's when my 'talent' was discovered by the humans. I became a hitman. It was easy, real fucking easy. These people I was killing, they were just as evil and dirty as I was; I was doing the world a favor. And one day, someone would come for me, and then everything would be okay." Dakota shook his head. "It's not okay. It will never be okay, never again. Even if I manage to die some noble death, if there is such a thing anymore, it will never undo what I've done. What I've seen. What I've forced others to do. That's why I need to find redemption, through you or someone else. I need to find salvation so I can live with myself, so I can stop pretending I'm okay." He rubbed hard at his face, the tears dried on his skin. He noticed Nathan staring then, watching him with unguarded eyes, open and deep as he'd never seen before. "What? You've never seen a murderer cry before?"

Nathan just shook his head. "I've never seen anyone like you before." He didn't understand the want running through him, but felt that maybe there was hope there. Before he could talk himself out of it, he pressed his mouth to Dakota's in a warm kiss.

Dakota pushed him away as soon as Nathan's tongue touched his mouth. "Nathan ... "

"I wanted to do that," Nathan said firmly, simply. "I still want to."

After a moment, Dakota pulled Nathan into his lap, pressing their mouths together in a heated frenzy. It was hard and sweet and wonderful, and Nathan never wanted it to stop. He could sit there forever, on the stone floor of Hell with Dakota. Straddling Dakota's lap felt safe and exciting, thrilling in a way he had never known life could be. It was terrifying, being so real with someone; it was frightening to him that he wanted Dakota when he had kept himself from wanting anything.

He ran his hands over Dakota's arms and chest, as he nipped and sucked at his mouth. He felt Dakota grip his hips in response, applying firm pressure to the soft skin and sharp bones beneath.

Nathan rolled his hips, and the friction between their covered cocks was so delicious and unexpected that they both moaned loudly. Nathan went to do it again, but Dakota stopped him, fingers tight on his hips.

"No ... " Nathan whispered. "I want to ... "

Dakota just shook his head, about to lay it all on the line. "Not tonight. I need to be sure this isn't because I told you my story."

But it is, Nathan thought. You trusted me. You shared that with me. Instead, he nodded, and for the first time, he didn't run away from Dakota. Instead, he spent the night with him. It was a first for both of them: the first time Dakota had slept beside another person since Laren's death, the first time ever for Nathan. For the first time in a long time, they didn't feel guilty, dirty, or alone. They felt whole.

~~*

278

"You are the weirdest hitman ever," Nathan remarked, stretching the next morning.

Dakota raised an eyebrow. "What'd I do this time?"

"It's the way you talk ... the way you act. You're not like ... people."

"Good. This community is full of assholes."

"See? Like that. One minute you're all street or whatever, and the next you're all, like, holy or some shit."

Dakota shot him a wry smile. "I'm trying not to be an asshole."

"And being a God-nut is better?"

"I'm trying for redemption. I don't think being an asshole will help." He shrugged off Nathan's doubtful look. "I haven't found a happy medium, yet. If you stick around, you might see it someday."

~~*

"The sea life is about to be killed and the water poisoned."

Nathan blinked at Amber from across the table. She certainly didn't beat around the bush, that was for sure. "Yeah?"

"I've been counting signs." Her usual pastime. "It won't be long now."

Nathan hummed, but that was it. What else was he supposed to say? It wasn't like they hadn't known this was coming.

"I heard you spent the night with Dakota Walker." Nope, Amber didn't beat around the bush at all.

"We didn't fuck."

"I— That's not what I was asking."

He raised an eyebrow. "Isn't it?"

She smiled. "Maybe. What's up with you two? Some angel-angel mind meld?"

Nathan snorted. "It's not because he's an angel." Amber gave him a look. "Okay, maybe it is, a little. I don't know. When he's not out to save my fucked up soul ... I don't know. It's different with him. I don't know what it means."

Amber gave a knowing smile and laughed. "Oh, you are just too precious! You sound like a love struck high school boy."

"I don't know what love is."

"Duh. You gonna let Dakota teach you about loving?"

Nathan got up. "I'm gonna go."

"Gonna go see your boyfriend?"

He flipped her off and shut the door on her laughter.

~~*

Since being outcast from the Lord's army, Nathan had believed that anything good in his life was too good to last and that this ... this thing with Dakota was just one more of them.

The Savior sent Dakota out on a job, having a man he needed Dakota to track down and kill. Dakota offered Nathan his house to stay in while he was away and took Nathan's silent 'no' as a 'yes.'

Dakota and Nathan had made a lot of enemies in Civilization. Mostly, Dakota had made enemies and those enemies got back at him through Nathan. All those brutes who liked it rough, all those men who had accidentally damaged Nathan, they had all been punished by Dakota, and now that Nathan's protector was gone, they were going to exact their revenge.

The men came one at a time, offering food and clothes, and fucked Nathan raw, took him apart and scattered the pieces. It was clear why they were doing it: to punish Nathan, to hurt Dakota, to remind Nathan of his place.

He got the memo, loud and clear, as it was carved into his body and written in his blood.

When Dakota came back three days later, Nathan was gone. Not understanding what was happening, sure that he had finally gotten through to Nathan, Dakota went to look for him. He found him standing—seeing as sitting was too painful—in an alley, leaning against a wall. His face and neck were bruised, as were his wrists. Dakota couldn't see the rest of him, but he could imagine that the rest of Nathan's body looked worse.

"Nathan ... "

Nathan shook his head, wincing as he pushed away from the wall. "Don't."

"Nathan, what happened?"

Nathan's eyes grew hard and fierce. "What happened?" he asked softly. "What happened? You left and took your little 'circle of protection' with you! I told you not to do that; I told you not to get involved with me. As soon as you left, every fucker you beat up for me came to take his share." He stared Dakota down, not enough of himself left to be ashamed. This was his life, damn it; he knew how this world worked. Dakota, it seemed, couldn't get it through his head and was going to drag Nathan down with him.

"Why didn't you fight back? You're an angel."

Nathan glared. "I want to live. You kill people and I let them fuck me. We do what we have to do to survive."

"You can't honestly tell me you're happy as a whore."

"Happy?" Nathan snorted; the idea was ridiculous. "Of course I'm not happy. This is the Apocalypse, not the party hosted by the one and only Jesus Christ."

"Then why don't you do something about it instead of being passed around like a fucking slut?" Dakota was furious with Nathan's willingness to suffer.

Nathan's eyes gleamed with rage and maybe, just maybe, a hint of tears. "If I'm such a 'fucking slut,' why don't you go find someone else to preach to?" He pushed past Dakota, unable to believe himself. He'd actually believed Dakota could care about him? He was even more of an idiot than he'd been telling himself.

Dakota fumed all the way back to his house. At first, he was furious, but that quickly turned to guilt. Nathan had been right: in trying to defend and protect him, Dakota had only made things worse.

In the beginning, Dakota's sole interest in Nathan had been redemption: help Nathan and God would take away his guilt. Somewhere amid all the fighting, however, that had changed. He still wanted to save himself, and Nathan, but it was more than that; there was something about Nathan to which he felt connected and drawn. Nathan stood up to him, called him out, and that in itself was something. He didn't seem to fear him, even if Dakota made him uncomfortable at times. There was this beautiful spark, this amazing will to survive that Dakota could barely imagine. He had made himself a whore, giving up his body and numbing his mind, instead of giving up. There was some ember of hope deep within him.

He actually listened when Dakota spoke. He didn't shrug off Dakota's past or judge it; he understood. Dakota had never met anyone like him before and he found himself wanting Nathan in a way he'd never wanted anyone. Laren had been beautiful—physically, spiritually, mentally. Everyone had been attracted to his light and Dakota had considered himself lucky when Laren had loved him. He had been almost too perfect to bear. Nathan was far from perfect; he was beautiful, yes, but also flawed. He lacked self-worth and had some kind of bitter animosity toward God. He was rude, he was damaged; he was real and Dakota couldn't help falling for him.

~~*

"I want Nathan Homestead to work for me." It was Dakota's brilliant plan: get Nathan out of whoring and get him closer to Dakota. Two birds, one stone. He just needed the Savior's go-ahead.

"No."

Dakota blinked at him. "Excuse me?"

"I said no."

"Why not?"

The Savior turned away from his view of Civilization. "Do you see them out there? Two hundred and sixteen people, all depending on me to protect them, feed them, keep them alive. Everyone has their place, fulfills a role to keep the community alive. The soldiers protect us. The farmers feed us. My women pleasure me—and one is carrying my first child."

Dakota narrowed his eyes, certainly not about to congratulate the Savior on knocking up some brainwashed girl. "Nathan's not protecting you, feeding you, or bearing your children. What 'role' is he 'fulfilling'?"

"Why, he's keeping the public entertained, of course." The Savior's thin-lipped smile was sickening; Dakota wanted to rip it off his face. "And he keeps them in check. Without Nathan to satisfy them, the people would turn on each other. Assault, violence, and chaos would ensue."

"Or they could just keep it in their pants."

The Savior looked at him as though he was a naïve child, a look Dakota was getting regularly from him, and he didn't like it at all. "I don't know what it's like for you angels, but we human men have needs. It has to be someone's job to provide it for us."

Dakota's lip curled in disgust. A million insults ran through his head, but he bit them back, searching for one that wouldn't get him kicked out of Civilization.

The Savior knew, somehow, and smiled smugly. "You can go now."

Incensed, and dismissed on top of it, Dakota strode from the room before he could give in and slit the Savior's skinny throat.

~~*

The Savior returned to his window. Dakota and Nathan? He hadn't foreseen a romance; he'd thought Nathan was completely under his thumb. No matter. Nathan had his place and he would do well to remember it. He belonged to the Savior.

He wouldn't step in, not yet; just watch from afar. There was a lesson to be learned by Nathan and the Savior would let him figure it out on his own.

And if he didn't ... the Savior would teach it to him the hard way.

~~*

Nathan went back to his life in the gutters of Civilization, schmoozing his way back into his former clients' good graces and erasing the damage Dakota had done, returning to his unpredictable lifestyle. He did his best to forget about Dakota and erase him from his mind, but then he started seeing him in his dreams.

It did no good, Nathan told himself, to think about what he could have had with Dakota. Dakota was one of a kind, it was true; he was the only man in all of Civilization who looked at the world not as a game to win, but as something to make better. He looked at Nathan that way, too, as though Nathan was something special, something worth cherishing—not a prize to be taken and traded. Nathan was sorely missing that, and now that he had had a taste of Dakota's cherishing, he realized just how much he had longed for that connection. Dakota trusted him, cared about him, and Nathan found himself actually caring for a change, about Dakota and life itself.

But it couldn't be. He and Dakota could never be together. He needed to work for a living, needing to continue the trades Civilization demanded. Even if he gave in to Dakota's ridiculous demands, let Dakota provide for him, there was still the rent to pay to the Savior and only one way for Nathan to pay it. Dakota deserved better than that, deserved someone who could still see the beauty in the world. He deserved someone like Laren, and Nathan realized that he would willingly trade his life for Laren's, just so Dakota could have something he deserved. He certainly didn't deserve to be saddled with the damaged, filthy, inhuman thing that Nathan had become.

How had he fallen so completely?

~~*

"Shortly, all living sea creatures will die and our waters will be poisoned."

The citizens in the town hall gasped in shock and fear.

"This would be a lot more impressive if it hadn't been foretold about a thousand times," Amber muttered to Nathan, who sat beside her.

"No shit. And if you hadn't predicted it a week ago."

"We must stockpile water!" the Savior continued. "Barrels and containers must be built and water must be collected—quickly, while we still can!"

The community entered a frenzy after that, everyone devoting themselves to building water storage units. Nathan was outcast, again. His only job was to be ready for a fuck, and even the threat of dehydration—and then death—didn't persuade anyone to give him a job. On top of that, everyone was too busy for sex.

Nathan wondered if he might starve to death while the community worked to keep everyone alive.

Not for the first time, Dakota found himself wishing that Laren was there to advise him. He had been so strong and forward, and blunt with his honesty, and these were things that Dakota was sorely missing in his life. Laren had been so much smarter than he, could read people so much better. Dakota needed him there to tell him what to do, how to win Nathan over. He wondered what happened to demi-angels when they died, if Laren was somewhere up there looking down on him, waiting for the day Dakota would rejoin him. He wondered if Laren was guiding him still, helping him to make the right decisions.

Even if he wasn't, Dakota would have to make the right decisions, because he was not letting Nathan get away from him. He had tried to talk to Nathan a few times and failed. Nathan had avoided him, walked away, or sworn at him before walking away. Dakota thought that if Nathan could avoid all of the bad things in life the way he avoided Dakota, he'd be the happiest man on the planet. As it was, Dakota was pretty sure that Nathan walked headfirst into all of the bad things, took them in with open arms, and convinced himself that it was his lot in life. Maybe he saw it as penance for what he'd done; maybe he saw it as the only option for him because of the way he'd been created. Either way, he pushed Dakota away with a fierceness that took Dakota by surprise.

When Dakota found Nathan lying on the street, half-asleep and freezing in the cold spring rain, Dakota picked him up and took him home. This half-conscious, half-frozen Nathan was much more pliable and willing to do what Dakota wanted, and Dakota most certainly made a note of it. He hoped that he would never have to use that piece of knowledge, but he assumed that Nathan's stubbornness was part of his character. If Dakota wanted to spend the rest of his life with Nathan, then he was probably going to have to get used to the pig-headedness.

It was definitely a sacrifice he was willing to make.

~~*

When Nathan woke up the next morning, he was nestled in soft sheets and a warm blanket. His clothes were dry ... and they weren't his clothes. He was not on street corner where he'd fallen asleep.

He sat up, head swimming when the motion overwhelmed him, and tried to orient himself with his surroundings. He quickly recognized Dakota's house, the simple, open rooms and plain curtains for privacy. He should have known.

"Dakota ... "

His voice was a warning, but Dakota ignored it, bringing him a cup of coffee and a breakfast roll. "No, no warnings," Dakota ordered. "Have your breakfast."

"Dakota—"

"I said no warnings!" Dakota's voice was firmer than it was sharp, but Nathan bit his tongue and took the offered items. Dakota didn't speak until Nathan was done. "How do you feel?"

Nathan shrugged. "'m fine."

"No," Dakota said, as though talking to a small child. "You didn't even think about it. Take a moment, think, and then tell me how you feel."

Nathan narrowed his eyes, but took a deep breath anyway. He took stock of his body, which really was no worse off than usual, and then thought briefly of his mental and emotional state.

"Shitty. I feel shitty."

Dakota seemed pleased with Nathan's answer, that he was being honest with Dakota. Suddenly, Nathan was spilling out his feelings.

"I feel like shit, all the time. I feel so worthless and useless. I can't even do anything useful in this town. I'm just a hole; that's all I can be. That's all I can do. The physical shittiness ... it's ... it's fine, it's whatever. I can deal with that. But the rest ... I don't want to feel this way. I don't like it. I hate it. I hate it." He stopped suddenly, eyes widening as he realized what he'd said.

"Why haven't you done anything about it? Why not leave?" Dakota asked.

Nathan snorted. "And go where?"

Dakota gave him a look, not letting him off the hook that easily; not when he was finally opening up. "There are other communities out there and you know it."

Nathan looked uneasy. He glanced away, warring with himself, and finally blurted out, "Because I deserve what I've got, okay? This is punishment; this is what happens when you disobey God. I'm not right, Dakota; there's something wrong with me, something I can't fix. I've tried, believe me, I've tried to be the way I'm supposed to be, but I can't, okay? This is the life I have to live."

"No, it's not." Dakota's voice was soft, but firm.

Nathan sighed. "I don't ... I don't want to live like this, even if it's what God wants."

"Have you ever thought that God wants you to be happy?"

"I don't know what God wants." Of everything in life, that was the one thing of which Nathan was always sure. "I don't understand God's will. I never have. But I want ... "

"What do you want, Nathan?" Dakota asked softly. "What do you really want?"

Nathan did think, but just for a moment, because he really didn't need to linger on it—he already knew. "You. I want you, Dakota. You're ... you're the only good thing in Civilization; you look at the world like you can make it better. You look at me like you can fix me, and I want you to. I want you to make me feel good again, feel whole. I want you, Dakota. I want you."

"Finally," Dakota whispered, climbing onto the bed and pressing his mouth firmly against Nathan's.

It was slow and deliberate ... well, it was supposed to be, at least. Nathan was desperate and hungry, swiping his tongue in Dakota's mouth, sucking hard on his bottom lip, rutting up against him with a fierce desire, as if salvation could be found in Dakota. Dakota, however, met his desperation with a deliberate passion, trying to draw out the moments and enjoy every feeling of Nathan's skin beneath his, of his gasping breaths, of his racing heart, trying to memorize them all and store them in his mind forever.

Nathan immediately went still when Dakota reached for his shirt and Dakota pulled back a bit, panting. "What is it? What's wrong?"

Nathan looked away, not meeting Dakota's eyes, ashamed of something for the first time in a long while. He was ashamed to be lying here in front of another angel, a beautiful wonderful angel, and show him that he was less than Dakota, that he wasn't even a full angel anymore and had the scars to prove it.

"Nathan? Did I do something wrong?"

Oh, God. How perfect was that? Nathan had done something wrong and Dakota was worried that he had done wrong by Nathan? "No. God, no. Dakota ... "

"What is it, Nathan? Tell me what's wrong. Please."

"I ... I have scars," he muttered. Nathan allowed himself to look at Dakota out of the corner of his eye, trying to gauge his reaction, and saw Dakota's dark eyebrows pull together in confusion.

Dakota shrugged hesitantly, still not sure. "I have scars, too. We were soldiers; we all have them."

Nathan quickly shook his head. "That's not what I'm talking about. I mean, I have those scars, too. Plenty of them. It's just ... "

"It's just what, Nathan?"

All in the space of one quick breath, Nathan whispered, "When I questioned my commanders about wanting to leave, they ripped my wings out and the burn left scars."

Dakota took a moment to comprehend what Nathan had said. "They ... "

"Yeah," Nathan whispered, unable to look at him, unable to face the disgust he was sure to see in Dakota's eyes.

"Nathan ... " Dakota's voice was pained.

Nathan was so surprised that he looked up, seeing sympathy and hurt in Dakota's eyes.

"Will you let me see? Will you show me?"

Not quite sure why Dakota wasn't forcing him out of his bed and house, Nathan pulled his shirt over his head, and then slowly turned, revealing his back. Dakota gasped, unable to help himself. When Nathan tensed at the sound, it only pulled the skin of his back tighter, making the image more visible. Between his shoulder blades was a vaguely wing-shaped, rust-colored burn, a color that only came from being burned by angels.

"Dakota?" Nathan finally managed in a strained voice. "Do you … ?"

"Can I touch it?" Dakota whispered. "Will you let me touch it?"

All Nathan could do was nod, so unsure, so lost, so desperate.

The gentle pads of warm fingers slid down his back, tracing over and across the shape in his skin. Nathan couldn't help but arch his back toward Dakota, whimpering when Dakota leaned forward, sliding his tongue across the damaged flesh.

"Oh, oh, God," Nathan whimpered, and Dakota immediately pulled back.

"Fuck. Fuck, I'm sorry. Was that wrong? Did I hurt you? Nathan?"

Nathan shook slightly and turned toward him. "No one … I didn't think any angel would even be able to look at me when he saw the mark and you … you *like* it."

"God, Nathan, I'm sorry." Dakota leaned forward, trying to show Nathan just how genuine he was, that he wasn't turned on by Nathan's suffering. "I didn't mean to hurt you; I didn't want you to—"

"That's why they like it," Nathan mused softly. "They like to see the burn before they fuck me; it makes them feel better, like I'm less than an angel, less than human. They won't touch it, though; it terrifies them. But you … "

"Nathan ... " Dakota didn't know what to say. He couldn't believe this, couldn't believe that after all this time of wanting Nathan, of wanting to protect him, he had blown everything just like this.

"I like it." Nathan's voice was rough, heavy with want. "I like that you're not afraid of it, of me."

Dakota was so relieved that all of the tension went out of his body.

"Do it again? Please?"

"Oh, fuck, yes."

Dakota turned him and pushed him forward, so he could drape over him and lick across the burn, trace it with the pads of his fingers until Nathan was trembling beneath.

"Yes, Dakota. Yes."

Dakota's pants were tight; he needed more. More than that, though, he needed Nathan to enjoy this, needed this to be good for Nathan, even if Dakota himself didn't even get to come.

"Dakota ... Dakota ... "

"Yeah? What do you need?"

"You. I need you. Clothes off?"

"Oh, thank God."

They pulled apart just long enough to strip, and then they were back on Dakota's bed, their bodies pressed firmly together with Dakota on top. The kiss was messy, hot, open mouths and firm, slick tongues, too much teeth, too much spit, but so perfect that if his cock hadn't been nearing a state of explosion, Dakota could have spent the rest of his life kissing Nathan just like this.

When Nathan jerked his mouth away to gasp for air, Dakota forced him over and began an assault of his burn, lips, tongue, and teeth sliding and scraping over the shiny, rusty skin. Beneath him, Nathan whimpered and trembled, alternated between bowing and arching his back, trying to get away from the intense feeling, but wanting to get more of it, never wanting to leave this spot. In the past, he had always thought that the sensitivity of the angel-fire burn was punishment from God, His way of constantly reminding him of his sins, but for the first time, he wondered if maybe the hypersensitivity of every angel's body was instead a gift.

Dakota's hand slid down Nathan's back to touch him, and then stopped.

Nathan noticed. "What? What is it, Dakota?"

"I ... Do you want to fuck me?"

Nathan blinked at him for a moment, and then looked over his shoulder at him. "What?"

"Do you want to fuck me? You can."

"I ... Dakota ... " All of the blood in Nathan's body had left his brain and he could make no sense of Dakota's words.

Dakota was loath to bring up Nathan's hurts here and now, but he did anyway. "What they've done ... They've hurt you. I don't ever want to hurt you, Nathan. Ever. I don't want to hurt you."

Nathan stilled beneath him, the final walls in his eyes coming down when Dakota said that, and turned around to face Dakota. "Kiss me," he demanded in a whisper.

Dakota complied, their mouths meeting in a deep, probing kiss that was sweet and tender. When Nathan pulled away, he whispered, "Now fuck me, on my back. I want to see you. I want you to see me. Fuck me. Please."

Dakota prepped Nathan thoroughly and gently, which was completely unheard of in Nathan's experience. As Dakota slid into him, locking eyes with him the whole time, it dawned on Nathan that this was the first time he'd ever had sex without a tradeoff ... and most importantly, he was okay with that.

It didn't take long for Dakota to set up a rhythm, thrusting in and out, the drag making Nathan's eyelids flutter. He found Nathan's spot quickly and focused on making everything as good for Nathan as he could possibly could.

It didn't last long. Past experiences suggested that all good things came too an end faster than was desired, but as Nathan came with Dakota inside him, Dakota was the only thing on his mind.

After Dakota pulled out and cleaned them up, they lay together in the bed, Nathan's head on Dakota's chest with Dakota's arm wrapped loosely around him.

"Nathan ... " Dakota began tentatively. "I'm not trying to witness to you, not anymore. I just ... I want you. I want to be with you. It's not about redemption. It's—"

"Okay."

Dakota paused for a moment, certain that Nathan didn't mean what he thought he did. "What?"

"I get it," Nathan answered softly. "I really do."

Dakota smiled, pulling Nathan tightly against him as he kissed the top of his head, sure that he'd never been this happy before.

~~*

The Savior felt the bottom drop out of his stomach; he thought he might throw up. Shame, disappointment, and rage erupted in his chest and spread like wildfire throughout his body. These were schoolboy feelings, Thomas Ackley feelings, not the feelings of the Savior.

"You're what?" His clipped tones were so soft he could barely hear them.

Emily heard, however, and burst into tears. "I'm not pregnant. I'm sorry, so sorry, I am. I don't know what happened ... We'll try again." She sniffed back the tears, her large brown eyes bright with hope. "Let's try again. It'll work for us, it will."

The Savior jerked away when she reached out to him. "Don't touch me."

Emily choked on a few sobs. "It's not my fault—don't blame me. I don't—"

Humiliation burned in his veins. "This is my fault?"

"No! No, of course not. It's no one's fault. It just takes time—"

"Get out, you stupid girl. Get away from me."

She wailed. "No! You don't mean—"

"Get out!" he roared at her, and with a fearful squeak, she ran crying from the room. As embarrassment turned to rage, the Savior threw a vase at the wall, watching the pieces shatter and clink as they hit the floor.

He was fucking three women regularly; he should have been surrounded by half a dozen wailing brats. Clearly, something was wrong, and the odds were against him. He didn't want children—far from it—but the fact that he couldn't was shameful, another taunting jab at his masculinity. What kind of man couldn't knock his women up? What did his people think?

Furious and ashamed, he opened the door, looking down the hall until he spotted his personal guardsman. "Get the hell over here. What good are you doing over there?"

There was no complaint, only instant obedience. "Sir?"

"Get me Nathan Homestead—now."

There was no shame to be had with Nathan—no one in the world could get him pregnant—and the Savior needed a distraction.

~~*

When the Savior was done with him, Nathan slowly returned to Dakota's. He was sore and tired, and he just wanted to lie down and sleep it off.

"What the fuck?" Dakota got to his feet as Nathan closed the door and Nathan flinched at his tone.

"Whatever." Nathan tried to shake him off.

"What happened?"

"Nothing. I'm fine. I fell."

"You fell? And, what, a tree rammed itself up your ass?"

"It's nothing."

"The fuck it is!" Dakota got close, rage coming off him in waves. "Tell me what happened."

"The Savior, okay? Get out of my face." He shoved Dakota backward.

"Get out of your face? You didn't have a problem with me being in your face last night when I was fucking you. What, was I not enough for you? You needed someone else to finish you off?"

Nathan gaped, wide-eyed and furious. "That's shit and you know it. Fucking grow a pair."

"A pair like the Savior's, you mean? That's why you needed him to fuck you not hours after I was in you?"

"I didn't need him. He needed me, wanted me, what the fuck ever."

"Oh." Dakota's voice was snide and taunting. "He wants you?"

"Fuck you. You wanted me just fine last night—enough to let me fuck you, if I wanted."

"Because I didn't want to hurt you! Stupid me, cuz apparently you just love when people fuck with you."

"Fuck you, Dakota! I don't like it; I put up with it."

"You don't like it? Then stop."

Nathan's eyes widened. How dare Dakota waltz in and tell him how to live, as though he knew him at all? "I can't. I need to pay to stay here. I need food. I need somewhere to fucking sleep."

"Then do something else!"

"I can't! They won't let me!"

"Then leave! Go somewhere where you don't have to whore yourself, play cheap and easy."

"Why don't you leave? Why don't you leave me alone? Why don't you go somewhere you don't slit throats on command?"

"You're the one who's the Savior's bitch!"

"You're such a fucking hypocrite!" Nathan couldn't help screaming, couldn't help being red in the face with shame, rage, and hurt. "You kill people on the Savior's say so and that makes you better than me?"

"That's different."

"Why? Why is any different for you to kill people than for me to fuck them?"

"Because I want redemption." Clearly Dakota had told himself that before.

"And you're going to get that by killing assholes?" Nathan sneered. Dakota was just as messed up as he was; he just wouldn't admit it to himself. Delusional idiot.

"They're bad people. They deserve it. It's different."

"I'm a bad person, you fucker. You have no idea what I've done. You gonna kill me?"

"That's different." Dakota had nothing to stand on but the lie he kept telling himself; Nathan could see it in his eyes.

"No, it's not. You just can't admit you're wrong."

"I'm wrong? You're a whore!"

Nathan felt himself flush. People called him that all the time; so why was Dakota any different? "I'm trying to stay alive."

"You're not living." Dakota's tone was full of condensation.

"And you are?"

"You don't understand," Dakota spat.

"No, I do understand. You think I'm a dirty slut? Fine; I am. At least I know it. But you're a fucking murderer."

Dakota went pale. "You have no idea what you're talking about."

Nathan took a step forward, his smile an empty victory. "No, Dakota, I do know. You're just a fucking hypocrite." He spat at Dakota's feet, turned, and left.

~~*

Nathan wasn't allowed to go with the groups heading outside the community to collect water, but he wasn't surprised. He was a whore; that was his place in society. Besides, with his luck, he'd be assigned to the same crew as Dakota, which would be awful.

Amber let him stay in her house while she was gone. Technically, she asked him to stay there and guard her shit, and help himself to her food and bed, but she was as opaque as glass. He stayed, anyway, too pissy and annoyed to fight her. He wasn't sure why he felt as though Dakota had betrayed him—Dakota didn't owe him anything. Had he really let himself think that just because he wanted Dakota, Dakota would want him back? What had he expected, happily ever after? Apparently, Dakota wasn't the only delusional one.

~~*

Nathan was startled one day by a sudden banging on Amber's door. He quickly shut the book he'd been reading—doodling in the margins—and was dumbfounded to see Dakota standing outside.

"Dakota?"

"Oh, thank God." He pushed his way in and looked Nathan over. "Are you okay? You're okay, aren't you? Nathan? I came as soon as I heard ... "

"Dakota, what are you talking about?" Why the hell was Dakota here? "I'm fine. Why wouldn't I be?"

"The Savior." Dakota's pale green eyes were glowing brightly, intensely. "He left, two days ago, to come back to Civilization. I thought he ... " What he thought was written clearly in his eyes.

"I'm fine. I take care of myself. I haven't even seen the Savior, so ... "

Dakota didn't take the hint, lingering even though Nathan was just fine. "I had to know you were okay."

Nathan stared, searching, his voice more desperate than he intended. "Why do you care about me?"

"I ... " Dakota seemed to be searching for answers, too. "You yell at me."

"I yell at you?" Nathan repeated doubtfully. "What does that—"

"You don't treat me like a child or like I'm going to break, and you're not afraid of me. You tell me exactly how it is, whether I like it or not."

"I ... " Nathan shook his head helplessly.

"It's fine," Dakota said quickly. "I'm not looking for declarations."

Stubborn, Nathan replied, "I can make fucking declarations if I want to."

"Yeah?"

"Yeah." His voice softened to a tone he'd never heard himself use before. "You make me think and feel, and ... I want. For the first time in ages, I want." Life, freedom, Dakota. It was fucking terrifying.

"You want ... me? Or something else?"

"Everything. I fucking want everything and I don't ... I can't ... "

Dakota cut off his stuttered ramble with a kiss, mouth hot and firm, but so damn soft, and Nathan was filled with feelings he'd never before felt—lust, fear, guilt, joy, comfort, safety, terror, worry ... They were overwhelming and he moaned into Dakota's mouth.

Dakota pulled back and Nathan couldn't help the needy sound that slipped out. "There a bed here?" Dakota's voice was low and rough, and it made Nathan hot all over.

He snorted, though, remembering where he was. "No sex in Amber's bed. She'll never shut up about it."

Dakota actually laughed, leaning down to press his forehead to Nathan's shoulder, breathing hard. Nathan's hands were in Dakota's jacket ... When had that happened?

"What about my bed?" Dakota raised his head to look at him.

"You probably won't shut up about that, either." Nathan gave a small smile, for some reason pleased that by stalling, he could make Dakota want it more.

"Then shut me up," Dakota challenged.

Nathan pressed his thigh between Dakota's and rolled his hips. Dakota didn't shut up; he gasped, but no words came out, so Nathan counted it as a victory. "Take me to your bed."

"Fucking finally."

Dakota and Nathan were in bed together when the smell finally reached the community—death, decay, and putrid rot. Their heightened senses made them the first to be aware, but within a day, even the most ignorant citizens could smell the reek. They all knew what had happened. The water-life had been killed; the water had been poisoned. There was no living outside the community, anymore; there was no leaving Civilization without a guaranteed haven somewhere else. Never before had the walls felt like such a barrier, caging the people within and holding back the death outside.

~~*

"What are we doing?" The question had been eating at Nathan for some time, and finally, lying in bed with Dakota, he dared to ask.

Dakota wasn't sure where this question was going. "What do you mean?"

Nathan sighed. "You and me. What are we doing?"

Dakota rolled onto his side to face Nathan. "More declarations?"

"No, I don't mean—I don't know what we're doing there, either, but—Things aren't going to change. I'm always going to be at the Savior's beck and call; it's just the way it is. You're always going to be hunting people down. It's not ... Nothing will change here. Can you live with that?"

"What are you saying?" Dakota asked hesitantly. "You want to end this?"

"No, fuck no, that's not—" Nathan huffed out a breath and pushed the hair out of his eyes. "You hate what I do. You've said it a million times; you'll say it a million more. And every time you do, I'll call you a filthy hypocrite. We'll fight, we'll fuck, we'll make up, and we'll do it all over again. That's never going to change and you need to know that."

Dakota was quiet and Nathan got nervous. Nathan had said all this so Dakota could back out if he wanted, but he wasn't actually supposed to leave. He was supposed to make some more of those grand declarations that made Nathan feel. To make him feel so many new and huge things, and then kiss him some more. He wasn't supposed to—

"Dakota? What ... what are you thinking? What ... ?" He trailed off helplessly, waiting.

"Things can't change here; I get it." Dakota quickly added, "I hate it, but I get it. But there's nowhere else to go. I've been to other communities and they're just like this, or worse. Drugs. Rape. Violence. They're no better."

Quietly, Nathan said, "And it wouldn't matter. Anywhere we go, I still have to work. This is what I do."

"No," Dakota said, eyes and voice firm. "You could do something else, something better. But ... I won't take you out of here just so you can get raped or beat up by some drug addicts or made into a killer. We could try to find somewhere safe, but we'd die out there before we did." He looked away, and said, "But there's something you should know."

His tone put Nathan on edge, and his silence only made it worse. "What? What is it?"

"There's somewhere we could go." Dakota's tone was emotionless, as though he didn't want to sway Nathan one way or the other. He wasn't looking at him, either. "A community I've heard of but never seen. It's ... it's all angels."

"No!" Dakota's head snapped up at Nathan's hard and fearful tone. "God, no!" Nathan's eyes were wide. "Angels? Fucking angels? Do you know—? I've— They'll hate me. They'd string me up or worse. Angels? Angels? I can't— God, I—"

"Shh, shh. It's okay." Dakota wrapped his arms around Nathan, trying to calm him down. "We won't go."

"No!" Nathan pulled back. "You go. If it's better than here ... I'm not going to hold you back."

Dakota snorted. "I sure as hell don't want to go. I hunt angels all the time. They'd probably shoot me as soon as look at me."

"Then why'd you say it?"

"I don't know. To give you a choice."

"Some choice. You're an idiot."

"You love it."

"Whatever."

Dakota was quiet. "I wouldn't go anywhere without you. It sucks here, but nowhere is better if you're not there."

Nathan rolled his eyes. He secretly loved Dakota's lame lines and the way they made his stomach tingle, but there was no way he was letting Dakota know that. "Where do you come up with these lines, seriously? Do you read old-world chick magazines? Were you always this lame?"

"Shut up." Dakota shoved at him, but he was smiling.

"Make me."

"I will."

Nathan snorted. "You're all big talk, no action."

"I'll give you action." Dakota rolled on top of him, pressing down with all his weight. "What you going to do about that?"

"Get off me, you idiot." Nathan shoved uselessly at his shoulders. "You're crushing me!"

"Not what you said this morning."

"Fuck you."

"I'm down with that. It's going to be hard for you, if you can't move."

"Asshole." Nathan squirmed, but he wasn't going anywhere.

Before Dakota could reply to that, there was a knock at the door. "Come in!" he shouted, and then began sucking on Nathan's neck. If someone was looking for a hookup, they were going to get an eyeful.

"Christ, guys, it's the middle of the afternoon. Don't you ever get your asses out of bed?"

Dakota glanced over his shoulder to see Amber standing in the doorway. With a groan, Nathan dropped his head back and squeezed his eyes shut. She was never going to let him live this down. Ever.

"I'd leave you to it, but I want to talk to Nathan, when he's done hiding under you."

Nathan groaned again and shoved at Dakota's shoulder. This time, Dakota rolled off and Nathan sat up. "Can you give us a minute?"

Amber rolled her eyes. "Like I haven't seen it before."

"Out!" He pointed to the door. "Other room, now!"

"Fine. Whatever makes you feel better."

Nathan reached for his pants.

"She's seen your dick?"

"Not cuz I was fucking her with it! We're—She's—It's not like that for us." Nathan stood up, zipping his pants.

"Huh."

"What?"

Dakota eyed him thoughtfully, but said, "Nothing."

"Fine. Keep your secrets." Nathan pulled his t-shirt over his head. "Are you getting dressed or what?"

Amber was waiting for them with a new book a raider had brought back for her. It appeared to be written from an angel's point of view about the war and she needed Nathan to clarity a few slang terms.

Nathan wasn't sure how it happened, but before long, he was hiding his face while Amber told every embarrassing story about him she knew. Apparently he'd done a lot of humiliating things in the past year and a half—besides the glaringly obvious ones—and she was getting a laugh out of sharing them.

"I like her," Dakota said, after she left. "She's funny."

"You only think so cuz she's dishing dirt on me. If she was talking about you, you wouldn't think so."

"She's a sweet girl."

"That girl knows four ways to kill you with just her thumb. She's as sweet as my ass." He walked toward the bedroom, stripping off his shirt.

"Where are you going?"

"To bed."

"With me?"

"Only if you get your ass in here."

~~*

Nathan tried to bury Amber's stories safely in the past, but Dakota kept bringing them up, mentioning them offhand or sneaking them into jokes and snide comments. Nathan had thought Amber was bad, but at least he didn't live with her. There was no shutting Dakota up, unless he punched him or threatened to sleep under the table. Those only worked for so long, before Dakota had some lame line to reel him back in.

~~*

"Why did they take your wings, Nathan?" Dakota whispered, as they lay naked together in bed, partially covered by the blanket. Dakota was propped up on one arm watching him and Nathan closed his eyes for just a moment.

"I wasn't a good soldier … " he began, not really looking at Dakota. He mostly stared up at the ceiling, and then it all came out. He hadn't told anyone the whole story of his existence, barely mentioning parts of it to Amber, and was surprised at just how good it felt to let it all out, to trust Dakota with his every imperfection and the story of his past.

"That was the life I had to live to stay here," he finished. "That's just how I've lived until … until I met you." He gave a small smile, glancing away, and then met Dakota's eyes. "When I met you, I changed. You took away my off-switch. Before, I could just tune everything out, but then you came and I couldn't anymore. I was feeling things I hadn't let myself feel, things I had had to shut out or I would've destroyed myself. You made me feel, made me someone else, someone better."

Dakota kissed him, hard and full, a long probing kiss filled with love and strength and promise.

"What was your name?" Dakota whispered when he pulled back, voice rough with the lack of breath in his lungs. "Before, the name they gave you when you were created."

Nathan shook his head. "I'm not an angel anymore."

"Yes, you are," Dakota countered firmly. "You're still an angel. You're even more of one now."

Gazing at him with level eyes, considering for a long moment, Nathan softly said, "Ephraim." It felt weird to say; he hadn't let himself even think the name since he had been exiled, much less say it aloud.

"Ephraim," Dakota repeated, trying the name out on his tongue, testing it. He nodded, not passing judgment of any kind.

"What was yours?" Nathan asked eagerly, and Dakota was pleased that Nathan wanted to know more about him.

"Azriel."

"Azriel." Nathan nodded. "It fits you."

Dakota shrugged. "Azriel wasn't really strong enough to deal with the life I had. Hopefully Dakota is."

"I know you are," Nathan replied softly, reaching up to run his fingertips down Dakota's warm cheek. "You're so strong ... "

"So are you. Stronger than you let yourself believe."

Nathan didn't argue and Dakota considered that to be a triumph, a step in a better direction, the right direction.

Nathan's tongue swiped over his bottom lip, almost as if he was about to speak, but then turned away ever so slightly.

"What?" Dakota asked. "What is it?"

Nathan shrugged. "I was going to ask ... Never mind. It doesn't matter."

"Ask me anything, Nathan," Dakota said firmly. "Anything."

Nathan glanced up at him with a burning hope in his eyes. "Can I see ... Will you show me your wings?"

Dakota smiled. He didn't reply, but he moved over Nathan to stand naked on the floor. One moment he was just a naked man and the next ... The next, glorious black wings, the feathers tinted with the iridescent green of Dakota's eyes, appeared seemingly out of nowhere to rest between his shoulder blades. Even though Nathan had seen angels draw out their wings countless times, even though he himself had done it since the day of his creation, he was still struck with awe at the sight before him.

Without conscious thought, Nathan found himself standing in front of Dakota, fingers tremulously reaching out to touch the magnificence of Dakota's wings. He hesitated, eyes glancing to Dakota's for reassurance, and then felt Dakota draw his wings forward so that Nathan's hand rested against the soft, downy feathers, feeling the strong muscles rippling beneath the surface.

Then Nathan's arms were around Dakota's neck, his body bowed so that the two of them were almost one skin, and his mouth desperately and feverishly started devouring Dakota's own mouth.

~~*

Nathan walked beside Dakota, hauling loads of lumber from the mill to the southern corner of Civilization, where a new guard tower was being built. Nathan was a volunteer, since he wasn't allowed to be paid for any real job, but Dakota was getting paid in food tokens, which would be shared with him.

On the way back to the mill for another load, Dakota asked, "What's up? You're quiet."

Nathan shrugged. "I feel shitty."

Dakota drew them both up short and his eyes were worried. "What's wrong? Do you feel sick? What?"

Nathan shook his head. "Not like that. I ... " He sighed. "I feel like I'm taking advantage of you."

"How?"

"You're taking care of me all the time. What the hell have I done for it? You're supplying the house, the food. I can't even tell myself that I'm giving you sex cuz I know I want it just as much as you do."

"It is pretty great sex."

Nathan gave him a look. "I'm serious. I feel bad letting you take care of me. I feel so helpless."

Dakota shrugged. "That's just how it is right now. It's not forever."

"Isn't it?"

"I don't have all the answers." More than ever, lately, it seemed; Dakota didn't have answers for anything anymore.

I don't have all the answers ... but I serve a God who does. How many times had Nathan heard that? It hit him then: it was time.

~~*

The next morning, while Dakota was still sleeping, Nathan eased out from under him, pulled on his jeans and hoodie, and headed outside. Just outside Civilization was the community's farm territory, constantly guarded by soldiers. Nathan headed there, needing the peace of wide open space. He found a hill above the fields, watched the few people already working for a few minutes, and then turned his eyes skyward.

"I don't know if You're listening," he began unsurely, "or if You even want to hear from me anymore, but I need ... I need to hear from You. I need You. God ... I'm so lost. I don't understand Your will. I never have. I guess that's always been pretty obvious ...

"But for the first time in my entire existence, I'm happy. Dakota ... Just being with him, being around him, it makes me feel good again, like I could be whole again. I want to thank You for that. I know that You have a plan for me. Maybe I didn't follow it and this has been my punishment. Or maybe this has been Your plan all along. I don't know. I don't understand You. I will never understand You, I don't think.

"But that's okay. I don't need to be all-knowing; I don't want to be all-knowing. All I want to know ... all I want to know is Dakota. That's all I need, and if You'll give it to me, if You'll let me have this one good thing ... I'm not trying to make a deal. I know it doesn't work that way, but I'm begging. I've done horrible things, to You and to the world, but I'm asking You, begging You, let me have Dakota. Let him turn my life around. Let him make me good again. Please, let me have this one good thing. Please."

Nathan could feel tears sliding down his face, warm and wet, feel the rough ground digging into his knees, and he let himself cry for the first time in ages. He let himself mourn his own pain and suffering, let him mourn the hurt he had caused to others, let himself mourn the life he'd been living.

When he finally cried himself empty, when it felt like the plague inside him was pushed back and healed, he looked up to find Dakota walking up the hill toward him. He staggered to his feet. "How ... ?"

"You were gone when I woke up. I asked around for you."

"I'm fine."

Instead of giving him a lecture, instead of getting angry, Dakota simply said, "Nathan, I'm always going to need to know that you're okay, not just hope."

When Nathan threw his arms around him, buried his face in Dakota's chest, and murmured, "Thank you," Dakota knew Nathan wasn't just talking to him.

"C'mon. Let's go home." He took Nathan's hand in his, eyes warm. "I want to make love with you, for the rest of my life."

Lame lines be damned, Nathan thought. He would never get sick of them.

~~*

The Savior sat in a velvet upholstered chair—more like a throne—at the head of a long table, deep in thought. He'd given Nathan ample time to return to him on his own; he'd been more than generous in that aspect, he thought. He'd let Nathan have his fun, let him play house with Dakota. He'd even refrained from fucking him on more than one occasion.

Nathan belonged to him. From the start, he had denied the other citizens the right to pay Nathan for any job other than sex, making Nathan his toy and ensuring that no one could take Nathan away from him. Every time he saw Nathan limp, wince, or walk bowlegged, it made him smile, a physical manifestation of his power. He had created that.

There was a lesson to be learned here and it was simple: Nathan was his, his to treat as he pleased, his to control. Dakota had no claim on him. The Savior had allowed Dakota into his graces and this was how he was repaid?

Nathan had had his chance to learn this on his own, but it was time for the Savior to teach it to him the hard way. He would show once and for all that Nathan belonged to him, remind everyone of their place in Civilization and his power over them. Nathan would come running back to him, former angel or not, just as soon as Dakota was out of the picture. The Savior would make it that way.

~~*

Before leaving on the Savior's mission, Dakota had instructed Nathan to stay in the house, not wanting any horny assholes to get their hands on him while Dakota was gone. He'd thought about asking Amber to check in, but figured Nathan would hit him—or worse, be insulted.

It was a short and easy mission—knock off three mentally unstable, and therefore violent, men camping a day's flight beyond the walls, according to the Savior's spies. Quick and easy, two days tops.

When he got to the area, the campsite was deserted. He followed the trail a ways, but was caught completely unaware by two dozen trained soldiers who captured him and took him away.

~~*

Nathan worried about Dakota; he couldn't help it. He had no idea where Dakota was going, no idea whom he was after … but it wouldn't have mattered, anyway. What would Nathan have been able to do about it? It was almost laughable when Nathan thought about it. Besides, Dakota was a specially trained angel who still had his wings. He was practically invincible.

Dakota didn't come back the first day or the second. Nathan didn't sleep and barely ate, just paced back and forth, waiting.

By day three, Nathan had to face the fact that Dakota might not come back. He tried not to think about it, but it just kept coming back to him in dreams and waking fears. Maybe it had all been too good for what he deserved.

By day five, he had to accept the fact that Dakota wasn't coming back. No one was invincible; everyone died. Maybe Nathan had dragged Dakota down or maybe this was God's plan. Maybe it was just the way it had to be. The why didn't really matter; Dakota was gone, he was never coming back, and everything cured in Nathan began to relapse.

After spending the night of the sixth day sobbing, Nathan realized it was time to move forward—or back— and put his life back together. He needed food. He needed water. He needed protection from the certain death waiting beyond the walls.

There was only one way to get it. It was clear what he had to do—what he had always done, what he had done before Dakota had come and picked him out of the dirt, giving him back his heart and soul and his very life. He had to trade for food and clothes. He had to pay to be allowed to stay in Civilization. There was no safety outside the Savior's protection. There was no life for him outside the walls.

Nathan had to go back to the Savior.

~~*

The Savior looked Nathan over, making him squirm uncomfortably. Reclining lazily on a couch—a full, plush, luxurious couch that couldn't have looked more frivolous—the Savior stared at him, enjoying the power his eyes had over Nathan. His Nathan.

"Can I do something for you?" the Savior asked, voice light, almost taunting.

Nathan swallowed. "I want to pay my rent."

The Savior casually raised an eyebrow. "I haven't seen you here in a while. Not since you and—"

"You're right," Nathan interrupted, jaw tightening, eyes squeezing shut for a moment. "I'm sorry."

The Savior would have laughed outright if it wouldn't have ruined the scene he had created. Little Nathan couldn't even stand to hear the name of his lost angel? It was too precious, too valuable, something the Savior would use to his advantage for a long time to come.

The Savior smiled gently, although the emotion couldn't have looked emptier and out of place on his unfeeling face. "It will be all right. When one goes astray, forgiveness must be sought and penance paid. I am merciful."

Nathan swallowed hard, forcing down the horrible taste in his mouth. Why didn't the Savior just quote Scripture outright? Why didn't he just declare himself the Father incarnate? Nathan was tempted, terribly tempted, to spit at the Savior's feet and leave … but he couldn't. He couldn't and they both knew it. He had nowhere else to go. He would die on his own outside Civilization. Dakota wasn't there to protect him anymore; he would never protect him again. Nathan would never see him smile, never feel his arms, never hear his laugh, never—

He shook his head furiously, pushing back tears as he tried to shake the horrible thoughts out of his head. Nathan was on his own again and he had to take care of himself, whatever it took.

Slowly, he raised dying eyes to the Savior, and whispered, "I want … I'm ready."

The Savior gave another condescending eyebrow rise..
"Ready for what?"

Why did the Savior play with him like this? "I'm ready
for you."

A sharp grin spread over the Savior's face. "You better
be—because you've kept me waiting too long."

As soon as the Savior slipped inside him, Nathan felt
his switch flick to 'off' for the first time in what seemed
like an eternity, a beautiful eternity of feeling. Just like
that, it was all gone, all feeling shut off, all emotion
blocked out. There was nothing but whatever Nathan let
in through the thick walls of his mind and he didn't let
anything in—not the feel of the Savior, not the memories
of Dakota, not his pain or fear or hopeless despair. He
couldn't.

One thought, however, slipped in before he could stop
it and it sent a single tear sliding down his face. This is
what I defied God for? This is what I threw everything
away to protect? This is what I thought was right?

"You're mine," the Savior hissed, just before he came.
"I'm never letting you go, ever."

When the Savior let him leave, Nathan stumbled
blearily to Dakota's home—his home, now—and collapsed
to the floor by the wall, crying for everything he had lost,
everything he had let himself become again, and
everything that formed his life now. For the first time
since Nathan had met Dakota, he wished he was dead.

~~*

Nathan spent hours just sitting and staring blankly at
the wall. What else was there to do? Why even bother? It
didn't matter, anyway. Nothing mattered. He didn't
matter.

Amber found him like that and held him even though
Nathan kept himself stiff, unable to feel any comfort. She

talked softly to him, running her fingers through his hair, but he didn't really notice until she said Dakota's name.

"Don't." His voice was hoarse and he turned dead eyes on her. "Don't say his name. He's dead and gone."

"You don't know that! He could still be—"

Nathan snorted humorlessly. "What, lost? It's been more than a week. He's not coming back."

"Maybe he would if you didn't give up on him," she accused.

"Give up? Give up?" Finally, an emotion—anger. "When have I ever been allowed to give up? I'm here, getting fucked by strangers, so I can stay alive. I'm not giving up. I'm keeping myself alive. You're just like Dakota, thinking you need to save me, like you're God or some shit! Well, you can't. He tried and look what happened! He's fucking dead and I'm even worse off cuz now I know I had a chance for it to be different. But now it's gone and—"

"I'm not God," she satiated firmly, not fighting. "I'm not all-powerful or all-knowing. I can't save you. No one can. We have to save ourselves now."

Nathan could feel the pieces inside him sharp and slicing. He was too broken to save himself, and with Dakota gone—

The door opened suddenly and one of the Savior's guards appeared. "The Savior wants you."

With no other choice, he went.

He knocked on the Savior's door, came inside when ordered, and sat on the bed.

The Savior sneered. "On your knees. I'm not your angel. I don't want to see your face."

Nathan froze. No one wanted to see his face—not the Savior, not the butcher, not the guards or the farmers or the traders or any of the men he had let fuck him over the last eighteen months. They didn't want to see his face or hear what he had to say. They didn't want to hold him and fall asleep afterward. They didn't want to kiss him or laugh with him or just talk to him.

Dakota was the only one who wanted any—all—of those things. None of those fucks mattered, but every kiss with Dakota had been special. What they'd had together was real and Nathan had given up on Dakota, given up on himself, by going back to this life.

"No."

The Savior raised both eyebrows, not as part of a scheme, but because he was honestly surprised. "What do you mean, 'no'?"

Nathan got to his feet, a fire in his eyes that the Savior had never before seen, a light he had thought he'd quashed completely. "No, I won't let you fuck me. No, you don't own me. No, I'm not staying here."

The Savior gave a sharp, humorless laugh. "Where will you go? You're a whore and you always will be. There's nothing for you out there."

"Dakota's out there."

"Dakota's dead."

"Maybe."

"Not 'maybe'. For sure!" The Savior had lost his cool demeanor, suddenly afraid that Nathan was about to take his power away from him. "He's barely recognizable, beaten to death and left in the woods to rot, just another angelic casualty!"

Nathan's breath hitched. "How do you know that?"

"I'm the Savior. I control everything."

"Not me, not anymore."

"I do! I control you! I killed off your precious angel and you came crawling back to me, begging on your knees for me to fuck you and protect you!"

Nathan's eyes went wide and he couldn't breathe. The Savior … no … "You bastard!" He leapt forward, knocking the Savior to the ground, and straddled him, holding a hand to the Savior's throat. "You killed him!"

The Savior laughed breathlessly, the angel in Nathan terrifying him just as much as the sudden threat, but fought to remain in control. He was the Savior. He controlled everyone and everything. "You can't kill me."

"You think so? I've killed a lot of people—I can add you to the group."

"But you won't—you need me. You need me to keep you safe, to give you a purpose."

"My life meant nothing to you," Nathan spat, his hand gripping instead of resting threateningly.

"What about Civilization? The people here need me. If you kill me, you kill them."

Nathan shook his head. "They just think they need you. Anyone could do what you do and do it better. Amber can read signs before you even see them. She can prophesize for the community."

The Savior gasped for air. He was running out of excuses for Nathan to let him live.

Nathan gripped his throat harder and the Savior clutched uselessly at Nathan's arm. As thin as Nathan was, he was still stronger, and for the first time, they both knew it. "You are never going to touch me again. I'm not your toy. I'm not yours. God will judge me, not you."

The Savior's eyes went wide in terror, his fear so palpable that Nathan thought that he could get high from it. It scared him, just how much he wanted the Savior to suffer, how much he wanted to hurt him.

The Savior began to cry beneath him, terror overwhelming and pulling him apart, breaking him down, even as he begged, promising never to fuck Nathan again, offering him anything he wanted.

Nathan couldn't sink to the Savior's level, wouldn't allow himself to torture another the way he had allowed the Savior to torture him. He couldn't and he wouldn't. Hadn't Dakota showed him that he was better than this? Hadn't he tried to show Dakota the same?

"You will never hurt anyone again."

Reaching up to a small table, Nathan grabbed the lamp and slammed it into the Savior's temple.

It killed him instantly.

~~*

Nathan said goodbye to Amber and wished her luck with the community, before setting out. He couldn't stay in Civilization, couldn't face the people or the horrible memories. Most importantly, Dakota wasn't out there. He was somewhere beyond the walls and Nathan would find him, alive or dead.

~~*

Three days later, almost two weeks longer than he had expected and told Nathan, Dakota was returning to Civilization, bruised and battered, but alive—which would surprise the Savior, no doubt. He'd been captured, beaten, and had had to fight his way out of a stronghold of a camp, but he'd done it. Nathan needed him and he needed Nathan—there was nothing that could keep him away.

A few days walking distance beyond Civilization, he flew over a familiar-looking body. When he landed, he realized that it was Nathan.

"No ... " he whispered, stumbling in shock. He had forced himself to prepare for the worst, for Nathan to have been brutalized by the townsmen, fucked again by the Savior, but to find him dead beyond the walls? Dakota dropped to his knees, reached out to touch Nathan's face. It was then that Nathan stirred, exhausted eyes cracking open and filling with surprise and wonder.

"Are we dead?"

Dakota just shook his head, pressing his lips tight together to hold back tears of relief and fear. Nathan carefully sat up, and Dakota choked out, "How?" How are you? How are you here? How are you alive?

"I came looking for you," Nathan said softly, voice cracked and dry. "I couldn't stay in Civilization without you there. I killed the Savior. I had—"

"You killed the Savior?" Dakota's tear-filled eyes were wide.

"I had to. I had to do it. I couldn't let him live after what he did to me, after what he did—tried to do—to you. I couldn't."

Dakota wrapped Nathan in a tight hug, letting the tears fall now that he had Nathan safely in his arms.

"I'm sorry," he whispered some time later.

"For what?"

Dakota pulled back and looked away from Nathan's eyes. "I … I thought that when I didn't come back, you'd … "

"I did. I did at first and I'm sorry. I gave up. I went back to him. I went back to who I was before." His eyes grew stronger, more self-assured. "Then I remembered what you said, that I had to save myself. I couldn't stay there and be nothing, not when I'd seen what it could be like with you, not when you could have been alive out here."

Dakota hugged him again. "God, you're so strong. All this time … I never … " He pulled back. "If you can be this strong, if you can save yourself, I can, too, if you'll help me."

"Always."

Always. Dakota liked the sound of that. "I'll take you to that angel community. I don't know what they'll think of us, but we can start over there. I'll take you there with me." He realized then that he didn't make decisions for Nathan anymore, that Nathan was no longer taking anyone's orders. "If you want to, that is."

Nathan smiled. "I'm ready to start over. With you."

Dakota smiled back.

It took the better part of two weeks to find the city, but when they did, it was everything they'd ever dreamed it could be. Children ran in the streets—Nathan couldn't remember the last time he'd seen a child—while men and women worked side by side. Dakota held his hand tightly.

Nathan had thought he would be terrified in the presence of angels, thought he would feel lowly and worthless and wretched. He'd thought they would look down on him for what he'd done ... But if they were here, if they were no longer in the Lord's army, then they had made the same choice he had. The other events of his past might be uglier than theirs, but the events that led to their departure from the army was the same. He held his head high beside Dakota, feeling stronger than ever before.

They were met by a young woman with bright red hair and a man with bottomless brown eyes. The pair introduced themselves as Sara and Ben, the founders of the community. They were welcomed and informed that they would have to work hard to keep the community alive and well. The wellbeing of the community was everyone's responsibility.

When Dakota told the founders what community they had lived in, Ben's gaze immediately turned to Nathan. When Nathan looked into Ben's eyes, he recognized something in them, and realized that Ben knew and understood. He nodded once, confirming their shared history, and noticed when Sara reached out to link her fingers with Ben's. "What happened before is no one's business but yours," she told Nathan firmly. "We don't condone that here. No one owns anyone else. We belong to ourselves and whoever we choose to share ourselves."

Later that night, in the safety of their new home, Nathan and Dakota made love for the first time in freedom. It was a fresh start, a rebirth. They could choose to leave the past behind, allow it to have shaped and formed them, but not allow it to control their future.

"I love you," Nathan whispered, knowing it was the first time he had said those words.

"I love you, too."

"What she said, about belonging to ourselves? I belong to me. No one owns me or controls me. But I choose to give myself to you, Dakota. Forever." They smiled together, watching as one world ended and a new one began.

On Wings Not My Own

Evie Kiels

Prologue

Dowd leaned against the door jamb, watching the captured angel in awe. The stone room was so dimly lit by the torch in Dowd's hand that he could barely make out the prisoner's features. His white hair glowed, but the rest of the prisoner was in shadow. Dowd sighed. Surely nothing was as beautiful as this heavenly creature of God. Even his name, Sobal, was both gentle and fearsome. Sobal moved and the chains dragged and chinked as he tested their strength.

"How long are you going to stand there, *Bishop* Dowd?" The venom in the angel's voice was surprising. God was merciful and just—not angry. Why would He give such a human emotion to His holy emissaries? Never mind, it was not for Dowd to question.

The angel looked down upon him, even though he was chained to the ground and Dowd stood tall above. It was proper, of course, that the angel should be so superior. Dowd was far beneath this magnificent being of God. Dowd mentally shook himself from his contemplation of awe and bowed. "I am honored that you know my name."

"I make it my business to know those who are a threat to me."

Dowd walked into the room and lowered himself to sit on the damp floor in front of the angel. He wasn't a threat to the angel, not in the slightest. In time, Sobal would come to understand that. Dowd simply needed his cooperation to gain credibility with the Assembly of Bishops. Then he'd be granted a city, and the city would grow. The people would come, and he could share the beauty and teachings of God with them. Who better than a creature of God to want the same thing? It was such a pity the angel granted cooperation so reluctantly.

"I know this must seem a terrible inconvenience to you," Dowd said. "You have my most heartfelt and sincere apologies." Sobal raised his face and the light fell upon his body. No emotion was present, only a sneer of condescension. His chest was bare except for the stained cloth that wrapped around his torso and flattened his wings to his back. Dowd decided to extend an olive branch. "May I undo your bindings?"

"Do not touch me." Sobal rattled the chains attached to his wrists.

Dowd shook his head in awe. Sobal must be in terrible pain with the bindings still in place. Mortification of the flesh was something even Dowd could not tolerate. He was very lucky to have acquired such a holy being. "Very well. The shackles will be removed in a month. You can unbind yourself then."

The chains rattled constantly and with increasing volume. "I'm not alone, you know."

Dowd suppressed the urge to laugh. That would have been rude and inappropriate in the presence of a holy creature. "Of course not. I am here with you, and you will always be in my thoughts." Dowd cocked his head to the side as if in thought. "But you mean your boy?"

"Aive. Yes, I mean Aive."

Dowd nodded in agreement. "Of course. We took care of Aive."

The first hint of genuine emotion crossed the creature's beautiful face. "What did you do to—if you killed him, I swear, wrath unlike you've ever known shall rain down up—"

"No, no." Dowd raised his hands and bowed his head. "To kill is a mortal sin. We helped him go home." And what a chore that had been. He'd had to call in every favor owed for the resources to deal with that particular thorn.

"He will find me."

"I very much doubt that, your eminence."

"He will."

"In the unlikely event that your boy was to show up, it will not matter. By that time, you will have seen the wisdom of my plan and agreed to aid me."

Sobal's eyes widened. He tensed, but the fear was quickly replaced by a mask of ennui, and he relaxed. He could feign optimism, but they both knew that after a year or so in the cave, Sobal would break. Then Dowd would have his holy slave well in hand, and it would be too late for anyone, much less a merchant-class boy, to steal his heavenly creature of God.

Six months later ...

Aive sat in his chair. The back faced the fire and, as a result, the chair warmed to a comfortable and cozy cocoon. He loved curling up within its arms and wings where he felt safe and cradled. In this chair was the only place he could snatch this small bit of calm.

Across the room, his sister quietly hummed to herself while flipping through the store's account books. Lina closed the book with a quiet thud and her humming stopped. "What are you thinking over there, so dull and mopey?"

Aive lifted his head and uncurled his body. He had been thinking about his most recent dream. He looked at her. Her lips drew into a thin line, and her eyes bored into him. He sighed and composed the words in his head. When he thought he had the right ones to do the dream justice, he took a breath and spoke.

"Last night I dreamt of the ocean. Its blue waters stretching from the land to the sky. I dreamt I had wings that carried me from here in the plains, west over the desert, over mountains, over forests, and finally to a massive city pinched between mountains and sea. The wings took me over the water. I could smell the salt in the air, feel it stick on my skin. There were gulls and sea birds fishing. I even saw a pod of whales. But then the wings were gone, and I was falling."

The dream had profoundly disturbed Aive for reasons he couldn't name. It set off an emptiness in him that festered and ate at the core of his being. Even now, at this very minute, he needed to understand it, fill the terrible chasm gnawing at his insides, and vanquish it. Instead he took a deep breath, trying to calm and soothe the panic bubbling below his thin facade of calm.

Lina, his sister and sometimes friend, sat silently, running her finger along the shell of her ear—a sign she was deep in thought. "Do you think," she said slowly, "that you were actually there?"

Aive shook his head slowly. "That's absurd. The ocean is a six-month journey. How could I get there and back here in just a year and not even remember it?"

Lina shrugged. "You were gone for a year."

"I think if I were to go to the ocean, I'd stay a little longer than three minutes before turning around to get back in that amount of time."

"Maybe you should go." She tapped her pencil slowly on the table. "If you've never been, but you're having vivid dreams ..." Lina looked down at the table.

Aive had thought of that. That something waited for him at the edge of the land. "It's so far away. I don't know if I'd ever make it home again."

"Is that so bad? No one expected to see you again after you left last time. Yet you're here and ... Are you even happy?"

Aive didn't need to think about his answer, but he paused anyway, out of courtesy. "No."

Chapter One

Four months later ...

Aive stood hidden in the shade of a large tree, observing the small village he was supposed to pass through. It had been over a month since the dreams had taken him through any sort of community. Normally they steered him around villages and, after the unfortunate incident when he had gone to one anyway, he was happy to follow the dreams and avoid strangers as much as possible. However, this time, they told him to go through the small farming community, and he was desperately in need of supplies anyway.

The sun was high in a cloudless blue sky, and few people were outside in the heat of the afternoon. None were on the dusty dirt road between the edge of the forest and the village gate. Heat rose in waves off the pebbles covering the ground, and no trees grew along the road to provide any kind of shade from the bright sun. The grass flanking the road was yellow, brittle, and dry. Maybe he should wait out the sun, take a nap and make sure this was what he was supposed to do, but it would be nice to talk with people. Share a meal with someone. Joke.

His pack was weighted down with goods to trade: animal pelts, dried meat, and dried mushrooms. He'd even found some raw amber in the ridges of the last mountain range he passed through. He planned to keep the amber to sell at the coast, but unloading the rest would be a great relief. He would trade it for food and two new sets of clothing. Aive adjusted his pack, trying to distribute the weight better, and then touched the blade on his side for reassurance.

Wariness of people was another one of the many things that had changed between the hole in his life and now. Before, he'd have seen the village and run to it. He had loved meeting new people, seeing new places. He touched the blade again, adjusted the hilt, and then began walking to the village gate.

The top of his head quickly heated and sweat dripped down his forehead and neck. After several minutes traveling on the open path, he stopped and set his pack down, scowling at himself. He'd been traveling through forest for so long that his hat was buried below all of his other possessions. He rummaged around the cloth and pelts and dried food until he felt the coarse brim and pulled out the bent and misshapen hat. Aive put it on his head and sighed. The brim in front was bent like the steep roof of a house. One more thing he needed to replace. At least his eyes were protected from the harsh glare of the sun.

He sneered in disgust at his spare clothing as he stuffed them back into the pack. They were torn, faded, and stretched—not at all respectable. The clothes he wore were in no better shape. He had run out of thread weeks ago, so several rips gaped open and exposed his skin. Luckily, traveling had made his skin dark brown with the sun so he wouldn't burn. Old Aive, before he'd woken up after a year of events unknown, would have burnt and blistered. New Aive? He was a little more impervious to the sun. He hoisted his pack onto his back and walked on.

Fear and excitement warred within him. People! The high heat of the day was beginning to wane, and the inhabitants of the village were venturing outside to resume their activities. There were no brawls in plain view going on, which Aive took to be a very good sign. Children ran through the streets playing a game with a bushel of straw and several long sticks. Adults walked with purpose, deftly avoiding the weaving children and flying bundle of straw.

Carts pulled by large draft horses left the village and turned towards the fields to the east. Fields upon fields upon fields stretched out, flourishing with hearty crops. Aive was surprised that such a small village maintained such a large tract of land. Provided there were no disasters, they would have an excellent yield come harvest.

Harvest. By that time, Aive would be at the coast and the gnawing emptiness that consumed him would be gone. He hoped.

A man passed through the village gate and walked with intent towards Aive. He carried his rotund figure with a self-assurance that could only belong to a sheriff or a bishop. Aive sighed. Of course the villagers had sent someone to interrogate him. He kept walking and said a quick prayer that this village—and the welcome committee—were friendly.

"Well met, traveler." The man, still a good distance away, called out and waved a hand.

Aive waved and gave the appropriate reply of "Well met" in return.

Far too soon their paths met, and he found himself standing in front of a man dressed in the modest black attire of a bishop. "What brings you to our village, traveler?"

This welcome committee asked questions first—another good sign. "Just passing through," Aive said. "I have goods to trade and supplies to obtain." He looked for hints of malice in the bishop, but found none. The presence of the bishop was a surprise. Villages this small had, at best, a priest. Usually, though, it was a poor acolyte training for his final orders who was stationed in such a remote place.

"Where are you going?" The bishop took up most of the small road and blocked the village from view. He clearly had no intention of moving until he was satisfied with Aive and the answers he provided. He also had a mace attached to his belt. It was part of the uniform, so not out of the ordinary or particularly threatening ... but it was still a mace, and it could still maim.

Aive smiled and relaxed as he tried to appear non-threatening and at ease. "The coast."

The bishop whistled. "You've a long way to go."

"Not as far as I've come." Aive held out his hand. "The name's Aive."

The bishop grasped his hand. "Mine is Gray."

"Bishop Gray. It is an honor to meet you."

"How long do you plan on staying?"

"A day? Two? Just long enough to make some trades."

The bishop clapped him hard on the back. "I hope we can provide what you need. Welcome to our village, young Aive."

Aive mentally snorted. Young. He'd recently spent his twenty-sixth birthday trying to cross a river. Damned if he could remember birthday twenty-five. Young was behind him and moving farther with every step westward.

They walked to the gate together chatting almost companionably. Aive talked of his travels, and Gray of the village life. Once in the village, Gray led him along more dusty paths and past several merchant shops, the market, and finally to the inn.

Aive got a room for the night. He hadn't had a proper bath in weeks, so he took advantage of the inn's bathing chambers. After the bath and a shave, his limbs were warm and languid and his mind was calm, and once he lay on the bed with the softest blankets he had felt in what seemed like an eternity, he couldn't bring himself to move again.

The sun was setting and the light growing dim. He should get up. Get some supper. Talk with the locals and find who would be best to trade with. But he didn't. Instead, his eyes grew heavy.

~~*

Aive dreamed.

He flew high above the ground. This was nothing new. After the first few terrifying dreams, he looked forward to the freedom of flight while his body slept. He loved the feel of being aloft and soaring through the azure sky. He loved the ability to see far across the land, and the feel of the wind running through his hair and rushing over his arms.

His body was light as a feather and he soared and swooped on the whims of the wind and the power of his wings. During moments like this giddiness overflowed his heart, and the emptiness that plagued him during his waking hours was blessedly absent. He laughed with the sheer joy of life and spun in the air.

It was a pristine spring day. The air was cool, but the sun was warm. Verdant green fields stretched out with the new growth of crops. Little blue flowers dotted the landscape in patches, and pink blossoms on the trees made them look like large balls of sugar wisp candy.

Below him was the forest that, awake, he'd come out of the day before. He slowed as he approached the village. Several birds swooped up and away. His winged friends often joined him for spots of play, and he enjoyed their company. He spun in the air and dove down then up, veered left then right, around and through the tiny birds. Nature embraced his presence in the air, and he wanted to give joy back to her small creatures that flocked around him.

A beat of his wings and the weather changed in a snap. That often happened in his dreams. Where a moment ago it had been a warm spring day, now it was winter and the fields and rooftops of the village were white with fresh fallen snow. He thought it quite strange after he woke, but in the dream world it was natural. As if it should have been winter a moment after spring. He flew over the village slowly, looking at the people and considering whether or not to land. He saw a man below, tattered clothing marking him as a traveler, who looked very much like Aive.

He decided not to stop and continued to fly westward, instead. After he had passed over the village, the perfect spring day from before slid back into reality, replacing the icy grasp of winter with a quick shock of warmth. He was going to the coast, and he wanted to follow the North Road. He angled slightly so he would meet up with the road that would eventually take him to North High Pass. He flew over a herd of wild horses and slowed to watch them run. He followed them all the way until the horses crossed the North Road, then he left his horse friends and followed the road. He flew over a forest, veering towards the mountain range. When the flat land transitioned to steep terrain, he ascended with the slope of the mountain. The gray and brown path was marred momentarily by a colorful caravan slowly plodding their way up the mountain.

The chill of the high air made him nostalgic for home—the cold, crisp mountain-top city where he had grown up. After five years in the lowlands, he was ready to return. He only had to go to High City to make one final report, and then he would be allowed to return home. His missed his parents and friends and longed for the spiritual connection to Nature that the humans in the lowlands failed to recognize, despite its constant presence in their lives. It pained him to watch as the humans perverted the gifts Nature gave to them. And, selfish though it was, he was tired of hiding among them. It hurt. It was annoying.

He flew onward, the sense of nostalgia growing profound. Upon reaching the summit of the mountain, he descended to a rock ledge and settled down for a brief rest. The sky was streaked with swirls of orange and pink. Below him, High City sprawled obscenely between the mountain range and the ocean. He wondered, not for the first time, why the humans found it necessary to squeeze into every possible inch of the land and gobble more of it up with each passing year. The city was visible from his mountain-home, and the sprawl saddened all of them greatly.

Soon he would no longer have to witness the humans' follies. Soon he would go home.

He pulled an apple out of the small pouch attached to his belt. His right arm lay across his leg and his hand hung limply towards the ground. He studied the black lines on his skin. It was one of the more complicated birthmarks he'd seen among his people. It curved and traveled along his hand in a way that reminded him of brisk wind. The elders said it meant he would be a great man and would bring fortune to himself and their people. He thought the elders were being fanciful rather than rational. He made a fist with his hand to watch the lines pull taut. Then he made a fist with the other hand, frowning at the blank canvas of skin.

He had hoped to find a partner by now, someone to live and love with, who would place his mark on their hand and give him a mark in return. As soon as he got home he'd ask his parents to find him a companion. If he was going to find one on his own, he'd have done so by now, and he was lonely.

He was uneasy about returning to High City, but it was the last hurdle to home. He couldn't pinpoint the source of the bad feeling, but it nagged at him all the same. The chill of the air, combined with the sweetness of the apple, helped to soothe his anxiety. A small mountain bird swooped in and perched above him on a rock. It chirped happy notes, telling him about the wind and the ocean and the sun.

~~*

Aive woke.

Bright shafts of light from the rising sun spilled into Aive's room and illuminated all but the darkest of shadows. The soft mattress cradled his limbs, still weary despite a full night's sleep. Dust motes swirled lazily in the sunbeams, birds sang outside. It was such a lovely morning, and loveliest of all was the comfortable bed. Aive breathed deeply and smiled. He looked forward to a day of company and staying in one place for more than an hour or two.

He swung his legs over the edge of the bed and sat up. Pulling his pack to him, he extracted the rough map that had been his companion for the last four months. His direction had been more or less due west, and he'd covered several inches since the last time he'd been in a village. His dreams occasionally had him detour north or south to avoid rivers, gorges, villages, or sometimes to meet those obstacles head on.

He found the place where he believed himself to be. There was no village noted on the map, but the forest was there. A small line indicated a road that cut diagonally northwest to meet with the North Road, which ascended to become the North High Pass and then descended into High City on the coast. It wasn't the easiest route to the city. The easiest route was to continue due west, take the easier Middle Pass, and go north on the other side of the mountains. But the dreams directed him north, so north he would go. He was so close he could almost smell the salty ocean air, or so he imagined. One more month and it would be a reality.

He conducted his morning ablutions and then rang the bell for breakfast. While eating the most delicious meal he'd had in weeks—due in large part to the fact he hadn't made it himself—he wrote a short letter to his sister. The letter might reach her. It might not. Mail was uncertain this far from his home in the Eastern Plains.

He arrived at the mail office shortly after noon. A young man—a boy really—sat behind the counter reading. So engrossed was the boy in his tattered old book, he failed to realize that Aive stood at the counter. After waiting a good three minutes, he took the "Ring Bell for Service" sign at its word and flicked the top. The ding echoed off the bare walls in the empty room. The boy jumped and fell forward off his stool.

"S-sorry, sir. Didn't see you there."

Obviously. Aive affected a benign smile and the boy relaxed.

The boy fidgeted with papers on the counter, probably trying to appear productive. "Traveling through? Have a letter to send home?" he asked.

"I am. And I have a letter to send back to the Eastern Plains."

The boy's eyebrows rose into the uneven black bangs hanging over his brow. "Wow, that's ... uhm, I need to look up how much that'll be." He rummaged below the counter and emerged with a massive tome of loosely bound papers. He flipped through the pages once, and then once again. "Well ..." he said, running his finger over rows of letters and numbers. "The closest I have is the Eastern Coast ... and that's five coin. So ... five coin."

Five coin. Heaven high, the price had gone up since the last mail office. Aive extracted the necessary amount from his coin purse and placed the money on the counter.

The boy leaned forward and whispered, "Don't tell anyone I said, but nice tattoo."

Aive looked at the black shapes inked into his left hand. "It is. Don't remember getting it, though." Aive pulled back his hand and hid it from sight.

"Can't imagine not remembering something like that."

Aive shrugged. He hated talking about the lost time and the absence of memories. Tattoos weren't common, and the people who got them were considered a little off in the head. What in heaven had he been thinking to do such a thing? Old Aive would never have done that. Not only would his family and friends have been scandalized, *he* would have been scandalized.

Sadness washed through Aive. He directed his thoughts away from the mark and onto ... Lina. Yes, Lina, who was both his sister and friend. She hadn't minded the tattoo. She never mentioned it because she, at least, seemed to understand how much it bothered him and how much more acute the emptiness became when he dwelled upon it.

Lina, Lina, Lina.

It didn't work. Aive eyed the tattoo, and his good mood seeped out of him and into those black lines. He sighed.

The boy took the letter Aive had set onto the counter and placed it in a small empty cubby on the back wall. "Well, um. The carrier comes by for letters every other week. Doubt it'll get to the Eastern Plains anytime soon."

Aive forced himself to give the lad a smile. "I appreciate your honesty. Enjoy your reading." Aive nodded at the book and left.

He no longer wished to socialize with the citizens of the village. He changed his plans to include only trading, eating, sleeping, and leaving. The quicker, the better.

The villagers were kind and fair. He was able to unload all of his tradable items and get all of his necessary supplies in return. He even got rid of his old clothes, giving them to the innkeeper, who was happy to have them for cleaning rags.

After one more night in a comfortable bed and one more delicious breakfast, he resumed his long walk to the ocean.

~~*

Aive sat on the summit of a relatively short mountain. It wasn't the same spot where he'd sat in his dream, but the view was equally as stunning. He bit into a pear—the last piece of food in his pack. He'd met a traveler earlier in the day and traded all of his dried meats for fresh fruit. The succulent pear was a welcome change from the salty dried foods that had sustained him through the last leg of his journey.

In the distance to the north, there stood a peak at least twice as high as any other in the mountain range. Was it possible that was the peak Heaven sat on? The prestige of High City came not from its pristine sandy white beaches, nor from its majestic mountains, but from its proximity to Heaven, home of God's angels.

If he couldn't find what he lacked in High City, maybe he'd try Heaven next.

But one journey at a time. The current one was almost over. He could *see* the ocean. In fact, most of his view was of ocean. The city packed in from the base of the mountain range to the coast, and its lights shone far to the north and south. How it was able to be governed as a single city, Aive couldn't guess. It would take a week to walk from the south end to the north.

He still wasn't sure why he needed to come to the Western Ocean, but with each mile closer to the coast, the more the panic and the emptiness in his heart receded, and the unease became tolerable to the point where it might almost be possible to be content with life. Almost.

The dreams had changed, too. If Aive had to pick a word, he'd say they were more urgent. In the beginning, they were slow, luxurious flights west. Now, they were still fun, they were still joyous, but they were *fast*. They took him faster and faster over greater distances to the city. As if that would enable him to walk faster. It didn't.

He idly looked at the tattoo on his left hand. Even that didn't distress him as much anymore. Maybe the stress of the journey had dulled his feelings towards everything. The black lines swirled in a way that reminded him of clouds and snow. He had yet to come across anyone with similar markings. Then again, he'd only crossed paths with maybe two other people with markings on their skin. He wasn't artistic enough to come up with the design, or even to conceive of getting such a design. Where had it come from? What had possessed him to have it done in the first place?

He licked the sticky sweet pear juice from his hands, enjoying one last moment of sweetness and peace before gathering his things and preparing to resume his trek. He had to make it to the city that night. Fall had moved in, and night on the mountain would be too cold for him to safely sleep.

~~*

Aive dreamed.

The dream felt so real. It always did. He wasn't traveling anymore. He wasn't high above the ground. He wasn't even outside. Instead, he was in a dark room that smelled like the air never moved. It was cold but so humid he could feel the air pressing against his skin. He reached out and his fingers encountered chilled rock slick with condensation. He was in a cave.

"Hello?" His voice echoed and faded. He doubted anyone would answer him. Who in their right mind would be there?

As his eyes adjusted to the dim interior, he realized there was an ever so slight glow coming from … where? He couldn't find the source of the light, but somehow he could see. He was standing in front of a door. He tried the handle, but it was locked. He looked around for a key, felt along the wall and on the floor. There was no key, just uneven rock with rivulets of water running down the dips and crevices.

He turned around and walked. And walked, and walked, and walked. And as he walked, the light went away and he could only hope not to trip as he put one foot in front of the other in pitch black.

~~*

Aive woke.

Despite the chill of the dream, he was covered in sweat. At some point in the night he'd thrown the covers off. They spilled off the bottom of the bed and onto the floor, creating a pool of white that stood out against the dark floor. He leaned over and pulled the sheets over him. Through the window he could see the predawn light glowing over the mountains.

He was at a loss. The dreams had guided him quite well thus far. Now, however, they put him in the dark, and he wasn't sure how he was supposed to go to the dark place. He was too awake and too unsettled to return to sleep. Since the dream hadn't told him where to go, or how to find his destination, he would continue on to the ocean.

He ate a hearty breakfast and set off across the city. Along the way, he traded the goods he'd picked up since the last village for coin and a new hat. Another difference between before and after: Old Aive never wore hats. New Aive never ventured out into the sun without a good hat. He looked like an idiot, but he didn't care. Was it an important detail? He had no idea. Aive only knew that it was a difference.

It took all day to cross the city. The buildings had no space between them. The streets were narrow and filled with merchant stalls and shoppers. Countless peddlers knew exactly what Aive needed to improve his life, mood, and power in society, and, lucky him, they could sell it to him at a discount. Throngs of people shouting and pushing in their hurry to go about their own daily tasks kept hindering his progress, and he had to push through the hot, sweaty bodies before reaching the quieter west neighborhoods and eventually, the ocean.

He stood on the beach, his bare feet in the foamy waves washing on the shore. He had hoped that the simple act of standing in the cold blue water would cure him of the emptiness and the panic. It didn't. But what a sight! Never had Aive seen so much water. It was intimidating but so soothing. The salt smell was the same as in the dreams and so was the sticky, humid feel on his skin.

Aive enjoyed the wet sand between his toes and the antics of a sea bird running back and forth along the beach. He stayed to watch the sunset, and then he set off for an inn on the ocean front. He wanted to hear the waves while he slept.

~~*

Aive dreamed.

The city was bustling. The high heat of the hot sun meant it was summer. His arms were still pale, though; so pale that he hid them under long sleeves. On his head was a wide-brimmed hat that blocked the sun from his face and neck and kept his skin cool.

He had no goal, no destination. He was out enjoying the day and a brief respite before returning home once and for all. He told himself that many years from now he'd look back fondly on moments like this. It would be interesting to see if in years that actually happened. The only taint on the day was that his back ached, but he was well used to that.

He walked idly through the market and bought a ripe pear from a lad behind several small mountains of fruit. He bit into the most perfect pear he had ever tasted and continued on through the market. A trickle of juice flowed down his hand and he licked it up. He wished he had bought more than one because the fruit served only to whet his appetite. He changed his task from that of idle observation to a search for an inn or tavern. He walked past a tavern that had a roach scurrying inside, and then an inn that he knew from experience to contain employees who were unsavory. Finally, he found a respectable looking place tucked in the recesses of a neighborhood. The aroma of bread and rosemary drifted out the door and he went in.

A harried woman told him to sit wherever, so he chose a seat by a large window cracked open to let air in. He set his hat aside and gazed out the window, observing the humans walking slowly and looking straight ahead or to the ground. Occasionally one would face the sky. Smart human.

A throat cleared near his seat. "Excuse me, sir, would you like to hear our menu, or would you like me to come back?"

He turned his head and smiled pleasantly at the— himself? His body went tight with shock and an unexplained terror. He, the other him, smiled serenely at him as if nothing were amiss.

Something was wrong. He needed to wake.

He needed to wake now.

Wake. Up.

Now!

Chapter Two

Aive shot out of his bed and scrambled across the floor like a crab. What in the name of Heaven? A deep sense of loss and sadness trudged through his body like a massive invading force; it was oppressive and heavy, and when it had consumed him completely tears sluiced down his face and neck, and sobs erupted uncontrollably.

What in God's name was he doing in his own dream?

Pieces started fitting together, even through the consuming sadness, and for the first time he didn't want to know. He didn't want to analyze. He didn't want to understand, but the pieces knit together into understanding anyway.

The long, pale limbs. The odd dressing habits. The flying. *Flying.*

He looked at his own sun-darkened arms streaked with tears. These were his arms, dark, lanky, but muscled. *Not* pale and not thin. He hiccupped as the tears slowed to a steady trickle.

They weren't his lost memories. They weren't his dreams. They were someone else's. Which made no sense, yet he knew with certainty that it was true. His weird thoughts in the dreams were not his own, nor were his odd actions. Another wave of sadness and loss and pain engulfed him and the sobs returned. He needed it to stop, needed everything to stop. To sleep. To not dream. *Oh God, please no more dreams.*

He crawled in a wretched heap back to his bed, tears falling and shoulders heaving. He pulled the quilt around him and wrapped himself in a dark cocoon and prayed selfish prayers: Let the pain go away. Let the dreams stop. Let everything stop.

Eventually the darkness took him and, mercifully, he had no more dreams.

In the morning, Aive woke, overheated and uncomfortable. He was soaked in sweat and his hair was matted and crusty. He tried to throw the blankets off, but he was trapped. He pushed out at his jail in vain. It took several minutes of struggle before he managed to extract himself limb by limb, rolling around and out of the blanket.

The desolation was gone. He poked and prodded at his feelings and, yes, it was definitely gone.

He finally had a destination, and he was utterly terrified to go there. Even more terrifying, however, was the prospect of having that dream again. He knew the market he—the dreamer—had passed through. He—himself—had passed through it the previous day on the way to the ocean.

He rose, shaky and weak, stretching out his stiff and sore muscles. He took a towel and a fresh change of clothes to the bath. The soak helped his body. It also helped take away the edge of panic that still lingered on the periphery. The shock of seeing himself. The inexplicable, terrifying reaction. The loss.

He got out of the bath and put on something simple and presentable. The area where he was headed seemed too nice to tolerate his ragged clothing.

It took an hour to return to the market from the dream. The fruit stall wasn't there, and it was the wrong time of the year. The produce and meat available were appropriate for fall, not spring. Aive's stomach growled unhappily, but he walked on, intent on finding the inn. It took him an additional hour to locate it buried in a nearby neighborhood.

He wasn't sure what to expect. What if he actually had been there before? Would these people know him? This could confirm whether or not the dreams were real memories or imagination. His heart galloped as he stepped over the threshold.

"Aive!"

He swung his head in the direction of the voice. A plump woman behind the bar stared at him, her hands frozen around a mug and a dishcloth. An enormous giant of a man standing in the door to the kitchen had a similar expression, eyes wide and mouth hanging open.

The woman set the towel and mug on the bar. "Aive! Angels to Heaven, boy, where have you been?" The woman ran up and hugged him tightly. "You've never been gone *this* long."

"I ... " How would he even start to explain? "I'm sorry, but I don't remember you." Aive tensed for any number of possible reactions.

The woman stepped back, her hands lightly grasping his arms. As she looked at him, her head tilted to the side and a frown spread down her face. "It's me, Rachel. Don't you remember us?"

Aive shook his head. "I'm sorry. No."

Rachel guided him to the bar and up onto a stool. The man brought out a bowl of stew and a mug of water and set them in front of Aive. He inhaled his food while Rachel and the giant looked on with expressions of concern.

"Hey Aive! You're back." A young man, the same one who had sold him—the dreamer—the pear, bounded in from outside. "Where's Sobal?"

"Sobal?"

"Uh ... Yeah. Sobal." The kid cocked his head to the side. "You know, tall guy, long hair, white as a sheet, practically attached to you?"

A gentler version of the sadness rolled through him. "Sobal." The word sounded foreign to his ears, but it *felt* right. There was meaning there, somewhere. "Sobal."

The young man continued to look at him as if he'd completely lost his mind. Aive probably had.

"Paul," Rachel said to the young man. "Go get Aive's old room ready."

Aive held his hand up. "I couldn't possibly—"

"Nonsense, and if you need it, you can have your old job, too."

Aive considered the offer. It would be nice to have a place to stay while he dealt with the dreams. These people seemed nice. They seemed to care about him. "What exactly was my old job?"

"Oh, you helped where it was needed. Whenever you were around, at least! Served patrons, helped in the kitchens, cleaned a bit." She leaned forward, a twinkle in her eye. "We thought you wouldn't be back. I'll give you a raise?"

He had so many questions. Everything these people said only reinforced how much he didn't remember. "How long have I been gone?"

Rachel put her finger on her lip in thought. "We last saw you and Sobal, oh, what was it dear?"

"April." The giant nodded his head.

"That sounds about right." Rachel climbed up onto the next stool over. "So a year and a half ago?"

"And what about ..." He hesitated. "Sobal?"

"Same time." Rachel frowned and lines of worry creased her face. "So you don't remember Sobal, either? He's not with you?"

Aive shook his head. "I think ... I think I need to find him."

~~*

Aive dreamed.

He sat across the table from himself. His subconscious felt this was really bizarre, the dream self only felt annoyed. Like the Aive across the table was a bothersome, bratty burden.

The Aive across the table leaned forward with a grin on his face. "Sobal! Come on, it'll be fun."

He looked out the window. The sky was overcast; red and orange leaves floated down from oak trees. "It's going to rain." He could feel it.

"You don't like rain?"

He shrugged. "I prefer not to be rained on." Aive looked on the verge of a question, one Sobal probably didn't want asked. Not in public. Hopefully Aive knew that. The door opened, bringing a cool gust of air swirling through the room along with a young, haughty looking acolyte. This was the fourth time he'd seen that particular acolyte in a week. He was now positive the young man was following him.

Sobal angled and leaned his back into the wall. He set his elbow on the table and his ankle on his knee, trying to look casual. His disguise was fine. He wouldn't be recognized, but he still didn't want the acolyte to see him. Although, if the acolyte was following him, he probably already knew what Sobal was.

"What about after it rains?" Aive was annoyingly persistent today.

"Fine." He would say anything if it meant the brat would be quiet. Sobal kept his eyes on the acolyte. He wanted the acolyte to leave.

The dream changed.

Sobal followed Aive down the street. The air was crisp, cold, and snowflakes drifted down from the sky. His back ached. The left wing had shifted into an awkward position and was cutting into his skin. He really needed to redo his bindings.

They passed shops decorated for the winter holidays. Even the locksmith had decorated, which Sobal thought odd. What could a locksmith offer as a gift? A new trunk lock? Aive, however, didn't dismiss the place so idly. He veered off towards the window and examined the display case.

"What's caught your eye in there? Fancy key rings?" Sobal asked.

"Um ..." Aive looked around. "Don't really need one of those."

Sobal climbed a single step to stand behind Aive. He wrapped his arms around Aive's middle, leaning into the warmth and comfort of his body. The snow reminded him of home, and he wished for the hundredth time he and Aive were already there. But Aive, stubborn, *stubborn* Aive, wasn't ready, had places to go, legendary monuments to see. Sobal shifted, trying to adjust his bindings so they didn't hurt so much.

Aive huffed. "Sobal, you have got to stop that."

Sobal stilled. "Sorry." He kissed Aive's head and rubbed his cheek against the soft brown hair. In the window there were a couple of sturdy looking key rings. There were also lock picking sets and giant skeleton keys.

"Can we go home?" Aive asked. A desperation that Sobal loved to hear threaded through Aive's voice. He ground his hips back, as if Sobal needed extra persuasion. "Please?"

The dream changed.

He was in the cave again, staring at the door. The locked door. Dripping water in the distance. Darkness except for the glow that came from nowhere. He tried the handle, even though he knew it was locked.

~~*

Aive woke.

He ran to the fireplace, fumbled in the matchbox on the mantle for a stick, and then stuck it in the dying embers. The smell of sulfur filled the space and a small flame danced on the end of the matchstick. He lit two of the wicks in the large candle on his nightstand and picked up his journal and pencil.

He wrote down as much of the dreams as he could recall. No analysis, just recording. It was peculiar dreaming and writing as Sobal. Aive mined the dreams for information about the man he'd loved and forgotten. Some parts made him very uncomfortable. Like kissing himself. It was so very wrong. Although he was pleased to notice that Sobal enjoyed kissing him, which was an even weirder thought in a great series of very weird thoughts. Grateful though he was for every tidbit of information about Sobal and their former life together, what Aive wanted most of all was to see Sobal with his own eyes and touch him with his own hands.

After detailing as much as he could remember onto the pages, he read over the first dream. He had trouble identifying what was important there. Was it the autumn trees? Perhaps it was the unknown place where he had wanted to take Sobal. The rain? The uneasiness about the acolyte? Or was it the fact that Sobal thought he was a little twerp?

The second and the third dream—he needed to go to the locksmith. Locked door and a lock picking kit? Aive didn't have to be a genius to piece that together.

There was one last thing Aive puzzled over. Sobal's emotions of annoyance and irritation directed at the dream Aive had been strong. He wondered what had happened in the three or so months between autumn and winter to change Sobal's feelings so completely. It probably didn't matter, only the fact that they had changed was important. Sobal *loved* him. Ever since Aive had appeared in the dreams, they were filled with a pervasive sense of love and contentment. Aive desperately wanted those feelings and Sobal outside of those dreams.

Unfortunately, Aive had no idea where the cave was located. He had explored the coast soon after he'd arrived two weeks ago. There were at least a hundred entrances to caverns that went deep into the cliffs. He returned and picked a cavern to explore every couple of days, but so far he'd found nothing. He needed a hint. He needed directions. What he really needed was a map.

Aive opened the window curtain. The sun would rise soon. He was wide-awake, so he went to check if Rachel needed any help preparing breakfast.

~~*

It was going to rain. The sun had never quite burned through the early morning fog, and a slight but constant breeze rustled the orange and red leaves of the trees. Aive pulled on a thick jacket and grabbed his rain gear off a peg. The inn's morning rush was over and he was free for the remainder of the day.

He patted his side, touching his coin pouch and dagger. He left his room, shutting the door behind him. As he descended the back stairs, he peeked into the kitchen to make sure Rachel didn't need any more help. She waved him on, so on he went.

The weather was fast turning cold. The children running about were twice as puffed up with clothing as they had been just two weeks ago. Aive smiled to himself. He'd hated when his mother layered clothing on him as a child. She would get so mad when he returned in his undershirt and pants.

He began winding his way along the streets using the memory of the dream as a guide. People he'd met in the past couple of weeks waved and stopped to say hello. Aive talked politely with them until they moved on with their business, rushed by the gray, drooping clouds moving swiftly across the sky.

Aive reached the neighborhood square he and Sobal had gone to in the dream. This time, though, the storefronts were decorated in celebration of harvest.

Instead of fake cotton snow, little blocks of hay sat in windows and bright red leaves colored the displays. Aive had yet to visit the fields attached to the city, they were too far away, but the harvest had been good it seemed. High City was well prepared for the winter and maybe even the following one.

Aive climbed the three steps to the locksmith's door and hesitated. He wondered why the dream had directed to him to this particular shop. There was a locksmith three blocks from Rachel's inn. Aive shook his head. Oh well. At least the shop was on the way to the caves. He'd already walked half the distance to the coast and would go there afterwards to explore more.

He opened the door and stepped inside. Behind a counter, a red-haired man was hunched over a collection of metal parts. The door slammed shut behind Aive, and the man jumped, his hand flying over his heart. "Oh! Aive, sorry! You startled me." The man smoothed his vest in a nervous gesture. "Didn't think we'd see you again. Where have you been?"

Aive smiled, trying to hide his surprise at being remembered by name. He waited for the man to find calm. When he seemed sufficiently recovered, Aive said, "I need a lock pick."

Seemingly unperturbed that Aive completely ignored his question, the shopkeeper said, "What happened to the last one I gave you?"

Aive sighed. Apparently this was yet another person Aive had known well once upon a time. "I, err, lost it."

The man raised an eyebrow. "Too bad."

Aive watched as the man bent down, hefted a large box from behind the counter and dropped it next to the pile of parts with a loud *thunk*. "What have you and Sobal been doing this last year?"

"Traveling."

The shopkeeper rifled through the box and started setting pick sets in a pile to his left, not asking for any more details. Slowly he curled over into the box and his head was in danger of disappearing completely. "Ah hah!" The man's voice was muffled behind the thick wood. His thin, spindly arm emerged from the box, extended towards Aive, and in his hand was a very comprehensive lock picking set. Aive took the set. The man gripped the sides of the box and levered himself upright.

"There! That should do you just fine." The man looked at Aive, and then with a slight pout said, "Although the other one was better."

Aive wished he could remember that man's name, but he didn't want to lose the hour it would require to explain what had happened, so he'd pretend nothing was amiss. Aive turned the kit in his hand. He extracted small pieces of jagged metal and looked at them from every angle. They would work very well indeed. "This is great," Aive said. "How much?"

"Don't worry about it. I figure I owe you five times its worth for your help last year."

Aive shifted on his seat, a sense of unease moving through him. "I ... see. Thank you. That's very kind."

The man smiled. It was awkward not knowing what he had done to help the man out. He almost asked—almost, but the nagging distrust he had of *everyone* held him back. Instead, he placed the pick in an empty pocket and stood. "I must be on my way. It was great seeing you again."

"Stop by anytime, Aive. And bring Sobal with you next time. It would be good to catch up on old times."

When Aive found Sobal, he'd ask about this particular man. Assuming Sobal still had his memories. He must, right? If he sent the dreams, he must still remember.

~~*

Fat raindrops plopped on Aive's wide hat as he continued westward to the ocean. The streets were clearing fast, and soon Aive was alone, walking down the dark, dirt roads matted down from the rain. He was severely frustrated with the lack of progress in finding Sobal. It shouldn't take so long, and Sobal so clearly needed Aive to find him now. Last week, even. The clues from the dreams came in a slow trickle. Why couldn't they show him how to get to the cave? Why, after they had become so urgent, had they become so infuriatingly tedious?

Aive still anticipated and treasured every little detail. He'd picked up some interesting facts about Sobal in the dreams. Just the day before he had learned what Sobal's favorite soap was and had gotten some for himself, as well as few extra bars for when he found Sobal. A tiny detail, perhaps, but precious because there were so few.

Aive kicked a rock out of the road. It rolled and skittered to a stop in the gutter. Gradually homes and trees gave way to sand dunes and the ocean. He wandered north along the beach to where the cliffs began. The tide was low, so the beach was wide. Birds picked at the sand where little sea creatures had been abandoned by the water. At high tide, there would be no beach, only waves crashing against the rock face. After walking an unknown amount of time, he came across a large piece of driftwood embedded in the sand. He sat and wished that he'd brought lunch. Sobal would have had food. He always seemed to have a piece of fruit with him.

The air was thick with moisture, and the rain and humidity dampened and weighed down his hair. The clouds had broken in the distance, and blue was quickly overtaking the gray over the water. The ocean's rhythmic push and pull of water over the sand mesmerized Aive, and he inhaled the salty, fishy smell. Eventually, meaningful thoughts ceased, and he simply existed on the piece of driftwood. He was just another piece of debris scattered about the beach waiting for the tide to come in, cover him with water, and pull him back out to sea.

He shifted to lie down on the smooth, sea-bleached log. Dampness seeped through his jacket, but Aive ignored it. The clouds flew by overhead in translucent strands of gray. Eventually the gray became white and patches of blue shone through. Shadow and light alternated over his face. Warmth and chill, light and dark. And then, instead of clouds, there was a man.

Aive's hand flew to the hilt of his dagger. The man quickly stepped back. He cocked his head to the side and raised an eyebrow. "Well met, Aive."

Aive swung his legs around and sat up. Distrust came immediate, irrational and strong. He regarded the man, and there was something familiar about him, but Aive couldn't quite place where he'd seen him before. It must have been in a dream. The man shifted a large, soaking black cloak in his arms. Aive nodded and gave a "Well met" in reply.

"What are you doing out here in this weather?" There was no accusation in the man's voice, only genuine curiosity.

Aive shrugged. "I like to watch the ocean."

The man looked over the ocean as if looking for something interesting, but finding nothing. "I see. Not very good weather for it."

"I come when I can." Aive racked his memory for how he knew the man. And then it came to him. He was the acolyte whom Sobal suspected was following him. "And what about you, acolyte? Or have you taken orders?"

The acolyte laughed softly and sat down next to Aive. "Still an acolyte. I have not *proven* myself sufficiently to earn my ordination." The acolyte looked at the water and shivered. "I thought you were gone."

"What do you mean?" Aive tried not to tense, but he couldn't prevent it. His body readied for a fight even as the acolyte relaxed further.

"Well … I was just told … I mean … weren't you taken home?"

"And what do you know about *that*?" Aive leaned forward, not bothering to appear non-threatening. He gripped the dagger hilt. He wanted to be threatening. Hell, he was a threat.

"I, erm … Nothing? I just heard that—" The acolyte coughed. "I mean. What I *mean*, is that you left … To go home." The acolyte shifted as if he were nervous.

"Of course I did."

The acolyte frowned, his brow wrinkled in concern, and he leaned close. The man was an idiot. Would he stick his head into a lion's mouth, as well? "You know, Aive. My bishop … he'd be very upset to see you here."

"I do not care what your bishop thinks."

The acolyte leaned back and his frown deepened. "But … the bishop is the voice of God on Earth."

Aive sighed. This was nothing he wanted to hear. "Why are you here?" he demanded of the acolyte.

The acolyte shrugged. "I'm just taking a walk, enjoying the beauty of God's creation." Right, and Aive was the crown prince. The acolyte threw his robes on the log and stretched. "My bishop would be very interested in what *you* are doing here. You should leave High City, Aive. You're a good kid, but you're not welcome here. Go back home." He picked up his robes and trudged through the wet sand back towards the road.

Kid. Aive snorted. *Kid*. He was one to talk. There was no way the acolyte was a day over twenty. He had a bad feeling about that acolyte. Sobal didn't like him in the dream, and it was clear that the man knew too much about Aive's past not to be involved somehow.

Aive stood, glowering in the direction the acolyte had disappeared. The clouds had cleared. The tide was coming in. He had a good three hours before he needed to either leave or drown, and he was most certainly not going home. He passed the entrances to several caves he'd already explored and went into the first unexplored one.

Like every cave, it was dark, cold, and he could find no evidence that anyone or anything lived in its bowels.

He returned to Rachel's, tired, cold, hungry, and very discouraged.

~~*

Aive dreamed.

Sobal sat with his arm around Aive. Spring had moved in for good, and the meadow was lush with life reasserting itself after the thaw. Wildflowers and trees bloomed, showing off their best and brightest blossoms. Sobal already missed the cold. Aive, however, was happy as could be. They sat facing the mountain range to the northeast where Sobal's home was. He desperately wanted to return home, but not as much as he desperately wanted to keep Aive.

"Which one's Heaven?" Aive snuggled into Sobal's body.

"Hel F'Nin."

"You say Helfnin, I say Heaven."

Sobal rolled his eyes skyward. The moment they came down and introduced themselves to the humans, centuries ago, the humans took the name of their city and bastardized it into the name of the holy home of God. "Hel-Fuh-Neen," he enunciated every minute, phonetic detail, "is atop the tallest peak over there." Sobal shifted them so they directly faced his home.

"Tell me again what it's like?"

Sobal settled them in a more relaxed position. "It's cold. The air is crisp. The sun is bright. I miss it."

Aive tensed, sighed, and relaxed again. "I ... I'm not ready to settle. My parents—they had such great plans for me. Not that great really, but plans. I would take over their grain store. *Grain!* What do I care about grain?"

"Nothing." Aive was a mechanic at heart. He loved holding things and fiddling with them, taking them apart and putting them back together in new and different ways. Running a grain store? Sobal half-believed Aive's parents intentionally tried to drive their son away.

Aive turned his head and kissed Sobal's neck. "Let's travel just a little more. Then we'll go to Helfnin."

"Hel F'Nin."

"Hey. I'm trying."

Sobal smiled and rubbed his cheek in Aive's hair. "I know. Thank you."

"Are there many of us there?"

"You mean humans?" Sobal asked. Aive nodded. "One or two. Not many make it, and those who do cannot leave. We can't carry you, and the trip up is hazardous enough. But the humans there are happy, and they blend in well with our society. I don't imagine much has changed since I've been gone."

Sobal fell backwards against the ground and cradled Aive as he fell too. "Aive. I know you aren't ready to leave but … it would make me feel better if we went through the bonding ceremony down here."

"What about your family?"

Sobal kicked the twin doubled edged short swords he'd dropped by his feet just to hear them. They clanked against one another and flashed a brilliant shaft of sunlight onto Aive's hair. The noise and the light reminded him of days spent with his father learning to defend himself. "I do wish they could be present, but if anything was to happen to me down here and another of my kind saw you, they'd protect you."

Aive scoffed and waved in the general direction of the blades. "Nothing will happen to you. You've got your fancy swords and technique like I've never seen. Anyway, I've never even seen another angel down here."

"You probably have and just don't know it."

"I suppose. I don't need *protection*, though." Aive sat and turned to lean over Sobal. "Here or there, makes no difference to me. When do you want to perform the ceremony? It's not going to require blood or some animal sacrifice or something is it?"

Sobal laughed. "No blood and no dead animals. We can do it with only the two of us. I could get a witness, but that would be … it would remind someone I'm here. I don't want that. Then I'd have to go home, or at least live in an embassy, and you wouldn't like that, would you? Being cooped up in some monstrosity of a house?"

Aive shook his head, grinning. "Not at all."

"Tomorrow. On our beach."

And then they were on the beach.

Aive carried Sobal's pack, and they walked up the beach hand in hand. They walked through shallow, calm water to skirt a jut of the cliff and on the other side was a large, clean, wholly sheltered beach.

Aive stopped and looked around. "This is such a wonderful place. So secluded."

"I like it. Not many people know they can come here. I imagine they think the water is deeper than it actually is."

"Pfft. Not like it matters to you. You can fly."

"Ah, but you have to walk. I prefer places you can go, too."

Sobal led Aive to a little table they'd constructed out of driftwood. Aive set the bag on the table, and Sobal began extracting the items one by one. Aive raised an eyebrow when he saw them.

"Uh, Sobal, I thought you said no blood."

"There shouldn't be." Sobal held out his right hand to Aive, palm down so that his mark faced upward. "I'm going to make this on your left hand. If that's okay? It's required actually, so please don't say no."

"You're going to put a tattoo on my hand? Angels to Heaven, what will people think of me?"

"*My* people will know we are bonded."

Aive sighed. "Anything for you, but *my people* are going to think I'm a bad person. They'll hide their children, bolt their windows, bar their doors."

Sobal scoffed. "It won't be *that* bad. Your people have wedding rings. We share markings."

Aive leaned over and kissed Sobal's lips gently. "Then by all means, mark away."

~~*

Aive woke.

He hurried to the fireplace and lit a match. He then lit two of the wicks in the large candle on his nightstand and picked up his journal and pencil. He wrote down the dreams, fighting the urge to stare at his hand.

The beach. That was it. That *had* to be it. Please, God, let that be it.

The sun wasn't up yet, but Aive couldn't wait. He pulled on his trousers, socks, and shoes as quickly as he could. He didn't bother changing out of his nightshirt. He packed extra clothes and the lock pick set. He didn't know what else he'd need. He stopped by the kitchen on his way out, added food and a flask of water to his supplies, and then he grabbed a lantern with enough fuel to last several hours.

He ran. He ran until he couldn't run any longer, then he slowed to a fast walk until he could run again. In the empty streets, without the myriad people going about their business, the journey went faster than usual. He was out of breath when he reached the beach. He bent over, sucking in great lungfuls of air until he could breathe normally. He couldn't afford even this small break, but he needed air. The tide was only half out, and the water was deeper than in his dream.

The sky was lightening with the dawn, but the sun itself was hidden behind the cliffs. Aive carefully made his way along the cliff by touch and the weak light. When he reached open beach again, the bottom half of his trousers was soaked through. He barely noted the discomfort.

He hadn't noticed any gaps in the rock face in the dream, but he searched for anything that could be an entrance to the caverns anyway, confident it would be there. The sun was still in the wrong place in the sky, and the cliff walls were entirely obscured in dark shadows. The lantern illuminated a scant three feet in front of him. He walked close along the cliff's edge, trailing his fingertips lightly along the rough rocky surface.

And there it was: a dark void among the shadows of the cliff and a small gap, barely wide enough for a large human.

Holding the lantern as far in front of him as he could, Aive carefully stepped through the hole and made his way through the meandering cave, ducking and sliding where rocks hung low or jutted out. He came to a split in the path. There was nothing on which to make an educated guess. Not a thing. There was never a choice in the dreams, only darkness. He squashed the panic that arose from not knowing where to go.

He chose right, because that was the hand Sobal's own mark was on.

Before going forward, he made a deep gouge in the sandy ground indicating the path he'd taken. He came to two more splits and picked the right path both times for the same reason he had previously. He fully expected to be retracing his steps and trying other paths.

The farther into the cavern he got, the more acute his desperation became. He hated enclosed spaces, and that fear was not helping things at all. The echo of his footsteps grew shorter. He was coming upon something. God, let it be Sobal. He stopped at the wall. It looked like an ordinary section of cave wall, but Aive felt around for any hint of door or a keyhole anyway.

Nothing was there.

Aive sighed and turned around. He retraced his steps to the most recent split. After obscuring his original mark, and creating a new one, he took the other path. This probably wasn't the way, and he most likely would not find Sobal. He kept telling himself that so he would not be disappointed. He reached the end of the path. There was no door.

His heart sank a little more, and the ever-present panic spiked dangerously.

There were still more paths he could try. He retraced his steps again and followed the nearest path not taken. No door.

Aive leaned his forehead against the cool, damp rock. If Sobal weren't in the cave, how long would he be able to go on like this? All the fruitless searching, and he had nothing. Nothing.

Aive took deep breaths, trying to ignore the close walls that seemed to be getting closer each second.

It's okay. It's only a cave. There are no monsters. The walls are not moving. Sobal is here. He has to be. If he's not, then you'll look in a different cave tomorrow, the next day, however long it takes. One more path.

His eyes burned, and he thought the best thing in the world he could do right then would be to huddle in a ball on the ground and cry.

Aive roughly ran his hands over his face, straightened his back, and squared his shoulders. He returned to the first fork and took the remaining path. There was another split. Since the right paths had led him to dead ends, he took the left. When he arrived at the dead end, it looked like all the others. Didn't the paths have to connect somewhere? Wasn't that some sacred rule of caverns? Panicked laughter escaped from his throat and reverberated in the small area, his own voice mocking and laughing at him.

Aive felt along the wall. His fingers brushed over something different. It was so small, so subtle, that he almost missed it. He moved his hand along the slick rock and felt again. It was a tiny metal plate, and in its center was a tiny hole.

He dropped his pack to the ground and dug out the lock picking set. After placing the lantern on the ground, he had barely enough light to manipulate the thin crinkled spikes of metal in the hole and patiently poke and twist them. After at least three eternities, the lock clicked and the door sprung open so hard it knocked Aive on his butt.

He stared in shock through the black opening. The door had actually opened. He scrambled to his feet and picked up the lantern. His whole body shook in anticipation. Two steps and he was inside, and the small room filled with the dim glow of lantern light.

He scanned the room quickly. There were chains attached to the wall, the shackles empty and hanging limp. He scanned the floor. A dirty gray blanket lay over a mound on the floor. Hope overcame him, and he rushed over.

The blanket was, in fact, dull, gray, dirty feathers that were attached to the lump. Stringy brown hair hung limply over a face. Aive carefully brushed the hair away, and his heart stopped for a moment only to race in his throat in the next.

"Sobal?"

Chapter Three

The lump—Sobal—moved, groaned, then shuddered. Then he was lifeless again, or at least unconscious—Aive hoped he was only unconscious.

The panic was closer than ever. His body shook with it, but Aive couldn't give in to it. He needed to get Sobal out of the cave, but Sobal was so much taller than Aive. It would be an impossible task to carry him any meaningful distance. Aive should have brought help. He was so stupid to think he could do this alone.

"Sobal? Please wake up."

He didn't move.

Aive positioned his arm under Sobal, braced himself, and pushed upwards. Aive overestimated Sobal's weight and they shot into the air. With no hope of staying upright, Aive pulled Sobal's body against his. They fell to the ground, but Aive was able to protect Sobal and cushion his body from the impact. Aive took ragged breaths. He stared in shock at the lantern several feet away. The condensation on the floor glowed in the light of the fire.

"I hope it's normal for you to weigh the same as a sack of grain."

Aive ignored the dread in his chest when Sobal didn't say anything. Of course there would be no response. He carefully propped Sobal against the knobby wall and picked up the lantern. He looked between the light in his hand and Sobal, trying to figure out how he could carry both at the same time. He didn't want to hurt Sobal further, but he needed the light to see by. The only way seemed to be to carry Sobal over his shoulder.

Aive knelt in front of Sobal and, as gently as possible, maneuvered the frail body into place. He braced his arm around Sobal's legs and carefully stood. Sobal was so light that Aive easily carried him. The only difficulty was the dusty, rotten smelling feathers that kept brushing against his face and under his nose.

The sun was bright in the sky when they returned to the outside world. Aive felt like the worst bastard in existence each and every time he jostled Sobal's body. The whimpers had gone from sporadic to constant somewhere between the cave exit and the water. Aive peered into the distance, trying to discern shadows or movements that should not be present. Now that he had Sobal, he wasn't letting anyone else near him. Especially since he didn't know why Sobal had been captured or who had taken him. Aive had a few suspicions with that acolyte appearing several times.

The sand kept trying to swallow Aive's feet, but he trudged as steadily as he possibly could onward. He took them to the makeshift table of driftwood and then supported Sobal's weight as he slid Sobal onto a wooden stool. Aive dropped onto the beach, staring at the still unconscious angel. He had no idea where to go or how to help. Sobal was so light. In the dreams he was thin, but this was emaciation of the likes Aive had never seen.

"Sobal?" Aive reached his hand forward and picked up Sobal's hand with the mark that was identical to his own. He traced the swirls of light charcoal colored lines that seemed like a natural part of the skin. He wished he knew what they meant. He wished that Sobal would wake up and tell him. He squeezed Sobal's hand.

Sobal shifted. "Aive?"

"Yes?" Aive sprung forward onto his knees and leaned in closer to Sobal, touching his face, his neck, his hair, his arms, his hands. The odor emanating from him was putrid, even in the open air. "Talk to me. What do you need? I have food. Water."

With obvious effort, Sobal lifted his head and let it fall back so that his face was bathed in sunlight. "Sky ... need to be outside."

Aive stroked his fingers up and down Sobal's arm. His skin was coarse with dirt. "Is there ... I can take you to Rachel's?" He wished Sobal would look at him. After all the dreams, the searching, he wanted to see Sobal's face. See his eyes open and alert. See him smile. Hear him laugh. Talk. "Sobal, please?" Aive hated the whine in his voice. What if he was too late to save Sobal? The thought was too much, and it became harder to breathe. Aive clutched Sobal's hands. "Sobal? Tell me what to do."

"Embassy."

Aive stared at Sobal in shock. Never had it entered his mind to go there. It was the obvious place to take an injured angel, of course, but *no one* went there. Much less a merchant class nobody. He had no place there. He was no one. Nothing.

"Please. Embassy."

"Okay." The guards would toss him out on his ear, but if that was where Sobal needed to go, go they would.

"You need ... hide ... wings. Or ... night."

Aive looked at the poor wings. He saw at least one place where a bone had broken and knit at a funny angle, and the other wing hung limply down. Aive caressed a feather; the wing flinched and Sobal gasped. There was no way to hide them without harming Sobal further.

"We'll go at night. But we need to hide for now. Come on." Aive lifted Sobal to his feet and together they walked through the wet beach where the tide was coming in and would wash away their trail—Aive walked, Sobal stumbled while leaning on Aive, one wing dragging behind him. Aive took Sobal farther north until they were well away from the prison in the caves. Eventually they came to a grove of trees that bordered the beach. Aive took them deep inside, guilt eating at him with each snag and snap of twigs against Sobal. They spent the rest of the day hidden under the canopy of leaves.

Aive thought he would jump out of his skin at every little chirp of a bird or rustling from within the bushes. They drank warm water and Aive ate the dried berries and nuts he'd brought from the inn. Sobal didn't say another word. After he drank, he slept, his face turned up to the sky. The minutes and hours ticked by slowly as the sun crossed east to west. The sunset seemed to take days, but finally it was dark.

Aive lifted Sobal over his shoulder again. It was a relief that Sobal remained unconscious. Aive walked in the direction of the road. They passed the same branch shaped like an arrow three times, and the worry and panic fought a terrible battle in Aive as he forced himself to keep trying to find the forest exit. At last, they came to the road. After miles of careful movement, they reached the outskirts of the city. The moon was new and the night dark as could be. Luck was on their side. No one was still out and all the windows were black—a small miracle in such a large city. They came in from the north—another miracle since that was where Heaven's embassy was located. Still, it took ages to reach the embassy. They arrived at its foreboding twelve-foot-tall cast iron gates as light was creeping into the sky from the east.

The guards straightened and grabbed the hilts of their swords as Aive approached. In the dark, Sobal looked like an indistinct lump. The guard said something to him, but Aive was too tired to understand. He slid Sobal around, being as careful of the wings as he could, and held him in his arms so the guard could better see his face in the dim light the torches cast from the gate. Third miracle of the night: The gates swung open with surprising speed and the guards ushered them in. The gates closed with a loud clang that resonated along the ground. They were led towards a large entrance flanked by two stone lions. On the left, the lion looked over the stairwell, regal and alert; on the right, the lion napped peacefully.

The two stories of stairs Aive needed to climb with Sobal in his arms? Not so much a miracle.

"May I assist you with the angel, sir?" A guard tried to take Sobal, but Aive held on tight, still trying to be as gentle as he could.

"No!" he snapped. "Don't touch him." The guard took a step back, and Aive focused on the lions. His goal was to get Sobal to the sleeping stone lion. No, that was wrong, to the door. He needed to get Sobal inside.

The door swung open, smashing against something on the other side. Instead of a butler, as would have been proper and expected, a very grumpy man—no, an angel—stood in a deep blue dressing gown. "This had better—gods above! Sobal?" The angel looked from Sobal to Aive and back again. "What happened to him? Come in. Hurry."

When he was close enough, the angel also tried to take Sobal, but Aive wouldn't let Sobal out of his grasp. Not to a stranger. Aive shook his head and said, "I've got him." His mother would kill him if she knew he had denied anything to one of God's creatures, but he needed to be sure that Sobal was safe, and that was more important than making some perfectly healthy angel he didn't know feel respected.

"This way." The angel sighed and led the way inside. "It might rain, but there's no helping it."

Aive carried Sobal up three more flights of stairs, trying to figure out what rain had to do with anything. He followed the angel down a long hallway and into an atrium. In one corner was a large bed, in the opposite corner, a large armoire. Topiaries and planters filled with green and deep red plants edged the walls. It was a bedroom with no ceiling.

"Lay him face down on the bed. I'll return with my wife in a moment."

Aive carried Sobal to the bed and laid him down as the other angel instructed. Dust from Sobal's body floated down onto the bedspread that had, until that moment, been a pristine, pure white. Aive turned Sobal's face away from the fluffy pillows so that he could breathe easily.

Every time Aive looked at Sobal, he was alarmed to find further signs of distress. There were deep purple bags under his eyes that appeared sunken, hollow almost, above cheekbones that jutted out, sharply angled; his lips were dry and cracked. His skin was gray tinged and reminded Aive of a corpse. At least there were no cuts or injuries to the skin itself. He placed his hand on Sobal's back between the wings and relaxed when he felt the slight rise and fall of breath.

The angel returned with another, also in a dressing gown. She rushed to Sobal and began running her hands all over his emaciated body and tattered wings.

"What are you doing?" Aive moved to stop her, but the other angel pulled him back.

"That's Isela," the angel said. "She's a doctor. He needs her." Aive watched her very closely.

"Where did you find him?" Isela spared a moment from her examination to look at Aive.

"Cave." Aive still struggled to move towards Sobal, but the angel held his arm and he couldn't move forward far enough.

"We lost track of him over a year ago," the angel holding his arm said.

Aive stopped trying to reach Sobal and looked at the angel. "Forgive my rudeness, but who exactly are you?"

"Jolden. I'm the official ambassador in High City."

"I'm honored to be in your presence, your eminence." Aive's mother would have been so proud at him parroting the correct greeting, even while watching Isela.

Jolden picked up Aive's left hand and inspected the marking, turning it this way and that. "You don't need to be so formal in private. You're Sobal's husband. You are part of our family."

Aive yanked his hand out of Jolden's grip and shrugged, trying to appear unaffected. *Husband?* How could he forget something so important? "I don't remember." This man, who in his dreams, loved Aive, cared for Aive, put Aive's wishes above his own. This man who Aive didn't know and yet loved more than the air he breathed. This man was apparently his husband and Aive remembered nothing.

Jolden raised an eyebrow. He opened his mouth, and Aive mentally braced himself for the onslaught of questions sure to come. But then Isela finished whatever she was doing and straightened up, distracting Jolden. A small wrinkle of concern marred her pale brow and the deep frown looked wrong on her perfect angel face.

"His wings are broken in three places. I want to clean them before setting them. Other than that? Open skies, food, water. The ... real damage won't be apparent until he heals."

"What damage?" Aive asked.

Jolden gripped Aive's shoulder. "You're tired. I'll have some food sent up. Eat something. Help Isela clean Sobal's wings and try to get him to eat. When he's patched and you're rested, we can talk about things that aren't quite so pressing."

Aive huffed in frustration. After being awake for over a day and carrying Sobal around, he didn't have the energy to argue or demand to know what they weren't telling him. He was tired, and he wanted to help Sobal. "Okay. But tomorrow, I want real answers."

~~*

The next day, Aive found himself on a short stool next to a large, shallow porcelain tub half filled with water. The tub was made so that a person could lie front-down and be immersed in a small depth. He poured another bucket full of warm water over Sobal's head, wings, and back. The water had turned deep brown with grime. Sobal's hair had lightened considerably to an almost white, but his wings were still brownish-gray. Isela rubbed the feathers carefully, dislodging rocks, sand, and other debris.

The bathing chamber attached to the bedroom, and it too had no ceiling. The sun was at the highest point in the sky, and though the season was turning cool with the coming winter, the room had grown warm and almost too hot under the bright sun. Aive scooted his chair so that he cast a shadow over Sobal's back. He'd been through so much discomfort already, a sunburn would be like rubbing salt in a wound.

"If you're shadowing him so he doesn't burn, it's not necessary. We don't burn."

One more thing Aive hadn't known about Sobal. How long would it take until he felt like he knew this man? He watched Isela's hands work, studying the simple but beautiful tattoos on her own hands, and his gaze wandered up her arms to her wings. "Your wings are so white."

She looked up at him quickly and gave him a reassuring smile. "Don't worry. His will be. Once he molts they'll come back in white."

"Molts?" That was ... really strange. Birds molted. Angels did, too? That seemed too messy for something that was supposed to be God's most holy creation.

"Of course. We can't keep the same feathers our whole life. They break and fall out. We'd be grounded by age ten." That made sense.

"I think we've done as much as we can for these." Isela rubbed a dingy gray feather between her fingers. "Do you remember when he last molted?"

"I don't remember anything about Sobal."

Isela set Sobal's wing gently down. "Nothing?"

"I woke up back home and a year was missing from my memories. The only reason I came here was because the dreams led me here. Everything I know is from the dreams, which amounts to almost nothing. Except flying is fun."

Isela gave a light laugh. "Indeed it is. Perhaps after Sobal is settled and healing we can talk about your missing memories, see if anything can be done." She briskly wiped her hands on her apron. "Two more buckets and then we'll dry him and move him back to the bed."

Aive didn't bother telling her it would be no use. He'd seen doctors back home, and they couldn't help him. The lost year was no longer the terrifying hole in Aive's life. He still felt vulnerable and wary, but he had gotten used to it, hating it all the same. He poured two more buckets over his still sleeping Sobal. Aive was beginning to grow worried; Sobal hadn't uttered a sound, or even moved, since the grove, and surely he would have woken by now. Right?

Aive grabbed Sobal under his arms and gently lifted him. As he held Sobal up, Isela dried him with fast, sure, yet gentle swipes of a towel. They carried him back to the bed and laid him on his stomach, still naked. Someone had replaced the dusty sheets while they were in the bathing chamber.

"Why don't you get some rest?" Isela said. "The bones in his wings have been broken so long, waiting another couple hours won't do any more harm."

Aive nodded. "I can stay with him, right?"

"Of course." Isela gathered up the damp towels and left the room. Aive curled up next to Sobal on the bed. The sun was warm on his skin, and there was a gentle breeze of fresh air circling the room, making the leaves of the plants rustle quietly. He touched Sobal's shoulder and ran his finger down the pale skin. The gray tinge was turning to the healthier ivory tone that Jolden and Isela had. He combed the damp, almost-white hair with his fingers until it was dry and silky, falling in strands about Sobal's face.

Aive's eyes grew heavy as he watched the rise and fall of wings with Sobal's breathing. Finally, he closed his eyes and had the second bout of dreamless sleep in a year.

~~*

Aive woke and reached out. His hand brushed Sobal's arm and Aive let out the breath he'd been holding. He closed his eyes and opened them again, just to make sure Sobal was there. He was. Aive smiled and threaded his fingers into Sobal's hair and drew them down. He plucked a leaf resting by Sobal's ear away and dropped it on the bed.

The sun no longer shone directly through the open ceiling. Little white puffs of clouds moved serenely across the blue sky. Aive felt well-rested, but anxious still. He stretched and shifted, looking lazily around the room, and startled when he saw they weren't alone. Jolden and Isela sat on stools next to the window. Aive sat up on the bed and stared at them.

"Nice nap?" Jolden asked. Aive blushed and nodded—feeling much like he'd been caught kissing another boy behind the barn by his mother. "Isela called for a colleague from Hel F'Nin. He should be here soon." Jolden gestured to the plate of food on the window seat being used as a table. "Would you like something to eat?"

Aive shoved off the bed and dragged his feet over to the window-seat-table. "Can I sit here?" If it was a table, and never a window seat, he didn't want to be rude and sit there, but the only chairs were occupied.

Isela patted the hard wood surface. "Please."

Aive sat and slowly cleared the food of mostly fruit and nuts from the tray. He took a long drink of tea and was beginning to feel a little more alert. Somewhere in the house a bell rang out.

"Ah," Jolden said. "That will be Isela's help. Come with us to greet him, Aive?" He glanced at Sobal. "Sobal will be fine. We'll just be a minute."

Aive frowned, but Jolden was right. Sobal was asleep and likely wouldn't wake and know that Aive wasn't with him. He hesitated and tried to comb out the tangles in his hair. "I'm really not presentable. I could wait here."

Jolden shook his head. "I insist that you join us. Come."

Aive followed Isela and Jolden out of the room. He didn't want to leave Sobal; in fact, he never wanted to let him out of his sight ever again. He didn't turn and run back, though. He continued to follow the angels farther and farther away from his angel. When they came to the main staircase, instead of taking the stairs to the ground floor, they continued walking. Eventually the hallway widened into a large foyer far more ornate and impressive than the downstairs entrance. There were large pots of flowers outside the door, and inside stood large golden vases with elaborate flower arrangements.

Two guards opened the doors as Jolden approached. On the other side of the door another angel was brushing off his clothes and shaking his wings. Jolden walked forward and clasped forearms with the newcomer. "Welcome to our home, Alexis." Jolden led the newcomer inside. "Isela you know, of course, and this is Aive, Sobal's husband."

Alexis grinned at Isela and clasped her hand. "Great to see you again, Isa. It's been forever since I've come down here."

"We greatly appreciate you making the trip. I wish it were for a happier reason, though." Isela turned the handclasp into a quick hug and ruffled Alexis's already very messy hair. "You look like you flew through a flock of geese."

"I was in a hurry." Alexis extricated himself from Isela's hold and turned to Aive. "Aive, I'm very sorry to meet under these circumstances. I'm Alexis, Sobal's brother, which I guess makes you my brother-in-law." Alexis gave a small smile that didn't reach his eyes. "We've been worried about Sobal, so we thank you for recovering him. My mother also sends her thanks on finally getting him to settle."

Brother-in-law?

Aive took Alexis's offered hand and ended up in a fierce hug. "We'll get Sobal right as snow, okay?"

His reassurances did nothing to ease the constant worry that had plagued Aive since finding Sobal. He nodded anyway. He turned to follow Isela and Alexis back to Sobal, but Jolden touched his arm. "Why don't we take a walk?"

Aive watched Isela and Alexis disappear into Sobal's room. He really should go back too. What if Sobal woke up? Aive needed to be there. "I made it a request to be polite," Jolden said. "But I insist you take a walk with me."

"Like you insisted I come out here?" Aive couldn't help the panicked edge that elevated his voice. "Why don't you want me to be with Sobal?" Jolden raised a brow at him. Aive stifled a sigh. "Fine."

They went out the door, and it was suddenly obvious this was the real main entrance. Stone tiles in varying shades of cream and taupe covered the ground creating a meandering path that disappeared around the building corner. Flora of ferns and hedges grew as if they were a part of the house. Jolden led them around, following the lazy path of the tiles. The view of the mountains changed to a view of the ocean. The vast blue water stretching to the horizon reminded Aive of that very first dream.

"I dreamt about the ocean," Aive said. "That's why I came." He walked to the white stone banister and leaned over, as if that could bring him closer to the distant waves.

"Isela mentioned something like that. It shows your bond with Sobal is strong."

"So Sobal *did* send the dreams?" Aive turned to face Jolden.

"I doubt he knew he was doing it. He probably was unconscious for the last four months, at least."

"Why four months?"

"We *need* open skies. The gods above send us nourishment." Jolden leaned against the railing next to Aive. "Angels are proud and stubborn. *If* you manage to capture one, the only way to get them to cooperate with you is to starve them of the sky. Eventually they break, and they can be controlled."

"What about Sobal?"

"We'll see when he wakes up."

The panic which had lessened since finding Sobal built again to new levels. He had found Sobal, but from Jolden's words it sounded like Aive was too late. "But he was there for almost a year, maybe more. What if—"

"Don't jump ahead of yourself. We've been known to last longer than that."

"How will you know if he ..."

Jolden's frown deepened in a way that caused dread in Aive. "It's not very simple, unfortunately. The true test is whether or not he will do his captor's bidding. Since I have no intention of seeing Sobal in the same room as whoever imprisoned him ... time will tell."

"So there's another way to know?"

"If he can't fly, but his wings are so damaged he couldn't fly anyway. We will see. If we find he has been so badly damaged, his recovery will be ... difficult."

"But he can recover?"

"To a point." Jolden pushed off the banister and resumed walking on the pathway. Aive hurried to catch up. If Sobal was injured, Aive would help him heal. Just like Aive had learned to accept the missing memories, Sobal could learn to live with the after effects of his ordeal. Aive hoped that it wouldn't be necessary, though.

They walked in silence and came around to view the mountains again. Aive was struck with how profoundly different the land was here compared to his home in the Eastern Plains, where if he looked, even as far as the eye could see in all directions, there was nothing but golden fields of wheat. Not a tree, not a lake, not a hill.

Jolden clasped his hands behind his back, drawing Aive's attention to the tattoos on each of his hands. "You have two marks." Aive winced. That was probably an incredibly rude statement.

Jolden chuckled. "Yes. One is mine. I was born with it. The other is Isela's. When we marry, we give our spouse our mark. If you were an angel, you'd have two, and so would Sobal. His mark is particularly elaborate. It must have been … irritating getting the twin." Aive shrugged. He'd give almost anything to be able to remember how irritating it had been. "Don't worry. When Sobal wakes, he can tell you all about your time together. He'll be recovering for a while, yet. You have time."

"Time," Aive spat out. The worry morphed to fury. "There's been too much time. Sobal looks like death warmed over. I don't even know this man who … " *The man who was in my heart.* "Whoever did this to us, I'm going to kill him."

Jolden stopped and faced Aive. "Is that really wise?" he asked calmly. "It would be better for you to go to Hel F'Nin where this can't happen again."

Just as quickly as worry had turned to fury, fury turned to guilt—acute guilt. Sobal had wanted to go to Hel F'Nin long ago, but Aive had refused. *Why* hadn't he gone? None of this would have happened if Aive had only *listened* to Sobal. Remembering the dreams, he was furious with himself. He wanted to strangle the Aive of over a year ago and tell him to go to Hel F'Nin as fast as they could. But he couldn't change the past. Instead, he had to be content with the knowledge that they probably saw some nice piles of rocks that were monuments to long-dead men, but he couldn't be certain they were nice or interesting or worth it because *he didn't remember.*

Aive took a breath, trying to calm himself, but he felt no calmer. "Aren't you supposed to want justice?" Aive asked. "Aren't you the infallible arbiters of human affairs or something?"

"Of course, and I intend to see the man who wronged you eviscerated, but Sobal needs to heal. I will take care of this."

Aive shook his head. "Well I need to know that whoever did this is not going to do it again. Ever."

Jolden considered Aive seriously for a long moment and nodded. "That is fair. You do have claim, too. I don't suppose you know who we're looking for?"

"Not really." Aive kicked at one of the squat pillars holding up the railing. "I think Sobal knows. I ran across an acolyte in the dreams and on the beach. It can't be a coincidence, especially since he was on the beach so close to Sobal."

Jolden sighed. "Gods-damned human religion. They supposedly revere us, but then they capture us and use us to assert their claim to power. It's absurd. We. Are. Not. Their. God's. Creatures." Jolden spun around and walked briskly on. "It wouldn't work." He sliced his arm through the air. "Do they think we're stupid? We ensure the angels who aid the human leaders are there willingly. If we found Sobal under the control of a human ... that human would die a most excruciating death."

"Good." Hopefully, it would be a slow, excruciating death.

Jolden slowed and lowered his arms into a more relaxed pose. "We are very lucky you found him, Aive, and very thankful. It's a tragedy when one of our own is lost."

They reached the rooftop entrance again. Jolden led Aive inside and back to Sobal's room. Alexis and Isela sat in the chairs by the window.

On the floor was a bucket full of bloody bandages, and Aive's stomach rolled dangerously. Sobal had bandages covering his wings. The one that had been dragging on the ground was angled properly, and the wings were symmetrical on Sobal's back. The white bandages only highlighted how dirty the feathers still were and made the spots of blood seeping through them seem redder in contrast.

Aive looked away, nauseated. "I thought you were just setting the bones?"

Alexis shook his head. "We had to re-break them first."

A shiver of horror traveled down Aive's arms. "Is he in pain? When will he wake up?"

"He's unconscious," Isela said. "In cases like this, sometimes it takes up to a month."

"A month!" That was too long. What if he never woke up? What if— "Will he fly again?"

Alexis frowned. "It's hard to say at this point."

Aive bit his lower lip and looked at the poor wings. Sobal had to fly again. Flying was Sobal's joy. Without it, he wouldn't be Sobal. Aive knew that as sure as he needed his next breath.

"He'll fly again." If Aive had to will Sobal to levitate with his mind, Sobal *would* fly.

Isela smiled at Aive and touched his shoulder lightly. "Of course he will."

Chapter Four

The sun slipped above the wall of the open-ceiling room and woke Aive with bright spots of light heating his face. He opened his eyes, reached out, and touched Sobal. Several red-orange leaves had drifted in overnight and fallen to rest on Sobal's pale skin. He plucked them off and let them drop to the floor. The leaves would stop coming in soon; the trees were almost entirely bare.

Two weeks had passed since Aive had found Sobal and brought him to the embassy, but Sobal was still asleep. The dreams had stopped. Aive's quality of sleep had improved dramatically, yet he missed the dreams and the knowledge of Sobal they brought him. Knowledge that Sobal loved pears, but hated peaches. That he preferred to read books on geology rather than politics and law, but he read the books on law anyway. That he adored Rachel and took great amusement in teasing Paul. That he yearned to go home except he couldn't stand to leave Aive behind.

Now Aive had to extract small tidbits of information from Isela and Jolden, and they seemed to know very little. Jolden had only met Sobal a handful of times, and Isela met him only in passing many years ago. Alexis, who was a much better source of information, had returned to Hel F'Nin over a week ago.

Aive inhaled Sobal's scent one more time and slid out of the bed. He washed his face and put on the same clothes he'd worn since arriving. He really needed to return to Rachel's and get the rest of his belongings, but he didn't want to leave Sobal. He also needed to find that acolyte again. Yet, that too would require leaving Sobal. His stomach growled, and he had to leave Sobal anyway to go eat breakfast.

The carpet cushioned Aive's feet as he made his way to the outdoor eating area. The table was laid with a breakfast of pastries, nuts, and cheeses. Isela took occasional sips from a steaming cup of tea while staring in the direction of Hel F'Nin, and Jolden sat hunched over cradling his head in his hand.

"Morning," Aive said, his voice dull and lacking any enthusiasm for the world. He sat and picked slowly at a sweet roll. It was delicious, melt-in-your-mouth goodness that Sobal would love, but Aive barely tasted. He was growing more and more worried about Sobal. Isela had said it might take up to a month for him to wake, but Aive hadn't expected it would really take so long. Sobal's health had improved over the past two weeks, but he was so still, almost like a sculpture. Maybe Aive could tempt him awake by placing sweet rolls by his nose.

"We have a problem," Jolden said, sitting up and looking at Aive.

Aive set the sweet roll down onto his plate. Was it a problem with Sobal? Had they found who took him? Were they making Aive leave the embassy? He tried to keep the panic off his face and out of his voice. "What's that?"

"Another one of the angels down here has gone missing. I need you to show me the cave where you found Sobal."

~~*

"Walking is such a tedious mode of transportation." Jolden was in quite the mood after walking the several miles from his home towards the ocean. He continued to grouse. "How you humans deal with it, I will never know."

Aive studiously kept his eyes forward and mouth closed. He knew very well how the humans dealt with it:

they put one foot in front of the other and kept going. To Jolden's point, flying would have been much faster.

The day was cool, but the sky had remained clear. The salt feel in the air grew thicker as the dirt road transitioned to sand. Aive stopped, took off his shoes, and dug his toes into the sun-warmed beach. No matter how many times he felt the sand under his feet, saw the ocean with his own eyes, he still couldn't believe that he'd made it to land's end. Apparently he'd done so twice. The birds and insects around the water were so different from the ones he had grown up with back east.

Jolden cleared his throat with unmistakable impatience. Aive felt a pang of guilt in that he felt no sense of urgency in returning to the caverns. He didn't want to see the place where Sobal had been kept the past year, nor did he want to reenter the dark, tight spaces. He tried pretending that the latest missing angel was someone he cared about. It didn't work, but Jolden was standing there, looking more and more irritated by the moment.

"This way," Aive said. He turned and walked in the direction of the protected beach. Jolden and the guards who'd accompanied them followed silently. The tide was low, so getting around the jutting cliff was easy. Aive spared a glance for the driftwood table where he could see in his mind's eye the image from the dream of him and Sobal preparing to commit to each other.

Aive forced himself to focus on the caves. "This is it." He waved at the small entrance in the cliff face. In the daylight, several more entrances to the caverns were visible. There was nothing that marked this entrance as special in any way. The only footprints in the sand were his, the guards', and Jolden's, so it was clear that no one else had been in the area since the last high tide.

"It looks rather tight." Jolden's wings pulled back against his body. "If my feathers get stained someone will suffer."

Aive pulled two torches out of his pack and lit them with a lantern that one of the guards had brought. After handing a light to Jolden, Aive led the way to the cell Sobal had been imprisoned in. It took very little time now that he knew which paths to take. The door was open and the room empty. "This is it. No one's here."

"Indeed." Jolden walked around the room, kicking at little bits of straw and brown cloth on the ground. He frowned at the shackles on the wall. Pinching the chain between his fingers, he picked it up, shook it, and looked at it with distaste. "You found him alone? No one else here? Not even a guard?" He dropped the chain and strode out of the room.

"No," Aive said. He had stayed back in the doorway. Nothing could induce him to enter that cell again. "The only person I've even seen on these beaches was that one acolyte."

Jolden's brows furrowed. "There's nothing to learn here. Let's go."

Aive led the way back out of cave. Once they were on the beach and in daylight again, he extinguished the flame from his torch. He should have been with Sobal, even though he was sleeping and effectively dead to the world. Instead, Aive was playing tour guide for a man who found nothing of importance at any of the stops. This trip was a waste of time.

Jolden put his hands on his hips and looked around. All he would see was sand, rocks, and ocean. "Show me where you met the acolyte."

Aive led them south, out of the protected beach, and to the large driftwood log. This beach was also deserted.

"I suppose just happening upon him would be too easy." Jolden kicked at the sand.

Aive's clothes felt damp and heavy from the humidity in the air. The need to return to Sobal was turning into desperation, and Jolden seemed content to poke and prod along the coast. There had to be a faster way. Then it occurred to him, of course there was a faster way. "Maybe we should go to the bishop," Aive suggested. "The acolyte definitely worked for the bishop ... and there's only one in the city."

"Yes. You're right. We shall go to the cathedral." Jolden rubbed his forehead with his fist. "This was utterly fruitless."

Jolden continued to grumble on the long walk back to the cathedral, which was conveniently located within walking distance of the embassy. Convenient if one left from the embassy, not very convenient from the coast.

"Do you mind if we make a small detour?" It wasn't really small, but Jolden didn't need to know that.

"Detour to where? Is there a chair?"

"Yes." Aive quickly sidestepped a small boy running in the street. "It's an inn and tavern. I stayed there. Actually, I think I met Sobal there. I haven't gone back since I found Sobal, and I need to get the rest of my things."

Jolden shrugged. "Why don't you tell one of the monks where it is and they will fetch your things?"

"Monks?"

Jolden gestured back to the guards. "Them. These guys who follow us around, the monks." Aive had thought they were just guards. Jolden went on, "You met Sobal there? Do you think any of the workers would know about Sobal's disappearance or the acolyte?"

Aive shrugged. "The acolyte, maybe. I'm not sure when Sobal was taken, but I get the feeling we had already left the inn."

Jolden turned back to the guards. "Please fetch the ... Aive, who would be best to talk to?"

"Rachel."

"Please ask Rachel to accompany you to the embassy and bring Aive's belongings," Jolden said. Aive told the guards where the inn was located and two of them left. Jolden stopped about a block away from the cathedral.

"I'd like to talk to Rachel first. Let's go back to the embassy."

Aive was relieved that he could return to Sobal. He didn't know why, but it was vitally important to him that he was present when Sobal woke. Maybe it was because he'd been gone when Sobal had truly needed him. Maybe he hoped that his memories would return. Maybe it was a million little things that coalesced into the overwhelming need to be present when Sobal reentered the world.

~~*

Aive had an hour with Sobal, who was of course still asleep, before Rachel and Paul arrived. They had been shown to a parlor on the main floor of the embassy. Aive had only spent time in the bedroom he shared with Sobal and outside on the rooftop. Until that day, the angels had not used any of the enclosed rooms. The parlor was tastefully decorated in creamy blues and whites. The artwork depicted scenes of Hel F'Nin and avenging angels carrying out justice on the mortals of the earth. Aive thought it was rather arrogant, but perhaps that was the intent.

Isela sat next to a large window that stretched from floor to ceiling, and Jolden stood behind her. Rachel and Paul sat on a couch finer than Aive had ever seen. It was cream colored and looked to be made of silk with small subtle flowers embroidered in an even lighter shade of cream. Aive would have been terrified that if he sat on the couch he'd end up leaving a dirt mark in the shape of his rear. Paul sat tense on the edge of the seat, and Aive suspected he had a similar worry.

Rachel gave a nervous smile when she noticed Aive had entered the room. "Aive, we wondered where you'd gotten off to again. Imagine the shock at having the guards of Heaven show up. At my little inn."

Aive rubbed the back of his neck, smiling sheepishly. "Sorry about leaving like that. I hope it wasn't too surprising—the guards, I mean."

"It'll be great for business!" Paul piped.

"You're probably wondering why you've been brought here," Jolden said.

"Yes," Rachel said. "Other than to bring Aive's belongings, yes."

Aive sat—on the very edge of the cushion—next to Rachel and placed his hand over hers. "I found Sobal."

She faced him again and gave him a tight hug. "Thank Heaven. Is he okay?"

Aive shook his head. "Not right now. He's in a deep sleep. Would you mind talking to the ambassador about Sobal?"

"Of course not." Rachel turned to face Jolden and Isela, though she waited to speak while a servant brought tea and pastries. She took a sip of the tea and smiled fondly at Aive. "Aive came first. He showed up on the doorstep one day caked in so many layers of dust." Rachel chuckled. "He said he was an explorer come to unearth the wonders of the coast. We offered him a job and lodging while he in the area."

Aive tried to remember ever being an 'explorer' and failed.

"He was with us maybe two weeks when Sobal came. Our Aive—" she ruffled his hair "—he was immediately smitten. My husband and I thought it quite sweet, really. Aive tried so hard to flirt with Sobal, and it was met with complete disinterest."

"Do you know why he wasn't interested?" Aive hadn't meant to interrupt, but he was still puzzled over that odd beginning.

"Well ..." Rachel said, "You did come on a bit strong. But ..." Rachel turned back to Jolden and Isela. "Aive is more stubborn than Sobal, and by the winter festival Sobal was just as smitten right back.

"Anyway, once Sobal and Aive had found themselves mutually taken with one another, they disappeared for long periods of time. Sometimes they'd be gone just two nights; one time it was two months before they came back." She ruffled Aive's hair again. "Our Aive here wanted only to explore the coast and mountains, and Sobal, besotted as he was, went with him."

Jolden turned away from the window and nodded at them. "So that's why, when they didn't return, even after seven months, you weren't overly alarmed."

Rachel nodded and smoothed away the mess she'd made of Aive's hair. "That's right. We figured they'd gone really far this time." She turned and gave Aive a sympathetic look. "I do hope Sobal will be okay."

"How often," Jolden asked, "do you get acolytes in your inn?"

If Rachel was surprised by the change in topic, she didn't show it. "Oh all the time. Seems like there's more every year. Bishop Black brought in another bishop a couple years ago to build up the theology department at the university, and since then we've seen a flood of young hopefuls come into the city."

"Was there one that you saw often when Sobal was around?"

"I'm sorry." Rachel shook her head. "I really don't remember. Paul?" Paul shook his head. Jolden raised an eyebrow at Aive.

"There was one in a dream," Aive said. "It was autumn."

"Did you speak with him?"

"I don't know. The dream changed, but Sobal didn't like the acolyte. He took extra care to hide his back."

Jolden turned back to Rachel. "What is the name of the bishop that Bishop Black brought in?"

"Uhm ..." Rachel tapped her lip. "Dour or Dove or ... Do-something. We've only heard of him from the acolytes. Never seen him around."

Jolden stood. "If you'll excuse me, this conversation has brought to mind several matters I need to attend." He bowed his head slightly to Rachel. "Thank you for taking the time to come and talk with me."

"It is our honor, your eminence."

Jolden left. Aive, Rachel, and Paul stared after him. The departure was abrupt, bordering on rude, but as one of God's creatures, it wasn't possible for Jolden to be rude. Isela set down her cup with a loud clink. "May I offer you a tour of the gardens?"

~~*

After Rachel and Paul left, Aive returned to Sobal. He sat on the bed reading a book that discussed the basics of the angels' native language. Apparently it was a book the monks studied. While trying to memorize the months as they corresponded to the months in Aive's own tongue, he heard Jolden's voice carry in from the hallway and growing louder as he neared.

"I cannot believe that I, the supposed most holy being in this entire city, consulted in all things spiritual, did not know that the bishop was building up the theology school. Much less that he was amassing acolytes in my own city!"

"We will have to find out what is going on and put a stop to it. This can't continue," Isela replied as they walked into Aive's room.

"Black and I are going to have words," Jolden said. "This is completely unacceptable."

Isela turned from Jolden and looked at Aive and Sobal. "Any change in our sleeping beauty?"

"No."

Jolden frowned as he looked at Sobal. "We won't worry for another two weeks. In the meantime, tomorrow, actually, you will accompany me to the cathedral to visit our good friend, the Bishop Black."

The next day, Jolden, Aive, and several guards walked the short distance to the cathedral. Jolden's mood, if possible, had descended into a foulness unrivaled by any Aive had witnessed before. Aive stayed silent and breathed a sigh of relief when they reached the cathedral doors. A mousy little initiate led them to the bishop's office, and Aive was surprised to see Bishop Gray present.

"Bishop Gray? I thought you were the bishop in ..." Aive couldn't remember the name of the village. Did he ever even know the name of the village?

"Indeed I am, my boy." Gray grinned and clapped Aive on the back. "Bishops Black and Dowd are away on business. I am overseeing their duties while they are gone."

The bishop shifted his focus to Jolden, bowed slightly, and gave the appropriate words of greeting.

Jolden nodded; he'd managed to school his features, but the flush and throbbing vein on his temple belied the anger he'd built up on the walk over. "Bishop Gray, it is a pleasure to meet you. Thank you for seeing us so quickly."

"It's not every day that Heaven's emissary comes to the door. I am humbled that you find me worthy of your presence." Gray gestured to an overstuffed stool in front of the desk. "Please, have a seat."

Jolden sat and gave a strained smile. Aive couldn't imagine how Jolden dealt with the groveling. No wonder Sobal hid himself. "Well," Jolden said, "I'm afraid I haven't come on a social call."

"Oh? That sounds serious." Gray walked around behind the desk and settled in the shiny, mahogany colored, leather chair.

"Yes. I've come to you as a man close to God. If anyone can help me, it is one of our allies in the church."

Gray settled his hands on his stomach and leaned back in the chair, his smile wide. "Of course, your eminence. Please tell me how I may help you."

"Well, you see, this is a rather delicate matter. You probably know that we—angels—periodically travel through your lands. Usually disguised."

"Yes, I have heard that, though I've never seen one that I know of."

"Well, one of those travelers hasn't been heard from in several weeks, and that is unusual for him. As the representative of all angels in the city, naturally, I'm concerned. Have you heard anything about an angel named Rothel?"

"Hmm." The bishop frowned and steepled his fingers together under his chin. "I'm sorry I don't have better news, but I haven't heard of any traveling angels in disguise. It has been a long time since rumors of one reached me."

Jolden stared at Gray for several minutes and finally stood up. "If you hear anything, you will notify me immediately."

"Of course." Bishop Gray rose and Aive hastily stood as well.

Once outside again, Jolden breathed a huge sigh. "Someone knows where Rothel is. At least we have learned the identity of the other bishop in the city. I still can't believe the audacity—" Jolden took another deep breath. "We need to find this Dowd."

They walked in silence back to the embassy. Once they were inside the embassy gates, Jolden stopped and looked directly at Aive. "Don't tell anyone, but I hate bishops."

Aive nodded. "Me too." He really did. They took Sobal, and for what?

"Aive!" Isela bellowed from the roof above. Aive looked up and shielded his eyes from the sun. "Aive!" Isela waved, beckoning him up. "Sobal woke up!"

Awake? Sobal was awake! Aive ran into the embassy and up the three stories of stairs to the top floor as if he had wings on his feet. He skidded on the landing and turned sharply towards the main entrance.

"Over here, Aive," Isela called from the other side of the open doorway.

Aive rushed over. Sobal sat on a stool, resting his weight on the table. His wings were still bandaged, and any feathers not covered by the wrappings hung limp and gray as if they'd drop off at the slightest breeze. "Sobal?"

Sobal turned his head slowly and smiled at Aive. "Hey there." It was the most beautiful smile Aive could remember seeing, even outside the dreams. Sobal was *awake*. There were deep purple bags under his eyes. After sleeping so long, Aive thought they would have been gone. He stared at Sobal, nervous and uncertain. Should he touch Sobal? Hug him? Kiss him?

"Come, sit next to me." Sobal nodded to the empty space beside him.

Aive pulled his high-back chair close to Sobal—close enough to touch, if either of them reached out—and sat down, suddenly feeling very shy. Aive couldn't take his eyes off Sobal. He was so very alive. His eyes were open, and his breaths were deep. He sat mostly upright. He talked. He was present. "How do you feel?" Aive finally asked.

Sobal smiled wanly. "I've felt better. I hear I owe you my gratitude."

Owe? Gratitude? Aive frowned. They were lovers. So why was Sobal speaking with such formality? Maybe Sobal didn't remember. Maybe whatever had taken Aive's memories had taken Sobal's too. Aive had assumed that Sobal would be able to tell him about their past. If he couldn't, that would be all right, but it would make Aive sad. "I, uhm, you do remember me, right?"

"Of course." Sobal grabbed Aive's left hand with his right and gave a weak squeeze. "I'm feeling a little off."

Sobal didn't let go. Aive looked at Isela, concerned. Sobal's thumb softly caressed Aive's skin and he relaxed slightly. "Where were you and Jolden off to?" Sobal asked.

Aive was surprised Jolden had not joined them. "We went to the cathedral to meet Bishops Black and Dowd. However, they weren't there. Only Bishop Gray was there, and that was a surprise. I thought he was ... back east."

"I don't know Gray, but Dowd is a bastard." Sobal's grip around Aive's hand grew tighter, but not to the point of pain. Aive wondered if that was because Sobal was so weak or because he was being considerate.

"Is he the one who ..." Holding Sobal's hand reminded Aive of being young and with his first innocent love again. He didn't want to talk about bishops or illness or all the bad things that had been happening around them.

"Yes."

Jolden came through the door and settled on a stool next to Isela. "Sobal. So glad that you're awake."

"It's been a long time, Jolden." Sobal gave a half-hearted smirk. "I planned to return home without ever seeing you again."

"That clearly worked out well," Jolden said. They chuckled together. There was some history there, and Aive felt acutely how much he didn't know Sobal. He had gotten the impression that Jolden and Sobal weren't well acquainted, but that was clearly false. They shared a camaraderie that spoke of being close. Aive wanted that so badly. Yes, he loved Sobal, but he didn't feel like he knew Sobal, like they were friends.

Jolden sighed and his face turned serious. "Another angel has gone missing. Given what happened to you, we need to find him and the Bishop Dowd as soon as possible. Any idea where they are?"

Sobal shook his head. "If the missing angel is not where I was, then I have no idea. Probably another cave. As for Dowd ... I'm surprised you didn't find him at the cathedral."

"Yesterday was the first I heard of Dowd. The bishops have tried to keep their activities from us, which is troublesome. Aive mentioned you were worried by an acolyte last autumn. What of him?"

Sobal gazed at the mountains looking pensive. He continued to caress Aive's hand. "Ah yes, him. If you find the acolyte, you'll find Dowd. I think he's grooming the boy as his successor."

"All right. I have some monks watching the cathedral. Hopefully one of them will show up."

Aive and Sobal sat quietly while Jolden told Isela about their unsuccessful visit to the cathedral. Sobal slumped closer and closer to the table. Finally, afraid that Sobal would fall asleep in his chair, Aive stood and tugged Sobal up with him. "Sobal needs to rest. Is there anything else that needs to be done today?"

Jolden shook his head. "No. Thank you for your help, Aive. Someone will fetch you when supper is ready."

Aive walked slowly next to Sobal down the hall. Sobal moved stiffly, but otherwise seemed to move okay. He didn't let go of Aive's hand, even after the door to their room closed. The sun was high in the sky and shone directly into their room.

Aive put an arm around Sobal when he leaned against him. "I'm still so tired," Sobal said. "Will you lie down with me?"

"Of course." Aive made sure Sobal got onto the bed without incident, and then Aive slipped off his shoes and shirt before joining him. Lying on their sides, they faced one another. Aive was struck once more with uncertainty. What should he do now that Sobal was awake and they were alone? What would he have done before the missing year?

Sobal reached across the divide between their bodies and clasped Aive's hand. He brought it briefly to his lips as he draped an arm around Aive's waist and pulled him in to his body. Aive rested his forehead on Sobal's chest, breathing in his scent and listening to the soft puffs of his breath.

"Thank you for finding me," Sobal said, placing his hand on Aive's cheek.

"I'm sorry it took so long." Aive's voice came out muffled, but Sobal must have understood. Aive felt fingers comb through his hair. Relief and happiness at the simple touch overwhelmed him as he finally experienced for himself one of the gestures Sobal was so fond of in the dreams. The fingers on his scalp seemed to take away the stress of the past year and gave only love and contentment in return.

After several moments, Sobal said, "Isela told me how it happened, with the dreams."

Aive nodded, rubbing his forehead against Sobal's skin. He couldn't seem to get enough of Sobal's touch. "I liked the dreams you sent. I liked flying."

Sobal laughed softly and hugged Aive closer to him. "It's fun. I wish I could really take you flying." He sighed as he rubbed his chin on Aive's head. "I doubt I could send you the dreams again if I tried. I had no idea we could do that."

"It's okay. We found you."

"*You* found me."

Aive moved back so he could look up at Sobal. They gazed at each other in silence. "You thought I was a brat."

Sobal's eyes widened in surprise, and then he laughed. "Well, you were."

Aive tried to keep his face stern, even as he fought a smile. He was overjoyed to hear Sobal's laugh, which was completely different in the waking world. It had a melodic cadence that filled Aive's heart with happiness, and he couldn't help his own laughter that bubbled out. "You don't have to be quite so ... honest about it."

Sobal reached his hand up and threaded his fingers through Aive's hair again. "What can I say? You grew on me." Sobal frowned. "But you're different now." The joy drained out of him and Aive tensed. "It's not a bad thing," Sobal rushed to say. "It just is."

After the lump of fear dislodged from Aive's throat he said, "I don't know anything. I don't trust anyone. I second-guess everyone, except you and Jolden. And you, the most important person in my life, I know nothing about." Aive took a deep breath. "I love you, and I have no idea why." Sobal's fingers running through Aive's hair continued to soothe him. "Why didn't I agree to go to Helfinin when you asked? All of this would have been avoided." Aive buried his face in Sobal's chest. "I feel like such an idiot."

"Hel F'Nin."

"Sobal!" Aive pushed lightly at Sobal.

Sobal laughed. How Aive loved that sound. He was already addicted to it. "You'll say it correctly yet. It's my mission in life."

"Really?"

"One of them," Sobal said. Aive wondered what Sobal's other missions were. Had he known before? Had they changed?

Aive drew little patterns on Sobal's skin. "Once we find Dowd ... I want to go there."

Sobal's hand stilled and he said in a careful, measured voice, "Are you certain? Once there, you can't return."

"Yes. I've had enough traveling, and you were right. It's too dangerous here."

"Do you want to go see your family one last time?"

Aive thought of his parents who seemed to feel his only value was to work in the store. No, he didn't need to see them again, but Lina. They knew when he left that he might not return. Aive wasn't willing to stay any longer and risk Sobal's safety again, but it still made his chest ache knowing he'd never see his sister again. "No. It would take a year to go, only to say goodbye. I can still write, though. Right?"

"Yes, you can." Sobal's voice was slurred in almost sleep. His fingers, still trying to touch Aive as much as possible, had grown sloppy and slower.

Aive closed his eyes and wrapped his arm around Sobal's waist, carefully avoiding the damaged wings. He took a deep breath, feeling odd. The emptiness was gone. The panic was gone. The worry was also gone. Aive breathed in Sobal's scent and fell into a content, dreamless sleep.

Chapter Five

For three weeks they waited on word of the acolyte or Dowd. Sobal slowly regained strength. Each day the bony ridges of his body smoothed out just a little more, and after the second week, Isela removed the bandages from Sobal's wings. He walked around flexing them open and closed, ruffling his feathers, and then flexing them more. He refused to attempt flight—the feathers were too damaged, he claimed.

The day was more winter than autumn. Thick clouds hung over the city and obstructed the view of the mountains. It seemed the angels were in a particularly foul mood when their home was hidden from their sight, or maybe they were in a foul mood because they couldn't find Rothel. Maybe it was both.

Isela glided around the embassy snapping at the servants for not polishing this table, or for letting dust collect on that tapestry, or reorganizing her medical texts, which had previously been in perfect, logical order. Jolden took out his aggression by sparring with Sobal, and Sobal was just cranky.

Aive sat on the top level of the roof watching Sobal go through exercises with short swords. There were several training areas, and Aive was beginning to wonder if there was anything the angels had not put on the roof. He turned the page in the book he was reading on the history, law, and lore of Hel F'Nin—another book that had appeared from the mysterious monastery in the mountains.

"These are terribly balanced," Sobal groused. Aive scanned briefly over a table explaining food allotment practices from five hundred years ago and turned to the next page.

"You're just not used to them," Aive replied, not for the first time. He was glad Sobal focused his foul mood on Jolden. While Aive wasn't willing to let Sobal far from his sight, he was growing impatient with the excessive complaining from the winged contingent of the household. It was all the better if they focused on each other.

"I want mine."

"Too bad," Jolden yelled and rammed into him from the right. "Practice!"

Aive felt bad for the loss of Sobal's swords. From the dreams, he knew that Sobal had adored his blades— almost as much as he adored Aive. If they were lucky, they would find the swords among Dowd's possessions. Sobal was attached to them in a way he was attached to very few material items. The blades had been a gift from his father and imbedded over time with jewels that each carried a special meaning—meanings which, incidentally, were covered in chapter forty-five of Aive's book.

Eventually Jolden excused himself and a guard took his place. Sobal put forth a good effort, but he was too weak and too slow. He kept the guard out of his sphere for a time, but the guard was still able to penetrate gaps in the flashing swords. Once he touched Sobal everything was over. Sobal was slammed to the ground or flung across the practice space. It turned out that being so light-weight put the angels at a severe disadvantage in close-range combat. Frustration made Sobal reckless, and the guard trounced him quicker and quicker each round.

Aive winced as Sobal went down, yet again. The guard held out a hand and lifted Sobal off the ground with an apologetic look.

Isela, who had apparently decided to take a break from overseeing her staff, sat next to Aive. "Don't worry," she called to Sobal. "It will come back."

Sobal grumbled inelegantly. "Says you. You can fly. You can fight. You don't have to walk your spouse up to Hel F'Nin, more or less unprotected. If not humans, there are bears."

"I can take care of myself," Aive pointed out matter-of-factly. "I've walked twice across the country. I'm not incompetent."

Sobal raised a brow at Aive. "I never said you were." Sobal turned back to the guard and raised the swords again, preparing to defend. He looked so tired and his limbs were shaking. Aive wasn't sure how he was holding his arms up.

"Aive," Isela said. "I wanted to talk to you about your memory loss."

The topic was unexpected. "Okay."

"It took a little while—" Isela sighed "—but I finally found the medical book I was looking for. With your permission, I'd like to use a … meditation technique to unlock the memories."

Cautious hope bloomed in Aive. "Yes, of course. Anything." He set his book aside. "I want to remember."

"It might not work, especially if the memories were taken unnaturally."

"What does that mean?" How was it possible for one's memories to be taken unnaturally?

"There are tonics which are known to permanently affect memory that nothing can overcome."

A sinking feeling in Aive's stomach told him what he had known deep down from the start: the memories were gone. But he had to try. He'd tried everything else available to him. Perhaps this would give him a sense of closure. "I understand. When do you want to start?"

"Now is fine. Just listen to the sound of my voice and relax." Isela began speaking low and steady. The words were not in Aive's language, but he thought he recognized a word or two he had learned from the book of the angels' native language. As Aive listened to her voice, his limbs relaxed and his eyes grew heavy. In his mind's eye there was fog, and under the fog was Isela's voice. He felt Sobal's presence, but saw him nowhere. There was only fog and a constant quiet sound, like the rushing of water.

Though Sobal was not there, Aive felt his love surrounding him, like in the dreams. The fog thinned in small patches, revealing scenes of the two of them together. Reading. Lying in a meadow. Staring at an ancient ruin that was once a castle. If only the fog would lift he could go to that moment and be there again with Sobal.

But the fog did not lift. Instead, it returned thick as ever and the glimpses of those moments were gone. The scenes became obscured, and nothing was left for Aive to see. He opened his eyes and blinked against the harsh outdoor light.

Sobal sat across from him, his hand on Aive's knee. "Are you all right?" he asked.

Aive nodded. "I … I don't think it worked." Sobal brushed Aive's hair to the side and ran his long fingers down to Aive's neck.

"Why do you think that?" Isela asked.

"I saw moments. We were looking at a castle in ruins and in a meadow in the spring and reading somewhere. But the moments were distant, and I only saw images, like a painting. I don't remember them. I remember seeing them, but not living them." His eyes ached. He wanted so badly to remember. He wanted to hope that someday he could remember.

"I'm sorry Aive." Isela briefly touched Aive's knee. "It is not impossible for the memories to return, but very unlikely."

Aive took a deep breath. "It's okay." He didn't need the memories. He had Sobal. Sobal was who had filled the emptiness inside of him, not memories. "They've been gone a long time, and Sobal can remember for both of us and tell me."

Sobal pulled Aive into his lap and held him tightly. "I look forward to many nights recounting our time together." Aive sighed at the feel of Sobal's cheek resting on his head. "We are lucky there are nights to be had. You are an amazing man. I can't think of anyone else who would have come all this way based on a dream."

"They were insistent dreams." Aive pressed his face in the crook of Sobal's neck, burning into memory the scent and softness of his skin.

~~*

The skies had cleared and so had the foul tempers of Jolden, Isela, and Sobal. They sat around the supper table laughing at a story Isela was telling about Alexis and some animal Aive couldn't fathom.

The angels seemed impervious to the harsh chill in the night air and wore the same lightweight clothing they normally did. Aive felt as if he was five years old again. He wore not one, but two heavy, wool coats so that he could join the angels outside for dinner and not freeze. Aive had borrowed the coats from the guards, and he hoped some poor monk wasn't on duty without a coat. Moving his arms to eat was difficult under the stiff material, but the extra effort was worth it to be able to watch Sobal. Even after three weeks, the site of Sobal happy, laughing, and awake felt new and precious.

A throat cleared to Aive's left, pulling him out of his musings. The conversation around him abruptly ceased. A guard dressed simply in monk's robes stood with his hands folded in front of him.

"Yes, Oren," Jolden said.

"A bishop has returned accompanied by an acolyte. Based on their descriptions, I believe them to be Dowd and his acolyte."

Jolden dabbed at the side of his mouth with a napkin. "Please take the acolyte quietly and bring him to the interview room. Let me know when he is ready." The tone of Jolden's voice caused Aive's stomach to turn. He looked at Sobal, whose face had become hard and expressionless.

An hour later the monk returned. He had a small splatter of what looked like blood on the left side of his face. "The acolyte is ready, your eminence."

Jolden stood, as did Sobal. "Aive, would you like to be present when we question the prisoner?" Jolden asked.

"You do not have to be there," Sobal said.

Aive stood as well. "No, I'll go." He wanted to know what the acolyte had to say for his actions, what could have motivated him to have taken part in harming a creature of God, whom he supposedly served.

The interview room was on the ground floor. Aive caught a glimpse of the kitchens, a food pantry, and a large linen closet before walking down a long, dimly lit hallway to a heavy wooden door at the very end. It was reminiscent of being in the caves.

Inside, the acolyte he had spoken with on the beach was tied to a chair. His nose was at a crooked angle and blood flowed from it down onto his chin and shirt. He looked otherwise unhurt.

Aive stayed by door. There was a table several feet from the acolyte where Jolden and Sobal sat. "Only two?" Jolden asked the monk, nodding at the table. Aive followed Jolden's gaze and cringed. On the table were two fingernails. Perhaps he should have stayed with Isela.

The monk nodded. He stood next to the prisoner, who leaned away towards the other side of the room. Jolden looked at the acolyte for several long moments. Sobal still had his expressionless mask well in place.

"An angel is missing," Jolden finally said. His voice echoed against the bare walls. "Where is he?"

The acolyte looked at the monk then quickly back at Jolden. "Dowd is moving him," he said. "I don't know where they are." The monk kicked the acolyte's chair when he did not continue. "There's a cave. I think his holiness is taking the angel there."

"Where is the cave?" Sobal bit out.

"It would be faster for him to show us," Jolden said. "Unless it's the same one Sobal was kept in?" The acolyte shook his head.

Aive felt a hand on his shoulder. Isela stood behind him. He stepped aside and she walked past him with a basket full of bottles and bandages. There seemed to be a fine-tuned system at work, and Aive wondered how often people found themselves in the angels' interview room. Isela stopped in front of the prisoner. "Untie his arms, please, Oren." Oren did as she asked. "What's your name, acolyte?"

"C-Christopher."

"I'm going to fix your nose. Please blow into this." She handed him a square cloth. Christopher blew and the square became red and soggy. Aive really wasn't sure he wanted to watch. Isela placed her hands on Christopher's face. "Deep breath, through your mouth." Isela moved her hands quickly and Christopher cried out. Oren reached out and kept Christopher upright. Isela placed a cloth in his nose to stem the blood flow. "There you go," she said. "Right as snow."

Tears streamed down Christopher's face, and Aive felt pity for the boy, even though he was taking part in the abductions of angels.

Isela left and Oren untied Christopher's legs. "Let's go," Jolden said. To a guard outside the door, he added, "Please get Frederick and Trival and meet us at the gate." The guard hurried away.

"Aive," Sobal said, touching his arm. "I would feel better if you stayed here."

"No. I'm not letting you go anywhere without me ever again." Aive hurried through the door to walk next to Jolden. No way was he being left behind. He had every intention of killing Dowd with his bare hands, or maybe with fire.

Silence hung over the group as they walked through the almost empty streets of the city. Those who were out had stared at the two angels walking through the city in the dead of night. Aive could imagine how odd the site was since he'd not seen an angel in his life until he returned to high city—not counting the dreams or the year he couldn't remember.

About an hour after they had left the embassy, Jolden asked, "Christopher. How old are you?"

"Twenty." Christopher's voice was an odd mixture of hoarse and pinched. He cleared his throat once and pulled the cloth from his nose.

"And how long have you been with Dowd?"

Aive wondered what the point was of the questions. Who cared about Christopher's past? They had an angel to rescue and a bishop to kill. Acolytes didn't matter.

"Eight years. My parents were dead. I was living in barns. He adopted me."

"You warm his bed?" Jolden asked.

"Yes," Christopher whispered.

"How long?"

Moments passed and Aive thought the acolyte wouldn't answer. Christopher shivered and Aive wasn't sure it was from the chill, though Christopher only had on a light shirt. Finally, Christopher looked quickly at Jolden then away again and said, "Six years."

Sobal made a noise of disapproval. Jolden went on. "How did he know the way to capture an angel?"

"We ..." Christopher sighed and his shoulders sagged. "We were in Honoria. A new archbishop had been seated and we were present for the rituals. And—"

"That was six years ago," Sobal said.

"Yes." Christopher paused, probably waiting for another interruption. "Another bishop was there accompanied by an angel. The angel was ... surprisingly agreeable. Bishop Dowd asked how they had established such an easy partnership."

"I see. Their names?"

"I don't know. I wasn't present at the time. He told me of it afterwards."

"That's just fantastic." Jolden's wings tightened to his back. "We're going to have to visit every single angel down here to find ... whoever." Jolden didn't ask any more questions, and Christopher didn't offer any more information.

Dread moved through Aive. What if they asked Sobal to help? What if Sobal was taken again? "Sobal, I want to go to Hel F'Nin, now."

Sobal looked at him, his eyes wide. He opened his mouth several times. Aive stumbled over a rock in the road, but Sobal's arm shot out and caught him. "Why now? Don't you wish to settle any affairs you have here?"

"It's safer up there. I want to go to Hel F'Nin tomorrow."

Sobal smiled and put his arm around Aive. "There are logistic concerns to the trip. Let's talk about this later. I think we're almost to the beach."

The scent and feel of the ocean was thick in the air. The waves washed ashore in their slightly unsteady rhythm. Christopher, flanked by guards holding torches bright with flame, led them to a cave entrance with two sets of footprints in the sand disappearing inside and one set coming out. "Aive," Jolden said. "You have your lock picks?" Aive nodded. "Please go with the guards and bring Rothel out. We shall wait outside."

Aive's dinner had never quite settled over the course of the evening, and the thought of going into another cave did not help his churning stomach. But he had to go—an angel was being held in there, just like Sobal had been. He took a deep breath and nodded. Sobal pulled him into a tight embrace. "Thank you."

The guards and Aive went through the caves. There were very few branches in the path, so they found the door quickly. This lock was harder to disengage than the one to Sobal's prison, but Aive eventually succeeded. The guards entered first, flooding the room with light. Sitting on the ground, limbs bound but wings free, was a very angry angel. He held out his hands, silently demanding to be freed. Aive knelt in front of him and removed the manacles from both wrists and ankles.

"You're Rothel, right?" Aive asked.

"Yes. I assume Jolden is here?" Rothel stood up and shook out his wings. Other than appearing angry, he looked to be fine.

"Yes. He and Sobal are outside."

They left the caves. It had been so easy, so much easier than fetching Sobal. If Aive hadn't been sent home and his memories taken, would they have found Sobal so quickly? Probably.

Rothel immediately went to Jolden. Aive couldn't hear what they were saying. Eventually Rothel and Jolden parted and Rothel flew off.

Jolden walked to where Aive and Sobal stood. "He's returning to Hel F'Nin. We shall return to the embassy. Well, I am flying. Sobal, you suit yourself. Aive and Christopher should be perfectly fine with the monks."

Sobal tightened his hold on Aive, shook his head, and said, "We'll see you at lunch tomorrow." Jolden shrugged and took to the air. Sobal looked down at Aive. "Shall we go?"

"Stop! Christopher!"

Aive turned in the direction of the yelling. A bishop ran towards them, torch waving in one hand, a mace in the other.

"Bishop Dowd?" Christopher said and started to move towards the running man. Oren reached over and grabbed the back of Christopher's shirt, yanking him back.

"What have you done?" the bishop bellowed.

Bishop Dowd, the man who had taken Sobal from him. The same man who had most likely taken Aive's memories. The man who might, at that very moment, have control over Sobal—who could command and exploit him. Aive lurched out of Sobal's arms and ran towards the bishop. A guard tried to stop him, but he veered out of reach.

"Aive!" Sobal called. "Stop!"

Aive didn't listen. He kept running. Fury coursed through his veins. Aive was going to kill that man for everything he had done to them and the time he had stolen. No one would feel that pain again. Aive's feet pounded and slipped in the sand, but he stayed upright, and in a few more steps, he would strangle Dowd.

A white blur passed overhead, and then Sobal stood behind Dowd, holding a blade against his throat. Aive stopped, barely keeping his balance, and stared.

Sobal had flown.

"Sobal. Let me go immediately," Dowd commanded. If Sobal flew, then surely he wouldn't obey. Aive watched. Waited. A trickle of blood ran down Dowd's neck, and Aive wanted to weep with relief. Sobal was all right. He had been rescued in time.

Three guards surrounded Dowd. They bound his arms and put a gag in his mouth. Aive ran to Sobal and threw his arms around him. "You flew!"

Sobal hugged Aive in return and buried his face in Aive's hair. "I would never let him touch you." Dowd struggled against the guards, futile though it was. "Let's wait a few minutes to leave."

Dowd was led away, while he, Sobal, Oren, and Christopher stayed behind. "What will happen to him?" Christopher asked.

Sobal answered, "Tomorrow you will both be judged for your crimes. Do not be afraid to speak against your bishop. In fact, it is in your interest to speak the entire truth." Christopher paled and remained silent the rest of the night.

~~*

The following day, Aive sat in the front pew of the cathedral. He sat next to a priest who kept his head bowed, silently moving his mouth in prayer. The sanctuary was filled with acolytes, priests, and several bishops who were all dressed in their most formal robes. Aive guessed there were at least two hundred of the clergy present, perhaps more. Quiet murmurs of speculation filled the room with a buzz of possible reasons why they had been summoned to witness a trial and what exactly Bishop Dowd and the acolyte had done to draw the attention of Heaven.

Sobal, Jolden, and Isela sat in front of the altar. Their wings were spread wider than normal, and as a result, they looked majestic and intimidating. Dowd and Christopher knelt prostrate in front of them on gleaming marble tiles. Guards stood to the side, ensuring they remained on the floor.

In their laps, Sobal held a book, Jolden a gold scepter with the symbol of the church on the end, and Isela a sword. Only Jolden spoke. "Bishop Dowd." His voice boomed throughout the sanctuary and the murmurs of the clergy ceased. "You are accused of the abduction of the holy angel Sobal, the holy angel Rothel, and the human Aive. You are accused of holding the holy angel Sobal prisoner for one year. You are accused of holding the holy angel Rothel prisoner for one month. You are accused of poisoning the human Aive and transporting him against his will. What do you say to these accusations?"

"I am innocent." Dowd's voice was muffled, as his head faced the floor. "Christopher did all of those things."

Christopher's back tensed, but he did not say anything. Aive couldn't imagine how anyone would believe Christopher to be capable of executing the complex series of events that had occurred. He was barely more than a boy.

Jolden turned his head to look at Christopher. "Christopher, acolyte of the holy church, you are accused of aiding Bishop Dowd in the matters stated. You are further accused, by the bishop, of having conducted those crimes. What do you say to these accusations?"

"I assisted the bishop. I did not do those things, though." Christopher's voice was quiet and barely discernible. He trembled in the formal robes of his station.

"What is the difference between assisting and executing the tasks?" Jolden asked. He did not sound very impressed.

Christopher shuddered, and in spite of himself, Aive felt pity once more for the young man. Everyone knew that crimes against God's angels were punished with death. Aive hoped it would be swift for Christopher. He had only been aiding Dowd, who had been a rescuer and lover to him. But somehow, Aive didn't think the angels would see it that way; they were not known for seeing actions and crimes in shades of gray.

"He is my bishop," Christopher said. "I do as he says. I never touched either of the angels. I never saw them. I only prepared the cells and checked that the cells were closed."

"You were aware angels were being harmed. You should have brought this matter to the embassy. Your loyalty to Dowd was misplaced."

"Yes, your eminence."

Sobal, Jolden, and Isela exchanged a glance. "We have made our judgment," Jolden said.

Isela stood, sword in hand, pointed at the floor. She stepped down three steps and stood above Christopher. "Acolyte," she said. The congregation of bishops, priests, and acolytes shifted and stirred. Her voice was melodic and starkly contrasted with Jolden's harsh tone and manner of speaking. "You are guilty of assisting the bishop Dowd in crimes against God's holy angels. You are exiled to the Monastery of the Betrayer where you will spend the remainder of your days." She nodded to Oren, who stepped forward, lifted Christopher, and guided him out of the sanctuary. Aive breathed a small sigh of relief that Christopher was spared death.

"Bishop Dowd." The congregation stilled. Isela stood where Christopher had been, and her sword rested directly to the right of Dowd's face. Unless his eyes were closed, he would see the blade. "You are guilty of abducting God's holy angels, attempting to gain their favor by imprisonment, and harming one of God's beloved children. Your status as bishop is revoked. You will be unwelcome in God's kingdom. You will die by decapitation. Your head will sit atop the cathedral steeple to remind God's children that sins against Him and His holy angels will be met with justice."

In under the time it took to take two full breaths, Isela braced the sword in her hands, raised it high, and swung. Dowd's head slid off his body and blood sprayed against Isela. She looked over the congregation while the blood pooled at her feet. "Remember this well. Harming a holy angel of God will be met with swift justice. It has been brought to our attention that one of God's holy angels has been assaulted by another bishop." She looked slowly over the clergy present, as if measuring the merit of each person individually. "Confess what you know of the matter and we shall be merciful. Protect your brother of faith, and you both will meet the same fate."

Jolden and Sobal stood and joined Isela. They walked around Dowd's body and down the center aisle of the sanctuary. The congregation was silent. Aive didn't know if he should follow Sobal or wait. A guard approached him and held out his hand, indicating Aive should follow. They left out a side door. Sobal stood waiting for him and pulled him into his arms as soon as Aive was free of the building. "Are you all right?"

"I'm fine," Aive said. "I didn't expect Isela to ... to do that."

Sobal slid his arm around Aive's waist and began walking back towards the embassy. "A lot of that was for effect. To intimidate. The clergy think that women especially are weak. They do not expect violence from them. It adds a nice touch, I think. Makes the whole thing a little more horrible and the angels different from humans."

"But the blood was all over her."

"She's a doctor. She's perfectly at ease around blood and dismembered body parts."

Aive shuddered. "When can we go to Hel F'Nin?" He wanted to leave this behind—the bishops and the danger.

"We can go as far as the Monastery of the Betrayer—"

"Isn't that where Christopher is going?"

Sobal petted Aive's hip as they walked along the quiet street. "The Monastery of the Betrayer is the name of the monastery where our monks reside. It is not a bad place. In fact, it's quite nice. We hope that Christopher will find peace there."

"So, it's not much of a punishment?" The whole thing had sounded so ominous.

Sobal shrugged. "That depends on your perspective. It was the gentlest punishment we could give him. He will have to leave everyone and everything he knows behind, never able to return. Much like you, once we leave for Hel F'Nin."

"And what were you saying about when we could leave?"

"Well, we could leave immediately for the monastery and then resume the journey come spring. Or we can stay here several more months and complete the journey all at once. Oren and Christopher will be leaving immediately."

Aive wanted to leave as soon as possible, but his wishes had not been helpful before. This time, Sobal would choose. "What do you want?"

Sobal looked to the mountain range. "Honestly, I am still weak. I can't fly very far. I'm uncomfortable traveling with you while I'm so defenseless, and I'd rather not take the monks for protection because it's hard for them, too. I would like to wait."

Aive squeezed Sobal's hand. "Okay. We will wait. As long as we don't leave the embassy again."

"Not even to see Rachel?" Sobal teased.

"Rachel can come see us."

The embassy gates closed behind them. Reality was better than the dreams of his past. Sobal's wings spread wide and one wrapped around Aive, pulling him in, close and loved.

Made For You

Megan Derr

Charlie pulled the broken glasses from the pocket of his corduroy jacket and carefully unwound the kerchief in which they were wrapped. He stared at the bent frames. One lens was shattered, the other gone entirely.

He didn't know why he kept looking at them, as though they would somehow, magically, be fixed. Magic would not fix them until they were returned to their owner, and he first had to find Jed. Despair clawed at him, but Charlie fought it back.

Jed was alive and he was close, Charlie could feel it like cold rain on too hot skin. He drew a deep breath and let it out slowly, then tucked the glasses away again. The clock on the wall ticked softly, and Charlie sighed, looking around the fancy office where he had been sitting for the past half hour.

It was handsome, classy, but a waiting room was a waiting room. He wondered miserably if Sable Brennus would even see him; he was still tempted to walk out and just find Jed without permission to be in the territory—but if he caused even half the havoc he suspected he would, then it was better to do it with the demon lord's approval (or at least his knowledge).

Charlie reached up to touch the collar around his throat: butter-soft, dark brown leather embossed with runes. The sound of a door opening drew his attention, made him drop his hand and stand up—only to see it was Brennus' secretary again. Disappointed, shoulders slumping, Charlie resumed his seat.

He'd been told that Sable Brennus was good so far as demons went. Charlie had hoped that meant that Brennus would not look down on him, as so many others had, for failing his master. He flinched, fingers twitching with a need to reach again for Jed's glasses, but he refrained. He caught the secretary's sympathetic look and felt dejected all over again. "Should—um—should I just go?" he asked.

"Go? Oh, no, honey. Don't go. Sable will be seeing you shortly. He's downstairs putting out fires—figuratively speaking. If you'd come yesterday, it would have been literally." She rolled her eyes, and then smiled warmly at him. Charlie was again reminded of how much she looked like someone out of the old movies Jed liked to watch. "You sure I can't get you something to eat or drink? You name it. I can get it, honey."

Charlie shook his head. The only sustenance he craved was the presence of his master, to see Jed healthy and happy again. If his wings were out, they would have fluttered restlessly, but as it was, he could only fist his hands in his lap and try to keep himself together.

Six months he had been trying to find Jed, six months since that djinn had thrown him so hard Charlie swore sometimes his head and back would never stop aching. Six months since he'd heard Jed screaming his name as he was taken away.

Charlie fisted his hand so tightly his nails bit into his skin.

He heard the door open again and looked up—and then stood up when he saw a tall, broad-shouldered man in an expensive-looking, dark-gray, pinstripe suit with a dark blue tie secured by a sapphire tie pin. Demon radiated off him; he wore his nature as arrogantly as he wore his wealth. His eyes were the color of a stormy summer sky as he glanced at Charlie. "I was told there was an angel waiting for me," Sable Brennus said, and he extended a hand. Startled, Charlie shook it. "A pleasure to meet you, angel."

"Um—Charlie. That's what my master named me."

Sable smiled and rested a hand lightly on Charlie's shoulder, guiding him toward the double doors that proved to lead into an office that was larger than Jed's house had been. Fire and smoke filled Charlie's mind, and he hastily pushed the memories away. He focused on the floor to ceiling windows that lined two sides of the office, the magnificent view beyond of cloudy skies, afternoon sinking rapidly into evening, and the glitter of city lights rising to beat back the growing dark.

"Would you like anything to drink, angel?" Sable asked.

Charlie tamped down a flicker of annoyance that no one ever seemed to want to use his name. Jed had assured him many times people used 'angel' more as an honorific, a sign of respect, but he would rather they used the name his master had given him. "No, thank you. It was not my intention to detain you, my lord. I only came to inform you that I would be in your territory. I—" He swallowed because it was always so painful to speak of Jed; every time he did so, the wounds tore open anew. He had failed when Jed most needed him because he had let the damned jinn get the best of him. "I am searching for my master, who was kidnapped six months ago. I have been on the trail of the kidnappers, but never managed to get close. But I think they are holing up here because the signature stops. So ..."

Sable strode over to him and pushed a glass into his hand. Wine, Charlie saw, a rich merlot in a stem-less wine glass. He took a sip of it from habit, not wanting to be rude by refusing it now that it had been given to him. He loved wine; how had Sable known?

He remembered sitting with Jed at so many tiny motel tables, drinking wine and food obtained from whatever restaurant they had picked that day. The few precious months they'd had in Jed's old home before they'd been forced to go on the run. Italian food had been their favorite, and he would always remember best the night Jed had overindulged in the wine and fallen asleep against him, soft hair falling in his face, snoring quietly, relaxed and warm in Charlie's arms.

It made his eyes sting, made the back of his throat ache, and he drank more wine just to keep from saying something stupid.

"Do whatever you must, angel," Sable said, and Charlie was strangely comforted by the fierce glint in his eyes, like lightning behind black clouds. "Thank you for coming to see me. I do appreciate the courtesy. I know of your master, though I've never met him. I have always heard that he is a good man, and now I know it's true."

Charlie frowned, confused. "But you haven't met him."

Sable smiled. "I am over three hundred years old and never before have I seen an angel so well and lovingly made. Go find your master, angel. Do whatever you must to get him back. If you require assistance, simply call for me or my consort. His name is Christian. We'll hear you."

"Thank you," Charlie said and finished his wine. He would not ask someone else to save his master; it was his duty alone. "Your generosity is greatly appreciated."

"Generosity has nothing to do with it," Sable said. "I don't like trouble in my city, and anyone strong enough and stupid enough to kidnap a descendant of Solomon without killing his archangel first is trouble I definitely don't like."

Charlie nodded and sketched him a brief half-bow, then turned neatly on his heel and left. In the elevator, he slumped against the mirrored back wall, allowing himself to finally feel the exhaustion he'd been resisting. He reached up to touch his collar once more, aching to feel Jed's fingers trace the runes, calloused fingers just brushing his skin as he pulled away.

He would give anything—do anything—to see his master again, hold him tightly, and never fail him again.

The elevator dinged, drawing his attention back to the present, and Charlie slowly left the casino to make his way into the dark depths of the city to find his master and finally kill those who had taken him.

First, however, he needed rest. As if the thought triggered physical response, Charlie yawned. He could not remember the last time he had slept—sometime before he had almost gotten to them in Blue territory. He'd been so close that losing him again had left Charlie in tears. He was closer than ever, though, and would not fail again.

If he had to destroy himself to save his master, he would. Those damned djinn and that bastard sorcerer who had called them. They would learn to fear Jed's angel— and die with that fear still stuck in their throats. He flexed his fingers, restless, and shoved them into the pockets of his coat as he slipped outside into the dark, rainy night.

He walked briskly back to his cheap motel room, covering the six blocks easily, grateful to reach the still and quiet of the room after the bustle of the city and the cacophony of the casino. Sitting down on the edge of the furthest bed, he shrugged out of his jacket and then pulled off his boots. He pulled his legs up and folded them under him, resting his elbows on his knees.

More than anything, he wanted a nap, but if he fell asleep and they managed to slip away again he would never forgive himself. Not that he would forgive himself, anyway. Jed had created him for protection, and Charlie had failed to protect. He just hoped that Jed did not decide to dismiss him when it was finally all over.

Charlie curled his fingers around his collar, seeking the comfort it always offered, terrified of the thought of being banished and never again seeing or smelling or touching Jed. Of losing forever the chance that he might be able to touch Jed the way he had always wanted...

Lying down on the bed, Charlie tucked his hands behind his head and stared up at the ceiling, meaning to rest for only a few minutes before he went off to pick a fight with the djinn holding his master captive.

The smell of incense, pungent and sharp. Beeswax and roses, fresh spring air.

His eyes fluttered, then slowly opened, and he stared into the most beautiful face he had ever seen. The man's warmth and magic he had felt, sensed, for a very long time. He had touched it, caressed it where he was able, but always the source of it was ultimately out of reach to a being that had no form.

Except ... suddenly he did have form. He stared down at himself, the trim body, fair skin hairless except around the ... he looked up again, into that beautiful face, cheeks flushing as he comprehended that he was naked.

"Hello, angel," the beautiful man said softly.

"H-hello," the angel replied and smiled. "It is an honor to finally meet you."

The man looked at him in surprise. "Finally?"

"All can feel your warmth and magic. It's very lovely. I am honored that it was to me you gave a form." He stretched and tested his limbs, pausing when he felt something on his neck that seemed like it should not be there.

Reaching up, he felt the soft leather and the runes embossed in it. He traced each rune that he could reach, putting together what the whole meant. "I am an archangel, made for you."

The man's cheeks turned the loveliest shade of pink. "Made to protect me since I am no longer able to fight my enemies on my own. They've killed nearly every other member of my family, and those who remain are normals of no use to them. I am sorry to summon you for such a selfish purpose—"

"No, I am happy to protect. I am made for you. I will do whatever you want, master."

"Jed, my name is Jed. You don't have to call me master."

"Jed," he repeated, tasting it, liking it, but he still preferred, "Yes, master."

Rolling his eyes, a smile tugging at his pretty mouth, Jed said, "You need a name as well."

He brightened, smiled widely, at the idea of that. A name. A name made something real, above and beyond simply being given a form. Something with a name was carved into reality and could never really be taken out of it again. Even should he be dismissed again someday, his name would remain and a piece of him would linger forever. "I would be honored to be given a name, master."

Jed smiled again, reaching out to lightly trace his collar, then reached up more slowly to stroke his cheek—then he abruptly jerked back, cheeks going from pink to red. "Uh. How about Charles? It was my grandfather's name. He was a good man and the one who gave me the Ring of Solomon." He held up his left hand, where an innocuous-looking copper ring carved with a six-point star in a circle shone in the light.

The ring radiated a power at complete odds with its humble appearance, and Charles thought that if the ring was that powerful, it would take a sorcerer of considerable power to wield it properly. But he already knew his master was incomparable. "Charles," he repeated and nodded. "I like it, master."

"Good," Jed said softly, and he held out a hand. "You can step out of the spell circle now, Charlie."

"I like that better," Charlie said and took the offered hand. It was warm, rough with callouses, and there was a long, red scratch across the back of it. Without thinking, he lifted Jed's hand to his lips and kissed it softly. "I hope you feel no pain."

Jed's face turned red again, but he did not pull his hand away. "No, I'm fine. Thank you. There, uh—there are clothes there on the sofa for you."

Charlie looked where he indicated, then went over to the sofa and picked up the clothes there and slowly put it all on. He looked much like his master in terms of dress, though his jeans were darker and the sweater blue rather than black. The boots took some work, and he flushed when Jed finally came over to help him lace them up.

He stood up once he was done and pushed away the hair that had fallen in his eyes. "Do I look acceptable, master? I would hate to look unfit to be your archangel."

"You're perfect," Jed said softly, pushing at his glasses, cheeks turning pink again as he looked away. "Come, I will tell you all that you need to know. I have been in this location too long. Soon we shall have to leave, and you must be prepared for what is coming after us."

Charlie nodded and followed as his master led him out of the room they were in, smiling in quiet happiness that he had been made real and given such an important purpose.

His eyes snapped open as he felt a powerful presence trying very hard not to be noticed. He sneered at the ceiling, wondering why djinn were so powerful, but so stupid. Sitting up, he slid off the end of the bed and went to stand beside the door.

A couple of minutes later, the door chimed and unlocked. The silver handle turned, and the door slowly pushed open. Charlie slammed his clasped hands down on the back of the djinn's head, sending it falling to the floor. He dragged the djinn into the room, slammed the door shut, and then slapped a spell of locking on it.

Whipping back around, he only just avoided the blow swung at him, feeling the scorching heat of the djinn's body. Magic alone kept the djinn from incinerating everything around him. He was, as djinn often were, handsome. Dark skin and dark hair with eyes the color of a blue flame. "Greetings, angel," he said and lunged again.

He collided with the shield Charlie had erected, creating a shower of rainbow sparks that singed everything they touched. Charlie smirked and cocked his head. "Where's my master?"

"Sucking my master's cock," the djinn taunted—then roared in pain as Charlie filled the room with blinding light. The djinn had gotten him once, and he would always bear the scars of that terrible night. But he learned quickly, and in the endless months since they had stolen Jed, he had learned how to deal with the djinn.

Charlie moved easily amidst the blinding light. He held out his hand, fingers splayed, and then slowly closed them around a hilt. As the light faded, he retained a sword of light. In the moment where the djinn still recovered, Charlie drove the sword into its gut, yanked it out, and then did it again. The djinn screamed in agony and fell the floor. Charlie drove the blade down into its throat, and the djinn dissolved into ashes.

He let the sword fade back into nothing and used the sleeve of his shirt to wipe sweat from his face.

Stupid djinn.

Glancing at the alarm clock on the bedside table, Charlie saw he'd been asleep only two hours. So much for getting real rest—but he supposed something was better than nothing. He dismissed the need for more rest and focused on his duty. The djinn he'd killed had been powerful, but young. It hadn't been summoned very long ago. Likely, it had been summoned for the sole purpose of stopping him, or at least slowing Charlie down.

Charlie smeared his fingers with the djinn's ashes then began to draw a spell circle with them. He worked slowly, meticulously, painting every rune with the utmost care. Spell work, as his master often said, was a matter of patience more than of skill. Anyone could make a spell circle, but to get it perfect the first time was a trick some witches and sorcerers never mastered.

When the circle was finished, he held his splayed hand, still smeared with ashes, over the spell circle and spoke the activating words. The spell burst to life in flames of flickering blue fire, pulling on the remaining pieces of the djinn's spirit that lingered and forcing from them where it had last been.

At last, the spell circle dissolved, leaving only a single glowing blue flame. Charlie wiped his hand off then flicked his fingers, indicating the flame should show him the way.

It led him on a merry chase through the dark city, taking a meandering circuit through the business distract, into a cluster of small shops that often had private apartments on the top floors, then into the neighborhoods that were almost strictly residential. Eventually, those too faded away as the little flame led him into the industrial areas by the river, into the depths of the harbor.

When it stopped and went out, Charlie found himself standing in front of an enormous warehouse. It smelled of blood: werewolves, dragons, and dozens more. So it had once been an arena, including the d-pits where dragons were fought. But those smells were old, meaning they'd been driven out a long time ago.

The only fresh-smelling blood was human and goblin; he could also smell roasted human flesh, which matched with the scent of goblin blood. Somewhere in the warehouse was a processing operation for the human meat goblins loved so much.

It churned his stomach thinking about it and made him fear for his master. He could guess why they might take Jed to the goblins: the ring of Solomon. It would not come off his finger unless Jed desired, but goblins were adept at removing such things.

Charlie slowly approached the warehouse and was not at all surprised to find it locked. A stupid padlock, however, was no match for him. He etched a single rune on the front of it and activated it with a word. The lock separated into two pieces in his hand, and he threw them aside. Pushing open the door, he slipped inside.

The smell of human flesh, both raw and cooked, was stronger than ever. It made him gag, but he forced his stomach down and pushed onward, slipping easily through the dark.

He heard them long before he saw them and slowed his steps, before stopping completely. Let them think he was hesitating, lost ...

And when they had formed a half-circle around him, he let out a burst of blinding light. After that, the half dozen or so goblins were easy to take care of. He broke three noses, one arm, and bruised several ribs. When he finally stopped, he was panting lightly. Lifting a hand high above his head, he slowly closed his splayed fingers into a fist, snuffing the light.

"Where is my master?" he asked the groaning, whimpering goblins. "Give my master to me, or stay out of my way."

When they gave him no useful reply, he knocked them all unconscious one by one before moving on further into the warehouse. His next challenge—honestly, was he in a game or a bad movie, did they expect such childish one-by-one antics to work on him?—was a vampire.

The little bastard was quick and threw a mean punch. Charlie grunted at the first one and wiped glistening, red-gold blood from his lips. He heard the vampire laugh and managed to dodge the next swing, but tripped over something on the floor that he didn't see until too late. He went down hard, grunting at the painful jolt, and swore as the vampire grabbed him up and threw him into a stack of crates. It sent him crashing right back down again, and he bashed his temple on a piece of pipe. Damn it.

When he tried to summon his light, the ultimate weapon of an archangel, the vampire punched him again, and it landed dead on his jaw. Charlie's vision swam, but he dragged himself to his feet and wiped more blood from his lips. Ah, idea.

"Come here, pretty bloodsucker," he purred tauntingly. "Even the djinn don't give me this much trouble."

"Young djinn," the vampire said, voice soft, sultry, and came at him again.

Charlie didn't resist. He let the vampire grab him, shove him into a wall—then he kissed the bastard, forcing him to take a mouthful of blood. The vampire jerked back and spat out the blood, but too late.

While he was choking and twitching on blood he could not handle—blood that was too rich, too potent—Charlie summoned a dagger of light and slit his throat. Since that was not nearly enough to kill a vampire, he finished the job with more light, pouring it into the vampire until it leaked out, and with a flash, the vampire was only dust.

He wiped sweat from his brow, panting more heavily. A two hour nap was not nearly long enough for all the energy he was pouring out. At least he was almost there.

Charlie pressed on, weaving through the last half of the warehouse until he finally reached the rooms at the back. He ignored those on the ground level because he could just barely feel the signature of Jed's magic higher up.

Reaching the rusty metal stairs in the far right corner, he climbed them, but as he reached the first landing and turned, a figure appeared at the very top. The taste of magic was acrid on his tongue, making him gag. Stolen magic was foul magic, even if humans never seemed to notice.

He didn't give the witch time to make the first strike, just flew up the stairs, grabbed him by the throat, and swung him out over the railing to choke and dangle helplessly.

An earring gleamed in the man's. Carved from imp horn, it was despicable. Charlie reached out and tore it from the man's ear, unmoved by his snarl of pain. "Those who steal do not deserve what they take," he said and let the man fall.

From the sounds he made as he landed, he would be sore, but little else whenever he woke up. Charlie pressed on, breaking the lock on the door at the tap of the stairs. Inside, four men pointed guns at him, but the bullets only died as they reached the shield that Charlie threw up.

He used most of what remained of his rapidly diminishing energy to summon another burst of blinding light, and as they screamed in agony, he drew it back into a shining blade. After that, it went quickly. Four piddling humans would never be a match for an archangel, not when they finally had nowhere else to run. Charlie killed them quickly, angry that the man responsible for it all was not there. But he would find the bastard later.

First, always first, he had to take care of his master. Charlie's eyes stung with tears when he finally let go of his battle rage and allowed himself to focus on the man huddled in the corner.

He was rumpled, dirty, and exhausted looking. There was a bruise on his jaw, another at his right eye, and a cut on his lip. Charlie didn't doubt his clothes hid far more of the same. "Master," he said softly as he crossed the room. Dropping to one knee, Charlie dipped his head and said, "My apologies, master, for taking so long to find and retrieve you. Whatever punishment—" he broke off with a surprise grunt as he suddenly found his arms full of Jed, the force knocking him over to lie on his back.

"You're alive!" Jed said, looking and sounding close to tears. "I couldn't feel you, and I saw that djinn throw you into the banister. I saw the blood, saw you weren't moving as the flames—you're alive, I can't believe you're alive, Charlie."

Before Charlie could get a word in edgewise, Jed kissed him. Charlie froze, shocked, but when Jed started to draw away, he curled his fingers into Jed's hair, twined an arm around his waist, and held on tightly. He kissed Jed hard, deep, and tasted blood as the cut on Jed's lip reopened.

He drew back only to avoid causing further injury, licking away blood and the taste of Jed on his lips. "Master ... "

"Sorry," Jed muttered, and Charlie fought disappoint that the kiss was already being rescinded. "I'm so happy you're alive, Charlie. I thought I'd gotten you killed."

Charlie got them standing then hugged him tightly. "I would never die without first ensuring you were safe, Master. I exist for you. I am sorry that I took so long to find you."

"You came, Charlie. You're alive. That's all that matters to me. We should go before the others come back. They're working on a way to steal my ring, but they had to go speak with an alchemist and did not dare take me."

"I would imagine not, Master," Charlie said softly and, ignoring Jed's cry of protest, picked him up and carried him down the stairs and out of the warehouse.

Though he'd half expected more trouble on the way out, no one bothered them.

"Let me down, Charlie," Jed said once they were outside. "I'm exhausted and malnourished, I admit it, but I can walk."

Charlie reluctantly obeyed, but kept hold of Jed's hand as they walked back to Charlie's rented room.

Jed hugged him again once the door was closed, held tightly, and Charlie thought he felt tears soaking into his shirt. "Thank you, Charlie. I was beginning to think I was stuck forever in hell. They kept me too weak to use my magic—most of the time I was asleep. I only woke this time because they've been at the alchemist's for so long. And you're alive, I can't stop being awed—"

He stopped talking, buried his face against Charlie's chest, and just clung. Charlie held him, soothed him as best he could, his own eyes stinging, throat raw, with his own relief.

Whatever happened later didn't matter. He had his master back.

Sniffling one last time, Jed drew back and wiped his eyes on the dirty sleeve of his torn and frayed long-sleeved t-shirt. "I think first I need a shower before my own stench kills me. Then food. And I need to get new glasses—"

"I have your glasses, master," Charlie said quietly, and he pulled out the broken glasses wrapped in his handkerchief. "I'm sorry the house burned, I should—"

Jed's fingers covered his mouth. "Charlie, you're wonderful. You've done more than anyone should ever have had to. You are more than I deserve. Thank you for saving my glasses. Let me shower, eat, and rest, and I can repair them."

For a moment, Charlie thought he was going to get another kiss, and his heart thudded in his chest. He leaned his own head down slightly—and tried not to show his disappointment when Jed drew away and headed for the bathroom.

Charlie went to his suitcase and pulled out the clothes he had carried for Jed from the start, certain that eventually he would save his master. He set them out in one of the two armchairs in the room and put the glasses on the table between them.

Out of things to do, he toed off his shoes, shucked his jacket, and lay down in bed to rest until Jed came out of the shower. He was asleep before his head hit the pillow.

He woke up to the smell of food and the sound of his own stomach growling. Looking up, Charlie blinked sleepily and asked, "Food?" Jed's laughter washed over him, warming Charlie all the way through. Everything came rushing back, one thought blazing in his head: he'd gotten his master back.

After six long months of agony, he finally had his master back. Charlie sat up and swung his feet over the edge of the bed. His body ached from being pushed so hard, and he could feel all the cuts and bruises he had acquired in the warehouse.

He also reeked.

Ignoring the tempting food on the table by the window and smiling brightly at Jed, he dragged himself into the bathroom. He started the shower then stripped off his clothes, throwing them on top of Jed's discarded clothes.

Steam poured out of the shower, and Charlie groaned as the hot water struck his skin, washing over him and sluicing away the dirt, blood, and sweat. The worst of his aches eased slightly, and after a few minutes of simply soaking up the wet heat, he finally picked up a bar of soap and began to scrub.

Three thorough scrubs later, he finally shut the water off and climbed out, toweling roughly as he returned to the main room. Shuffling over to his suitcase, he quickly pulled out clean jeans, a black long-sleeved t-shirt, socks, and underwear. He dressed hastily, towel-dried his shaggy blond hair some more, and then finally joined Jed at the table.

"Good morning, Charlie," Jed said with a smile. "Well, good evening, really. But you know what I mean."

Charlie smiled and reached across the table to lightly touch his fingertips to Jed's cheek. "Good morning, Master," he said softly. "Are you well?"

Jed's cheeks flushed pink as they always did at so many of the things Charlie said and did. Charlie had missed it, feared he would never again see his master smile and flush in that way.

It reminded him of their kiss, and with an effort, he pulled his hand back. He wanted more kisses—wanted much more than kisses—but he sensed if he pushed, Jed would only push back and close the matter forever. Charlie was tired of his resisting, but patience and persistence would go farther than pushing.

Patience and persistence he had.

"So," he prodded when Jed did not reply, "are you well, Master?"

"Oh! Quite well, thank you. Well enough, I think, that I can finally fix my glasses. Sit and eat, Charlie."

Charlie did as he was told, or at least started to, but he had always loved to watch Jed work. Even the most trivial of spells were made fascinating just because Jed was so good at what he did.

Jed cleared a space on the hardwood floor, wiping everything away so that it gleamed and not a speck of dust remained. Then he reached into his pocket and pulled out what looked like a cigarette case at a glance. Charlie was not surprised that Jed had retrieved it so quickly. Opening the case, Jed extracted a piece of chalk.

It took him twenty minutes to draw out a small spell circle and weave the runes together into a spell of repair and durability. In the center of the circle he placed his broken glasses. He checked the circle over thoroughly, then held his hand out over the circle and spoke the activating mark.

The room filled with a flash of gold light. When it faded away, Jed laughed with pleasure and removed his repaired glasses. He slid them on his face and smiled brightly at Charlie. "All set."

"Yes, Master," Charlie agreed with a smile, though to him Jed still looked strained. There was a touch of trying-too-hard behind his smile and lines of strain around his eyes. Shadows lurked in his eyes as well, and Charlie hated the men who had made Jed's life miserable for so long.

He waited until Jed had resumed his seat at the table, then said, "Are you sure you're all right, Master?"

"A shower, rest, and now food are doing me a world of good. I can almost forget—" he stopped, fork slipping from his fingers. His eyes slipped shut and he pressed his fingertips to them, shuddering. "Well, I did say almost," he said eventually, trying so hard to be flippant, but there was an unmistakable tremble in his voice.

Charlie stood up, moved around the table, and scooped him up. He sat down in Jed's chair and settled Jed in his lap, holding him tightly. He dared to brush a soft kiss to Jed's cheek. "I won't let them have you again, Master. Let me have your shadows, and I will burn them away with holy light."

For once, Jed didn't say anything about propriety, not being right, and advantages being taken. He leaned into Charlie, curled a hand around his neck, and held fast.

The only thing that could have made it better was a happier reason, but Charlie was just relieved Jed was accepting his comfort for once. "Master," he breathed against Jed's skin, lips ghosting over his cheek again. Jed smelled like wildflowers and sunshine, with that underlying tang that was his magic. "Let go of your shadows, Master. Give them to me."

Jed clung to him, buried his face in the hollow of Charlie's throat, and obediently let go of everything: the murders of so much of his family, six months of abuse, the agony of believing Charlie was dead, and the fear that someone would finally wrest the ring of Solomon from him.

Charlie held him tightly, pressed soft kisses wherever he could reach, caressed and soothed, absorbed all the agony pouring out, and turned it into energy he needed, pouring back out healing energies. It surrounded them in a soft, hazy, rainbow of light, and everything around them vanished. The world was reduced to just the two of them.

It reminded Charlie of all their nights together, just the two of them against the world. A quiet meal of turkey sandwiches in the house where he had first gained a form, burgers in a motel that had smelled like sex and cabbage, and steak in a nicer hotel, one with soft beds where Jed had slept without dreaming for the first time in a long time.

So many nights spent with just the two of them. Wandering from place to place, barely staying ahead of those who so desperately sought Jed's power.

Charlie just held him, healed him, served his master, and reveled in being the angel lucky enough to have been granted form and given Jed's collar. There was nothing he wouldn't do to remain Jed's angel forever.

Eventually, Jed went slack in his arms, breathing evening out into sleep. Charlie stood up, holding Jed tightly, and carried him over to the bed. He lay Jed down and removed all but his jeans and t-shirt, then settled the blankets over him.

He brushed a soft kiss across Jed's mouth and said softly, "Sleep well, Master." He rubbed his thumb along Jed's fingers and the lights around them dimmed. Returning to the table, he filled a plate with chicken, mashed potatoes, and steamed carrots and broccoli. It never failed to impress him how adept Jed was at obtaining food; whatever else they had occasionally lacked in their frenzied attempts not to get captured, they had seldom gone hungry.

Charlie looked at the bed, the last of his fear and guilt easing as he saw his master sleeping peacefully. He turned his attention back to eating, and then piled everything back on the tray when he was done and set it outside for the cleaning staff to take away.

Returning to the bed, he put the lights out entirely and simply lay there in the dark, soothed by his Master's presence and the soft, steady sounds of his breathing. Reaching out, he twined their fingers together and slowly allowed himself to go back to sleep.

He woke to the smell of something burning—and the acrid taste of djinn magic. Snarling, Charlie threw a protective shell over Jed then surged to his feet. The entire room was burning, but there was no djinn.

It was likely they had trapped them... But they would not simply let Jed die while he still wore the ring of Solomon. If he died wearing it, then on his finger it would stay until a suitable heir came along to remove it.

Charlie moved to the door and jerked back when the doorknob burned his hand. He stared at the burned flesh, beginning to feel real worry. Mere fired should not burn him so easily. It could burn him, eventually kill him, but it was hard.

Demon magic, however ...

Fear chilled his veins, to think that the bastards chasing them had resorted to summoning a demon. Surely they had not been that stupid—especially as they were in demon territory. Sable Brennus would not take lightly the presence of another demon in his domain.

Smoke began to fill the room in earnest, and Charlie shook off his momentary fears, gathered his magic, and filled the room with shimmering rainbow light.

"Charlie?" Jed asked then inhaled sharply. "Damn it, I knew we held still for too long. Hang on." He climbed out of bed and, as Charlie's light began to fade, rapidly drew a spell circle. "Come, Charlie."

Obeying immediately, Charlie joined him in the spell circle. Jed held on to him tightly and spoke the final words of the spell. With a faint tugging sensation and a burst of blue light, they vanished.

They reappeared on the street and stared in momentary dismay at the hotel burning down right before their eyes.

"Angel ... " A soft, sibilant voice said. Charlie whipped around, summoning his sword and throwing a new protection around Jed, just as the figure who'd spoken came slinking out of the shadows across the street. "They do not lie. The powers of Solomon overcome even demon workings. But then again, Solomon did command hundreds of demons ..."

"Yes," Jed said. "Leave us in peace, or I will show you how."

Charlie froze, surprised. He had forgotten that. How could he have forgotten that? But then again, he hated the ring. Every bit of misery in their lives could be laid at the feet of Solomon's damn ring.

He knew Jed's heart would break if he lost the ring, however; it was a family legacy, bestowed to them out of trust, out of faith. Charlie would not betray that faith.

The demon laughed, sneered. "No watered-down descendant of Solomon can ensnare me. Did you think they summoned a child? No, you will not take me, descendant of Solomon."

Charlie was sick of the talking. With a roar, he lunged at the demon, light arcing as he swung his sword. He snarled in frustration when the demon countered easily, their powers clashing in a shower of black and gold sparks.

Before Charlie could regroup and strike again, the demon moved—fast, nearly too fast to follow, and definitely too fast to counter the hit. It landed hard, broke Charlie's nose, and sent him falling back on his ass. Shimmering red-gold blood poured down his face and across his shirt. Charlie snarled and got his feet under him and then sprang forward as the demon came at him again.

They collided full tilt, the power of the demon like acid against his skin. Charlie screamed, but ignored the white-hot pain and simply countered with his own power until the demon finally threw him off. He laid on the ground, panting and bleeding, dizzy with pain.

The demon's cold laughter made him shudder, and he forced himself up, getting as far as his elbows and knees before the pain simply made it impossible to continue. He saw Jed, who looked angry and miserable, and found the strength to stand.

He stumbled, turned, and gathered his power. "You will not have my master, demon."

"Oh, I'll have him, angel. Over and over and over again." The demon touched his tongue to his lip then smirked. "Shall we go round three?"

"Enough!" Jed shouted, and he held out the hand bearing the ring. Then he began to speak in a language Charlie did not know—the language of Solomon, the language of days long past.

The demon paled. Charlie didn't wait for Jed to finish the spell. Summoning all of his remaining strength, he surged toward the demon and drove his sword through its stomach. The demon dropped to the ground, and Charlie slit his throat to be sure he was dead. When the demon was gone, driven back to the hell by the loss of the body to which it was bound, Charlie summoned a last shred—

"I'll do it," Jed said softly, covering Charlie's outstretched hand with his own. Charlie relaxed, stepped back—and sank to his knees, too exhausted to stand, while he listened to Jed's smooth, deep voice recite an incantation for burning.

He looked up when gentle hands touched his face and stared up into the sad, watery eyes of his master. "Oh, Charlie. I can't—you shouldn't—I never meant for you to suffer this way."

Charlie tried to smile, but it hurt. He did not bother to try speaking. He simply covered the hands cupping his face with his own, squeezed lightly, and curled into Jed as he was pulled close.

Gentle magic washed over him, smelling and tasting of his master. Charlie tried to stay awake, stay alert, but the warmth and the recent battle were too much to fight and once more he felt himself slip away into the mercies of oblivion.

When he woke again, he did not recognize the fancy-looking ceiling painted in ornate swirls with lamps shaped and set to blend into the design. He sat up in a bed that was big enough for ten, the sheets dark blue silk with a warm, down duvet and a satin cover in a myriad of shades of swirling blue and silver.

He looked around the room, stunned by the opulence of the furniture, the floor to ceiling windows, the lavish breakfast set on the kitchen bar. Where were they that it had its own kitchen?

There were powerful wards on the place—some of them were Jed's, but the rest had the flavor of demon magic. Familiar demon magic, he realized: Sable Brennus.

Realizing they must be in one of Sable's casinos, or at least some building that belonged to Sable, Charlie relaxed. He slid out of the bed and padded over to the windows, gawking at the city below.

They'd been on the street; he'd been broken, battered, and exhausted. Jed had been crying again. Charlie wished he could give Jed something, anything that would make him happy and banish the tears forever.

Where was Jed? Charlie frowned, suddenly anxious, but even as he started to panic he saw Jed's clothes in a pile at the foot of the bed. So he must be around somewhere—and, he remembered idiotically, Jed had placed his own wards around the room.

Rolling his eyes at himself, he went into the bathroom to use the mirror. His nose looked as though it had never been broken, though it was still a bit tender when he touched it. There was a faint scar on one cheek, and he felt sore all over, but Jed, or someone else, had healed the majority of the damage.

Going back out to the main room, Charlie approached the kitchen bar and helped himself to buttery croissants and slices of apple and pineapple. He licked crumbs and juice from his fingers before washing them at the sink. Then he poured a cup of coffee from a tall, black thermos pitcher and wandered back over to the windows.

How long he stood there admiring the view, he wasn't sure, but the sound of the door opening finally drew him away. Jed stood there, staring at him, before he all but flew across the room to him. Charlie barely was able to set his coffee cup aside before he caught Jed up. "Master ... "

"Charlie," Jed said softly, breathing the words against his skin.

"I'm fine, Master," Charlie said, frowning in concern at the way Jed was trembling. To distract him, Charlie asked, "How did we wind up here? Where are we, besides in the domain of Sable Brennus?"

Jed laughed every so faintly. "Your fights tend to be very dramatic, Charlie. And the presence of an uninvited demon ... " he smiled up at Charlie. "You also appear to have made quite the impression on Sable Brennus. He says you are the finest angel he has ever seen."

Charlie smiled. "He said that I was well and lovingly made, Master."

"You are very lovingly made," Jed said tightly, and he rested his forehead against Charlie's chest, his trembling returning. "I'm not sure I can take seeing you almost die in front of me again. I did not summon you just to see you battered and abused over and over again. I never should have—I'm so sorry—you deserve more—"

"NO!" Charlie burst out, sudden real fear cutting through him. He drew back, reluctantly leaving the warmth of Jed's arms, and dropped to his knees. Holding fast to Jed's hands, he said, "Master, please. Do not send me away, do not send me back to exist as practically nothing."

Tears fell from Jed's dark, weary, sad eyes. "But an angel is a gift, and I have done naught, but see you hurt time and again, Charlie." His fingers caressed Charlie's cheek. "I don't deserve you."

"You summoned me, you gave me form, you hold all of me," Charlie said, capturing his hand again, pressing it to the collar around his throat. "I am yours, willingly come from the light and bound to the form you made for me. I am yours and want only that: To protect, serve, and love you. Please, Master, if I am allowed one boon, it would be that you not dismiss me."

"Charlie ... "

"Please, Master, I beg—"

"No!" Jed cut in, voice shaky. "Don't beg. You, above everyone else in the world, should never have to beg. I'd be dead without you, Charlie. Worse, I'd be alive, but as good as dead. Don't—don't beg."

Charlie smiled then kissed the backs of Jed's hands. "All I want is you, Master. You gathered my light and gave it form, and so I shine for you."

"You say the most ridiculous things," Jed said and tugged him to his feet.

"But you like them," Charlie said.

"But I like them," Jed agreed softly and cupped his face. And to Charlie's astonishment, drew him down and kissed him softly. Charlie whimpered, hardly daring to believe it, but Jed really was awake and aware and not just free from recent danger.

He drew Jed closer, held him tightly, and took the kiss deeper. Jed tasted like coffee and magic, and the way he moved into and with every touch that glided across his skin sent a hot thrill jolting through Charlie. He drew back just enough to lick those addictive lips and nuzzle against his cheek. "Master ... "

Jed shivered in his arms and whispered his name like it was a fragile thing. "Charlie."

It was all the invitation—permission—that Charlie required. Hot with anticipation and satisfaction, he took another hungry kiss, then tore away long enough to drag Jed over to the bed.

He stripped off their clothes as quickly as he could manage, then swept Jed up and deposited him on the bed. Climbing on top of him, Charlie swooped in to steal another kiss as Jed's arms twined around him, pulling him closer, their legs sliding and tangling together.

Charlie just knew he was dreaming. Knew he was going to wake up at any moment, alone and exhausted in a grungy motel room still aching to find the master he had lost.

Tearing away from Jed's mouth, Charlie just held him close. "Am I awake, Master?"

"You had better be," Jed said with a laugh that held only a faint tremble in it. "I'm going to be displeased if this is all your dream."

Charlie laughed with him and drew back again, nipping Jed's jaw, his nose, before sliding his mouth back over Jed's and taking his mouth in a slow, burning kiss.

Jed's fingers slid along his collar, and when Charlie drew back, Jed reached up to press soft kisses to his skin just below the collar. "My angel," Jed whispered, warm breaths giving Charlie goosebumps.

"Yours," he agreed and began to drop kisses at random points across Jed's body, determined to cover every last inch of it. Eventually his explorations ended at Jed's cock, which was hard and wet. The soft, whimpering noises Jed made were the sweetest sounds Charlie had ever heard.

His master was safe. His master was finally admitting to what he wanted. What they needed. Charlie closed his mouth around Jed's cock and began to suck, slowly working his way down the length of it as far as he could manage.

"I don't—" Jed broke off with a groan, hips moving, pushing his cock deeper. The fingers of one hand sank into Charlie's hair as the others tangled in the sheets. He tried to speak again, the words falling out between pants and gasps for more. "I don't remember including that sort of talent in your making spell, angel."

Charlie just sucked harder, taking Jed as deep as he possibly could, tongue and throat working, his jaw aching, eyes watering by the time Jed finally succumbed and came down his throat with a ragged cry. Charlie swallowed it all down, licked remaining traces from his cock, and then wiped his own chin. He crawled back up Jed's body, rubbing his own cock along all that smooth, warm skin.

Jed's mouth latched onto his throat, just above the collar, sucking up a mark as he wrapped hot, calloused fingers around Charlie's cock and began to stroke. "Master," Charlie moaned, moving into that knowing, talented hand, angling his head to grant him better access, happy to be lost in the thrall of his master.

He muffled his shout in Jed's mouth, shuddering in his arms until at last, the orgasm eased. "I do not think I have managed to leave bed for more than a few minutes since regaining you, master."

"I hope that's not a complaint," Jed said with a grin as he began to lick Charlie's come from his fingers. Like his blood, it held a faint, gold shimmer. Unlike the vampire who had suffered drinking Charlie's blood, Jed showed no ill effects.

Charlie flopped back on the bed, dragging Jed to lay half on top of him, nuzzling against him, and breathing in his scent, happy to laze about and doze as Jed fell into slumber.

The sound of something tapping on glass drew his attention some time later, and Charlie resentfully dug himself out of the warm nest of blankets and Jed. His gaze was immediately drawn to movement—and a figure standing outside his window on some magic-made platform, slowly breaking through the wards.

Not just anyone, but the bastard responsible for the nightmare of the past three years, the bastard who had kept Jed from him for the past six months. Elmore, a powerful sorcerer and head of a group—a cult, so far as Charlie could tell—determined to take the ring of Solomon and put normals in their place.

Charlie had killed many of them while protecting his master and later trying to find him, but he had not seen their bastard leader since the night Elmore got the better of him, nearly killed him, and stole Jed.

"I won't fail a second time," he said. Outside the window, Elmore continued to work diligently away, a cold smile on his face as he briefly met Charlie's gaze.

Striding up to the window, Charlie loosed his magic and drove his fist through it. The glass shattered, and he grabbed Elmore by the scruff of his shirt and dragged him inside the room.

"Hello again, angel," Elmore greeted—and slammed his hand over Charlie's face, speaking the words of a spell.

Charlie screamed as agonizing pain tore through him, as something crawled and clawed through him, scraped at his innards, and seemed to try to tear him apart from the inside out. It went for his mind, oozed over it, stung it with burning barbs—

His screams filled the room, spilled out into the night, and his own world reduced to that unbelievable pain.

Then it stopped, leaving him panting. Charlie fell to his knees, doubled over, barely catching himself in time to avoid smashing his face into the floor. His body was soaked in sweat. It dripped from his hair and down his face, plastered his clothes to his body. He stared up at Elmore, exhausted and drained, body still shuddering, wracked with memories of the recent pain. He licked dry lips, tried to clear his raw throat, and asked, "What did you do to me?"

Elmore scowled at him. "Stand up."

"No," Charlie said.

"Obey me, angel!" Elmore snarled. "Obey me and stand up!"

Charlie sneered at him. "I do not obey any, but my master."

"I am your master now!"

Jed's laughter drew their attention as he walked toward them, slipping from the shadows of the bed and into the light closer to the windows. "Nobody steals my angel."

Is that what the bastard had tried to do? Steal him from his master? Charlie's world went white hot. He barely remembered moving, remembered only a handful of actions and sensations. There was the surge of power and fury and the rush of his wings and the weight of his blade in his hand.

There was Elmore's fear, in the breath before Charlie took his life.

Then he felt Jed's arms wrap around him from behind, and the white hot rage cooled, faded. Charlie shuddered, all of his strength going out of him. He sank to his knees, covering his face with his hands. "Master—what did I do?"

"You're an archangel," Jed said softly. "You've never managed to tap the full breadth of that power because you're gentle at heart. But I made you to be the strongest of angels, and so the power was always there."

"He tried to take me away from you," Charlie said. "I lost you once, but you were still my master. I won't tolerate any master but you."

Jed let him go, and Charlie almost whimpered at the loss, but then Jed moved to kneel in front of him, drew Charlie back into his arms, and rested Charlie's head on his shoulder. "No one else will ever have you, angel. I made you, and even if I'm a terrible master—" He broke off, swallowed. "I don't care. You're my angel, mine alone. I made you for me."

"Yes, master," Charlie said, slowly unfurling. He lightly touched Jed's cheek, letting his fingers curl into his soft hair as Jed leaned forward. "Made by you, made for you, for all eternity."

Angel Eyes

Debora Day

Chapter One

Disorientated blue eyes shot open to gaze at the glaringly bright sun. Thick drifts of pristine snow surrounded him, the chill seeping into the very core of his being. An unfamiliar body shivered as sensations he'd never experienced rolled through him. What was this feeling? Was it cold?

He had never been privy to such a sensation before. Pain, hunger, and thirst were unknown to him. He understood the principle behind them, but as a member of the Celestial Hierarchy, they were strange to him. Such experiences were reserved for the Fallen and humans dwelling upon the earth.

Until now.

The new sensations rippling through him sent the sensory portions of his brain into a state of near overload. He could barely process them all as they drilled into him.

His consciousness was not prepared to deal with such a torturous blend of human awareness.

The crystalline glare of the sun reflected off of the snow and burned painfully into his human eyes, forcing light into previously unused orbs. It was a different light from that of the Creator. There was an underlying harshness present in the gleam. There was no comfort, only detached illumination.

Brightness poured down upon him, cold and without the life he always felt when gazing upon the Creator. What he felt made no sense. Why was he in this place? Was this freezing hell some sort of punishment for an unknown transgression?

Each exhaled breath brought forth small wisps of smoke. Thoughts swam together as he attempted to understand his surroundings and his reason for being placed in such an environment. Something of great importance must have occurred in Heaven for him to be lying amidst the white powdery flakes and freezing temperatures. If only his mind could focus enough to access the blocked parts of his memory.

His head ached from the strain of searching the lost memories for some explanation as to why he was in his current location. Trying to force the memories was not bringing forth the desired results. Instead of helping, it was creating a throbbing pain originating from behind the lids of his closed eyes. It radiated outward so quickly and painfully that he was left gasping for breath.

Where were his memories? Why was he lost upon this sea of loneliness without the integral connection to his Creator? Until this moment, it had always been a strong whisper in his mind—warm and constant. Now only silence existed.

Time could later be spent attempting to find the lost fragments of his psyche. For now, he needed to remove himself from his current circumstances before his soul expired in the frigid atmosphere. His core temperature was rapidly dropping, which meant the window of survival was short.

He rolled shakily to his knees only to realize his balance was severely distorted. Something crucial was missing from him. He felt wrong. His internal compass seemed off.

Sudden and inexplicable fear wound tight in his abdomen. It was a truth he'd pushed as far away from his current thoughts as he could manage. His body began to shake with an emotion unfamiliar to him—fear so powerful it ate away at his core. He had never experienced fear or any powerful emotion before this moment.

Lifting a trembling hand to his shoulder, he nearly collapsed in the agony of what he felt. There was nothing there. Fear was replaced by a pain so keen he could barely withstand the force of it. Crippling agony washed through him in thick waves, leaving him nearly drowning in its wake.

Instead of the downy composition of feathers usually present, he felt nothing but cool, numb skin. Gone from him was that which set him apart from the Beloved. His wings were taken from him.

Wings were his status as a servant of the Creator—proof of his existence in the hierarchy of angels. Without them he was nothing. He was lower than all creatures created by his Father.

A Fallen.

Shaking, he cried out weakly into the white wasteland of snow creating dunes around him. His voice seemed to catch on the wind and echo through the nearby wood. So great was his distress, he believed he might expire from the sheer pain of loss and betrayal working through him.

"Why?" he cried out into the snowy surroundings. "Why am I here?"

Had his transgression been so terrible? Without his wings, he could not survive. He was human but without his Father's love. He was Damned.

"Hey! Is someone there?"

Pale eyes flickered upward from the white drifts of snow. He heard the voice but was unable to pinpoint its location. His first instinct was to hide but his body betrayed him by collapsing into the freezing flakes. He felt frozen where he sat, unable to defend himself should danger approach.

"Holy God—"

The crunch of footsteps in the snow was closer, allowing him to pinpoint the direction. He shifted his gaze until it landed on a tall, slender man bundled thickly in a fleece coat and hat, the material collecting fallen flakes of snow. The small bits of ice glittered with the caught sunlight, giving him an innocent, almost angelic quality.

This was a man—a human.

Realization struck him. This pristine and icy landscape was not Hell—the pit where demons writhed, seeking only for the torment of others. This was far more bitter a fate.

Knowledge burned his mind with a fiery brand. The truth was now as plain as the snow falling around him. He could neither run from it, nor deny it. His earlier assumption was correct. He was Fallen—lost forever from his Father's love. There was no worse fate he could imagine in all his millennia of existence.

Closing his eyes at the feeling of deep-set remorse, his body heaved a great shudder. Darkness threatened his consciousness, calling him to abandon all thought and succumb to the Fall. Hell was preferable to what had happened—what he had no memory of. Only betrayal against Father brought on this most bitter of punishments. To be Fallen was to be devoid of the Father's love. He possessed no memory of his crime, making his Fall all the more bitter.

Shocked words tumbled from the human's lips, yet he could not hear. Any dialogue fell on grief and shock-clogged ears. His only salvation was to stare into a pair of the most exquisite green eyes he had ever seen and pray for a quick death. There was nothing for him as a Fallen. Whatever had forced him to such a choice was lost in the Fall.

He, Uriel, Guardian of Eden, wished for the finality of death. There would be no rebirth or Hell, only the abyss of nothing. Angels possessed no soul because they were a soul. In human form, he was still naught but a solid soul. To die was the end of everything.

Glove-clad fingers shook him with jarring force, tearing him from the edge of the abyss. "How did you get here? Where are your clothes?"

The hands latched onto his chilled shoulders and forced him to face the stranger. He couldn't speak. He was barely conscious. The cold and shock were taking their toll on his normally resilient body.

"You're freezing. We've got to get you warm or you'll go into shock."

Something thick and warm was draped across his shoulders. "My cabin is just over that drift."

Hands forced him to his feet and kept him aloft during the walk across the frozen land towards a small quaint cabin nestled against the edge of the forest. "Just a little farther."

Pain shot up the soles of his feet with each step. The snow appeared soft but when walked upon with tender, bare feet, it felt as if needles were being shoved into his soles. His teeth bit deeply into his lower lip, breaking the skin and filling his mouth with surprisingly warm blood considering he was now shaking violently with cold and barely able to remain standing.

Warmth radiating from the cabin beckoned them inside. The stark difference in temperature did little to stop the violent shakes rocking his body. It was an experience he equated to death, though with no practical knowledge in the area. His muscles jumped of their own accord, spasming in wild jerks. A haze began to creep into the corners of his vision, narrowing it.

His very being seemed frozen where he stood. Had he been of his normal strength, he would have found the attention of a human distressing. Instead, he was left swaying in the middle of a one room cabin, every passing moment bringing him closer to oblivion.

"I'm going to draw a bath. You need to stay awake."

The statement fell upon deaf ears as Uriel collapsed to his knees, body shaking in a seizure-like motion. He would never feel warm again. The cold had become a part of him—ingrained into his very being. From the tips of his ears to the soles of his feet was nothing but frozen flesh. Even the pain had ceased to register in his mind.

It felt like an eternity before warm arms wrapped around his body. His frame shuddered with the effort to burrow closer into the warmth. He soaked up every ounce of the heat yet continued to shake with uncontrollable jerks.

"Damn, you're heavy." Darkness pricked Uriel's vision, making it difficult to respond, let alone assist the human. "Help me a little, damn it."

He tried; he truly did. His muscles simply refused to obey even the smallest command. He was as helpless as a newly whelped infant. The simple act of remaining conscious took every ounce of his rapidly dwindling strength.

With a hard tug and pull, Uriel found himself transferred to a tub of cool water. As the water settled around him, his teeth chattered violently. Gradually, the cool water was drained and replaced with heated. The warming process was painfully slow, but soon the shudders gradually retreated into only the occasional tremor. The stranger's hands ran up and down on the flesh of his feet and fingers in almost violent motions so to keep circulation flowing through the chilled limbs.

"That's strange," murmured the human as his fingers traced Uriel's smooth, creaseless palms. "I'm sorry, but this is probably going to start to hurt."

The comment confused him until he realized the purpose of the action. Feeling returned to his extremities, and with it, excruciating pain. No amount of torture could compare to the sensation of having blood resume its trek through previously oxygen-starved flesh. Nails were being driven into his hands, fingers, and feet. Each passing minute was filled with an infinite torture.

Uriel's voice cracked as he screamed in pain. None of his jerking and flailing prevented the man from continuing to massage his frozen extremities. He was left to suffer the attention, lacking the strength to push him away.

"I don't think they are frostbitten. You're lucky you aren't dead."

Uriel could not respond to the comment. The agony caused by the ministrations took on a life of its own. When it appeared to be easing, another wave of fresh anguish would siphon through his system. He was caught in the maelstrom, with his only connection to life being the human currently chasing away the cold from his body.

An eternity might have passed before the pain receded and with it, the touches of the human. The water grew cool around him, bringing forth small tremors. They in no way resembled the wild spasms caused by the freezing snow, but were like small aftershocks following a large quake.

The human drained some of the cooling water, replacing it with renewed warm. "I'm not sure how long you should stay in here. I'm not a doctor, but you were so cold."

With the pain passing, the warmth emanating from the water relaxed him. His eyes drifted closed and a temporary sense of peace washed over him. For a brief moment the earlier emotional overload faded away, leaving him in blissful relaxation.

"Don't go to sleep. I'm not sure I could drag you from the tub."

Uriel's eyes fluttered open. The stranger disappeared upon issuing the order, returning moments later with a large plush towel. He stood quietly with assistance and allowed the man the task of drying his body. Exhaustion weighed heavily upon him. His body swayed back and forth, threatening to collapse beneath him despite his most stringent attempts to remain aloft.

How he reached the bed was a mystery. He could have walked or been carried. Nothing could explain it and his mind was too exhausted to attempt the chore. Perhaps this was a dream—a nightmare from which he would awake and be returned to his place in the Creator's service.

He could no longer fight to remain conscious. Exhaustion won the battle, causing the worries and pain to fade into nothingness. In slumber's domain, he remained dreamless for an apparent eternity until memories flitted to the edge of his consciousness— teasing him with the promise of knowledge.

In each instant, they slipped from his fingers like water. Each memory brought to the surface was quickly replaced by another until they seemed to merge together in insanity. Retrieving those he sought was a seemingly insurmountable task.

He recalled the moment of his creation and the development of his consciousness. He could remember basking in the love of his Creator and being assigned the duties upon which he was devoted. Those memories were ingrained so deeply in him that expelling them would be impossible. Only in death would they be wiped from him.

He was looked on with favor by the Creator and given the task of guarding the Garden. It was his honor to do so. He performed the job with all his strength. His bare hands had assisted in the burial of the First. He was older than the Earth and younger than the sun. He existed only to serve his Father in His will. There was no greater purpose for his existence.

The dreamlike memories faded to more recent days. A stolen tome. The Fallen's search. Acceptance of a task. The complete truth was an inevitable tide washing away all evidence from his eyes. Never before was the truth hidden from him in such a way. The Father had gifted him with prophecy. He was to lead all into their fates.

Why couldn't he recall his ultimate purpose in this nightmare? Why was he on Earth in the body of a Fallen? He needed to escape this darkness and return to his rightful place.

Screaming out in the dark recesses of his mind, he cried out for answers but received only silence in return. None came to relieve him of his suffering. It seemed all he held dear had abandoned him.

He drifted endlessly until the burning came. He was no longer amidst his brethren but rather in a fiery lake surrounded by the Damned. There was no ceasing of the all-consuming heat. He was forsaken and left to roast in the deepest depths.

Hellfire lapped at him, burning away his skin in rippling waves only to have it grow anew. It enveloped him in wave after burning wave. Any sense of peace he might have found was washed away by the soul-devouring heat.

"It's alright." The words rushed over him in his suffering, soothing away the fire while offering a reprieve from its heat. "Drink this."

Cool liquid was dribbled over his parched lips and tongue. The life-giving fluid sustained him in his fevered madness. Was he forgiven of the unknown transgression he committed to earn him this eternal suffering? To have even the smallest drop of water while in the deepest pits of Hell was to be granted forgiveness.

Dry, cracked lips parted in desperation for more of the cool refreshment. He needed it badly, just as he needed the soothing voice. One of his brethren? None other could provide such gentle care.

"Raphael?" His brother's healing touch would soothe away his suffering. "I am burning, Brother."

"Rest. You're feverish. This will help."

He parted his lips to accept the offered brew, grimacing at the foul taste spilling across his tongue. He didn't want this vile liquid. He needed more of the deliciously cool water.

"Water," he rasped.

The smooth rim of a cup was pressed to lips which opened readily for the liquid. Delightfully refreshing water filled his mouth and trickled down his throat to coat his stomach. It was a temporary ease to the fire eating away at his insides, but one he welcomed.

"More," Uriel demanded.

"I don't want you to get sick."

The reply was not that which he desired. Pale eyes shot open and a strong hand reached out to wrap tightly around the forearm of the one who denied him the soothing refreshment. He was not Raphael.

"You are not my Brother." Fevered eyes, glazed with illness, stared wildly at the man before him. "Human."

"You have a high fever. The roads are snowed in so I can't take you to the hospital." The cloth from his brow was removed. "I've prepared a cool bath. Your fever is dangerously high and we need to get it down."

"Who are you?"

"Stephen Trent," he answered. "I found you naked in the snow on the edge of my property. What is your name?"

Eyes clouded with fever blinked slowly before he answered. "Uriel."

"Uriel." Stephen rolled the name around on his tongue. "That's a strange name. It sounds foreign. How did you end up naked in the snow?"

Uriel remained silent. Humans might be beloved by the Creator, but they were notoriously devious. The First Fallen had seen to that with his influence. Light and darkness were allowed to flourish inside them at the Creator's wish.

"Well, Uriel, I need you to help me. I don't think I can pick you up and we really need to get you cooled down. Can you walk?"

Uriel tested his limbs. Moving his body was difficult. His muscles rebelled against each mental command but seemed sturdy enough to keep him aloft for a short period of time.

"Yes. I can walk."

Stephan nodded in satisfaction before tugging at Uriel's arm, forcing him to rise from the soft mattress and to his feet. His hold was firm as he led the swaying and trembling body towards a tub filled with cool water. It tempted him, offering respite from the burning.

"Get in. It will feel cooler than it is because your fever is so high."

Fight though he might to gain complete control of his body, illness robbed him of every ounce of his strength, forcing him to lean heavily on Stephen. In his weakened state, he was vulnerable. He could do no other than obey the spoken directions until he was fully submerged.

The water seemed icy as it closed around him. His breath gasped in and out rapidly under the chill. The temperature wasn't freezing, but compared to his feverish body, it felt as if he was surrounded by glacier-chilled ice. Almost immediately his teeth began chattering and his muscles clenching as the water proceeded to slowly drop his core temperature from dangerous levels.

Uriel's chattering teeth barely allowed him to speak about his discomfort. "Cold."

"Just a little while longer. I told you, it only feels cold because your fever is so high." Stephen pressed a hand to Uriel's brow. "Your temperature is dropping. I want to get it far enough down that you're out of danger; at least until the roads are cleared. We've had unusually heavy snow lately."

The seconds ticked by slowly. Uriel shivered in the water longer than he thought he could bear until finally he was allowed to ascend from the tub. His body protested the treatment it was receiving, causing him to struggle to even stand.

His body trembled as if it would collapse as he pulled himself from the water. Streams of water ran down his long frame in rivulets, pooling on the floor around his feet. His body continued to shake and tremble, only lessening in degrees under the stroking of the thick terrycloth towel.

The touches stroking over his body had a surprisingly calming effect. His muscles ceased their trembling and relaxed under the care. His mind, weakened by the fever, followed quickly in suit under the touch. Relaxation caused his eyes to drift closed and a sound of purring escaped from him. He nearly drifted to sleep while standing.

"That is an amazing tattoo. The artist who did it does astounding work." Stephen's fingers traced along Uriel's shoulder blades and down towards his hips. "I've never seen anything like it."

Uriel's eyes slid open lazily, his mind still hazy with a mixture of contentment and fever. The touch felt strange, as if his wings were being stroked in a long, delicate caress. "Tattoo?"

Stephen brushed aside the long dark hair draped across Uriel's shoulders so as to allow his fingers to trace lightly over the expanse of defined shoulder blades. "The wings on your back. You look like an angel."

Formerly hooded eyes flared wide in immediate awareness. He felt as if the human had stroked his wings. The sensations were there, though the wings were not. His eyes darted around the small bathroom until they landed on the small utilitarian mirror hanging above the sink. Surprisingly strong hands pushed Stephen aside in a desperate and instinctual need to see what he thought had been taken from him. The sight shocked him to his core, causing previously untapped emotions to rise to the surface.

Flattened against the skin of his back were his massive raven-hued wings. Instead of their normally billowy girth, they laid parallel down the length of his spine. It was not the mark of a Fallen. This was something entirely different.

The sight caused Uriel to become much more curious as to his reasons for being here. Why was he stranded on Earth with his direct connection to the Creator taken from him? He was marooned with no apparent hope of returning to his previous post, yet he retained his wings—if only sketched across his back.

And then there was the mystery of his memories.

For a creature whose existence was older than even the moment of Earth's creation, memories were not formulated as a string of events. He had lived too long to recall every instant of his existence. He simply knew what needed to be done.

He existed for his Creator. Every order he ever received from burying Adam in Eden, to guarding its gates was fresh in his mind. His reason for being here on Earth in the presence of one of the Beloved was not in the forefront of his memory. His mission was hidden beneath the shock of the transition into a human body.

"What's wrong?" Stephen moved quickly to his side. "Don't pass out on me. I don't want to have to drag you to the bed."

His pale eyes shifted from their locked position on the mirror, sliding to the human standing nervously at his side. "I shall not."

"Famous last words," said Stephen.

Uriel blinked in confusion. The comment baffled him. Had he more time, he would have attempted to decipher the statement but the weakness in his body prevented him from focusing on such trivial matters. He allowed himself to be led toward the bed before he collapsed.

He would attempt to understand this human later. To be placed here ... with this human, Stephen Trent, must be connected to his mission. If he understood why Stephen was the nearest human, he would discover his mission.

They reached the soft mattress just as Uriel's strength left him, forcing him to collapse haphazardly upon the crisp sheets. Despite his weakness, his eyes never left the human who attended him.

Stephen paused in the task of covering Uriel's weary body. "You should rest."

It was another order. Were his strength returned to him, Uriel would have resisted. Rest was an activity rarely allowed to celestial beings. He was always aware; yet, in his human form, he felt the exhaustion tugging at his consciousness. There was no choice but to obey the pull, and fall into the darkness once more.

Uriel rested deeply, until a glass rod was shoved beneath his tongue, dispelling sleep and causing him to fight to force out the intrusion. Any attempt was ignored and the glass quickly replaced. His efforts only resulted in the human named Stephen becoming more forceful about the object remaining inside.

"Hold it under your tongue, damn it. I need to check your temperature to make sure the fever has mostly passed."

"Do not shove things into my mouth." Uriel glared at his human attendant with as much force as he could, given his current state.

Stephen rolled his eyes skyward. "Heaven help me, you're as stubborn as a mule. I'm not trying to poison you."

"You ask the Creator for help with me?"

The words apparently gave Stephen pause. "Huh?"

"You asked Heaven for assistance."

Confusion played across Stephen's features. His palm flattened on the flesh above Uriel's brows. "You don't feel as feverish."

"I am well enough." Uriel pushed away the hand with a scowl. He did not require the assistance of a human. He was not a Fallen and only needed to wait until the Creator realized his absence and retrieved him or until his memories returned so he could complete whatever task he had been placed on earth to fulfill.

"Just to be sure, hold this under your tongue." A glare nearly equal to that of the darkest demon in Hell had Uriel staring in shock at Stephen. "Don't bite it, and don't take it out."

Uriel did as commanded, sitting quietly with the small glass rod beneath his tongue. It was shameful to be subjugated so easily. The fever was apparently taking more of a toll than he originally suspected.

The minutes passed in strained silence before the thermometer was removed. Stephen nodded towards Uriel. "Your fever is almost gone."

Uriel withheld comment, continuing to stare. With the fever nearly abated, he was able to focus his thoughts. He needed to recall why he was on Earth and find a way to return to Heaven. If something happened in his absence—

"You still look pale. Maybe some food will help." Stephen looked expectantly at Uriel. "Are you hungry?"

"I do not feel hunger." As if to deny the truth of his statement, his stomach chose that very moment to rumble loudly.

The sound amused Stephen, causing him to chuckle at the expression of annoyance spreading across Uriel's face. "I think your body disagrees with you."

It was strange listening to Stephen laugh. The sound rolled pleasantly over Uriel's senses, unlike anything he had ever experienced. It was as beautiful as the voices of a thousand angels. Each small chuckle calmed his soul while at the same time causing his heart to thump erratically in his chest. That a human could create such varying responses in him was disconcerting.

His pale eyes followed Stephen as he moved away, internally bemoaning the end of the laughter. Now that he felt better, he took in his host and surroundings. The cabin was small, consisting of only one large room and a bathroom. The space was divided into different functional areas by the furniture. A small sofa that had seen better days was pushed against one wall with an equally small table beside it. A small, wood-burning stove was tucked against the wall near the sofa, and provided warmth for the entire space. The kitchen possessed only an oven, a refrigerator, and a few cupboards filled with a variety of canned goods.

His gaze dropped to the bed he reclined upon. It was the nicest piece of furniture with its sturdy wooden headboard and comfortable mattress. Atop him laid a down-filled comforter and hand-sewn patchwork blanket.

The living space was small, but comfortable. Its owner's essence was stamped into every inch. Even without his celestial gifts, Uriel could sense Stephen in every part of this cabin. It was a testament to the time he had spent there.

Uriel's gaze slid to his companion. He was unused to dealing with humans. Stephen Trent was the first in many centuries. He seemed compassionate—a trait Uriel thought long removed from humanity. There was a spark inside Stephen that warmed him in much the same way of his Creator's light. They felt the same and yet they didn't.

There was a definite connection between Stephen Trent and his unknown mission. He felt a protective instinct rise in him. It echoed faintly familiar in his lost memories.

Physically, there was nothing special about the tall, slender man. His build was lean, bordering on gaunt. Compared to the physical perfection of the residents of Heaven, he was nothing, possibly not even considered overly attractive by human standards. It confused Uriel that he could find him so intriguing.

Steven's hair was a sandy blond, shaggy and unkempt. The bridge of his slightly crooked nose was dotted with freckles and the lips below thin and slightly chapped. The only exceptional feature was his eyes. They were an amazing emerald hue, speckled with tiny flecks of gold—unique and expressive. In all his existence, he had never seen such a startling color scheme.

"I just have canned soup. I don't think you should eat anything solid for a day or two." Stephen approached the bed carrying a small bowl of clear broth.

Uriel accepted the offered bowl dubiously. He had never tasted human food. As a celestial being, there had never been the need.

The smells wafting from the broth caused his stomach to rumble loudly once again. The clenching feeling in his abdomen was an unfamiliar sensation, as was the pooling of saliva in his mouth. He was unsure how to react to the new needs of his body in its human form.

In his current human body, he felt hunger and thirst all too keenly. He couldn't stop himself from bringing the bowl directly to his lips and swallowing the contents as quickly as possible. The liquid scalded his lips and tongue, causing him to yelp and cry out at the pain radiating through his mouth.

"Careful!" Stephen moved quickly to tug the bowl from Uriel's hands. "You burned yourself."

Uriel lifted surprised fingers to his lips. The sensation was a strange mix of stinging and numbness radiating outward. It was the most recent in a series of new experiences since his transformation into human form, each one both unique and baffling.

"Here." Another bowl was placed in his hands. "Use the spoon and sip it so you don't burn yourself again."

The delicious fragrance was just as pungent as in the previous bowl. This time Uriel was more cautious. He took the advice of his companion and used the utensil to slowly spoon small sips of the still hot soup into his mouth. Nothing could have tasted so wonderful. Each spoonful coated his stomach in warmth, making him want to devour it in a single gulp while demanding more.

Now he understood the reasoning behind the human sin of gluttony. Already he was falling prey to its temptation. Barely five minutes passed before he was handing the bowl back to Stephen in anticipation of more. The small amount of soup he ingested barely touched the hunger still gnawing at his insides.

"More," he demanded.

Stephen chuckled at the command. "You probably shouldn't eat too much. It might not sit well on your stomach."

The apparent denial didn't sit well with Uriel. His stomach still clenched and rumbled in demand of more of the delicious soup. "More."

"You'll make yourself sick."

Uriel clenched his jaw in frustration. He had never dealt with many humans. His role as the Guardian of Eden had limited his contact with the Creator's beloved children. With his current bizarre circumstances, he was adrift in uncharted waters. His own naturally aggressive personality demanded some semblance of control.

"You will give me more."

The previously compliant aura left Stephen. His arms folded across his chest and a scowl pulled across his face. "No. You'll get sick."

Frustration worked through Uriel. "By the Creator, do not deny me, Human."

Confusion spread across the angular face. "There you go with the human shit, again. Has your fever returned?"

"I am not feverish."

A hand brushed against Uriel's brow. "You're cool."

Uriel longed to lean into the touch. There was a calming aspect to the stroking fingers running over the smooth skin of his brow. He heaved a sigh, keeping his expression as neutral as possible. "You humans and your mistrust of things you do not understand."

"Why shouldn't I be mistrustful? You're a stranger who showed up naked in the snow outside my cabin. I have no idea how you got there or what you were doing. It's a wonder you didn't end up dead." Stephen began pacing beside the bed. "Who are you really? What are you doing here?"

The questions gave Uriel pause. He wanted to answer but couldn't because the truth of his presence on Earth eluded him. He, too, wanted to know why he was placed in this precise locale with this lone human.

Though he could not feel it, he instinctively knew he still possessed the love of the Creator. Falling was not his reason for being on Earth. It was something else.

If he knew at least part of his mission, he would be more able to fulfill it. Pain splintered through his skull when he attempted to access the hidden memories. It sent him crashing back into full awareness of Stephen's presence.

"Well?"

He was not Lucifer and as such, could not lie. To lie to one of the Beloved was to lie to the Creator. "I am Uriel, cherub guardian of Eden. I cannot say for what reasons I was sent to Earth, only that I do not recall my mission."

"Cherub?" Disbelief spread across Stephen's face before laughter erupted once more. "Either the fever has given you brain damage, or you were insane to begin with."

Annoyance spread across Uriel's features. It offended him that Stephen thought him a lunatic with no sense of reality. "I do not lie. It is you who does not see the truth."

"And what is the truth?" Stephen arched a brow. "You expect me to accept your word at face value?"

Humans! Uriel was torn between exasperation and frustration. It never failed to confuse him as to how the Creator could consider them his most precious creation. "The proof is before you."

"All I see before me is a fever-deranged man with tattoos who thinks he is an angel," scoffed Stephen. "As soon as the snow is cleared, I'll call the hospital to come pick you up."

"Cherub. Do not lump me with all celestial beings."

"There is a difference?" Stephen wasn't even attempting to hide his mirth.

"Yes."

"Oh, forgive me. I thought cherubs were fat little babies with wings," snickered Stephen. "You don't look like a baby to me, unless you're one of those people into infantilism. I just can't seem to picture you wearing a diaper and sitting in an adult-sized playpen."

Uriel snorted; Humans and their mythologies. Cherubim were second only to seraphim in the Hierarchy of Heaven. Not even the archangels could compare to his position and this human thought he should be a fat infant with wings.

"Humans. You know nothing."

"There you go with the human comments again." Stephen crossed his arms. "I hate to tell you, but you're human too."

Uriel leaned back against the headboard, closing his eyes. If only the human realized just how wrong he was with that comment. Something dangerous crackled in the air. Unless he could recall his reasons for being on earth in a human body, they would be nearly defenseless when the unseen force teasing the edges of his thoughts arrived.

Chapter Two

Uriel stood, unmindful of his nakedness and began to explore the confined area of the cabin. He spotted a robe thrown over a chair, but ignored it. It would barely cover anything. His shoulders were simply too broad for it to fit properly.

An icy breeze entered the cabin, causing him to glance towards the door. Uriel watched his companion stomp his feet on the doormat and step into the cabin.

"What are you doing out of bed?" Stephen shook the snow from his jacket before hanging it on the coat rack nearby.

Uriel ignored Stephen and began moving about the cabin. It had been many years since he had moved about on Earth. Much had changed since that time.

A small gasp erupted from Stephen's lips as he noticed Uriel's state of undress. A flush spread across pale cheeks and he began digging through the set of drawers near the bed. The flush seemed to grow brighter with each passing moment.

"Here are some clothes. They are old and stretched, so they should fit you. If you're going to be out of bed, you need to wear something or your fever will return. Not to mention, I'd rather not see your hairy ass every time I turn around." Stephen handed him a carefully folded pile of gray sweats while being certain not to glance down at the flaccid length of Uriel's manhood. "They'll probably be a little tight. You're a lot bigger than me in the shoulders."

"I do not have a hairy ass." Uriel snarled at Stephen, his eyes flashing dangerously. "Celestial beings have very little body hair."

Stephen snorted loudly. "There you go with the angel stuff again. Why couldn't you be normal? The first man I've had alone in my residence in over two years and you're as crazy as a loon. Just take the damn clothes and save me the hassle."

Uriel accepted the clothing with a blank expression. He missed the flush once more spreading across Stephen's face as he pulled the tight cotton pants into place, followed by the shirt. "Thank you."

Turning his face towards Stephen, Uriel watched the darkening of the skin around his ears and cheekbones. He found the red stain working across pale cheeks surprisingly appealing. His intent gaze only seemed to intensify the spreading of color. The tint worked across a stubble coated jaw and down a slender neck before disappearing from view in the collar of his shirt.

An unfamiliar warmth began to settle in Uriel's chest. Where before there was nothing, now there was a sparking flame that rose from the abyss. It filled the empty void and brought to life hidden emotions. He had no idea that humans could have such a rapid and strange effect on angels.

"Not that I believe you, but what's Heaven like?" Stephen glanced from his position in the small kitchen. "I'm curious."

Uriel folded his arms across his chest. "It is not what you humans think. We do not walk on fluffy clouds with harps. We train and plan."

Confusion spread across Stephen's features. "For what?"

Uriel did not answer. He took up position near the window. It was a dangerous game he was playing, remaining in a stationary location. There was no point in moving when he was unsure what role Stephen played. He refused to leave him alone.

Unable to prevent it, Uriel found his gaze drifting to his human companion as he puttered around the small cabin. He was amusing to watch, and doing so caused the strange warmth to build in a slow simmer. The heat was small and fragile, yet it filled him. He felt an increase in the need to protect Stephen.

He forced his gaze to shift to the world visible through the window. The quiet created by the pristine landscape drew his attention. It provided the perfect distraction from Stephen. He could use it as an escape from the burgeoning unfamiliar human emotions spiraling through him.

His brother, Rafael, would laugh at his predicament. It was strange to think of his laughter compared to Stephen's. Emotions were practically nonexistent to his kind. Laughter was expressed, but possessed no true feeling except for a select few. The emotions experienced by those few were muted to such a degree that they were barely comparable to those of humans.

Stephen's laughter was an intriguing sound. Where most emotions were lost on angels, humans possessed them in spades. They changed everything. The sound of Stephen's joy was more than enough of an example.

Uriel gritted his teeth in frustration. Instead of escaping thoughts of Stephen, his attempt only served to bring his focus directly to him. Stephen Trent was quickly becoming a dangerous obsession—one he was finding it difficult to ignore.

"Would you like some coffee?"

Uriel turned from his place at the window, watching the thick flakes create mounds of snow. His eyes slid to the brown brew steaming in the blue mug. Its appearance was unappetizing, but the smell wafting upward made his tongue tingle for a taste.

"Consider it a peace offering. I shouldn't have laughed. What you said surprised me." Stephen's almond-shaped green eyes regarded Uriel earnestly. "It's hot, so sip it."

Accepting the cup, Uriel brought the liquid to his lips. The flavor was bitter, but contained a sweet and creamy undertone. He could not say it was unappealing, just different from the soup the previous evening. He enjoyed savoring the variety of tastes playing over his palate.

"I fixed it like I drink it. I've been told I add a little too much sugar, but I have a bit of a sweet tooth." A lean hand lifted to run through mussed locks of sandy hair.

Stephen was slightly embarrassed by the admission. Strangely, Uriel found the faint blush playing across the pale, freckle-dotted cheekbones appealing. It caused a softening in his normally hard armor. "Thank you for this."

"What are you thinking about?" Stephen offered a friendly smile. "When I look in the snow, I'm always thinking about something."

A small smile curled Uriel's lips upward. "I am searching for my purpose."

"You're in an odd place looking for a purpose." Stephen's gaze drifted out towards the thick snow formed drifts just outside the cabin. "I've been trying to escape mine. Or what everyone told me was mine."

"If you know your purpose, tell me it." Stephen was somehow interwoven into Uriel's lost purpose. Understanding his companion might in turn help him recall what was lost.

An uncertain look spread across Stephen's face. "I was a biochemist. The company I worked for was hired by the military to construct a chemical that could be used in the war on terrorism. It was my job so that's what I did. I thought in the hands of the military, my research wouldn't be abused."

"But it was?"

"A few months later, I heard from some of my co-workers that the substance we'd created had been stolen from the army and been used in a bombing that killed hundreds of people." Green eyes lowered to stare at the dust covering the windowsill. "I killed hundreds of people."

A solemn look spread across Uriel's face. He shook his head slowly and placed a hand on Stephen's shoulder. "Humans and your wars. Do not assume you are the only one to bear guilt. You are not completely innocent, but I cannot find you guilty of actions that are not fully your own."

Before Stephen could respond, a loud crash rocked the cabin. The glass in the windows shook and pans were thrown from their places on the wall. The earth shuddered as if it was preparing to devour them in one great gulp and thick clouds darkened the sun.

"An earthquake?" Stephen fell to the wooden floor as another vibration rocked the building.

Uriel knelt beside him, assisting him to his feet. It was no earthquake disturbing them. Something much more deadly had risen into being just outside the walls.

Where, previously, he had felt nothing but the hint of a darkness whispering on the edge of his mind, now he sensed the creature in its fully incarnated form. It circled like vultures over a rotting corpse. The smell of rotting flesh and suffering was nearly overwhelming. Only one sort of creature could bring forth such a sense of death and decay.

"Stay here," Uriel said as he walked barefoot from the cabin and into the snowy clearing surrounding the area.

"What's this? I thought I sensed you hiding inside, Uriel. My, how the mighty have fallen. Have you decided to join us, Brother?"

He didn't need to look in the direction the voice came from. It was as melodic and beautiful as any celestial being, yet possessed such hatred and scorn that it could never belong to one of the Celestial Brotherhood. Only the Fallen possessed such speech because only the Fallen held the wide array of emotions needed to develop such hatred.

"Do not call me Brother, Abaddon."

A beautiful man leaning languidly against the cabin shrugged his broad shoulders. His long crimson hair flowed around his body like silk. Small white flakes landed, framing his stunning visage in pristine innocence. "Still such a Bitter Betty. You never did know how to have fun."

Uriel's gaze remained on the Fallen. Nothing they did or said was to be trusted. To do so

was to invite despair and destruction. "Why are you here, Abaddon?"

Surprise, quickly followed by delight, spread across Abaddon's face. "Oh! Don't tell me He didn't tell you? This is rich. Send a cherub to Earth and don't tell him why. That doesn't sound like Him."

"Abaddon—"

"It really is a shame that He left you in the dark." Abaddon folded his arms across his chest. "What to do?"

Uriel clenched his jaw at the mocking tone. "Leave or I will have to destroy you."

"Destroy me? Tell me something. Where are your wings, angel? I'll show you mine if you show me yours." Black wings streaked with crimson exploded from Abaddon's back, creating a great whoosh of air. Small feathers drifted down between them to land on the snow while a smirk played across angelic features. They were not the wings given him by the Creator. The darkness oozing from them proved where his loyalties now lay.

"Wings?" Uriel nearly stumbled at the sight of the beautiful, yet deadly appendages sprouting from his former comrade's back. "You should not possess wings. You are a Fallen."

Arrogance mixed liberally with sadistic delight spread across Abaddon's cruelly beautiful features. "Oh? Didn't He tell you? His power over us is finished. We are completely free of His yoke. Why should our wings be sacrificed? Should we give up our power to live as humans? What do you take us for?"

The tension rose between them, causing Uriel to widen his stance at the menacingly slow approach of his former comrade. Abaddon's approach was heralded by the crunch of snow beneath his feet—step by step until his black, soulless eyes were clearly visible. It was a shame to see the once beautiful blue eyes now eclipsed with the taint of darkness.

"To think the great Uriel has been demoted to mere guard duty. For shame," taunted Abaddon. "I can feel the taint growing in you. You're already Falling and don't even realize it. Poor Uriel."

"Leave this place, Abaddon, before I strike you down." Uriel's flaming blade materialized in his hand. The fire was designed to strike down the wicked, while leaving the innocent uninjured. Divine flame licked at the air, but left the delicate flakes floating down around them untouched.

False hurt spread across Abaddon's face. With a swish of his thick red hair, he halted his approach. "I'm hurt that you would brandish your weapon. Or, perhaps guard duty has made you weak."

"The only weak one is you who have Fallen from the grace of the Creator."

Abaddon's features grew fierce. His hair flared wildly around him and his eyes sparked in challenge. A dark scythe materialized in his hands, containing all the darkness the world had experienced since Creation.

Pain and sorrow were his allies. Destruction was his weapon. "Join us, Uriel. You were always the strongest after Gabriel. It's not like you have any love for these humans. They are worthless ants running around with no purpose other than their own desires. Why give up the ability to feel for the simple honor of serving Him?"

"Emotions impede our judgment. It is the first lesson taught us. We cannot guard Creation without having impartial judgment. I would never betray the Creator. I serve only Him. Not you, and not he who first Fell." Uriel brandished his blade, sliding his feet apart in preparation for an attack.

Abaddon's eyes rolled skyward. "Always spouting that load of bullshit. You don't even know your purpose and you're still defending Him like the good little soldier you are. Fine. Have it your way, Uriel. Die with your false sense of honor. You could have tasted power, but instead I shall bring you your death."

An instant of stillness passed—no wind blew or animal cried. Even the snow falling in slow waves seemed to stop in midair between the two celestial beings. It was a perfect moment to reflect on things past and those to come. Time halted for only a moment preceding their desire to destroy each other.

The first attack came swift from Abaddon. His scythe swung in wide, precise swipes, seeking Uriel's blood with its blade. Back and forth, the movements were a deadly dance of skill and will. One false step and all would fade to black. The blade called all living beings to the abyss. There could be no mistakes in this deadly battle.

Uriel felt the power rise up in him. His wings, symbols of Heaven, burst outward to curl around his body like a shadowy shield—effectively blocking Abaddon's attack with divine strength. He jabbed his sword forward, barely missing a critical hit to Abaddon's abdomen. If not for the Fallen's quick adjustment to defend himself from the jab, the battle between the two would have been over almost before it began.

"Sneaky, Uriel." Abaddon stumbled back several steps, the ringing from the collision of weapons still echoing in the cold. "You've grown in strength since we last spoke."

"When we last spoke, I considered you a friend." Uriel's wings parted to reveal his faintly shimmering frame glowing with divine light. "No more."

Abaddon ran a thumb over the dull curve of his black scythe. "We could be again. Kill the human and join us."

A gasp reached Uriel's ears and his eyes darted from Abaddon to the entrance of the cabin where Stephen stood looking on in shock. Green eyes widened with a mixture of awe and fear. His skin was so pale that the green of his irises seemed even brighter.

Uriel moved with the speed of those created to serve Him, shielding the sight from Abaddon's amused gaze. Fear ran thick in his veins, something he had never experienced in his existence. He feared for Stephen's life. One nick was all it would take.

"Stephen, go inside." Uriel's wings extended wide to cover him.

Stephen blinked as if waking from a trance. His hand reached outward for his fingers to stroke along the tips of dark feathers. "You have wings."

"Go inside, now!" shouted Uriel in a near panic due to how open his human companion was to an attack by Abaddon. "I can't defend you and battle him."

Stephen's mouth opened as if he wanted to argue. He looked at the smirking Abaddon before he nodded and did as he was commanded, disappearing into the cabin. He appeared once more at the window, prepared to watch the unfolding events between the two angelic creatures. A palm pressed into the pane while another clenched into the wooden frame. "Uriel—"

"Hmm. Do I sense fear in you?" Abaddon moved with unnatural speed, appearing behind Uriel. His voice purred softly in his opponent's ear. A tongue darted out to flick at the shell before being forced back by the blaze of the fiery sword. "You're closer to Falling than I would have ever thought, Uriel. Is it the human? Do you want to fuck him— to bury yourself inside him until you come? Why don't you? Fucking feels so much better with emotions."

"Cease spouting your venom. I will never become a Fallen."

Abaddon chuckled, swinging his weapon as casually as if he was twirling a baton. "So you say. It's a shame I simply can't sit back to watch your Fall but orders are orders The human must die."

The attack was swift, catching Uriel by surprise. Only his speed allowed him to evade the powerful swipe of Abaddon's blade. Even with the return of his wings, his movements felt sluggish, as if thick mud clung to his feet.

He was on the defense from Abaddon's attacks. Each swing of the black scythe seemed to increase in speed and force. Each block with his sword reverberated up his arm, causing it to tremble and ache. If he remained too long on the defensive, he would fall beneath the ever increasing onslaught. The games between them were at an end.

Only calming the inner turmoil rising in his mind would save him from destruction at the hands of a former comrade. He needed to still his mind and shed the human emotions rumbling through him in waves. There was little time.

Droplets of sweat trickled down the side of his face and splattered on the icy ground below. If he failed, death would be his reward—his and Stephen's. It was an outcome he refused to allow.

With the ease of desperation, the tumultuous ocean in his mind smoothed to the calmness of a crystalline pool. His eternity of training and knowledge returned to him. He recalled his relationship with Abaddon and the time spent honing their skills. He knew Abaddon's abilities. Even with their advancement during the many eons apart, they remained based on those of the past.

Eyes, as keen as those of a raptor, followed each slashing movement of the scythe. One. Two. Three. Strike.

Uriel's blade darted in the opening created after the third attack. It was an opening Abaddon had possessed long before his Fall from grace. Even after millennia, he could conceal the weakness, but not remove it.

The fiery blade long used to guard the Garden slid easily into Abaddon's warm flesh, burning the soul as well as the body. The scream erupting from him shattered the shards of ice dangling precariously from the roof of the cabin. It reached into Heaven and to the ears of all celestial beings. The pitch forced a wince from Uriel and a cry from Stephen.

"No!" Abaddon stumbled away and fell weakly to his knees on the snow covered ground. The blade created a sickly gushing sound as it was extracted from his trembling body. "I am Death. You cannot destroy me."

"You are not Death. You are merely his servant. Only one may hold that title." Uriel approached, his gaze holding apathy for the Fallen before him. "Lucifer is your god now. Do you wish to face your demise praising only his name?"

Abaddon spat at Uriel. His normally exquisite features pulled down into something horrible. There was no trace of the once quiet angel—only the monster created from his descent into despair.

Blood and spittle dripped slowly down Uriel's emotionless features. A pale hand lifted to rub at the fluid before closing his eyes and driving forward the blade. "So be it."

There was no scream, only the sound of flesh being rendered followed by the gurgle of blood filling a throat. The body before him twitched and spasmed, eventually going still. And then, silence. Not a sound was made, not even that of snow shifting beneath Uriel's bare feet.

"Oh—" Stephen stepped from the house, his eyes as wide and lips parted though no sound escaped.

Uriel felt his presence despite his gaze never leaving the body of a former comrade. Lifting his flaming weapon, he sliced a downward arc in the air above the Fallen angel. Flames rose and licked at the still form, leaving no trace of his fallen comrade. All but the untouched snow was reduced to ash, and then to nothing.

Just as quickly as his strength returned, it failed him and Uriel collapsed into the snow. His large raven wings returned to his body and his sword faded from sight. The touch of the icy wind against his cheeks and the numbness in his extremities returned him to the reality of his current situation.

"Uriel!" Familiar warmth was wrapped around his body, lean arms chasing away the cold. "You're freezing."

Uriel allowed this small display of weakness. With Stephen, it was different. He had healed him—seen him in ways few had. His human body was weakened under the strain of wielding the flaming sword and needed to recuperate.

Looking into Stephen's worried gaze, realization sparked in his dark memory. The memory of whispered instructions and the outrage of his brethren flashed before his eyes. It was as if a key had turned the lock on his mind. He knew and fully understood his mission.

As the Angel of Prophecy, his responsibility was to ensure fated actions were upheld. His duty was clear. He had to protect Stephen at all costs. His life would change the face of the world, be it by direct or indirect contact. He must not die until his appointed time on earth was at an end.

Arms tugged at his shoulders. "Get up. You'll die out here."

He couldn't move. Weakened as he was, he was vulnerable to the cold. "I—"

"Get up!" By sheer force of will, Stephen pulled Uriel to his feet.

He was forced to bear nearly all of Uriel's weight. Their feet crunched through the snow towards the cabin. They nearly crashed to the floor as they entered the warm interior. Both panted from the exertion as they collapsed on the sofa located directly across from the stove.

Stephen's eyes were wide, his gaze filled with a mixture of shock and awe. His tongue darted out to lick at his suddenly dry lips and his throat bobbed repeatedly. His lips parted to speak but no sound escaped, forcing him to draw several deep breaths before trying again.

"You're an angel, a real angel. You aren't delusional." Stephen began to shake as the shock from the recent events took over. "Or, maybe I'm the one who is delusional. Perhaps I've finally lost it."

"I told you, I do not lie."

"I didn't believe you. It just seemed so incredible." Stephen stood and walked towards the small wood-burning stove he used to heat the cabin. His hand shook as he added additional wood to it before returning to the small couch where Uriel sat quietly.

Uriel winced as the heat from the metal stove began to provide warmth to his tortured feet. "That is understandable. Few humans truly believe what they cannot see."

"What happened out there?" Stephen ran a frustrated hand through his messy blond hair. "I want to know. He wanted to kill me. I've never met him before and he wanted to kill me."

Uriel remained silent, considering his options before speaking. He glanced at his palm, the perfectly smooth skin seeming pale in the lamplight. Stephen was a good man. He deserved to know his life could end at any moment from the hands of a Fallen. "His name was Abaddon. He was a Fallen."

"A Fallen?"

"Falling results from an angel being corrupted by human emotion. Celestial beings were not created to feel, but to protect. Emotion cannot easily be forgotten." Uriel frowned into the fire. He could feel the beginnings of his own corruption. Abaddon was correct in his assessment. If he remained in this form for much longer, he could never resume his place in Heaven.

Stephen laid a hand upon Uriel's arm, pulling him from his thoughts and into the present. "Why would they want to Fall? What could be gained by it?"

"I cannot say for certain. For some it is emotions and the desire to feel them; for others it is jealousy towards humans." Uriel lifted Stephen's hand to trace the creases on his palm. "It is different for each."

"What does being human have to do with anything?" asked Stephen.

Uriel lifted a lineless palm, displaying it for Stephen. "Once there was only the Creator."

Stephen arched a brow. "You mean God?"

"He has been called that. But He is not like you humans portray. He is more—an infinity of knowledge. He is good and evil—the balance of all things. The universe—all universes—are kept in synchronicity because of Him. When He created the cosmos, He desired guardians to defend them and Heaven was their residence." Uriel thought back on his inception. Everything was too perfect. "But the Guardians were not of Him. They followed His command with no thought to disobey. And so He chose to create a being of Himself with the potential for both good and evil."

"That's not what I was told. I was led to believe humans were corrupted by Satan," interrupted Stephen. "You're telling me God created humans with evil already in them?"

"Is it so hard to believe you were born with the capacity for good and evil? Lucifer only tempts the darkness into prominence." Uriel's lips twitched with humor.

Humans were so certain their beliefs and thoughts were correct. Those who believed differently were considered outcasts and eventually, enemies. "Humans were so loved upon their creation they received the title of Beloved amongst the residents of Heaven. But one was not pleased. Until that moment, none stood above him but the Creator. He was the first to Fall. His own desire for power brought him into the darkness and he took a book with him—my book."

A sudden chill seemed to sweep through the room. "What's in the book?"

"Everything. The book is the reason you are hunted by the Fallen." There was no way to explain to Stephen what the book represented. It was too much for the human psyche to comprehend. Even those of celestial origin had difficulty truly understanding. "Because the book was in my care, I am to protect you."

Stephen gasped. "Protect me? Why? I'm no one. What importance could I be to angels?"

"You have a purpose. One day, you will save someone important and he will change the world. That is all I know. The book foretold this and the Fallen seek to prevent it coming to pass. As the Angel of Prophecy it is my duty to ensure its completion." Uriel watched as Stephen paled, his hands clenching in the loose material of his jeans. Unable to stop himself, he took the hand in his and rubbed the skin. It was surprisingly strong, the palm coated with calluses. "Your purpose is important and I will protect you until you fulfill it."

"Do you even know when I'll save this person? Or who he is?"

Uriel shook his head. "I do not. Prophecy isn't exact. There are always variables to take into account. Things change and in turn, so do the outcomes predicted. Chances are the Fallen can't decipher anything but your name from the text. It is an amazing feat that they were able to even pick your name from the tome. The pages are infinite."

Stephen's expression hardened. "Does this mean there will be more angels coming to kill me?"

"Yes."

Stephen began to laugh hysterically. "I'm a dead man. This is my punishment for all those people."

"No!" Uriel's hand latched onto Stephen's wrist, forcing him to face him. "I will protect you."

"You can't protect me from a legion of fallen angels." He futilely attempted to jerk his hand from the punishing grip. "They'll send more. You barely survived that one. What happens when two or three or more come?"

"I will protect you." Uriel lowered his gaze to the wrist he gripped. The smooth skin drew his attention. He found himself unable to resist stroking a thumb across the flesh, savoring the warmth radiating from it. He was falling too rapidly. The surge of emotions threatened to overwhelm him and he had no defense against them.

"Don't promise things you can't deliver." Stephen's eyes stared at where their hands were joined. "That's your first lesson as a human."

"Are all humans as pessimistic as you?"

Stephen chuckled faintly, the sound dry and weak. "I prefer the term pragmatic."

"You have my vow. I will protect you or die." Uriel watched Stephen's green eyes flicker with an array of emotions.

They closed before he spoke again. "Don't die for me."

"If that is my fate, I will meet it willingly." Uriel didn't understand what he was experiencing. It was a building of emotion to such a degree, his grip tightened on the flesh beneath his hand in response. "Stephen—"

Stephen's free hand latched over their joined flesh. The action brought Uriel's head up to meet the desperate green eyes. They were filled with fear and something else—longing perhaps.

Uriel had to fight the urge to pull him into his arms and soothe away every fear. It was an irrational thought, but still there. A connection was formed between them—one he was loathe to break.

"I've only known you two days, but the thought of you dying hurts." Stephen leaned forward suddenly, catching Uriel completely off guard.

Stephen's lips were pressed against his, seeking something unknown from him. They moved softly, creating a subtle heat inside him. It curled through his insides, spreading the warmth in increasing increments.

And just as quickly, the lips were gone, leaving a strange longing for more.

"I'm sorry." Stephen stood, took his jacket from the door, and walked out into the glittering, snow-coated landscape.

Uriel lifted fingers to his lips. Sensations he had never felt before were coursing through him. They warmed him with small electrical explosions along his nerve endings. Emotions sprang from where there had been none.

He understood kisses though he had never experienced one such as that. Celestial beings were not above finding physical pleasure with each other, but that is all it was. Companionship without true emotion was all they understood.

With the kiss Stephen had placed upon his lips, short though it was, he was affected inside his chest. Somehow his armor had become cracked. His heart thrummed a quick beat and his stomach lurched into his throat. He needed to find Stephen. He needed to understand what it was about Stephen that could turn his existence on its ear.

Standing, he followed Stephen into the snow, uncaring about his lack of footwear. The discomfort was nothing compared to the need to comfort his companion. "Stephen—"

"It's funny. I don't know anything about you and yet, I have to entrust my life to you." Stephen shoved his hands into the pockets of his down-filled jacket. "I'm sorry for the trouble."

Shaggy blond locks swayed back and forth as he shook his head. "Why after so long alone do I find myself willingly turning over everything to you? You are the most dysfunctional man I know. I shouldn't be attracted to you.

You're good looking, but that's not the reason. Make me understand. Tell me why I feel like I'm meant to be with you when you're not even human?"

"I don't know."

Stephen looked towards Uriel. His fist shot out and slammed against a hard chest. "Why don't you know anything? Why can't you explain it to me? What is it about you that draws me like the moth to the flame?"

Uriel couldn't answer because he was feeling the pull just as strongly, perhaps even more so. They were tied together by some invisible string. The loss of Stephen was going to be a bitter medicine once he returned to Heaven. The more attached he became, the harder it would be to let him go.

"Celestial beings don't feel as humans do." Uriel frowned at his attempt to explain the unexplainable. Until recently, he felt only the need to serve his Creator. His devotion and the light shining on him as a servant had always been enough until now. "Perhaps you feel that way because I saved your life today."

Stephen shook his head emphatically. "That's not it."

Uriel sighed. An entire new world was opened for him and he was adrift in the tempest of emotions. Each passing moment created a stronger tie to the human state. "We were created as guardians. We were not meant to experience emotions. Fear and love have no place in a celestial warrior."

"I understand." Stephen turned to leave, forcing Uriel to wrap a hand around his arm.

Pale eyes bore deeply into green. He could not leave it at that. To do so would be a disservice to both of them. "Wait. As I am, I am not as I was."

Confusion spread across Stephen's face. "What do you mean?"

"I feel. It's difficult to explain. I am fighting to force the emotion back but it's different with you." Uriel's throat bobbed several times. Explaining his emotions to Stephen was proving to be much more of a challenge than he had first thought. "I am not who you want. When you are safe, I will leave you and return to Heaven. Do not seek to find what you long for in me."

He said it as much for himself as for Stephen. Already he was too entangled in him. He longed for things he could not have. He could sense himself slipping away, drowning in the sensation of Stephen's presence.

Stephen dropped his gaze. "I know. It's just—"

Uriel released his arm and turned to stare out over the white plains. Small birds fluttered through the air, diving to capture small bits of twigs or insects braving the winter air. It was peaceful here. The environment suited Stephen. "Human emotions are strange to me. When I am with you, I can't help but notice at the way your eyes remind me of the grass in the Garden or how I need to protect you even were you not in danger. I long for things I should not."

Stephen clenched Uriel's shirt. "You don't sound emotionless to me."

He wasn't. He felt the emotions running through his veins. He felt affection towards his charge and hate towards those who sought to kill him. Lust and confusion raged through him along with the lesser understood love and longing.

Though he knew it was wrong, he could not lock away the new sensations. "While I am with you, I am not."

"You could stay." Stephen pressed his head to Uriel's back. "After the angels are gone, you could stay with me if you wanted."

Uriel turned to face him. He wished it was as easy as simply not returning home. The human body he resided in would not last. Eventually it would begin to decay under the force of his divine essence. Knowledge didn't stop him from wanting.

He lifted a hand, placing it at Stephen's nape. "Will you give me this, Stephen Trent?"

"What?"

Uriel smiled at the confusion on Stephen's face. "A kiss. Even knowing there can never be anything between us, would you give me a kiss?"

He wanted to experience a real kiss once more. It would be perhaps the last time he would allow himself to savor the forbidden. The urge was undeniable and he would act on it.

His fingers tipped Stephen's head back so their eyes could meet. Perhaps it was selfish of him, but he could not deny his need to experience what it was like to feel love. It wasn't the pure love of his Creator, but the unique and sometimes painful love humans were allowed. Just this once, he wanted to claim it for his own.

Uriel pressed forward with his claim. His lips brushed across Stephen's cheek and jaw before sliding below to the trembling flesh. "Are you cold?" he whispered.

Stephen jumped slight, his breath catching in his chest. "No."

"Good." Uriel slid his lips across the moist flesh. It felt as if he was being ripped apart and reassembled in one instant. He didn't want the moment to end, didn't want reality to rear its head.

The kiss was both innocent and provocative. It warmed the soul and ignited the body in a single action. For this too short instant, time stood still. There was naught but the two of them.

Stephen gasped as Uriel flicked his tongue over his lips before regretfully pulling back. Any more was too risky. "A kiss to remember."

Stephen shifted nervously in the snow. His brow pressed against Uriel's shoulder and his chest heaved with the weight of what he had experienced. "What do we do now?"

"I would like to return inside." Uriel glanced down at his bare feet turning blue in the snow. His thought of stopping Stephen had overwritten any other concern, including the pain his feet would suffer from the cold.

"Oh my God! Uriel, you're going to get frostbite standing out here like that!" Stephen linked their fingers together and tugged him towards the cabin.

Warmth rushed through Uriel, having nothing to do with the immediate heat coming from the stove as Stephen shoved him onto the sofa he had earlier vacated. Lean hands began to rub briskly along the cold extremities in much the same way he had done the day Uriel had arrived. The pain was worth the care given to him.

"Thank you."

Stephen kept his attention focused on his task. "You should be more careful. You can lose digits from the cold."

Uriel lowered a hand, brushing it over messy locks curling faintly around Stephen's cheeks. "I was worried for you."

"Stop doing that." Stephen brushed away the stroking fingers. "I can't think when you do that."

Uriel sat back to watch his charge. He found himself doing so often. He wasn't like an angel. He was full of imperfections from the lack of symmetry in his features to the almost gaunt frame. Stephen's body should be carrying at least twenty additional pounds.

"You should eat more."

Stephen sat back with a growl. "And you should mind your business. I eat when I'm hungry."

"Your body is hungry. It is crying out for nourishment," said Uriel determinedly. His hand ran over the shoulders down to the tight abdomen.

Stephen's stomach chose that moment to rumble loudly through cover of his sweater. "Damn it."

A sound rose in Uriel's throat. He fought against the strange sensation but it burst through despite his struggle. Laughter—another new experience. It rolled from him in waves, eventually forcing him to double over in mirth.

"I don't see anything funny about it." Stephen's face drew down into a pout, his own lips fighting the urge to turn upward. "I might have lost a little weight. I just haven't been hungry."

Glancing at the stove and then to the cupboards, Uriel was determined to see Stephen eat more. If he was to be his protector, he would do so completely. Food was the first order of business for both of them. "We should eat now."

"Is that an order?" teased Stephen.

Uriel smiled, enjoying the warmth spreading through him. "Yes."

"Well if you're going to be ordering me around, then might I pose a request?" Stephen flushed slightly, shifting his gaze to the wall behind Uriel's head. "Now that your fever is gone I wanted to know if we could sleep together."

Uriel froze. "What do you mean?"

Stephen's flush intensified dramatically, spreading across every inch of visible skin, from his hairline to the collar of his shirt. "Not like that. It gets cold in the cabin at night. Getting up constantly to put wood in the stove is exhausting."

Uriel hadn't realized. His mentality was that of a celestial creature. He wasn't used to the needs of the body and definitely not those of a human with infinitely expressive eyes. "You wish to share my bed?"

"You don't have to make it sound so lurid." Stephen stood and began to cook a meal. "The mattress is specially insulated to keep the occupant warm. It gets pretty cold at night. On some nights, I have to leave water running in the faucets to keep the pipes from freezing."

"Forgive me." Uriel felt heat rushing to his cheeks. "If you like, we can share the bed tonight." Stephen relaxed, sending a pleased smile in Uriel's direction. "Thank you. You won't even notice me."

Uriel very much doubted it. He would notice Stephen from across the room.

Chapter Three

The night was torture for Uriel. Although their bodies started apart, gradually the two gravitated towards each other's natural warmth. Stephen was so close, Uriel could feel the faint fluttering of his heart and each breath pressed their chests together. Being in such close proximity returned the ache to his chest. It made him long for the things he was not allowed, such as love and affection.

He edged away from Stephen, only to have him shift close once more. This time he moved a leg over Uriel's thighs to hold the warmth he sought in place. It created an intimate embrace—a natural molding of frames. Stephen's leaner physique fit perfectly against him.

Before he realized it, his arms were wrapping around the body, tugging him closer. It felt natural to hold him like this. Their skin rubbed where Stephen's shirt rose up. The delightful friction created caused Uriel to hiss in pleasure.

"Even in sleep, you're bothersome," he whispered into Stephen's hair. Yet, he couldn't release him. Some integral part of his being needed this connection that had formed between them.

Uriel brought a hand to his chest where an all too human heart thrummed in a slow and easy beat. The longer he stayed in this form, the more emotions he experienced and the less connected he felt to who he was. But he wanted more of them. They filled him with a sense of completion and gave him reasons to fight. How could something that felt so good be wrong?

"Uriel—" Stephen nuzzled closer in his sleep.

A softness gentled Uriel's features and he raised a hand to stroke the mussed blond locks falling against his chest. He wanted quieter, simple moments like this. "I'm here."

There was some unintelligible mumbling before Stephen settled into a deep sleep. Sleep came easily for him, but not for Uriel. With the new emotions came fear. Would he truly be capable of defending Stephen alone and in a human body?

Doubt coursed thickly through his veins, stealing all the good and replacing it with shadowy thoughts of less pleasant outcomes. Abaddon had nearly killed him. Uriel doubted Abaddon was strongest of the Fallen; therefore, if they came en mass, he would be unable to defend himself and Stephen. It was likely he would die on this mission. If Stephen survived, it was a choice he was willing to make.

The same circuit of thoughts circled through his mind until dawn. If left alone, there was nothing he could do but pray for deliverance for himself and Stephen. The Fallen would not stop at one loss. Disconnected as he was from Heaven, he doubted his brethren would hear his call and they could not watch over them at all times.

"You're awake?" Stephen mumbled, his sleep slack face burying deeper into Uriel's chest.

Uriel couldn't halt the rumbling chuckle at his companion's attempt to resume sleep. "Yes."

Quickly, reality returned as Stephen realized his current position. "Sorry—"

It was amusing for Uriel to watch the flush of color spreading across skin before Stephen slid from the warm cocoon created between the two. The play of emotions across his companion's face pleased Uriel. For an instant, he wished he could see that same series of expressions every morning. It was an irrational and fruitless yearning, but one he could not halt.

Silently, Uriel rose from the bed, his gaze shifting to scan the cabin's living space. As used as he was to wide spaces and freedom, he was content to remain in the small enclosed cabin as long as Stephen was in his presence. So long as the Fallen sought to destroy Stephen, he would remain and defend him with his entire being. The need to protect nearly over powered him.

"I thought we could go into town today. The snow has stopped, and the roads were probably cleared by the county's snowplows earlier. We could get you some clothes that fit and some shoes." Stephen exited the bathroom and pulled a pair of worn bedroom shoes from beneath the bed. "You could wear these and our first stop will be the shoe store."

Uriel was dubious about venturing into public. He wanted to stay away from humans. It was dangerous for him to become saturated in human company, but he could not deny Stephen his request. Being amongst a large number of humans for too long would push him closer towards Falling. He would simply need to remain vigilant while in town. "As you wish."

Stephen noticed the uncertainty on Uriel's face. He stood quietly for a moment before speaking. "This might be the only chance I have. If I might die, I'd like to get some things in order."

Anger and frustration rose quickly to the surface causing Uriel's vision to go red. He stormed across the living space and pressed Stephen against the nearest wall. He could feel the intensity of his emotions building inside him, triggering his eyes to glow with an otherworldly light. "Do not talk in such a way. I will not allow you to die."

"What if more angels come?"

"I will fight them all." Uriel's body quaked with the force of emotions he couldn't tamp down. "Your death will not be on my hands."

Stephen was thoughtful for a moment. "Why do you care so much?"

The question burned through him, leaving a trail of destruction in its wake. How did one answer such a loaded inquiry? It asked him to analyze his emotions, something he dared not do. Fear of what he would find held him back. "It is my mission."

The body in his arms sagged slightly. "I see."

Baffled at the response, Uriel lifted a hand to force Stephen to meet his gaze. There was hurt reflected in his green eyes. Seeing such pain expressed, Uriel was at a loss for the words that could dispel it.

Uriel's fingers grazed Stephen's slightly stubbly jaw, marveling at the texture of newly grown hair. "Why are you doing this to me? Since my inception, I have lived and never once longed for what the humans were gifted with until now. Tell me, Stephen, why do you torment me with what cannot be mine?"

Stephen swallowed thickly, his pulse picking up speed at the base of his throat. "What do you mean?"

The kisses they shared the previous day had opened up an untraveled gateway. With little experience in emotions, Uriel could not appropriately verbalize what he felt. All he could think of was having those lips against his—his tongue driving inside. Despite his mind screaming at the futility of acting on the human emotions coursing through him, he was under the control of his instincts.

And they were telling him to act.

Lowering his head, he did the only thing he could think of; he captured Stephen's lips in a breath-stealing kiss. There was no gentleness, only possession. He didn't know how to give with a partner. Before Stephen, it had been about one's own pleasure—two beings seeking physical relief only for themselves and not for each other. Angels were not capable of feeling deep emotions such as love. The depth of their emotion consisted of mild regard for comrades. Only one of the Celestial Brotherhood could boast of possessing a full range of emotions.

As their lips slid over each other, Uriel was on fire from the taste of him. His mind became hazy as a heady dose of lust enveloped him. His tongue plundered inside, desiring more while his hands pulled Stephen's legs around his waist to better feel the rising desire in him. He wanted to take—to devour this gift.

Stephen moaned into the kiss, his hips arching and grinding in search of more friction. His hands tore at Uriel's hair, burying themselves in the thick locks while his lips parted in equal desperation. Exploring hands slid beneath Uriel's tight shirt and across the tattooed wings spanning down the length of his back.

As quickly as the desire came, it dissipated with the realization of what they were doing. Uriel tugged Stephen's legs from his hips and took a step back. A small voice in the back of his mind quickly drove him away from the welcoming arms. "No. This cannot happen."

Stephen parted his lips to argue, forcing Uriel to silence him with his fingers. "I am not human. I cannot love you and to continue like this would only hurt you."

Stephen appeared as if he might debate the issue but instead, leaned wearily against the wall. "I see. Are you still alright with going into town?"

Uriel nodded slowly at the subject change but allowed Stephen the small escape. "I would like clothes that fit."

Stephen's lips quirked, though his smile did not quite reach his eyes. "I kind of like you in my clothes."

Uriel chuckled. Humor was an emotion he would miss upon returning to Heaven, but not the only one.

It did not take long for them to wash up and exit the house to a small garage where Stephen's pickup truck, custom fit with snow tires, sat. "I would have taken you to the hospital the other night, but the snow was too thick. We would have likely stalled and frozen to death before getting far."

"What is that?" Uriel took a step back upon seeing the small, claustrophobic cab.

"You've never ridden in a car, have you?" Stephen's lips twitched and his hand clenched on the door handle. The rising laughter caused him to shake in the effort to avoid releasing it.

Uriel was not amused. "You find my lack of experience in a human contraption amusing?"

"No," snickered Stephen. "It's just that the look on your face. I thought you might draw your sword again and slay my truck."

"That is a tempting suggestion." Uriel clenched his teeth in frustration. "Can we not walk?"

"It's at least a thirty-minute drive. Walking would take a couple of hours in the snow not to mention your lack of footwear. Stop being a pussy and get in." Stephen's eyes twinkled. "I'll buy you something nice if you do."

It wasn't the promise of something nice that had him sliding cautiously into the cab, but the fear Stephen would leave and be assaulted by another Fallen while away from his guardian. He tamped down the fear and closed his eyes to keep from becoming sick at the sight of the rapidly passing countryside. Moving at high speeds seemed different from within the interior of the vehicle.

"I wanted to ask you something, since I have a bounty on my head." Stephen's gaze remained on the road, though his eyes seemed distant. "You say you're from Heaven. Is that where our souls go when we die?"

Uriel turned his gaze to the white fields visible from his window. "No."

"You're not helping. What happens to us?" Stephen hazarded a glance at his companion. "Tell me."

"Souls are reborn. I don't know how or why it happens. Residents of Heaven are not privy to all that is the Creator."

Stephen nodded sagely. "Reincarnation. That seems plausible. I'm sure the Church wouldn't be happy to receive this news."

Uriel smiled at the thought. The Church, in all its incarnations, was a comfort to humans. It gave hope to an otherwise seemingly ignored creation unable to sense the presence of their creator.

"What about angels?"

"What of them?"

Stephen snickered. "When you die, are you reborn?"

He shook his head. "No."

"That's your answer?" Stephen shot Uriel a disbelieving glance. "What happens?"

"Nothing. We are simply gone." There wasn't anything to tell. Celestial beings are a soul in a tangible form. When they die, it is the end. Extreme longevity possessed a definite weakness.

Stephen slammed his foot into the breaks, causing the vehicle to swerve dangerously close to the snow banks lining the road. "I want you to leave."

Uriel cocked his head, slightly confused at the look of horror and fear playing across Stephen's features. "I do not understand."

"I want you to go back to Heaven. I don't want you to stay here." Stephen's hands gripped the wheel so tightly his knuckles began to whiten.

"I cannot. It is my mission to protect you." Uriel was beginning to understand. Stephen feared for him.

Stephen turned off the engine. "It's my life. If I don't want your protection, you can't make me take it."

"You sound childish." Uriel shifted his gaze once more to the environment so as not to see the hurt and fear displayed across Stephen's face.

"I don't care. I refuse to let you die so I can save someone I don't even know." Stephen turned flashing green eyes towards Uriel. "I won't allow it. Go back to Heaven."

Uriel's heart gave a thud in his chest. It seemed Stephen was constantly having that effect on him of late. "I could not in good conscience allow such a thing. You should trust in my abilities. I would not have been sent to die."

"Uriel—"

"Do not worry about my death. I struggled with Abaddon because of my current state. It is a mistake I will not make again." Uriel inclined his head toward Stephen. "Thank you for caring for me."

Stephen lowered his gaze, his jaw clenching from withholding his words. "If you die—"

"I won't."

There was a pause before Stephen nodded stiffly and turned over the engine. "I'll hold you to that."

The snowy countryside transformed into periodic houses, and then public buildings. The town wasn't a large collection of humans, but a small modest grouping. The Main Street buildings seemed weathered, some in dire need of cosmetic repair, and the road contained its fair share of potholes. As they pulled into one of the few open parking slots, several people waved to Stephen.

"You're well known?"

Stephen shrugged. "People here are friendly. They welcome newcomers as if they were family."

He pointed towards a building. Glass windows displayed various clothing and shoes along with matching accessories. The exterior was well kept, showing the love the owner put into upkeep. "We'll get you some clothes in there."

"Stephen!" A middle-aged woman behind the counter waved in his direction as they entered the store. "It's been a while since you've come to town."

"Can you blame me?" he teased. "Just shoveling a path from my door exhausts me."

Her eyes narrowed on his thin frame. "That's because you don't eat enough."

Uriel couldn't stop the smirk pulling at his lips. He'd told Stephen the same. Having his opinion validated brought on a sense of satisfaction.

"Who's your friend?"

"Martha, this is Uriel. He's been staying with me at the cabin, but we need to pick up some shoes and clothes for him. He's a bit big for mine." Stephen said.

Uriel cocked his head at the woman. It was obvious she wanted to ask more but kept her opinion to herself. She eyed him closely before waddling down several isles and coming back with a stack of clothes.

"Here, dear. Why don't you go try these on while I find you a pair of good work boots. What size are you?"

At Uriel's confused look, Stephen quickly stepped in to answer. "Let's try him with a thirteen and go on from there."

Uriel glanced at Stephen who pointed him to the curtained room. Inside was a mirror, a small bench, and several clothing hangers. It was a small space and immediately a sense of claustrophobia rushed through him.

Giving a small shudder, he began stripping the tight cotton from his body. The splash of dark reflected in the mirror caught his gaze and caused him to glance over his shoulder into the reflection.

The detailed raven feathers of his wings arched across his shoulders and curved gracefully over his hips and buttocks. A sense of loss enveloped him. He missed the solid feel of them on his back. In this state, they seemed almost unreal—a dream.

"Uriel? Are you alright in there?"

"I am fine." He slid a hand over his shoulder until he reached the marked skin. His body gave a final tremor of longing before he tugged on the jeans and turtleneck provided for him.

He stepped from the curtained room. "Well?"

Stephen gave a satisfied hum before handing him a pair of socks and brown boots. "Put these on. I've had Martha bag up a couple of outfits. She's uncanny at judging size. I've rarely seen her wrong."

Uriel watched as Stephen paid for their purchases. Human currency had changed from bronze coins to plastic cards. It was both confusing and intriguing.

"I'm going to go to the bookstore. If you like, you can wait at the truck. Once I'm done, we'll run to the grocery and then home."

Uriel was about to follow when the hairs on his neck stood at attention. He nodded to Stephen, glancing slowly across the street until he spotted two shadowy figures.

His eyes narrowed as he approached the men standing beneath the awning of one of the specialty shops. "Rafael. Michael. Why are you here?"

"Your predicament has come to our attention, Uriel." Rafael's short pale locks seemed to capture the rays of sunlight as he moved from the shadows.

Michael, the dark Archangel and general to the army of Celestials, stepped forward as well. "You're Falling. We've come to take you home. The Creator was foolish to send you in a human form."

Though they appeared human to his eyes, he knew it was an illusion. Neither was in a human form as he was. Both glowed with the inner light all celestial beings contained.

"You know it was the only way for me to remain as his guardian. The order came directly from Gabriel." Uriel felt a wave of true affection for the two. They were the closest thing to friends he had. For the first time, he was truly able to understand the depth of his affection for the two. It seemed a loss that neither would experience what it was to truly care for another.

Rafael's gaze never wavered. "Still, it was a mistake. We will find another way."

"There isn't one." Uriel released a small sigh. "You know that celestial beings cannot remain on earth for more than a few hours before our power begins to wane. For me to be able to fully guard him, I must be in his presence at all times."

Michael wasn't willing to accept that answer. "It doesn't matter. You will return. We will not lose another to the temptation of human emotion. Already you've felt too much. I can barely sense the Celestial in you as we stand here."

He extended a hand to grasp Uriel's forearm. "If you remain much longer, there will be no returning."

"Is that so bad a fate?" Uriel knew the risks. When he accepted the mission, he had known he could possibly lose everything. It was a calculated risk. There were no other options.

"Please, Uriel. We've lost too many and you are too important." Rafael always was the voice of reason in Heaven. As the Angel of Healing, it was his nature to seek to aid those who were injured.

"I am sorry, Rafael. I cannot leave Stephen unprotected, even for the time it would take to devise an alternate plan. There has already been an attack on him." Uriel refused to even consider abandoning Stephen in order to save his place among his fellow angels. It was his choice to remain, and remain he would.

Michael's eyes narrowed, the wheels in his analytical mind spinning. "You would give up your rightful place in Heaven for a human?"

"A human who will change the world simply by his actions. I won't leave him."

Rafael's shoulders sagged. "Is that your decision?"

Uriel nodded. "It is."

"Rafael, we cannot—"

"It is his decision." He turned his face towards Michael. "All we can do is respect it."

Rafael's piercing gaze returned to Uriel. "If you truly wish to return to Heaven, you must temper your emotions. Do not allow them reign over your being or you will be corrupted beyond repair. Do you understand?"

Uriel nodded, though he was certain he was already too corrupted to return. All he could hope for was that his celestial strength would withstand until the appointed time came. Only the Creator could have knowledge of when that day was, and He was not talking.

Michael shoved Rafael aside. "I refuse. It could be years before his duty is complete."

"No." Rafael shook his head. "It is close. It is why they are attacking now and why the Creator sent an angel to the human."

"But likely not close enough to save Uriel from being ruined."

"Thank you for your concern, Michael." Uriel clasped his hand on Michael's shoulder. "But I cannot allow harm to come to Stephen. Not even at the risk of Falling."

Michael's jaw clenched tightly, the small muscles jumping under the strain. "The Creator should have protected you from this. You are one of His most loyal."

"That's not how it works—not how He works." Uriel's lips creased in a smile. "But protecting Stephen is something I must do and I am grateful to Him for allowing me the honor."

"You're in love with him ... with a human." Michael's expression didn't change. "How could you allow such a thing?"

Love? Was such a thing even possible? "I do not love the human."

"You cannot lie to us." Michael's dark eyes seemed to shimmer as he spoke. "You are Fallen. You will never return to us."

"Uriel, is this true?" Rafael frowned at Michael's words. "If you return now—"

Uriel slammed his fist into the wall. "I cannot return until Stephen is safe."

"As you wish." Rafael took a step back. "There is nothing more that can be said."

Guilt washed though Uriel. "I am sorry."

"The choices we make define us." Rafael placed a hand upon Uriel's shoulder. "I will miss our discussions."

"You're talking as if he's died." Michael glared at his companion. "I still feel him. Perhaps there is still time if he returns now."

"Uriel?" Stephen called to him from several feet away.

Uriel turned at the call. He could sense the fear rolling off of Stephen. He feared Michael and Rafael were Fallen. "Do not worry. They are my brethren."

"This is the human?" asked Michael.

Stephen approached cautiously. "My name is Stephen Trent."

Rafael's lips twisted upward in a small smile. He was privy to slightly more emotions than other Celestials, though they remained muted to a large degree. It was why he possessed the ability for laughter. "Hello, Steven Trent. I have heard much of you. Your life is now very precious."

"Because of this person I'm supposed to save?"

Rafael's gaze slid to Uriel. "No. It is precious because of what was freely sacrificed so that you might live."

Michael did not speak immediately, his eyes never leaving Stephen. He appeared so intense; Uriel instinctively stepped in front of Stephen.

"You've become quite the defender."

"Michael—" Rafael placed a calming hand on his companion's arm. "We must leave."

"This isn't finished, Uriel. You would be wise to abandon the human before you are completely lost. It would be a shame for you to harm your human instead of protecting him." Michael held his ground for several seconds before turning and fading as if he were never there.

A sad smile played across Rafael's features. "I hope this man is worth what you are giving up."

"He is."

Rafael nodded. "Then I will aid you in protecting him. Call upon us if you require our aid. You might not hear us, but we still hear you."

"I will." Uriel nodded, watching as Rafael faded from sight.

Stephen glanced at Uriel. "What did he mean?"

"You do not need to worry." Uriel moved towards the waiting truck.

"Uriel—"

He smiled, wondering at Rafael and Michael's visit. It was pleasant to know they cared. Their aid would be invaluable should more than one Fallen attack.

"Don't you ignore me!"

"Forgive me." Uriel turned his gaze to Stephen. "Do not worry. They only think of my well-being. You should be more concerned with your own life."

There was a pause. "They didn't look happy. What did they want?"

"For me to return to Heaven."

Stephen visibly paled. "Why didn't you?"

Distress was plain on Stephen's face. It was obvious that he was torn between what he wanted and the danger posed should Uriel remain. Perhaps Michael was correct in his assumption, but for now Uriel wanted nothing more than to ease the worry playing across Stephen's features.

"I made a vow to protect you. It is my only duty at this moment." Uriel spoke with conviction. He would not abandon Stephen for any reason, even a direct order from the Creator.

"Why did they want you to return? If you're in danger, why not send more angels? Are angels really in such short supply?" Stephen ran a frustrated hand through his hair.

Uriel shifted his gaze away. "They have their reasons."

Stephen grabbed Uriel's arm in a surprisingly strong grasp. "Tell me, damn it."

"Celestial beings don't feel." That wasn't exactly true. They were diluted and extremely muted emotions, but emotions still.

"You mentioned as much. You said the emotions put you off kilter at first but that you're adjusting." Stephen sent Uriel a look of doubt. "You adjusted quickly."

Saying the words were harder than he'd first thought. "I am on the cusp of Falling."

"What?"

Uriel moved towards the waiting vehicle. "Being in a human body causes the strong amplification of emotions. To become saturated with them makes it impossible to revert to little or no feelings. Few Celestials can adapt. They longs for what was once experienced. The stronger the emotion, the harder it becomes to break the ties to the human world. That is when we Fall."

"Why don't you remain here as an angel? Why take human form? There aren't many people where I live if you're afraid of being seen."

"We can't remain on Earth for longer than a few hours while in our true forms." Uriel thought of how odd Michael had looked, as if his insurmountable strength was waning with each passing moment. "But being placed in a human body carries risks. The emotions that make humans special are addictive. It was known I would not survive this mission unscathed."

Stephen stopped walking. "That's cruel."

"The truth often is."

"But—"

Uriel lifted a hand to Stephen's lips. "Do not argue. I have made my choice."

Stephen's eyes closed and he nodded. "Let's just go get the food and go home."

Uriel spoke no more as he climbed cautiously into the cab. He forced his focus onto the passing buildings and people rather than Stephen.

Chapter Four

After purchasing groceries, they headed home. The return trip towards the cabin was completed in silence. It seemed deafening.

Stephen focused on the road before him and Uriel on the pristine white of the passing fields. Both were lost in their thoughts of what the future held for them.

"Uriel, I'm sorry for this." Stephen clenched the wheel. "I'm sorry for what you are losing so I can live."

Uriel's lips curved upward. He took one of Stephen's hands in his. "A most willing sacrifice."

A flush stole across Stephen's face and his eyes cut sideways to glance at Uriel. "If you Fall, will you stay with me?"

Uriel met Stephen's gaze, the smile on his face broadening. Before he could respond, the road before them exploded. Debris flew into the windshield, shattering it.

"Stephen, look out!" Uriel threw up his arms to shield himself from the splintering glass.

Stephen spun the wheel as hard as he could to evade the clumps of rock and asphalt spewing from the dust-clouded road. Try though he might, he was unable to maintain control over the vehicle and the truck skidded across the road before rolling like a child's play toy toward the snow banks lining the road.

The sound of crunching metal and busting glass filled the cab. Equilibrium was lost as the world spun around in a seemingly endless whirl. Even when all was still, there was a haze over Uriel's senses. The world seemed to freeze, moving in slow motion before coming to a halt.

Pain shot up Uriel's arm as he came back to his senses. The ringing in his ears passed in moments and with its passing returned his wits. Blood dribbled into his eyes and the scent of hellfire permeated his senses. He realized that the truck was upside down and both he and Stephen dangled a foot above the flipped roof. Then, he felt the overwhelming sense of foreboding coming from the direction of the massive crater created in the road.

Pushing aside the pain, he freed his body from the seat belt Stephen had insisted he wear and collapsed to the glass-scattered ground. "Stephen?"

Coughs wracked his body from the mixture of smoke and dust permeating the air. He wiped at the blood clouding his vision and crawled towards where Stephen still sat locked in his seat. Reaching up, he brushed his fingers across Stephen's brow. "Stephen, can you hear me?"

There was no reply. Stephen's body, held in place by the seat belt, hung unresponsive in his seat. His arms dangled towards the roof and a small trickle of blood dripped from a cut on his brow caused by striking the steering wheel.

Uriel was forced to tamp down the pain and panic eating away at him. Stephen was unresponsive, but breathing. It was too dangerous to leave him in the truck. He needed to move him to safety before he could deal with the dark presence waiting almost patiently amid the chaos.

Smoke and brimstone swirled around the area. Fluid dripped from the underside of the truck and added to the disruption of the air with its deadly fumes. The slightest spark was likely to send the entire truck into flames.

There was a shifting in the atmosphere before a chiming voice rang out. "Come out, Uriel."

Uriel ignored the taunt, focusing on moving Stephen from the death trap the vehicle had become and to safety. He pressed the buckle's snap, catching the limp body as it fell from the seat. "Stephen—"

Stephen's head lolled like a rag doll's and his skin was the color of parchment. He needed a healer's aid. The sooner he took care of their current problem, the better.

"If you don't come out, I will destroy you both without allowing you the chance to fight back. There is no fun in that but I do have a schedule to keep."

Uriel slid from the vehicle, cradling the unconscious Stephen against his chest with his uninjured arm. "Belial."

Standing before him was one of the darkest beings in existence. Belial—a demon born of fire and death. He was sent for only the most important cases. Short of Lucifer, Belial was the most dangerous being in creation. He was formed from pure darkness and had nothing of the Creator in him. The First Fallen was tired of playing if he sent his second-in-command to handle the issue.

"You've caused quite a bit of trouble, Uriel. Abaddon was a useful creature and now he's dead." Belial stepped forward in the guise of a child. He was the epitome of hopelessness and despair.

"Abaddon chose his fate when he Fell. He knew he would be hunted and destroyed." Uriel pulled Stephen closer to his body.

Belial cocked his small head. "But to do so to a former lover. For shame."

"We have no lovers." Uriel's jaw clenched tightly. "Only comrades."

"Ah, yes. You are like me, lacking in emotion. I suppose it is for the best that I was sent to complete the task Abaddon failed. I don't have emotions to cloud my skills." Solid black eyes stared forward with emotionless intent. "Prepare to die."

"I won't die at your hand." Uriel placed Stephen on a large boulder several feet away from the destroyed road.

"You're wasting your time saving the human. It only delays his inevitable fate." Belial's head cocked slightly as his gaze followed the two.

Uriel snarled under his breath, his hands running over Stephen to ensure he wasn't badly wounded. Other than the cut across his brow, he couldn't find any life threatening injuries. It was good that he slept. This battle would not be a pleasant sight.

Belial shrugged his small shoulders. It was a taunt to take the form of a child. Children represented innocence, but Uriel could see the truth in what stood before him. This creature was no child but a spawn created of pure darkness. The purpose for his existence was simply to follow the command of his master.

"Don't think that form will stop me from destroying you."

Unblinking eyes stared neutrally. "No?"

"I'm not human. I am not fooled by a demon in the guise of an innocent." Uriel stepped forward, his eyes as crystalline as the calmest lake. "It's you who will face an inevitable fate."

"Then I shall simply have to choose a different form. Perhaps this one will interest you more?" Belial's body warped, a dark shadow engulfed him, and his frame wavered. The horrible odor of brimstone and sulfur rose in the air, tainting it with a sense of decay.

Bare moments passed while his body elongated to that of an adult. His dark hair lightened and grew shaggy. Faint stubble sprouted on his cheeks and his lips parted in an easy grin. If not for his pitch black eyes, he would look identical to Stephen. "And now? Do you want to fight me still? Or would you rather fuck me?"

"You aren't Stephen." Uriel's jaw clenched. "Taking his form won't stop me from killing you."

"True, but I'll consider it a pleasure to kill you while wearing it. To think the last thing in this world you will see will be the one you love stabbing you through the heart."

Belial's arm extended to pull a fiery black blade from the air. "It will be the sweet appetizer before I finish off this loose end."

Fury erupted in Uriel. He had never felt the likes of it before. It burned and ate away at his being. All he could think of was ripping Belial's head from his shoulders for daring to even hint at harming Stephen.

A myriad of emotions ran powerfully through Uriel, all competing for dominance. The threat of emotions once held him on the cusp of the abyss, but now he welcomed the rush spilling through his bloodstream. His fury would power his blade as he struck down this monster and rid the world of his taint. If Falling meant he could accomplish that, he would willingly embrace the descent.

"Ah—" A fire seemed to light behind Belial's eyes. "Embrace the anger. Savor it and destroy me, if you can."

Uriel's flaming sword materialized in his hand and his wings burst forth in a flash of dark feathers. His eyes burned with hate for the creature standing before him wearing Stephen's face. His blade longed to taste its blood. Emotion heightened his senses and influenced his attacks.

He was the first to strike, his blade and wings sending the demon stumbling backwards. An otherworldly glow enveloped Uriel, culminating in his blade as it struck repeatedly. Determination and anger whispered in his mind. He would kill this abomination.

Belial defended himself from the attacks. Sparks flew from their weapons as Uriel's attacks came in fast succession. He was a beast. The bloodlust roared loudly through him.

Attack after attack sent Belial staggering across the debris-strewn highway. He wasn't even attempting to counter the attacks, merely taking them. Each blow sounded through the area in sharp clarity until Belial collapsed beneath the force of a blow.

Power rushed through Uriel due to his dominance. This was what it felt like to conquer. It was addictive. He wanted his adversary to suffer. He was the Death and Belial would fall under his assault.

And then realization washed through him.

This was the reason angels possessed few tangible emotions. The power was addictive. In his current state, he felt as if he could conquer the world. He could destroy all those who stood in his way. If he called upon his brethren, they could free the humans of their floundering existence. He could become a dark god.

As if struck, he stumbled away from the sprawled Belial. "No—"

"What is the matter, angel?" Belial moved smoothly to his feet. "You tasted it, didn't you? You know the true power of the Fallen. Kill the human and it can be yours. Even I shall bow to you if you do this."

The words tempted him. He felt Belial's power worming inside his skull. It forced his gaze to where Stephen lay unconscious. He could kill him mercifully and quickly.

Instinctively his hand tightened on his sword and he took a hesitant step in Stephen's direction. "No. That's not what I want."

"Oh?" Belial stepped forward, his blade flashing darkly at his side. "Then what do you want, Uriel? Tell me."

Uriel watched as Stephen's eyes blinked open to reveal the rich green he had come to love. A hand was lifted to probe the wound on his brow before their gazes met. He didn't want to kill Stephen, he wanted to take him. He wanted to lay a claim to him so that none other could deny that he belonged to Uriel.

A cold hand placed itself on his shoulder. "Pity."

"Uriel!" Stephen sat up, his eyes wide with fear.

The warning was just enough to force sense back into Uriel. He evaded the piercing blade, but at the cost of his arm. The pain throbbing upward was so intense, he was sure his arm was seared to the bone and left hanging useless at his side.

Belial turned emotionless eyes to Stephen. "I would spend your last moments sending pleas to your maker, human. After I finish here, I'll be sure to send you to meet him post-haste."

"You will not touch him." Uriel swung his blade, the crimson fire singeing Belial's hair as he ducked the attack.

Belial's hand lifted to stroke his cheek. Though the attack missed, the fire burned enough of him to force his true features into light. Dark skin, the color of pitch, shimmered into view. His hair vanished, leaving a smooth head.

"You will not touch him," repeated Uriel.

No witty comment followed. Talk was finished.

Belial's attack was instantaneous. He swung his weapon with the accuracy of millennia of experience. Each stroke was precise, a true dance of blades. It caused Uriel to pause to wonder if his previous defense was nothing more than a ruse.

Uriel was now on the defense.

His injured arm was worthless, throwing his balance completely off. It was all he could do to block the barrage of slices and jabs. Each stroke sent his hair flying. His wings were singed, feathers drifting around them with each attempt to deflect the attacks with his uninjured arm. If another blow landed, it would be over.

Unlike Abaddon's blade, Belial's fiery weapon wouldn't kill with a single touch. It was meant to cause the most pain possible before he chose to dispatch his prey. The blade was made for suffering.

His wings were taking the brunt of the damage as he was forced to use them as a shield over his unguarded side. Each blow sent feathers scattering. If not for his wings, he would have long since fallen. Belial's blows were too quick and accurate to allow a moment to rest and reevaluate the situation.

The unthinkable happened when Uriel stumbled over a small bit of debris. Belial took the advantage and snared a black hand into the thick feathers of Uriel's left wing. With a quick blow, the wing was sliced off, hellfire cauterizing the wound instantly.

Uriel screamed in agony, his body writhing on the ground. It wasn't solely losing a limb. For an angel, the wings were their link to the Creator. To have part of that link severed was akin to having a portion of their soul sliced off. It was more than physical agony; it was a pain in their very core.

"A one-winged angel, how appropriate. While I would love to stay and play longer, I have a task to finish." Belial lifted his arm to deal the final blow.

Stephen acted in Belial's distraction. He wrapped his hands around an uprooted fence post and charged. The blow landed with a sickening crunch atop Belial's head.

Instead of falling, Belial's lifeless obsidian eyes shifted. "Human. Did you really think you could take me down with a stick when an angel of the highest order falls before me? I am Death, crown prince of Hell and all it entails. Nothing can defeat me."

Belial's hand shot out to wrap around Stephen's neck. His fingers tightened, cutting off his oxygen. Eyes watched dispassionately as the human in his grip struggled futilely before slowly going limp. There was nothing in his gaze. No compassion. No triumph. Nothing.

"Stephen!" Uriel struggled to rise. His heart cried out in agony. He couldn't be dead.

Belial tossed Stephen to the side as if he were nothing but a discarded piece of garbage. The body skidded across the road to land harshly against a drift of snow. "Now that the human is dead, all that is left is cleaning up the mess."

"Stop, Belial." Rafael stepped from the veil and into the light. "It ends at this."

"This Celestial could not stop me, why should you be able to?" Belial raised his sword, dark flames licking at the air. "I am stronger than one angel."

"Perhaps so, but we do not abandon our brethren." Rafael looked to his side as his brethren in full battle regalia stepped into view. Countless numbers surrounded the small stretch of highway. Not even Lucifer could withstand such a mounting of forces alone.

"What's this?" Belial's eyes scanned the massive gathering. "All this for a Fallen? Is his life that important to Heaven?"

Michael stepped forward, his flaming sword flaring brighter than any other. "He Fell for the right reasons."

"There are no right reasons." Belial's eyes showed no emotion, though he took several steps away from the enclosing angels. He might not fear death, but he was wise enough to know when to retreat from the futility of his actions. "It is of no consequence. The human is dead. My mission is complete."

"No!" Uriel stumbled to his feet despite Rafael's hands attempting to hold him down. "Fight me, coward."

Belial's gaze slid over Uriel's tattered form. "No. I do not waste what is given me by doing anything other than the task I am given. Finishing you off is not worth my life."

Uriel charged the fading form, his sword swinging wildly. It was to no avail. Belial returned to his domain of fire. Only his destruction remained as testament to his appearance.

"Uriel, you must rest. You're badly injured." Rafael sought to wrestle Uriel to the ground, only to have a blade pressed to his throat.

"Where is Stephen?"

Rafael's gaze lowered before drifting to where a score of angels stood watch over the crushed body. "There."

Uriel stumbled towards where Stephen lay. Celestial warriors stepped aside as he fell to his knees before the body. Dark bruising circled Stephen's neck and his skin was the color of wax paper. The beautiful green eyes he had come to love stared blindly forward. No life remained in them.

He was gone. And the pain nearly destroyed Uriel. His body shook as he cradled Stephen against his chest. Never again would he hear Stephen's rippling laughter or feel the soft brush Stephen's lips against his.

He felt the gazes of those who watched his suffering but found it difficult to care. No amount of whispered comfort could ease the hell he was now a part of.

His silent anguish ripped through the ranks. That he possessed the capacity to feel such depth for a human baffled them. They could only watch as one of their own sat staring blindly while rocking the cold body he clasped tight against him.

"I'm sorry," he whispered into Stephen's hair. Tears trickled down his cheeks to splash against the still features. He closed his eyes, unable to bear the pain. It was worse than a thousand injuries. If he were forced to go on with this agony inside him, he would self-destruct.

"What about his wing?" Michael gestured to the leaking stump where once grew a massive raven-hued wing. "What are we to do now? Is he one of us? Is he a Fallen?"

Rafael shook his head. "He's not a Fallen, not completely. I can sense remnants of the Celestial inside him."

"But he isn't an angel either. What do we do? Do we leave him here or do we take him with us?"

Uriel's mad gaze turned on the two. "Is that all that matters? What to do with me? Stephen is dead. My mission is a failure and it's—"

"Who said your mission was a failure?"

All eyes turned to the golden-haired angel standing apart from the rest. His golden hair fell in a long braid over one shoulder. Small braids framed aristocratic features and upon his back curled the only golden wings in existence.

"Gabriel." Michael fell to his knee, sword piercing the ground before him.

Instantly all who stood fell to their knee before the voice of the Creator. When Gabriel was sent, all listened, including Lucifer. He spoke for the Creator.

Gabriel ignored those lining the way to Uriel. His white and gold robes flowed around him. At his side hung a sheathed blade none had ever seen drawn. He was the oldest and wisest. Above all other Celestials, he possessed the full range of emotions. His voice was pure and clear, demanding both respect and awe. "It has been a long while, Uriel."

"Gabriel." Uriel lowered his head in respect. Not even he could deny it to one such as Gabriel.

"Why do you weep?" Gabriel focused on the drying tears creating tracks amidst the soot and dirt painting Uriel's face. "The Creator is grateful for your sacrifice and offers you a boon. Shall I restore you to your place in Heaven? Your wings and your life can be yours again."

Uriel's heart thudded in his chest. "And Stephen?"

"His purpose has been served. He will be reborn as all humans are." Gabriel's lavender eyes slid over the fallen human.

"You said I could have any boon. I want Stephen back." Uriel tightened his arms around the cold body. "That is what I ask."

"No!" Michael stepped forward. "Uriel, the gifts of the Creator are not to be squandered on humans. He will eventually be reborn. You have a chance for your status to be returned to you. Would you throw it away for fifty years with him?"

Gabriel's lips quirked in amusement. "Ah, that is the question. You may have any boon you wish, even this human's life. Think carefully on the offer, Uriel."

There was no need to think. Even if his position were returned to him, he would never forego the emotions he'd experienced. He would choose the nothing of death before he would choose such a life. Stephen was his only hope for salvation now. "I choose Stephen."

Gabriel crouched beside Uriel. A smile curled the corners of his mouth as he spoke. "Wise choice."

A hand extended, brushing over Uriel's shoulder. The gaping wounds healed and his single wing faded. Instead of disappearing completely, both wings in their entirety were inked once more across the length of his back.

Gabriel's eyes turned their focus to Stephen. "Time to wake up, little human."

The air surrounding them charged with static. The hair on every angel present perked up under the atmospheric change. Uriel's eyes shifted quickly to Stephen.

The wound on his brow faded and the bruising around his crushed throat healed. It wasn't until his chest expanded in a deep breath that every being knew he breathed again. Coughs wracked his frame and his hands clawed desperately at Uriel's arms.

"Stephen?" Uriel's eyes focused on the man in his arms. "Stephen, can you hear me?"

Stephen's eyes closed before fluttering open, revealing the pasture-green eyes enriched with life once more. "Uriel? What happened?"

Uriel's eyes closed and he lowered his head in silent prayer. "Thank you. Thank you."

Stephen's gaze scanned the score of angels surrounding them. "Uriel—"

Uriel remained seated as Stephen pulled away and stood. His gaze landed on each kneeling being. "What's going on?"

Gabriel moved from a crouch to his knee before Stephen. "You have the gratitude of every being in the heavens."

Stephen's eyes widened at the show of respect. "Why? What did I do?"

Gabriel smiled so radiantly, nothing in Heaven or Earth could compare. "You saved Uriel, as you were meant to do."

Uriel's gaze jerked upward. "Me? I thought he was supposed to save a human."

Gabriel arched a brow. "You foresaw it, didn't you, Angel of Prophecy?"

"It doesn't work like that, and you know it." Uriel struggled to his feet despite his healed body. "Deciphering prophecy is nearly impossible."

Rafael nodded slowly. "And why the Fallen were mistaken in seeking to kill Stephen Trent."

Gabriel's lips twitched. "Fate is an amusing thing. It can't happen without free will. If they hadn't sought to kill the human, Uriel would never have been sent and therefore would not require rescue. By doing nothing, they would have achieved what they wished for. And now Lucifer knows it."

"I wouldn't want to be in his court tonight," commented Rafael.

Michael latched firmly onto Gabriel's arm. "You sacrificed one of our own knowing this would happen?"

Every breath caught at the impudent action. Gabriel's gaze never left Stephen. "Once the Fallen chose their path, we were bound by it."

Rafael stepped forward with a respectful bow. "What of Uriel? Is he Fallen? Will we one day face him in battle?"

Gabriel paused, a small smile teasing his lips. "Uriel has more important things to accomplish on Earth. He will not return to Heaven."

Gasps rang out. Angels glanced at each other in distress. It wasn't until Gabriel lifted his hand that they silenced. "He made his choice and is Beloved by the Creator for it."

"Human?"

Gabriel shook his head. "Not exactly, but no longer an angel. Returning was not his wish. To remain with the human, he must change."

Uriel gazed down at Stephen in awe. "I can stay?"

"There are things you must do." Gabriel clasped a hand to Uriel's shoulder. "Not fulfilling them goes against the current plan."

"What are they?"

"That I cannot say. It's for you to discover," said Gabriel.

Stephen began to shake. His hands latched onto Uriel so as to allow him to bury his face in warm neck. "What does all this mean?"

Uriel closed his eyes and basked in the warmth radiating from Stephen. "It means I can stay with you for the remainder of your life."

Stephen's eyes widened and his breath stuttered in his chest. "With me? You want to stay with me?"

"You have become precious to me." Uriel traced his fingers across Stephen's cheek and down to his lips. "I can't imagine being without you."

"What about when you die?" Stephen became panicked. "I don't want you to fade away to nothing."

Gabriel stepped forward. "You need not fear that. Uriel's life span is still celestial. He will not die and will always find you when you're reborn."

"He won't die?" Stephen glanced at Gabriel.

"The Creator needs an angel on Earth. He has long considered how but it would require gifting emotions and emotions lead to Falling." Gabriel threaded his fingers together. "This works out well."

Stephen shifted nervously on his heels. "You'll stay with me even though I'm a man?"

"Gender is of no consequence. We are not prejudiced as you humans are." Uriel sniffed indignantly at being compared to humans.

Stephen chuckled as he wrapped his slender arms around Uriel's waist. The Church would shit if they knew what I do."

Uriel snickered under his breath while his heart lodged in his throat at the look of joy spreading across Stephen's features. "Let's keep that small bit to ourselves."

"You know you'll only have me for fifty or so years." Stephen nibbled nervously on his lip. "Is that enough time?"

Uriel nodded, his arms tightening around the warm body cradled in his arms. "For now."

"And later?"

There was a pause before Uriel lifted a hand to angle Stephen's head. Their lips met in a slow kiss, expressing every ounce of passion and affection they held for each other. He did not speak until they pulled back slowly. "I'll always find you. I am an angel."

Stephen's face glowed with his happiness. "My angel."

"Thank you for giving me this life, Gabriel." Uriel nuzzled his face against Stephen's jaw. "I am forever in your debt."

Gabriel nodded and turned from the two. "It was not I. We shall speak again, Uriel. There is much that needs to be done on Earth. He has plans for you, but for now, enjoy a short vacation with your human."

Uriel pulled back so he could stare into Stephen's eyes. For the first time since accepting a human body, he welcomed the rush of emotions. He accepted each one in turn, relishing in them. He knew what he felt for Stephen was real. This was their fate.

"Thank you," he whispered.

Stephen linked their fingers together. "For what?"

"For existing." He sealed his lips over Stephen's slightly parted mouth. For the first time in his eternal existence, he felt at home. This was where he belonged.

Angel Fever

May Ridge

The orphanage was gloomier than Mal remembered, grayer somehow, as if too many overcast days had imprinted themselves on the smooth concrete walls. There had been talks of murals and communal painting projects when he'd lived there, but either funding or enthusiasm had waned, and they were just slabs of stone. It looked like there were fewer windows as well, but Mal was reassured by the rough, noisy sound of the orphans floating up over the perimeter wall. He'd chosen the right time, somewhere between the beginning of lunch and the start of afternoon classes, so there would be no younger orphans to see his arrival.

He had definitely come to the right place, though. The name was still carved in the concrete next to the front gate, *Angel's Orphanage: Patience*. There were six other orphanages scattered around the country, each with a specialized virtue from the Holy Book of Law itself.

The receptionist was human, her face lined with too many wrinkles to count. "Can I help you, dear?"

Mal smiled and cocked his head charmingly. "I was an orphan here three years ago. I was wondering if I could have access to my personal files."

She blinked and cocked her head back at him, a stray wisp of grey hair falling over her eyes. She brushed it back impatiently, and then tapped her fingers on her desk as she considered him. "Are you eighteen, dear?"

"Yes," Mal lied, keeping a perfectly straight face. He would be in two months, and that was good enough, he was sure. Additionally, given his rank and status in the Healing Academy, he was almost as good as legal.

The receptionist was obviously adept at telling lying boys from honest ones, however, and only partly tried to hide her dubious expression as she turned back to her ancient computer. "Well, our priest has a free slot now, as it is lunchtime. You can go talk to him if you want and he'll do his best to authorise you for the file transfer … if he can."

Mal barely hid a wince. He'd been hoping to avoid any and all authorities on this search of his. In his experience, authorities did little but get in the way of an honest attempt to find information. It was personal information he was after as well; nothing that could threaten the status quo—not even potentially. Still, if it was his only chance. "That would be great, thank you."

The receptionist allowed herself a smile at his lie this time and nodded him towards two uncomfortable looking chairs under the window by the door. He declined the seat, feeling too restless to sit at first, and stared at the bland artwork on the wall while he waited for her to finish her quiet call to the priest. Mal sat once he'd listened to her resumed typing for what felt like hours, but according to the clock on the wall, was really only just ten minutes.

The side door opened and Mal turned to look, blinking a little bit in surprise. The last orphanage priest—the one he remembered—had been a typical desk sitter, old and fragile looking. This new one looked young and healthy and more than fit enough to be able to punch Mal through a wall and not even struggle with the effort. It didn't reassure Mal, or make his task any easier, but he was bound and determined to follow through.

The priest met his eyes. "You're here to see me about accessing some personal records?"

"Yeah," Mal replied and got to his feet automatically. Even if this priest only looked a few years older than him, his own years of childhood training were still ingrained deep enough that the move was hardly optional.

The priest looked briefly startled by his sudden move then waved a hand dismissively, as his gaze gave Mal a swift once over. He was obviously well trained in his field; the corner of his mouth curled in a smirk as his eyes met Mal's again and he inclined his head slightly. "You outrank me, if those markings are real." He glanced at the receptionist, who was caught obviously trying to categorise Mal's markings, and then he waved Mal towards his office. "Come in, sit down."

Mal shot the receptionist a sweet smile and moved past the priest into his office. There was only one piece of art on the wall in this room, a rather obvious painting considering where the priest was stationed. It was a massive canvas of St Paul's Cathedral, the original headquarters for the priests. It was now too small for all the members of the priesthood, but it was still one of the largest Church buildings in Western Europe that the government still held. There was a distinct lack of angels featured in the painting, a point that Mal felt sure had been done on purpose. The art had the essence of human painted all over it, and certainly no angel artist would ever focus on such a topic with that size of a canvas.

The priest saw Mal looking and smiled secretly to himself, not even bothering to hide the expression when Mal turned back to face him. "So how may I be of assistance?"

"I am Malachi," Mal replied, tiring of this first step but needing to go through the basics before he could get to the real business at hand. "Class A, rank 2, formerly Class D, rank 1. I want access to my personal files held by this orphanage."

The priest hummed quietly under his breath. "Well, Malachi, of Class A, rank 2, my name is Tobias and I'm afraid I can't help you."

Mal certainly hadn't expected it to be easy—in fact, he'd *expected* to have to fight for the information, but the instant and unequivocal refusal stunned Mal into forgetting his strategy for a minute, and by the time he had his wits and composure back again, Tobias was tapping on his keyboard.

His brow was furrowed, but only absently, as if he couldn't remember the final word needed to complete a crossword puzzle. It wasn't a big deal to him, but Mal needed to know. He didn't have time to start a protest though, because Tobias spoke before he had a chance, leaving him to watch the human with disgust. "And anyway, if the orphanage records of my predecessor are correct, you're not meant to have any access to any records or files until your twenty-first birthday."

That news was completely unexpected, a blow from nowhere, and Mal gaped at Tobias. "But—"

"You could never pass for twenty-one, I'm afraid," Tobias told him, seeming more sympathetically amused by his attempt than angry at his audacity.

"But—last time—when I left the orphanage three years ago, he said I only had to wait until I was eighteen!"

Tobias arched his eyebrows, looking briefly surprised by the desperation of his voice, then grinned. "Well, you're not even quite there yet, so why don't you wait a couple of months, and you can try an appeal. Mrs Hamilton will—"

"No!" Mal exclaimed, the sheer disgust at the idea and the changing of the rules sending him to his feet, his shoulder blades prickling painfully under his loose white top.

Tobias eyed his forearms cautiously, the whorls of light starting to show under Mal's skin, and then he sighed and sat back in his chair. He looked remarkably calm for having an angry angel in his face, and granted, priests were chosen from their own priest orphanages for their nerve and dedication, but the sheer boredom on Tobias' face was enough of a damper that Mal didn't go any further in his rant. He almost felt ashamed of his outburst, but there was no way the priest could understand just what the information meant to Malachi.

"Well, all right then. Let's try this. Tell me what information you're trying to access from your files specifically and I'll see if I can give it to you," Tobias offered and arched his eyebrows.

Mal hesitated, his brow furrowing as he studied the human, watching for signs of lying. The old priest had lied, obviously, had taken his quite innocent request for information to the Council and had his legality pushed back an additional three years. Twenty-one was obviously an age the arch angels believed they could control better because Mal *knew* the age had been set at eighteen before he'd left.

If this priest told the council the same request had come in from the same angel, again before he was technically allowed to access any of the information even before the push back ... who knew how many years they'd add this time. And yet, it wasn't as if Malachi would be able to find out on his own—or even wait the three years and two months until his twenty-first birthday.

Mal dropped his eyes, licking his lips nervously as he stared down at the priest's desk for a minute before he lifted his gaze again. "I'm looking for information on my mother."

Tobias blinked, his fingers hovering over his keyboard. "That's it?"

Mal frowned. "It's all I want to know."

It was Tobias' turn to frown, his brows furrowing again as he turned his attention back to his computer screen. "That shouldn't take me more than a minute, really. Do you remember your orphan number?"

"M3862."

"Mm," Tobias hummed, his fingers moving over the keyboard even as Mal felt his shoulder blades start to itch, a burning feeling of exultant triumph swelling in his chest, threatening to explode it from the inside. So close. He was so close to the information that he'd been searching for since his tenth birthday, and the anticipation was so hard to bear, he almost thought his heart would stop from the sheer pressure of it. He didn't even notice he'd been holding his breath until Tobias frowned and said, "That's odd."

Those weren't exactly the words Mal had been hoping to hear, and after three years of actively waiting for his birthday for the permission to check, he wasn't sure if he wanted to know what was odd.

"It says," Tobias went on, his voice sounding as if he was imparting a great puzzle, "that the information is classified." He gave Mal a narrow, accusing look, as if it was Mal's fault that they were barred from the information. "I have rank two security clearance, so the question, Malachi, is this: Who *is* your mother?"

Rank two security clearance gave access to all but the Council's most private documents. Mal swallowed and lifted a hand to scratch his cheek, trying not to show his disappointment as another obstacle jumped into his way. It looked like his search for his mother had just gotten far more complicated than just his age.

~~*

The whorls on his arm glowed like dying embers even as the Master Healer walked slowly around the lab room, talking them through the process even though they weren't even remotely beginners anymore. Broken bones weren't usually a problem at their skill level, but ribs were a special case as it meant they had to be careful of the human lungs as well as set the bones correctly. It was also a point of pride to leave as little a mark as possible.

"Now feel the pain release," the Master murmured, its voice quiet to lessen the interruption and the focus of its students. Malachi closed his eyes for a moment as he concentrated a little harder. Releasing the pain was his least favourite part, but it was ingrained into all healers in an attempt to prevent any possible corruption from the human taint.

His patient was a female human, mid twenties, and she bit her lower lip when Mal pressed his hands harder against her side. There was a quick gasp and a pained sound, but Mal ignored it. He couldn't let it deter him. Instead, he closed his eyes again to try and heal through the slow flow of pain creeping up his arms, burning as it went.

He'd heard female angels healed with cool energy, and the sexless ones with a neutral, light warmth. Male healers, rare as they were, were meant to heal with something akin to the sun, a blaze of white heat. Mal agreed with the heat part, but it felt more like molten lava to him—and he mentally apologised to the human female on the table in front of him. It was just her bad luck that had gotten her assigned to him rather than to one of the cooler female angels in his class.

On the other hand, he was the better choice, if only because his own raw talent made up for the flaring heat. There wouldn't even be a hairline crack to show where the breakage had been, and her lungs felt completely healthy as well. There'd been no accidents this time. Malachi rarely had accidents.

There was another soft pained sound; the markings on his arms flared once, like sunlight through a cloud, and then the heat vanished. The light remained in patterns on his skin for a few lingering seconds afterwards, and then winked out. Mal breathed a soft sigh and pulled his hands away.

The human female didn't move at first, recovering from the final blast of heat, and then the Master Healer came to stand next to his table. It didn't even ask permission, just laid a hand on the girl's forehead. She was asleep or unconscious in an instant, and the Master smiled at Mal, a brief expression that flickered away almost as soon as it had appeared. "Not bad," it said.

Mal smirked and inclined his head respectfully. He knew he was learning the lessons too fast for the comfort of his trainers, and he took great delight in straining his intelligence to learn even faster to spite their pompous jealousies. It was easy for him, the knowledge clicked in his head almost as soon as he'd tried the lesson one or two times—and he had a knack for remembering it.

It was well known, after all, that when a male master healer was born, he outshone the sexless masters as easily as those masters outshone the far more common female masters. Male healers didn't come very often, especially not those capable of a master rank ...

And Malachi enjoyed showing off what he could do.

"I humbly request permission to leave," Mal replied quietly, bowing slightly with the words.

The Master frowned. "It is highly irregular to leave before the class is complete."

"I have an appointment with the Council office, Wise One. It would be most impolite to be late to such an official affair."

The Master frowned harder before its expression smoothed out. "Very well. You have my permission to leave early—after the appropriate rituals."

Rituals after healing mainly consisted of having extra hot showers to wash any sickness or germs off after leaving the lab and the Healing Academy. Mal rather enjoyed the extra hot showers; his own shower at home couldn't quite achieve that kind of heat. He wasn't sure if it was a side effect of his own healing talent, but it was difficult to have a shower hot enough for his own full enjoyment.

The Master might have meant for the ritual to delay his appointment, and thus get him in trouble with the Council office on his eighteenth birthday, but since the excuse had been a lie, Mal didn't mind the restriction. He'd need to be extra clean to get into where he was trying to go that night anyway.

~~*

"Are you ready then?"

"I don't know how you humans wear these things—they're terrible," Mal complained in a whisper, rolling his shoulders under the unaccustomed, heavy material. It was hard to get completely comfortable. He was too used to the short sleeved or completely sleeveless shirts that felt a lot freer.

"It's easier when there's no wing shadow to deal with," Tobias replied calmly and adjusted his collar again, the strip of white standing out brightly against the black of his priest suit. "Remember, you're a *human* orphan now, Mal. Try not to stand out too much. I know it's hard for you ..."

"The idea is outrageous," Mal muttered, shooting Tobias a swift glare. "One only has to look at my arms to see—"

"Which is exactly why you're wearing that jacket, Mal," Tobias reminded him. "You don't think you're going to get in there as an angel, do you?" He nodded at the Cathedral as he spoke.

"No," Mal muttered. "But they'll know by my face as well."

Tobias scoffed as he dropped to his haunches to shine his shoes again with a little cloth he pulled from his pocket. Hopefully it was the last such cleaning—Mal had counted it happening four times so far and goodness knew how many times Tobias had done it before he'd even arrived. "Right, your heavenly features—"

"No," Mal hissed and flicked his pale, strawberry blond hair out of his eyes with his hand. "Although I'm not denying the fact that I'm gorgeous, I also happen to be the only male heal—"

"—er of this generation, I know," Tobias finished for him. "That doesn't necessarily mean that most priests who haven't the pleasure of your friendship would know that, though. Shall we go in, if you're ready?" he added before Mal could retort.

It was just as well, really. Mal couldn't actually speak at that point. Everything had been leading up to that point—the last three years, the past two months of planning with the orphanage priest—now he was finally going to find out who his mother was. If everything went according to plan, at least.

"Right," Tobias said when no reply came. "Let's get this over with, shall we?"

Mal graced the priest with a cool nod and straightened his shoulders, preparing to walk right in— until Tobias caught his arm to hold him back. "Priests first, little orphan," Tobias murmured, giving Mal a distinctly smug smirk. Mal rolled his eyes. The priest was only a few years older and the airs were really not doing any favours for Tobias' reputation, but he let Tobias go first to humour him. He was also trying to remember how the human orphans had acted as opposed to the more privileged angel orphans. They hadn't met very often, but there had been a few inter-orphanage events planned so that they would at least know some of who they would be dealing with when they grew up and took their places in the Council or in the Cloth.

The stairs leading up to the front entrance of the Cathedral were full of priests coming and going, and although Malachi got a few obligatory glances for his orphan's outfit, nobody looked twice. Mal was somewhat relieved; the Cathedral was imposing enough without trying to hide the fact that he was an imposter, and an angel one at that. The columns and the main door made him feel uncomfortably small, but if he'd hoped to feel more at ease once inside, the hope quickly expired.

"This place is huge ..."

Tobias shot him a slightly incredulous look. "What did you expect, the orphanage chapel? And please stop looking around like a Neanderthal, you're embarrassing yourself. Do you want them to think you've never been in a proper church before? At your age and supposed training?"

"No," Mal replied, stung by the implication that he was as backwards as that. "Maybe not the orphanage chapel, but I did expect something ... less ... elaborate," he eventually supplied and smirked. "I thought you priests were meant to be simple creatures. It would fit to be a Neanderthal, too."

Tobias scoffed at that, rolling his eyes. "Simple? Maybe several hundred years ago," he said and jerked his head, indicating a new direction. "Times have changed a little."

It didn't look like times had changed all that much to Malachi, at least as far as the building itself went. It was even more impressive from the inside, the stained glass windows throwing coloured light over the priests currently at worship in the pews at the far end of the Cathedral. The sheer *age* of the building was breathtaking, and that didn't even touch upon the carved wood or the painted ceilings or the candles burning everywhere.

"This way," Tobias murmured, and Mal followed, amused at the seemingly automatic quiet mood that had fallen over Tobias. He wondered if it was an ingrained response and decided it was simply because the mood was everywhere he looked. It felt stiffer, somehow, more formal, and Mal was gladder than ever that he wasn't one of them. It looked like they never had any fun, and if they did, it would be against protocol.

Case in point: Tobias was even walking differently, his footsteps quiet and barely audible through nearly visible effort. It looked like he was actually trying to hold most of his weight in the air, too scared to let it come out in a loud footstep to relax while he walked. His shoulders were more squared, with his eyes staring straight ahead as well. They were walking towards a small door on the right of the pew, and Mal had almost thought they'd arrived safely when Tobias stopped.

"What—" Mal started to ask, and then blinked when the priest simply glared at him over his shoulder. He didn't get a chance to respond indignantly to the look because they were interrupted.

"Tobias Callahan," somebody—purred, was the only word Mal could think of. Like a cat that had found a dish of cream, the tone was entirely self-satisfied—and Mal disliked it instantly. "What a ... pleasant surprise."

"Eli," Tobias said back. His tone was blank, just like his face as he stared at the stranger. Mal looked between the two of them and decided to stay out of it, whatever it was. The decision was made harder, however, when the other priest dragged him right into it.

"Carting around orphans now, are we?"

"Somebody has to protect the welfare of our youth," Tobias said calmly and arched his eyebrows. "Even you were an orphan once, remember?"

"But I, thankfully, rose high enough to leave that unfortunate situation behind me."

"I'm not unfortunate," Mal retorted, not entirely sure what the conversation of barbs was for, but he felt somewhat bound to defend Tobias, who was not a bad priest by any means. He'd known Tobias for two months, and even thought them friends sometimes; after all, he was helping Mal find his mother. "And Tobias makes a very good chaplain."

Tobias looked pained rather than gratified at that comment and Eli just laughed. "A very good chaplain … how the mighty hath fallen, Tobias Callahan."

Mal opened his mouth to reply somewhat heatedly to that comment as well, but Tobias shook his head at him, and Mal subsided sulkily. He didn't like this new priest at all, and what was worse was the fact that Tobias wasn't even arguing or fighting back. The only thing he eventually said, in a pleasant voice, was, "As nice as it is talking to you, Eli, we *do* have some business to attend to here."

Eli's smile turned mean; Mal actually found it fascinating to watch. "You'll have to explain it all to me, I'm afraid, if you need to use the records room." His nod indicated the room they'd been heading for. "So prepare to impress me."

~~*

"Nothing," Mal sighed and slumped in an almost human way on the uncomfortable wooden chair that was in the corner of the records room. Eli had eventually let them in after about forty-five minutes of the most pointless, trivial questions he could come up with. Tobias had answered them all, silently forbidding Mal to answer any by cutting in with the answer every time Mal opened his mouth.

It had been boring to watch, and now with nothing to be found in the room, Mal was feeling just a little annoyed. Tobias wasn't even paying attention to him, just nodding absently as he scanned the ledger he was currently looking through. Mal rolled his eyes and huffed out a sigh, not entirely impressed with the plan as a whole anymore.

"Right, not that this hasn't been a fascinating experience, but I think I'll go have a look around whilst you—"

"No, you won't."

Mal stared at Tobias, somewhat stunned by the quick shutdown. "What?"

Tobias lifted his head, arching his eyebrows as he watched Mal. "I said, you're not walking around in St. Paul's. What do you think I am, stupid? You'd be found out. In *minutes*—seconds, even. "

"Clearly you think I'm stupid," Mal retorted, narrowing his eyes at Tobias as he straightened in the chair. It was just as uncomfortable when he sat on it like an angel would, but that didn't improve his mood.

"No, just young and restless," Tobias replied and smirked a little, his dark eyes understanding even as they mocked. "They'd discover you, Mal, and then how would you find the information you're looking for?"

Mal stood and bit the inside of his cheek sulkily before shaking his head. "I suppose you're right, but it's not exactly what I'd planned when we agreed to disguise me so as to get in here."

"I understand that, but you have to realise the danger you're in. If they catch you in here without the proper arrangements ... it wouldn't be a good thing, Mal. I've seen what they do to angels who disobey the laws of the Cathedral."

"They wouldn't dare do anything," Mal retorted and flicked his hair out of his eyes. "I'm—"

"Just trust me, would you? Sit down. We're almost done here."

"We're doing the Council records next, right? Maybe they'll have the right information. Can't count on priests to keep any information correctly," Mal smirked and sat down again, shifting restlessly in the chair. The room was starting to feel stuffy and closed, but if they were really nearly done, then it wasn't so bad. He could last a few more minutes. His shoulder blades itched.

"Hey now, be nice," Tobias reprimanded, but he was smirking as he dropped his gaze again, and they sat in silence for a while.

Malachi wasn't sure when during that time it started, but he was suddenly very aware that his heart was pounding and his skin felt clammy and cold. His own breathing seemed to be echoing in his ears and his vision was blurring a little. Mal blinked, then lifted his hands and rubbed his eyes, shaking his head to try and clear his eyes, but the movement made his head ache, and Mal winced instead.

"Are you all right?"

Mal jumped a little at the unexpected question and blinked at Tobias, his expression almost piteous. "I feel sick."

Tobias cocked his head, then furrowed his brow, his eyes taking in the look on Mal's face. "Sick? But—"

"I *never* feel sick," Mal told him and shoved a hand through his hair. His skin was damp, with sweat on his forehead, and he stared at his hand for a second before lifting his gaze back up to Tobias'. "I'm an *angel*."

"Not so loud," Tobias soothed, pushing up from his spot and moving closer to crouch in front of Mal's chair, his eyes searching Mal's face. "When did you start feeling sick?"

"Now," Mal replied and tried not to act so pathetic when he could handle being sick. It was a rare occurrence; *Angel Fever*, they called it, and if he had caught it— "I need to get home. Now."

"You don't know if it's anything serious—"

"If it's the Fever, I need to go home *now*, before anyone else can catch it," Mal told him as firmly as he could when his voice wanted to shake. The Angel Fever struck fast and hard, and it was a good thing he was in priest territory because if he breathed too hard in any one angel's direction, the sickness would spread and so would the panic that followed. It inhibited the natural talents of angels, as well as some individual problems depending on which strain it was. If Mal had it ...

"Fair enough," Tobias said after a moment, his voice quiet. He got to his feet and held out his hand to help Mal up. Ordinarily Mal might have ignored it, but that time he took the offer. Tobias' hand was warm in his, at a distinct difference to his own clammy hand, but to his credit, Tobias didn't pull away. "Do you need any help getting home?"

Mal debated the question, and the consequences, and then just nodded.

Tobias' mouth curved in a small, understanding smile, and he nodded back. "All right. Let's go."

~~*

He didn't leave the apartment for three more days, when the most contagious part of the fever was over, according to most standards from the past. The first place he went to once he'd left were his classes, but he found a large crowd of angels gathered around outside the Healing Academy. Mal stared at all the whorled arms and necks, the faint gray tinge of the wing shadow on their backs, and pushed his way to the front.

The Master Healer was standing there in the doorway, looking decidedly flustered at all the cold demands and the calm anger on the other angels' faces. The Master looked a little relieved at the sight of Malachi though, and reached out an arm to pull him in. The door slammed shut behind them, and the Master shook its head. "Third time in two years," it said. "It's disgraceful."

Mal glanced around at his classmates; they were all nodding along, and Mal nodded as well after a moment. There had been a particularly bad strain of the Fever a few months ago that had caused a larger amount of panic than might ordinarily have happened. It was only supposed to strike once a generation statistically, so for it to be three times in two years ...

There had even been an angel that had *died* from that sickness, which had really panicked everyone because it had proved that the angel's natural healing had failed in the most ultimate way possible. Everyone feared their own resistance failing like that. Even Mal had tested his own abilities on himself every day to check that they still worked.

They hadn't, not until he'd recovered.

No humans had ever stepped forward to take responsibility for the outbreak, and in the end, it had only served to heighten tensions already simmering. Angels being so resistant to any *natural* sickness, they had seen no other option but to blame the humans, and the priests had denied all knowledge and responsibility, and there had been a lack of proof and evidence for any of it.

And now it was happening again.

The Master Healer shook its head. "As far as I am aware, symptoms started for most of the populace two days ago, in the early morning."

It sounded a little later than when Mal had first felt sick, but it was possible there had been no reports previous to that. Mal debated admitting that he'd been sick sooner than that, but feared the quarantine and the blame he would get for spreading it when he hadn't seen any angels that day on his way home and had spent the rest of the time locked in his apartment. After a brief moment of hesitation, Mal moved to the side of the room to take his usual seat at one of the examination tables, not saying anything. The Master gave him a distracted frown, and then continued. "Symptoms include sneezing, headaches, fever, fatigue ... and the most concerning of all: evidence seems to be coming through that the healing gene seems to be defective."

There was a silence for a few minutes, and then one of the females quietly lifted her hand. "Please, I don't understand."

The Master stared at her, then shook its head. "What that means is that we are in a dangerous time. If a second sickness were to hit right now, another fever or anything like that, we would have no immune system to fight it."

"But our own healing—we'll be fine, won't we?" asked one of the other girls, her forehead hitching.

"Try it and see," the Master replied morosely.

The class looked around at each other, and Mal could almost see the brimming fear even as the second girl cleared her throat and held out her hand, palm down, over the table. She looked like she was concentrating, but there was nothing. No light under the whorls on her skin, not even when sweat broke out on her forehead—and then she gave up with a slight pant, slumping down on her chair like a common human.

"It doesn't work, either," said one of the sexless ones, sounding terrified. Mal knew better than to admit to the fear himself, but he couldn't help the urge to check his forearms and fingers for any hints that the sickness had progressed to an advanced state without him completely realising it.

"What we have to remember," the Master said, its voice breaking the buzz of increasing panic amidst the students, "is that we have to remain calm. Let nobody know the full implication of the problem here. Do *not* go to human healers, or recommend that anyone go to human healers. They are unequipped and quite ill-trained. There's nothing that they can do that we haven't tried already. And above all else—do not let the humans realise how serious the problem is."

Malachi nodded along with the rest of the class.

~~*

Tobias was waiting for him when he got home, and of course, the first thing Mal did after letting him in was tell him what the Master had said.

He had frowned, but hadn't responded to the news, seemingly more concerned with how Mal himself was feeling. "Because I've had a thought, Mal—maybe we're looking in the wrong places for your mother. Maybe we should start simpler, in some ways. Do you know who your father is?"

"Cassiel," Malachi responded nonchalantly and turned to go into his kitchen to start making supper for them. "I think. I mean, I'm as sure as I could be. Really, it's not like they're all that open about who they father in the Council—"

"The—the *Council*? Mal, are you saying that Cassiel Firebrand is your father?"

Mal shot a smirk at Tobias over his shoulder. "Yeah, I think that's what I said. But it's not like I care. He certainly doesn't."

"I can imagine not. Well, that's almost intimidating," Tobias teased, and Mal grinned at him before turning back to his fridge to pull out some vegetables. "How do you figure he's your father, if you don't mind me asking?"

"Well, he's the one who had me pulled from the orphanage when I was fifteen to join the Healing Academy," Mal replied and smiled. "He was the only one that really showed interest and—" he hesitated, shooting Tobias a swift glance before smirking, his eyes dancing with amusement. "When I was twelve I snuck into the orphanage records room to check. The priest before you wasn't that big on security."

"Clearly not," Tobias replied dryly, and then laughed. "And Cassiel's name was there, hmm? Well, that's rather like waking up and finding you're royalty."

"Sort of, I guess. I didn't really care. I was more interested in who my mother was."

Tobias frowned and moved closer, leaning against the counter and folding his arms across his chest. "Her name wasn't on the same record?"

Mal shook his head and pulled out the cutting board and the knife, pulling two bell peppers out of the bag before putting it back in the fridge. "I really snuck in to find her, you know, but she wasn't there even then. It's kind of like my own personal mystery, really. It's exciting," he told Tobias and smirked again.

Tobias simply arched his eyebrow. "Mm hmm. Why did you start looking in the first place? I don't think you ever told me why the search is so important."

Mal blinked at him and cocked his head. "Well … most of the other kids knew who their mother was."

"I didn't know either of my parents," Tobias mused and ran a hand through his hair before he tilted his head. "I never tried to find them though …"

"Exactly," Mal replied and pointed the knife at Tobias in agreement. "That seems to be the way most people think of it. Whenever I asked about her, or mentioned trying to find her to anyone, all I got was a bunch of naysayers and people thinking I was crazy for wanting to find a woman who had abandoned me in the first place—"

"Mal—that wasn't anyone's fault. All angels leave their children in the orphanages. It's in your nature—"

"My father didn't."

Tobias didn't say anything to that.

Malachi scowled and started cutting faster, the quick thud of the knife hitting the board sounding louder as anger made him push harder through the peppers. "My father has one of the hardest reputations of the council, and he was still the one to pull me out of the orphanage and give me what I deserved, what I *earned*, and she gave me *nothing* …"

Tobias didn't reply for a moment, but then he sighed and picked up the kettle, starting to fill it with water. "I'm going to make some tea and boil some water for rice; is that okay with what you're planning?"

"Yeah," Mal muttered, his thoughts still distracted even as he tried not to linger on the fact of his mother's complete disinterest in him, because maybe there was a good reason. Maybe she wasn't in the country anymore, or she had forgotten which orphanage he'd been placed in, or maybe—

The sharp pain was unexpected, and Mal hissed as he jerked his hand back—the hand holding the knife. It only registered after a minute that he'd pulled it back along the palm of his other hand, and he stood staring down at the cut for a second before reaction kicked in. He'd seen blood before, of course, but not usually his own, and never when it was flowing like it was currently doing. "Tobias." Malachi looked down at his hand while he waited for a response, blinking as the cut seeped blood out over his palm, revolted and fascinated by the sight.

Tobias didn't look over immediately at Mal's soft query, but he looked when Malachi hissed in pain, staring at the tip of the knife as he poked it against the pad of his fingertip. "What are you doing?"

"I'm *bleeding*," Mal replied. He sounded childishly excited even to his own ears, but it didn't stop him from poking another fingertip with the knife. "How am I doing this?"

He could almost hear it when Tobias rolled his eyes and came closer. "You're poking yourself with—Jesus Christ, you're really *bleeding*."

"I *know*," Mal replied, lifting his blue eyes to meet Tobias' gaze. Tobias was not smiling. He was frowning, and then he was grabbing Malachi's hand like he had every right to do so. "Wait—"

"You're bleeding," Tobias said again and pulled on Mal's arm, dragging him to the other side of the counter to grab up a dishrag. Mal tried to yank his hand away, not wanting to touch what looked like it had once been white but was now a dirty shade of gray. "That's not good."

"But how am I doing that?" Mal asked again, losing all fascination with the prospect because it was starting to hurt and he wasn't sure he liked that part as much. "I mean ... I'm not supposed to *bleed*. Only humans *bleed*."

"Well, then—" Tobias started and cut himself off, frowning again as he looked at Mal. "Why are you bleeding?"

"I've been asking you that all along. Angel blood congeals in the wound; it's not supposed to—"

"Flow," Tobias finished, arching his eyebrows. "I know."

He wasn't supposed to know, Malachi remembered. It was something only the healers were supposed to be privy to, and he opened his mouth to ask why Tobias would know that kind of information when his ranking wasn't nearly high enough, but all that came out was another pained sound as Tobias lifted the cloth a fraction of an inch. "Ow," he said instead, after he'd had a moment to rethink the question. Tobias never answered anyway, and it would go a lot easier on the both of them if Mal didn't try to make him. "That hurts."

"You're still bleeding."

"Of course I'm still bleeding. I only just cut it—"

"Why," Tobias interrupted, with the same lack of respect he'd shown Mal since they'd first met. "Why are you still bleeding when you're supposed to be congealing?"

Mal stared at Tobias for a moment, his brow furrowing as Tobias' eyes narrowed at him. "Maybe it's the sickness?" Mal ventured after a moment, but he didn't have any particularly high hopes for that. They would have mentioned the thinner blood side effect in class if only to warn them that in order to avoid showing additional weakness, no physical injuries should be risked. "Maybe it's one of the side effects."

"I don't think so," Tobias replied and looked down at Mal's hand again. He was still holding it between his own two, the cloth pressed against Mal's palm. Mal could feel Tobias' skin, warm against his own oddly cold hand, and he felt a little dizzy. He swayed. Tobias immediately dropped one of his own hands, the warm one, and used it to catch Mal around his arm, steadying him. "Hey, you okay?"

"I feel funny," Malachi complained and scowled down at his hand. "I don't like bleeding. Make it stop."

He almost thought he saw the corner of Tobias' mouth tilt up, but the expression was gone before he could comment on it—if it had ever existed in the first place—and Tobias ducked his head to apparently examine Mal's hand more closely. "You're the healer," he told Mal. "I'm not sure what I can do to make it stop."

Malachi frowned and then lifted his own free hand, covering the cloth—along with Tobias' hand as well. Tobias flinched a little, but Malachi was ignoring him, invoking the powers that made him a prodigy amongst his healing peers, waiting for the warmth of the healing to first light the whorls on his arms and then travel into his palm to seal the skin closed.

Nothing happened.

Malachi frowned again. "Move your hand, you're ruining the spell," he snapped at Tobias, but Tobias didn't move. He was staring down at their fingers, his own curled tightly in the cloth as he pressed it harder against Malachi's hand. "Tobias, move your hand."

"I don't think it's going to help, Mal," Tobias replied quietly, not even pretending to obey him. "You know none of your healing has worked since the sickness started."

"Well, I'm bleeding," Malachi replied, pointing out the obvious in the hopes that it would make Tobias realise there was no other option.

"I know," Tobias said quietly, so quietly that Malachi wasn't sure he would have heard him if he hadn't been standing so close. "You're bleeding." A thought seemed to hit him, and he lifted his head to stare at Malachi again, his brows furrowed even as he lifted his hand and pulled Mal's uninjured hand away. The cloth sat pressure-less in his palm, dark stains already seeping through the faded gray material in a pattern that was ragged at the edges. "I almost want to take you to hospital, it looks that deep, but—Mal."

"I refuse to be treated by humans."

That had Tobias' eyebrows arching up, derision in his cool eyes. "That should be the least of your worries, Mal. You're an angel and you're actively bleeding."

Malachi looked at Tobias, his only ally in his current mission in life, and mourned the fact that he seemed to have acquired a witless one. It could have been anyone, but Tobias was just stating the obvious facts right then, and that wasn't doing anyone much good. He was an angel. He was still bleeding. If he didn't get it fixed, who knew how long this was going to last. He'd never really heard of angels bleeding before, he wondered how much blood they had to lose before they died from it. Humans died from blood loss once they'd lost 40 percent of their total capacity, but how much was he losing now, and how much—

"Mal."

Malachi blinked and looked up. His fingers were squeezing down on the cloth, and Tobias' voice brought him back enough out of his calculations to realise how painful the motion actually was. "What?"

Tobias was looking at him and there was something in his eyes that Malachi definitely did not like. "We have to consider the possibility ..."

He didn't want to consider anything. It felt like a part of him already knew what Tobias was going to say, and Malachi's whole system rebelled against hearing the words, of having them spoken. He felt ill and light headed, but Tobias' hand was still on his arm, still steadying him *physically* and short of leaving the room, Mal couldn't actually stop him. It didn't mean he couldn't try, though, and Malachi shook his head. "No. It's just the sickness. I'll be fine once the fever and the other symptoms have passed; I'll start congealing like a normal ang—"

"I don't think you're an angel. Not a normal one, at least."

Malachi stared at him, suddenly terrified of the next words that he was going to say. "Please don't."

Tobias continued, looking almost like he couldn't stop, not at that point. "You don't know who your mother was, Mal."

Malachi closed his eyes in a last attempt to avoid the words, the mere idea; there was total mute denial in the gesture.

"What if she was a human?"

~~*

Tobias eventually had to stitch him up himself, with Mal complaining every step of the way, but he'd had to admit that Tobias had been right. He hadn't wanted to go to the hospital, and he certainly hadn't trusted his own wound with an angel healer—if any of them were even still able to heal during this time. He'd kept up the string of complaints simply to avoid thinking of the point that Tobias had brought up.

The mere thought was impossible.

Interspecies breeding was the unholiest of all the sins, and if there was a case, then all three were either put to death or exiled to one of the prison camps out in the middle of nowhere, separated until everyone forgot about them and their scandal. The last case Mal himself knew about had happened over forty years ago. Angels had no interest in diluting their blood with human taint, and whilst humans didn't seem to really have a problem with the blood, Malachi was fairly sure that any half breed would grow up to be completely ostracized by both angels and humans if they even lived or escaped the prisons and now Tobias was claiming he might be one of them?

It was impossible.

He didn't want to think about it; but there was no denying the fact that he was bleeding a lot. Every time he thought the blood had congealed, or even clotted like a human's would have, it would prove to have only slowed to an ooze, but would continue as soon as he moved his arm and got his circulation pumping harder again.

Tobias proved to be rather skilled with the needle, and he let Mal talk himself into a shocked silence as he finished up cleaning the skin around the wound. He even made Mal some hot, sweet tea, and forced Mal to drink it all, and he was washing the cup before Malachi felt ready to talk again.

"It's impossible," he said again, but his own voice was quiet, begging for reassurance on that point.

Tobias set the mug down on the drying rack and turned to come closer, kneeling down in front of Mal and meeting his eyes with his own. Mal's breath caught in his throat; panic, he told himself even as a small part in his mind denied that. "Mal, it's only a theory. If you don't want to accept it, we can search for other options." He hesitated and dropped his eyes for a moment before his brow furrowed. "What we have to consider is the rate at which you bled. I've only ever seen one other person ever bleed like that—"

"But he was a human," Mal said, matter-of-factly. "I told you, mine was only a result from the fever. I'm still sick, you know."

"Did your Master Healer mention anything like thinned blood in the symptoms?"

"No," Mal replied reluctantly. "But maybe it just hadn't been caught at that point."

Tobias sighed. "Mal, I understand your reluctance to accept the point, but listen to me. There was a boy in my orphanage, a pretty clumsy lad, I always thought, until we learned that he actually suffered from a blood disease. It thins the blood, makes it easier to bleed, and harder to clot—or possibly to congeal."

"I've never bled like that before," Mal argued. "Are you trying to suggest I have a disease?"

Tobias actually smiled at Mal's insulted tone, then shook his head. "All I'm saying is that maybe without your natural angel ability to heal yourself, maybe the disease—*if* you have it—finally could show enough for us to diagnose it."

Mal narrowed his eyes at Tobias, blaming him and all of his kind for one bitter, resentful moment before he looked away and bit his lip. "We did learn about human blood diseases. There used to be one in particular that the Healing Master mentioned as a part of healing history." Mal stared at Tobias again, tilting his head. "Haemophilia, right?"

Tobias nodded slightly. "That's what the boy had. He got it from his mother, Mal."

Malachi bit his lip, not sure what he was meant to feel at that kind of news, and he shook his head after a minute, not wanting to talk about it anymore. He needed to think about it; what it would mean for him—what it said about him, really. It was like the world had started spinning counter-clockwise under his feet, and he had to readjust his entire balance in order to make sense of the change.

Tobias dropped a hand on Mal's knee, squeezing his fingers down lightly. "Mal, if that is the case—if any of this theory is right—there is one more records room we can check at St. Paul's. It's the medical records. We didn't look at those ones last time; we didn't think to look. But if we can get a list of haemophiliac carriers and compare it to the pregnancy and birth records that we already checked, we might come up with something, especially if we check the human mothers rather than the angel ones. That has to be why we didn't find anything, Mal."

"Fine," Mal replied dully. He didn't want to find anything if it meant he'd have to be a half-human. He was the best male healer in a generation! He was supposed to be all angel; it couldn't be any other option! "Will we have to get past Eli again?"

"No, probably not. We'll have to sneak in," Tobias replied, as if that option was easier, and he arched his eyebrows at Mal. "The medical records are kept in the upper gallery of the dome. They're more private than birth records, have far more detailed information as well. We'll try and go through the back way."

Mal blinked at him, surprised by the smirk on Tobias' face. "You know of a back way into St. Paul's?"

Tobias just smiled. It was a sly smile and had an alarming feeling swooping in Mal's stomach, somewhat resembling a flock of butterflies performing acrobats. "Mal, there are a lot of things I learned in my training … and only some of them are legally smiled upon."

Malachi just grinned back in response.

~~*

A week later and they had perfected their plan. They'd sneak in through the cemetery on the east side of the Cathedral and climb up the stairs from there. They left late, shortly after dusk, so the sky was dark by the time they made it to the cemetery. The tombstones and statues decorating the yard looked ancient and unsettling, making Mal feel even more nervous than he did already. There was a little iron gate leading into one of the chapels that was their goal and Tobias used his set of keys to unlock it.

The whole thing only made Mal more desperate to understand just why Tobias knew what he knew, but he knew that Tobias would never answer those questions, especially not when they were both trying so hard to be quiet.

When they were safely in the chapel, however, Tobias turned to him and smirked triumphantly even as he stretched out a hand to turn on the light. The sight that greeted Mal, though, had Tobias turning around and staring just as blankly.

Instead of the chapel they had been expecting, there was a clean looking room that had nothing similar to the original chapel that Mal assumed had been there except for the architecture. Instead of alters and pews, there were tables and stools, beacons and other glass equipment of a scientific lab. Mal blinked, and then blinked again, but nothing changed, and it still looked exactly the same. Tobias looked equally surprised for a minute before he managed to regain control of his expression.

"Well ... this isn't what I expected," he said and glanced at Mal.

Mal shrugged. "I thought it would be a chapel," he replied and moved forward, curious as to the different coloured liquids in the glass containers. "Is this a new addition to St. Paul's? I hadn't thought priests the scientific type."

"We're humans," Tobias replied shortly, following Mal's lead and starting to inspect some of the tables closest to him. "We do a little bit of everything."

"Clearly," Mal replied, amused. "I have to admit though, I never thought of priests as the scientific, scholarly types. Don't you mostly deal with law and policing and such?"

"Yeah," Tobias replied and shrugged. "For the most part. Maybe we're branching out."

"I guess so," Mal started to say, then stopped, a certain table catching his eye—or rather, the case of vials on the table. It was labelled quite clearly, and Mal moved forward quickly, lifting a vial and frowning at the pale green liquid inside of it.

"What's that?" Tobias asked, coming to stand at Mal's side. Mal silently pointed out the label and ignored Tobias's sudden grip on his shoulder. "Mal—you're not fully healed; if they're trying to make a vaccine—"

"Do you really think that's what it is?" Malachi asked, shooting Tobias a look even as he shrugged Tobias' grip off his shoulder. "Angels have suspected priests as the instigators of Angel Fever for a very long time. This is only the proof," he added, waving his free hand at the case labelled *Angel Fever III*. "Angel Fever, three," Mal continued and carefully put the vial back into its slot. "Three times in the past two years, the Master Healer said. He said it was disgraceful, that most Fevers take over fifty years to naturally create a strain that affects angels again, and yet, in two years—"

"Mal—I think you need to—"

"No!" Mal yelled and whirled around, glaring at Tobias. "An angel *died* a few months ago because the strain was the strongest we'd ever had to face before. I got sick in this very Cathedral just the other day—and now I know why my symptoms struck early, too! This place is the real source!"

Tobias opened his mouth to reply, but a slow clapping interrupted him, making them both whirl around. Eli was standing by the entrance to the room, his head tilted, and a satisfied smirk on his face. "Well done, little orphan … who, it turns out, is not a priest orphan after all."

"Eli—" Tobias started, but Eli cut him off with a wave of his hand. A small troop of four guards came in passed him, and Mal took a step back to run through the back way, the same way they'd come in, but Eli shook his head.

"Uh uh, little angel boy. You know quite a bit of information now that it might be dangerous to let loose, and, well, I do so enjoy our reunions, Tobias Callahan."

"You can't do anything, Eli," Tobias said sharply, sounding angrier than Mal had ever heard him sound before. "I doubt this lab is sanctioned by the Priesthood at all—"

"Ah, but you're mistaken. The Head of the Lab is very high up the chain, and she will be quite pleased to talk to you, I imagine. Until then—take them to the crypt," he ordered the guards. Mal thought about fighting back, but Tobias shook his head in response to the look Mal gave him. Mal hesitated, and then obeyed. He trusted Tobias— but he sure hoped he knew what he was doing.

The crypt was dark and dank, lamps flickering on the walls to increase the general atmosphere of the place. There didn't appear to be any electricity, so Mal had to concentrate as they wound their way down the stairs, trying not to trip and fall, not when there was nothing to soften the landing. The cell they got thrown into was not very hospitable, and neither was the way they landed. Tobias managed to stay on his feet, but Mal got an extra rough shove through the door and stumbled and fell on his side. His wrist caught most of his weight, a sharp pain shooting up his arm that had Mal sitting up and cradling his arm against his chest as he glared at Eli, who was smirking at them through the bars as the door slammed shut.

"Make yourselves at home," he told them and smiled pleasantly. Mal rolled his eyes and pushed himself to his feet, looking down when a small sound attracted his notice to the floor. There was just enough light to see the nail as it rolled away from his toe where he'd accidentally kicked it, and Mal stared down at it for a moment before he blinked—and then looked at his arm.

It was starting to feel like a usual occurrence, but after a moment, Mal moved closer to where Tobias was involved with trying to bargain with Eli to let them go. Mal distracted him, though. "Tobias ... I fell."

"You're pretty weak for an angel, aren't you?" Eli taunted. "Oh, but I forgot. You're suffering under the latest strain of the Fever, aren't you—?"

Mal shot him a glare, and then held out his arm for Tobias' attention. It wasn't bleeding as much the cut on his hand had been, and it certainly didn't look deep, but it was long, a sizable cut from the bottom of his wrist to halfway up the inside of his forearm. Tobias looked at it, and then frowned, and the words slipped out of Mal before he had a thought to stop them.

"I'm bleeding—Tobias—I—"

"Shh," Tobias murmured, his arm slipping around Mal's waist, steadying him even as their guards looked on suspiciously. "It'll be okay—we'll need some bandages." He addressed this to Eli, who was still standing there watching them.

Eli just smirked on the other side of the bars and came closer. "You expect us—*me*—to believe that? It's just a little cut."

"A little cut that won't stop bleeding," Tobias retorted sharply, and Mal would have marvelled at the fact that his priest sounded genuinely angry rather than calm had he not been the one bleeding. If it was anything like what had happened after the knife had sliced his palm … He hated the thought of Tobias giving him stitches again. "It violates all the rules to deny aid at a time like this," Tobias went on, and Mal had to hide a smirk that threatened to appear when Tobias' speech turned more formal again.

Eli scoffed. "You honestly think we care about tiny little rules like that when there's no need? We have—"

"Sir," one of the younger guards behind Eli spoke up. "Sir, he's right. The boy's bleeding quite hard."

Even feeling a little dizzy, Mal objected to the term. "I'm not a boy, I'm an adult, I turned—"

"Yes, shh," Tobias muttered placatingly, his arm squeezing a little tighter around Mal's waist. "Just stay calm, all right?"

Mal bit his lip and nodded, closing his eyes to avoid the sight of his own blood dripping down his fingers. If it had been anyone else, he would have been able to handle it, wouldn't have even blinked, but because he knew it was his own ... The sight sickened him, had his stomach lurching in panic, and somehow, it made him dare to nestle in closer against Tobias' side.

His priest was warm and felt good, and Mal concentrated on staying conscious and not embarrassing himself by fainting like he had the last time he cut himself. The full effort of the attempt had him missing most of the rest of the argument as it went on over his head, but he got the gist well enough to know that Tobias was winning. Eventually the guards left, and he and Tobias were alone to wait it out.

"How are you holding up?" Tobias asked, and Mal was scared for a moment that he would remove the warmth and the comfort and the support that he was supplying. All Tobias did though was shift a little until he could see Mal's face more clearly.

The concern in his dark eyes made Mal tell the truth. "I'm cold and dizzy and bleeding and I feel sick, and I'm probably going to die."

Amazingly, the words made the corner of Tobias' mouth tilt up, the expression absurdly affectionate, and it certainly couldn't be healthy to have his heart beat that much faster when he was bleeding. "Stop being so dramatic," Tobias told him. Even his voice sounded affectionate.

"I'm bleeding," Mal pointed out tragically. "I might need stitches again."

"I highly doubt that. They've gone to get you a bandage, so you'll be all right in a few minutes. It's not as deep as the cut on your hand was."

"I'm going to get a horrible disease from that nail and die. Who knows what kind of germs are on that thing."

"Oh for the love of—you're not going to die, Malachi. Stop saying such stupid things."

Mal was silent for a moment, then sighed sadly, unable to resist. "I might have known not to expect sympathy—"

Tobias made a sound that was a mix between frustration, exasperation, and amusement, and then he turned on the spot. The next moment, Tobias was kissing him, and Mal stood motionless with the shock before kissing back wholeheartedly, his uninjured arm creeping up to curl around Tobias' neck.

Tobias pulled away at that contact though, pulling Mal's arm down at the same time, and Mal blinked at him silently. Several things to say ran through his head, endless possibilities based on the very unusual circumstance, but none of the thoughts made it out. Tobias looked as calm and collected as ever, and Mal resented him for that fact even as Tobias smiled at him and made his pulse race faster.

"That's better. Now stay calm and be quiet, or the guards will—"

The rest of his words were cut off at the sound of approaching footsteps, and Mal could only blink as Tobias moved forward to collect the medical supplies from the young guard who pushed them through the bars. Tobias worked quickly with the bandage, his brow furrowed thoughtfully as he wrapped Mal's wrist securely. It was rather awkward, especially as Malachi, for once in his life, didn't know what to say. Tobias had just kissed him. Mal had *liked* it, quite a bit really, but that didn't mean he knew what to do about it.

In the end, though, he couldn't bear the silence any longer. "So ... what do we do now?"

Tobias glanced up, arching his eyebrows at Mal, and then proceeded to ignore what Mal was really asking about. "Well, I suppose we wait until we can try to figure out a way to escape." He kept his voice low as he spoke, moving in close enough to whisper the words in Mal's ear, and Mal was both fascinated and a little nervous about the shiver that ran down his spine, prompted by the close proximity of Tobias' voice.

He rolled his eyes to avoid the reaction as best he could, desperately hoping that Tobias hadn't noticed even as he prepared to ask the same question again. Slower footsteps interrupted him this time, the pace easy and assured, and Tobias sighed and straightened up, giving Mal's arm one last pat. "Here we go," he said.

Eli appeared around the corner a moment later, smirking his detestable smirk. "The Lady Caroline is ready to see you now. She is most interested in hearing what the bleeding angel thinks about her lab."

Mal was standing too close to Tobias not to notice how he stiffened at the words, and then Tobias turned his head to stare at Mal, his eyes wide. Mal stared back, confused, then looked at Eli. "Who is Lady Caroline?"

"You will not speak her name," Eli snapped, slamming a hand on the bars and glaring at them both. "She is too high to be tainted by an angel such as you. And you, Ex guard Tobias Callahan—"

"We understand," Tobias inserted quickly, inclining his head and shooting Mal a warning look from under his eyelashes. "We are honoured by her indulgence in seeing us."

Eli scoffed and laughed, a mean sound. "Don't try to mock me, Tobias Callahan. You're not going to fool me with your formal talk. Regardless, she wishes to see the two of you. I'm here to escort you and warn you both that you will show her respect, or face the consequences."

"Fine," Tobias agreed easily and arched his eyebrows. "Are we going then?"

Eli narrowed his eyes and stared at them for a minute before unlocking the cell door. He waved Mal out first, his gaze still narrow and locked on Tobias. Mal shot a glance at Tobias over his shoulder, and then continued on his way up the stairs and out of the crypt when a sudden loud clanging sound had his foot slipping in the dark. He jumped and spun around, almost frightened by the thought of what he would find. The firelight from the lamp in front of their cell was flickering, and the sounds of a desperate struggle echoed up the stairs before Tobias' voice broke through the confusion.

"*Run*!"

If it had been anyone else to shout the command, Mal would have hung back and hesitated, unsure whether to help the struggle or not—but it was Tobias. Just Tobias: his priest, whom he trusted, and Mal scrambled up the stairs, his breathing coming faster with the rush of panicked adrenaline.

There was nobody around the entrance to the staircase to the crypt, but there were priests by the altar and the pew—and probably in the separate meditation chambers along the side of the main hall of the Cathedral. Mal debated running immediately further, but he wasn't about to leave Tobias alone to handle all of those priests all at once—but then Tobias was there, panting. His throat was bruised and he had a hand pressed to his stomach but there was a kind of fierceness in his expression that might have scared Malachi if Tobias hadn't been on his side.

Then time seemed to speed up again, and Tobias grabbed his arm, yanking Mal forward even as the priests in the pews started to turn, their attention attracted by the loud noise of Eli yelling from down the stairs. There was an almost hysteric note in his voice that made Tobias sound astonishingly calm when he spoke again. "Run. I'll be right behind you, Mal."

It was so quiet and calm that it actually took a few moments for Malachi to register that Tobias was talking to him. Then he obeyed automatically, sprinting for the doorway. There was a brief silence for a few moments as the other priests took in the fact of their escape, and then chaos broke out behind them. Pounding footsteps echoed all the way to the arched ceilings, and Mal could only hear the aching sound of his own breaths over the noise. Voices were crying out commands, and Mal was forced to duck and dodge around grasping hands. Thankfully he only had to dodge the priests coming out of the meditation chambers.

The ones behind him had their head start to contend with, and Tobias seemed to be doing a well enough job of keeping most pursuers away as he ran. The priests that had been in the meditation chambers seemed to be mostly older than a certain age, which made it easier for Mal to duck and dodge their attempts to catch him. Guards, they had obviously not been.

He could hear Tobias behind him, the command to keep running ringing in his ears even as he made it to the tall heavy door that was the entrance to the Cathedral. He dodged passed priests who were coming up the stairs, passed all the ones that just looked shocked and confused. He only looked behind him once to check, and Tobias was still there, a few metres behind him, and keeping pace even though it looked like it was a little painful for him.

They ran for four more blocks before ducking into an alleyway that Mal had hoped was a shortcut, but only turned out to be a dead end. Tobias held his arm though, preventing Mal from taking off to search for another exit, and Mal obeyed the clasp of his hand to take the time to breath, heaving in breaths that felt like they didn't help at all. It took a few minutes before Mal had his breath back enough to try talking again. "What—what *happened* back there?"

"Right," Tobias replied, shoving a hand through his hair. He sounded less out of breath than Mal, and Mal resented him for that alone, because Tobias had been fighting on top of running, and it just wasn't fair that he was more fit. "Perhaps I should explain some things ... but not here."

Mal could readily agree with that, and he managed a nod, but somehow he couldn't look away from Tobias' mouth. There was a slight discolouring around the corner, as if Eli had punched him—or maybe one of the other priests, but it only served to draw Mal's attention to Tobias' lips and maybe that would be explained as well.

He could only hope.

~~*

He hadn't thought about it before—they'd always used his own apartment to plan, but when Mal thought about it, it made sense. He could remember the old orphanage priest living on site as well, but it hadn't occurred to him that Tobias would obviously do the same. The little cottage attached to the orphanage chapel was more cheap than charming, but the furniture looked comfortable and homey enough. Mal had just selected a promising looking armchair when he was interrupted before even sitting down.

"Don't sit. We're not staying."

"But you were going to explain—"

"At your apartment, Mal. They all know I live here; hopefully it'll take them longer to find you. I'm just picking up a few essentials, like—this," he finished triumphantly, holding up a small bag full of bandages and disinfectants.

Mal gave it a dubious look, and then turned the look on Tobias. Tobias merely grinned. "In case you cut yourself again. It was hard enough finding a bandage at your place the first time, and you definitely seem clumsy enough that we'll probably have need again."

"I'm not clumsy," Mal argued and scowled. "I'm just not used to not being able to heal myself."

"Clearly," Tobias teased, and Mal looked at his smile, and then looked away again. He wanted to understand about it all—and he could only hope that Tobias would give him all the answers.

They maintained a watchful eye on the way back to his apartment, Mal suspecting every person of being someone who could sell them out to the rest of the priests. None did, of course, but it didn't make him feel any more relaxed until they were safe in his apartment, his door locked and the curtains drawn in case of spies. Tobias refused any refreshment, although the bruising around his throat was starting to take the shape of fingers, and Mal wished he had his full healing abilities back.

He'd have been able to fix that without any problem, and Tobias was going to have to talk to explain things, and he didn't want his priest to be in pain. He'd tried in the cell though, and his abilities were still out of reach, thanks to that damned fever.

It was a moment before Tobias started talking and his voice was so raspy that Mal got up to get him a glass of water. Tobias accepted it without thanks and just went on with his story. "Back ... when I was first initiated," he started hesitantly, his eyes darting to Mal's and then darting away again. "You might have already guessed this, but I was initiated as a guard."

Mal eyed Tobias, taking in the bruises on his throat and face as well as the swollen knuckles before he cocked his head. "The possibility that you weren't always administration had occurred to me, yeah."

Tobias grinned, a quick flash of teeth. "Pretty observant, aren't you. Well, I started early so I was pretty young for a guard trainee. Thirteen," he replied in response to Mal's look. "I was sixteen when I was set to elite guard and twenty when I was completely initiated into the ranks."

"So, what ... two years ago?" Mal asked, a little surprised by the timeline. "You didn't stay a guard for very long."

Tobias' expression darkened, his eyes dropping to his water. "No. I was set to guard an angel called Loki."

Malachi blinked—then sucked in a sharp breath. He remembered that name, the circumstances surrounding the fame of it. "That—that was you?"

Tobias hesitated, and he lifted a hand to rub over his face. "It wasn't my fault," he said mechanically. It sounded like something he'd been telling himself for a very long time. "It had been a long week and he'd been pushing harder than usual on my hours. That night, I had been relieved of duty a few hours before it happened. They had been preparing a new guard so we could go alternate shifts on him, and I thought they had it under control."

Mal watched, silent. He couldn't think of anything to say to the news, not with the enormity of the situation. It was beyond his experience to talk about.

Tobias looked up again when Mal didn't say anything, and he shot Mal a wry smile. "I can say it as often as I want, but it doesn't change the fact that I failed. I should have been there and I wasn't; his blood is on my hands because of it, but—well, anyway. After that I had a brief stint in jail while they tried to figure out if I'd left my post on purpose to aid the attackers. My relief that night had disappeared. By all accounts it should have been me protecting him."

"But you weren't," Mal said softly. "I remember the news. They all said that the guard responsible had been dealt with."

"And I was," Tobias replied. "I went to jail until proof was found to back me up—I *had* been relieved that night, and he had all the right credentials. I couldn't have known they were faked, and so I couldn't be blamed—not legally, anyway."

"What happened then?" Mal asked, itching to move closer and comfort the desolation so obvious in Tobias' voice. He didn't move though, sure that it would be unappreciated at the moment.

Tobias looked at him again, and then shrugged. "I went to jail until the Pope had enough evidence presented to clear me and free me again. I couldn't be trusted as an elite after that, though—no angel wanted me. So they shot me down into administration and that's how I ended up at the orphanage."

"I'd want you," Mal blurted out, and he felt his face heat up as his own words registered and Tobias stared at him, wide eyed. "As a guard, I mean."

"Of course," Tobias said after a miniscule pause, and Mal continued to talk, trying to come up with enough reasons why he had meant that perfectly innocently so that maybe his face would stop blushing.

"I mean, I trust you. That is—you've protected me well so far, and I—I'd request you as my guard when I'm a healer so—"

"Mal," Tobias said quietly, interrupting the flow of embarrassment from Mal. Malachi slammed his mouth shut, staring at his priest with wide blue eyes as Tobias continued. "I understand. Thanks," Tobias went on, a small involuntary smile playing around the corners of his mouth. "I'd even accept the offer if you made it."

Malachi smiled back, a genuinely happy smile because he couldn't conceive of a more perfect future than having Tobias' guaranteed company for the rest of his priest's life. They smiled at each other in silence for a few seconds before Tobias blinked and cleared his throat, looking away again. "Anyway. What I was saying was that in jail, there's not much to do but repent and gossip. There were a lot of rumours going around, about priests and angels alike. There were some ... unpleasant rumours about the head of the lab, Mal. I didn't know what the lab was back then, but I do now—and it makes more sense. Caroline is the head of the lab."

Mal blinked. "*Lady* Caroline? She's the head of the lab? The one where we found—"

"Yes," Tobias replied and cocked his head, considering Mal closely. "And there were more rumours, Mal. From some of the older priests in there," he added and hesitated a second before continuing. "You know the rule against the top priests having families, that they have to dedicate their lives to the work?"

"I heard something about it," Mal replied, his brow furrowing. "All the females above a certain rank have to give their child to the priest orphanage like the angel mothers to the angel orphanage. It's why most priests come from orphanages as well, right?"

"Right. Mal, there were rumours that Caroline had a child—out of wedlock—and nobody ever knew who or where that child was."

Mal stared at him and lifted a hand to run it through his hair. His fingers were trembling a little, his face pale. "She—she had a child? When was this?" he asked, his voice a bit higher. "How old would it be?"

Tobias bit his lip. "If the old priest is to be believed, then ... about your age. And it makes sense, Mal," he added quickly, before Mal could say anything to refute the news. "She wanted to see you. The bleeding angel, Eli said. As far as most priests are concerned, angels bleed like humans, but the upper security ranks would know the truth—and so she'd ask to see you, specifically calling you by that term?"

Mal was shaking his head. "No. No, it can't be her. The lab was—she wants to *kill* us, Tob. The angels, everything. She—"

"You don't know that," Tobias replied sharply, and Malachi eyed him dubiously. "We don't know why they were researching the fever. Maybe they're looking for a cure."

Mal laughed at that, at the thought that the priests would care that much about an angel problem—one that could successfully weaken a species that had been repressing them for centuries, if certain lobbyists were to be believed. Mal honestly didn't think angels were that bad. Most of them helped more than the few that hindered, but that was the same with every humanoid species—but there would always be priests who believed the worst against all of them.

Tobias was watching him though, and then drew in a deep breath, like a diver about to take the plunge. "Mal ... she's also a haemophiliac."

Mal blinked, and then shook his head. "So are lots of other humans—"

"Not as many as you might wish to think. I researched it a little bit after your hand was cut, Mal, and I have to admit it all fits. Why else would she be so interested in the bleeding angel?"

Mal shook his head again silently in mute protest and dropped his eyes to watch his own fingers pluck at the upholstery of the couch defensively. Tobias sighed and moved forward to switch his seat to sit on the couch next to Mal and leaned back, relaxing slightly. There was a silence for a minute longer before Tobias spoke up again. "So what do you want to do now?"

Mal bit his lip and debated asking about what he most wanted to know about, but he wasn't sure how Tobias would take it or even if he'd want to answer questions about the kiss. Eventually he shied away from that topic and chose to focus on the suddenly easier problem of his parents, supposed or not. "Let's ... go see if Cassiel is available to talk to me. He never replied to any of my queries before, but maybe now—if I go talk to him face-to-face ..."

Tobias was nodding. "Sounds like a good plan to me. If he's your father, he should definitely know who your mother is, and it won't take more than a minute to tell you at least a name or something. We'll have to figure out a disguise for me to get in safely, though. I'm still persona non grata with the Council."

Mal smirked and stretched, putting arrogance into every line of the move. "Well, I guess it's my turn to take the lead then."

Tobias scoffed, and then laughed. "Yeah, sure. If that's the way you want to look at it."

Mal grinned at him in reply, and there was that silence again, the one that *should* have felt awkward, but really just felt easy and comfortable. Mal basked in it, thrilling in the feeling of finding a genuine friend and possibly more, but Tobias' expression started to get increasingly nervous. When they spoke, it was at the same time.

"Mal—"

"Tobias—" Mal hesitated, but then continued before he could avoid the question, before Tobias went on. He didn't think he'd be able to bring up the topic again if he didn't say anything about it now; and if he didn't, he had a fair guess that Tobias never would, and then he would never know. "Back there, in the cell—"

"Yes?" It wasn't an encouraging tone, nor was Tobias' expression particularly pleased with the conversation.

Mal did his best to ignore that part. It was hard enough to talk about already without Tobias making him even more nervous about the fact. "When I was bleeding ... you kissed me."

The words sounded like they rang out louder into the quiet of his apartment, echoed in his thudding heartbeat which then continued in a rhythm that Mal almost couldn't bear. *You kissed me, you kissed me—* "You—"

"You know," Tobias interrupted him with no apparent regret, his expression blank. "In my fourth year in training, we learned different tactics to deal with certain stressful situations."

Mal blinked. "I don't understand." He didn't want to understand. He was starting to hate the fact that Tobias delivered bad news almost every time he got that same sort of sympathetic look in his eyes—the same look that was starting to creep in now. It made it look like Tobias hated the fact that he was the one who had to break the news to Mal, which made Mal feel guilty about having asked in the first place.

"Mal … you were starting to panic. I had to calm you down, and it was either slap you … or kiss you."

Mal stared at Tobias for a second, trying to read more in his expression, before he dropped his eyes and closed them. The easy silence that had happened only a few minutes earlier now felt like it had never even existed.

The worst was possibly when Tobias cleared his throat in the definitely awkward silence and then continued to talk when Mal made it clear that he didn't want to hear anymore. "It didn't mean anything, Mal." He hesitated, then started again in a quick rush. "I'm sorry for—"

"Let's go," Mal said, shooting to his feet. He wasn't about to listen to more of that particular speech. He was Malachi—far above feeling hurt at a rejection when he hadn't even wanted the kiss before it had happened. It was just another part of their adventure at this point, and he would view it as such from that point on. If it hadn't meant anything to Tobias, then it hadn't meant anything to Mal either. "We'll go see Cassiel."

Tobias looked at him, and then looked away—but he didn't say a word; he only nodded.

"I was thinking," Tobias started as they made their way into the Kensington Palace gardens on their way to the Council headquarters, "that even if we can't trust some of the upper ranks of priests in relation to that lab we found … we should still let someone know about it."

"I've been thinking the same," Mal agreed and frowned. He was wearing full healing gear, which left his arms entirely bare as well as his upper back. It left the whorls and his wing shadow exposed; in stark comparison, Tobias was wearing his old guard uniform, without the stripes on his shoulders. "I was thinking we could report it to Cassiel, or possibly Raphael and they'd take appropriate action."

His voice sounded hard even to himself, but Mal let himself be pulled to a stop when Tobias put a hand on his arm. "Mal, she could be your mother."

"And she's trying to kill us all," Mal replied, tilting his head at Tobias. "You're honestly okay with what she'd doing?"

"Of course not," Tobias retorted sharply, and the insult in his voice was enough to relieve Malachi of an unacknowledged fear that maybe Tobias was sick of angels as well. "I just think there're better ways to deal with the issue than turning them in to angels who ... you know it'll happen, Mal—they'll kill them all."

"Well, what else are we supposed to do?" Mal asked, but his concentration was splitting between the conversation and the heat of Tobias' fingers still wrapped around his arm. Angels passing them by were starting to give Tobias odd, warning looks, shocked by his nerve. "I certainly can't let nobody know about the lab."

Tobias hesitated for a moment, then shook his head. "When I was in jail, the Pope cleared my name, Mal. He was fair and he listened to my side of the story. He'll do the right thing when it comes right down to it."

Mal shrugged and continued staring at Tobias' hand. After the whole 'it meant nothing' speech, any contact was suspicious, at least to him. Tobias stared at him in return, his face confused at Mal's silence at first, and then slowly growing increasingly aware of just how close they were and the contact that lingered. He pulled his hand away, his face going a little red, and Mal stared at him for a minute before trying to shrug the feeling in his chest away.

"Anyway," Tobias said after an uncomfortable moment of just looking at each other, "that's what I think you should do. We can continue, sir," he added, with a little bow that showed Malachi just how well Tobias had been trained as a guard. He grinned at the sight, then turned to continue on towards the Council headquarters.

The grand entrance was quieter than Mal had expected, with fewer angels milling around than there had been priests, and Mal frowned at that before going up to a female angel working quietly at a long mahogany desk with a discreet Receptionist plaque sitting next to her computer. She looked up as he approached and Mal watched her eyes take in the patterns on his arms before smiling. She ignored Tobias, silent behind Mal.

Mal smiled back, his best arrogant look. "Good morning. My name is Malachi, Class A, rank 2, formerly Class D, rank 1. I'm here to request a meeting with Cassiel, should it please his lordship."

She looked almost comically dismayed, enough that Mal might have laughed at her expression if he hadn't felt a sinking of his own hopes for the meeting. "I'm sorry, Malachi," she told him formally, her expression miserable. "Cassiel is out of commission with Angel's Fever and he won't have free time until after he's fulfilled his Council responsibilities once he has recovered. I can't guarantee when he'll be able to get back to you, but I can add your name to a list if you don't mind waiting a few weeks."

Mal didn't dare shoot a look at Tobias to see how his priest was handling the news, but it hadn't been what he'd wanted to hear. "I see. Yes, that'll be fine. I can also come back and check on his status before then, right?"

"Of course," she replied helpfully, her eyes wide with her sincerity. "There's no telling how long the sickness will last, after all. He could be recovering as soon as tomorrow."

"It's true," Mal agreed and thanked her quickly before turning to leave. He waited until they were out of the Palace grounds before turning to Tobias and arching his eyebrows. "What now?"

Tobias shrugged. "You already know what I think we should do."

Mal furrowed his brow, confused. "And the Pope will handle it properly?"

"You know he'll probably consult the angels on the matter. He does have good relations with them, regardless of the tension of the lower ranks."

"I suppose you're right," Malachi sighed and shook his head. "I just wish there was something we could do *now* to fix it."

"Well," Tobias cocked his head and grinned a little, the expression prompting a similar one from Mal. "I happen to know where the Pope lives. We could always drop by for a personal visit and get his advice on the matter ourselves. I'm sure he'll know what to do from that point."

"You just know everything, don't you," Mal told Tobias, inserting a large amount of awe into his voice. Tobias laughed, but Mal noticed he didn't refute the claim and that fact made him grin back.

Their improved mood lasted until they arrived at a charming little townhouse in the centre of London. It wasn't a bad area, but it wasn't what Mal had expected from the Head of the Priesthood, not when Council members lived in houses almost as large as Kensington Palace in and of itself. Mal stared at the building, then turned to Tobias. "Are you sure this is the right place?"

"Positive," Tobias replied. "This was where they took me when they proved that I wasn't involved with the whole plot against the angel. I got a personal apology from the Pope, but he also explained that I wouldn't be able to be a guard again until an angel requested me, and we all know how well that went."

Mal bit his lip and refrained from saying anything because he knew very well how he wanted that particular part to end. He arched his eyebrows and smirked at Tobias instead. "You're pretty high up in the world, aren't you?" he teased, and Tobias laughed.

"Just a humble orphanage priest," Tobias replied and knocked on the knocker. Mal fidgeted with his formal healer uniform. He'd wanted to go home to change, but Tobias, possibly scared that he'd have to reconvince Mal about this errand, had told him it would be better to prove their point if he had an angel along with him.

The door was answered by an elderly lady who looked down her nose at them. "May I help you?"

"It's very important that we see him," Tobias spoke up. "It's urgent. It's—about the Angel Fever."

She arched her eyebrows haughtily, then her gaze shifted sideways to take in Mal's obviously exposed forearms, and her brows furrowed in a thoughtful frown instead. "He is eating his afternoon tea at the moment, but I will let you in to see him as long as you are quick about it. He has a meeting in an hour that he has to prepare for."

"Thank you," Tobias replied and bowed again, shooting Mal a look as he did so. Mal hurriedly murmured thanks as well and copied the bow. The lady just sniffed and turned on her heel. Tobias carefully shut the door behind them, and they followed her into a decently-sized parlour with ancient furniture that would probably fetch thousands in an antique store. The Pope was sitting on a comfortable looking chair, his glasses perched on the end of his nose as he read over some documents that he set aside when the lady announced them.

"Tobias Callahan," the Pope said, sounding surprised as he looked at Tobias, and Mal was actually impressed that he obviously remembered Tobias. "And this is—?"

"Malachi," Mal replied and bit his lip, not quite sure what to say. He looked to Tobias for help, and Tobias shot him a tiny smile before explaining. He didn't mention anything about the search for Mal's mother, just made it sound like they had been looking for some medical records of an important human who had enough money to pay for the angel healers.

He explained about the lab and about the Lady Caroline, and the Pope nodded along with the story enough that Mal felt quite hopeful—until Tobias was finished and the Pope sighed. "It's a delicate problem," he started, and Mal scowled. Tobias seemed to sense the outburst before it happened though and shot him a warning look.

"What do you mean, sir?" Tobias asked, all politeness.

The Pope shook his head. "I have had suspicions, Tobias. She's had a bit of a rough time with angels, especially about a decade or so ago. I've seen her lab," he said shortly. "It's actually doing some pretty good research for humans. Her last filed report indicated she was helping Oxford University research a potential cure for Alzheimers, so we stand fully behind her in that regard. The thing is," he seemed to hesitate, and then heaved a gusty sigh. "The thing is that I've had her lab searched before. A year or so ago, when the Council was sure that Angel Fever was of human origin, but nothing was found and it angered quite a lot of the higher ranks that I'd catered to the Council."

Tobias ran his hand through his hair and shook his head. "But, sir—this is—"

The Pope held up a hand, looking a little more like a leader of men than a friendly looking uncle. "I am willing to orchestrate another search—but first I must have proof. You know how important evidence is," he told Tobias, who nodded glumly. "I would not be able to achieve anything without the evidence, and Caroline is such that there would be no evidence left when a search is started. Bring me proof and I will handle the rest. If you do not think you can handle it alone, might I suggest presenting the information to a fourth level ranked officer?"

Mal cocked his head, but Tobias shot him a look before nodding in agreement. "We understand, sir."

~~*

"So what's a fourth rank?" Mal asked, settling down at his dining table with a cup of steaming hot tea. It helped ease the sick, tired feeling in his gut at all the problems this whole search had put him through from the very beginning. It felt like his whole life had passed whilst they'd been going back and forth and running from priests and trying to implicate the source of a sometimes fatal fever—it was just very hard to settle down.

So Tobias had made tea, and now they were both staring into their mugs as they pondered what to do next. But first, Tobias had to answer the question. He tilted his head and stared at Mal, then smiled. "The five ranks of priesthood. You didn't learn about that?"

"Not really," Mal replied, blushing a bit because when Tobias looked at him like that, it felt like it meant a lot more than just a teasing smile between friends. "It didn't have anything to do with healing."

"The five ranks, commissioned by angels to be the keepers of laws and justice. There's the first level, which is what I currently am: administration. Then there's the second level, which is the peace keepers, who are mainly there to keep the peace between humans and angels. Third rank, law officials: the judge and jury of trials; fourth level is the police service. They'd be our best bet to ask for help, the Pope was right about that. They carry out punishments, but they also aid the third rank in finding evidence."

"And the guard," Mal said quietly, tilting his head and staring at Tobias across the table. "Fifth rank. Guard the angels that require protection or can afford it."

"Pretty much."

Mal started to grin. "So you were the best of the best?"

"Like I told you, I started young," Tobias replied and smiled back. "I skipped four levels in my demotion. It was pretty hard, but the Pope's done his best for me. I honestly think that this is the best option."

Mal sighed and pushed to his feet, unable to sit peacefully any longer. "I know—and I can see your point, but she'd be willing to kill us, Tobias. With all those vials— there had to be at least thirty in that case—it would be the easiest thing in the world for her to wipe at least most of the Council out. Without them, there'd be chaos. We're not *that* bad," he added desperately. He wanted Tobias at least to understand that; that angels were doing the best they could, and if the priests would just understand that—

"Shh," Tobias told him, his voice quiet and soothing even as he got to his feet and moved closer to Malachi. Mal stared at him, then turned away, shoving his hands through his hair.

"And how can your Pope *know* she'd cause such trouble and still do nothing without proof? Isn't it enough that we saw it?"

"He needs to see it, Mal," Tobias said calmly, lifting a hand to rest it on Mal's shoulder. "It's only to be expected. She's a hard woman by all accounts, Mal. The Pope better have all information ready and waiting, because she'll fight him. Rumour says that she doesn't let anyone take anything from her that she doesn't want to give."

"No," Mal replied, his voice oddly toneless. "Even her child, obviously."

Tobias sucked in a breath, obviously realising his misstep, but that didn't make Mal feel any better. "If I'm that child, Tobias, why would she give me up? Angels usually abandon their children; humans rarely do—"

"I was abandoned, too, Mal. It never bothered me as much as it obviously does you, but I can promise you, the fact that you're an orphan says *nothing* about you that you don't want it to say."

Mal shot Tobias an unfriendly look. "And yet, people seem to enjoy not wanting me. Cassiel, my mother— whoever she is—and—" He stopped and narrowed his eyes. "You."

Tobias blinked and then paled. "Excuse me?"

"You," Mal shot back and scowled. "You kissed me and you don't even want me. And I didn't want you until you kissed me, and now I can't think of anything else and you—"

He stopped and blinked, shocked because Tobias was right there again, his mouth crushed to Mal's as his hands buried themselves in Mal's hair. It took a second to register the contact before Mal made an embarrassingly weak sound in his throat, his hands coming up to hold onto his priest because if Tobias tried to pull away again— but Tobias pressed closer, the kiss deepening even as it got a little rougher for a minute. When he broke the contact, Tobias still didn't move away. His breath was ragged against Mal's lips. "You little fool. How could I not want you? But you're an angel—and only eighteen—"

"It's only four years," Mal argued, his fingers clenching in Tobias' guard uniform. "And—and I'm half human—"

Tobias laughed, a slightly desperate sound before he dropped his head to start kissing Mal again. It was delightfully warm in the room, or maybe it was just his body's own reaction to the contact and the flush of triumph that maybe it was possible that Tobias did want him after all, and that perfect future seemed to be crystallizing into a reality except for the fact that there was a loud banging sounding in his ears.

It took a full minute for Mal to realise that it wasn't his own thundering pulse, but Tobias recognised the fact sooner and pulled away, shooting Mal a simple but genuine smile before he moved to open the door. Then there was a loud crack, and Tobias was stumbling backwards, a hand lifted to his face with blood already dripping down his chin. Eli grinned at the sight then shoved Tobias further into the room.

He was flanked by two other guards who grabbed Tobias before Eli moved further into the room, coming closer to Mal and making Mal back away, desperately checking over his shoulder for an escape route before he realised that there was no conceivable escape, not when there were two guards holding onto Tobias. Mal wouldn't run without him—and he didn't think he'd be able to dodge Eli without Tobias' help.

"Well," Eli said, and his voice was gleeful and delighted enough that Mal wanted to punch him. "It looks like Tobias Callahan found an adequate substitute for an angel to guard, even without the Pope's help. Who knew you went for the young and mongrel type," Eli shot over his shoulder. Mal narrowed his eyes and prepared to punch Eli regardless of the consequences when Tobias' look reined him in.

"It's just a bit of fun, Eli. I'm sure you understand. If it's me you want, leave him out of it," Tobias told Eli, looking away from Mal and avoiding his gaze from that point on. "I'm the one who went to the Pope earlier."

"We know," Eli replied and stepped forward to wrap his hand tightly around Mal's wrist. Mal didn't move, couldn't move because Tobias was making it seem like the kiss had been another excuse to calm him down—and all his words during it had only been to aid the process. "We saw you visit the old man—and we saw the bleeding angel go with you, and so we went to Lady Caroline and she gave us the address. It seems she's been watching you for a very long time, angel."

"Then I'm *very* eager to meet her," Mal snarled, and lifted a hand to try and punch Eli just in case he could succeed. Eli barely even flinched; he simply lifted his own gun. The butt of it thudded into Mal's head, and then the world went black.

~~*

Mal discovered he didn't like staying in cells with humans very shortly after they were forced into the crypt again. It was a different cell than they'd had before; this one was shaped in an L, which made it a hell of a lot easier to avoid Tobias. Mal wasn't sure what to think about anything to do with him, so he tried not to think about it at all. He could still almost feel the warm press of Tobias' body and his hands in his hair and—right. He wasn't thinking about it.

They stayed in silence for a very long time, locked in the cell for several days. The kiss made things awkward because they could have been planning another escape, or exactly what awaited them with the upcoming confrontation. Eli came down with every meal, smirking and gloating over the fact that they had been so easy to catch in the end, and Tobias always replied politely. Malachi just ignored them both. He'd had enough of priests to last him a long time.

Eli eventually came down to bring them up to the lab again; this time, Lady Caroline was apparently to have her wish and meet the bleeding angel. Malachi didn't think he'd ever looked forward to anything less. Dread felt like a live thing in his stomach as he climbed the stairs out of the crypt, the footsteps of the two humans following him. There was another guard stationed at the top of the stairs, probably to prevent another escape, and he grabbed Malachi's arm roughly. "Follow me," he told Mal, and Mal didn't even try to pull out of his grip.

They walked back along the length of the Cathedral to the side chapel that housed the lab, and Mal was surprised to see that the Cathedral wasn't as busy as it had been before. "Where is everyone?" he asked his guard and only got a frown in reply before Eli laughed from behind him. Mal twisted his head around to look at Eli and blinked when he saw that Tobias was being escorted by four other guards, including Eli. They were elite, if the stripes on their shoulders were anything to go by, and Mal wasn't confident of any attempt at escape. Tobias wasn't looking anywhere but at the ground as they walked, and Mal bit his lip and hoped in spite of himself that his priest was okay.

"Most everyone has gone to conduct their sermons and attend to usual Sunday business," Eli answered Mal eventually. "Or did you forget that it was Sunday?"

"I didn't forget, because I didn't exactly know," Mal snapped back, refusing to show how nervous he really was. "It's hard to keep track when you're stuck in a cell."

Eli just smirked. "It was better than you deserved, angel."

Mal just rolled his eyes and stumbled when his own guard pushed him forward again, muttering for him to move faster. "The Lady Caroline does not like to be kept waiting," he said. Mal made a humming, non-committal sound and tried not to think too hard about what else the Lady Caroline did not like—besides angels.

She was standing in the centre of the lab when they stepped through the door, looking as if she'd arranged herself in that place quite on purpose to achieve the maximum effect. And Mal, looking at her for the first time, couldn't look away. Her hair was a glossy black, pulled back into a bun so tight that it pulled at the skin of her face; but aside from that—aside from that, and the strange, distant look in her eyes—it was like staring into a mirror. Still, Mal hoped. "Lady Caroline, I presume?"

She arched her eyebrows haughtily and gave him a once over look that had Mal straightening, lifting his chin, and smirking arrogantly in response. He refused to be judged by a human, no matter who Tobias suspected she was, and Mal immediately tried to prove that he wasn't scared or even affected by the sight of her. "Well, my name is Mal—"

"Malachi," Caroline said and tilted her head, an odd expression flicking across her face as she moved closer, deliberately ignoring all the other humans in the room. She wasn't a tall lady; her eyes were an inch below Mal's, but she made up for her lack of height with sheer self-confidence. Her eyes locked on Mal's face as if she were trying to memorise it, and Mal didn't move, watching her stare at him. "Yes," Caroline murmured after several minutes had passed. "Yes, I see now."

"See what?" Mal asked, half without meaning to say anything.

He was surprised to see a slight smile cross her face before she turned away from him, looking past him and arching her eyebrows. "And who is this?"

"Ex-guard Tobias Callahan," Eli promptly replied, and Mal twisted around to look at them as well. Tobias was well within his guards' grips, with both his arms being held and a guard behind him, with Eli standing in front proudly. "He's been helping the angel."

"And what have you been trying to accomplish?" Caroline asked Mal, her attention turning back to him and seeming to lock onto his expression. "Why are you here, Malachi?"

Mal bit his lip and wanted to look at Tobias for a hint as to what he was supposed to say, but he couldn't make himself look away from Caroline. Her gaze burned into him and seemed to demand equal attention back, and if she was— "I'm looking for my mother," Mal blurted out and the claim embarrassed him a little, but he made no attempt to take the words back, even after Eli scoffed behind him. He was about to turn around to sharply reprimand the priest, when Caroline did it for him.

"Quiet, Eli."

"But, Lady Caroline—"

"Quiet," she repeated and looked at Mal again. Then she tilted her head. "You found her, Malachi. What now?"

Mal blinked. "But—I—you can't—"

Caroline arched her eyebrow at the stuttered attempt at denial. "Yes, I am your mother."

Mal stared at her, taking in her bright blue, almond-shaped eyes, the slight uplift at the outer corners that were so like his own, and couldn't make himself believe the news. "But this lab. The angel fever … you were going to kill us … me."

She simply watched him for a moment, her face utterly expressionless. "Yes," she said after a minute. "I was."

"But … you don't want to now, right? Kill your son?"

There was a brief moment when emotion flickered through her eyes, but Mal couldn't quite tell what it was. It softened her features to a kind of warmer beauty, and Mal hoped—but then her face hardened again, cold and unapproachable. "There was a time when I might have done anything—given anything—to keep you. That is no longer the case."

"Mal—her past—" Tobias managed and grunted when one of the other priests slammed the butt of his gun into Tobias' stomach. Mal wanted to go to him to help, to do something other than stare into the face of the woman who claimed to be his mother, but would still kill him as if there was nothing at all to it. But Tobias was being held by a host of elite guards and if they had rendered Tobias helpless, then there was not much more that Mal would be able to do to help—especially not when he was still recovering from Angel Fever.

"Only rumours, Ex-guard Tobias. Only rumours—for the most part."

"What happened?" Mal asked, partly to stall. He was desperate for some more time to think up some kind of a plan to get himself and Tobias out without injury … But there was still a large part of him that wanted to know just what had happened to make him not worth searching for. Everything he'd heard about her past had hinted that she wouldn't have let them steal her baby, even new to the Cloth. The thought that she might *never* have wanted him made something in his throat tighten and his chest constrict.

Something of the tightness must have shown on his face and it seemed to soften hers again briefly. "Avert your eyes," she snapped at the guards.

"But, Mistress Caroline," one of them protested and she cut him off with a glare. Mal kept his gaze on his mother even as the guards shuffled to face the wall of the laboratory, forcing Tobias to turn with them. "The angel?" one of them asked, and Caroline looked back at Malachi, ignoring the question completely.

"You wish to know what happened?"

Mal glanced over his shoulder at Tobias' back. Tobias' shoulders were tensed. Mal knew him well enough by now to notice the fact and to know that he was simply biding his time, waiting for the right opportunity. It made Mal relax just a little; Tobias was also trying to think up a plan, and when they were both aiming for the same goal ... there wasn't any real way they'd lose this fight ... right? He looked back at his mother to help get more time as well as the answers he'd been searching for his entire life. "Yes."

She nodded, her face expressionless, her eyes distant. "I suppose it's natural for you to want to know." She shifted her weight and looked around aimlessly for a minute, looking vaguely uncomfortable before she returned her attention to Malachi. "I was young when I met your father—at the Initiation Ceremony."

"Cassiel," Mal said, and Caroline nodded.

"Right," she hesitated for a moment, as if she wasn't quite sure how to continue before she shook her head slightly. "He was the most beautiful thing I'd ever seen." It sounded like she was discussing someone else's life, a second- or even third-hand story that had had no contact with her own life whatsoever. "He obviously liked what he saw as well, and—well, we started to spend more time together. I initiated as a third level priest—the law officials," she supplied at Mal's blank expression. "You know, I hope, about the five levels of priesthood?"

"Yes," Mal replied and tilted his head. "Tobias explained it to me."

She looked briefly surprised at this, and then tossed her head dismissively. "Good. One thing led to another and I fell pregnant. With you," Caroline frowned. "I wasn't old enough to handle a baby, let alone an illegal one, but I couldn't stand the thought of visiting the healers for them to deal with you, either. A law official, pregnant with an angel's baby—and not just any angel, but a member of the Council ... I was young, though, and foolish enough that I thought I'd be able to keep you. Perhaps hide your true breeding, but I didn't take your father properly into account."

"My father?" Mal said, his voice barely above a whisper. He couldn't seem to make it go any louder, but he was desperate to hear the rest of the story.

"He found out I was pregnant several months in ... and he reported it."

Mal blinked. He hadn't expected to hear that kind of news, and he shot a glance at Tobias' back instinctively, hoping to maybe see what his priest thought of that news because he had been convinced that Cassiel actually cared, and if he'd reported him— "Why am I still alive then?" he asked quietly.

Caroline's expression faltered, an arrested look on her face as she stared at Mal before she turned away and started moving around the lab, straightening things on the tables and neatening the area up quite needlessly. "They took you instead. You were raised in that orphanage from a baby with no record to your mother's name, and I—the Council had to ensure my silence on the matter of your heritage."

"But *why*? Angel and human interbreeding is illegal; I should be dead," Mal asked, stepping forward before jerking himself to a stop. He didn't want to get too close to her. She was standing right by where the vials labelled Angel Fever had been on their last visit, and if she did still want him dead—

Caroline shook her head in response to the question, though, her expression sad for a moment. "That, I do not know. I can only suspect that they wished to study the effects of human qualities in an angel. They didn't expect me to be the carrier of that disease, and I was punished for that too when it was discovered."

She said the last bit a little quieter, enough that Mal had to strain to hear her, and he was feeling completely bewildered by this point. "Punished? I—I don't understand."

Caroline looked at him for a few seconds, and then moved closer again, standing in front of Mal and lifting her hand to cup his face. She was wearing thin leather gloves, and Mal didn't like the sensation of it against his face, but he didn't move, barely dared to breathe. "I was young," she told him. "I was young, and I wanted to keep you, and then they took you away before I'd even gotten to hold you. Of course, I looked for you," she went on, her voice sharpening with anger. "I asked everyone I could think to go to. The current pope had me shunted into administration, but it wasn't enough to stop me. I went to visit Cassiel."

She stopped talking, her eyes vague with a kind of horror, and Mal hesitated before lifting his own hand, curling his fingers lightly around her wrist in an instinctive and natural urge to try and take some of the pain from his mother—but she shook him off, her eyes cold and distant again, icy in their anger. "All I found when I went to visit your father—to see if he knew where you were—were angels. Council flunkies that captured me and took me to Council headquarters and tortured me to stop me from asking questions."

Mal blinked, his brows furrowed. He hadn't expected that kind of answer. The silence in the room was deafening; he couldn't tell if this was all fresh news to the priests behind him, or if this was something they'd heard before. Possibly this was the extra bit in her past that Tobias had tried to warn him about a few minutes after their entry to the lab, but—but had it really been that bad? Had they really tortured her?

Caroline sighed and closed her eyes for a moment before opening them again, looking at her hands before flicking her eyes back up to Mal's. "This ... is only part of what they did," Caroline went on after a minute. Her expression was politely disinterested, detaching herself emotionally from the story even as she pulled off one of her gloves.

Malachi bit his lip. If he hadn't been a healer, the sight would have disturbed him more. As it was, he just felt sorry for her. The skin of her hand was mottled and scarred; ridges of the scar tissue threaded over her skin. The scarring went up her wrist and under her sleeve so that there was no telling how bad it had been or how high it went.

"Every time," Caroline said softly, rubbing the ruined skin with her other hand as if trying to remember what her skin had felt like before the torture. "Every time I ever asked about you, they would burn me. Every time I asked for you back ... That is why they have to pay. That is why we have to break free from the angels: if they were cruel enough to do that to a woman who was barely more than a girl, there is no pity in any of them. Any of *you*," she spat at Mal, and for a minute, she wasn't pretty at all.

Mal knew it wasn't his fault. He knew there was no possible way he could have helped her at that time, but Malachi still felt guilty. That hadn't been her fault—and even more than that, she *had* wanted him back. He hadn't been completely worthless to her, not then—and maybe, maybe not now either, regardless of her apparent hate for him and the other angels. "I can—" he started to say, and then stopped, shooting a look over his shoulder. "I can't understand what you went through—but you seem to have kept track of me regardless of those consequences. Maybe you already know I'm the most talented healer of the Academy at the moment. If ... if you promise to let Tobias and myself go free," he offered, ignoring the short scuffle of sound that came from behind him, "then I can heal you."

Caroline stared at him, looking genuinely shocked for the first time. For a moment, he thought he had a bargain she would agree to, but then she shook her head. "I've been to healers. The scars are too old."

"Human healers," Malachi argued, dismissing the attempts of people who didn't have the pure healing talent he did. It was the one thing he was most confident in, the one thing about himself he was absolutely sure of, and he knew he would be able to help her, even if it was only a little. Even a little would be more than the human healers had managed, by the looks of her hands. "I'm the best healer of the Academy," he repeated and arched his eyebrows. "You ought to know that."

"I gave up watching you when you left the orphanage," Caroline retorted, then stopped and narrowed her eyes, seeming surprised by her own mini-outburst. She appeared to be considering it; she looked over Mal's shoulder at the huddle of guards around Tobias. "If I let you both go?"

"Yes," Mal promised and licked his lips nervously, biting his lip a moment later. If there was a single way out of this whole mess, then this had to be it. It seemed like she really wanted to be healed, and surely he could think of a way to help her and yet still gather evidence to prove to the Pope that this was the real problem he'd always thought it would be. Yes, some angels were cruel, but most of them were not. For most, their besetting sin was arrogance and ignorance, but it was no worse with them than it was within the human ranks of priesthood.

She considered him then walked past him to the guards behind him. Mal spun around to watch her as she walked past them to the door and pulled it open, eyeing her guards sharply. "Get out."

"But Lady Caroline—" Eli started to protest and fell silent under her glare. Eli shot Mal a dangerous glower, warning him not to try anything, and Mal just shot him a cocky looking smile, the expression wiping clean when his mother turned to look at him again. Eli closed the door behind the guards, and Mal licked his lips again, running a hand through his hair as he tried to draw upon all his lessons to at least give off a professional healing air.

"How high does the scarring go up?"

She tilted her head as she looked at him again, and Mal was astonished to see a slight smile on her face, one that, if it had been on anyone else, he would have labelled as pride. The mere idea made him uncomfortable, and he had to resist the urge to squirm out of embarrassment. It seemed a lot more awkward when it was just the two of them in the room, and Mal was actually grateful when her expression to settled back into its distant look again. "All the way up to my shoulder and down my back."

Mal winced and tried not to think about how much that had to hurt before trying for the mentality that it was just another human—like a final test before his initiation. "I'll need to see most of it to heal you," he told her and wracked his brain for something that he could do to enable Tobias' and his escape as well as see that his mother paid for her crimes concerning the Angel Fever outbreaks. He could understand her hatred, but he couldn't condone it, and she would have to be dealt with. But how to get the Pope in the lab before they cleaned it out again?

"Very well," she said and didn't even hesitate before starting to unbutton her priest robe. She was wearing a thin undershirt on underneath it, and she draped her robe over the nearest table as she turned back to him. The shirt was sleeveless, and Mal could see a lot more of the scarring. It was as bad as she'd said, and Mal's brow hitched at the obvious distaste she had for her own body now that it looked the way it did; a constant reminder as to what she had gone through and a very physical goad to her own hatred. Maybe if he eliminated the visible effects of what those angels that had done this to her, somebody from the priesthood would be able to lessen their internal mental effect.

"You should have a seat," he told her softly. Caroline didn't reply, simply sat on the nearest stool and watched Mal as he moved closer, willing his own healing to work. The fever symptoms had abated during their stint in the jail, so he was hopeful that his more basic talents had returned to normal. It was still a relief, when he put his hands on her back under her shirt and concentrated, to feel the familiar warmth and the soft glow under the whorls on his arms as the pressure and heat built to a strength that would be able to handle the task he had set for himself.

He'd only ever dealt with a few burns, and none of them had been this old, but scar tissue was scar tissue, and he'd done well in those lessons. It couldn't be too much harder to achieve this goal, and he fell into a silent trance-like state as he concentrated. The heat flooded through him in hot waves that left them both sweating, but she didn't make a sound, even when he had to release the pain, the white hot ritual happening often enough to leave both of them shaking with exhaustion.

He felt his knees begin to weaken and buckle by the time he'd made his way to the curve of her shoulder. The thought of taking a nap crept into Mal's head, making his fingers tighten on her shoulder as the idea spread from that simple thought. If he could possibly knock her out—if he could knock her out and grab some of the vials that they had seen last time—maybe help break Tobias free as well so he could talk to the Pope and explain ...

It might work.

The comfort of having an actual plan made Mal relax, and he concentrated harder on healing his mother's arm. The skin he left in his wake looked red and raw, peeling like a sunburn. It was a little shiny, like fresh skin, but it wasn't scarred any longer. There might be a faint discolouration left behind, but compared to the ridges that had been there before, Mal didn't think it would bother Caroline all that much. He was proud of himself for doing such a fine job even with the odds stacked against him from the age of the scars.

He was doing the final stretch of skin, from her hand to her wrist, when she turned her head to look at her arm, and then at him. The expression in her eyes had Mal's throat tightening, and for a moment it felt like they could ignore the years and everything else that had happened to both of them. It prompted him to speak, quietly so as to not disturb the healing process and also so as not to force an answer if she didn't want to answer. "What happened to the angels who did this to you?"

Caroline was silent for a long time, enough that Mal was in the releasing pain stage when she answered, her voice little more than a gasp. "They are dead."

Mal blinked at that then frowned in concentration as his fingers splayed over her skin, forcing the scar tissue loose and relaxed, to start peeling off properly. "How?"

Caroline was still watching his face, but the look in her eyes sent a chill down Mal's spine, and he had to drop his gaze to avoid it, pretending to stare at her hand instead. "I waited years. Many years. The first was attacked by someone who should have protected him two years ago, the angel Loki. Eli impersonated an elite guard and fooled Loki's original guard."

Mal had to concentrate very hard on her skin to avoid doing something that would ensure his recapture, but it was hard. It was so very hard not to pull away from the healing and open the door and attempt to beat Eli at his own game. Mal knew how to fix broken bones as a healer, but he was sure that the talent could be used the other way round, to maybe break them instead, and if anyone deserved it, it was Eli.

And his *mother* had been the one to organise the downfall of Tobias. He'd just been an innocent bystander, and what would he think of Mal after he'd found that out. He'd never kiss him again, or even want to talk about it, and Mal wouldn't be able to blame him, not when his mother had been the one to ruin Tobias' life.

She didn't seem to notice his sudden tension. Her eyes were back on her hand when Mal dared to look up again. There was a tiny smile on her face as she stared at her arm, and Mal hoped it was for the healing rather than for the death of the angel that had hurt her. "The second died a few months ago, from the Fever. It was what I had been aiming for." She was quiet a moment, seeming to debate whether or not to add more for Malachi's benefit before she seemed to judge it only as his due. "This time ... this time, it will be your father I aim for. And then the list will be complete."

Malachi swallowed and released the pain. The whorls on his arm glowed red, and Caroline made a small sound this time, her eyes squeezing shut to cope with the heat of it. Mal saw his chance and took it; he didn't want to listen to her anymore. He didn't want to have to face Tobias afterwards. He was familiar enough with pain release to know how long it took, and just as soon as it was safe to lift a hand, he did so, pressing his fingers to Caroline's cheek.

Her eyes flew open to look at him, bright blue meeting bright blue as they stared at each other, and then her lashes fluttered, her eyelids sinking as all the tension left her body and she slumped over, collapsing into his arm. Mal pulled her off the stool carefully and laid her on the ground. He hesitated before pulling her robe off the table behind him and covered her prone form, hoping to keep it at least a little warm until he could find some way to keep Eli out whilst bringing the Pope in.

Of Lady Caroline, he had no more real worries. She would sleep for a few hours with the effect of his talent, and if he and Tobias hadn't sorted the mess out in those few hours, then they probably deserved to be caught again. Mal liked to think that they weren't distracted or stupid enough to be caught a third time.

He only had to think of a way to help free Tobias—but he hadn't gotten past the point of opening the door before the door opened suddenly, thudding against the wall with a loud crash. Malachi jumped and prepared to fight back, but it was Tobias, bruised and bleeding Tobias, with the beginnings of a black eye and a slight limp as he rushed into the room to stare at Mal and then at Lady Caroline, fast asleep on the floor. Tobias blinked.

"Well, I guess you don't need a guard anymore."

And for some reason, even in spite of everything they'd been through in the past week, and knowing what they had left to go through, Mal couldn't help but smile. "Doesn't matter. I'd still want you."

Tobias stared at him and started to smile, but Mal remembered the fact of what his mother had done, and turned away to stare down at her again. "I think we should go get some authorities. Like the Pope, or something."

Tobias didn't reply for a moment, but then he agreed, his voice a little flat.

~~*

Malachi didn't leave his apartment for several days afterwards. The news that he had caught the instigator and creator of the most fatal strain of manufactured Angel Fever that had ever been seen had rendered him somewhat of a star. Malachi had used to like attention, but only when he felt he deserved it—such as being the best male healer of his generation. The fact that he'd caught somebody intent on doing real damage just saddened him and left him feeling drained and undesiring of any kind of company

Lady Caroline had been put into jail, along with Eli, and Tobias' name had been completely cleared. Malachi hadn't seen his priest since it had happened, but he was missing him more than he'd ever thought possible. He missed Tobias' smirks at his overreacting and he missed Tobias' calm, collected way of dealing with all sorts of problems, large or small. He missed the way he could surprise Tobias into giving him that kind of look and affectionate smile that made Mal's heart start to pound— but he couldn't bear the thought of seeing Tobias and knowing that his priest knew his mother was responsible for the worst period of Tobias' life.

He'd thought about their last kiss often over the past few days, and now that the most emotional part of the adventure was over, he could admit to himself that Tobias had said what he had when Eli caught them to try and get them to take only Tobias. It had been a noble, if stupid, thing to attempt, but Mal could understand why he'd done it. He would have done the same thing if Eli had been prepared to accept anything less that Tobias' utter downfall.

Ordinarily, the knowledge would have made Mal search Tobias out again, but he hadn't. He couldn't.

There was a knocking at his door as Mal was making himself some dinner, and Mal hesitated before moving slowly to it. He kept the chain on as he opened the door, just in case it was another Eli waiting to burst in, and then he stood and stared at the priest on the other side. Tobias stared back solemnly. He was wearing his elite guard uniform, with the stripes on his shoulders and all, and Mal blinked at them before shutting the door again, taking a moment to breathe as he undid the chain and opened the door properly.

Tobias' mouth curled up slightly at one side, a lopsided smirk that Tobias managed to wipe clean when he bowed formally. "I humbly request an interview for your guard position."

"You have your timing wrong," Mal replied blankly, still feeling a little shocked. He hadn't gone to look for Tobias, and he certainly hadn't expected Tobias to show up before he felt ready to deal with him. "I don't qualify for a guard until I'm initiated properly. That's two years away."

"I realise that," Tobias replied and cocked his head. "It'll take me two years to learn how to guard a healer, though. Apparently it's a whole lot of new things to learn about who I'm supposed to let through to you to see and—" he broke off as Mal wandered aimlessly back towards his kitchen. There was silence for a few seconds before Tobias spoke again, and Mal nearly couldn't stand the confused misery in his priest's voice when Tobias was supposed to be the calm and collected one always. "Mal ... what happened? Is this about what I said to Eli when he broke in—"

"No," Mal replied and turned to shoot a small smile over his shoulder at Tobias. "I understood why you said that. I just didn't think to examine it until after everything else had happened." He was regretting it now. That time in the cell could have been spent in a lot nicer ways had he not felt wounded and defeated enough to refuse to listen to Tobias.

"Then why are you avoiding me?" Tobias asked, sounding implacably calm again. "I expected to see you at the trial, but you weren't there."

"I was told I wasn't needed," Mal explained and shrugged. "That it would give other angels ideas to break into St. Paul's, which I suppose it might, but I—"

"Mal."

Malachi sighed and turned to face Tobias. "You were at the trial. You heard what she did."

"Your mother?" Tobias asked, his brow furrowing.

Mal nodded. "Yeah. You heard them testify about what happened ... two years ago."

Tobias looked blank for a second before his expression shifted to anger so fast that it shocked Mal, and he backed up a step instinctively. Tobias advanced quickly, slamming his hands onto the kitchen counter on either side of Mal's hips. "Are you serious? You've been avoiding me because of *that*?"

"It was her fault," Mal tried to explain, but the words got tangled in his throat, and he couldn't say anymore as he watched Tobias' face with wide eyes. Tobias seemed genuinely mad, and Mal licked his lips and his gaze darted away, biting his lip after a second. "I just thought—"

"Mal," Tobias interrupted, and his voice sounded a little amused again. Mal dared to look back, and the corners of his mouth curved up a little because Tobias was watching him with such a look of exasperation on his face that it couldn't fail to be amusing. "Stop being so noble. I don't give a damn that it was your mother who created the whole Loki situation. It happened two years ago; I'm over it. And furthermore," he went on before Mal could think of something to say, "if I hadn't been demoted, I would still be working for him, and I would never have met the best male healer in a generation. And if I hadn't met you, how could I have found out that I'd rather work for you than for anyone else?"

Mal searched Tobias' face, his smile growing into a lopsided, happy grin. Tobias meant what he was saying. His dark eyes were steady on Mal's, and Mal tilted his head. "You don't mind waiting two years for me to be initiated?"

"I think I can handle the wait."

"And you don't mind being overshadowed by my sheer ability?"

Tobias shrugged and somehow his hands found their way from the counter to Mal's hips. "Somehow, I think I have talents to rival yours."

Mal grinned. "Your bruises are going down already."

"Sheer natural healing," Tobias replied and arched an eyebrow. "Unless you'd be willing to help with that."

"Can you afford my services? Humans have to pay for angel healing, you know," Mal murmured as a final question, and Tobias just grinned, a boyishly happy grin that made him look younger.

"Shut up, Mal," he said and kissed him. Wise as ever, Malachi could only obey.

The Book of Judgment

Sasha L. Miller

Reza waited impatiently, drumming his fingers against the arm of the chair in which he was sitting. He was a little early for this meeting, but he'd expected the High Chairman and the leader of the mercenaries he'd hired to already be there. That neither was meant this meeting would take longer than Reza had anticipated.

Stifling a sigh, Reza glanced disinterestedly around the High Chairman's office. It was neat and tidy, richly decorated in tones that would offend no one. It was a bureaucrat's office, and it showed in the sleek wood, the neatness, and the stately, unscarred desk that was planted dead center in front of the large windows.

It was larger than Reza's office—workroom, really, since Reza did barely anything that could be considered "office work." His workroom was in the west wing, with the offices of the other mages who studied the more volatile arts. Understandable, but it meant a long walk whenever Reza had to meet with anyone in the administrative or teaching sections of the university.

Debating the merits of skipping the meeting and returning to his workroom and his latest experiments, Reza scowled at the polished wood of the High Chairman's desk. No, unfortunately, he couldn't skip the meeting. It was too important that the book the meeting was about be secured as soon as possible, and while Reza wasn't particularly thrilled about accompanying the book to the temple in Carimchi, he was the best person for the job.

The door to the High Chairman's office opened then, thankfully, and Reza stood, turning to meet the High Chairman and the mercenary leader. Reza's sarcastic greeting died on his lips, and he clamped his mouth shut before he could fumble something stupid out.

The mercenary was striking—not handsome, not in a traditional way. He was tall, lean, and wore the sword at his hip as casually as if it were simply another limb. His hair was longer than most of the mercenaries Reza had seen; it fell messily to the tops of his ears, shadowing his eyes in the front. His eyes were dark, probably brown, but it was impossible to tell from across the room. His gaze, however, was piercing, as though he knew all of Reza's flaws and mistakes and was weighing each of them.

"Ah, Professor," Bernard Charbonneau, High Chairman of the University of Magesterial Studies in Giroux, greeted as he shut the door to his office behind him. "Good to see you."

Reza nodded shortly, focusing on Charbonneau because that was easier than looking at the mercenary. Reza fervently hoped that the mercenary wasn't going with them, that he was only there to negotiate and sort out the travel minutiae that needed to be hashed out to transport the book safely to Carimchi. Then he wouldn't have to deal with the man's unsettling presence for too long.

"I'd like to introduce you to Edmé Herriot. He'll be helping us determine the best way to transport the book to Carimchi, as well as accompanying you there," Charbonneau continued, dashing Reza's hopes.

"Nice to meet you," Reza said, sounding anything but happy. He wasn't, but he could usually summon better manners than that. Reza forced a smile, but Edmé didn't seem too impressed. He inclined his head a bare inch, acknowledging Reza's statement but not returning it.

Charbonneau laughed, taking a seat behind his massive desk. "Professor Tremblay isn't convinced we need an armed escort of this book."

"It doesn't matter what I think," Reza replied curtly. The administration wasn't going to change its mind, so there would be an armed escort of the book. The more Reza learned about the book—and the more threats he received—the more he agreed that it was a good idea, but the administration was still hung up on his initial opinion.

Charbonneau gave him a stern look, but Reza ignored it, sitting down in his chosen seat again. "In light of the problems we've had in keeping information about this book contained, Master Herriot and I have agreed that as few people as possible should know the details of your journey. Can you handle coordinating the details, Professor?"

"Yes," Reza replied, startled by that. In retrospect, he conceded it made sense. No one was supposed to know about the book in the first place, but its discovery had somehow gotten out and there were far too many people interested in it.

Transporting the book to the temple in Carimchi—and keeping the book secure—was going to be much more difficult with all the people after it. At least the book would be safe at the temple in Carimchi, and given the book's nature, Reza couldn't blame Charbonneau for being impatient to make the book their problem.

It shouldn't have been their problem, but the Church had disbanded the combative corps attached to the priesthood. The angels, as they'd been called, both for the good they did and the terrible destructive power they wielded. Reza hadn't cared much about the matter previously, having little to do with the Church. It had been a good number of years since then; they should have come up with a better solution than 'wing it' for dealing with books of power.

"Your office should be a good place for that discussion," Charbonneau said, the tone of his voice making it an order instead of a suggestion.

"Right," Reza said, standing again. "I'll make sure my reports are filed before I leave."

"Very good," Charbonneau said, then looked at Edmé. "Good luck."

Edmé nodded, but didn't voice a reply. Reza scowled, hoping the man wasn't mute or willfully refusing to speak. He doubted the former; why would the mercenary group send someone who couldn't speak to discuss the job?

Reza strode across the office, passing in front of Edmé. He refused to go out of his way to avoid the man. He wasn't *that* intimidating. It was disconcerting, however, the way Reza could feel Edmé's presence behind him even as he couldn't hear his footsteps on the soft carpet that coated the floor of Charbonneau's office.

Charbonneau's secretary was busy filing something in one of the massive cabinets that lined the walls in the outer office. She looked up when Reza and Edmé entered the room and set down the folder she was holding. "Oh, Professor Tremblay, wait a moment." She crossed the room briskly to her desk and picked up a portfolio that was sealed magically. "This arrived for you a moment ago."

"Thank you," Reza said, taking the portfolio. The magical seal felt familiar and Reza nearly set the thing ablaze then and there. Instead, he tucked it under his arm and left the secretary's office, picking up his pace when he and Edmé reached the main corridor between the wings. "My office is on the other side of the building."

Edmé gave no reply, and Reza made a note to pack a lot of headache powders. He was going to need them if he had to beat his head against the brick wall of Edmé for the next two months. The trip across the university seemed interminable between Edmé's quiet, intense presence behind him and the letter he was carrying. Finally, though, they reached Reza's office.

It was a small room, tucked among a handful of others. Reza had only been a professor at the university for a few years, and he wouldn't be promoted to a larger office until he had been there at least a few more years, unless he took on a project that the university deemed important enough for a larger office. He'd already skipped past the worst offices simply because he was one of the strongest mages in the university—something that had not endeared him to his colleagues—and bumping him up further would do nothing to help that.

Reza stopped in front of the door, but didn't open it. He could feel the familiar pulse of his magical signature thrumming from the walls, soothing and pleasant, like the warmth from a hearth after being outside in the cold. No one had tried to enter while he was gone, Reza noted as he pulled the portfolio out from under his arm.

For all intents and purposes, the magical seal on the portfolio was simple and harmless. It was too strong, though, and Reza wasn't going to let it anywhere near the book and its protections. Setting his hand across the inscription of the seal, Reza felt out the catch that would allow him to break the seal. The inscription was false, Reza noted, shifting his hand a few inches to the left where the seal really rested. If he'd broken the fake inscription, whatever spell lurked behind the seal would have been free to complete.

Smothering the portfolio with a strong barrier, Reza broke the seal and quashed the underlying spell, unsurprised to note it was intended to cause harm of some sort to him. Magic dispelled, Reza handed the portfolio to Edmé, who was still watching him with that unsettling and intent gaze.

"I've been getting these regularly since I informed High Chairman Charbonneau of the book's content," Reza said, passing the portfolio to Edmé without opening it. He knew roughly what the letter would say, and it wasn't as though the letter's contents were the important part. Edmé took the portfolio, flipping it open. Reza left him to it, focusing on the magical barrier he'd erected around his office.

The barrier spell on the office was the first layer of spellwork he'd put in place when he'd realized what the book was. It was spelled to keep out anyone but him, using the unique pattern of energy every person had in order to determine whether they were allowed inside. Reza hooked himself into the spell, pressing a hand against the door to make the changes needed to allow Edmé inside. "Put your hand against the wall," Reza ordered, half-distracted by the spell threads he was manipulating.

"Why?" Edmé asked, and Reza nearly dropped the spell, startled by hearing Edmé speak. His voice was low and rough, as though it scraped over gravel before it left Edmé's mouth.

"So I can let you in," Reza said flatly, debating the merits of giving Edmé a nasty shock when he let Edmé into the room.

"What does that entail?" Edmé asked, obviously not caring about Reza's impatience.

"You put your hand against the wall to register your energy pattern with my spell so I can let you through the barrier," Reza rattled off, expecting more protest or more questions. Edmé stared at him for a moment, then simply lifted his hand and set it against the wall.

Edmé's energy signature was strong, thrumming with power. Reza would bet he was the mage strength for his group of mercs—every group worth the money had at least one mage, though it was strange Edmé led, since mages didn't usually do that. Dismissing that thought, Reza focused on weaving Edmé into the spell quickly. Disconnecting from the spell threads, Reza opened his office door and led the way inside. The room was a mess, but Reza refused to make excuses for that. He *worked* here and it showed.

The book was sitting in the center of the table in the middle of the room. It was encased with a solid sheet of energy that glowed even to the eyes of those who didn't use magic. It prevented the book from being touched, teleported, or moved in any way from the space it occupied. Even were the table to be removed from beneath it, the book would hang in mid-air, encased in the spell Reza had constructed around it.

It would take a mage stronger than Reza, or Reza's death, to break the box—hence the booby-trapped letters, since there weren't many mages stronger than Reza. Reza scowled at the book, slipping into the room and edging around the massive table that took up most of the space in the room.

"What do you know about the book?" Reza asked, deciding that was the best place to start. If Edmé wasn't aware of the gravity of what they were dealing with, then he wouldn't take any of Reza's suggestions for protecting the book seriously.

"It's *The Book of Judgment*," Edmé said, approaching the table. Reza suppressed a shiver at the tone of Edmé's voice as he pronounced the title of the book. "You're taking it to Carimchi so they can archive it in the Goddess's tomb."

Reza nodded, startled. Had Charbonneau told Edmé that much? The plans for the book had been kept strictly between himself, Charbonneau, and the priests in Carimchi who would be putting the book out of reach forever. Edmé would need to know where they were going, though, so it made some sense that Charbonneau had told him that.

"I can maintain the spellbox for the duration of the trip," Reza said. Edmé nodded, but he seemed distracted by the book, and a shiver of unease snaked down Reza's spine. Charbonneau had outsourced the protection of the book partly because of the threats and attempts to steal it—threats and attempts that had come from within the university. What if Edmé was working with them? Or working on his own? Stealing *The Book of Judgment* would be a pretty feather in any mercenary's cap, after all.

"Can you make it more discreet?" Edmé asked after a moment, looking up and subjecting Reza to that intense stare again.

"The book?" Reza asked, then felt immediately stupid because of course not the book. Shaking his head, he frowned at the spellbox. "You mean make the spellbox invisible?"

"Yes," Edmé said without explaining himself further. Reza stared at the spellbox for a long moment, pondering the request. The spellbox was only visible because it was such strong magic. Reza hadn't much cared that it was visible; it made it obvious that the book was protected and not easily removed. To make the spell invisible, he should simply be able to weave in some masking elements.

Reaching out towards the spell cage, Reza latched into the spell. It took a moment to weave the masking into the spell cage, and Reza was careful to not interfere with any of the protective qualities of the cage. Detaching from the spell, Reza glanced at Edmé. "Like that?"

Edmé nodded. "Can you make a duplicate?"

"No," Reza said flatly, scowling. "I'm not copying that book."

"Duplicate in appearance, only," Edmé clarified, somewhat impatiently, as though Reza should have divined that.

"You want a decoy," Reza said, then shrugged. "I can do that, sure. What do you have in mind?"

"Two groups, one real and one fake," Edmé said, frowning at the book. "The decoys will leave first, taking the standard route to Carimchi. We'll follow a day or two later, taking a less travelled route."

"Are you going to get a decoy for me, as well?" Reza asked. "I have to accompany the book in order to maintain the protections around it. No one will believe the university would just hand it off to a group of mercs and allow them full access to it. No offense."

Edmé smiled. It relaxed his stern features, making him seem more handsome and more approachable. "Yes, there will be a decoy of you, as well."

"Good," Reza said, somewhat annoyed that Edmé had thought of that. Better he was thorough than not, however. A second-rate mercenary would never do for this trip. "I need a day to clear away the rest of my projects, but after that I can leave whenever. The sooner, the better, obviously."

"Two days hence," Edmé said, decisively. "I'll meet you here."

"Fine," Reza said. "Is there anything I need to authorize for supplies?"

"No, the High Chairman has provided me with everything we'll need," Edmé said dismissively. "Make the decoy and be here at dawn in two days. I'll handle the rest."

"Fine," Reza repeated, somewhat annoyed that Edmé was taking over all of the plans and preparations. Edmé did seem competent, however, even if he was lacking in manners, so at least Reza could be reasonably assured he'd be able to handle the preparations without oversight.

"If you need to reach me before then, send a message to *Greenhouse on the Bay*," Edmé said, listing an inn by the harbor that was often frequented by mercenaries passing through the city. Reza nodded, unsurprised when Edmé turned and strode from the room without further ado. He cut as fine a figure from behind as he did from the front.

Reza rolled his eyes at himself, waiting until the door shut behind Edmé to latch himself into the barrier spell around the office. He removed Edmé's permissions to enter, then turned to study *The Book of Judgment*. It wouldn't be difficult to make a facsimile. The leather was simple but hardy, worn with age. The only sign it was a book of magic was in the text embossed on the front cover. It was as bright as the day it had been placed, the white lettering almost shining against the dark-dyed leather.

The Book of Judgment had been buried deep in one of a dozen crates of miscellaneous books that had been donated to the university after an earl had passed away without any heirs. Reza was positive that *The Book of Judgment* had been in the earl's possession unwittingly; knowledge of its existence and whereabouts would have been common knowledge had the earl been aware.

It had been pure, dumb luck that Reza had been the one to work on cataloguing the crate in which the book resided. He didn't doubt most of his peers would have hidden the book away to figure out how to use it to their best advantage. Reza wasn't that stupid. There was more than one story about overly proud mages who thought they could manage the spells in *The Book of Judgment* and had perished or caused catastrophes instead.

The Book of Judgment contained some of the worst and most dangerous spells known to mankind. They were vengeful and destructive and could cause no end of damage in the wrong hands. Reza hadn't let himself succumb to curiosity, caging the book without looking past the first few pages to ascertain that the book wasn't a prank or forgery from one of the younger professors.

Reza glared at the book, wishing it had stayed missing. He didn't want its responsibility, its hassle. He wanted to continue his research and his studies, not take a months-long journey across the country to settle a book in the most secure place on the continent. Scowling, Reza stepped away from the book, moving to gather what he'd need to make a decoy of the book.

~~*

Edmé knocked on the office door, glancing up and down the hallway while he waited. The hallway was deserted, however, and Edmé refocused his attention on the door in front of him. Hopefully Reza had followed his instructions and was waiting for him. He had the right office, at least. There was no mistaking the aura of mage energy surrounding the room. It made his forehead itch, but Edmé ignored that.

The door opened after a moment, the small gap framing Reza's face between the doorframe and the doorway. The office behind him was much brighter than the hallway, casting Reza's face into shadow and obscuring his face.

"Just a moment," Reza said, not giving him a chance to reply to that and shutting the door in Edmé's face.

Edmé cracked a reluctant smile, amused despite the slight. Probably unintentional—Reza had reset the barrier spell so that Edmé was no longer allowed through, so it wasn't as though he could wait inside the office. Still, it was not often people closed doors in his face or were rude to him. Cautious, yes. Rude, no. Edmé took a few steps back, leaning against the wall opposite Reza's office door and waiting.

True to his word, Reza opened the door again after a few moments. The hallway was shadowy, but there was enough light to make out Reza's silhouette and the shape of the pack he carried over his shoulder. It was easily large enough for the two books he'd be carrying as well as some additional supplies. Edmé stepped away from the wall, silently leading the way down the hallway. He could hear Reza's footsteps behind him, soft and quiet.

It didn't take them long to reach the street. The section of the university where Reza's office was located was in the outer edges of the building. They passed few people, mostly servants, and Edmé kept a close eye on them. A servant was often easier to bribe than anyone else; Edmé was sure that it would get back to the wrong ears that Reza had left, book in tow.

Reza had at least been smart enough to leave the barrier spell up on his office. It would fade the further Reza got from it, but it would stay in place a few days. Between that and the confusion Edmé hoped to sow with his decoy, hopefully they'd have a clear window in which to depart.

The sun was barely peeking over the horizon as they reached the street. It was cool at the moment, but the day would quickly heat up. The streets were busier than when he'd entered the university, people hurrying about to complete errands before the day got too hot. It was a risk, escorting Reza by himself, but one he was willing to take. Too much of an escort would attract attention, and unless Reza had let something slip, no ambush would be ready to spring on them.

"Stay close," Edmé said quietly, pausing to let Reza catch up when a group of laundresses split them.

Reza gave him a look that spoke volumes about how much of an idiot he though Edmé was, but he didn't elaborate on that, falling into step behind Edmé easily. It took nearly a half an hour to traverse the city and reach the inn where Edmé and his group were staying. The

Greenhouse on the Bay was painted a hideous shade of green, managing to be a bright, yet sickly shade of green that reminded Edmé vividly of dying grass. It was a large establishment, four stories tall and a city block wide.

Edmé strode inside without pause and took the stairs up to the top level. The rooms he'd rented were tucked under the eaves that gave the top floor fewer rooms. Edmé had rented them all, preferring the security over the frugality of renting rooms on the cheaper, lower-level floors. The noise of the kitchen and dining room receded as he climbed the stairs, leaving the noise of Edmé and Reza's boots on the stairs as the loudest sound.

Reaching the top of the stairs, Edmé paused in front of the first door on the left. He slid the key into the lock, unlocking it and stepping inside. He held the door for Reza, then turned to face the two men in the room. Aubin and Jean were settled at the small table on the far side of the room, discussing something; their conversation broke off when Edmé entered the room.

Shutting the door behind Reza, Edmé gestured towards him briefly. "Give your cloak and pack to Jean. Quickly."

Reza didn't reply, crossing the room to the bed that was shoved under the slope of the roof. In all, the room was small, hosting the bed and the table, a small set of drawers and a single window facing the bay. Reza quickly divested the pack of its contents, setting two identical books on the bed alongside a few shapeless parcels wrapped in cloth. He also removed clothing and some other personal effects, then put one of the books back into the bag.

Jean stepped forward; he was about Reza's size, maybe a little stockier and slightly taller. Jean's hair was darker and shorter, but the cloak should obscure that. Edmé didn't think the deception would work for long, but it was worth the day or two it would buy Edmé and Reza.

"I want the cloak pin back," Reza said, watching Jean critically as he swung Reza's cloak over his shoulders.

"Yeah, you'll get it," Jean said dismissively, fastening the silver leaf into place with only a little fumbling. Reza scowled, but didn't press the point, and Edmé made a note to get the pin back. He didn't doubt Reza would insist on its return after their journey was complete, and he didn't seem the type to be nice about it. With the magic he had at his disposal—and the ease with which he used it—Edmé didn't doubt that Reza could make Jean's life uncomfortable easily.

Aubin quickly filled out Reza's mostly-empty pack with some of the things from the over-stuffed bag he'd been sitting next to, splitting the load between them. Jean pulled the hood of the cloak up over his head, obscuring his features. He took the pack from Aubin and swung it over his shoulders, then looked at Edmé.

"Out the back, keep covered," Edmé said, as though they hadn't thoroughly discussed the plan the previous evening.

"Yes, boss," Jean said, heading for the door. "See you in a few months."

Edmé didn't reply to that as he opened the door for Jean and Aubin to leave. Hopefully they'd be safe enough, but they knew the risks. They didn't know what it was they were carrying a decoy of, but they knew it was dangerous and coveted. It wouldn't take long for the deception to be discovered, since Aubin and Jean would only ride a week out before turning around, but any time bought was good. Shutting the door, Edmé turned back to Reza, who was fidgeting with the book that was on the bed.

He wasn't sure what to make of Reza yet. He didn't seem to have any concept of the danger he was in, but he knew what *The Book of Judgment* was and how dangerous it was. Perhaps he thought his magic was enough to protect him?

That was another oddity—Edmé hadn't met very many people who were as comfortable casting and using magic as Reza was, especially after the scandals that had rocked the mage divisions of the priesthood the last five years. Using magic so openly had been on the decline. It was a rarity to see anyone outside the King's men and mercenaries so comfortable using magic.

Especially someone so young. Edmé would peg Reza as maybe twenty-five, perhaps younger. From the High Chairman at the university, Edmé had gotten the impression that Reza had breezed through his schooling and was on a fast track as a professor, which certainly explained why he was so reluctant to take this journey. It would take two months, at a minimum, to get to Carimchi. Add to that however long it took for Reza to do his part in securing the book and then two months back, and that was at least a half a year's setback to Reza's plans.

"What now?" Reza asked, looking away from the book and meeting Edmé's eyes. He didn't look away, and Edmé appreciated that. Edmé was well aware of how intimidating he could look, and it was refreshing that Reza didn't seem to care about that.

"We'll leave tonight," Edmé said. "We'll be accompanied by two others. Don't speak of the book with them." Reza gave him a flat look that plainly said he thought Edmé was an idiot for telling him that. "You can ride, yes?" Edmé asked, as it occurred to him he didn't actually know that. Reza seemed fairly capable, but there was no telling his background. If he'd lived in the city his entire life, it was feasible he hadn't had the means or reason to learn to ride.

"I'm not stellar, but I'll manage," Reza said, shrugging. "Faster than a carriage."

Better than nothing, Edmé supposed, though he would have preferred stellar. The faster they could ride, the better. The decoy would buy them time, but Edmé knew it wouldn't be long before that ruse was uncovered and efforts redoubled to find them.

To find the book and Reza, in any case. Edmé doubted Reza was aware that he was half the appeal. The spells in *The Book of Judgment* were terrible, horrible spells, but they also required a mage with no small amount of strength. Reza was more than strong enough, magically, to handle all of the spells in that book. There weren't many mages out there of his caliber—which was why Reza was accompanying the book: to put additional protections on it to prevent anyone from getting to it.

Edmé would have been happier if the book and Reza travelled separately, but there wasn't time to sort that out, and Reza was the best chance of keeping the book magically protected while they travelled. Edmé wouldn't be happy until they reached Carimchi and the book was stored safely in the Goddess's tomb.

"Don't leave the room," Edmé said, breaking away from his thoughts. "I'll bring you food later. In the meantime, get some rest. We'll be riding all night."

"You'll be getting me a new pack and cloak?" Reza asked, not objecting. Edmé gave him credit for that; he'd had to protect spoiled young people more often than he cared to remember and they often objected to the simplest security measures because they didn't like them.

"I'll bring them later," Edmé said, then turned to head from the room. He'd managed to get most of the supplies they'd need for the trip, but there were a few more things that he needed to ensure Jacques and Serge had or were getting.

Reza made no complaint as he left, and Edmé was confident that Reza wouldn't do anything stupid enough to blow their decoy. Edmé had sown a few rumors that he'd taken a few jobs that would split up his men; he was supposedly heading towards the coast with important papers for the Crown, whereas a few of his men were doing a standard escort for a university professor.

With luck, his ruses would buy them a few days. The alternate route would help. It would be a rough ride and would add another few weeks to the trip—the standard route to Carimchi took six weeks—but Edmé wanted the journey to be as easy as possible. He didn't doubt they'd encounter trouble, but the less trouble they met, the better.

~~*

There wasn't supposed to be downtime. Reza stared at the ceiling, wishing he could turn his brain off and sleep as Edmé had suggested. It was going to be a long day, and an even longer night. Reza had never been good at forcing himself to sleep, however, and he hadn't thought to bring anything along to pass the time. He hadn't thought there would be time to pass, not as fast as he'd thought they'd be travelling.

Giving up on the idea of sleep—maybe he'd be tired enough come afternoon to manage it—Reza shoved off the bed. Pacing across room, Reza sat down at the small table. *The Book of Judgment* sat in the center of the table. Reza could feel the spell of protection he'd wrapped around it, strong and reassuring. Swinging his feet up onto the other chair, Reza hooked himself into the protection spell and slowly traced the lines of the spell, searching for weak spots. He added a few layers of obfuscation, then broke away.

If for any reason the book fell into the wrong hands, it would take a strong, smart mage to crack the protection spell, and even then it would take weeks. Reza stifled a sigh, running his hands through his hair. What on earth was he going to do for the rest of the day? He'd almost prefer an afternoon of Edmé's taciturn company over the boredom that loomed before him.

When was the last time he'd had nothing to do? Reza couldn't remember. Even on his infrequent days off he often ended up in his office or on some errand or another to support his research. Before that had been school and all the assignments and coursework that involved. Probably his last true day of having nothing to do had been before he'd come to the city, Reza decided, making a face as he thought about those days. He'd been lucky, Reza would acknowledge that. The second son of a bookkeeper, he'd had nothing but accounting in his future until a priest travelling to the city had noticed Reza's latent power.

Magic had always interested him more than bookkeeping, and Reza was plenty happy with it. Most of the time, when he wasn't discovering ancient books that held spells that could wreak untold havoc across the country. Frowning at *The Book of Judgment*, Reza squashed the urge to drop the protections and give the contents of the book a quick glance.

The protections would stay until he reached Carimchi and they could be replaced with the protection of the Goddess's tomb. Reza didn't need to know what the book actually held; the glimpse he'd gotten of the first few pages had been more than enough to know that the book held nothing good. He didn't need to know more than that.

Standing, Reza paced back and forth across the room, wishing he'd thought to ask Edmé for *something* to do before he left. He didn't like that idea, though. The idea of asking Edmé for anything grated. Reza was well aware that it was a childish reaction, but something about the way Edmé looked at him—as though he thought Reza was incapable of any practical tasks—made Reza want to prove he could handle himself.

Reza scowled, agitated and wishing they could *leave* already. Unfortunately, it had only been maybe an hour since Edmé had left. That left far too many hours before nightfall, when Edmé had said they *would* leave. Reza wasn't particularly looking forward to the travel, but anything was better than having nothing to do. He was passingly familiar with riding, but not so much so that a months-long trip was going to be fun.

Hopefully he'd be able to keep up with Edmé and the other two mercenaries who were accompanying them on the trip. With luck, those two would be friendlier and this trip wouldn't be a complete disaster. Reza highly doubted it, however; friendly and Edmé didn't seem to know each other's names, let alone work together, and Reza didn't think anything would go right on this trip.

Returning to the table, Reza took a seat and propped his feet up again. He could be patient. It wasn't as though he had another choice. He wasn't going to leave the room. Edmé would come back eventually, and Reza might get tired and bored enough later in the day to actually sleep.

The morning dragged on slowly, and Reza spent far too much time wandering the room, exploring every nook and cranny. He managed to fall asleep late in the afternoon, waking from a fitful sleep when someone knocked on the door. Reza barely had the chance to sit up when the door opened. He struggled free of the blanket that had tangled around him and stared sleepily at Edmé.

"We'll leave in about an hour," Edmé said, his rough voice pouring over Reza pleasantly. Reza blinked at the tray Edmé held, trying to shake the fog of sleep.

Edmé didn't wait for a reply as he crossed the room towards the table. He set the tray on the table, reaching out to move the book out of the way. Reza opened his mouth to warn him, but too late—Edmé jerked back as the protection spell zapped him. It was a nasty shock, and Reza winced, impressed that Edmé hadn't lost his grip on the tray. "Sorry," Reza said, shoving a hand through his hair and crossing the room. He picked up the book and slid it out of the way. "It's spelled so only I can touch it."

"Good," Edmé said, though he didn't sound particularly thrilled about it. "Eat."

Edmé turned and left then, and Reza rolled his eyes at Edmé's departing back. Sitting down, Reza glanced out the window, unsurprised to see the sun was setting. Reza wasn't particularly hungry, but he started eating anyway. He doubted Edmé would let them stop in a few hours when Reza did get hungry.

He'd gotten halfway through the soup when Edmé entered the room again, this time without knocking. He carried a cloak and a pack, both very different from the ones Reza had left the university with that morning. He tossed them on the bed, then turned and left again, and Reza took that to mean they were for him. Finishing the soup, Reza wrapped the bread in a handkerchief for later.

He drank half the cup of ale, then stood to pack his belongings again. The book went in first, followed by the clothing Reza had brought. The university was shipping a chest behind him; it should arrive a week or so after Reza. Maybe before, Reza realized. Edmé had said they were taking an alternate route, which meant it wasn't the standard, quickest route to Carimchi. Hopefully it wouldn't take much longer; Reza had already been dreading a six week trip.

Reza finished packing and set the bag on the bed next to the cloak. It was poorer quality than Reza's had been, but seemed sturdy enough. Reza gave the room a last look-over and then settled on the bed to wait Edmé's return, anxious to be underway now that the waiting was nearly over.

Edmé showed up what seemed like ages later, but was probably closer to twenty minutes. He was wearing a cloak now, though it did little to obscure the sword around his waist. He held another sword, complete with belt, and Reza stared at him, confused. "This is for you," Edmé said, which didn't help explain anything.

"I can't use a sword," Reza said, refusing to feel inadequate for that. "I don't want it."

"You won't be using it," Edmé said impatiently, entering the room. "It's camouflage."

"Camouflage?" Reza repeated, confused. "For what?"

"You," Edmé said, crossing the room. "Do you know how to put it on?"

"No," Reza snapped, scowling at Edmé. "Why do I need camouflage?"

"If you're the only rider without a sword, it will be readily apparent you're the one we're protecting," Edmé said, pulling the sword belt apart with a few quick motions. He stepped in close, and Reza's mind stopped working for a moment, scrambled as Edmé leaned close and fastened the sword around his waist. Reza tried not to notice the way Edmé smelled almost sweet, with a hint of something sharper that Reza couldn't put his finger on.

"Anyone watching will notice I don't know how to even walk with this," Reza said when Edmé stepped away. The sword belt felt heavy and awkward around his waist, and Reza fidgeted with it, restlessly trying to settle it around his hips in a way that didn't feel odd.

"You'll get used to it," Edmé said, his dark eyes staring at Reza critically. They were brown, Reza noted, then scowled because he didn't care.

"I doubt it," Reza muttered, carefully setting a hand on the hilt. It was rough and felt heavy in his hand.

"Don't draw it. You'd probably stab yourself." Edmé looked as though he thought Reza would somehow manage that without drawing it.

"I'm not that stupid," Reza muttered, turning and barely avoiding knocking Edmé in the shins with the sword. He bit back the question of whether it was really necessary, but it was better to be annoyed and safer than less annoyed and easy to pick off. The protection spell on the book would die when he did; of course he was a target.

"I've known many would-be swordsmen who have lost a hand or foot with that attitude," Edmé said.

Reza grabbed his pack and turned back towards Edmé, angry that Edmé honestly seemed to think him stupid. Reza wasn't stupid—naïve on occasion, yes, but he'd long grown out of the worst of that. "I'm not stupid enough to draw it, but thanks for the concern. Are we leaving now?"

Edmé stared at him a moment before apparently accepting that. He didn't apologize, just turned and headed for the door, and Reza barely kept himself from chucking his bag at Edmé's back. It was going to be a long few months, he felt. Edmé led the way down the hallway to a narrow, poorly lit staircase on the opposite side of the inn from the one they'd climbed earlier that morning.

They somehow managed to make it down without killing themselves or seeing anyone. The staircase ended next to a door that led outside, into the stable yard. There were four horses waiting, accompanied by two men who had to be the two others who would fill out their party.

"Can I touch your bag?" Edmé asked quietly, shutting the door to the inn behind him.

Reza didn't comprehend for a moment before he remembered that the book had shocked Edmé not that long ago. "Yes. Only the book itself has that protection."

Edmé nodded, holding out his hand. Reza obediently handed the bag over, somewhat uneasy it was out of his grip. The book was his, not Edmé's. Shaking that thought away, Reza adjusted the sword around his waist and followed Edmé across the yard to where the horses waited.

"Jacques," Edmé said, pointed to the tall, broad-shouldered man to the left and then gestured to the other tall, broad-shouldered man to the right. "Serge."

"Nice to meet you," Reza said dryly, observing that it wouldn't be very difficult to pick him out amongst the mercenaries at all. He was a good half a head shorter than all of them and much less stocky to boot. He didn't bother to mention that, however; Edmé wasn't likely to want to discuss that at the moment. Jacques grunted in acknowledgement and Serge nodded. Reza stifled a sigh, hoping that wasn't going to be the extent of communication for the next few months.

Edmé moved to one of the center horses and attached the bag behind the saddle. Reza waited, eyeing the horse reluctantly. It was huge, but that wasn't really saying much. All horses were huge. It seemed bigger than most, however, and Reza wondered if he could really manage riding it.

"Your horse is over here," Jacques spoke up, directing Reza to a slightly smaller beast. His accent was strange, with a dark, rough sound to his words that Reza couldn't place. Reza stared at the horse a moment before reluctantly conceding defeat and mounting.

Edmé only wanted to keep the book safer. As Reza had noted, it would be easy enough to pick him out amongst them. If the people after the book managed to separate Reza from the mercenaries, they'd be no closer to having the book. He didn't want the book near him, Reza reassured himself, settling himself in the saddle. The sword was an uncomfortable weight at his hip, hanging oddly, and Reza really hoped he could talk Edmé out of that when they stopped.

Edmé gestured for Serge to lead the way out of the stable yard and sent Reza after him. Reza awkwardly urged his horse after Serge, refusing to contemplate how tired and sore he was going to be by the time they stopped.

~~*

The forest was quiet, but it was a peaceful quiet, not the too-quiet stillness that heralded more ominous tidings. Edmé watched the treeline nonetheless, in no hurry to be ambushed because he let his guard down. With the exception of a few storms that had drenched them, they'd travelled uneventfully for the last three days.

Serge and Jacques had borne the bad weather without complaint, but while Reza hadn't technically complained, he'd grown increasingly ill-tempered with every downpour. Part of that, Edmé conceded, was likely the riding as well. Reza was obviously inexperienced at it, and doubly so when it came to making long journeys. Still, while he was quick to scowl and stomp and swear, he hadn't yet demanded that they go slower or stop for longer periods of time.

Edmé wasn't going to slow their pace, not even if it made Reza more pleasant to travel with. They were stopping only long enough to rest the horses and when fatigue dulled their senses to dangerous levels. The heavy rain wasn't helping their progress, however; the horses couldn't travel as quickly on the muddy, sodden paths, but Edmé wasn't going to force them to do so, since he didn't want to deal with the delay of a crippled horse.

As if on cue, his horse stumbled, slipping in the muck beneath its hooves. Edmé slowed the horse's pace, twisting in the saddle to check the others had followed his lead. Jacques rode behind Edmé, close to Reza, with Serge following at the rear. Reza had thrown the hood of his cloak back and was scowling at everything, his face pinched in annoyance. His hair was sopping wet, and Edmé did feel a little bad that the cloak he'd procured for Reza was obviously not doing the trick against the inclement weather.

Satisfied that all was as it should be, Edmé righted his direction and surveyed the path ahead of them. It was more mud than dirt, which was the only reason Edmé noticed the tracks. Hoof prints, recent ones, sunk into the very edge of the path, both facing the woods and not, as though someone had ridden out of the forest and then changed their mind and returned to it.

Edmé could see no hint of the men in the woods, but that meant nothing. His horse stumbled slightly again, and Edmé used the movement to mask giving the *be alert, possible danger* signal. He could be reading too much into it, but he doubted it. Careless of them to leave such obvious tracks, and Edmé brought his horse to a stop, wondering if that was a trap. Certainly if their attention was on the eastern part of the woods, they wouldn't be paying attention to the western side.

"The path is getting worse," Edmé announced loudly, giving any listeners a good reason for them to stop. Heading back the way they'd come would incite an attack, but pressing forward would as well. Edmé had led them too close to where the men would be hiding.

Edmé loosened his sword in its sheath casually, disguising the movement by leaning forward to study the mud below. He was about to give the order to move forward, slowly, when arrows began flying from the trees. He drew his sword, his magical energy pulsing through the runes inscribed on its blade. He threw up a barrier to block the arrows—but too late, as an arrow buried itself in his horse's chest. The horse bucked, then collapsed, and Edmé barely had time to kick his feet free of the stirrups as it screamed and fell.

Freeing himself from the saddle, Edmé cast a quick glance behind him. Jacques was staying close to Reza, Edmé noted with approval. He paused long enough to slice Reza's bag free from his horse's corpse, as half a dozen riders poured from the trees. Edmé looped his hand through the strap of Reza's bag, grimacing at the unwieldy weight of it. That would be a hindrance, but he couldn't leave the book lying about for anyone to grab.

The riders were almost upon them and Edmé set his stance, feet sinking into the mud. On foot versus riders didn't give him great odds, but he could handle it. His sword thrummed with power, anticipating the fight.

A wash of magic brushed past him, making the hair stand up on the back of his neck, but it slid by without more than a brief caress, and Edmé belatedly recognized Reza's magical signature. The spell wasn't so kind to the riders bearing down on them. It hit them like a wall, stopping the horses in their tracks. The horses panicked, and four of the six riders were knocked off their horses. Another of the horses wheeled and took off into the woods, and the last rider barely kept his seat and control of his horse.

The men wore dark, unmarked leathers, Edmé noted as they stumbled to their feet. Mercenaries, like himself, and experienced enough not to give up at the display of magic. Did they have a mage with them? Edmé scanned the group as they pressed forward, three heading for him—including the rider—and the other two moving to contend with Jacques, Serge, and Reza.

They had powerful, spell blocking amulets, Edmé realized when one of the men got close enough. He was a bear of a man and wielded a large ax. A bright gold amulet was pinned to his leather chest plate. Such amulets, meant to keep most magics from affecting the wearer, were expensive. It made Edmé wonder what Reza's spell would have done had they not been wearing them.

Edmé didn't get the chance to wonder further as the large man reached him and all of his focus was redirected to the fight. The large man relied far too much on his reach and strength—he was all offense and no defense—and it was an easy thing for Edmé to slip under his guard and bury his sword in the man's side. The magic in his blade overrode the amulet easily, poisoning the man's heart and consigning him to death.

The other two were smarter, warier, working together to try and get to him. The mud hindered them all, and keeping Reza's bag close wasn't doing Edmé any favors. The two mercenaries bore swords. They wielded long, thin blades with experience. Edmé parried a strike from the rider, quickly turning to drive off the mercenary on the ground. Blade work alone wouldn't win him this fight—he was outmatched by a rider alone, never mind the accomplice on the ground.

As though on cue, a hot, sharp flare of magic slapped Edmé in the face—Reza again. It startled the two mercenaries, as well, and Edmé recovered quickly, taking the advantage to drive his sword into the unhorsed mercenary's side. The mercenary managed to get his blade around enough to mark Edmé's arm, where the armor jointed, but it was a small wound and in the next moment he was dead, the magic in Edmé's sword stopping his heart.

Edmé pulled his sword free, redoubled his grip on Reza's bag, and turned to face the rider. The man didn't wait for him to attack, however, turning his horse and forcing it to gallop down the road. Thankfully, he was heading back the way Edmé and his group had come, so he, at least, wouldn't be coordinating another ambush ahead of them.

Keeping his sword at the ready, Edmé turned around. The two mercenaries who had gone after Reza were down, dead or unconscious, and Reza seemed fine. None of the horses were around—Reza, Jacques, and Serge were all on the ground. Unfortunately, Jacques and Serge did not appear to have weathered the attack as well as Reza had.

Edmé jogged over to them quickly, his feet slipping and sliding in the mud. Serge was lying face down on the path, still in the unmoving, stiff way of all dead people. Jacques was sitting up, sword resting beside him. Reza was pressing a wadded bunch of cloth to his leg, above the knee. They were both covered in mud, though Reza wore more of it.

"Serge was working with them, boss," Jacques said as Edmé approached. Edmé scowled; he'd thought Serge more dependable than that. He'd been with the group nearly a year and had always been trustworthy, if a little reticent. Edmé preferred reticent—it was much better than dealing with endless questions.

"How bad?" Edmé asked, glancing around. The horses were scattered; only Reza's had lingered. It waited nearby, at the trees to the west.

"Broken, definitely," Jacques said, grimacing. Edmé glanced at Reza, who glared up at him.

"I don't know healing magic," Reza said, angry and somewhat defensive.

"No, you know combat magic," Edmé replied, and that was interesting, but it could wait for the moment. "Are you injured?"

Reza shook his head shortly, his gaze dropping to the bag Edmé still held. Some of the tension left his face, and Edmé set the bag down next to Jacques, moving to collect the things he'd need for a splint.

He'd have to send Jacques back—there was a small village a day behind them and not another for a week ahead of them. He and Reza would push on, and that left only him to guard both Reza and the book. Edmé didn't like those odds, even if Reza had proved to be less useless than Edmé had initially calculated.

How had Reza become so proficient at practical magics? From what little Edmé knew of the universities, they tended to focus on more esoteric studies, rarely doing more than theorizing and writing papers on magic. Granted, his knowledge of the universities was limited, so perhaps it was common practice for the professors to cast such spells regularly? That would certainly explain why Charbonneau hadn't mentioned Reza's practical skills. He may also have assumed that Reza would tell Edmé himself.

It was a good thing Reza hadn't mentioned it, and anger burned through him as he was once more reminded of Serge's betrayal. Serge had earned his just desserts, at least, sparing Edmé from the task of dealing with him.

Returning to Jacques' side with the supplies he'd gathered, Edmé knelt in the mud of the path. Reza shuffled slightly away, giving Edmé more of an opening without letting up the pressure against Jacques' leg. "See if you can't track down some of the horses."

Reza looked doubtful, but he nodded, leaving the wadded cloth resting on top of Jacques' leg. Edmé set to getting Jacques' leg taken care of, already running through different plans to get Reza and the book to Carimchi with a minimum of danger.

"Sorry, boss," Jacques said as Edmé wrapped a length of cloth around Jacques' leg and the sticks he'd scrounged for the makeshift splint. "I'd thought Serge was acting a bit funny, but you know how he gets his moods sometimes."

"It's fine," Edmé said. He hadn't noticed even that much, too preoccupied by Reza and the book. Edmé needed to get his head out of his ass, or this entire job would end in one big dead end. "I'm sorry you were injured."

Jacques cracked a wan smile at that. "Reza's doing. He spooked my horse real good with whatever spell he used to zap Serge. He was really annoyed about it. I think—" Jacques flinched when Edmé tied off a strip of cloth, pressing the sticks firmly against Jacques' leg, "—he's not used to working with people."

Edmé grunted in agreement. Reza had certainly struck him as independent, if nothing else. Tying off the last strip of cloth, Edmé surveyed his handiwork, then looked around for Reza. Reza was nowhere in sight, and Edmé tensed, wondering how far Reza had gone. He picked up Reza's bag, intending to search Reza out. Jacques eyed the bag curiously, but he didn't ask about it.

Before Edmé could do more than stand, Reza stepped out of the trees. When he saw Edmé, he shouted, "How am I supposed to find horses? I don't have a spell for that!"

Edmé cracked a smile, amused despite the less than ideal situation. He waved Reza over while Jacques snickered. Reza trudged through the mud, brushing ineffectively at the front of his mud-caked shirt. He'd lost his cloak and sword, Edmé realized, making a note to at least find his cloak or steal one from the dead men before they left.

Reza had tied his horse to a tree, so that was one horse for sure. Hopefully, he could find two more, or else the journey forward was going to be even more troublesome.

"Stay here, keep an eye on Jacques," Edmé said, slinging the book over his shoulder. No sense leaving the book and Reza together, unguarded but for Reza's magics and an injured Jacques. Reza watched the movement closely, then abruptly sat down next to Jacques, heedless of the mud. He grumbled something under his breath, then stared at Jacques' broken leg broodingly. Edmé left him to it, sure Reza wouldn't be happy to know how amusing Edmé found him.

Tracking down two more horses took longer than Edmé liked, but at least he had found them. If they'd had to walk until the next town, it would have put them even further behind than the time it took to track the beasts down. When he returned to the path, he found that Reza had moved Jacques off the path, over to the shelter of the trees. It was raining again, a light sprinkle, and Edmé wished the weather would clear. Everything seemed to be against them—surely they'd earned some sort of luck?

Reza had changed, though there was still mud smeared across his forehead and his hair was darker than usual—whether from the rain or mud, Edmé couldn't tell. He'd also spread the belongings of the dead mercenaries across the ground next to Jacques, including their weapons.

"Pack up what you think we'll need," Edmé ordered while he tied the horses to a nearby, low-hanging tree branch. He checked over their tack carefully, making sure everything was as it should be, then moved to join Reza. Night was starting to fall, but that wasn't going to stop Edmé from pushing forward.

"Where is it?" Reza demanded when he approached.

Edmé stared uncomprehendingly before realizing Reza was talking about the book. He wordlessly pointed to the horses, wondering if Reza was being pulled in by the book's spell. Probably not, Edmé decided when Reza turned back to the detritus he'd scattered across the grass. Reza had been in possession of the book for long enough that it would have taken hold of him by now.

"Head back," Edmé said, moving to help Jacques to his feet. "Find a healer, get that leg set properly. Use whatever funds you need from the company account until you're healed."

Jacques gritted his teeth, his breath coming sharp and pained as he leaned heavily on Edmé. They crossed the ground to the nearest horse slowly, laboriously. "Be careful, boss." Edmé nodded, focusing on getting Jacques into the saddle. It took some doing, but Jacques managed to pull himself up side-saddle style, and then swing his leg over awkwardly.

"If you don't hear from me in the next four months, the company falls to you. You're in charge until I get back."

Jacques snorted. His face was too pale in the fading sunlight, and Edmé wished he could send someone as an escort with Jacques to ensure he made it to the village. "I'll see you in four months, then."

Edmé quirked a smile, even if Jacques' faith was optimistic. There were full saddlebags on the horse he'd given Jacques; that should see him set until he reached the village they'd left behind. Edmé untied the horse and Jacques took the reins, heading off without further delay.

"He'll be fine, right?" Reza asked, staring after Jacques' horse.

Edmé nodded his confirmation, giving the piles of belongings a quick sweep for anything Reza might have missed before dismissing them. "Mount up."

Reza wrinkled his nose, but headed over to his horse without voicing protest. A few moments later, they were on the road again, heading towards Carimchi as night fell.

~~*

Reza glared half-heartedly at Edmé, his annoyance increasing when Edmé dismounted without a hint of stiffness. It was bad enough that Edmé had made them ride through the night, but to add insult to injury and make it clear he was only stopping because Reza couldn't continue was uncalled for.

The horses were flagging, at least as much as Reza was, so he didn't feel too bad about needing to stop. Honestly, what did Edmé expect? Reza was a professor at a university. He studied and experimented with magic, and the most physical exercise he got was lugging books between his office and the main library.

If he had studied healing magics, even a little, he might have been able to bolster his energy, but healing had never interested him. He also had no books of magic with him; the weight was unnecessary and the monastery in Carimchi had its own vast library to draw from.

He did have access to one book of magic, Reza thought, his gaze sliding to the bag secured to Edmé's horse. There could be a useful spell in there ... Reza shook his head, frowning. Even if he were stupid enough to look in *The Book of Judgment*, there were no good spells in that book, only spells of destruction.

Reza didn't know that for sure, though. The dangerous spells were the lure, what everyone wanted and what everyone talked about. There could certainly be tamer, helpful spells in the book, and he would never know unless—

"Reza." Edmé's rough, gravelly voice scattered Reza's thoughts, and he realized belatedly that he was still mounted. Edmé had already tied his horse to a tree with a long lead so it could reach the small creek nearby. The creek ran alongside the small clearing Edmé had found for them a good distance from the beaten path.

"Are you going to leave the area?" Reza asked, feeling thick-witted. That was probably the exhaustion, he decided. "For firewood or anything?"

"No fire. Too risky," Edmé said. That didn't answer Reza's question, and Reza stared at Edmé, willing him to elaborate. Edmé returned the stare, his eyes shadowed by the length of his hair. It covered the mark on his forehead neatly, and the mark certainly explained why Edmé, so practical and focused in everything related to his job, put up with the longer hair.

"Great," Reza said, caving because he was tired and didn't want to stay on the horse all day. "So you'll be staying in the clearing?"

"Why?" Edmé asked.

He was being aggravating on purpose, Reza knew it. "I was going to cast a spell around us to shield our presence from ... whomever might come looking. Going out would break it."

"Shield against people and wildlife?"

"Both," Reza confirmed and made himself move finally. He nearly fell on his face, as stiff as he was, but he managed.

Edmé studied him, then nodded, taking the reins to Reza's horse. "Do it."

Reza bit back a retort, too tired to push back against Edmé's bossiness. He'd push Edmé in the creek or something later. That would make him feel better. Reza put his back to Edmé, taking a deep breath and focusing on the spell he was about to cast. He created the focus in the center of the clearing, then slowly built it up, expanding it out towards the edges of the clearing and up towards the tree tops.

Setting the spell, Reza spent a few moments tinkering with its strength and fine-tuning the *look past here* setting. When he was finished with that, he tested its stability with a few sharp pulses of energy. It held, and Reza unhooked from the spell slowly.

Edmé was still settling the horses, so Reza started getting the campsite set up. No fire meant cold dinner—or breakfast, Reza supposed, glancing towards the sun rising through the trees on the eastern edge of the clearing. Cold food was all to the good; it was quick and easy, which meant that Reza could pass out that much sooner.

Reza set out the bed rolls, then dug through one of the packs that his horse had carried to find something to eat. He found some travel bread that didn't seem too stale and a few apples. That would do well enough, and if Edmé had complaints, he could sort out his own meal.

It seemed like ages ago that they'd stayed in a town and slept in real beds, but it had really only been two days prior. Everything that had happened—the attack, the riding, having *killed* a man and injured another—made it seem much further in the past.

Resolutely, Reza pushed those thoughts away. He didn't want to remember the grim, resolved look on Serge's face when he'd faced them, sword drawn. He didn't want to remember the way Serge's face had changed when Reza had fired the spell to stop Serge's heart, a mixture of fear and relief. Reza's stomach turned, and he sat down heavily on one of the bed rolls. He wasn't thinking about it. Serge had meant to kill him. Reza had beaten him to it. End of story.

Edmé joined him, sitting down on the other bed roll. He'd removed his sword belt and had set it on the ground beside him, within easy reach. He didn't look any worse for the wear, minus some dirt and mud staining his trousers. Reza scowled, half-heartedly picking at the chunk of bread he'd taken for himself. Why couldn't Edmé be less than perfect at something?

"Tell me about your combat magic," Edmé said, picking up one of the apples Reza had pulled out.

"What about it?" Reza asked, startled. Had the High Chairman not told Edmé anything about that, either?

"What can you cast, what experience do you have," Edmé said, his face creasing in frustration. "I don't like the idea of the two of us travelling alone, but I need to know if we can do it."

"Can't you hire more men?" Reza asked, stalling for time. He wasn't sure he could quantify his magic, not in the way Edmé expected.

"If I can't trust men I've known for months, how can I trust men I've known for minutes?" Edmé asked, his voice rougher, deeper. Reza's stomach churned sourly, reminded once more of Serge.

It took Reza a moment to realize Edmé was staring at him expectantly, and Reza shrugged. "I don't know what to tell you."

"What were the spells you cast earlier?" Edmé asked, biting into the apple he held with a loud crunch. He was watching Reza intently, and Reza fought the urge to squirm. It was an odd feeling, knowing that he was the focus of all of Edmé's attention, and he wasn't sure he liked it.

"Spook spell, I guess you'd call it," Reza said. "Targeted to their horses, which is probably why it took you so long to find them."

"And the other?" Edmé asked, his gaze and voice never faltering.

"A killing spell," Reza said, hoping his voice didn't give anything away. He didn't want to seem weak, not in front of Edmé.

"Could you do it again?" Edmé took another, smaller bite of his apple, giving Reza a reprieve. Reza's anger flared at that; he didn't need coddling.

"Yes," Reza snapped, glaring at Edmé. If Edmé was at all moved by the expression, it didn't show, and Reza set down the chunk of bread he wasn't eating before he succumbed to the urge to chuck it at Edmé.

"What other spells do you know?"

"I don't know specific spells," Reza said, huffing out an annoyed breath. It was stupid to be frustrated that Edmé didn't know the particulars of Reza's studies. Most people didn't—even at the university, his experiments fell under the vague title of 'compound studies.' "It's what I'm studying: building spells on the fly. I guess I'll be getting a lot of practical work in."

"That's an unusual field of study," Edmé said, and if he was impressed, it didn't show. It *was* impressive, Reza knew it was. Spell casting was difficult enough when there was a strict set of instructions to follow. One wrong spell segment and the entire spell could collapse. Winging it, so to speak, increased the risk of that exponentially. "How did you come to study that topic?"

"The university was interested in it, and I had the experience," Reza said, shrugging one shoulder. He leaned back on his palms, staring up at the sky through the trees.

"Experience?" Edmé asked, finishing his apple and tossing the core towards where the horses were tied up.

"I did it a lot growing up," Reza explained, recalling the days he'd spent hiding in the fields from the village— especially his parents and their chores—making up spell after spell. "There wasn't anyone in my town to teach me magic, so I fumbled through it myself."

"No priests?" Edmé asked. Priests sometimes sponsored the cost of sending young mages to a larger city for training, with the expectation that they would serve the Church for a time afterwards to pay off the debt.

"No priest, just a monk who I don't think was officially affiliated." Reza paused, considering. "Was that how you joined the priesthood?"

Edmé went so suddenly, perfectly still that Reza was half-afraid that he was about to lose his head for that question. Reza tilted his head to meet Edmé's eyes, refusing to be cowed by the response to his simple question. It wasn't as though Edmé tried to hide it—that sword and its magics were practically flaunting it.

"Yes." The single word slammed the door in the face of more questions, as did the stony set to Edmé's face.

"Whatever," Reza muttered, giving up on trying to hold a conversation. What had he expected, really? Edmé had never tried to talk to him before. Everything he said or asked about was related to his job of getting Reza to Carimchi. He wasn't interested in anything more than that.

Picking up the apple and the bread he hadn't eaten, Reza shoved them into the pack he'd pulled them from, fully intending to go to sleep since talking was obviously a waste of time.

"It's not something I care to talk about," Edmé said, as though that excused being rude. "I assure you that I will see this job through, no matter what my past position may indicate."

"What?" Reza asked intelligently, before it clicked. The sword meant Edmé had been an angel. The sword was distinct, crafted with magic and deadly at the slightest touch of blade to skin. It had other uses, as well, if Reza recalled correctly, but he didn't know much about it. He also doubted Edmé would tell him, as closed-mouthed as he was.

The angels had been at the heart of a huge scandal nearly five years ago, when travesty after travesty at their hands had come to light. Stories of people—men, women, and children—tortured and killed for sport, gross robberies and bribes ... Reza had never heard a good thing about the fallen angels. The entire troupe had been disbanded, their magic stripped away, and the mark of the church inked into their foreheads. The worst offenders had been executed and all of them as a whole had been barred from serving the Church or Crown again.

So why did Edmé still have his sword? Maybe because he wasn't as terrible as the rest of the fallen angels? Edmé was watching him, silent and tense, and Reza realized he was staring like an idiot.

"You would have sold me out or left me already if you were going to," Reza said dismissively, rolling his eyes. Something in Edmé's expression eased, and Reza turned away, discomfited. "I'm going to sleep."

Edmé didn't reply to that, but Reza hadn't expected an answer. Pulling his cloak tightly around him, Reza stretched out on his bed roll. Despite the way his head was buzzing with thoughts, exhaustion quickly won out and he was asleep in seconds.

~~*

Everything was going smoothly and Edmé didn't trust it. It had been over a week since the attack that had halved their number. Edmé had them taking even more precautions—traveling during the night, taking an even more circuitous route, avoiding towns and villages. He'd expected more trouble. The decoy was found out, with Serge's betrayal, but so far they'd seen no further sign of pursuers or ambushers. Edmé was thankful for it, but he didn't trust it.

Reza wasn't happy with the pace, but his happiness wasn't a priority. His safety was. Edmé wasn't sure which was worse: dealing with spoiled, entitled brats who didn't listen to a single of his directions, or dealing with Reza, who never outright protested an order, but grumped and grumbled as he followed them.

Glancing in Reza's direction, Edmé was unsurprised to find Reza leveling a glare at the small cook pot resting next to the tiny campfire. Reza's skills did not lay with cooking—at least, not in cooking travel fare—but nothing he'd made so far had poisoned them.

Edmé furrowed his brow, watching as Reza's lips moved. He was muttering something to himself inaudibly, a habit he'd picked up a few days prior. Probably complaining again. In no mood to deal with it, Edmé stood and pulled off his cloak, leaving it in a heap where he'd been sitting. He picked up his sword and strapped it into place, securing the belt in place with long familiar motions.

Reza watched him, but returned to poking at the soup he was making without a word. Edmé left him to it, heading towards the river they were camping next to.

He'd wash up a bit, then see if the soup was finished. It was more work than they had been putting into their meals, but there were no other foodstuffs to fall back on.

They would have to stop for supplies soon, much to Edmé's displeasure. It had been part of the original plan, to stop every so often, but Edmé had also counted on having two more men to handle that. He and Reza were easily recognizable, but he couldn't leave Reza without protection and they couldn't survive on what they until Carimchi.

Not much he could do for it, Edmé thought dismissively. He'd handle it when it became an issue. Kneeling next to the river, Edmé grimaced at the water soaking the knees of his trousers and started washing his face. The cool water felt fantastic; if there was one thing Edmé missed when travelling, it was the luxury of bathing. Lingering at the river bank, Edmé watched the water flow until he couldn't justify dallying any longer.

When he turned back to the clearing, Reza was nowhere in sight. The pot was sitting, undisturbed, next to the fire, and there were no signs of anyone else having been there. Edmé would have heard them, in any case; the river wasn't so far away or so loud as to drown out sounds directly behind him. The hair on the back of Edmé's neck rose, and he heeded it, drawing his sword. He walked carefully over to the clearing, keeping close to the few trees that were between him and the open space.

Reza was still in the clearing, and to all appearances, alone. He was kneeling next to Edmé's horse, digging through the pack that had been strapped to the back of Edmé's horse—the pack that held *The Book of Judgment*.

He hadn't noticed Edmé, and Edmé waited, wanting to see what Reza was up to. There was nothing in that bag Reza could need as all of his belongings had been transferred to other bags the horses carried. If Reza was planning something with the book, as Edmé's instincts suggested, better to nip that in the bud.

Reza sat back, pulling the book into his lap. His movements were quick, hurried, as he pushed the pack out of his way. So the book wasn't properly warded after all. Edmé stepped forward, at the same time Reza glanced around. He hunched over the book, as though to hide it from Edmé's sight.

There would be no reasoning with Reza, not if the spell had taken hold, so Edmé didn't even try. Reza scrambled to his feet, clutching the book to his chest. His eyes were wide, his face pale, but he took off into the woods without any hesitation. He moved faster than Edmé would have credited him to be able to move, especially after how slowly he'd been moving after their last stretch of riding.

Edmé followed, feeling out the appropriate runes in his sword. He just had to get close enough and be precise enough not to kill Reza ... the barrier spell on the book crumbled, and Edmé stumbled as its malevolent magic washed over him. How much power did Reza have that he could suppress such magic and still have so much energy left over?

Too much, Edmé thought grimly, sprinting as Reza ducked behind a large oak. Edmé was right behind him and nearly slammed into the barrier spell Reza had erected. It was strong—stronger than Edmé's magic could break, but Reza would know that. He grinned at Edmé slyly, sitting down at the base of the tree and making himself comfortable.

The shield spell was tainted, Edmé noted. The book was exerting too much influence to keep from spilling into Reza's energy. Reza flipped open the book, and Edmé stepped up to the edge of the barrier.

"Not going to try to talk me out of it?" Reza asked, taunting him as he ran his hand down the front of the page he'd opened the book to, caressing the page lovingly.

"No point," Edmé said. He ignored the way Reza watched, curious but not alarmed, as Edmé lifted his sword and brought it down against the barrier. He pushed his magic through the purifying runes on the blade when it touched the barrier, and a flash of light exploded through the air from the point of contact.

Reza's spell shattered, the taint from the book weak under the power of Edmé's purification. Reza's eyes went wide, and he scrambled to move—but too slowly. Edmé averted his swing, bringing it around to score a line in Reza's arm. He cast the spell again, coursing the rest of his energy through Reza and hoping it was enough to break the book's influence.

The book fell from Reza's hands, tumbling unheeded to the ground. Edmé stepped back, holding his sword to the ready in case it hadn't worked—little good that it would do him in the face of Reza's magic. Reza lifted a hand to his arm, where blood was rapidly soaking the sleeve of his shirt. Edmé watched closely as Reza blinked, looking dazed. His gaze lifted to Edmé, his brow furrowing, before dropping to the book.

"Oh, god," Reza said, scrambling up and away. "What—" He didn't continue, and the malevolent energy abruptly disappeared as Reza slapped the spell shield back in place.

"Did you account for the book?" Edmé asked, lowering his sword.

"Account for it how?" Reza asked, none of his usual bite in the words. His eyes were still wide, his face too pale, and Edmé didn't like it. He didn't think the book still had its hold on Reza, but he didn't like Reza without his bite. "It's the same spell."

"The book has its own ... presence," Edmé said. How had Reza not known that? Why hadn't Edmé thought to double-check that he did? "It's part of why it's so dangerous. It taints the minds of anyone—any mage—and lures them into using the spells in it."

"Why now?" Reza asked. He crossed his arms, hunching his shoulders as though to ward off the book's influence.

"It takes prolonged exposure," Edmé said, but Reza was right. It shouldn't have taken so long to affect him, as strong as the book was. "How long did you have the book at the university?"

"A month or so." Reza's brow furrowed as he stared at the book.

"It should have affected you sooner." Edmé sheathed his sword, stepping close to rest a hand on Reza's shoulder in what he hoped was a reassuring manner. "What changed in your spell?"

Reza didn't answer, though he did lean into Edmé's touch. His expression shifted from worried to thoughtful, and Edmé waited. If Reza couldn't figure out the hole in the spell … Edmé wasn't sure what he could do.

The spell around the book flared to life, glowing brightly, as it had in Reza's office. Reza shook his head, muttering something about intersections as the light of the spell fluctuated. The light died out and a second later, something Reza did snapped the lingering tension from the air. Edmé hadn't noticed it was there until it was gone, and Reza relaxed under his shoulder, maybe feeling the difference and maybe just relieved he'd fixed it.

"Better?" Reza asked, turning to look at Edmé.

Dropping his hand from Reza's shoulder, Edmé drew his sword. Reza's eyes widened, but to his credit, he didn't move. Edmé offered the sword to Reza, holding it by the pommel so Reza could easily grasp the hilt. Reza took the sword slowly, cautiously, as though handling something incredibly fragile. Edmé couldn't feel anything from the book, but he hadn't before, not really. He approached the book slowly. It still lay spread open to a random page, face-down in the grass.

"I think so," Edmé said, kneeling close to the book. He didn't touch it, remembering all too well the shock it had given him the last time he'd touched it. Without the immediate presence of his sword, the book could easily target him, but there was no subtle whisper of magic, nothing to suggest the book was more than a book.

"You can touch it," Reza said. When Edmé looked up, he continued, "I had to remove that part of the spell. It was overriding another, more important piece. A small part. I hadn't noticed before I looked for it."

Edmé nodded, gingerly picking up the book by its spine. True to Reza's word, it didn't shock him, and Edmé let the book fall shut. Straightening, he walked back over to Reza, who handed back his sword, holding it out awkwardly.

Reza didn't say a word as Edmé led the way back to the campsite. Edmé tucked the book back into its pack, securing it in place behind the saddle once more. He paused briefly to find some clean rags in the bottom of his bag, kept for instances such as these where there was a minor injury to tend. Thankfully, the cut hadn't been too deep, and Reza barely seemed to notice it.

The fire had nearly burned itself out, and Reza was busying himself building it back up. He'd set the cook pot aside, out of the way, and he didn't look up when Edmé rejoined him. Edmé removed his sword belt, setting it down before taking a seat next to Reza. He waited patiently while Reza continued to fuss with the fire.

"Take off your jacket," Edmé said when Reza finished. Reza glanced at him, questioning without a word. Edmé held up the rags for Reza to see. "I need to bind your arm."

"Ah," Reza said, still too pale for Edmé's liking. Honestly, he knew better than to question a trip going well. Something always immediately went wrong, and he wasn't sure if it was fixed this time. Hopefully Reza's spell was fixed; Edmé doubted that Reza would make the same mistakes twice. Reza shrugged off his jacket, then simply tore the sleeve off his shirt. It was ragged and torn already, Edmé noted, so no great loss.

Reza held still as Edmé cleaned his arm, slowly and meticulously removing the blood that had stained Reza's skin. He managed to re-open the wound cleaning it, but it was a slow, sluggish bleed that would close up soon enough. He tied the scraps around the wound, securing them tightly, but not so tight they'd cut off blood to the rest of Reza's arm.

"I'm sorry," Reza said. Edmé knotted the last bandage in place and sat back.

"Don't be. I should have asked, not assumed." Edmé bore at least equal blame—he knew better than to make assumptions, especially where books of magic were concerned.

"Your sword blocks it?" Reza asked, a redirect if ever Edmé had heard it. Edmé went with it, in no way inclined to linger over the subject. "What was it you cast on me?"

"Purification spell," Edmé said, with only the briefest hesitation. He didn't like discussing the spells in the sword, but he'd make an exception for Reza. Certainly, he'd want to know the spell if it had been cast on him. "It strips all alien magics from the target. It shouldn't have any lingering effects."

"Do you deal with books like this a lot?" Reza asked. He stared at Edmé, some of the spark coming back to his eyes. His expression dared Edmé not to answer that, and Edmé almost didn't out of reflex.

"It's what I did," Edmé said. "When I was with the Church."

"Anything as dangerous as *The Book of Judgment*?" Reza asked, leaning over to grab his bag. He riffled through it briefly, coming up with a bowl.

"Sometimes," Edmé said, though that wasn't true. He'd come close, but *The Book of Judgment* was the single most dangerous book on the Church's registry. If they could destroy it, Edmé had no doubt they would. "It's one of the reasons I was hired for this job."

Reza nodded, and Edmé didn't doubt no one had told him that. There seemed to be some major communication gaps going on and part of that was his fault. He'd made too many assumptions at the beginning of the job, and that was coming back to hurt them. Between Serge and the improper seal on the book, Edmé was beginning to wonder if they would make it Carimchi. He doubted they'd seen the last of their attackers, either.

"Is the lure of the book why you keep it away from me?" Reza asked, dishing out the soup into the bowl he'd pulled out. He dropped a wooden spoon into the bowl and passed it to Edmé, then dropped a second spoon directly into the pot.

"No," Edmé said, debating whether to inform Reza of the rest of it. It was probably better he knew, however, especially considering the mess the job had become. "The spells in the book require a strong mage. The stronger, the better. You're one of the strongest—there are few in your caliber, from what High Chairman Charbonneau told me."

"You think they'll try to get me, too," Reza said. "I wouldn't cast—no, all they'd have to do is break the seal."

Edmé nodded. "If it looks like the book is captured, get as far away as you can. If we're closer to Carimchi, go there, otherwise head back to the University."

"It would help if I knew where we were," Reza pointed out, scowling at the trees. "Telling me won't help, so don't bother. I'll lose track when we move later."

"Hopefully it won't come to that," Edmé said, digging into the soup. It was done enough that none of the dried ingredients were crunchy, but it was as bland and tasteless as he'd imagined it would be. He didn't have a contingency plan for if he and Reza were separated. More than likely, he'd be dead and Reza would be captured. He doubted Reza could hide his tracks and he'd all but admitted he'd get hopelessly lost without a guide.

Reza finished eating quickly, collecting their dishes for a quick rinse in the river. Edmé watched him, wishing he was better at conversation. Reza didn't seem settled from the run-in with the book's power, for which Edmé didn't blame him, but he didn't know what he could say to make it better.

Edmé buried the fire, annoyed with himself. It was a job and jobs didn't require small talk. He shouldn't care that Reza was upset, unless it was going to affect the job. He couldn't even convince himself of that; he didn't doubt that Reza would continue to do what Edmé told him with no argument. He might even grumble less.

Moving his sword so it was within easy reach of his bedroll, Edmé stretched out. He listened as Reza returned, setting the dishes down before settling on the other bedroll. Reza set up the protection spell again, the magic washing mute and dull over Edmé—a side effect of using so much of his magic—and then settled down to sleep without a word. Edmé shut his eyes and made himself sleep before he could say anything he'd regret.

~~*

Reza stared broodingly at the wall of the tiny inn room. He was exhausted, but far too keyed up to sleep. Edmé was gone, ferreting out fresh horses and more supplies. He'd completely rejected the idea of Reza's coming with him on the grounds they'd be more easily noticed together—as though he was somehow less noticeable on his own.

He'd left the book with Reza, and Reza should have been happy that Edmé still trusted him after his massive screw up of the protection spell. Instead, he was unhappy the book was close and that he was responsible for it. At least the spell seemed to be working properly this time around. Reza hadn't thought even once that he should go anywhere near the book.

Get some rest, Edmé had said and Reza wanted to throttle him. He'd been less brusque and more conciliatory ever since the book had gotten to Reza. Reza hated it. He wasn't made of glass; he didn't need to be coddled. Scowling, Reza levered himself off the bed.

The inn room wasn't much, for all it had cost Edmé an arm and a leg. It was barely wide enough to fit the bed and slightly longer in depth. The room was at the end of the building, underneath the slope of the roof, and the bed—a thin pallet on a rickety wooden frame—was the only bit of furniture in the room. It didn't even have its own fireplace, and the only light streamed through the small, curtainless window above the bed.

Despite all that, it was the most secure room that Edmé had found. They hadn't had a choice about stopping—the horses were worn out and they were nearly out of food for themselves and the beasts. Edmé had rented the room for three nights, an attempt at misdirection, as he'd told Reza to be ready to leave after two nights.

That was certainly long enough to get their clothes laundered, Reza decided. For the price they were paying for the room, the innkeeper *would* take care of that. Reza kneeled down next to the packs stacked haphazardly against the wall. Edmé hadn't said to stay in the room, after all, even if it had been implied in his order to get some rest.

Reza would pick a fight with the stingy innkeeper, then try to sleep again. For some reason, he doubted he'd sleep well sharing the narrow bed with Edmé, even if it was a bed and therefore ten times better than sleeping outside. With his luck, Edmé would be a kicker or something. Reza's stomach did a funny flip, which he disregarded.

They might not end up sharing at all, Reza thought, yanking clothing from the packs—studiously ignoring the pack with *The Book of Judgment* in it. One of them could certainly sleep on the floor, though that seemed unfair after all the uncomfortable travel they'd done thus far. Why was he even worrying about it? Sharing or not, it wouldn't be anything more than another inconvenience.

Freeing the last of the dirty clothes from Edmé's pack, Reza gathered the pile in his cloak and stood. Reza left the room, sealing the door with a strong barrier spell, then headed downstairs. He'd pick a fight and distract himself from the stupid thoughts in his head. Hopefully then he'd be able to focus on sleeping.

~~*

Reza woke to a loud knock. His heart jumped into his throat and he all but fell on his face clambering out of bed. The tiny window above the bed showed that Reza had managed to sleep through the afternoon. The knock sounded again, louder and more impatient. There was something funny about the noise, but Reza wasn't awake enough to figure it out.

Stumbling over to the door, Reza yanked it open, belatedly recalling to the fact that he'd never dropped the sealing spell when he found Edmé standing on the other side of the door. Reza blinked at him, wondering fuzzily how Edmé had knocked when his hands were full—one was occupied holding a large sack and the other held a tray bearing food.

"Write me in, don't drop it," Edmé said when Reza reached out to dismantle the spell.

Reza nodded; that made more sense. He stepped out of the room, then hesitated. Writing Edmé into the spell required hooking his energy to the spell, which required him to either touch the spell or to touch Reza. Edmé's hands were full, so Reza instead reached out and wrapped his hand around Edmé's wrist, where the sleeve of his shirt had fallen back to reveal bare skin. If Edmé was surprised by the touch, he didn't show it, standing patiently.

Edmé's skin was cool to the touch, smooth under Reza's hand, and Reza's traitorous mind wondered if all of Edmé's skin felt the same. Reza flushed; he wasn't awake enough to deal with his wandering thoughts. Reaching out to the spell, Reza hooked in and carefully wrote Edmé's energy into the barrier so he could pass. Reza triple-checked everything, even though it was a relatively simple change.

When he was finished, Reza dropped his hand quickly, stepping back into the room. Edmé followed, kicking the door shut behind him. He'd kicked the door, Reza realized. Someone in the neighboring room thumped on the wall, but Edmé paid it no mind as he set the sack down.

"Sorry to lock you out," Reza said, crossing the room and sitting down on the edge of the bed.

"You protected the book," Edmé said, setting the tray on the bed next to Reza. It held two bowls that were still steaming, a pair of wooden cups with somewhat murky contents, and a small loaf of bread. The bowls held some sort of stew-like concoction made primarily with vegetables.

Reza picked up the closer bowl and settled it in his lap, suddenly ravenous. He tore the bread in half, leaving one end on the tray and beginning to eat. As Reza watched, Edmé removed his cloak, dropping it on the floor next to the sack. He removed his sword belt next, though he brought that over to the bed and popped it against the foot before joining Reza on the bed.

"The innkeeper is getting our clothes laundered. He said they'd be delivered late tomorrow morning," Reza said between bites of stew. For all its unappealing appearance, it still far outstripped anything Reza had eaten lately.

Edmé looked briefly surprised at that, but he only nodded before digging into his own meal. Reza finished his dinner first and sat quietly as Edmé ate. Edmé didn't take long, eating as though it had been years since his last proper meal. It had been weeks, Reza conceded, not looking forward to eating his own cooking again.

"I have a few more things to get in the morning," Edmé said, setting the tray with the empty dishes on the floor. "We'll leave in the afternoon."

Reza nodded. He should have expected that. "I take it I'll be staying here again?"

Edmé nodded. "Don't leave the room without me."

Reza bit back a retort. After all, he had proven himself useless with spell casting. It was little wonder Edmé didn't trust him to protect himself after Reza's spell on the book had failed. Edmé was watching him, his face impossible to read in the fading light from the window.

Reza stood, unable to take the scrutiny. He stacked his bowl on top of Edmé's, picked up the tray, and headed for the door. Setting the tray outside, Reza shut the door again and turned back to the bed. The innkeeper had been too cheap to provide candles or a lantern, Reza noted belatedly. If he'd noticed earlier, he would have badgered those out of the man when he'd gone to badger him about laundry.

He called up a quick lighting spell, not in the mood to skulk around in the semi-dark with Edmé staring at him. Edmé was still watching him, his expression impossible to read as always. Reza was vividly reminded of the day he'd met Edmé in the High Chairman's office, how he'd thought Edmé had been weighing his worth. Edmé's stare was different now, though Reza couldn't say how. Edmé opened his mouth, then shook his head and looked away.

"What?" Reza demanded, in no mood to be coddled. If Edmé no longer thought he was worth anything magically, let him say it instead of mincing about the issue.

"I'm afraid our presence in town may have been noted," Edmé said after a pause long enough that Reza almost threw a small spell at him to shock him into talking. "I'm trying to minimize the risk to us, not ..." Edmé paused, and Reza was startled to realize that Edmé was, if not nervous, at least not as confident as he usually was when he spoke. "... I believe you can protect yourself—"

Reza snorted. Was Edmé actually trying to reassure him? "Oh, yes. Why wouldn't you after the complete mess I've made of things so far?" Reza couldn't help but glance in the direction of the book, shivering as he remembered the weird right-wrong feeling of the book exerting its influence on his mind.

"Everyone makes mistakes," Edmé said, sounding awkward and stilted. Surely he didn't expect Reza to believe him when he didn't sound as though he believed himself.

"Like you'd know anything about making mistakes," Reza said. The words were out of his mouth before he could think through how terrible that sounded, and Reza flushed.

Edmé stilled, all expression disappearing from his face. Reza shifted uneasily, biting his tongue on saying anything more. Edmé stood, every movement slow and deliberate, but Reza refused to back down, staring at Edmé as he approached. Edmé stopped in front of him, close enough that Reza found breathing to be difficult. Distracted as he was by Edmé's proximity, he was too slow to get away when Edmé reached out and grabbed his chin.

"People make mistakes," Edmé said, his voice rough. He reached up with his free hand, his grip tightening briefly on Reza's chin as he swept the hair away from his forehead and revealed the mark on his forehead. It was inked in, the black stark against the paleness of Edmé's forehead. It was the perfect replica of the goddess's symbol—four overlapping diamonds surrounded by branches from the alimio tree—except completely inverted. "You can define yourself by your mistakes or learn from them and define yourself by the whole of your actions."

Edmé dropped his hands, and Reza swallowed, still feeling the touch of Edmé's fingers against his jaw. "I could have unleashed the spells in *The Book of Judgment*. That's a big mistake."

"It *was* a small mistake with potentially large consequences." Edmé frowned at him, frustration evident in his face. "Consequences that didn't come to pass."

"Barely. Only because of you," Reza said. Unable to hold still under Edmé's gaze, Reza paced away, putting space between them.

"There's no shame in relying on other people," Edmé said quietly. Reza only shrugged in response to that. How was he supposed to say he didn't know how to? He'd never had to before, and he was supposed to be the top of his field, not prone to mistakes a first year university student would make.

Reza jerked, startled when Edmé laid a hand on his shoulder. He hadn't heard Edmé approach. Reza's foot caught on an upraised board in the floor when he turned, and he nearly tumbled, catching his balance at the last second but getting far too close to Edmé in the process. Edmé steadied him, his brow furrowed in concern and Reza couldn't take it. He didn't need Edmé's sympathy or concern.

"Can we stop discussing this now?" Reza asked, swallowing hard when Edmé's hands slid away. He still felt unsteady, and he needed to focus on the discussion at hand, not on thoughts of what Edmé would do if Reza kissed him. Edmé stared at him as though trying to read every thought in Reza's head. Reza stared back, stubbornly lifting his chin in challenge.

"So long as you know I don't ask you to stay here because I doubt your ability to handle yourself."

"Yes, fine, whatever," Reza grumbled. That response was somehow the correct one, despite the flippancy with which Reza said it, as Edmé smiled and stepped away.

Rolling his eyes, Reza sat down heavily on the edge of the bed. He was tired again, though he doubted he'd feel rested until they reached Carimchi and he was able to spend a week in a real bed. Edmé crossed the room to the packs, and Reza frowned, watching as Edmé pulled out the bed rolls. He stacked them together, and Reza shoved away a feeling of disappointment. He'd sleep better not sharing a bed with Edmé, after all.

"You should take the bed," Reza said, standing as Edmé rolled out the first one. "I had it all afternoon, and I'll have it tomorrow while you're out."

Edmé looked up, and he was going to protest. Reza could tell, even if Edmé was still figuring out what he was going to protest over.

"You're taking it," Reza said, narrowing his eyes because it was stupid for Edmé to not sleep well. "I'll sleep on the floor tonight whether you do or not. Better to use the bed yourself than let it go to waste, yes?"

Edmé smiled again, and Reza barely kept himself from returning it. He was being stern, otherwise Edmé wouldn't cave.

"All right," Edmé accepted, rolling out the second bedroll on top of the first. "You'll take the covers from the bed, however."

Reza narrowed his eyes, debating the merits of debating the matter. His cloak was with the rest of their clothing, however, so he only nodded, turning and pulling the worn blanket from the bed. He crossed the room and settled onto the bed rolls—which were much more comfortable two deep, on a solid, mostly smooth surface—and waited until he heard Edmé settle in before dousing the magical light.

~~*

Edmé threw himself off his horse, hitting the ground with a jarring thump. He didn't pause, sprinting across the path to where Reza was sprawled in the grass after being thrown from his own horse. The latest attack had been weak—only three men, and no magic in any of them—but that would mean nothing if the fall from his horse had killed Reza.

He'd almost reached Reza when Reza finally moved, and Edmé felt like he could breathe again. Reza groaned, sitting up slowly and pressing a hand to the back of his head, presumably where he'd bumped it when he'd fallen.

"Are you all right?" Edmé asked, dropping down in the grass next to Reza. Nothing seemed too out of sorts and Edmé hoped Reza was only dazed.

"I think so. Maybe." Reza frowned, wrinkling his nose. He dropped his hand to his lap, blinking at Edmé.

Edmé wanted badly to linger, to give Reza time to collect himself, but they didn't have the luxury of time. The attacks were coming more quickly the closer they got to Carimchi; there were fewer ways that Edmé could take them to get to the city. They had almost a week of travel left, and staying where they were would leave them sitting ducks. "Can you ride?" Edmé asked, standing and offering a hand to Reza.

"Tie me to the saddle," Reza said, accepting his hand. He made a face. "At least then I'd stay on that damn beast."

Reza was fine, Edmé decided, smiling faintly at the familiar grousing tone. Reza started to stand, but tumbled back to the ground with a pained cry when he put his weight on his left ankle. The color had fled Reza's face, and Edmé winced. "Did you catch it in the stirrup?" Edmé asked, hoping like hell it wasn't broken. He couldn't fix that, and they couldn't risk stopping between here and Carimchi, which would leave Reza healing incorrectly for over a week.

"I don't know," Reza said. He gritted his teeth, yanking off his boot. The ankle was swollen, even under the stockings Reza wore. "One minute I was on the horse, the next I wasn't and everything hurt."

Edmé nodded, standing to return to his pack. He'd stocked up on some medical supplies when they'd last stopped in a town, since his original store of them had ridden off on the back of a horse during the first attack. He brought his horse over to where Reza was sitting, wincing as Reza poked at his ankle because that was the smart thing to do with an injury.

Digging through his pack, he pulled out the packet of herbs he'd acquired and one of the wider, long bandages. It didn't take long to bind Reza's ankle with some of the herbs meant to reduce the swelling. It wasn't obviously broken, but Edmé had never been a medic, so he couldn't be sure. Nothing he could do about it, however, and Reza seemed accepting of that, only complaining a little as Edmé wrapped it.

"Thanks," Reza said when Edmé helped him up. He balanced on his uninjured foot, wavering slightly when Edmé let him go, but keeping upright. Edmé reluctantly left him there, moving to collect Reza's horse from where it had wandered into the field bordering the road. When Edmé returned, Reza was sitting down again, one hand pressed to the side of his head.

"How is your head?" Edmé asked, frowning worriedly. They'd be slowed greatly if Reza couldn't keep his balance enough to ride.

"It hurts," Reza said shortly, glaring up at him. "But I'll live."

Edmé frowned, letting go of the reins to Reza's horse to kneel down next to him again. Reza watched him suspiciously, jerking back when Edmé reached for his head. Too slowly, so slowed reflexes ... Edmé sank his hands into Reza's hair, running his fingers along Reza's skull in search of a bump. Reza was still under his hands, and Edmé was pleased to have an actual excuse to touch Reza, even if he wasn't particularly pleased by the circumstances. Reza jerked away when Edmé's fingers brushed against the bump on the back of his head, and Edmé dropped his hands, frowning.

"I can ride," Reza said stubbornly.

"Are you sure?" Edmé asked. He trusted Reza, but he didn't trust that Reza would be truthful about his health when they were so close to Carimchi and after dealing with the third attack in as many days. "We can double-up. I don't want you to fall and break your neck."

"I won't," Reza said. He sat forward, shifting around so he was kneeling instead of sitting. He put his weight on his right leg, levering himself to his feet awkwardly. "If I do, feel free to tell me that you told me so."

"Not much point if you're dead," Edmé said, moving to help Reza limp over to his horse.

"I won't care at that point," Reza replied, his voice only slightly strained as he half-hopped, half-limped, leaning on Edmé heavily.

"I will," Edmé said, sounding far more serious than he'd meant. Reza glanced at him, a flush coloring his cheeks, and Edmé was grateful to focus on getting Reza on his horse before he said anything else to get himself in trouble.

It was difficult to get Reza back on his horse, but they managed it somehow, and Edmé mounted up on his own, leading the way down the path. They'd have to find a different route, Edmé thought as he rode, glancing back every so often to make sure Reza was doing all right. Reza made obscene gestures each time Edmé looked, so he probably was fine and Edmé was being overprotective.

Still, he'd rather be overprotective than have to explain how he'd gotten Reza so close to Carimchi only to have him die from falling off his horse. He'd rather Reza didn't die at all, let alone from something so preventable. Edmé glanced back again. Reza wasn't looking at him, but at the fields they were riding by. Edmé should have been doing the same, and he turned back, scrutinizing the road ahead.

He needed to focus on getting Reza to Carimchi, but he kept focusing on Reza instead. It was a mistake, and he knew it. The last week of the trip was going to be dangerous enough without splitting his focus as he was. Unfortunately, no matter how many times he thought it, it didn't keep him from watching Reza instead of the road, or keep him from wondering if he'd see Reza after they made it Carimchi, or if they'd go their separate ways and never see each other again.

A university professor and a mercenary with no other prospects weren't compatible. Edmé shouldn't have been thinking about how it could work, how he could perhaps convince Reza to join his crew—he'd proven himself more than capable with each subsequent attack and seemed to be getting more comfortable with travelling, even. No, Edmé needed to accept that they'd reach Carimchi and Reza would be sucked back into the life of a professor. Edmé would return home and continue his life leading his mercenary gang.

They rode deep into the night. Edmé called a halt when the first rays of dawn began to break over the horizon, making a camp near the river that had joined them to run along the path. Edmé hadn't decided yet whether to travel alongside the river, a more meandering and hopefully less treacherous path, or to break away from the river and head straight for Carimchi.

After tying his horse to a nearby tree, giving it a long lead so it could reach the river to drink, Edmé helped Reza down from his horse. If he held onto Reza a few seconds longer than was necessary, Reza didn't comment. Edmé let him go, watching critically as Reza limped away from the horse, sitting down heavily in the grass a few steps away.

At least he could walk on the ankle, even if he obviously couldn't put much weight on it. Edmé fetched the packs, dropping them next to Reza so he could get started on dinner while Edmé tended the horses. The familiar, bright and warm wash of Reza's magic flowed over Edmé as he finished settling the horses, and he smiled at the now-familiar sensation.

Joining Reza, Edmé accepted the stale bread and jerky Reza offered him. They'd been living off cold rations for the last few days. Edmé hadn't wanted to risk a fire since the smoke wouldn't be obscured by Reza's protective spell. Edmé ate quickly, then fetched the medical supplies again. "Let me see your ankle," Edmé said, kneeling next to Reza again.

"It's fine. Barely hurts," Reza said, but obediently shifted slightly so that Edmé could more easily get to his leg.

The swelling had gone down some, Edmé noted as he unwound the bandage. The dried herbs Edmé had wrapped in the bandage were crumbled, half disintegrated, and Edmé shook them free. Reza sighed, dropping back into the grass while Edmé worked on bandaging his ankle up with fresh herbs. "Looks like a nasty sprain."

"I figured," Reza said, not moving from his reclined position. Edmé smiled faintly, shifting Reza's leg off his lap and into the grass.

"How is your head?" Edmé asked, his fingers twitching to bury themselves in Reza's hair again.

"Hurts some," Reza said disinterestedly. "Sleep will fix it."

"Mmm," Edmé said, hoping that was the case. "Are you sleeping there?"

"Why not?" Reza muttered, sitting up slightly so he could glare at Edmé. "It's about as comfortable as those damn bed rolls."

"Suit yourself," Edmé said, standing to go fetch the bed rolls anyway. He dropped Reza's cloak on top of him, getting a half-hearted grumble from Reza. Edmé laid out the bedrolls, one next to Reza in case he changed his mind and another not too far away. Setting his sword down next to his bed roll, Edmé stretched out, pulled his cloak over himself, and was asleep in moments.

Edmé woke suddenly, registering the figure leaning over him. He acted reflexively, grabbing the person hovering above him and rolling, pinning his assailant to the ground. It took a moment for his brain to catch up, and Edmé stared down at Reza, who stared up at him with wide eyes.

"Ow," Reza said, though he made no move to extricate himself from Edmé's grasp. Edmé's forearm was pinning Reza's chest down with his other hand pressing one of Reza's wrists into the grass. Most of Edmé's weight rested against his forearm, and Edmé shifted his arm, leaning on his elbow in the grass next to Reza instead.

He'd had every intention of getting up, but movement to the left caught his eye. Edmé's heart skipped a beat—a pair of riders was only a few dozen yards away, down the river bank. They were watering their horses, but they didn't appear to have noticed Edmé and Reza, which meant Reza's barrier was still working. The leather armor and swords they wore indicated they were mercenaries; this close to Carimchi, they'd more likely than not be after Reza and the book. A quick glance confirmed the book was still in its place behind the saddle of Edmé's horse.

"They won't hear us," Reza said, but he said it quietly, as though afraid of being overheard. "The spell won't let them come this way, either, but they shouldn't notice it, either. It will influence them into going another way."

"We can't leave until they do?" Edmé asked, his eyes never leaving the riders. They seemed in no hurry to move on. It was mid-afternoon, judging from the position of the sun; Edmé would prefer to be riding, not hiding.

"I can't make the spell come with us," Reza said. Edmé glanced back to Reza, far too aware that he was still hovering over Reza. "There's only two of them."

"They're part of a larger group," Edmé said, wishing it were as easy as picking off the two of them. "Without knowing how close the others are ..."

"You don't know that for sure," Reza argued. "There were only the three yesterday."

"They were poorly outfitted and their horses weren't trained for combat," Edmé replied. "The armor they—" Edmé nodded to the two men, "—are wearing is more expensive. It's far more likely they're part of a larger group and not on their own."

"I guess," Reza said, twisting his head to scowl at the men and giving Edmé a lovely view of his profile. "So we wait them out?"

Edmé nodded, not thrilled with the delay. Though he could think of a few things to keep them occupied—and that was his cue to remove himself from Reza's proximity, like he should have done already. Pushing himself up, Edmé stood awkwardly, trying to keep from accidentally jarring Reza's injured ankle or lingering over Reza at all.

They would have to wait a while after the men left, as well, to make sure they weren't loitering out of sight. The terrain was flat, mostly meadows and fields, with a few trees here and there. The river was lined with bushes, but nothing that would obstruct their view of the men.

"How's your head?" Edmé asked, attempting to distract himself.

"Fine," Reza said, rolling his eyes. "My ankle is better, too. Doesn't hurt half as much."

"Good," Edmé said.

Keeping one eye on the two lingering mercenaries— who seemed to be arguing about which way to go, pointing and gesticulating in different directions—Edmé found his pack, intending to sort out breakfast while they waited. Reza shifted from kneeling to sitting on the grass, his legs stretched out in front of him, and he watched Edmé, a curious look on his face. Edmé ignored it. He couldn't afford to be distracted by anything, especially Reza, not this close to Carimchi and with the danger worse than ever.

Edmé brought the last of the stale bread over along with a few dried apples. Reza took the food, and Edmé took a seat next to him, watching as the men finally appeared to make a decision. They mounted and headed towards them, veering around the protective spell without seeming to find it strange. They rode along the river, and that certainly decided the path for Edmé, even if he didn't doubt there was more danger waiting for them in that direction as well.

"We're not going that way, are we?" Reza asked, taking a bite of one of the dried apples.

"No." Edmé shook his head, following suit. He ate quickly, watching the mercenaries ride further and further away until they were out of sight over the horizon. There was no sign of anyone else, yet, but if those two were scouts, then it wouldn't be long until they ran into the rest.

Edmé packed up the campsite quickly, admonishing Reza to stay where he was when he tried to get up to help. Reza made a face, but didn't push the matter, sprawling on the grass as though he were out on a picnic and not being hunted by hundreds for a book of power that could end the world. Reza managed to mount on his own, and then they were riding again.

~~*

Carimchi was a sprawling city, a maze of busy, hectic streets surrounding the temple at the heart. The center of the temple was the giant pyramid that housed the goddess's tomb, called so because the most favored of her children—mostly priests—were buried there alongside the most dangerous artifacts and treasures. *The Book of Judgment* would be interred in the deepest, most secure layer of the pyramid, far below ground. Like the goddess's symbol, the tomb was built as a diamond with the lower half of the building underground.

Reza had never seen it before. The pyramid was built out of white marble, glaringly bright in the sunlight. It was hard to look at, but that was all for the best. The streets of Carimchi were crowded, and Edmé had warned him to keep a sharp eye out and keep as close as he could until they were inside the temple walls.

It was difficult to believe the journey was almost complete. Reza was mostly relieved—he was tired of worrying where the next attack would come from. He wasn't completely happy, however, because reaching the temple meant he and Edmé would be going their separate ways. As far as Reza was aware, the contract only required Edmé get him and the book to Carimchi safely, not back. There was no danger on the way back, after all, and no doubt Edmé would want to be returning to his usual life.

Reza brooded, gripping the reins more tightly. He had his own life to go back to, even if it seemed somewhat dull. Reza scowled at himself. Honestly, what did he want? The ever-present threat of attack on the trip to Carimchi had been nerve-wracking and unpleasant, but what, returning to his office to complete more experiments was too boring?

Edmé was slowing down and Reza glanced around. They'd gotten much closer to the temple, and Edmé would yell at him something fierce if he'd realized how distracted Reza had let himself become. They were approaching a wall that seemed to wind its way around the temple grounds. It was about six feet in height with a huge, wide open gate that reached much higher.

There were fewer people inside the gates, at least from what Reza could see. Edmé didn't pause, riding straight through the gates. Reza followed, nervous and worried—what if they weren't ready for the book? What if Reza had screwed up the spell warding the book again? Reza glanced at the book, still secure on the back of Edmé's horse, but everything seemed all right with it.

If anything was wrong again, well, he'd done his best. It wasn't as though the temple priests had given him a lot of instruction in their missives. The ones Charbonneau had let him see, that was. Edmé was stopping in front of a large stable, and Reza hastily reined in his horse. Edmé dismounted and Reza followed suit, ignoring the brief twinge of pain from his ankle as he stepped down.

Edmé removed the saddle bags from his horse, and Reza fumbled to remove his own, his fingers working against him. Scowling in frustration, Reza was about to write the whole thing off when Edmé appeared next to him.

"Here," Edmé said, passing him the bag that held *The Book of Judgment*. Reza nearly dropped it, startled, but he supposed there wasn't much point in keeping him separate from the book any longer. Edmé deftly undid the fastenings holding his pack in place, swinging it up over his shoulder with his own.

"Do you know where we can find High Priest Blanc?" Reza asked the stable boy who came out to meet them.

"Um, the prayer hall?" The boy suggested nervously.

"Which is where?" Reza asked, turning to squint at the buildings over his shoulder in the shadow of the tomb.

"Closest building to the goddess's tomb, sir," the boy supplied, looking more curious than worried as he stared at Reza. "With the glass roof."

Reza nodded, slinging the bag over his shoulder. Edmé gestured for him to lead the way, falling into step behind him. Reza couldn't keep himself from watching everyone they passed with some suspicion, somewhat comforted by the way he could feel Edmé looming behind him. No one looked at them too long, so Edmé was being his usual inscrutable self.

There were half a dozen buildings in the shadow of the tomb itself, the biggest obviously being the prayer hall. It was built of gray stone with many windows filled with colored glass interspersed throughout the walls. The front doors were enormous; they could easily accommodate twelve men abreast.

The inside of the prayer hall was dark and shadowy, the sunlight occluded by the shadow of the tomb that stretched across the clear glass ceiling. The glass ceiling gave them a clear view of bright blue skies littered with small white clouds. The hall was one large, open room with long rows of prayer mats stretching across the floor.

It was mostly empty, with only a few people scattered about. The main prayer hour was noon, when the sun was overhead. Reza remembered that much from his childhood. At the far end of the hall stood two priests dressed in deep blue robes, the goddess's symbol embroidered over their hearts in white. Reza paused in the doorway, only stepping further inside when Edmé nudged him forward.

His boots clicked loudly on the tile floor, drawing the priests' attention. Reza hesitated, unfamiliar with the customs of the Church from this point. The monk who had served his village hadn't been much on tradition, and Reza had never bothered to attend any of the services at the university.

The priests saved him the trouble of making a decision. One of them split away from the other, crossing the hall towards them unhurriedly. He stopped in front of them, his eyes sliding from Reza to Edmé before settling on Reza.

"Good afternoon. The traveler's lodge is two buildings to the left if you'd like a place to rest before offering your prayers to the goddess," the priest said. He had an earnest, boyish face, and he smiled at them easily. "We provide hot meals and baths at any time and the prayer hall is open at all hours."

"What?" Reza asked, baffled before remembering that the goddess's tomb was a popular pilgrimage site. "No, we're here to see High Priest Blanc. It's a matter of importance."

The priest's pleasant expression didn't change a whit. "Do you have an appointment?"

Edmé snorted, drawing the priest's gaze. "Tell him the professor is here with his book."

"Oh, are you Professor Tremblay?" The priest asked Reza, curious. Reza nodded and the priest continued, "Come right this way, please. I apologize for the delay—we expected you two weeks ago."

"We had a few setbacks," Reza said politely.

The priest nodded, turning and leading them across the prayer hall. As they approached the back wall, Reza realized there was a small door, painted the same color as the wall. The priest took them through the door and a short walk down a narrow corridor before knocking on a closed, nondescript door.

The door opened after a moment, revealing a short, older man with gray hair and a black robe. He squinted at the priest. "Why are you pestering me, Francis? You know I don't like to be disturbed during my afternoon tea."

"The professor with the book is here, High Priest," Francis said, a smile flashing across his face. Reza stifled an amused grin, unsurprised to see Edmé glare at Francis for using his phrasing.

"Oh," Blanc said, sounding somewhat sullen about it. He peered past Francis's shoulder, then grudgingly opened the door wider. "See some rooms are prepared. In the tomb, not the traveler's lodge."

"Of course, High Priest," Francis said agreeably, dipping a slight bow before slipping back down the corridor the way they'd come.

"Come in, come in," Blanc said, stepping back so they could enter the room. The room was small. There was a single round table set in the center of it holding an open book and tray of tea and small pastries. There were a handful of chairs around the table, and Blanc crossed the room to settle into one on the far side of the table. "I take it the trip did not go smoothly?"

"Not really, no," Reza said, taking the seat opposite Blanc. He set the bag with the book down at his feet, eager to dispense with the pleasantries and be done with it already.

"Unfortunate," Blanc said, grimacing. "I had hoped otherwise ... No sense worrying over it now. You made it here safely and that's what counts. I won't keep you long. I'm sure you'd both like some rest before you destroy the book—"

"Wait, what?" Reza interrupted. "What do you mean, we're destroying the book?"

"Precisely that," Blanc said. He set down his cup of tea, looking startled at Reza's surprise. "*The Book of Judgment* is far too dangerous. Not even the protections of the tomb will keep it safe. Did High Chairman Charbonneau not tell you this?"

"No, he did not," Edmé said. He was still standing behind Reza, and the anger in his voice made the hair on the back of Reza's neck stand on end.

"I see," Blanc said pensively. He frowned at the table top. "I apologize on behalf of him, then. He was supposed to approach you about destroying the tome, not—what, escort?" Blanc peered at Edmé, who grunted an affirmation, a wealth of displeasure in that small sound.

"What am I missing?" Reza asked, irritated. He was missing something between Edmé's anger and Blanc's apology.

"Destroying a book of power requires a great deal of power," Blanc said, sitting back in his seat. His brow was furrowed, as though Reza and Edmé's not knowing they were meant to destroy the book was a huge setback. "It also requires a holy instrument through which to channel the power, and there are very few of those remaining."

A holy instrument? Edmé's sword, since he didn't think anything else they'd brought qualified. "Why didn't Charbonneau tell us this?"

"I don't know," Blanc said, and his scowl said he was going to have words with Charbonneau about that. "Perhaps he thought it would be easier to convince you after you'd completed the journey." Reza studied Blanc, but he'd never been particularly apt at reading people. If Blanc had been in agreement with Charbonneau on that point and was stringing them along now, Reza couldn't tell.

"What does destroying the book entail?" Reza asked. Perhaps there was a way to keep Edmé out of it. He hadn't spoken again, but Reza didn't think he was imagining the hostility radiating off of Edmé behind him.

Blanc started to reply, but was cut off by a frantic knock on the door. He stood and crossed the room briskly, opening the door to a priest barely out of boyhood. "What is it?"

"Aldric, sir, in the mess hall," the priest said, his voice wavering slightly. He didn't seem to notice Reza or Edmé as he shifted nervously from foot to foot as he stared at the High Priest with wide eyes.

Blanc nodded, turning back to Reza and Edmé. "There's a problem I must attend. We can discuss this further in the morning. Curtis will take you to your rooms."

"What about—" Reza started, lifting the bag that held the book.

"Your usual protective measures should be sufficient. We can discuss it further tomorrow," Blanc said. That wasn't the answer Reza wanted, but before he could argue the matter, Blanc was gone, hurrying off into the prayer hall and leaving Reza with a wide-eyed, baby-faced priest and an extremely hostile Edmé. Reza stifled a sigh; he'd hoped life would get simpler when they reached the tomb, not more complicated.

The rooms Curtis led them to were deep into the center of the goddess's tomb. There were no windows, but illumination was provided by a series of mage lights embedded in the walls and ceiling. Curtis stammered out quick directions for how to use the lights, then made a quick retreat. Reza didn't blame him—Edmé had been silent and glowering the entire trip, no doubt intimidating the poor priest.

The rooms were actually one large room separated into different sections with the use of floor-to-ceiling screens inscribed with the goddess's symbol and depictions of holy scenes. A quick inspection revealed two small sections set up for sleeping, a section with a steaming bath set up, as well as the large front area that hosted the fireplace, a writing desk and shelves, and a small table, meant for dining.

Reza dropped his bags next to a chair in the main area. The beds called to him—he swore he could sleep for a week—but Reza was all too aware that it had been weeks since he could call himself anything resembling clean.

"I'm bathing," Reza said, not bothering to offer Edmé the opportunity to take a bath first. Edmé could wait, especially if he was going to be angry and surly the rest of the evening. Edmé grunted and Reza left him to sulk. He could understand Edmé's anger to a certain extent— certainly Reza wasn't pleased that Charbonneau hadn't thought it important for them to know they were going to be destroying the book—but wasn't destroying it a good thing?

Sliding the screens shut behind him, Reza quickly disrobed. Sliding into the hot water with a sigh, Reza gave himself a few minutes to soak before reluctantly scrubbing himself clean. Lingering too long would only have him falling asleep in the bath. He could have a proper soak after he got some sleep. Climbing from the bath, Reza snagged a drying cloth and dried off quickly. There was a pair of robes hanging on a nearby wall, and Reza pulled one on. Hopefully, he could find something in his bag that didn't smell too strongly of horse.

Edmé wasn't in the common room when Reza entered it, but he emerged from the bedchamber on the right. He was no longer wearing his leather armor, though his sword belt was still fastened around his waist. He was dressed in just trousers and shirt, and Reza was suddenly recalled to the fact that he wore nothing more than a thin robe.

"There's clothing in the bureau," Edmé said. He seemed less angry, though not exactly happy—as happy as Edmé ever seemed to get, that was. "A meal is on the way."

Reza nodded, his gaze lingering on Edmé until he decided it was in his best interest to retreat before he gave Edmé cause to use his sword on Reza. Edmé had moved his bags from the common room to the other bedchamber and they rested on the middle of the bed. Reza ignored them for the moment, more interested in investigating the contents of the bureau. Each drawer was stuffed full of trousers and shirts, all the same color—a dark blue—and it took Reza far too long to sort out that each drawer held a different size.

Dressed, Reza turned to the task of securing the book. He stuffed the entire bag under the bed, out of sight, then set a spell on the bag that prevented it from being moved. Once Reza was sure they'd be uninterrupted the rest of the night, he'd secure the room itself, but with dinner on the way, there wasn't much point yet.

Returning to the common area, Reza settled into one of the low chairs, one that let him keep an eye on the entrance and on the screens leading to the bath. He felt vaguely guilty, waiting impatiently outside the bath to ambush Edmé, but Edmé was his best chance of answers at this point.

The sword had to be the key, but Reza didn't know how. He didn't know anything about destroying books of power—but Edmé did. That had been what he'd done, after all, before the angels had been disbanded. Why had they let Edmé keep his sword? Reza wasn't sure he could ask that question, not without earning Edmé's hostility for himself. Was Reza even necessary for destroying the book, or did Edmé have enough power on his own?

A knock on the door jolted Reza from his thoughts, and he stood, moving to answer the door. It was yet another unfamiliar priest. He bore a large tray with an assortment of dishes, and Reza let him in, watching the man's quick, nervous movements as he set down the tray.

"Don't worry about that," Reza said when he started to pour tea for Reza. "Thank you."

"Sir," the priest said, forcing a nervous smile that fell off his face when the screen to the bathing room slid open to reveal Edmé. He paled, and it suddenly struck Reza that Edmé's presence was probably what was making the priest nervous. Edmé was an excommunicated angel in the goddess's tomb—he didn't doubt that was the main topic of gossip at the moment.

"That's all we need, thank you," Reza said loudly, keeping his temper under control by sheer force of will. Edmé was no one to be feared, not the way this priest did. The priest nodded, beating a hasty retreat and accidentally slamming the door behind him.

He rolled his eyes, glancing at Edmé, but Edmé didn't seem to have noticed the priest's reaction to him. He was wearing the other dressing robe, but where Reza's had fit fine, Edmé's fit much tighter. It gaped open, exposing a tantalizing slice of Edmé's chest and it stopped a few inches short of Edmé's knees, showing off muscular thighs and sturdy calves—

Reza turned his head sharply, picking up the tea pot and pouring himself a cup of tea. He would have preferred wine, or spirits of any sort, but tea would do for the moment. The screens to Edmé's bedchamber slid shut, and Reza stifled a sigh. He needed to stop noticing Edmé. Edmé's part of the journey was done, unless he decided to help destroy the book, and no doubt he'd be on his way shortly either way.

He also, Reza thought a smidge bitterly, had no reason to be interested in Reza. Edmé seemed alternately indifferent and annoyed by him. Reza was good at magic, but that didn't seem to impress Edmé, and Reza had never had anything that could be described as 'physical prowess,' even if his riding skills had improved leaps and bounds the last few months.

Scowling at himself, Reza pushed the thoughts out of his head and began fixing a plate from the dishes on the tray. He drank some of the tea, wrinkling his nose at the grass-like texture of it. Edmé reappeared as Reza added a roll to the plate, dressed in the same outfit Reza wore. He carried his sword, which he propped against the chair next to Reza before taking a seat.

The mark on his forehead was slightly visible through the strands of his hair, which clung together wetly from the bath. Reza bit his tongue on his questions, forcing himself to eat instead. Edmé filled a plate for himself and poured a cup of tea, drinking half the cup in a swallow before turning to his meal. They ate in a familiar, comfortable silence even as Reza's mind whirled, trying to come up with an opening that wouldn't make Edmé glare at him.

"Ask," Edmé said when Reza set his empty plate down on the tray.

"What?" Reza asked, startled. He picked up his tea cup, taking a sip of the terrible tea.

"Whatever you're thinking of asking,' Edmé said, continuing to eat as though he hadn't given leave to Reza to interrogate him.

"Have you destroyed a book of power before?" Reza asked, deciding that wasn't *too* sensitive a question to ask.

"A few." Edmé set aside his own plate. "None as strong as *The Book of Judgment*. I could handle the others on my own."

"So I am needed for destroying it," Reza said, to which Edmé nodded. "How does it work?"

"Like casting any other spell," Edmé said, which meant absolutely nothing. Reza stared at Edmé, willing him to elaborate. Edmé smiled briefly. "It takes a destructive spell, usually fire, channeled through the sword."

"Why is the sword necessary?" Reza asked, eyeing it where it was propped against Edmé's chair. Edmé was silent, and Reza wondered if the sword was a taboo subject as well.

Edmé moved suddenly, picking up the sword and unsheathing it. The blade glinted in the mage lights above. Edmé stood, and Reza swallowed hard when he approached the chair Reza was sitting in. He laid the sword across Reza's lap, and Reza froze, shooting Edmé a startled look. Edmé knelt in front of him, and Reza wondered if he'd fallen and hit his head when he'd gotten out of the bath and didn't remember it.

"It took a year to make this," Edmé said, tracing the faint markings on the blade. "I don't know much of what went into its making. My part was to supply the energy for it every so often, but past that, the process is a secret."

Reza nodded—that didn't surprise him. From what little he knew of the priesthood and its mages, they were exceptionally protective of their magic. Given the power in them, Reza didn't doubt they'd keep the making of the angels' swords as secret as possible.

"There are a number of spells embedded in the blade," Edmé said, setting his fingertips against the blade, above the hilt. Spell marks flashed into existence, fading away to be replaced by others as Edmé cycled through the spells. The blade was warm where it laid on Reza's thighs, and he stared at it, wondering why Edmé had decided to share its secrets with him.

"But you said any destruction spell would work," Reza said. Edmé called up a fresh set of spell marks, most of which Reza didn't recognize. They were archaic, extremely old versions of the marks used these days, and Reza didn't know them. "Something to do with energy?" Reza asked, reaching out to touch the only mark he recognized. The blade sent a jolt of energy down his hand and Reza jerked away, startled.

"It only lets me use it," Edmé said, lifting the sword from Reza's lap. He stood, retrieving the sheath, and returned the sword to it. "The energy spell will suppress the energy in the book. If it's not suppressed, it finds another vessel to occupy."

"It doesn't dissipate?" Reza asked, baffled. All energy dissipated when it had no spell to shape it or vessel to hold it.

"Something about being trapped in a book of spells contorts the energy. It makes it act strangely—most often, the energy tries to find another vessel to occupy and the effects of that can be deadly," Edmé said. He set the sword down next to his chair, taking a seat again.

Reza nodded, accepting that. Edmé knew far more than he did about books of power, after all. "So you are going to help destroy the book?"

"I don't have a choice," Edmé said bitterly, glancing at the sword as though it was at fault.

"The other choice is to say no," Reza said, rolling his eyes at Edmé's dramatic proclamation. "I can keep the book safe until they get another of those made or they find someone else with one."

"They won't make more," Edmé said, leveling his glare on Reza. Reza stared back, unmoved. "And there's no telling when they'll find another person with a holy instrument."

"Why won't they make more?" Reza asked. "They're obviously necessary for tasks like this."

Edmé stared at Reza as though gauging the depth of Reza's stupidity. Reza glared back, silently daring Edmé to storm off without answering him.

"Because they made one of those for every one of us," Edmé finally said, anger and sadness flickering over his face so quickly that Reza would have missed it had he blinked.

"Oh." Edmé could only mean the angels, and Reza bit back the question of why Edmé still had his, not wanting to upset Edmé further. He was upset, though Reza doubted many others would have noticed it.

"They had to disband and mark us all," Edmé said. He stared at Reza, and Reza stayed quiet, not wanting to dissuade Edmé from telling him. "There were a few—very few—of us who were found to have done no wrong, and we were allowed to keep the swords. Probably so that something like *The Book of Judgment* could be destroyed if necessary."

"So you do have a choice," Reza said. "Make them find someone else."

"No." Edmé shook his head, scowling at Reza. "It needs to be destroyed as soon as possible."

"It can wait," Reza said. He shouldn't have been arguing with Edmé; it would be better to destroy the book with all possible haste. The idea of Edmé doing it grudgingly didn't sit well with him, however. "It's already been around for centuries, after all."

"It's in the open," Edmé snapped. "We kept it safe this long only by the grace of the goddess. Keeping it safe for as long as a year—if not longer—would be impossible."

"You don't think I'm capable?" Reza asked. That wasn't what Edmé was saying, and Reza knew it, but he didn't particularly feel like cutting Edmé any slack.

"Your skill won't matter." Edmé sat forward, glaring at Reza as though he wanted to throttle Reza. "Are you really prepared to give up years of your life to protect that book? What about your research?"

"I'm not—" Reza hesitated, then shrugged, looking away. "I'm not exactly in a hurry to return to a place run by a man who deceived us about the reason we travelled here. I'm also not in a hurry to force you to do something you don't want to do." Edmé was quiet, and Reza leaned forward to pick up his tea cup. The anger and tension had drained out of him and all he felt was tired. Taking a sip of the lukewarm tea, Reza glanced at Edmé.

"I wouldn't burden you with the task of protecting the book until they can find someone else to destroy it," Edmé said quietly. "I don't know if Charbonneau took that into account, or if he believed I would agree because of the distance we travelled."

"Probably the distance," Reza said, straining to keep his voice steady. Edmé cared enough that he'd destroy the book for Reza? He was likely reading too much into that, but it certainly sounded that way. "How long does destroying it take?"

"Not long," Edmé said. He was giving Reza a strange look, so Reza probably hadn't succeeded in keeping his cool. "Recovery will be longer. The spell will take all of our energy."

"*All* of it? Lovely." Reza winced. He hadn't used all of his energy since he was a teen and far too overconfident about his skills. It had left him exhausted for weeks and taken months to replenish his energy to a respectable level. Reza yawned, his eyes watering with the force of it. Swallowing the rest of his tea, he stood. "I suppose I should become acquainted with my bed in that case."

Edmé nodded, absently wishing him goodnight. Reza headed towards his bedchamber, glancing back as he slid open the screens. Edmé had drawn his sword again and was staring at it pensively. Stifling a sigh, Reza stepped through the screens, shutting them behind him.

~~*

Edmé had been in dozens of casting rooms in his life, but none compared to the one High Priest Blanc brought them to near the top of the goddess's tomb. It was huge, nearly three times the size of rooms he and Reza shared, and reached at least three stories up in height. The walls were painted a bright white with spell marks inscribed in black. The spell marks would keep any casting done in the room from leaving the room. The floor was a dark, porous tile—if spell markings were needed, they could be inscribed on the floor in chalk.

Reza carried the bag that held *The Book of Judgment* and Edmé wore his sword, but none of his armor. Reza had been quiet all morning, and Edmé couldn't tell if it was his normal lack of vigor in the morning, or if something about the previous night's discussion had put him off.

"You should wait outside," Edmé said, addressing Blanc. The fewer people in the room for the casting, the better. If something went wrong, goddess forbid, Blanc would be necessary to contain the damage.

"I'll watch from the observation deck," Blanc said, gesturing to the wall behind them. Edmé hadn't noticed the small balcony there, closed off from the rest of the tomb by glass. He left, leaving Edmé alone with Reza in the large room.

"Walk me through the casting?" Reza asked, heading for the center of the room. Edmé followed; technically, it didn't matter where the spell was cast, but the center was as good a place as any.

"The protection spell on the book will have to be dropped," Edmé said, watching as Reza removed the book from the bag and tossed the bag away carelessly. "Don't remove it yet." Reza gave him a withering look and Edmé couldn't help his smile. Reza dropped the book to the floor, its thump echoing loudly through the room.

Stepping forward, Edmé drew his sword. He turned it so the point was directed down, towards the book, and wrapped both hands around the hilt below the pommel. "Wrap your hands around the hilt, above mine."

"This isn't walking through it," Reza muttered, but obediently stepped forward. He placed his hands where Edmé had directed. There wasn't much room on the hilt and the edge of Reza's hands ended up pressed firmly against Edmé's, sending a thrill through him.

"You drop the protection spell on the book, we stab the book with sword, and I cast a fire spell and the energy dampening spell, pulling in your energy," Edmé said. "That's all there is to it."

"All right," Reza said, glancing down at the book briefly. He looked up at Edmé, took a deep breath, and dropped the protection spell. Even with the protection of the sword, Edmé felt the difference immediately, the malevolent energy of the book washing over them. It couldn't affect them, and Edmé steadfastly ignored Reza's wince.

Lowering the sword slowly—they only needed the slightest touch of the sword, technically—Edmé made certain Reza's grip didn't slip. Casting the fire spell took only a thought, as did activating the energy suppressing spell in the sword. Edmé's energy rushed out of him, through his brightly glowing sword, and channeled into the book. Reza's energy followed after, rushing through Edmé, then the sword, burning hot and clear.

The book burst into flames, flaring white hot for a fraction of a second before exploding into ash. Reza stared at him, wide-eyed; his harsh breathing matched Edmé's own and Edmé wished they'd been doing something more fun than destroying a book. Reza's hands slipped away from the hilt of the sword, and Edmé sheathed it, his hands trembling slightly as he did so.

Exhaustion crashed into him, heavy and hard, and Edmé grimaced. He hated this part, and Reza didn't appear to be faring much better. His skin was pale and he held a hand up to his head as though it was paining him.

"I'm never destroying a book of power again," Reza said, wrinkling his nose. He sounded fine, so the spell hadn't affected him more than they'd anticipated. That was good. Reza took a step forward, but stumbled. Edmé immediately reached out and steadied him, putting himself closer to Reza than he'd intended.

Reza fit well in his arms and Edmé wished he didn't know that, as it made it impossible for him to let Reza go. Reza made no move to free himself from Edmé's hold, looking up and opening his mouth as if about to say something. Edmé didn't bother to fight the urge, ducking his head and kissing Reza instead of letting him talk. Reza jerked back, nearly unbalancing them both because Edmé didn't let him go.

Edmé opened his mouth, intending to apologize, but Reza glared at him and snapped, "Why didn't you do that before we destroyed the book?" Some of Edmé's confusion must have shown on his face because Reza scowled, his fingers tightening their grip on Edmé's arm. "When I could actually *do* something about it?"

"I'm sorry?" Edmé stared at Reza, trying to gauge whether *do something* meant something magical and possibly violent or something physical and relating to kissing.

"You should be," Reza grumbled, tugging Edmé down for another kiss. That answered that question, Edmé thought hazily, far more interested in Reza than anything else. Reza kissed as sweet as his tongue was sharp, tasting of the tea with honey he'd drunk before they'd come to destroy the book. Edmé slid an arm around Reza's waist, dragging him that much closer, dizzy from more than the after-effects of the spell—

Reza jerked away suddenly at the sound of someone clearing their throat and Edmé was belatedly recalled to the fact that they were still in the casting chamber, with High Priest Blanc observing. Letting Reza go reluctantly, Edmé brushed at the front of his jacket, turning to face the High Priest.

"Do you need an escort to your rooms?" Blanc asked, acting as though he hadn't broken them apart.

"We can get there on our own," Reza said, his voice remarkably level. Edmé nodded his agreement, not sure he could manage Reza's steady tone.

"Very well," Blanc said, glancing between them before adding, "Thank you again for your assistance in destroying the book."

Reza waved it off, stepping forward and taking Edmé's arm as though it was perfectly normal and natural for him to do so. Edmé smiled, reminded once more of the way Reza never seemed to care what anyone thought about him. They left the casting hall, walking slowly, and made their way back to their rooms in a comfortable silence.

The remnants of the breakfast tray were still laid out on the table, and Reza poured himself a fresh cup of tea, adding enough honey to make it undrinkable. Edmé took his usual seat, facing the door with his back to the bathing area. He poured his own cup of tea and sat back, wondering if he should have gone straight to bed instead of sitting down. He wasn't sure he had the energy to get back up.

The tea was almost warm and Edmé drank it slowly while he watched Reza think. He wore the same expression he usually wore when he was thinking too hard about something or had a question he was trying to figure out how to ask. Edmé left him to his own devices for the moment, trying to not overthink kissing Reza himself.

He didn't regret it. Reza was smart, capable, and not easily intimidated. He didn't seem to care about Edmé's past as an angel, nor did he seem to care that Edmé was best described as 'unapproachable.' He wasn't sure what to do about it. He and Reza lived very different lives, no matter what doubts Reza had about returning to the university—but he wasn't going to worry about that yet. It would be a month, at least, before they could leave the goddess's tomb.

"What happens now?" Reza asked, setting down his cup of tea and staring at Edmé seriously.

"Whatever you want," Edmé said, shrugging.

Reza snorted at that, giving Edmé a heated look. "I know what I *want* to do, but I don't think I'd make it further than standing up before I passed out."

"You mean now the book is destroyed?" Edmé filled in, even though that was obvious. "We'll need to stay here at least a month before attempting travel, maybe longer. I need to return to Giroux to check in with my men. I assume you'll be accompanying me."

"Probably," Reza agreed, making a face. "I still don't know if I want to return to the university."

"You have time to figure that out," Edmé said, sliding down in his seat. A mistake—he definitely wasn't getting up anytime soon. "And you're more than welcome to join my group. We pay decently and your mage skills would be handy."

"I'll add it to my list of options to consider," Reza said dryly, yawning so widely that Edmé could hear his jaw crack.

Edmé nodded, his eyes slipping closed. He'd probably regret falling asleep in a chair, but he couldn't bring himself to care. He could finally relax and there was plenty to look forward to when he woke.

Author Profiles

LJ LaBarthe

L.J. is a French-Australian, who was born during the Witching Hour, just after midnight. From this auspicious beginning, she has gone on to dabble in many things! She wrote a prize-winning short story about Humpty Dumpty wearing an Aussie hat complete with corks dangling from it when she was six years old. From there, she wrote for her high school year book, her university newspaper and in her early teens, produced a fanzine about the local punk rock music scene. She loves music of all kinds and was once a classical pianist; she loves languages and speaks French and English with a teeny-tiny smattering of Mandarin Chinese, which she hopes to relearn properly very soon. She enjoys TV, film, travel, cooking, eating out, abandoned places and researching.

L.J. loves to read complicated plots and hopes to do complex plot lines justice in her own writing. She writes paranormal, historical, urban fantasy and contemporary Australian stories, usually m/m romance and featuring m/m erotica.

L.J. lives in the city of Adelaide, and is owned by her cat.

Publications include an essay written for the now-defunct Veinglory publication produced by Emily Veinglory, in the 2003 issue and a short story for the 2004 issue. A research paper on medieval women that L.J. wrote has been used extensively as a reference guide for other writers at 'All About Romance Novels' in their 'Ask An Historian' section. L.J. has had fiction published by Dreamspinner Press, Noble Romance Press, Freaky Fountain Press and Less Than Three Press. Her blog is at http://misslj-author.livejournal.com/profile.

Isabella Carter

Isabella has been torturing her players for years with character breaking plot twists and loving reminders of suffering to come. Now that she had retired from her illustrious career as a GM, she's turned to making her characters suffer just as much. The time she isn't writing she spends at her job as a computer technician wishing she was right back at home, writing.

Despite this, Isabella continues to be a self-proclaimed romantic. A childhood of Disney movies has taught her that there is no ending as satisfying as a happily ever after.

Sylvia A. Winters

Sylvia grew up in a seaside town that was popular in the Victorian era and has been in decline ever since. Most of her childhood was spent riding donkeys or horses, running through fields, or sat in a quiet corner with a book.

She has always been making up stories and was often in trouble for daydreaming and not paying attention in school.

These days, Sylvia still lives in the South West of England, which she rarely ventures away from, and spends most of her time in a darkened room, bent over her laptop.

Sylvia both writes and copy edits for Less Than Three.

She hopes to continue to improve her writing throughout her life, providing she doesn't run out of tea.

You can keep up with her through Sylvia twitter account (http://www.twitter.com/WintersSA) or her website (http://www.SylviaWinters.wordpress.com).

Elizah J. Davis

Elizah Davis has lived in various parts of the United States, but currently resides in the Pacific Northwest, enjoying the abundance of coffee readily available there. She earned her degree in creative writing after she realized journalism involved too many facts and not enough unicorns. She loves stories of all kinds, but has a particular fondness for romance and fantastical adventures. When she isn't busy making things up, Elizah enjoys reading, laughing at cats on the internet, buying girly shoes, and trying to come up with world domination plans that don't require the donning of pants (her endeavors towards which have thus far been unsuccessful).

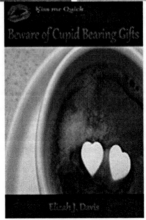

Kayla Bain-Vrba

Ever since she was a little girl, Kayla has been living in daydreams. They started out innocently enough—little dreams of being a world class gymnast or Olympic figure skater—but quickly escalated to grand fantasies of star-crossed lovers, bad boys with hearts of gold, and far-fetched chance meetings with that perfect stranger. For as long as she's been able to read her own writing, Kayla has been writing short stories about anyone and anything that finds its way into her fantasy world. Her three loves are music, writing, and art, and the man of her dreams will both inspire her best work and encourage her crazy ideas, hopefully without getting to say "I told you so" too often. (She wouldn't complain if he was tall, dark, and roguishly handsome too.) When she isn't writing, Kayla enjoys late night conversations, cuddling, singing to the radio, and long car rides with no destination. Best of all is when she can have all four of these at the same time.

Kayla loves feedback! Please email any questions or comments to kaylabainvrba@yahoo.com.

Evie Kiels

Evie Kiels was born and raised in the Midwest, brainwashed into environmental friendliness in the Pacific Northwest, and now lives a hop, skip, and a jump away from the beautiful Rocky Mountains (where she laments the lack of community composting but adores the abundance of sunshine). By day Evie works to make the world a better place by making websites more pleasant to use. By night, she typically reads about heroes searching for their happily ever after and writes about the same. Evie enjoys hiking on warm sunny days and sewing quilt-tops on cold rainy days.

Why she started writing is anyone's guess. She did not write at a young age and never had any grand life-long dreams of writing the great American love story, she just started writing one day and found herself completely engrossed in her own stories.

Visit Evie Kiels at http://eviekiels.net, her twitter, or on Goodreads.

Megan Derr

Megan is a long time resident of m/m fiction, and keeps herself busy reading, writing, and publishing it. She is often accused of fluff and nonsense. She loves to hear from readers, and can be found all around the internet.

maderr.com
maderr.tumblr.com
maderr.livejournal.com
lessthanthreepress.com
@amasour

Debora Day

Debora Day's love of the written word began at age thirteen when she read a romance novel left on the kitchen table by her mother. From that day on, she devoured literature as if starving. It wasn't until she was almost thirty did she decide to stop living in the fantasies of others and try her hand at creating her own fantasies. Much blood, sweat, and many frustrated fears were shed as she taught herself the unfamiliar art of transforming a mental fantasy into enjoyable prose. With the encouragement of her friends and family, she finally began to take a serious look into publishing her work. She loves to know her stories are appreciated and hopes that the enjoyment she had writing them is passed on to her readers. Romance has always been her love and she prides herself on being able to impress the emotions of her characters onto the readers. All her stories will be dedicated to her father who always knew what to say, even when she did not want to hear it.

May Ridge

When she isn't writing or reading, May Ridge potters around libraries looking for ideas to spring forth from the shadows between the stacks. When she has time to break from her imaginary world to take part in real life, she involves herself in work surrounded by books. She started writing slash as fanfiction, and expanded to creating her own characters to torture with love. Her greatest dream is to have a home library like the one that was showcased in Disney's Beauty and the Beast.

Sasha L. Miller

Sasha L. Miller spends most of her time writing, reading, or playing with all things website design. She loves telling stories, especially romance, because there's nothing better than giving people their happily ever afters. When not writing, she spends time cooking, harassing her roommates, and playing with her cats.